Into the Realm of Time

Recognition for
Into the Realm of Time

Imagine being asked out of the blue by a longtime friend—one who was trained as an environmental scientist and engineer and whose only writings you've seen are in technical reports and proposals—to read and comment on his first novel. Given that he never mentioned any interest in writing, and the story involves Roman generals and legions and all matters of things I never had much interest in, you can understand why I said, "Sure, I'd be happy to do so," after which I made a mad dash to the drugstore for NoDoz. Day 1: Twenty pages. Only two to three weeks to go. Day 2: Sixty more pages. My gosh, he knows how to carry a plot along. Day 3: Done.
Amazing.

— Gregory R. Buckle, Director of Data Management,
Locus Technologies

Scott weaves a masterful story where the lives of the characters collide in the crucible of a moment in time. *Into the Realm of Time* is fun to read, action packed, and well written. At the end I could not put it down as it moved to a climactic conclusion.

— The Rev. Dee M. Anderson, West Granville Presbyterian
Church, Milwaukee

The story has something for everyone: love, war, deceit, religion. I enjoyed the character development throughout the story: the honor and pride of a Roman General who serves the Empire; a Christian priest struggling with his faith while journeying in a land of polytheism; the greed and thirst for power of kings and tribal rulers; and a former queen to be forced into marriage. All the main characters struggled to overcome their own internal conflicts. The characters kept evolving as the story progressed. It seemed like I was reading three separate stories at once, but subconsciously I knew these storylines would weave together into a climax. Once I was engaged in the book, it was hard to put down.

— Christopher W. Barden, CWB Consulting, LLC

This was a great story and a fast read! The ending is wonderful! This book will make a blockbuster movie!

— Mark McCluskey, Claims Manager, Milwaukee
— Karen McCluskey, Agency Services Representative, Milwaukee

Into the Realm of Time brings to life the clash of kingdoms, religions, and culture at the end of the fourth century with a gripping intensity. Honor and valor, treachery and the lust for power are timeless themes that Prill illustrates through characters that I will remember for a long time.

— Mark Chelmowski, M.D., FACP

Totally captivated by the story. It is obvious that the author spent considerable time and effort researching the period, allowing the reader not only to get a historical perspective but also to enjoy a compelling tale built around a very engaging hero. I enjoyed the book immensely.

—John E. Bergstrom, Chicago

Into the Realm of Time is a fast-moving adventure, packed with many diverse characters (thanks to the author for including a "cast of characters" at the beginning). The complex interrelationships become clear as the story evolves. There are sometimes violent struggles between good and evil, both within and between the characters, as well as a sweet subplot of mature love. This story reveals the dangers and interpersonal power struggles of a fictional ancient Roman Empire.

— Nancy M. Adams, Retired Licensed Marriage and Family Therapist
and Registered Yoga Instructor

Scott Prill's first novel combines the historian's eye for seeing the details of an era with the storyteller's gift for weaving subplots into a bigger whole. He gives us the bygone names of Roman weapons and armor and military strategies, and he also gives us characters moved by the timeless motives of courage, loyalty, faith, and love.

— David G. Hanson, Attorney, Milwaukee

INTO THE REALM OF TIME

A Novel of the Fourth Century Roman Empire

Jan -

Savor the Victory
Hunger for More!

8-13-15

Scott Prill

SCOTT DOUGLAS PRILL

Cover design by Drew Maxwell
Cover photograph by Robyn Adair
Edited by Carolyn Kott Washburne
ISBN: 099086040X
ISBN: 9780990860402
U.S. Copyright Office Certificate of Registration Number: TXu 1-902-795

For

Marcie, my wife,

and

Jeff, Emily, and Christy, my children,

and

to those who came before us

Table of Contents

ACKNOWLEDGEMENTS

The production of any project such as this one is dependent upon the talent, work, and efforts of others. These fine people include:

Paul Stockhausen—reader and advisor

Lance and **Mary Ellen Panzer**—scriveners and editors

Conor Ekstrom—map illustrator

Steve Bogart—reader and commenter

John Principe—document producer and advisor

Jim Oldham—IT specialist

Dan Kattman—copyright and publishing advisor

Arnold Gutkowski—proofreader and reference provider

Carolyn Kott Washburne—copy editor

Drew Maxwell—cover designer and web designer

Robyn Adair—cover photograph

David Nichols—proofreader

Paula Haubrich—final proofreader

Lindsay Dal Porto—reader

and **Marcie, Jeff, Emily,** and **Christy Prill**—for support, advice and inspiration

Cast of Characters
(By Group and in General Order of Appearance)

ROMANS

Marcus Augustus Valerias: Roman general, Master of Soldiers, Magister Militum, serves both Western and Eastern parts of the Roman Empire

Braxus: Roman general, second-in-command to General Valerias

Cratus: Roman general, third-in-command to General Valerias

Bukarma: A North African and primary bodyguard to General Valerias

Revious: An Alan and chief intelligence officer to General Valerias

Joseph: Roman citizen and Christian priest

Jacob: Chief administrator to General Valerias

Olivertos: Chief physician/surgeon to General Valerias' legions

Agri: Roman deserter

Gius: Roman tribune

Maximus: Roman centurion

Casio: Christian bishop

Protius: Roman nobleman

Anguillo Claudius: Valerias' lawyer

Hyperion: Roman general who adopts Valerias as a young child

Marcellos: Junior Roman officer

Semelis: Junior Roman officer

Gratus: Roman officer

Perocitus: Roman nobleman

Proterous: Roman physician in Britannia

Bradicus: Former administrator to General Valerias, retired to Britannia

Titus: Roman general in Britannia

Tentrides: Roman tribune and engineer

Pyrin: Officer for General Valerias

Hermides: Officer for General Valerias

Trojax: Roman general

Proctur: Roman general under Trojax

Alan: Scout/spy for Revious

GOTHS

Mostar Gulivus: Goth king

Sivas Gul: Son of Mostar Gulivus

BRITONS

Gerhard: King of an area in central Britannia, killed by Saxons

Claire: Queen of Britons, wife of Gerhard

Douglas: Son of Claire and Gerhard

Anne: Oldest daughter of Claire and Gerhard

Elizabeth: Youngest daughter of Claire and Gerhard

Argus: Became King after death of Gerhard

Flavius Magnetious: A Roman, but officer to Argus

Mary: Chambermaid to Claire

Erik Longwilder: Captain of guards for Gerhard and Argus

Eustice: Brother of Claire

Edgbart: Briton village leader

Ruth: Briton villager

Garth: Father of Ruth, village leader

Edith: Druid priestess

Stephen: Briton retained by Flavius

Morguard: Officer to Argus

Kretawac: Scout for Morguard

Alpha: Village leader

HUNS

Drago: Leader of the Northern Huns

Uldric: Son of Drago

Rao: Son of Drago and fraternal twin of Uldric

Zestras: Leader of the Southern Huns

Braga: Son of Zestras

Produgas: Advisor to Uldric and Rao

Dimondes: Hun chieftain

Jutikes: Hun chieftain and appointed general

Borgas: Hun chieftain and appointed general

Oxanos: Hun chieftain and appointed general

Turskon: An Alan appointed Hun general

Radic: Hun general

Sardich: Hun general

Arb: Hun spy

DANUBE AREA VILLAGERS

David (Isaac): False rabbi

Orses: Village leader

Anastasis: Grandniece of Orses

Barca: Village leader

GLOSSARY

Certain Roman terms are used in this book. Definitions of these terms are noted below. These definitions are from the resources listed on the References page at the end of this book.

Bucellarii: Private bodyguards to Roman generals

Comitatenses: Roman mobile field army forces; some placed centrally, some on the major frontiers (Danube)

Gladius: Roman legionnaires' characteristic short sword

Limitanei: Roman frontier garrison troops in permanent stations, paid less than the Comitatenses

Magister Militum: Master of Soldiers; one of the most senior military commanders—second only to the Emperors, from the fourth century onward

Pseudocomitatenses: Roman units promoted into the field army from the Limitanei

Solidus (pl. Solidi): From Constantine onward, the standard Roman gold coin, minted at seventy-two to the pound; half- and third-Solidi were also minted

Spatha: Longer Roman sword; used by cavalrymen and, in later years, by infantrymen

A Note From The Author

When I walk through a cemetery and gaze at the old headstones, I think to myself: what stories those people could tell if they were alive, stories of people and events that are now lost forever. On a more personal note, I look at old family photos and listen to tales of this relative or that one. I know soon they will be forgotten as well. Even prominent persons who leave a record of their presence will have that record subjected to conjecture and interpretation or theory of what that person really meant or why that person acted the way he or she did. Only that person who is now gone could explain the reason why something was done.

Maybe there is a great Timekeeper somewhere who records all of what we do so we can review it in the afterlife. For now, we need to enjoy the time we have.

This is a novel that takes place in a time almost two millennia ago. It is not a novel based on a true story, nor is it intended to be based on historical depictions of actual persons and events. It is simply a story. Yes, the Roman Emperors referred to in the novel were real. It is also a likely fact that the Huns first appeared in Europe toward the end of the fourth century, and their migration pushed the Goths west to the Danube, where they encountered the Romans.

I have used current American measurements in this story. Thus, you will see references to distance, weight, and time as yards, pounds, and hours, respectively. A cast of characters is included immediately after the table of contents, as well as a glossary of several Roman terms used in the novel to assist the reader with the story.

Lastly, I want to say, enjoy your life *now*. The future becomes the past far too quickly.

Scott Douglas Prill

2015

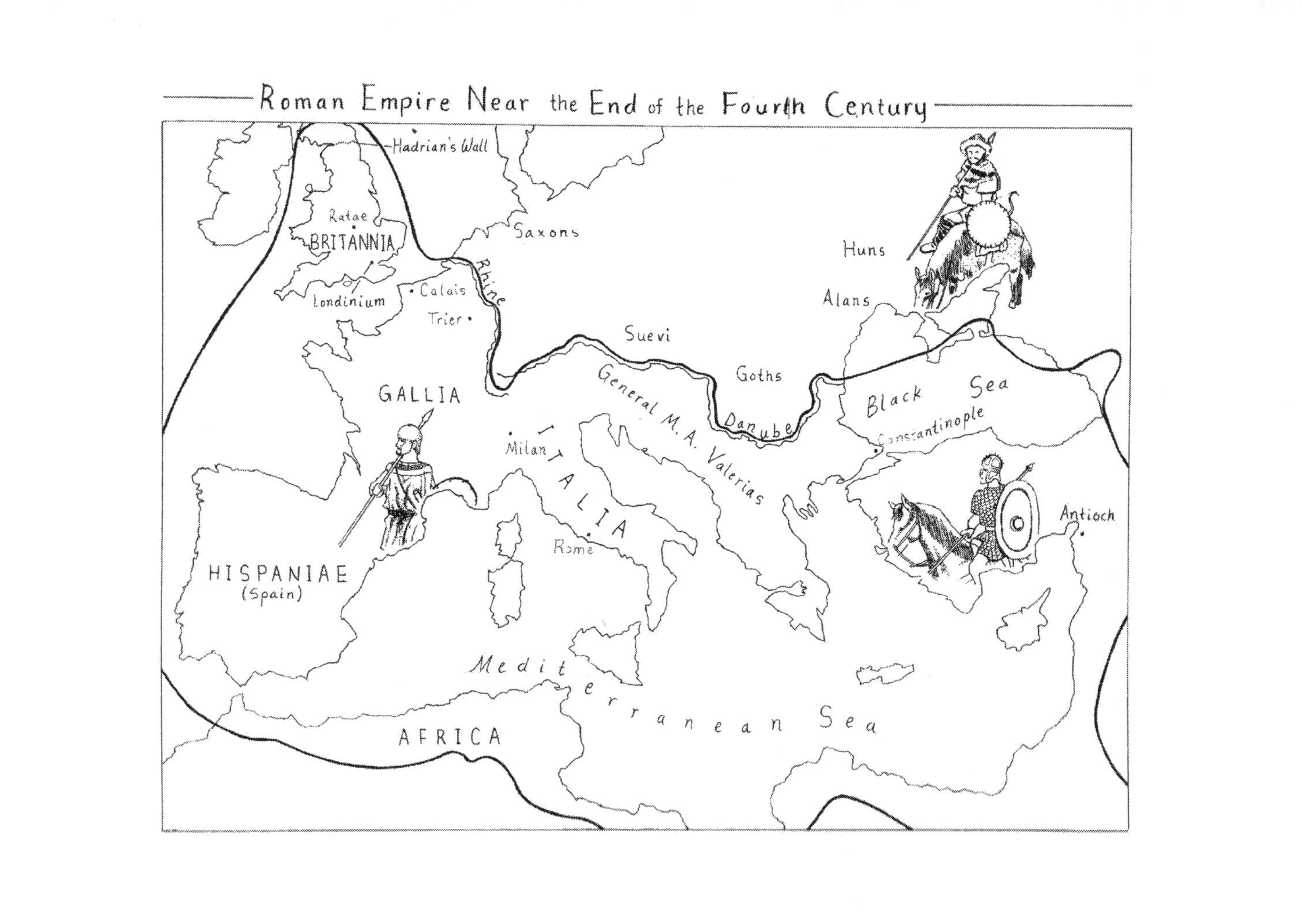
Roman Empire Near the End of the Fourth Century
Hadrian's Wall
Ratae
BRITANNIA
Londinium
Calais
Trier
Saxons
Rhine
Huns
Alans
Suevi
Goths
GALLIA
General M.A. Valerias
Danube
Black Sea
Constantinople
Milan
ITALIA
Rome
Antioch
HISPANIAE
(Spain)
Mediterranean Sea
AFRICA

PART I

"Reflect upon the rapidity with which all that exists and coming to be is swept past us and disappears from sight. For substance is like a river in perpetual flow . . . and ever at our side is the immeasurable span of the past and the yawning gulf of the future, in which all things vanish away. Then how is he not a fool who in the midst of all this is puffed up with pride, or tormented, or bewails his lot as though his troubles would endure for any great while?"

— Emperor Marcus Aurelius, taken from *How Rome Fell* by Adrian Goldsworthy

I

Reflection

Dawn had long since passed its relevancy as the afternoon sun perched overhead like the hawk scanning the meadow for prey. Shadows swarmed across an area below the canopy of trees. There by the brook a figure hunched, not moving. The brook was about ten feet wide. It was shallow at the point nearest to the figure, and then it gradually deepened on the other side. Even at the deepest point, a rat would have difficulty drowning.

Summer was approaching its end as the insects flying about portrayed a sense of urgency to get done whatever they needed to accomplish. Fall would soon come, although the point separating summer from fall was murky.

All this mattered little to the figure. He was completely lost in the thought of the reflection in the shallow part of the brook. The water was still, and the face in the reflection looked old and tired. The beard added years to the face. Every now and then a slight breeze blew across the water, creating a ripple effect. When this happened, the face reflected on the water grew older. If one used imagination, the face took on the appearance of a dead man.

Occasionally the ripples created a current that allowed the clearness of the stream to take on reddish tinges. The combination of the tiny waves and the reddish hue in the creek gave the old, reflected face of the man a grotesque and angry appearance. The cyclic changes in the reflection caused consternation in the man, and yet his gaze was frozen on the reflection. He became convinced that the reflection was an accurate portrayal of his actual features.

A breeze blew by the head of the man, but there was no movement on the now-still stream. The man ignored the breeze until a second breeze pushed on his ear, another puff of wind more forceful than before. This breeze had a human voice. The man, forced out of his trance, was irritable. "What?" he growled. The whispered response was short and direct. The man brusquely uttered "yes" and slowly stood up. He picked up the sword that was lying on the bank of the brook and rubbed it clean with a cloth. The man placed the sword in a worn leather shoulder harness strapped to his back. During these actions he never took his eyes away from the water.

The man turned away from the brook, then stopped and looked back at the spot where his reflection had been mocking him. He took his foot and forcefully splashed the water toward the other side of the bank. He muttered an angry curse under his breath and kicked the water again. At that moment even the insects stopped their search for nirvana.

The man whirled around in one motion and began walking up a short, steep hill. A wall of rock ran along the inner side of the path, and a tree growing out of the rock wall caught his attention. As he looked for the origin of the tree in the rock, the outside part of his right foot caught the edge of a round stone, causing the man to roll his ankle. Pain shot through the man as he slipped sideways on the path. This time he did not curse.

A hand that seemed to emanate from the wall reached out to grab the man to keep him from falling. The man, though, had caught his balance, and he pushed the extended arm back.

Pulling himself up, the man stood straight and gingerly took a step forward. He took another stride; this time his full weight was on the ankle. The man felt the pain in the ankle, but he made no change in his facial expression. He took several more steps, and this time he avoided putting his full body weight on the injured ankle.

General Marcus Augustus Valerias, the revered and feared Master of Soldiers, the Magister Militum, Regional Commander of the Roman Empire, ascended to his military camp.

On his way there, a passing Roman soldier shouted to the General, "*Sapor est victoria! Adhuc esurient!*" [Savor the victory! Hunger for more!]

The General nodded to the soldier without an observable expression.

The year was 372 AD, and the Roman Empire was divided into two parts. The Emperor Valentinian I ruled the Western part of the Roman Empire from Milan; the Eastern part of the Empire was ruled by the Emperor Valens based in Constantinople.

II

Gul

The General's walk back to camp was slower than normal and almost aimless. The ankle bothered him, but the face in the stream was more troublesome. Did he really look like that? Was he that old? Was he now unfit to lead his army? These questions filled his mind as he walked. Normally the General was a brisk walker, his gait noticeable to anyone near him. Today his walk was more deliberate. An officer approached the General and stopped directly in front of him.

The soldier saluted the General and said without pause, "General, your council awaits your presence."

The General did not look directly at the soldier. Instead, he stared off into the distance as if he were looking for something that was not there and without emotion said, "Inform the council that I will be there shortly."

The soldier saluted and left for the main command tent—the General's tent. General Valerias had come to hate this part of the campaign—the post battle review. He always enjoyed the strategy planning, coordinating legion personnel and other involved parties, issuing battle commands, and the battle itself. After the battle he had the duty to address casualties, file reports with either Milan or Constantinople, and decide what would be the next course of action.

Today he also had to determine the fates of the prisoners. Managing prisoners of war was typically an easy task for Valerias, assuming there were prisoners. The General had a long history of either executing prisoners caught in the battle or selling them to local mining interests. He knew that sending a prisoner to a mine was just a slower form of execution. That was not his concern, though.

As the General arrived at his tent, his limp was largely gone and his normal, forceful stride had returned. Two guards opened the entrance to the tent, and the General strode inside. The large tent had been divided into multiple rooms. The main room was the council room. The General observed about ten men in the room. They included his second- and third-in-commands, several officers, and a large man with dark-colored skin. The dark man, named Bukarma, was the General's chief bodyguard. The General briefly glanced around the room and moved to take his chair near the west wall of the tent. The men moved forward and sat on the cushions arranged in a semicircle in front of him. Only Bukarma remained standing; he stood by the entrance to the tent looking directly at the General.

The General glared at the men assembled before him and spoke to the man still wearing a helmet. "Battle report."

Braxus spoke hurriedly, as if the battle was about to begin instead of it having ended at midday. General Valerias interrupted Braxus at the end of his second sentence and told him to slow down or go outside and relieve himself first. Braxus apologized to the General for his haste and continued with his report in a slower manner.

Braxus was the General's second-in-command and, like the General, a true Roman. He was tall and slender, thirty-five years old, his face hidden by a cropped black beard. Braxus was not a great warrior, but he had potential as a brilliant strategist. He had served with the General for over fifteen years and was close to the General. However, the General often picked on Braxus because of his mannerisms. The General knew at some point he would retire or die, and he wanted Braxus to replace him. Even at thirty-five, Braxus still was not quite the leader Valerias had hoped he would be. A general of the army not only had to be a good strategist but also a leader of men. Braxus needed work on the second part and thus endured the General's sometimes-pointed proddings.

Braxus finished his report, and the General asked him why the enemy was so easy to defeat. The enemy was from a large group of barbarians that the General lumped into one category—the "Goths." Historically Goths had proven at times to be a worthy foe to the General. This time they were no match for the might of his army, and they had been slaughtered on the battlefield. Braxus did not have a clear answer, yet he hinted that most of the Goths were young men and not seasoned fighters.

The General sat back in his chair and pondered other possible answers to his own question. He tended to focus on the reasonable conclusion that these men were a rogue branch of the Goths. Certainly, he thought, battle-hardened Goth veterans would not have been duped by his fake retreat strategy at the beginning of the battle. The General was a believer in logic, so he chose the most reasonable explanation: that this was a renegade band of Goths. Once this short debate was over in his mind, he requested the casualty report. He knew this would be good news.

The casualty report was to be given by the General's third-in-command, a man called Cratus. Cratus was not of true Roman origin but had been born of parents—reportedly of minor nobility—who had migrated to Italy from Spain when he was a young boy. Cratus entered the army at age fifteen and soon became an officer. He had served as an aide to the General for about ten years and was promoted to the command position of general, subordinate to General Valerias. Cratus was short and stout. He was bold and brash, and occasionally the General had to rein him in to prevent mistakes that could get out of hand.

The men liked Cratus because he was more like them than the aloof Braxus. Cratus was also the more skilled fighter, but he lacked Braxus' overall intellect. The General often thought of Braxus as the shadow and Cratus as the bull. If the General could combine both Braxus and Cratus into one man—then he would have his own double. The General was amused and at the same time troubled by these thoughts, troubled because neither Braxus nor Cratus stood out as ready to be his worthy successor.

Although Braxus and Cratus had differences, they had one common trait: their unquestioned loyalty to the General. In fact, all of the General's officers had been hand picked by the General and were very loyal. The General had to rely on that loyalty, not only because of the external enemies to the Empire but because of his own internal enemies in Constantinople and Milan. Valerias was as about as popular in certain circles in Constantinople as a serpent in the bath. The dislike and even hate of the General permeated certain sectors of the Roman government and the Christian Church.

Even though the Roman Empire had been divided into Western and Eastern parts, the General wanted and had more to do with day-to-day life of the Western Roman Empire. He even maintained a villa in Rome. The Eastern Empire was much less familiar to him. Consequently, he had fewer friends and more enemies in Constantinople. Yet he served both Emperors, Valentinian and Valens, equally and well.

The General did not care about that problem during the council meeting; he focused on the recent battle. He hurried Cratus through the casualty report. Only fifteen Roman soldiers had died, and about fifty-five had taken a variety of wounds. Casualties among the Goths were very heavy. Over five hundred Goths had been killed. This figure included badly wounded Goths who were killed on the spot. About sixty men were captured, and the rest of the Goth forces fled wildly into the countryside.

Valerias congratulated his council on the great victory and then led them in a toast to the victory. The men all shouted to the General, "*Sapor est victoria! Adhuc esurient!*" [Savor the victory! Hunger for more!] This was the motto of Valerias' legions. The General had become visibly more relaxed now than when he had entered the tent.

After the toast was finished, the General asked the assembled council their views of the Goths' aggressiveness. Braxus previously had said he thought it was a renegade branch of the Goths. Valerias silently agreed. "Cratus, what is your theory?" asked the General.

Cratus spoke boldly and without much thought: "It does not matter if they were renegades or not, the Goths must pay for their belligerence. I say we strike at the heart of the Goths now and burn their cities. It would send a statement to the Goths not to betray Rome."

"I do not agree or disagree with either of you," the General said. "However, we must obtain more information before we conclude and do anything about this matter. And I know how to get the information we need. Cratus, instruct the guard to bring me the prisoners. Dusk will be with us soon, and I want to deal with them."

The General ordered the Goth prisoners be lined up outside the tent.

When the General emerged from the tent, the prisoners had been placed into a line that was straight only if one did not look hard at it. Valerias noted many of the prisoners were just adolescents. The presence of the General intimidated them, as his reputation as a ruthless Roman general was renowned. The General stood almost six feet tall and weighed close to 180 pounds. Even at forty-five he had a fitness level of someone ten years younger.

His face wore a cropped brown beard with streaks of gray. "Old age" hairs, the General called them. To many people his most noticeable feature was his dark brown eyes. It was said that his eyes could stop a deer in full stride.

Bukarma accompanied the General outside of the tent. Bukarma posed an even larger figure than the General. A special characteristic of Bukarma was his huge forearms, which were partially wrapped in blue cloth braces. Whereas the General had eyes that glanced in what seemed like every direction, Bukarma held his visual focus in one direction usually for several seconds, before looking in a new one.

The appearances of the General and Bukarma terrified the young Goths. After looking down the line, the General focused on a youthful-appearing Goth. The young man had no facial hair, which gave away his age. The General had a good idea of his age but asked him anyway. The frightened boy hesitated for a few seconds before answering. He spoke softly and said, "Fourteen." The General asked nothing further of that Goth and stepped back to look at the entire set of prisoners.

After a brief pause, the General asked the line of Goths, "Who is your leader?"

There was no immediate response from any of the Goths, although the line shuffled, and several of the prisoners had perspiration beading on their faces.

Valerias repeated, "Again, who is your leader?" This time the General had a little more vigor in his voice.

Again, the Goths did not respond. The shuffling and perspiring were now more notable.

The General anticipated that the young Goths would be scared. He knew they thought they would be executed or sold to the mines as slaves. After all, that was the General's reputation. He could see fear in their eyes and in the way they fidgeted in line. The General, though, was not in a patient mood, and he wanted a quick answer to his question. After a few more moments of silence, he took out his sword and in one quick motion sliced the ear off a young Goth. The boy immediately fell to the ground screaming. The General stabbed at the ear with his sword and flicked it onto the boy.

Valerias then raised his voice to a level just slightly below a shout and said, "I will ask you one more time the question I just asked you, and if I do not get an answer, I will run my sword through one of you. Which one of you will feel my steel, I don't know yet. But I will promise you that there will be no recovering from the wound like your earless friend here. I promise, you will feel death coming for a long time as you bleed out. Now, who is your leader?"

The General knew he totally had the Goths. After a few seconds, a young-looking man in the center right area of the line stepped forward and spoke reluctantly, "I'm the one you want. Do not hurt any more of my men."

The General walked up to the man with his sword point held down and asked, "What is your name?"

"Sivas Gul," was the response.

"You are a flawed man, Sivas Gul. But you are also brave for not sacrificing any of your soldiers so that I could get the information I need. And yet I do not know if your bravery will save you or your men." The General's voice was cold and did not give Gul or any of his men within earshot much comfort.

The General looked closely at the features in Gul's face. They reminded him of someone from his past. He stepped back as his mind raced through his list of enemies from this area. Finally he remembered.

"Are you related to Mostar Gulivus? A clan king of the Goths?" the General asked impatiently. His sword moved to a position more parallel to the ground, striking a more menacing pose.

Gul answered quickly, "Yes, I am his firstborn."

"Does Mostar Gulivus know you are here?"

"He does, but he could not stop us from trying to free our land from Rome's tyranny."

"*Rome's* tyranny?" the General responded. "Did your father not tell you that it was I who gave your people the autonomy you enjoy today? That it was I who saved your people in the first place from a life of displacement and possible slavery, which Rome had decreed? That it was I who let you live in peace with the Empire? That it was I who saved your father's life?"

The General was becoming agitated with Gul. He appeared to be a spoiled son of a king who tried to take on Rome's power without a clue why or how to accomplish the task. Gul's misadventure had ended with the death of hundreds of Goths.

It was not clear to the General whether Gul was operating on his own or with his father's blessing. If it turned out to be the latter, the General decided he would unleash his army to punish the Goth kingdom. If it was the former, Gul would be executed and his fellow prisoners would also be executed or sold into slavery at the mines. At least his initial thoughts were in that direction.

Gul seemed oblivious to the disaster he had caused and its likely aftermath. The General thought Gul was worse than dumb. He had been careless and unprepared for battle. Worst of all, he had insulted the General by proceeding against him with this foolish effort. The General concluded that Gul should be executed. The General then debated whether to bring the matter up to the council for their "approval" or carry out his sentence of his own volition. His internal debate was short. The General decided to issue sentence and carry out executions of Gul and his men. He did not want to waste his time and bother with the mines' owners.

Valerias would execute Gul by his own hand. As the General started to pronounce his sentence, he looked down the roadway from where the prisoners had been brought. What he saw caused the General to momentarily forget about Gul and his sorry band of followers.

III

Joseph

A disheveled figure in chains was being brought up the pathway east of the main tent by two soldiers. The man walked sluggishly and offered no resistance to the soldiers before being placed before the General. He was midsized and appeared to be about thirty years old. The man wore loose-fitting clothes that were torn; dirt and grime masked their color. The man's hair and beard were scraggly and cut in a non-symmetrical manner. He had tired brown eyes. The General looked at the man from his head to his feet.

"You are a Christian priest, are you not?" inquired the General, based on past experience with such men.

"I am a servant of the Lord," the man answered calmly.

"Good," said the General in a tone such that the unkempt man could not tell if it meant a good thing or a bad thing.

The General looked at Cratus and ordered, "Take Gul and his band of pissants to the stockade. I will announce their fate shortly." To Bukarma he said, "Bring the priest inside the tent. I would like to question him further."

The General spoke those words ominously. The priest ignored the General's tone as his mind focused on what was to become of Gul and his survivors.

The General's men knew, though, that the shroud of death hovered over the priest as much as on Gul's men. Several of the men from the preceding council meeting had already returned to the tent. Darkness appeared, and a cool breeze prompted the rest of the men who lingered to also make their way inside. The General noticed a new face.

"Revious, glad you could make at least one of our council meetings," the General spoke in almost a light-hearted manner.

Revious acknowledged the General by responding, "I am more glad to be alive and in one piece than to have made all of your meetings."

Revious was clearly a favorite of the General. He was intelligent and fluent in several languages, including Latin and Goth dialects. Revious was not Roman but an Alan, a people who lived east of the Danube River. He acted as the chief scout for the General's cohorts, and in that position he provided intelligence to the General about whatever enemy was the center point of the General's attention at that time. Revious generally focused on external enemies, but he also kept tabs on potential internal foes.

Revious had a slight build and clean-shaven face. He liked to laugh and on occasion lightly tease the General, although he knew his limits and never exceeded them. When needed, though, Revious could be as cold-blooded as any of the Romans. Revious had a staff of a couple dozen scouts, many of whom were known only to him. Revious had served the General for over fifteen years and had earned Valerias' complete trust.

After speaking with Revious about the recent campaign, the General turned his attention to the priest.

"Tell me, priest, what is your name?" queried the General. His voice showed no feeling, at least on the surface.

"I am Father Joseph, faithful servant of Christ," answered Joseph in a direct tone.

"Good. I know you are a follower of the supposed son of God," the General said, and then added mockingly, "Do you know who I am?

"Yes, you are the Roman General Valerias," Joseph answered.

"That is correct, and how did you know that?" the General inquired again with a seemingly vague interest in the question.

"Because your reputation is well known in the land," Joseph noted without giving much thought to his response.

"What reputation, and what land are you referring to, priest?" The General's intensity in the conversation was now slightly on the rise.

Again Joseph responded rather ambivalently. "You are the commander of legions in this area, and the land I referred to is this area."

"Where are you from?" the General asked as he changed the subject. He already had obtained part of the information he needed from Joseph.

"I am from the southern part of Rome."

Before Joseph could add to his response, the General asked another question. "How far have you traveled outside of Rome?"

"Generally not far. I was a food merchant that stayed in the family shop. But I traveled some with my father. I also trained as a physician."

"Well, you are neither of those now, are you? And you are not close to Rome." The General's tone was becoming serious. "And when did you become a priest?"

"About three years ago."

"And what was the event that caused you to leave your reputable position as a store owner and physician to become a Christian priest?" The General was becoming agitated. Still, Joseph did not seem to pick up on these signals. The council members, though, became quiet, where formerly there had been some chatter. The room waited for Joseph's reply.

"God came to me in a dream and told me to become a Christian and be one who spreads the Good Word, and brings comfort to the oppressed."

"And how did you end up with the Goths?" the General sternly asked. The question was a loaded one, but Joseph gave it little thought in his reply.

"My bishop sent me to save the souls of barbarian Goths," Joseph answered in a matter-of-fact tone.

"Didn't you fear for your life traveling from Rome to outer areas of the Empire? Didn't you feel threatened?"

"Oh no, not at all. I was treated as a messenger of God and Christ and the Church. I was wholly accepted by the Goths." Joseph seemed almost like he was reading a report to his superiors.

The General did not like this condescending attitude and asked, "Then to be a good Christian priest, you must believe in peace among the people."

"I do believe in peace—"

Before Joseph could utter another word, the General pointedly asked, "Then why are you traveling with a band of Goths to wage war on Rome?"

"I—" Joseph began to answer, but he was immediately cut off by Valerias, who followed up angrily, "Did you not know this was a Goth war party that was committing itself to battle with my army? Did you not know that blood would be spilled here today when you left with the Goths? I want to know, priest, was Mostar Gulivus involved in this conspiracy against Rome, or was it the fool Gul's own plot?"

Joseph finally realized he was in trouble. The extent of the trouble was still unclear to him, but he was now worried. Joseph had heard about General Valerias and his infamous treatment of his enemies both outside and inside the Empire. Still, he did not believe he was in mortal danger. After all, he did not think the General would actually harm a member of the Church, regardless of what he had heard. Joseph assumed he would probably get a verbal reprimand and be sent packing back to Rome. So he decided to call the General's bluff.

"General, I am a simple follower of Christ on a mission to convert lost souls. I see no harm in helping show the non-converted the way of God." The priest tried to put his best effort forward by being persuasive and calm. However, the turbulence in his stomach was another story. Joseph's hand also twitched, and the General observed this. Joseph stopped talking and waited for the General to respond.

"So you decided not to answer my question, priest," the words slithered off of the General's tongue. "Refusing to answer indicates to me you are an enemy of Rome and Constantinople. Now, I will give you one more chance to answer—was it Mostar Gulivus or his son, Gul, who was responsible for this pathetic attempt today?" The General's manner was strangely calm.

Joseph, as a servant of God in a newly Christian Empire, again assumed nothing traumatic would happen to him. He knew, though, that as the questioning by the General continued, the dialogue had become more of an interrogation.

Joseph decided to be coy and nervously said, "What does it matter?"

"Because it will determine whether I attack the Goth clan of Mostar Gulivus. You will assist me in my assessment, or I will have no choice but to execute you as a traitor to the Empire and then destroy the Goth clan. The choice is yours, priest." The General spoke sternly as he issued those words.

Joseph noted that the council room of the General was eerily silent. All eyes of the council fixated on him and the General. Joseph concluded his only way out of this bad situation was to again bluff and see if the General would let him go.

Joseph summoned all his courage and forcefully said, "I am a Christian priest, a citizen of Rome, and a man of God. I have only to answer to my superiors in Rome and to God. You will now excuse me, as I need to tend to the wounded Goths."

With those words, Joseph turned and moved toward the entrance of the tent.

He had taken two steps when he felt a great weight on his back, and he went crashing to the floor of the tent. In one motion he felt an arm around his abdomen lifting him up about a foot off the ground. Something pressed against his neck. Joseph squirmed to get out of this grip, but he was pulled even tighter against a strong body. Joseph didn't know what had happened. Then he felt the General's hot breath and heard the voice in his ear.

The General's temper had engulfed him. "You answer only to God—that is what you said—now let God come and save you!"

The blade of a knife pressed up against the throat of the priest. "Where is your God, priest? Where is he?" To Joseph, the rage emanating from the General seemed to be everywhere. He was now completely terrified. The blade pushed harder against his throat and Joseph realized he was about to have his throat slit, like a sacrificial calf. He lost track of what the General was shouting except for the spit landing on the side of his face. He went limp like a deer when the lion had broken its back and would soon die. Joseph tried saying a prayer, but it went nowhere. His last thoughts were of home and why he had decided to become a priest. He was a weak man, and now he was going to die.

In full rage, the General shouted, "I curse you, your presence here, your fake religion! You are as worthless as the shit from my dogs! It ends now!"

The General pulled the priest's chin up. He would make one swift cut across the throat and then toss the priest out of the tent to bleed to death. He wanted to kill this obnoxious priest, and yet his anger was caused by more than the priest. Joseph was the handy target.

As the General began to initiate the cut, he looked to his left. A hooded figure stood in the background, out of the way, but still very much apparent. The General gazed at the figure and the figure looked back at him. After a few seconds, the General peered down at the priest who was now totally limp. Valerias pulled the knife away from Joseph's head. He lifted the priest off of the ground and kicked him toward the entrance to the tent. Joseph went sprawling on the ground.

The General shouted, "Get this piece of garbage out of here! Throw him in with the livestock! I will deal with him tomorrow."

The General's guards pulled Joseph from the ground and carried him out of the tent. As they were leaving, the General, still enraged, threw his knife into the tent post near the priest's head. It missed by inches. As he threw the knife, the General screamed as if his prey had escaped. The General then turned slowly and walked back to his chair. As he sat down, he shouted, "Out!" The council, which had not moved during this event, filed quickly out of the tent. After a few minutes of sitting in the chair and soaking in deep breaths, the General again turned toward the hooded figure and nodded slightly. The figure slipped out of the tent into the oncoming night.

IV

Jacob

Two Roman guards hustled a limp Joseph down the slope from the General's tent. He was aware of his surroundings but could not move. The Romans carried him with his full weight resting on their shoulders. It was a walk of several hundred yards, but Joseph was oblivious; he felt that he was on his old horse running through a meadow.

In his earlier life, Joseph had a horse, and he would ride, sometimes all day. A shallow smile peeked out on Joseph's ashen face as he thought of his horse. Joseph took turns between reality and dreaming as the three men passed by tents of the infantry and then a corral of horses for the cavalry. They kept moving down a trail, with branches from bushes waving in their faces.

The Romans took Joseph past a group of servants who ceased talking when they approached. Joseph appeared like a sack of grain to them. He didn't care, though, as he rode his horse and enjoyed the ride. Suddenly the ride ended when they stopped at a pen. A number of swine were milling about in the dark quiet. Joseph's jolt back to reality was numbing as the odor of the swine invaded his nostrils. His old horse now faded into the darkness.

Fear again began to permeate Joseph's thoughts. He remembered in his younger days that he had heard swine, when left alone with a wounded or weak person, would tear the person to shreds and feast on the remains. The Romans began to open the gate and push Joseph inside. His fear was now a panic, and he began straining against the Romans. Joseph's sole thought was that he would rather be killed by the monster Valerias than be eaten by swine. Just as he was about to be tossed inside the pen, a voice came out of nowhere and gave a command. "Stop."

The soldier on the right turned to face the voice.

"By command of General Valerias, do not place this man into the pen. Instead, take him back to the servant camp."

The soldier knew the voice, and as the figure came nearer, he recognized the man under the hood. The soldier did not complain or disagree with the order. "Yes," was all the soldier said.

They retraced their steps to the servant camp with Joseph again carried between the two soldiers. The hooded figure followed behind.

Once they reached the outskirts of the servant camp, the figure said, "Put him over by that tree." The soldiers complied.

The figure requested two servants who had been watching nearby, "Bring me bedding for this man and also a bowl of water and a separate cup of water." The servants disappeared into the dark.

The hooded figure turned to the soldiers. "Return to the large, smooth rock fifty yards up the trail and wait for me there. I will join you shortly and we will return to camp."

As soon as the soldiers were gone, the servants returned with the items the hooded figure had ordered.

The figure then spoke to the servants, "Prepare his bedding so that he may sleep tonight. Take a clean cloth and wash his face with the water from the bowl. Give him all the water he would like to drink in the cup."

He took out two coins and gave each servant a coin. He then walked over to Joseph and knelt by Joseph's head. He spoke softly into Joseph's face.

"I am Jacob, Chief Administrator to the General. You were very fortunate tonight, as you are still alive. Tomorrow the General's guards will come for you. You will then have another audience with the General. If you want to live another day and accomplish what you would like to do with the rest of your life, you will be humble, apologetic, and, most important, sincere in your response to his questions. Do not bring your Christianity in any form to the General. If you do what I tell you, you will live; if not, not even God will save you. It is up to you."

At that moment, two new Roman guards arrived at the site.

Jacob spoke to them. "Protect him from others and himself tonight. In the morning, the General's guards will come for him. For your sakes, I hope he remains alive."

Jacob left into the night, just like the horse Joseph imagined earlier. The two guards stood by Joseph, their long spears extended into the dark night. The two servants returned with more supplies. They prepared a sleeping area. Then they washed his face, gently dabbing the reddish area on the neck caused by the knife's indentation. Joseph was offered a cup of water, which he drank quickly. The cup was refilled and he drank, more slowly this time, enjoying each swallow of the very cold water. Joseph closed his eyes, heard the two soldiers talking first to the servants and then to themselves. He fell into a deep sleep, as he was exhausted.

Joseph's night was filled with images and dreams; many of them were nightmares, other dreams were bizarre. At one point he thought he heard an angel speaking, but not to him, or to anyone else he could see.

The angel said, "Your servant must obey the word of General Valerias." Then the angel turned in the direction of Joseph and said, "Your time has not yet come to an end—you have other tasks to fulfill."

Joseph woke briefly from this dream and saw that the two soldiers were talking to someone in the dark. At that time he could not remember if the conversation he had heard with the angel was actually with an angel or with the Roman soldiers. He was confused, troubled, and tired. For the rest of the night he lay awake, or thought he was awake.

When Jacob returned to the General's tent, he found the General in his chair slowly eating a slice of bread and drinking a cup of water. This was odd, because the General usually had wine before bed. Jacob observed the General in the same position as when he had left. The one exception was that the knife was no longer in the pole. Instead it was on a small table by the right hand of the General. When the General took a drink, the knife became exposed.

Without looking at Jacob, the General asked, "Is he alive?"

"Yes," answered Jacob.

The General continued, "Is he well cared for?"

"Yes," Jacob repeated.

"You saved this traitor to Rome, Jacob. I hope he knows how close he was to death and rethinks his tone and attitude with me—or I will personally end his time on Earth and believe me, his God will not save him. If he is fortunate and does live, you will be responsible for him."

"Thank you for your mercy, General. I too await his appearance tomorrow."

The General had had enough of the day. He stood up and started to his night chambers. After three steps, he turned around and walked back to the table and picked up his knife.

He glanced at Jacob and said, "Good night. Tomorrow will be interesting—a day of reckoning for our prisoners . . . all of them."

With that statement, the General went to bed. He too would experience a restless night.

Before dawn emerged from the cold night, the General had awakened and toured the camp. Most of his men were asleep, but the guards, in both the outer perimeter and the inner perimeter, were solidly awake. Whoever was on guard duty knew that to fall asleep meant death. To allow an enemy access to the camp meant likely death for camp occupants. Therefore, the General viewed a sleeping guard as equivalent to a breach of camp security, resulting in the forfeiture of the guard's life.

The General's aides, including his spies and even the General himself, would frequently inspect the perimeters and status of the guards. More than one guard who had fallen to the temptress of sleep had been put to death. The General engaged in small talk with several of the guards, some of whom he had known for years. The General returned to his tent at sunrise. There he was met by Bukarma, who was obviously upset.

"General, if I'm to serve as your guard, you must tell me when and where you go. There may be assassins in the ranks who would like to have the chance to kill you. I don't have to remind you that there are many in Milan and more in Constantinople who want and pray for your death."

"Your concern is warranted," the General responded, looking straight into Bukarma's eyes. "But don't tell me what I can or cannot do. I am the General. If you are to be my primary guard, you should be awake all day and night."

Bukarma took a slight step back and seemed bothered by the General's response. "Your safety is my sole concern, General. It would help if you let me or one of my guards know when you leave your command tent."

"Yes," was all the General said, his eyes never leaving Bukarma's eyes.

A very small smile appeared briefly on the corners of the mouth of the General as he turned to his chair. Bukarma knew what the General meant. He briskly returned to his primary guard location, at the entrance to the tent, in a less agitated state.

Jacob had also risen early. As Chief Administrator to the General, he had to attend to numerous tasks. One was to check on the wounded and give a report to the General on the state of any injured officers. Valerias was extremely loyal to his men, and the loyalty was returned. Jacob and those under him were also responsible for the supplies, including food, brought to the General's legions.

The General believed in keeping his men well fed and provided with the best weapons. Part of the responsibility of maintaining the armory was given to Bukarma when he wasn't acting as the primary guard to the General. It was known that Bukarma was a master with weapons. The General was well aware of Jacob's and Bukarma's assets, and he had given both of them appropriate staffs to manage all aspects of satisfactorily supplying his legions.

The General had a small breakfast, brought to him by one of his trusted servants. Poisoning was an ongoing concern with the General's staff. Thus, food safety was another of Jacob's tasks.

The General finished breakfast and called to Bukarma to leave his post and obtain his game. Bukarma returned with a small cloth bag and emptied the contents on the table. The contents were an odd mix of stones, bones, and polished sticks with a scattering of silver and gold pieces. Bukarma brought another chair over to the table, and they proceeded to play an odd game that only the two knew how to play. Jacob thought it was a game Bukarma had brought from Africa, but he wasn't sure. Whatever its origin was, it kept the General occupied for almost an hour. At the end Valerias called Bukarma too smart for his own game, and after a few friendly and boisterous comments between the two, Bukarma carefully placed the contents back into the bag and gave the bag to a servant. He then returned to his primary guard position at the entranceway into the tent.

Morning had become the General's best time of the day, a time when he appeared almost happy. As the day progressed, he became more serious and less accepting of anyone except his most trusted advisors, and even they had learned to tread softly around him in the afternoon and especially at night. If someone wanted to approach the General, it was best to do so in the morning. Unfortunately for Joseph, his initial time with the General had been in the early evening when the darkness was not just a feature of nature outside the tent.

V

INTERROGATION

BY THE TIME the game with Bukarma had ended, the morning sun had triumphed over the haze that blanketed the low-lying areas. The General knew the longer he kept the priest waiting, the more nervous Joseph would be.

However, he also knew it was time, and he spoke to Bukarma, "Have the priest brought to me. It is time to see what fate he has chosen."

Joseph had awakened at dawn. At first he was calm and said his morning prayers, thinking more of what was to come than of God. Joseph thought he was hungry, but by the time food was brought to him, his mind had wandered back to the previous night and his near-death experience. His stomach churned. He tried to eat and failed. The ensuing vomiting showed Joseph that he was in a state of fear. He knew he would die this morning, and praying did not help his situation. He felt sorry for himself. Why had he left Rome and his comfortable lifestyle? And why was his faith so weak?

While running these thoughts through his head, Joseph failed to notice his two guards from the night standing straight at attention. The General's private guards had arrived and walked over to Joseph.

"Up," was all one said to Joseph.

The other guard seemed annoyed and told Joseph, "Come with us now. The General demands to see you."

Joseph started to get up; however, his efforts were too slow for the guards and they yanked him to his feet.

The guard who had first spoken said to the night guards, "We have the prisoner. Your task is complete. You may return to your unit."

One could feel the soldiers' relief. If something had happened to the priest, they would likely have been severely punished. Once Joseph was up, the two guards gave him alternating pushes in the back. The faster they retrieved the priest for the General, the better it would be for them. Escorting a weak priest was not the favorite task of elite guards.

The sun turned bright as Joseph and the two guards made their way up to the General's tent. The wind was calm, and even the camp was fairly quiet. Joseph looked around and saw very little movement, giving him even more discomfort.

Joseph became lost in self-pity. *Why am I in this position?* he thought. *All I want to do is help people in a Christian way and not end up on the end of a madman's knife. Why did I come with that Goth, Gul, when I should have stayed in the Goths' village and provided assistance to Mostar Gulivus?*

Time seemed to go by too fast—like a hungry man devouring a meal after days of fasting. There was no taste and then the meal was over. Now they were at the General's tent. One of the guards entered the tent while the second guard stood on Joseph's right side. The guard was a large man who had a jagged scar on his right forearm. After a few moments the first guard emerged from the tent; then he and the other guard who had stood next to

Joseph tied the flaps back, creating a large entranceway into the tent. Joseph thought this was his path into hell.

Once the tent entranceway was secured, Bukarma emerged and the two guards moved to stand behind Joseph. Joseph had forgotten how big a man Bukarma was, as the daylight made him even larger. The two guards were also impressive in stature, but Bukarma was exceptional. In Bukarma's right hand was a spear that matched his size. Joseph was impressed and terrified at the same time.

Bukarma spoke without looking at Joseph. "General Valerias will see you," and, after a slight pause, he added with chilling effect, "now."

Joseph walked into the tent like a man clearly headed for his death. His shoulders stooped and his head looked down. Bukarma was right behind him, followed by the two guards. Most of the General's council members were not present. An officer stood to the side behind the General; it was Braxus. The room was half lit. The General was seated, and Joseph was brought in front of him. A small chair was placed behind Joseph. The General gruffly told Joseph to sit, and he did. Joseph's eyes were downcast. When he sat down, he saw the knife laying flat on the small table to the side and a little in front of the General. The blade of the knife faced Joseph, and the perfectly shined finish seemed to stand out in the gloom of the tent. Joseph knew the knife was meant for him, and he could not stop looking at it.

"You seem to like my blade, priest," said the General in an ambiguous voice.

Joseph knew he was doomed, but a small amount of courage returned and he looked the General in the eyes and said, "No" in a soft voice, "I do not."

Joseph thought those were the last words he would say, and he kept looking at the General. Then he noticed a smaller figure behind and to the right of the General. It was Jacob. Joseph remembered his conversation with Jacob during the previous night. As a result, Jacob had given something to Joseph that he had abandoned—hope.

"I trust you were safe and comfortable last night." This was a statement and not a question from both the General's and Joseph's viewpoints.

"I understand you were not put in with the swine, but had a location all alone, and servants brought you food, water and blankets," the General continued without giving Joseph a chance to reply.

"And I understand my guards protected you last night from any number of dangers. You lived the life of a general."

The General then sat in silence. It was time for Joseph to respond.

"Yes," followed by a short pause, "General."

Joseph decided this was not the time to engage in any kind of debate with the General, because he would lose with his life.

The General then said something that caught Joseph by surprise.

"Is today the day you become a martyr for your cause, priest? Because if you do, I promise your martyrdom will be over quickly. You will be forgotten on the day you became a martyr."

Joseph instantly saw this as a clue that he might not die today. He indeed did not want to become a martyr today. He was just getting started in his new calling. And he did not want to die.

Joseph answered, "I apologize to the General for my lack of foresight in accompanying the Goths when they came to make war upon you. I should not have done that. I also apologize for my tone with you yesterday and—"

The General interrupted him, "Do you apologize to Rome, as well, for your insolent behavior?"

Joseph was not prepared for this question, because he had focused on the General and not Rome.

"Ahhh," was Joseph's initial stammered response, followed by "I thought you were Rome?"

"Oh, I am, in many ways, and in many ways not."

Joseph had no idea what this meant. He gave the General a quizzical look, but he saw that the General's hand now held the knife up from its resting position on the table.

Valerias then asked, "Why were you with the Goth, Gul, when they tried to attack my army?"

"I made a mistake. I should have stayed behind at the main village."

"That is true, priest, and then you would not be here today, in front of me as I decide your fate."

The General continued, "Where was Mostar Gulivus when you undertook your fantasy adventure? Did he give the orders for Gul to launch his attack? I can't believe that he did, but I want *you* to tell me."

Joseph stated that was not the case. Mostar Gulivus had traveled to the eastern part of the Goth territory following up on word of a new threat to the Goth kingdom, from a people called the Huns.

"Why didn't you tell me this last night? That was not wise, particularly for an educated priest." The General's tone was scornful.

After a few moments of silence, the General conferred with Braxus and then Jacob. Then he spoke to Joseph.

"I will give you a choice, priest." The General was playing with the knife as he talked. "You can be a martyr right now, or you can serve as an assistant to my Chief Physician. And when he does not need your help, you will do whatever my Chief Administrator tells you to do."

The General looked deep into Joseph's eyes as he finished his statement. Joseph looked back at the General tentatively. He was clearly showing signs of nervousness. And he knew what he was going to say.

"General, I choose the latter."

A short pause ensued as the General fiddled with his knife, then he spoke. "Wise choice, priest. Jacob will take you to my Chief Physician, Olivertos, so you can begin your duties. And let me warn you, if you engage in proselytizing any of my soldiers, servants or anyone else, I will have you executed on the spot. I will then hang your corpse for sixty days or until your body rots from the rope. And just so you know, if your answers would have been unsatisfactory to me today, you would be dead at this time. I've also decided to let Gul and his pathetic Goths live for now."

The General sat back in his chair. "And here is another demand: you are not to engage in any contact with Gul or any of the other Goths. Guards, take the priest to Olivertos." He turned around and looked at Jacob and then at Joseph as he was being led out of the tent and made one final comment. "Priest, I find it ironic that you have a Guardian Angel and he is a Jew."

Joseph said nothing and was taken out of the General's tent by the same two guards who had brought him there. As they started down the trail, Jacob joined the group. The group walked for several minutes without a word. Finally, Joseph broke the silence.

"Why did you do this for me and save me from—"

Jacob cut him off, curtly saying, "Death. Because I could tell that you would be of assistance to the General."

Jacob had now moved parallel to Joseph and shook his head slightly at Joseph. Jacob knew Joseph was going to say something that would be unflattering or even insulting about the General. The two guards walking in front would hear Joseph's comment, report it to the General, and Joseph would soon be hanging from a tree. Joseph understood the error he was about to commit and quickly answered to get out of his potential predicament.

"I understand," said Joseph.

Jacob dismissed the soldiers when they were within a short distance of the Chief Physician's tent.

"I'll take the priest from here. Return to the General's tent; he will give me no problem." With that, the guards briskly walked away.

Joseph said, "I do not understand. Why did General Valerias spare me?"

"Two reasons. First, he thinks you can provide value to his army—with your experience in medicine and also as a merchant. Second, for me. I went out on a limb for you. Do not let me down. If you prove me wrong, you will die, and any future person like yourself will not be spared from his wrath. I will only receive a verbal reprimand on how he was right about you and I was wrong. But you will be dead. I hope you listened to the General very closely, because right now you are walking on an unsteady and slippery bridge, and a misstep would cause your demise at any time. Help Olivertos and help me and live."

Olivertos came out of the tent at that moment. He looked first at Joseph and then to Jacob. "Is this my new assistant?"

"Yes. His name is Joseph," answered Jacob. "He says he has medical training, so I hope he can be useful. Please provide him with sleeping quarters at the end of the day. I will send for him in five days' time to introduce him to our accounting methods."

"I see," Olivertos said. "I suppose if he is good, we will have to play the game in which the winner gets to keep him." Olivertos smiled at his remark.

"I think he will be a shared commodity." Jacob also smiled and turned to Joseph. "Do well and remember the General's words and incorporate that in your faith."

With those words, Jacob said good-bye to Olivertos and Joseph and started walking back to the General's tent.

Olivertos looked at Jacob and then at Joseph. "He is a good man. You are a fortunate man. Come inside my tent. We have work to do."

Joseph was tired, but he felt calm for the first time in several days.

VI

Olivertos

JOSEPH WORKED WITH Olivertos for five days. During that time Olivertos became impressed with Joseph's skill as a physician, although he lacked a senior surgeon's skills. He had been trained well in Rome. The patients during this time were mostly Roman soldiers, and their injuries were primarily minor cuts and bruises. After the Romans had been taken care of, Olivertos looked at a few of the Goths who could be helped. The Goths' injuries were on the whole much more serious than those of the Romans, which reflected the outcome of the battle. Joseph wondered why they were even helping the Goths. The General seemed to have no tolerance for providing aid to the enemy. This thought led Joseph to the question, *wouldn't the General execute Olivertos if he found out the physician was aiding prisoners?*

Olivertos anticipated Joseph's question and volunteered an answer. "Healthy prisoners will bring value to Rome when they are sold to the mine owners. I don't think General Valerias wants to execute them as long as they bring money to the army."

Olivertos asked why Joseph had given up being a physician and became a Christian priest. In his answer, Joseph was careful. He remembered the last words he had with Jacob and limited his comments to the effect that he had simply received a calling to his current position. Joseph did not know whether Olivertos was a spy for the General. If there was a hint of Joseph proselytizing to Olivertos, his staff, any of the wounded Romans, or even the Goths, he feared his execution would be imminent.

To change the subject, Joseph emphasized to Olivertos that he also had been a merchant with his family business and helped manage the accounting part of the business. Olivertos did not press Joseph further on the subject because he was not a spy for the General and because he didn't care; there were more important things to address. Thus, Joseph and Olivertos spent most of their time discussing medicine and practicing the best procedures for their patients. This resulted in lively discussions. Joseph had experience with several herbal remedies that were unfamiliar to Olivertos. And Olivertos used special surgical techniques that Joseph had not seen. Both men shared a strong desire for continuing improvement, and they began helping each other become better physicians.

Joseph found Olivertos to be a rough man. He was well into his late thirties, and he already had a premature white beard and hair. Olivertos, like Braxus, had served with the General for over fifteen years. In that time he had seen horrific scenes in his hospital. On such occasions he could not treat many of the wounded soldiers, as their injuries were too great, and as a result, they died, sometimes horribly. Olivertos had been around the thick rope of death so often that it had changed him. Much of his compassion for patients had been buried. He had assistants, but none of them lasted long. When he had begun military service, Olivertos' sense of humor was well known. Now it was a flicker of what it had been. The arrival of Joseph at the hospital had been a blessing. Their discussions on medicine and Rome had brought Olivertos slivers of feeling good about himself and his practice. His sense of humor returned.

Jacob appeared at Olivertos' tent early on the sixth day. The day was overcast, but the clouds would not yield rain. Olivertos and Joseph were already up and had examined the remaining patients in the hospital tent. There were no Goths in the tent, as they had all been sent back to the stockade at dusk of the previous night. The Goths were prisoners, and the hospital did not have guards, so for the safety of the hospital staff, the prisoners were taken back to the guarded area every night.

"Good morning, you two," Jacob said, announcing himself to Olivertos and Joseph.

"Well, look who is up. I thought one of the General's best could sleep in and watch the day away," countered Olivertos.

"No, we spend our days fixing all the problems, like the ones you cause."

It was clear to Joseph that the two men were friends and had known each other for a long time. Jacob had shown up at the hospital tent at various times over the previous several days, and he and Olivertos had gently sparred on each occasion. This time, though, Jacob wanted something.

"Old fool," Jacob said after their usual verbal jousting, "I need to borrow your partner for a few days. The General wants to see how Joseph performs with some of my duties."

"That is sad," noted Olivertos. "He could be here doing real work and you want him to help you, even though you have a very capable staff, while my staff is so limited. Sounds to me like someone needs more time to sleep, or even worse, daydream."

"We are busy all the time. You know, doing all the logistics for the General is very time consuming. Besides, I don't even see a patient—Roman or Goth—here with you. I think you are the one who is sleeping, or, worse yet, trying your potions on the unsuspecting."

"Good, then you won't mind trying a little something I conjured up last night. It turns ordinary men into jackasses—or is it the other way around?"

"No, I don't mind, but first you look in a mirror. I think I see some large ears forming—even larger than the ones on your head now. You are already there!"

Both men laughed and Joseph smiled. He liked these two men and wondered how good men like Jacob and Olivertos could work for the General, whom Joseph considered a tyrant at best and monster at worst. Joseph contemplated this contrast, but kept it to himself.

At the end of their conversation, Jacob told Olivertos that Joseph would do a split detail between them. For one week he would work for Jacob and the next week he would help Olivertos. Joseph's talents could thus be used by both men.

Olivertos feigned unhappiness with the situation and said, "I suppose I could complain, but that probably would not be the wisest choice."

"I too do not think 'complain' and 'wise' go together in this instance," answered Jacob. "I suppose I'm forced to agree with you on this one."

Both men laughed again. Finally, Jacob turned to Joseph and said, "You have an extra day here with the old physician. I will send a guard for you tomorrow at dawn. Be ready, and he will take you to our main supply tent. I will meet you there."

Jacob turned to Olivertos and took a slight bow. He then spoke to Joseph but aimed his words at Olivertos. "I trust you can survive his craziness until tomorrow morning."

"He will go crazy with your damn books. The real innovative work is here as a physician." And with that statement, Jacob bowed slightly again to Olivertos and exited the tent.

"He saved you, you know," Olivertos said, looking at Joseph, becoming serious. "Come on. Let's finish up some of the work we started. I won't see you for a week."

Joseph asked Olivertos what he had meant with that comment. Olivertos just shrugged and said he needed to get the answer directly from Jacob. Joseph had been around Olivertos enough to know that was the end of that discussion. After a few awkward moments of silence, Olivertos announced to Joseph he had some new herbal medicine that he wanted to show him.

Later Joseph had a restless night. He recalled his life being saved, although he had not seen Jacob when the General had the knife to his throat. He also had never heard a voice saying stop. Joseph knew he had to ask Jacob what he had done and to thank him for his help in persuading the General to spare his life. Joseph received his opportunity sooner than he thought it would happen.

At dawn the next morning the sun erupted from its nightly pause, showering the horizon with sword-like rays, a seldom-seen, brilliant morning. Joseph was up early with his possessions at his side as he waited for the guard that Jacob said would come for him. His possessions had dramatically increased due to Olivertos' generosity. Joseph now had a couple changes of clothing, better sandals, and various other items to make life more livable. At the same time he did not want to convey signs he had come upon better times. Joseph thanked God for his two blessings: the clothing and other material items and, most important, for being alive.

Joseph thought that maybe his fortune had changed when Jacob and not a guard showed up at Olivertos' tent. Olivertos was still asleep, so Jacob spoke quietly. "I thought I would walk you up to the main tent complex, because there are some things I thought we should discuss."

"I have a few questions that I would also like to ask you," countered Joseph, although this was spoken meekly.

"I know what you are going to ask," Jacob interrupted Joseph's pause, "and I'm asking you to hold off on your questions for a later time. I have more urgent issues to discuss with you that will determine your future. That is why I and not the guard came to escort you up to my main supply tent."

For the first time in several days, Joseph started to feel uneasy. He let Jacob continue without saying anything further as they began to walk to Jacob's tent.

"You are returning to the area near the General's main tent, but you will be staying in my quarters for now. The rules the General laid out to you last week are fully in force. He gives Olivertos more leeway to conduct his business than other army personnel. And that is why Olivertos is stationed in a different area, away from the General. That way the General can avoid some of the impertinence Olivertos sometimes expresses or does. If Olivertos was stationed nearer to the General and the General saw what Olivertos was doing, it could end badly for Olivertos. Besides that, the General knows Olivertos and his staff are an excellent physician and surgeon group, and he wants that excellence to continue. The General always puts his men first. And lastly, Olivertos is the General's friend. The General and he have been together for more than fifteen years.

"You, on the other hand, are still walking along the edge of staying alive or facing an ending that you may not choose. My advice to you is keep your head down and focus on the tasks that you have been assigned. And most important, do not start a conversation with the General, and never, never, never argue or debate him. I hope you understand what I'm telling you. If you do, you will be allowed to live and be of great assistance to Olivertos and me."

"How do you know this, that I can be an asset to you and Olivertos?" questioned Joseph.

"Because we can tell you have strengths—you are not a meek priest. Anyone who rides with the ill-fated Goths against the General has certain characteristics we do not usually associate with Christian priests. And you seem willing to learn from your mistakes."

"When you say 'we,' do you mean you and Olivertos? Do you also include the General?" queried Joseph.

"Now, that is for you to find out on your own—I do not speak for 'we,' I only speak for me. I do not speak for Olivertos, and I certainly do not speak for the General."

The remainder of the walk to the main tents proceeded in silence, with Joseph deep in thought.

VII

MOSTAR GULIVUS

As Jacob and Joseph reached the area of tents that surrounded the command tents, there was a flurry of activity. Several dozen soldiers moved briskly in what appeared to be a community based on chaos. However, from Joseph's singular view, the action was organized and purposeful. A large soldier several feet away from Jacob and Joseph was issuing straightforward commands. Joseph thought briefly that this action reminded him of bees swarming around the queen of a hive.

The men were putting on full dress armor with sword, spear, and oval shields. Joseph wondered what event had caused this activity—was the camp under attack? Was the General ordering a surprise drill? The men who occupied the tents nearest to the command tents were the General's primary bodyguards, and any action taken by them was an indication that something had or was about to occur.

A man, not a soldier, ran up to Jacob. He acted subservient and whispered in Jacob's ear for a couple of minutes, then took off up the hill to the command tents.

"What did he say to you?" Joseph asked quietly.

"That man is one of my servants. He had been down the hill by the creek when someone yelled that riders are approaching."

Jacob continued, "There are five riders coming from the east. The front rider carries a white flag. The second rider carries another flag, the flag of the Goths, the flag of Mostar Gulivus. We must hurry to the main command tent. This will be interesting for you, Joseph. But remember what we just talked about."

Jacob and Joseph arrived at the main tent area and noticed two lines of Roman soldiers in full battle dress flanking both sides of the main road that ran through the camp to the command tents. The reflection from their shields gleamed in sunlight that almost hypnotized Joseph. Jacob said, "The General's guard can mobilize extremely fast, as you are a witness to."

"How many soldiers are in those lines?" inquired Joseph, still tantalized by the formation. The Goths he had stayed with were highly disorganized compared to what he observed about the Romans.

"About four hundred soldiers," Jacob answered in a monotone. He had seen such events several times.

Mostar Gulivus and his four associate riders had arrived at the base of the camp. The men all dismounted in unison. Five slaves immediately rushed out and grabbed the reins of the horses. However, one of the Goths was still in the process of dismounting, and the fast motion of the slave caused the horse to jerk back and almost throw off its rider. The rider yelled something and hooked his leg back over the horse to regain his balance. A Roman guard who was not part of the formation appeared and gave the slave a quick hit with what looked like a small club. The slave fell to his knees as the guard cursed him. An order was given and the slave picked himself off the ground and grabbed the reins of the horse. The Goth then dismounted, and he too said something that must have been derogatory to the slave.

Joseph felt a tinge of sorrow for the slave, but Jacob interrupted his thoughts. "The slave is fortunate. There have been times when such an offense would be dealt with by flogging."

The five Goths proceeded up the road. Joseph noted the man in the front was older, his beard mostly gray. He was not particularly tall, but he was burly. Joseph could tell he was the leader by the way the other four men walked behind him and because of the very noticeable tunic draped on his soldiers. The tunic was made from the skin of a large predatory animal that that appeared to be a species of cat.

Jacob spoke the obvious to Joseph. "The front man is Mostar Gulivus, king of a clan of Goths, part of the nation of Goths."

Jacob observed Joseph's interest in the tunic and continued, "The tunic is lion skin." After a short pause and no response from Joseph, Jacob added, "From Africa."

Joseph followed the Goths up the road and outside the lines of Roman soldiers. He thought to himself, *Mostar Gulivus is fearless; I wish I had followed him instead of Gul when I stayed with the Goths.*

Just then Joseph's eyes caught movement to the left. General Valerias had emerged from his tent with Bukarma. Braxus and three other guards stood outside the tent and awaited the arrival of Mostar Gulivus. Cratus was observed down the hill escorting the Goths to the General's tent. The area had grown silent, when minutes earlier controlled pandemonium was the rule. As the procession grew nearer, Jacob whispered into Joseph's ear, "Come with me, *now*." Joseph turned and followed Jacob up a short path to the General's tent.

"I need you to be absolutely silent and stay in the background. You will want to see this."

Joseph nodded and followed Jacob to an opening at the rear of the tent where two guards were standing. Jacob said something to the guard on the right, who opened a small entranceway that was a little more than the size of a small man.

Joseph and Jacob squeezed through the opening and proceeded through a couple of rooms. As they entered the main tent, Jacob told Joseph to remain in a back corner. From this corner, Joseph could see the entire main area of the tent, but it would be hard to see him from that spot. Joseph was nervous. But his trust in Jacob was genuine, so he relaxed as much as his racing thoughts would let him.

At the main entrance of the tent, the Goths had arrived along with their Roman escorts. The General greeted Mostar Gulivus, and each grabbed the other's forearm in some sort of an arm salute. The General then invited Mostar Gulivus into the tent, while the remainder of the Goths settled outside. Braxus and Cratus also entered into the tent. The General offered the Goth a seat and a drink of mead. Jacob brought the drinks out himself and gave one to each man. Joseph was surprised to see Jacob performing a servant's work.

Suddenly Mostar Gulivus said directly to Jacob, "Greetings, Jacob. I hope the General here is treating you well."

"As always, King Gulivus, although I continue to wait for him to sign my retirement papers." Jacob smiled when he made that statement.

Mostar Gulivus' title had always been a question to the Romans—Chief or King? That didn't matter to the General; to him, Mostar Gulivus was the unquestioned leader of a band of Tervingi Goths.

"Then we will all be old men when that happens!" Mostar Gulivus laughed as he spoke.

"Hell, you are already old," the General said, looking at both men.

And they answered in unison, "Who?"

The three men then broke out into true laughter. Joseph didn't know what to think. Mortal enemies and the chief accountant, a Jew, acting like best friends—this did not make sense.

Once the laughter was over and the small talk between the three died out, the General spoke directly to Mostar Gulivus. "I know why you are here. You want to know if your son is alive or dead, and if alive, what is to become of him! And if he is here—you want to have him back, correct?"

"Yes, and the other men too," Mostar Gulivus replied.

"You are aware of what your son did, are you not?" the General inquired.

"I am. He directly disobeyed my orders. He came under the influence of someone who was not looking out for the best interest of my son or our clan."

"You wouldn't be referring to a Christian priest as that someone?" The General intensified his questioning as he looked briefly to the area in the back of the tent where Joseph was standing.

"Oh, no, the priest you speak of was like a child. He was more interested in trying to fit in than being a priest or a bad influence. I barely knew he was around. No, the person I speak of was an elder in the clan, and he is no longer with us. I took care of that myself."

"So you are saying it was this elder and not your son who—"

Before the General could finish, Mostar Gulivus interrupted, "No, he was stupid. He did what youths sometimes do—act without much thought. He was influenced by a so-called mentor, and that person took advantage of the situation. I was out east, away from my clan, when this happened. I heard of a strange and powerful enemy who had begun to advance in territories held by the tribes to the east. Have you heard of the Huns, General?"

"Vaguely," answered the General, as he tried to recall his scant knowledge of the Huns.

Mostar Gulivus continued. "When I returned, my son and some of my warriors had gone on a raiding party to find Roman soldiers."

"I don't think they counted on me to be here or the size and readiness of my army," the General responded.

"No, he didn't, and he broke the treaty that you and I had made. I have come to ask your forgiveness and to ask that you give me my son back. Please do not execute him—or his men."

"How do you know I have not already done that, or sold them to my friends that own the mines?"

"Because I know you." Mostar Gulivus had shifted from a position of strength and power, like a king, to one of an older man, pleading for his son. The General sat in his chair for what seemed an eternity, which was actually about five minutes. No one in the room moved. The General looked in the eyes of Mostar Gulivus and confirmed to himself that the king was telling the truth and his request was genuine. Further, the son did not seem like a smart man. How else could it be explained that Gul could lead a bunch of young men and boys, not warriors, into attacking a Roman position of strength?

The General spoke. "I have heard your request, King Gulivus, and it is the truth. Gul and the men that survived are still at my camp. I have neither executed them nor sold them as slaves because I believed you would come for them, not with the Goth war club but as a humble leader and father, and I have decided to let them live. However, as with all things like this, there is a price. No one attacks my army without penalty. Your son and half of his men at this camp are to be conscripted into my legions for a minimum term of ten years. The other half can return with you. The choice of who goes and who stays will be made by you. But your son stays here. If it makes you feel better, Gul will start out as a junior aide to Braxus. The others will become citizens of the legion. There the penalty for not following orders or being good soldiers is flogging or death."

Mostar Gulivus seemed relieved that at least his son and the Goth prisoners were still alive and being kept just a short distance from him.

"There is no negotiation, King Gulivus, this is it—and your choice. I assume because you are their king, your men will agree with you. They will do what you say. So what is your decision?"

Mostar Gulivus remained very still. He had no leverage and he knew it. In the end it was imperative that his son remain alive, as well as the remaining Goths who were prisoners. Mostar Gulivus knew that the General would attempt to keep his son alive. He would learn discipline, how to fight, and, most important, to be a leader. Gul, at present, was far from the man that Mostar Gulivus wanted for a successor. Finally, Mostar Gulivus said slowly, "I agree," in a tone that seemed unconvincing. He seemed pleased that his son was still alive but had a tinge of sadness that he would not be returning with him. He clearly loved his son, but that had little pertinence in this situation.

The General called for Cratus, who appeared almost immediately at the General's side. "Cratus, take King Gulivus to the camp of the prisoners. You may stay the night, King Gulivus, but you must leave in the morning. Afterward I will start the training program for your son and the others. And by the way, Gul will be safer in a Roman camp than anywhere else; maybe we can turn him into a soldier."

Cratus, three soldiers, and the five Goths made their way to the prisoner camp. The Roman soldiers who had lined the road when Mostar Gulivus first arrived were gone, giving the roadway the resemblance of a flat, curvy snake.

The General told all who remained in the tent to leave, even Jacob. As they were leaving the tent, Valerias spoke directly into the shadows, "Priest, I need a word with you."

Joseph did not know what to think. *How did the General know I was in the tent?*

Jacob spoke very quietly to Joseph as he left the tent. "Remember what we talked about. God be with you." Then he and the rest of the men were gone from the tent.

"Have a seat, priest. I know you were listening. Do you think I handled that well? Was it to your Christian liking?"

"You showed mercy, General."

"I did, didn't I? Why?"

"General, only you can answer that question. I do not know."

"I see." The General sat back. He appeared very calm. He looked older and more tired than when Joseph first arrived in camp. But he did not look frail. Frailty was not a characteristic that applied to the General.

After a few minutes of quiet, the General spoke almost in a monotone. "I know all about you, priest. I have friends and spies in many places, just as my enemies have—at least they try—on me. I know you are the only son of the spice merchant and his wife. Your father was fairly wealthy and well connected in certain circles in Rome and also Milan. You were to take over the business, as your father wanted. But you had your eye on bigger accomplishments, beyond selling spices. And for that, you needed more money, so you took money from your parents when they traveled to Milan. Gambling was also a habit of yours, was it not? Maybe you thought you could win at gambling and eventually pay back your parents with your profits.

"Unfortunately, none of that worked out. You got caught stealing from your parents when they returned to Rome. Also, representatives of your gambling interests came for you. They did not find you as you slinked away to whatever shadows you could find. They did find your father. They beat him senseless and took as much gold and other valuables as they could find from your parents. Your father died of his injuries and your mother died soon after that. She probably died from a broken heart.

"Disgraced and with nowhere to go, you joined the Christian Church. They didn't want you around either because of the bad smell you emitted, so they sent you to the camp of Mostar Gulivus' Goths, where hopefully you would disappear or die; I don't think they cared which. Then you ended up here, following a boy prince who doesn't even know which end of a sword to fight with. Is this an accurate summary of where you are today?"

Joseph was completely mortified. Somehow the General had found out his personal history. Joseph had a sickening feeling again, and his life seemed to pass before him as the General spoke. He again knew he was a dead man. He thought the General needed to satisfy his blood lust and he wasn't going to get it from the Goths. Valerias was going to kill him very shortly. Joseph saw the sword still sheathed on the back of the General. But where was that little blade?

The General looked hard into Joseph's eyes and spoke slowly with a low, soft voice, "Don't be concerned. I am not going to execute you or send you away to the mines for your past *sins*. Jacob and Olivertos have spoken for you—even Braxus. You work hard and work well with others, and you have not tried to spread your Christian faith around the camp, as I have asked. Your past is between you and me. But walk the path as I have demanded of you, or you will be visiting your God, or your Satan, and your secret will no longer be one. Are we clear?"

Joseph was first deeply shaken and then relieved. His palms were soaked with sweat. He had done what Jacob had recommended and was allowed to live. Jacob had saved his life again.

The General said sharply, "Return to Jacob's part of this camp. Get out!"

Joseph stumbled out of the tent, not thinking of what he was doing but of what the General had said. He felt relieved that he had not been killed. Yet he felt a pressing stress that someone else knew about his past. His worst nightmare had come true—the General knew his secret and might use it against him at any time.

Joseph tripped over an object he could not identify. As he fell, a strong hand reached out and kept him from hitting the ground. It was Braxus. He was alone except for several soldiers sitting in the background by a large rock playing some type of game. Braxus was not as intimidating as the General; however, he still was a first-class warrior. *How could he not be and be second-in-command to the General?* Joseph thought.

"I see you survived the General again," Braxus spoke in a quiet tone. "Many men in the camp have spoken highly of your work with Olivertos. You have many talents; just keep doing what you are doing and keep your faith to yourself."

As Braxus finished speaking, Jacob came quickly up a path to the left and behind Joseph. His appearance startled Joseph.

"I am pleased you are here. The General has a way of testing people to see how they respond. You are following our advice, and it is keeping you alive."

Joseph then spoke the obvious, "I owe both of you my deep, deep gratitude. Jacob, I know you have saved my life at least twice. General Braxus, the General spoke to you, and I know on my behalf, you have helped me. I promise to act my best so I don't let you down—"

Braxus cut off Joseph, "There is only one person you need to please, so just do that."

Jacob then said, "Let's go back to Olivertos."

When Joseph turned around, Braxus was already nearing the rock where the soldiers were sitting.

Jacob added sharply, "*Now*."

As they walked to Olivertos' camp, Jacob was at first silent and then spoke very quietly, "You must be careful to whom you speak and what you speak. Remember, Braxus is the second-in-command and reports directly to the General. He may think you are doing fine, but if the General asks him a question about you, Braxus will answer truthfully. Besides, some of Braxus' bodyguards are not Christians and may be indirect spies for the General."

"I didn't think I said anything that would cause anyone any alarm."

"You did not, but think hard about having a loose tongue. A devious man may take you where you don't want to go. And then you will be in front of the General trying to explain what you were saying. Just be careful. You are proving yourself a valuable asset around here, and the General knows that. However, following orders, even if you are not a soldier, is paramount to him. I have seen him execute men for not obeying his wishes."

Further down the trail Jacob asked Joseph, "What was it that the General wanted to speak to you about in the tent, by yourselves?"

Joseph thought for a few moments before speaking and responded that the General had some questions about Mostar Gulivus that he could answer from his time in the Goth camp. Jacob knew that wasn't the truth, but he did not press the matter further. The General at times kept secrets from his subordinates, soldiers, and civilians, and in that way kept power over them.

Once Jacob dropped Joseph off at Olivertos' tent, he returned to the General's tent. Olivertos was not there, so it had been a quick stop. Jacob was troubled. The General had looked older in recent weeks and was not acting like himself. He had always had a confident swagger, with a temper and meanness he exerted with purpose. Now he seemed somewhat lost, and there was a subtle feeling that he did not care as much as usual. The General was clear that he had a problem with Joseph and yet he let him live. This was an action that would not have happened in the past.

Jacob himself did not feel well, either. He thought it might be the turn in the weather or his age. Jacob was about the same age as the General, the mid-forties. Life in a perpetual fort or camp, away from family, was tough, and the older one became, the harder it was to persevere. It was also more difficult to get the same tasks accomplished in the same amount of time. That is why

Joseph had become so important. He had picked up the slack for Olivertos. Now it would be his turn.

In getting older, Jacob had learned through experience all the tricks that were needed to complete tasks. Still, there was nothing quite like the energy of youth, even youth that lacked experience. Jacob stopped his feelings of self-pity. He was alive and served a great man, and he had a fine family, but he was tired, and he knew the great man was also tired.

VIII

Passing Away

Several weeks passed with Joseph assisting Jacob more than Olivertos. At the end of this period, Jacob had a night of bad dreams. One in particular was a nightmare that seemed very real. In this dream he saw himself falling down into a deep well, plunging through an abyss of darkness. No one was there to stop his fall, and eventually he reached the bottom. The floor consisted of a material he was unaware of. He would sink and yet would always just hover above the bottom.

Voices called to him from the walls with names from his past. He was very confused and wanted to get out of this hole so badly that he tried to yell with full throat, but words did not come out of his mouth. A large being emerged from the wall. This being was immense, but had no discernible shape. He carried a large anvil like the ones used by blacksmiths. The shapelessness especially bothered Jacob because how could a shapeless being carry an anvil? The being slowly worked his way over to Jacob in a slow rocking motion. Jacob was now in a supine position as the bottom suddenly became hard. His face looked up at the being, trying with great difficulty to see if he recognized it. Many faces flashed through the top of the being in a blurry fashion. Faces he knew, or at least seemed to know, and others that he did not recognize.

Paralyzed, Jacob peered up at the shapeless being, exerting all his energy to see who this was. Then the being placed the anvil on top of Jacob's chest. The weight was crushing him, and he tried again to yell for help, but no one came to his rescue. The being just stood there, not moving as the anvil felt heavier and heavier. Jacob knew the end was near and started to cry, when he felt his shoulder moving and a voice called to him at the top of the well. "Jacob, Jacob—climb back up here." He could not, though, as the anvil was too heavy. He relaxed and prepared to die.

Suddenly out of nowhere a sharp voice pierced the blur and Jacob woke up. In front of him stood the General with several soldiers and servants at the side of his bed.

"What happened?" Jacob tenuously asked.

The General was concerned. "You were having a very bad dream. One of your servants came and got me, as I was outside your tent at the time. I heard you calling into the darkness. You were shaking and pouring sweat. That is not natural, even with a bad dream. I am concerned, as you do not look well and have not for a few days now. I have called for Olivertos. I want him to take a look at you tonight—just in case this is more than a bad dream. After he is done, he will give me a full report and then we will decide what to do with you. I need my Administrator." "*And friend*" was the unspoken end to the sentence.

The General walked out of the tent with Bukarma at his side. "I am concerned about Jacob, Bukarma. Maybe he is doing too much around here. I need that priest to do more, and he had better step it up or I will cut his heart out and feed it the wolves that seem to haunt these hills."

This was a harsh statement even for the General. Bukarma felt uncomfortable with this language as he too had become impressed with Joseph's skills as a physician and accountant and as a friend to Jacob and Olivertos.

Bukarma spoke in measured terms. "The priest, Joseph, is already contributing much to the camp. He is not the reason Jacob is in the state he is in. Jacob views him favorably."

A long pause followed Bukarma's statement. "I didn't know you thought of the priest in a kind way, Bukarma." Another long pause, "We will await the physician's evaluation. I will try not to reach any more conclusions that might upset you." The last phrase was etched in sarcasm.

The General did respect Bukarma's opinions because he spoke so seldom. In his conscience, the General knew Bukarma was right. He was not going to admit that though. Bukarma also knew he gave the General an opportunity to pause for reflection. *Maybe the General will be a little more reserved in expressing his opinions about Joseph,* Bukarma thought. Bukarma too had grown to respect Joseph.

Olivertos arrived at Jacob's tent in minutes. With him was Joseph. Both men entered the tent and proceeded to evaluate Jacob's condition. When the General saw that Joseph was there, he emitted a short sigh. He then looked at Bukarma and sighed louder.

The General sarcastically said to Bukarma, "Very well, if he can help Olivertos, he can stay."

Olivertos and Jacob both shot the General a glare that made the General back off a bit.

"Let me know what you find out, Olivertos. Maybe the priest can offer some aid." He added under his breath, "Though I doubt it." Then he announced in a louder tone, "I will be down at the main training area of the camp. Send me a runner as soon as you have news."

The General and Bukarma were gone into the morning light as the tent flap opened and then closed.

After they had left, Jacob spoke to Olivertos and Joseph, "I am concerned. I have not felt well for a number of days, and I was going to take a trip to Rome to visit my family. I fear that may have to be postponed."

"We will see about your trip when we conclude our examination. I hope you can take a trip down to my tent so you can pay me the wager you will have lost after we are finished with you. Now do what you are told, for a change, because I know that is hard for you. Even the General told me you are beginning to act more like a general than a simple accountant."

Both men then laughed softly, although Olivertos' laugh was more exuberant. Joseph smiled too. He knew the two men were close, and he could tell this was more nervous than genuine laughter.

When the laughter ceased, Olivertos looked at Joseph and said matter-of-factly, "Let us begin. You heard our famous accountant—he needs to go to Rome and find out that all his children have enlisted in the army."

Jacob smiled at Olivertos and said, "If you were any slower, my children would have already blessed me with grandchildren before you are finished."

And with that comment, Olivertos began his examination with Joseph at his side. A short time later, the examination was completed. Olivertos gave Jacob a cup of tea that produced a calming effect on him, and he was soon asleep. Olivertos motioned to Joseph to join him outside. Once outside Joseph could see the training area in the background. There was much activity in the training area, and Joseph looked for the General but didn't see him in the crowd.

Olivertos noticed that Joseph was watching the fields below, and yet Joseph never blinked. His mind had gone elsewhere. He was thinking of his time acting as a physician in Rome, when he had seen patients in the same condition as Jacob.

"Well, what do think, Joseph?" Olivertos' manner had become more urgent.

"I think his heart is not working like it should be. It is beating too rapidly."

"Rapid and irregular," added Olivertos. "I gave him a tea, which should help smooth his heart's rhythms. I need to return to my tent and do some research on what is affecting his heart. Then he had that bad dream. I think it all fits together. You will need to stay with him. He is not to leave his bed. Please tell the General about our preliminary findings and that Jacob needs to remain in his bed. The General must tell him, as Jacob essentially only listens to the General."

Olivertos left the tent—out the same entrance that the General and Bukarma had used earlier.

Before Joseph could return to Jacob's bed, Joseph saw a shadow that seemed to surround him. It was the General.

"I'm not interested in training today. Braxus can be the leader. Tell me, priest, what have you and physician Olivertos found out about Jacob?"

"We don't know yet, General. It may be exhaustion. Olivertos has said you need to order Jacob to remain in the bed. He listens only to you."

"Well, let me know when you know something then."

The General exited the tent brusquely. Joseph was concerned and nervous. He was concerned about Jacob and nervous about his own situation. If Jacob were to die, there was no doubt in his mind that the General would hold him responsible and likely execute him. Someone would have to pay the price, and the General would not lay the blame on Olivertos.

Olivertos later appeared at the entrance to Jacob's tent in a somber mood and with notes in hand.

"I fear it is his heart. I have watched him grow slightly weaker over the past several months. The General counts on him to do so much, and I just think at his age it is too much for him. I am going to tell the General that it is my opinion that Jacob needs to retire and spend as much time with his family as he can."

"I agree with you, Olivertos." Both Olivertos and Joseph turned around and saw the General standing in the corner.

"I didn't see you come back, General."

"That is because I never left—you just thought I did. Relax, I am not here to condemn either of you two. I too have sensed something is not quite right for some time now. I was going to order that Jacob take an extended trip back to Rome. I assume that you, priest, have learned Jacob's duties. Correct?"

Joseph started to respond when a quiet voice, like a whisper, emanated from Jacob. "General, I would like a word with you." Jacob's voice was clear and focused solely on the General.

"Return to your posts, whatever you should be doing," commanded the General to Olivertos and Joseph. Both men left quickly.

Jacob spoke slowly but in a remarkably clear tone. "Marcus, I have been at your side for many, many years and want to continue in my service to you. However, I want to visit my family in Rome. It has been well over two years since I have seen them, and it is time. I will return after a one-month visit."

The General nodded. Jacob was the only person besides a few other Generals that could get away with calling the General by his first name, and that was only done in private.

"Joseph is well prepared to perform my duties and could act as a competent substitute for me with my other staff while I am in Rome."

The General nodded again and agreed with Jacob's plan. He added, "I want you to consider retirement while you are on leave, just as Olivertos suggested."

"I will, but don't count on me retiring quite yet. Someone needs to keep an eye on you to make sure you don't make a mess of matters." Jacob chuckled softly.

"Well, I assume the priest could do your work, which makes you a simpleton because that is what the priest is, a simpleton." It was the General's turn to smile.

Jacob grew quieter. "The priest, as you refer to him, Joseph, is very capable. He has had excellent training and quickly picks up what is needed from both my and Olivertos' directions. If you give him a chance, he will surprise you with his talents."

The General was silent for a few seconds, and then he said, "I understand what you are trying to say. However, I make no promises regarding how I handle the priest. If he follows my rules, he will be fine. If he doesn't, then that will be his fault and his undoing. But I hear you and because you are asking, maybe I'll give him a little more rope. Of course, the rope can still hang him; it just may take longer."

Again the General smiled as he finished his statement. Jacob was pleased that he got the General to at least consider backing off from Joseph. It all seemed natural to Jacob. He and the General were friends, regardless of their positions in life. Jacob had also become friends with Joseph. Maybe there was hope for Joseph with the General, but that was something he could not control. Jacob was tired, and he reached for the General's arm. The General sat down beside him.

"Be well, Jacob."

"Do well, Marcus."

Jacob fell asleep. The General sat still by the bed for several minutes. His head was clear of thoughts of the present situation; instead, he recalled past times with Jacob. The General then slowly left the tent still focused on the past. He didn't want to think of the future. He called out to Bukarma about playing their odd game.

Later in the night Jacob died peacefully in his sleep. His heart had become too weak and could not carry on any further.

Dawn was not yet on the horizon. The air had a pleasant cool, fall feeling that was not cold enough to cause shivers if one stood still and not warm enough to leave the cloak behind. The General had been by Jacob's bedside for over an hour. He stared straight ahead as his mind switched from his memories of Jacob to the old man who had been watching his reflection in the water of the creek several weeks before. He eventually, reluctantly, returned to reality.

The General exited Jacob's tent. Bukarma was there along with a cohort captain and several of Bukarma's men, who formed the General's bodyguard. The General issued an order to the captain, but not in his usual robust, authoritarian manner.

"Get me Olivertos—quickly," he spoke in a monotone. Olivertos had been in the tent most of the night but had left to check on some soldiers who had come down with apparent food poisoning.

"Yes, General," was the reply. The captain and some soldiers left as the dawn sun emerged.

The General looked at Bukarma and Bukarma knew what had happened.

"What can I do, General?"

"Nothing yet. I will wait for Olivertos before committing to anything."

After several minutes, Olivertos appeared, followed by the captain and more soldiers than had originally left to find the physician. Olivertos was out of breath, as he had actually fallen into a restless sleep after checking on the ill soldiers. Upon being abruptly awakened by the captain, he quickly stepped up to Jacob's tent.

"He is gone, Olivertos—but please verify." The General knew what had occurred, he just wanted to hear it from one he trusted.

Olivertos disappeared into the tent. Valerias waited outside not saying a word. He noticed the sun was now just above the branches of the highest trees. *How fast the sun rises today,* he thought.

One of the soldiers was faintly hitting one of his boots with a stick in a slow, rhythmic motion. Finally the General heard Olivertos' voice from inside the tent. The General and Bukarma entered the tent. Grief had overcome Olivertos as his slumped figure stood by the bedside. He had been Jacob's best friend through all the years they had served together with the General, and he was not yet ready to let his friend go.

"I am saddened too, Olivertos—he was my subordinate, but he was my friend." The General had been trained to show little emotion, particularly sadness, as that would be seen as a sign of weakness. The General's enemies would be sure to pounce on any evidence of weakness he showed. Still, in the quiet of the tent, the General put his hand on Olivertos' shoulder and left it there for several minutes. Bukarma stepped forward and folded Jacob's arms across his chest. He inserted a small, carved figure in Jacob's right hand.

"To accompany him in the afterlife." Bukarma stepped back.

Braxus and Cratus appeared in the tent at almost the same time. Both bowed their heads, and Braxus muttered something to himself. Valerias thought the mumble resembled a prayer. Other men now entered the tent, so the General thought it was a good time to leave. Braxus followed him out.

"Braxus, it amazes me that after all the death and trials we have gone through, that we have not become too hardened to appreciate a truly good man. We must still be human." Valerias paused and then continued, "He was not very religious, but he lived his life as a religious man should—no matter the religion."

"General, I agree. He had many friends in our camp and I was one of them. He lived an exemplary life."

The sun was now well above the trees, and its warmth was impressive for a fall day. The General stared straight ahead for a few more moments and then returned to form.

"General Braxus, send out two groups of cavalry and go to the nearest villages. Find me a rabbi, or more than one rabbi, I don't care, and bring them here. I want a rabbi to lead Jacob's funeral service. I want this done quickly so that Jacob's service is conducted as soon as possible, which means in the next day or two. Jacob shall be buried over there by that large pine. It is an unusual tree for this area, and Jacob was an unusual man. I will personally pay for the rabbi's work—in Roman gold."

It was implied by the importance of the General's order that Braxus himself would lead one of the cavalry units. Cratus emerged from the tent.

"Good, General Cratus, I'm pleased that you are here now. You can talk to Braxus about carrying out my order."

It was also not-so-subtly implied that Cratus was to lead the other cavalry unit. Braxus and Cratus left the area, with Braxus talking until they were out of sight.

Bukarma had been standing behind the General during most of this time. The General didn't look—he knew who was behind him.

"Bukarma, bring me the priest."

Within minutes Bukarma returned with Joseph.

"That was fast. Where was he? Was he hiding in the tent with us?" The General was in a sour mood, and he was going to take out his unhappiness with Joseph.

"No, General, he was just down the trail awaiting news of Jacob. He had been there all night."

Just then, Olivertos came out of the tent and said to the General, "I need him. Joseph, come with me."

The General raised his right arm as if he wanted to say or gesture something in exasperation, but then lowered his arm and finally crossed both arms. He said nothing but stared out at the splendid dawn. Joseph joined Olivertos inside the tent.

Olivertos moved over to Jacob's body and said straightforwardly, "Joseph, I need you to verify the death of Jacob and assist me in determining the cause of death." Olivertos lowered his voice to a whisper. "I wanted to get you out of there. I didn't want you to be made a scapegoat by the General. He is looking for someone to lash out at, and I did not want that someone to be you."

Joseph nodded his understanding to Olivertos. He walked over to the side of Jacob's bed and looked at his face. Joseph had little experience with death, even in the Goth and Roman camps. Jacob's death face was serene. Joseph thought he looked so natural that he would wake up shortly and begin spinning another one of his stories or jokes with Olivertos. However, he was not coming back. After a few minutes, Joseph acknowledged that his friend was indeed dead. He knew the cause of his passing—his heart had given out. Olivertos had reached the same conclusion earlier. Olivertos went out of the tent to report to the General, but he was already gone, along with Bukarma.

A guard told Olivertos that the General and Bukarma had left to watch Braxus and Cratus depart. Olivertos sighed, relieved. *Hopefully, the General will cool down,* he thought to himself. He was also worried. He thought that the next few days would be difficult to manage.

Olivertos turned to Joseph and said, "Let's prepare the body for burial. Jacob recently told me how he wanted this task done, and I will follow his wishes."

When they returned to the tent, Joseph noted a small area had been cut away from Jacob's right sleeve. Olivertos followed Joseph's eyes. "The General took a small piece of the cloth. He will have it made into a band that he will wear around his wrist. He wants Jacob to remain with him."

Joseph nodded and thought to himself, *If true, that is the first humane action I have seen from that man.*

IX

Claire

Dawn came but without the sun. The clouds were even hidden by a thick drizzle that hung in the air like a dark blanket. The walls of the castle dripped with ooze from the moisture in the air. Claire looked out at those walls, wondering if the gloomy feeling both outside and also inside of the castle could be any worse. The inside gloom was mental, not physical, and Claire knew that was the situation.

For a long time Argus had wanted to become the new king of an area of Britannia north of Londinium. "Warlord" was a more accurate term for Argus than "king." To accomplish his goal, Argus had demanded that Claire marry him within the month. Nothing disgusted Claire more than the thought of marrying Argus. Argus was not only Claire's uncle by marriage, but she was sure he had planned the scheme that resulted in Claire's husband, Gerhard, being killed by a group of Saxon raiders.

Gerhard had been king for ten years, and Claire had been his bride and queen for nine of those years. They had three children, an eight-year-old boy named Douglas and two girls aged six and four, approaching five, named Anne and Elizabeth.

This was a time of turmoil in Britannia. Not only were Saxons and their opportunistic raiding proving to be a tenacious foe in the east, but the Picts and Scots to the west and north were in full rebellion. The Picts posed a particularly dangerous threat to the security of Britannia, and as a result, the Roman General Titus in Britannia spent a majority of his time fighting them. Hadrian's Wall no longer served as the formidable barrier that it did in earlier times when the Emperor Hadrian had constructed it.

The Romans had generally coexisted peacefully with the Britons during Gerhard's reign. Rome's influence on Britannia was waning, though, as the Empire became consumed with internal strife and the crush of the barbarian hordes along other points of the Empire. To keep control of Britannia, Rome needed the aid of the Britons. And to keep Britannia from falling into the hands of the Picts, Saxons, and other raiders from across the seas, the Britons needed Rome—even in its weakened state. It had become a synergistic relationship.

Argus increasingly hungered to be king, and he desired to have Claire as his bride. To accomplish these goals, Argus knew he had to either kill Gerhard, or better still, have someone else kill him. So he arranged to have Gerhard assassinated. The cost was five hundred gold coins. But the real cost was Argus allowing the Saxons and their allies, the Angles and Jutes, to access lands in the eastern part of Britannia. The Saxons, though, had other thoughts than living peacefully with the Britons under Argus' rule. After gaining a foothold in Britannia, they could then launch additional attacks against the Britons and bring reinforcement troops and their families from across the North Sea.

The Romans were a problem, though. The Saxons had fought Romans before in Britannia without much success. Their plan was to first fight the Britons, which included killing Gerhard, and then assume control of the land. Because the Britons and

Romans were not particularly good allies, the Saxons believed they could overtake the Britons, which would force Rome to withdraw from Britannia.

Claire knew it was time to leave the once-friendly confines of her castle and nearby territory. Gerhard was dead—this had been confirmed by an agent whom she trusted. She knew Argus was either responsible or at a minimum complicit in his death. Claire's younger brother, Eustice, abdicated any claim to the throne and fled deep into the western Britannia countryside. Douglas was next in line to succeed to the throne, but he was eight years old and too young. Claire knew Argus would not allow that succession to occur. Before Argus could act, Claire staged an "ambush" by a group of her allies who pretended to be bandits. These men kidnapped and faked the death of Douglas. The trickery worked, and Argus believed that Douglas was dead. Instead, Douglas had been taken by Claire's allies to an isolated village near the northeast coast of Britannia.

After the death of Gerhard became known, Claire entered into a long period of mourning for her husband and her son, to delay Argus and his marital scheme. Unfortunately, Argus had limited patience and he grew tired of waiting. He gave Claire one month to complete the mourning period and then the wedding would proceed. After the wedding he would be the King and Claire would be his queen. There was no doubt in her mind that he would then have her killed—accidentally—after the wedding. Thus, the thought of being with Argus was so repulsive that if she did not have her daughters to care for, she would have thrown herself off of the castle walls.

Claire contemplated her situation as she sat in the large chair her husband had used when there was time to talk, away from the affairs of the state. There he conversed with Claire and the children whenever he had the chance. She missed Gerhard, but had not been in love with him. This was also no time for her reflections of the past when the future was so uncertain and needed her full attention.

As she thought about what she was going to try to do, the door to her room opened and in stepped a well-dressed man. It was Flavius, Argus' leading enforcer. Flavius was a Roman. He shaved daily and wore fine clothes. He was calm and deliberate in his actions. However, his appearance was deceiving. Flavius was a killer who acted on behalf of Argus. Flavius was like the snake that without warning struck from an ambush's cover. He also reminded Claire of an attack dog that, on command, tore into the target. After he entered the room, Flavius seemed unusually pleasant to Claire.

"Argus, the future king and your husband-to-be, is coming and will discuss the wedding," he said in a bored tone, as if it were a bother for him to even speak to Claire.

Then he sharpened his tone. "Be ready—he wants to name a date, and the sooner the better. We all know you are stalling. Anymore perceived stalling and we shall see what comes of your two brats."

By the time he finished his statements, his sneer appeared to occupy his entire face. As Flavius spoke, Claire thought,—*Who is more grotesque—Flavius or Argus? Who is more malevolent? Maybe it is a draw? Either way, I would like to kill both of them and feed their carcasses to the bog southeast of the castle.*

As she finished this thought, Claire noticed that Flavius had stopped talking and was looking straight at her as if he was trying to read her mind. Claire reacted by nonchalantly making a waving motion at Flavius, acknowledging what she had heard.

Flavius stopped staring for a moment. "This time, Argus is serious, woman. Argus wants a date for the wedding or you will suddenly be childless." Flavius returned to staring hard at Claire, trying to get some emotion to show, but Claire held her ground and stared directly back into Flavius' eyes.

After a few moments Flavius ended the staring duel and briskly walked out of the room as if he had been summoned. Before Claire even had time to blink, Argus entered the room. He had obviously heard everything that Claire and Flavius had spoken, and his quick arrival gave Claire no opportunity to assimilate what had just been said and prepare a strategy for dealing with him.

Argus was about a half a hand shorter than Flavius. He had a short, well-kept beard that was a mixture of black and gray. He had a narrow face with a thin, round chin. The shape of the chin was even apparent through the beard. His eyes were a dark color and just as piercing as Flavius' eyes. He reminded Claire of a large, vulture-like bird. *The animals on the ground led by Flavius do the dirty work of wounding the prey, and he then flies in for the kill,* she thought.

Argus started off the conversation in a manner that was cordial for him, which took Claire by surprise. "Tell me, Claire, how are your quarters? I've tried to make them comfortable for you. After the wedding, you will move into the King's wing with me. Your living quarters will be much better then."

"You know, that is the wing where Gerhard and I stayed—"

Argus interrupted, "Yes—he died and now it's mine. As I said, after the wedding, you will be allowed to return there. Your daughters, though, will stay with nannies in the south wing. You can visit them in the mornings and on special occasions, like our wedding."

"My daughters will stay with me after—"

"Not if you want them to remain alive, or at least in a healthy condition."

Claire had few options. She knew if she wanted to keep her daughters safe, she would have to agree to Argus' terms.

"As you wish. My daughters mean more to me than your fantasy of being a king."

Argus didn't trust Claire, but he had her daughters, and that would be his leverage to ensure her cooperation.

Argus started to leave the room, but at the doorframe he stopped and pivoted around, facing Claire. His eyes appeared lifeless. "You will marry me twenty days from now. You have had your opportunity to provide me with a date and you have failed. I must set the date and you shall live with it. Have a good night, my wife-to-be."

He seemed to almost laugh when he made that statement, and then he left the room. As he walked down the hallway, at least one other pair of footsteps joined his. Now laughter rang along the castle's walls. *That had to be Flavius who joined Argus,* thought Claire. "I really want to kill them both," she muttered softly.

Claire was not a woman whose beauty attracted males. It was the way she carried herself that was attractive. She was born the daughter of a Briton chief who taught her to fight and defend herself at an early age in the event their village was attacked by other tribes—or worse, by raiders from across the seas. The bow was her best weapon.

At eighteen she was engaged to Gerhard, the son of a dead king. It was an arranged engagement, and they married two years later. Over time Claire had grown to accept her husband as a good man and as father of her three children. He had been a decent king, but it was difficult to keep all the kingdom's enemies at bay and deal with the treachery lurking inside the castle. Such responsibilities weighed on Gerhard. He became serious and quiet, susceptible to court intrigue. Not recognizing that Argus was a traitor had proved to be his undoing. Claire truly grieved for her husband when she learned he was dead. Then the grieving was replaced by protecting her children and considering ideas of getting revenge on Argus. If Flavius was part of her revenge plan, so be it.

Any plan for revenge would have to be implemented after she and her daughters were free from Argus. From the day she had learned that Gerhard had been killed, she began conceiving a plan to escape. Claire still had many silent allies within the castle and kingdom who retained loyalty to Gerhard. She would need these allies to successfully execute any plan that would provide safety for her children and help remove Argus from the throne.

Claire was wise enough not to contact anyone other than a few trusted confidants. She knew she was being watched by Argus' men. Some spies were readily identifiable, and others were more camouflaged. In time she learned to identify the spies. Twelve days before her wedding to Argus, she casually gave a note to one of her chambermaids. The chambermaid in turn gave it to a cook, who gave it to a captain of the King's Guards, Erik Longwilder. Years ago, Erik and Gerhard had had a falling out, and Gerhard demoted Erik's rank. Once Gerhard was killed, Argus promoted Erik to the rank of Captain of the Guards. Argus assumed Erik and Gerhard were enemies. Erik, though, had sworn an oath of loyalty to Gerhard. When Gerhard was killed, Erik immediately sought out Claire and declared his loyalty, in secret, to her. An oath was an oath, and Erik was loyal to the oath.

The next day when the chambermaid was brushing Claire's hair, she left the brush on the table. A rolled up note was attached to the side of the brush. The location of the note on the brush was difficult for anyone but Claire to see. When no one was looking, she moved the note by an inconspicuous motion, placing it inside her top. She kept the note there until bedtime, when she read it and burned it by candle. Just as she finished this action, Flavius barged in her room. His air of self-importance was almost comical to her, particularly in the way he seemed to march up to her. He also maintained a condescending attitude toward her. She sometimes wondered if Flavius and Argus were lovers.

"Argus has instructed me to tell you that he has decided to move the day of the wedding up to two days' time from tomorrow. You *will* be ready."

Claire answered, "I'll be ready" in a tone that suggested more than one meaning. Flavius was not listening, though, as he was halfway out the door. As he left, Claire thought, *One day, you and Argus shall know my vengeance.* She took the candleholder with the lighted candle and walked to the window closest to the northwestern corner of her room. Then she blew the candle out. The signal had been given.

X

David

General Valerias was displeased, but in reality, he did not expect a much different result. Braxus and Cratus had returned to the camp, not having found a rabbi in their travels to the nearest villages. The custom of a quick Jewish burial limited their search in both time and distance. Both men were uneasy when it was time to report to the General.

Braxus began, "General, we each traveled over forty miles and went to several villages. We could not locate a rabbi."

Cratus then spoke. "We knew there were Jews in these villages, but we could not get anyone to speak about a rabbi. We did not have time to properly *interrogate* people we thought could give us answers."

Braxus started to speak, but the General cut him off before he uttered a word.

"I don't fault your efforts—it is your results that perplex me. You two are my highest-ranking officers and you failed on this mission. I would think the fear of the Empire would loosen peasant tongues, but maybe that fear is waning."

The General walked over to a chair and sat down. However, he did not sit back; instead he sat up on the edge, his eyes looked straight ahead. "I suppose I could send a contingent of cavalry and torch a village. That would make the points that I think need to be made. I think the villagers are holding back because they do not want to help a Roman. They might appreciate us more if they had bands of barbarians pillaging their villages. Be that as it may . . ." The General now sat back in his chair, deep in thought.

After a few minutes, he asked his two generals, "What do I always tell you two when planning an attack, on both the physical and mental levels?"

"General, to always have an alternative," answered Cratus in an almost schoolboy-like manner to the teacher.

Braxus also added his thought. "Or two, three, or more alternatives."

The General rubbed the knuckles of his left hand with his right hand. "You are both correct from a simple standpoint. It is always good to have a back-up plan to the back-up plan, but too many plans would be confusing, and the person trying to carry them out would be lost in details of the many plans."

Valerias didn't want to discuss this topic anymore and asked Cratus to bring him Joseph. As Cratus was leaving the tent, the General said, "This is Plan B."

After Cratus had left, the General commented, "We shall see how good of a Christian the priest is. I will have him oversee the funeral. He won't say no to me."

As Cratus looked for Joseph, a messenger ran to the General's tent. Bukarma let him in after first speaking with the runner.

"A rider comes from the west who would like to speak with you," said the man, who was noticeably out of breath. The man was trying to impress the General.

The General, however, was more concerned that the speaker, this runner, was part of his legions and so out of shape.

"General Braxus, do you have any idea how this man could be so poorly conditioned? Are you following our strict training protocols?"

"General, I believe he is a new recruit, and we haven't yet had the opportunity to train him as we do to all our recruits."

"Good, make sure that this happens." And then turning to the messenger, the General's voice became low and menacing. "I will be asking for your training report and it had better be sufficient."

Although the consequences were not spoken, both the General and the messenger knew any penalties would be harsh.

Valerias then asked the messenger who the rider was.

"I don't know," answered the messenger, "but he comes from one of the villages Generals Braxus and Cratus visited. He wants to speak with you, General."

"So be it. Bukarma, be sure the visitor is escorted to my tent as soon as possible. He may be our missing rabbi."

When the General turned around, Joseph stood in front of him.

"Cratus is fast—trying to make up for failing to produce a rabbi." The General spoke at Joseph, but not to him.

"Cratus isn't here. I have just been outside, waiting to see if you needed anything," Joseph spoke to the General.

"Perfect timing, priest, I do have a task for you, one you will readily agree to."

At that moment Bukarma opened the tent entrance and announced to the General that David, a rabbi, was outside. With him was Revious. Revious entered the tent.

"I thought only one rider was seen. Revious, where were you?"

"That's the beauty of it, General. I don't want to be seen."

"Where did you find this rabbi, Revious?" the General inquired, partly annoyed and partly curious.

"Do I get the credit and reward if it was I who found him?"

"No," was the General's one-word reply. "Jacob is dead, Revious, and I am not in a light mood."

Revious sobered quickly, "He was on the trail that I was on. I just rode with him to the edge of camp and then met some of my men who are camped on the other side of the ridge." Revious paused and put his head down. "Jacob is dead? I'm truly sorry. He was my friend too." The General looked at Revious, but there was a hollowness to his expression.

He turned to Bukarma. "Bring me the rabbi."

A smallish man entered the tent. He almost looked like a dwarf compared the mass of Bukarma.

"Speak your name and your title, man," the General asked in a formal tone.

"I am David from a small village across two valleys from here. I heard of your quest for a rabbi and that is why I am here."

"Did you not see my men in your village?" The General's annoyance factor was showing.

"No, they did not stop in my village. But I heard about your need and came immediately."

Valerias was confused. Braxus and Cratus had said they had visited all the villages in the area. Why did they miss this rabbi's village? He gave Braxus a hard look that if it could have been conjured into acid, it would have burned a hole in Braxus' head.

"I stopped in his village, General, and there was no rabbi." Braxus spoke in a reflex response to the General's intimidating manner.

The General brushed off the response and then turned to David. "Are you a rabbi?"

"Well, yes and no—I had a career change and am in training to become a rabbi."

The General's fist slammed into the table, knocking off most of the contents that had been placed on the top. He was furious.

"I asked for a rabbi and I don't have one to preside over Jacob's funeral. Instead, I have a part-rabbi and part-priest." He slammed the table again.

Silence entered the room and remained there until Olivertos spoke. He had just entered the tent. He observed that the tent was now crowded, but all the occupants except the General had shrunk away to the edges—even Bukarma.

"General, I suggest that Joseph and the rabbi conduct a joint service. Jacob was well known and liked by all types of people both in and out of the army who were Christians, pagans, and Jews. Perhaps it should be a service for every man."

The General put his right arm up to his chin and after a few minutes of silence said, "That is what we shall do. Priest and half-rabbi, you shall prepare for and conduct Jacob's service. It had better be a satisfactory service—satisfactory to me."

Everyone stood around, not knowing what to do. The General's temper could be wicked, and based on prior experiences, anyone who left without approval would be castigated. But the General had calmed down quickly—for him. He felt that the silence and the lack of movement in the tent was awkward.

"Go," the General said finally and dismissively waved his right arm at Joseph and David. "Olivertos, you go with them—they need a nanny."

The tent emptied out its occupants like villagers fleeing an erupting volcano. Valerias laughed to himself. *After all these years I'm still the one they fear. And that is good.*

After Bukarma and he were alone in the tent, he nodded to Bukarma "Bukarma, get your bag. I need to play your game tonight. Maybe we should bet on the lives of our religious icons—a rabbi who is not a rabbi and a priest who pretends to be a priest. Liars!"

XI

Burial

The funeral was held the next day at dawn. It was a sunny late fall day, and the air was cool with a hint that winter was approaching. The General viewed winter like a god. In one hand the winter god held a ball of cold and in the other a ball of snow. The god could inflict the land with cold or snow, or both. That is what winter was to him—cold and snow. Valerias, though, did not care about the time of year, but he was pleased that whatever gods were present had arranged a proper day to send off his friend. A large crowd was present, as Jacob was well liked by soldiers and civilians. Olivertos stood with Joseph and David. Braxus, Cratus, and the rest of the General's command team were present. Gul stood far back in the crowd.

Surprisingly to the General, the service went well. Joseph and David conducted an acceptable funeral. It was clear that Olivertos had played an important, behind-the-scenes role. Jacob was interred on the east side of a small meadow at the base of a large pine tree surrounded by other large pines. Large rocks were placed on his gravesite, and special ointments were splashed among the rocks to keep animals away. A larger stone, brought in with the help of two horses, made a rough headstone. Someone carved Jacob's name into the stone. It was a simple marker. At the service Joseph noted the General wore the wristlet created from Jacob's clothing.

When the memorial was completed, David and Joseph walked by the General, who was standing by the gravesite. He nodded as they approached, indicating he approved of their effort. Both men felt some relief at the General's apparent approval. Joseph was first to pass Valerias. The General said in a hushed tone, "Come to my tent tonight after supper." When David passed Valerias, the General spoke, again in a hushed voice, "Come to my tent in thirty minutes."

David and Joseph briefly conferred down the trail from the funeral about the meaning of Valerias' requests. David was relaxed and thought there might be a reward for his part. Joseph was uneasy, though. He had been around the General enough to know that he could come from a direction that was unexpected and could produce a bad result. Joseph warned David of this and told him to be alert and wary.

Before the thirty minutes were up, David was let inside the tent. It was empty. Bukarma and a couple of guards waited outside. David waited for what seemed like hours, and he stood the entire time. The more David waited, the more nervous he became. He started to pace, and sweat began to form around his neck. *Maybe Joseph was right—this might not go well.* It was warm inside the tent, which was surprising, as it was cool outside. A drop of sweat fell off his nose. He noticed his body odor had become more pronounced. Now he was worried, and horrific images of what the General could to do to him sprouted as nightmares in his brain. Finally the tent entrance flap opened and in strode the General. Bukarma was right behind him. This order of appearance had been played out many times and always with the same effect—intimidation.

The confidence and sureness of the General's manner was in sharp contrast to David's nervousness, and thus weakness. This was a weakness the General intended to use against David.

The General started, "Tell me your real name, *David*."

"David" was caught completely off guard by this question and muttered, "I don't know what you are talking about."

"*What*?" the General mockingly responded.

"David" started to speak, but his nervousness caught up to him and he stammered incoherently. The General stopped him with a quick hand gesture across the General's throat. Both men were then silent.

The General looked hard at "David." "I know who you are and it is not, *repeat not*, David. You are Isaac, and you are no more of a rabbi than I am—or even a semi-rabbi. You are from the village you claim to be from, but you are no religious man. Now tell me why you came here, to my camp." The General spoke again as if he knew the answer to his question.

Isaac tried to answer, but his mind was more focused on how he would die today. He had heard the General could be quick with an execution, at least the decision to have one carried out. One awful thought after another raced through his mind. He now regretted his decision to pretend to be a rabbi, and the ability to conjure possible outcomes was rampaging through his mind. Isaac's knees were gone, and he started to collapse. As he did so, he felt the strong arms of Bukarma catch him. A splash of water revived him, only now he was face-to-face with the General.

"You came here for money. You thought you could ride in here, pretend to be a rabbi, collect your purse, and ride smiling out of my camp. It's as if you put a clever ruse on the dumb Roman. The trouble is, I am not a dumb Roman. There is no such person. I am General Marcus Augustus Valerias, and you are an ignorant, lost soul. You stand here in front of me, wondering how you are going to die. You are not so clever now, are you, *Isaac*?"

The General backed away from Isaac's face, not taking his eyes off of his captive. Valerias had watched orb weaver spiders catch prey. First they rush in on an insect stuck in the web. Quickly they wrap the insect up and then go for the bite that eventually kills it. Sometimes the bite is made to initially embalm the insect before the web is spread around the insect to slow it down. Valerias had performed this technique many times on captives and even on Roman soldiers who strayed from the Roman ideals. Now he was using it on Isaac.

Isaac was not a practicing Jew. He came from a village, though, where the teacher from the rudimentary school was Jewish. Isaac had helped the teacher from time to time and picked up a few Jewish customs. Some people in the village viewed Isaac as trouble, others thought he was a fool. He had talent and the ability to quickly pick things up, and yet he lacked ambition. He had learned no trade well enough to practice with any efficiency or quality. Isaac preferred to scrounge for temporary unskilled jobs that barely paid enough money to live on. His lack of ambition and tardiness in looking for a wife had caused turmoil with his parents.

Isaac began to wise up about what it takes to get by in life, and when the Romans came looking for a rabbi, Isaac knew this was his chance to make money and show his fellow villagers that he was worth more than what they thought of him. However, his plan was not well thought out, as he had vastly underestimated the Roman he was now facing.

Isaac was frightened as he had never been before. The General, both calm and intimidating, said, "The man you rode into camp with yesterday was my chief intelligence gatherer—or spy—you pick the word. He learned much about you, and for what he didn't learn, he sent a man to your village to ask about you. Your own villagers voluntarily told us what I needed to know."

Isaac became overwhelmed. He thought he would try to quickly repent to God, whom he had largely ignored. Isaac was more pagan than Jewish, so he did not usually acknowledge a god. At this moment he changed his philosophy. He closed his eyes to pray for the final minutes that he would be alive. When Isaac opened his eyes, the General was standing back in the tent whispering to Bukarma.

The General walked over to Isaac. There was no weapon in his hands, which was a minor relief. "Today is the day that you have been blessed. Fortune has found you. It is I, not God, who forgives you. I was pleased with your part at Jacob's funeral today. I have decided to let you live. Be warned—I do this as a favor to Jacob, not you. It is my farewell gift to Jacob that I spare your life. There is a second gift. I will let you leave here with your health. There is your horse outside this tent. You will get on your horse and ride out of this camp and return to your village. I suggest you accomplish something good for the rest of your life. Maybe become a leader in your village? I don't know and I don't care. One thing is for certain: if I ever see you again, you will be executed on the spot. *Now go!*"

Isaac was almost too weak to walk to his horse. Bukarma basically carried him to the horse and roughly put him on it. Isaac barely had enough time to grab the horse's mane before someone slapped its rear and it took off away from the tent and out of the camp.

Bukarma spoke to the General as Isaac disappeared out of view. "You are getting soft, to show mercy to that fake."

"I did it for Jacob—that is all."

The General thought about Isaac for a few more minutes. He did admire, in a small way, the courage Isaac possessed in his effort to try to deceive a Roman general. Isaac reminded the General of another wasted effort that he had seen in the past months. That person was the priest, Joseph. Both men had misplaced courage and ended up being his captives. It was only by his mercy that both were still alive. *What fools,* he thought. *How lucky they are, and that includes Gul as well.* The General returned to the command tent, as there were other issues to address.

At sunset Bukarma announced to the General that Joseph was present, as he had requested. The General was curt in his remarks. "You are going to be my Chief Administrator. It is a temporary position. You will train someone to take your place as soon as possible."

Joseph did not know what to make of this statement, as it led to the question: *What is to become of me, particularly in light of the death of one of my primary advocates?*

"You should also talk to Olivertos, because you will no longer be his assistant," the General continued.

Again Joseph was worried. This sounded like the General was going to get rid of him. With Jacob gone, that was what apparently would happen. The General knew he had Joseph. Joseph was so concerned about his future that he would do exactly what the General wanted.

"Are you thinking about what is to become of you, priest?"

Joseph did not look the General in the eye. Instead, his view wandered to the floor.

"Look at me when I talk to you, or are you some child who has just been scolded?"

Joseph looked directly at the General. This was difficult for Joseph, because for what now seemed like the thousandth time, the intimidation factor of the General was working on him.

The General had anticipated Joseph's thoughts. "Priest, I want to alleviate your concerns. Nothing is going to happen to you—so long as you perform your duties."

Joseph initially believed that meant conducting the administration functions that Jacob had overseen. He was familiar enough with these functions, because of his background with his family's business and because of his work with Jacob. Jacob had been a good teacher. However, something was gnawing at the back of Joseph's mind as to his real function as the General's new Chief Administrator.

XII

Chronicles

Joseph's mind churned through different alternatives for his future when the General said, "Look to your right, priest."

Joseph complied. There on a table were several bound parchments.

"Those are chronicles—or as I think of them, my history. I would dictate to Jacob and he would write what I said. I want to have written chronicles of my time in the legions. Battles, wars, enemies, strategies, preparation, and the rest that I want in written form. I want my story told by the only person who could tell it, and that is me. Not some crony of an enemy in Rome or even Braxus or Olivertos. They have not been with me the entire time I have been a soldier, officer, and general, and they do not know what I have experienced. My history must be accurate, not some lie or exaggeration."

The General paused, which prompted Joseph to ask the question, "You want me to be your scribe for your diary?"

"You catch on fast, priest, but you already have the terms wrong. It is not a diary. It is my *history*, where facts are not clouded by emotion or feelings. And you are not a scribe. I don't know what 'scribe' means to you, but you will be my assistant. After you finish your accounting duties and after supper, you will report to me here. I will then cover a section of what I want to cover and you will transcribe it on the page."

The General moved closer to Joseph to make his point. "Do this function well for me, and I will allow you to leave this camp alive and you can go wherever you want to go. Back to Rome, back to the Goths or anywhere else—to conduct whatever priestly things you do—I do not care."

He spoke quietly in a direct way that froze Joseph. "If you fail me or let me down, I will sell you to the mines and you can proselytize there for the remainder of your life, which usually isn't very long. Is that clear enough for you?"

Without giving any thought to his response, Joseph blurted out, "Yes."

"Good," the General responded. "We start tomorrow night. By the way, winter is whispering in the winds. We have been fortunate the past few weeks with good weather. We will be breaking camp in the next few days and moving toward my fort, where we will winter. You will conduct all—and I mean all—of your duties during the relocation of my army for winter. You have much responsibility; show me that you can do it, and I will reward you with your freedom."

With that, the General gave Joseph his leave. Once he had left the tent, Bukarma came in and asked, "Do you think he can handle what you ask of him?"

"I don't know. For his sake, I hope so. For what I need, I hope so."

The next day Joseph arrived early. No one was in the command tent, and only two guards were stationed outside. This was unusual, as the General's tent had a constant flow of legion personnel and civilians throughout a normal day. Joseph knew the General would appear shortly, so while he waited, he went over by the parchments. There were four parchments, each comprised of a series of papyri.

Joseph opened and scanned one and then another and finally all four. Three had been completed. Jacob's writing was clear, with a distinctive style that was easy to read. The fourth book was about one-half finished.

Joseph started reading the last entry when there was a commotion by the tent. Braxus came in first followed by Cratus, Bukarma, and Revious and then more commanders whom Joseph recognized but whose names he could not remember. Braxus spread gold coins on a nearby table. The General entered the tent and walked over to the table with the coins and split them into three piles. Each pile was composed of ten coins. The General took one set of the coins. Braxus took another pile, and one of the commanders Joseph had rarely seen took the last set. Words were spoken in a mixture of laughter and cursing. In a few minutes all the men had left the tent.

Only the General, Joseph and a servant were present. He walked over with a glass of water for Joseph. The General was presented with a large container of mead. He took a big drink. "We just finished our final fall contests, and I won, which is typical for me. I can judge a man and what he is capable of as soon as I see him. I see someone and know he is a winner." This was spoken so matter-of-factly that Joseph assumed it was a fact.

The General knew his involuntary guest had no idea what he was talking about, so he focused on the purpose for having Joseph in his tent. "Have you looked at my books?" the General asked.

"Yes," replied Joseph.

"Then you know what you must do. I will discuss a segment of my history and you will neatly write in the parchments what I say. In case you need to, you may take notes on the rough pieces of papyri and then later transcribe your final notes on the papyri in the half-empty parchment. I prefer that you take this approach. You may ask me to slow down or repeat something I say. However, you are not to render opinions or discuss what I say. What I discuss also stays in this tent, and you are not to talk to anyone about our time here. Is all this clear?"

"Yes," said Joseph.

"Then let's begin," the General said in earnest.

XIII

Escape

At approximately three in the morning, Claire heard a very soft tapping on her door and opened it. The chambermaid Mary stood there along with Claire's daughters Anne and Elizabeth. Claire hugged all three and made a sound for silence with her hand over her mouth. They quietly walked into Claire's room, and she softly closed the door but did not set the lock. She went over to a large painting. It was of some old relative of Gerhard's she did not know. There was a small lever on the lower left in the wall by the painting. Claire lifted the lever and a soft grinding sound came from behind it. After the sound stopped, Claire gave a tug on the right side of the frame of the painting. It then moved away from the wall by about a foot.

Quickly she motioned for Mary to enter, followed by the two children. Claire then followed inside. She brought with her the candle she had previously used as a signal. It was relit by the dying remnants from her fireplace. After she entered the tunnel, she pulled the painting back and reattached it to the wall with a sticky substance. She then used a lever inside the tunnel to close the entrance. Hopefully no one would know how they had left the castle—at least that was the plan. They were now in the belly of the castle and walking the line between freedom and certain death.

Years ago Gerhard had shown this tunnel to Claire in case there would be a use for it. And now was the time. The tunnel was narrow with a low ceiling. It first was part of the castle, and then descended into rock. Claire did not know who had carved the tunnel in the rock and when, except she thought they had to be smaller-sized people. To whomever did the work though, she was thankful.

Claire did not know how she would have escaped from the castle without the tunnel. She would have had to leave her room, go to the girls' room, and make it out of the castle through the gates without being seen. Argus and his dupe, Flavius, and their spies had eyes everywhere. It would have been impossible to leave the castle any other way.

The tunnel located outside Claire's room was dry and had a desolate feeling. It wound down and around in a serpentine manner. The farther it descended, the more damp the conditions became, with an increasing number of spider webs to cause an entanglement. The webs gave Anne and Elizabeth fear that attached to the webs was some enormous hairy spider that could suck the juices out of a girl. Both girls dreaded spiders. Claire knew this and spoke to them in a quiet, soothing monotone.

"There is no giant spider. The spiders that made these webs were smaller than my thumbnail, and have fled the area when we arrived—if they were even here at all. We are much larger and more ferocious than any of these spiders. What you should be afraid of is the King of the Spiders—his name is Argus. Would you rather go back up and be trapped in his web of lies and cruelty or have a chance for freedom?"

Claire was never one to mince words, but she took time to calm her children. They would have to be strong to successfully manage this situation. Anne and Elizabeth both looked at their mother's eyes as they flickered in the candlelight. The calm manner and resolve Claire showed seemed to relax them.

Anne started to speak, but at that moment Claire put her hand over Anne's mouth, a message not to say anything. Claire then continued in her hushed tone. "I promise we will get through this tunnel soon. We will meet Erik and leave the castle and Argus for good. She then reached for Anne's hand and held the candle in her other hand. She looked back and signaled for Elizabeth to grab Anne's other hand, and then Mary took Elizabeth's hand and they continued on.

They moved along the passageway hand in hand for several minutes in silence. The fear that Anne and Elizabeth previously felt was still there, it was just buried. They knew that any scream would alert the guards, which would not end well for them, specifically their mother and Mary. The last few steps of the tunnel floor were covered by water a few inches deep. Although shallow, the water was cold and uncomfortable. The girls' focus turned from spider thoughts to keeping warm. They also didn't observe that their mother had stopped in front of what appeared to be a solid wall. Claire handed the candle to Mary and carefully removed pieces of the wall until a small opening was present and fresh air circulated around the four females.

Claire made a low call that filtered through the wall and out into the darkness. It was the call of an owl. After a few seconds, she made the call again. This time a similar call answered. They waited in silence, and finally someone was pulling the wall carefully down.

Erik stepped into view. "Welcome to your freedom."

Erik was dressed in all black, and his face was covered in mud. He had four sacks filled with dark-shaded clothing. In a hushed tone Claire instructed her daughters and Mary to put the clothes on over what they were wearing. It was cold outside, and the clothes would provide extra warmth as well as help them blend in with the night. Erik had also brought a small bucket of mud, and all the women put a light coating on their faces and hands. The empty sacks were put in the bucket and placed inside the tunnel. Erik and Claire then silently placed branches and whatever native materials they could find over the opening to the tunnel. They wanted to make it as difficult as possible for Argus to track them. They also knew Argus would spare no effort to do so.

When this was done, Erik motioned for the group to follow him. There was no trail, and it was very dark as they moved through a wooded area. Erik, Claire, and the rest of the group stayed close to one another and held hands so as not to become divided. Every now and then a flicker of light from the half moon barely above the horizon would find its way down to the surface where they walked. This light, though, was just a temporary shade of dark gray that poorly exposed animate and inanimate objects on the landscape. There was no wind, and the only sound was the calls of owls from a distance. It was an eerie setting, and Anne and Elizabeth were edgy, wishing they could get out of it. The castle almost seemed like a better alternative.

After walking for what Claire thought was about one-half a mile, the group came to a small clearing. Once again, Erik made the owl call. A man with five horses emerged from the dark cover of the woods. Erik motioned to the women to go to a horse, where the two men helped them mount. Claire was an excellent rider, and she had taught her daughters to be good riders for their ages. Mary was the least experienced of the foursome, but she could ride a horse. Once the group of six was mounted, they walked slowly through alternating patches of shallow forests and meadows. Erik took the lead; the other man trailed the group. After about an hour, another man from up ahead joined the group and spoke quietly with Erik. Erik turned and told Claire they had passed Argus' final checkpoint. They could now go to the main road without worry—at least for the time being.

The daughters were relieved to be out of the woods, and the approaching dawn made them feel better. The others of the party were much more apprehensive—they knew there would be hell to pay when Argus found Claire missing. However, they were free from Argus for now and traveling on a well-constructed Roman road. The road ahead held promise, unlike the hazardous life in the castle with Argus.

The party of seven rode all night and into the morning, when they stopped for a rest by a small brook in an area surrounded by trees. The water was cool and refreshing. The girls and Mary fell asleep. The two men who were with Erik left as dawn broke. That left five members in the party.

Erik took Claire away from the sleeping trio.

"How long do you think before Argus finds you missing and comes searching for you?" whispered a concerned Erik.

Claire answered, "He has known since very early this morning and is trying to figure out how we got away, and *with whom.* I am pleased so few people were involved. That will make it harder for him to track us and make it less likely that he will harm someone. Are your two cousins safe?"

"I imagine they are at full gallop to the Roman fort at Londinium. They have worked for the Romans in the past and should be accepted there. Maybe we should have gone there too."

"No," Claire said, "the Romans may well turn us in to Argus to prevent a war with him. I am a big prize, too big a prize for the Romans to protect in the face of Argus' demands. On the one hand, I am so happy to be out of that damned castle—all of us—where some of us faced certain death. On the other hand, we will need good fortune to find a safe way from Argus. What you and Mary have done for us is so courageous. You are risking everything for us and asking nothing in return. I can never repay you for your courage and your heart."

Erik had taken an oath to Gerhard, and he felt compelled to adhere to the oath even after Gerhard's death. "You are our rightful Queen, Claire. Argus is a usurper. My loyalty is to the Queen." He also had unspoken feelings for the Queen.

Claire had a soft spot in her heart for Erik. She and Erik could have been lovers, but it was not meant to be—at least for the time being.

After a few more minutes of conversation, Erik said that they needed to continue to ride. They would head northwest in the direction Argus would least suspect them to take. Argus would think they were traveling to Londinium.

Claire roused Mary and the children and soon they were off, out of the forest and on the main Roman road. They would take the road a little longer before veering off and taking a less-traveled path, but a path familiar to both Erik and Claire. They would try to avoid the main roads as much as possible and work their way to the wild western part of Britannia, where they could hopefully join her brother, Eustice. He was in hiding from Argus, and under protection of western tribes. The tribes had been friendly to Gerhard but were hostile to Argus. Gerhard had been wise enough to give those tribes a large degree of autonomy.

XIV

Punishment

The General had just started talking. His tone was similar to a lecturer, or like a teacher giving a lesson to his pupils. Joseph was so nervous that he made several initial mistakes. He wasn't even considering the content of the General's story. The General saw the nervousness and slowed down. After a few more moments, the General gave up and found old papyri and placed them in front of Joseph. Surprisingly, the General was very calm and showed unusual patience. He had not seemed to be one with any patience, especially with Joseph.

"Priest, use the old papyri first and take notes. You can later flesh it out in final."

Joseph was startled by this behavior of a man who once held a dagger to his throat.

"Yes, General, I'll get better."

The General started at the beginning again, and Joseph quickly developed a technique he thought would work. The end of the first night came, and the General left the tent. Joseph then wrote the work in final on good papyri. He left the final version on the table and returned to his tent to prepare for the morning.

When the General returned, he read what Joseph had written and nodded, a sign that he was pleased with the effort.

During the following afternoon, Joseph was walking to the General's main tent when he saw an organized commotion in an open area at the base of camp. Cratus slowly rode into the area with several soldiers also on horseback. Joseph couldn't see all that was happening, so he walked down to the area. Behind the horses were several men walking in chains. Their heads hung down, and they looked like the rabble Joseph had sometimes seen in Rome. It was obvious, both from visual and olfactory senses, that none of the men had bathed in some time. Joseph's curiosity was strong, and he pushed forward. As he grew near, the men in chains looked like Roman soldiers. He thought he recognized at least one of them through his work in the camp as a physician and administrator. He couldn't understand why they were being treated in such a manner. Just then he felt a hand on his shoulder.

"You may stay and watch; however, I suggest you return to the camp and do something productive."

It was the General, who had come from the same area as Joseph.

"Why?" Joseph asked.

"You will not like what you see." The General moved down into the open area where the men stood. He ordered all of men down on their knees and they complied. Joseph counted eight kneeling men. A Roman soldier stood over each man. The men looked scared, and one was beginning to sob. Joseph now realized something bad was about to happen, and yet he could not take his eyes off of this scene.

The General spoke to Cratus quietly for a few minutes. He then turned to the eight men on their knees.

"You have been found as deserters from the army." Then, in a more biting tone, *"From my legions."* The General inhaled deeply.

"You all know from your training that I consider desertion a traitorous act. And such treason warrants the death penalty. What say you before I issue sentence and carry out the punishment?"

The General went down the line and brusquely listened to each man's version of the events, from their point of view. He appeared to have little interest in their stories, many of which he knew were lies. The whining from some of them was annoying to him as well. Cratus stood with the General throughout this process. Joseph had found Cratus to be more willing to act as the General's enforcer than Braxus, so he now knew that things would end badly for the eight men.

After each of the eight finished what they had to say, the General stepped back and conferred again with Cratus. He then moved away from Cratus and walked to the right end of the line of despair. Joseph observed, though, that instead of looking at the men, the General's view was toward a faraway mountain whose top was covered in snow.

The General soon formulated his thoughts and moved back in front of the eight men.

"In my past days, I would have you all—all eight of you—executed for your actions. I hold you responsible for your actions—you and only you."

Half of the men looked at the General, the other half stared at the ground and waited for their sentence.

"I find desertion despicable, an utter lack of courage, and a coward's action. We cannot have desertions and cowardice in my army. We must each rely on all of us, or we all fail. It is with that in mind that I find all of you guilty of treason, for your desertion of my legions. Desertion cannot and will not be tolerated. Normally your sentence would be death, by whatever means I find appropriate to your act of desertion. However, I have decided to give you a choice—death by the sword, or you will be sold to work in the mines. I will give you a few minutes to select your fate."

The General strode over to Cratus and whispered a few words into Cratus' ear. Cratus nodded and disappeared into the crowd of soldiers who had gathered. The General walked back to the center of kneeling men, stopped for a second, moved to the right end of the line, and stood in front of that man. He was sweating profusely and refused to look the General in the eyes.

The General stared at the man, and then, slightly raising his voice, spoke so all eight could hear, "There is one exception to my previous offer and that is to this man. Rise and state your name."

The man mumbled incoherently. The General did not ask him to repeat himself but instead said, "Agri of Spain, I know who you are. You are the messenger who came to my tent recently. I sent you to train and become a proud Roman soldier. Now you are a cowardly deserter. Not only are you not in any condition to be a soldier, you fled the army that you took an oath to protect—with your life. I gave you a chance—a choice—and you responded by letting me down."

At this time there was movement in the crowd. Cratus stepped forward; behind him were three Roman archers. Agri was terrified, and the only thing he could think of was how he should have hid better when the soldiers first came to the village four days ago looking for a rabbi. He didn't think the soldiers saw him—but one of the reasons Cratus had become a general was because he was very observant of what was going on around him. This included seeing men who watched from the shadows. As a result, Agri was caught along with the other seven men.

Agri hated the army and did not regret deserting. What he regretted was being caught. It did not matter now, as the General would surely execute him.

The General, though, did not have an immediate execution in mind. He had always tried to create a punishment to best match the event that had triggered the need for punishment. Thus he said, "In prior days, when they held the games, I would have liked to see you try to outrun a lion. Unfortunately—or fortunately for you—there is no coliseum here and no beasts, no lions, so we are going to improvise. And I will give you a chance to live, Agri. There is a catch. For you to have a chance, you must be in the physical condition I would expect any Roman soldier to be in. *Are* you in such a condition?"

Both men knew that Agri was not in such a condition. However, Agri also knew he would not have a choice in the matter. The General nodded and Cratus moved to the front with the three archers. They carried long bows and each had a quiver of several arrows.

"You each may select one arrow from your quiver," the General said to the three men. He glanced at Cratus. "Make it a good choice."

The General turned back to Agri. "Here is what we and you are going to do. See the forest wall to the north? It is about one hundred yards away. It is a little uphill, but for a man in the condition that I expect of a Roman soldier, you should be able to run this distance easily in quick fashion. If you make it to the forest, you are a free man. I promise, I will not send any man or beast after you. You just need to survive in the forest—also a trait of a good Roman soldier. There is one condition, though. At General Cratus' count of ten, these three archers will each shoot one arrow at you. If you are hit, that is the end of my mercy and you will die. I promise you a full count of ten. It is all up to you."

The General then commanded the three archers, "Prepare yourselves. If you miss, General Cratus will find a special duty for you. I also may have General Cratus join you, for he selected you for this task."

The General was dead serious when he spoke, and the gravity was felt by the archers and to a lesser extent by Cratus. There was pressure not to fail, something not new to the soldiers who served under Valerias. Expecting excellence was the way Valerias had been so successful in battle. The General walked over to a mostly terrified Agri. Mostly terrified because he would likely die, but there was that small hope of surviving. The General's word was true, which was well known throughout the army.

"It is this or decapitation. I thought you might appreciate my choice for you. At my command, General Cratus, start the count." Agri prepared himself as best he could. Unfortunately for him, the pressure was even greater and his muscles had become very tight. The General knew this, which was part of his plan.

"Are you ready, Agri the messenger? Are you ready, archers? Are you ready, General Cratus?"

"Yes," Cratus replied.

"Begin."

"One." Cratus began the count.

Agri tried to get off to a good start, but nerves and tight muscles caused him to slip in dirt.

"Two."

Agri quickly regained control of his legs and pushed off hard.

"Three."

Agri accelerated and began to increase his strides.

"Four. Five."

For the first time Agri felt he had a chance, as the forest wall became clearer to his vision.

"Six. Seven."

Cratus' voice began to fade, as Agri now ran in a full-out sprint. By the time Cratus reached eight, Agri could not hear him. He had become so focused on reaching the forest that the only sound he heard was his loud breathing. He silently counted nine and then ten to himself. The forest seemed right in front of him. A little more effort and he would be there and free.

The first arrow slammed into his right shoulder and sent a shot of pain to his brain. He thought this was only a slight wound;

he was out of range by now and the forest was his. The second and third arrows pierced his back. One pierced a little lower than the other. The upper arrow had penetrated his heart, and he was instantly dead. He hit the ground with a thud, but only the air around him heard the sound. His arms stretched back in an involuntary reaction of reaching for the arrows.

The General and those around him showed no reaction. What had to be done was done. The General turned to Cratus. "Good. Pay the men appropriately."

Joseph could not take his eyes off of the corpse. Agri had made it maybe forty yards, still quite a long distance from the forest. The General knew he couldn't make it, and this served as his execution. Joseph was amazed at how easily the archers had taken Agri down. However, upon further thought, it was not that surprising, as the archers were hand picked by Cratus. These archers could easily hit a slow-moving target running in a generally straight line at double and even triple the distance from where they had shot Agri.

Joseph stared at Agri's body, mesmerized, as the General walked back to the seven kneeling men. He approached the second man from the end where Agri had been placed.

"What is your choice?" The General said in a low voice that left no doubt as to the severity of the situation.

The man answered, "I would like to have the choice you gave that man, Agri. I choose that one."

Just as the man spoke his last word, the sword plunged into his back and out through his lower abdomen. The sword was withdrawn as quickly as it entered the man. The soldier behind the man stepped back and looked at the General. The General looked very briefly at the soldier and then at the deserter. He stayed in the kneeling position briefly before falling forward. Blood gurgled from his mouth and also pooled underneath his body before migrating out and into the dirt.

The General did not move at first as the blood spread further out. Like Agri, this man had died instantly. When the blood was within an inch of his boots, the General made his way over to the next man. He sobbed uncontrollably. He knew he would be the next man to play one of the General's end-of-life games.

The General spoke to the remaining six from this position, "Do you think I'm a fool who grants deserters what they want? No, the fools are you. You will obey me now, as when you were actual soldiers."

The General turned to the third man in from the right side of the line, "Gather yourself, deserter, quickly. You can have the two choices I initially offered you, or you can select the choice your friend to your left just made. I hope you know how that choice will end. Choose now or I will choose for you."

The soldier behind the man moved forward, blade drawn above the man.

The man's mumbling was barely audible, but clear enough for the General to hear. "The mines."

The General proceeded to go down the line. Every man chose the mines over execution. With this choice, they knew their execution would not be so immediate.

The General then ordered the six surviving men, "Dispose of the two bodies and clean up the area where the bodies fell. General Cratus will watch you to see that this task is conducted according to my standards. Afterward, you can have a meal, and tomorrow you will be sent to the mines. I have representatives coming in the morning to assure your transition is a good one."

Joseph watched this second execution in horror. He had never seen such a death at such close range. The speed at which this execution had taken place and the manner by which it had occurred made him almost vomit. Fortunately, he held it together, because at this time the General walked up to him as he headed back to his command tent.

"I told you it was a poor idea for you to be here." The General's eyes were cold as he spoke, and there was a snarl in his tone. And then he was gone into the crowd that parted to let him and his guard pass. The last guard to pass Joseph was Bukarma.

He, too, spoke in a swift manner to Joseph. "Don't be so quick to judge," was all he said and then he too was gone.

Joseph felt both fear and anger toward the General and also confusion at Bukarma's comment. He decided, though, to go to Olivertos' tent and speak his mind. When Joseph arrived at Olivertos' tent, he told the physician what he had seen. However, he did not receive the sympathetic response that he wanted.

"You came to me this time because you want me to say something about the General that I cannot discuss further with you."

Olivertos' response surprised Joseph. In retrospect Joseph recalled that he did have a whining tone.

Olivertos continued, "The General has rules that he demands all men under his command obey. They take an oath to Rome—to defend Rome to the death. He absolutely hates rapists, cowards—and most of all, deserters. What you saw today was something that you would not have seen years ago. Those eight men would have been executed in many ways that you do not want me to describe for you. Today, you saw mercy in action, at least as much mercy as the General can extend. Only two men died today, and one of those two deaths was the result of that man's own stupidity."

"But he still slaughtered two men," Joseph weakly answered.

"You still don't get the point, do you, Joseph?" Olivertos was annoyed and it showed in his tone. "So let me explain. An army or legion or cohort, even a squad, is only as strong as its weakest point. To be successful in battle, there can be no weak points. A deserter who has fled his comrades has created a weak point. Not just by his actions but by being an example to other weak-minded men when times are difficult that they too could flee. This leaves the army vulnerable and puts those who serve in the army as true soldiers in a weakened position. In turn, that puts the General at risk—a risk he will not tolerate." Olivertos sat back in his chair and gave Joseph a hard look. "Do you understand now?"

Joseph answered, "I do think it is wrong to take a life—even a deserter's life. We don't know what caused those men to desert. Maybe they had a good reason to do what they did. Maybe their families needed them."

"Did Jesus Christ desert his followers?"

Joseph was caught off guard. This was the first time Olivertos had ever spoken of Christ or Christianity to him.

"Well, no," was all Joseph could think of in his response to Olivertos. He was thinking about what Olivertos meant. *Was Olivertos trying to compare the General to Christ? How did soldiers of Rome compare to the disciples of Christ?* Joseph thought what Olivertos had said bordered on blasphemy.

Olivertos interrupted Joseph's thoughts. "I know what you are thinking and that is not what I meant. That was a crude statement that should not have been made. No matter what the reason, those who decide to leave the fight are hurting the cause. Enough of this subject. Let's have some wine."

After a couple of cups of wine, both men relaxed and the talk turned to other subjects, as they usually did with Olivertos. The man had a gift of talk. *No wonder the General likes him around,* thought Joseph.

Later Joseph walked back to his tent. The day's events were so etched in his mind that he barely gave thought to the commotion around him. When he arrived at the tent, Braxus was standing in front of it with several soldiers a short distance away.

"The General has ordered the camp to be struck. We are moving to the main fort, for winter approaches. The General wants you to take charge of certain items." Braxus handed Joseph a list.

It wasn't long and at the bottom it read, "See you tonight as usual." The note was not signed, although Joseph knew its author.

"Let me give you some advice, Joseph. When you see the General tonight, do not bring up today's events. If he wants to discuss them, fine, but you don't initiate the topic. If he asks you for your thoughts, keep your answers short and in agreement. Do not debate him. Many of us want you around for the winter."

With that, Braxus, turned and walked back to the soldiers, and then they were gone.

XV

RELOCATION

BY NIGHTFALL THE wind inherited a northern flavor and the resultant cold air flowed into the Roman camp. When Joseph made his way to the General's tent, he was surprised to find many of the top command present. Bukarma held Joseph back from entering the tent until the meeting ended. One by one the commanders or generals left. The last to leave was Braxus, who gave a quick stare at Joseph but didn't say a word. Bukarma stood by the entranceway.

Joseph entered the main tent and found it warm and with the odor of men in need of a bath. The General sat in his usual chair. A servant had just brought him some mead. Joseph needed no prompting and sat on his chair, which he maneuvered up to the table. He reached out and grabbed his usual writing instrument and ink. He looked at the General to start writing on whatever topic would be covered that night.

"Do you approve of the way I handled those men today?" asked the General.

Joseph was surprised that the evening's work had begun with the General asking such a question. However, he was prepared based on his earlier talks with Olivertos and Braxus.

"General, how you manage your men is up to your discretion. Not mine."

"But do you approve?"

"I do not like to see any man die, whether in battle, from a discipline issue, or at the whims of a leader."

"Are you referring to me at the end of your thought?" The General showed little emotion as he spoke, and yet Joseph was uneasy. He had been in a similar situation when he first met the General. And he knew he did not want to be caught in the same position.

"No, I am not. You are the General. Those were your men. It is up to you to choose how you should manage them."

"But they aren't my men when they desert my ranks."

"Yes, they are your men, even as deserters. I realize you must handle your men for the greater good of the army. I just don't like the punishment that you dispensed."

"Do you not think my punishment was fair? Would your God not think it was fair?"

"It is your army and your punishment. I am not in the army and can't comment if the punishment was fair or not. I also cannot answer for God."

The General stopped and stared at Joseph for a few minutes. He then spoke to Joseph in different manner than ever before. "Someone gave you advice about how I might talk to you tonight and how you should respond. I think I know who those advisors are." Another pause followed, and it seemed the General was using these pauses to try to get Joseph to say something that would get him into trouble.

Joseph stood his ground as much as he could by saying nothing and alternating between organizing the papers in front of him and glancing quickly at the General.

The General took another drink, and stared at Joseph. "You actually listened to someone. Good. You are more intelligent than

I thought." This was the General's final try. When Joseph said nothing, this topic of conversation was over.

The General continued, "Tomorrow we break camp and move to lower grounds at my fort to wait out the winter. You no doubt tonight felt a token of what winter can be. The list I gave you needs to be done, and done soon. Get whatever help you need. Ask Braxus and Olivertos; they can orchestrate just about anything that I can."

Both the General and Joseph knew what the mention by name of the two men meant.

"We will not do any of my history writings tonight. We will resume when we get settled in our winter camp. Leave now, priest."

Joseph left the tent. The General watched him leave and took another drink of mead. Bukarma came into the tent.

"What do think, Bukarma?"

"He is beginning to sound and think like a true Roman—doing what it takes to survive today."

Bukarma laughed at his own comment. The General smiled; it was the first time he had emitted a smile in weeks. The General ordered the servant to bring another mead for himself and one for Bukarma.

"Winter is here and changes are coming," the General noted as they waited for the mead. "Did you bring your game?"

The men played the game in the warmth of the tent. Joseph shivered in the cold as he made his way to the administrative tent to finalize details for the relocation of the camp.

The relocation occurred over the next several days and progressed smoothly. The good weather helped to facilitate the move. The lower camp, which typically experienced warmer weather, was housed largely in an old fort.

Winter progressed, and the snow seemed to come in batches. It snowed, melted, and snowed again. The cycle repeated itself over and over. Joseph, being from southern Rome, was not used to this type of weather. He learned quickly from his colleagues what clothes to wear. Yet when he saw the General outside, Joseph was struck by the light clothing he typically wore around camp. It was almost spring-like clothing. Nothing seemed to bother the General.

However, this show was not the truth. What was apparent on the surface did not signify the depth of the General's troubles. He was deeply bothered by several things. Yet exhibiting any weakness was not allowed. There are always rivals for the dominant bull's position. These rivals were not in the General's camp but in Milan and Constantinople. The General was well aware of his circumstance.

General Marcus Augustus Valerias was a twenty-five-year veteran of the Roman army. He rose fast through the ranks and had attained a general's rank before he was thirty. He had fought in countless battles and wars as an apprentice, an officer, and a general in several territories of both Empires. He battled the barbarian tribes that occupied the fringe boundaries of the Empires and the usurpers who tried to unseat the Emperor of the time. As a general, he had never lost a battle or war. That reputation was well known throughout the Empire. This in turn attracted the better soldiers and officers to his legions.

It was also well known that the General was especially ruthless toward Romans who rebelled against the Emperor. Few prisoners were taken from those campaigns, and that ruthlessness created enemies. His successes also created enemies in both the Eastern and Western portions of the Empire who were both jealous of his prowess on the battlefield and feared that he someday would turn his attention to becoming Emperor.

Nothing could have been further from the truth. The General had no desire ever to be Emperor. He was not a politician. He preferred giving orders and having them obeyed by troops and non-soldiers who conducted ancillary functions for the army.

The General knew that if he performed his job well, he would have loyal legions that would also consistently function at high levels. On the other hand, an Emperor must always be mindful of watching his back for assassination attempts and maintain constant concern over where usurpers would sprout up next. Those types of worries were not typical for the General, who surrounded himself with loyal officers and soldiers many miles from Milan and Constantinople.

General Valerias preferred a military organization based on that utilized by earlier Roman generals. Braxus and Cratus were legates whom he had appointed to the rank of general. The two were the commanders of the General's field army, the comitatenses legions. These legions (four thousand men) were composed of cohorts (four to five hundred men) led by tribunes. The cohorts, in turn, were composed of subunits called centuries (one hundred men) commanded by centurions. Besides the comitatenses, the General also controlled the limitanei legions. The limitanei were stationed in the border areas of the General's territories. The General employed a top-down command, simple in organization, yet effective in its implementation.

That command structure was evident to Joseph during the next several weeks, when there was a whirl of activity around the fort. Numerous generals, officers, bureaucrats, and even civilians visited the General's headquarters. Joseph also observed that several commanders escorted their troops outside of the fort during this time. He knew that the General had divided his command for the winter and sent cohorts to the many smaller forts and cities in the region and also to provide support for the limitanei. This action gave a sense of security to the local populace that the Roman army was nearby. It also provided his soldiers a warmer environment in which to pass the winter. Finally, Joseph heard rumors of a large mass of Goths heading toward the Danube River, fleeing an unknown force from the east.

Joseph picked up these facts in the General's command center while the General was attempting to dictate his history to him. During the interruptions Joseph had his ears pointed to the visitor conversations while steering his eyes to the manuscript he was preparing for the General. Joseph had learned to juggle several tasks at the same time.

The General, at first, never discussed strategy with Joseph or even the events that were transpiring. He still held a slight belief that Joseph was a traitor, which meant that he always had a feeling of distrust of Joseph. Over time, though, he came to trust Joseph with keeping his history, something that was very important to him. Gradually the General lost his adverse feeling toward Joseph, who became a fixture in the General's quarters. In this role, Joseph accomplished fewer of his administrative duties, which instead were being conducted by the large bureaucracy that seemed to be ever present in the Roman army. The General was not fond of the size of this bureaucracy, but he no longer cared to deal with the issue.

Because of the pause in the military actions and resultant no casualties, Olivertos spent most of his time reading or talking to other staff physicians about new medical techniques and practices. Joseph dropped in on Olivertos about once a day in his rooms at the fort to catch up with these new measures and other nonmedical matters. Joseph preferred medical work to the administrative aspects to which he was assigned by the General. Thus he was glad to be largely relieved from the bookkeeping tasks and telling others how to do their jobs.

One night after all the visitors had exited the General's command center, just the General and Joseph, with the always-present Bukarma, remained in the room. During dictation of his history, the General had been unusually pensive. He frequently lost his train of thought, and tonight there were several long pauses. The General commanded that a large glass of mead be brought to him. He did not offer Joseph any drink. After taking a large gulp, he sat straight in his chair and looked at Joseph, but his eyes seem focused elsewhere.

Finally his eyes and mind came together as he looked to Joseph. "Do you think I am evil?"

When the General spoke those words, Joseph took his eyes off the General and let them wander around the room, trying to think of something to say. He observed that Bukarma, who usually looked straight ahead, had diverted his eyes away from the General.

Joseph had become accustomed to odd questions and comments from the General as he provided his history. Yet the discussion up to this point was largely facts, figures, strategies, reasons for strategies, battles, enemies, etc. There was little humanity involved in his history. This question from the General was so unusual it took Joseph completely aback. Also surprising in the General's question was that he did not use the word "priest" in any part of the sentence. Almost every sentence the General spoke to Joseph began or ended with "priest." Joseph did not know if this was a trap, and the first night in the General's tent with the knife at his throat continued to haunt his thoughts.

The General said nothing after asking Joseph that question, and Joseph was equally quiet. Joseph knew the General would say nothing until Joseph responded, so he finally said, "It is not my place to say to you if you are evil or not. I cannot answer that."

"But you have read and heard much of my history, and you have seen me do things to men that have revolted you. Am I not correct?"

"You have carried out actions that . . ." Joseph stopped speaking and looked down.

"That you do not approve of? Did I finish your sentence? Would your God approve of what I have done?"

"I don't know. I can't speak for God. I just follow the teachings." Joseph returned the same answer he had repeatedly said to the General.

"You are a foolish being. You read your books and listened to your teachers and then try to judge me. As you have seen, if I did not do what I do, there would be chaos all over this territory, and you would likely be dead—with your head planted on one of your books by a barbarian. I am the instrument that brings order and peace to those territories that I command. And I shall do what needs to be done to maintain order, collect taxes, and support the Empire. Period."

"No matter the human cost?" asked Joseph.

"Yes." The General paused before continuing. "You do not understand what you think you understand."

The General sat back in his chair to think about the dialog that had just happened, and, more importantly, with whom he had spoken. Joseph was confused, as he usually was during these sessions with the General. However, for the first time since his first encounter with the General, he felt that the General had actually spoken to him as a person.

The General concluded, "That is it for this evening. I am going to travel throughout my region to the fortifications and encampments. Something tells me there is a change coming, and I want to be at the top of the glacier, not in an avalanche. I also want to see the preparedness of my men. Braxus will take command while I'm gone. We will resume my history when I return. Try to keep money in the Treasury and Olivertos from doing more autopsies than needed. We are almost done here, and then we go to the next stage."

Joseph left relieved but confused. What did he mean "go to the next stage?" And was he trying to be humorous or was he serious? Joseph could never figure out what the General meant. It was best to keep his head down and stay as invisible as possible.

The next morning when Joseph awoke, the General, Bukarma, and a large group of light cavalry were gone to the north. There were reports that he was to meet with the Emperor Valens at some point and then travel to other parts of his region. A meeting with Emperor Valentinian was also rumored.

The following weeks went by quickly for Joseph. Winter overall was proving to be mild, with temperatures warmer than usual. Joseph spent half of his time with Olivertos and the other half with the administrative branch of the army, including the Treasury people. It was a slow time for Olivertos, as he generally treated minor illnesses and an occasional wound.

The General sent constant reports by messenger to Braxus while he was gone. Cratus continued in the role of master trainer of the soldiers, a role he relished. Cratus liked to keep physically busy while Braxus stayed in the General's command tent and assumed the role of Supreme General.

The General stressed continual training for all his soldiers. Usually morning was spent doing various chores and tasks around the fort, and the afternoon was devoted to several types of training. The most popular were combat exercises that pitted one squad against another in contests. The General frowned when the end result of a contest was death, so the competitors used wooden weapons. That didn't stop combatants from trying to inflict damage on an opponent. Cratus liked to reward the winners with coins, so that the contests had a monetary flavor in addition to the recognition of the squad and its cohort for a victory.

An interesting development for Joseph was that Braxus frequently included him in the council meetings. Cratus once asked Braxus why Joseph was present, and Braxus replied, "Because I want him here."

That ended the discussion. Cratus held no animosity toward Joseph, as he had also been a friend of Jacob and was close to Olivertos. Cratus, though, gave Joseph little thought and viewed him as a novelty that could easily be discarded. Braxus' attachment was more spiritual. He liked the presence of Joseph as a kind of calming effect and to keep the men on better behavior at the meetings.

Almost two months had passed since the General had left the fort. Joseph went as usual to the command room to help Braxus' chief assistant prepare for the council meeting. As he entered the room, he saw the General sitting in his chair reading a chapter of his history.

He looked up as Joseph entered the tent and immediately said, "I heard that you have been everywhere, priest. One minute you are with Olivertos, then you are with the Treasury, and then in the council meetings. Maybe you are God—you are everywhere at once and in everything. Is that true?"

Experience with the General had taught Joseph well. When the General asked questions, such as this one, it was best to keep quiet, shrug a shoulder, or change the topic to a pertinent one of interest to the General.

"Would the General like to continue with his history tonight?"

The General sat back in his chair and pondered his next statement. He finally said, "No, we will do that tomorrow night. I am having a council meeting tonight. And you are not invited—this time."

Joseph looked into the eyes of the General. They were tired and showed no emotion. During the previous times, his closing remark to Joseph would have been in a strong sarcastic tone. Tonight it was delivered very plainly. Joseph could sense something was not right. Yet he had experienced this feeling with the General on many previous occasions.

XVI

No Small Matter

THE WIND DECIDED to take the day off from its usual pounding of the steppe in western Asia. In the summer, it typically came in hard from arid areas, desiccating all sources of moisture, human and non-human. But today the wind was calm, which some viewed as a bad omen. A calm day was thought to be a day on which the spirits were regrouping for an ominous assault in the future. It was very dry in this village on the steppe. Even the rocks had a tired and dry appearance.

Uldric and his fraternal twin brother Rao were in the main tent of the village with their father Drago. It was warm in the tent as the three men spoke of the weather, livestock, and other affairs of the nomadic village. Drago was the village leader, and he was an old man. His weathered skin was evidence of his many years lived in both the hot and cold times of the steppe. He was also a sick man. He had a strange cough that had hung on him for weeks. The village shaman could neither diagnose nor cure the illness, and he spent much time walking around the tent muttering his thoughts out loud about the source of Drago's condition.

Drago had always been focused on village concerns; his sons had not. When Drago asked them about the condition of the pasture north of the village and whether they should move livestock there, the sons answered yes. In reality, they did not have much of an idea either way. The sons presently had something else on their minds. During the discussion Uldric stood up and walked over to a container and retrieved three drinking cups from a basket. He then poured an alcoholic beverage into the three cups. Rao got his father's attention during Uldric's actions by bringing up a problem that he was having with one of his horses.

Uldric brought over the cups to Drago and Rao and made a toast, "Here is to more fruitful times, when the rains come again and there is a new order to nature."

The toast had a concealed meaning. The three men lifted their heads back and drank the contents of the cups in one swallow. Drago should not have drunk so aggressively, and he started to cough. Rao went over to his father and gently started to pound on his back. After a few moments of this, Drago coughed more violently. He tried to stand up, took two, bent-over, wobbly steps, and fell straight down with his chest and face hitting the ground hard at the same time. Rao bent down to check his father's breathing and after a few moments concluded that his father was dead.

Meanwhile, Uldric had picked up his father's cup and put it in a hidden compartment in his clothes. Uldric grabbed another cup from the basket and poured a little residue from what was left in his own cup into the new cup. He then placed the cup by Drago. Uldric looked at Rao and then Rao called for help. The shaman who was meandering close to the tent quickly came inside and ran over to Drago's body. After pinching, probing, and talking to the body, the shaman's face showed both worry and resignation. He knew that it was his position to save the village leader and this result would look bad. The shaman started to panic and began to run out of the tent. Instead, he ran straight into Uldric's sword. Uldric pushed the sword in deeper until it was protruding from the back of the shaman.

After a few convulsions, the shaman fell dead on the floor. One of Drago's guards heard the commotion and entered the tent with his sword drawn and a puzzled look on his face. Soon a second and third guard joined the group in the tent.

Rao immediately spoke up. "Father is dead and our shaman did nothing. Then when father died, the shaman changed into Father's servant. Uldric saw what was happening and had to stop him from leaving our father's tent. I saw it with my own eyes. The shaman was a shape shifter, and Uldric killed him before he could change again."

The three guards had quizzical looks on their faces. Their leader was dead. The shaman was dead and appeared to be a sorcerer. To the first guard, a burly man, the whole event seemed wrong. He spoke directly at Uldric. "What really happened here?"

Rao answered, "The shaman put a spell on father and started to extract his soul before he died naturally. The shaman forced us to watch his soul-snatching powers. Yet the shaman's power was not as strong as he'd thought. Uldric broke free and slew him before he changed shapes again. Tell us, how long has the shaman been treating father's illness?"

The guards were not initially convinced of this explanation; however, there was fear of shape shifters in the village, and the sons had never caused trouble for Drago. Additionally, Drago was feeble and ill. Thus, after a brief discussion, the guards concluded that Uldric's and Rao's explanation made sense. Also, how could they disagree with Uldric and Rao, as they had no evidence to argue against them, as Drago was dead? A few awkward moments of standing around followed, with the three guards looking at each other and then at Rao and Uldric. Finally the burly guard spoke. "Hail to Uldric and Rao, our leaders!" The other two guards responded in kind.

Rao appeared genuinely saddened by the death of his father and gave a command in a soft voice, "Go tell the elders of Drago's death and the shaman's treachery. Then get the undertaker. We must prepare a funeral that is fit for a man, a great leader, and our father." Uldric nodded.

With this command the three guards left the tent. Uldric spoke quietly to Rao, "The poison worked as well as you predicted. We will bury father and wait out the traditional time of mourning. We must be patient. Any signs that we had a hand in father's death would be taken very badly by the elders. In sufficient time, we will initiate our plan."

Rao was quiet while looking at his father, "I did not want to do this to him. But he was weak, and removing him was the only way to accomplish what destiny has cried out for our village, for our people, and for the Hun nation. He could have lived for a long time. Time is of the essence. We must show strength in the days ahead."

XVII

ARGUS

As expected, Argus was furious that Claire had disappeared. A servant entered Claire's room, which was, strangely, unlocked. Claire had always locked the door at night to prevent Argus and Flavius from entering. Now she was gone. Argus was one of the first persons to arrive in Claire's room. He roughly quizzed the servant about what she had seen. When he realized she knew nothing, he became more enraged. Flavius entered the room and Argus took his anger out on him.

"How did they get out of this room, Flavius?" was Argus' first question—and it was more of a shout than a question. This was followed in a rapid, angry sequence by, "Where did they go? Who was involved? How many were involved? How did they get away with the brats? Where were you?"

Flavius said nothing. He strode around the room looking for any indication of what had happened as Argus stood still, giving the death stare to anyone that looked at him. Twice Flavius walked by the painting that hid the tunnel; however, he did not suspect the painting as an escape route. The likely escape point was outside the door and through the castle. For Claire's scheme to work, there had to be several collaborators.

Argus was impatient. "They think I'm a fool, who can be tricked. Flavius, assemble anyone who had contact with that bitch Claire and take them to the outside wall. I intend to find the collaborators in this treachery."

Within minutes all the servants and staff who had any contact with Claire were marched to the outside wall. It was a cold morning.

Argus commanded that all servants stand on top of the wall. It was about fifty feet from the flats of their feet to the ground. Because their average height was a little over five feet, the distance from their eyes to the ground added at least another five feet to the dreadful view. In reality it really didn't matter much; it was a long way down. A fall would mean death. The wind whirled around those on the wall with a coldness that brought thoughts of death. Argus walked behind them in a slow, meticulous motion, talking as he walked.

"Tell me, which among you helped Claire and her spawn escape?"

When that prompted no response, Argus continued, "Which among you know something about this? If you point out that person, or persons, I will let you live and give you a reward."

Again there was no response. Argus' patience was tried. He walked behind one of the larger women and gave her a push off the wall. The woman screamed all the way to the ground. When she hit the ground she landed on her back. The sound of the impact was muffled by the wind that seemed to be calling for more. The dead woman's eyes were open, and they seemed fixated on those on the wall. The survivors on the wall were now crying and making panicky gestures to get off their perches. Another person, a small man, lost his balance, and he too fell the long, cold distance to the ground.

The cook who had helped Claire escape was a most fortunate person. At the time all this was taking place on the castle wall, he was safely out of harm's way purchasing supplies from the nearby village.

Argus' determination to find out who had aided Claire had peaked, and he shouted loudly, "Tell me what you know about Claire and her treachery to me and my kingdom, now! *Now!*"

Flavius, though, focused his thoughts on Claire's room. "My Lord, Argus, come with me. I think I know how they did this. I don't think these servants know anything. They would have cracked by now just watching their friends breaking on the ground."

A captain in Argus' guard approached Argus and Flavius. After a quick salute, the captain excitedly reported, "Erik Longwilder did not report for his shift today and is missing. We believe he is the one who helped your Queen Claire escape."

Argus struck the captain hard in the face with the flat front of his right palm. "She is not my queen, fool. No queen would ever leave me. She is a bitch and a traitor, and when I find her, she will more than pay for being a traitor."

The Captain answered meekly, "Yes, Lord Argus."

Argus turned to Flavius. "That may answer the question of how they scurried from the castle, but how did they get outside the castle? How do I even know they left the castle? Did any of your guards see the traitor Longwilder last night, either inside or outside of the castle?"

After pausing for a minute, Argus continued, "I still think it was one of the servants. Maybe I should continue my persuasive techniques on the servants."

Flavius cared little for those servants, except one, but he thought a better use of time would be to search Claire's room for clues.

"Lord Argus, before spending more time outside and in the cold, let's return to her room. Perhaps the story is there under our eyes."

"Dismiss the servants for now," Argus said to no one in particular. Then to Flavius, "Flavius, I hope you are right. Someone is going to pay for this treachery to me, and I hope it is not you for being careless. I'm holding you responsible for her leaving."

Flavius pandered to Argus, but he was not a coward and spoke back at Argus when his integrity was in question. "I was with you last night, Lord Argus, carrying on with matters of the kingdom."

Flavius knew that was only partially true. Actually, it was another nightly drinking affair. "Her leaving is no more my responsibility than the king's." Flavius was careful, though, not to say Argus' name.

Argus scowled at Flavius but did not say anything. He pointed in the direction of Claire's room and they made their way back there. Claire's leaving the door unlocked seemed odd to Flavius. He felt this was a trick, and he believed the escape route was in Claire's room.

Claire's chambers were unusually large and not well lit. The windows had been boarded shut to prevent any escape. Shadows seemed to rise and fall with the flickering candles. Argus walked in and looked around for a short time and cursed Flavius for his idea.

"I know at least one of those servants out there could tell me what happened."

Flavius entered the room. "It seems one of her servants is not present. She may have helped Claire get out."

"Really, Flavius! A woman, two children, and a chambermaid eluded the guards that should have been awake in the hall, walked through the castle unnoticed, and then left the castle grounds through the manned gates? Erik Longwilder was an outside guard, so there is no way he could have entered the castle grounds without someone seeing him. I suppose the chambermaid was a witch and turned them invisible and they flew out of here. Or maybe they were turned into rats and fled through the cracks in the walls. Or maybe they donned invisible cloaks and are watching us now from behind those invisible cloaks!"

At the end of his tirade, Argus' rage had turned sharply sarcastic, as he was at a loss to explain what had happened. Flavius had stopped listening and was looking hard at the walls. He had already searched the floor and did not find any sign there of an escape route. When scanning the north wall, he peered at the large painting. A nearby soldier was also gazing at the painting. Flavius walked over to the painting. The painting appeared to be valuable, as he recognized the artist's name in the lower right corner. He also noticed minor amounts of dust on the floor just below the painting.

Argus had stopped his talking, which was becoming a whine, and began watching Flavius conduct his detective work. Flavius looked at the painting, grabbed the right edge, and pulled it back to open a clear view of the wall. In front of him was a closed entranceway. Flavius gave it a slight push and nothing happened. He commanded a guard to come over, who gave it a much more forceful push. The walled entranceway suddenly gave way, and the guard fell down inside the tunnel. The fallen guard cursed loudly while another guard moved in to help him up. Argus pushed both guards out of the way and called for a candle. Once he had a candle, he peered down inside the tunnel. Flavius also had obtained a candle, and he too looked at the extent of the tunnel.

"Well, now we know how they escaped and why there were so few in their party." Argus announced the obvious. He then shouted excitedly to his guards, "Bring torches, now! Let's find where this tunnel goes."

There was a rustling around in the room as several of the men went in search of torches. Because it was daytime, the search took longer than if it had been at night. Finally several guards returned with torches, most of which were of poor quality. One burned out within minutes after being lit. Another burned with an acrid odor, and a third burned like the start of a fire of wet logs—with lots of smoke. In a different setting this scene would have been comedic, but not to Argus. He went into a rage and swore to all the guards that they would soon be reduced in rank to boot polishers and latrine cleaners or, worse, join the servants on the wall.

The group eventually organized itself and set a course down the tunnel. Two soldiers went first, followed by an anxious Argus, then Flavius and several more guards. Argus strategically put ordinary guards first in case Claire or someone else had placed a booby trap in the tunnel. Still, these guards wound their way through the tunnel cautiously.

Flavius spoke quietly as they ducked and walked. "Gerhard must have known about the tunnel and he told Claire. This was to be an escape route in case of raiders. Very clever."

It was clear from the broken spider webs that someone had recently been through the tunnel. Footprints were also evident in the dusty floor. As they walked, the smoke became so odorous from the one torch that two of the guards started retching. Because there was so little room in the tunnel, the smell from the vomit and odorous torch caused the entire group to become ill. Argus finally had had enough of the amateur expedition. He grabbed a torch from a bent-over soldier and pushed to the front.

They finally reached the tunnel's end. The light from day showed through cracks in the makeshift wall that Claire and Erik had erected several hours before. Argus let the lead guards disassemble the wall and then Argus, Flavius, and the other guards emerged to see a bright day. The wind had blown the fog away, and the area around the tunnel's entrance was clear for viewing. Argus ordered the men to search the nearby area for signs of how many were in Claire's party and in which direction they had fled.

After a few minutes, Flavius talked to several of the guards and reported to Argus.

"There were four persons who escaped through the tunnel. We assume they were Claire, her daughters and the chambermaid."

Flavius pointed to an area outside the entrance that had not been trampled by Argus and the rest.

Flavius then proceeded to that area, where a man's footprints were evident. "This is where Erik was waiting, Lord Argus."

"Summon my cavalry," Argus briskly spoke to one of the guards, "and find me my trackers. We will search all areas of my kingdom and even beyond until we catch these traitors. And we *will* catch them. When I do, they will undergo a death march that will take days or even weeks. It will be delicious. I want to see Claire's face when I put her brood to death."

Soldiers were already running back up the tunnel to carry out Argus' orders. Argus looked around with a twisted smile on his face. *They won't get very far,* he thought.

The most relieved man of the group was Flavius. He had a secret lover, a servant who could have been on the wall. He knew most of the servants likely would have perished in Argus' search for his truth had he, Flavius, not found the tunnel.

Argus now settled into a more confident personality. "We shall have the rats by nightfall."

Flavius wasn't as sure of capturing the fugitives before nightfall. He knew Claire would do anything to protect her children, and Erik was experienced in woodland travel. Besides, Claire still had many allies in the kingdom. And yet he did not want to upset Argus, so he said nothing, but thought, *He will find out soon enough that a rat can go in several directions to avoid being caught.* Then Flavius shrugged his shoulders. *Although, I have little experience with rats.*

XVIII

Suevi (Suebi)

On the following night when Joseph appeared at the usual time to conduct the General's history writing, there was much activity both inside and outside of the General's command center. Joseph didn't know what to think as his mind swirled as to the source of the commotion. Joseph observed both Braxus' and Cratus' arrival and entrance into the large room. Then Revious and three roughly dressed men followed. Bukarma stood outside and motioned for Joseph to enter the room. As he walked by Bukarma, the large man told Joseph, "Not a word."

Joseph entered the room, and the considerable number of men there surprised him. His focus stayed on Revious. He had not seen Revious in several weeks and wondered where he had gone. Joseph knew he hadn't been with the General; other scouts had conducted that work. But here he was standing by the left side of the General's chair. Joseph slowly merged into the background with other soldiers he did not know and the three ragged men.

The room was large and smelled of men. Talk echoed throughout the room. Joseph now recognized several men, including two tribunes, centurions, and other officers. When the General was satisfied with those in attendance, he raised his arm that held his sword and then brought it down with the flat part hitting the table. The room grew instantly quiet. Joseph observed that the General did not look in a pleasant mood.

After a brief pause the General said curtly, "Revious has just returned from his home. On the way back, he encountered a village just a few miles north of where we had our last summer encampment. The village had been burned and looted. Revious believes all its residents were slaughtered; none were even taken prisoner or for slavery. Revious tracked the killers and found they were a renegade band of Suevi. They allegedly did the same to other villages as well. They are now so burdened with plunder that they are moving slowly to the north. Revious thinks they are going back to their homeland." There was not a sound in the room as the General continued, "Do you know what angers me to the end of my limits concerning these killings and destruction of the villages?"

No one dared speak because they knew an answer was soon forthcoming.

"The village was under the protection of the Empire. It was under my protection. This is a slap at me. This is an insult to me, and to you. I will not tolerate such actions in any territory under my command. I do not care what Milan thinks. I do not care what Constantinople thinks. I care only for the pride of this army and that we protect what needs to be protected. These people pay taxes to the Empire for our protection." The more the General talked, the angrier he became—and he was very angry.

Finally Braxus asked, "How many Suevi, General?"

The General turned to Revious and nodded.

"My scouts and I counted around one hundred fifty Suevi, maybe a few more. We figured they struck this latest village at night, as this is not a particularly large raiding party, and word of their raiding was bound to reach this village. Still, the villagers never had a chance. These Suevi are moving north-northeast about ten miles a day. I think they are currently about seventy miles from our fort. They obviously do not fear a response from us. Why, I don't know. One more thing: they look more like raiders than soldiers, so they will likely flee if encountered by a real army." Revious stepped back to stand slightly behind the General.

"Any questions?" the General asked abruptly.

No one said a word. The General had Revious unfold a map on the large table in the room. It was a sketch by Revious. After flattening the map out, Revious pointed to the various locations, including the village that had just been slaughtered, where the Suevi were now situated, and the Romans' fort. Revious also showed the valley where the Suevi were headed. The General stepped in and noted two spots further east and drew lines from each spot to the Suevi's destination. He had pulled out his small dagger and slammed it at the point where the three lines merged.

"We will hit them here," said the General. "I know we will have to climb a few small hills to get to this point and I know it is winter, but we are Romans accustomed to accepting and meeting challenges. Traveling directly through the valley would take too long. We leave at dawn tomorrow. As we speak, I have ordered the stable hands and support people to prepare us for the journey. I have requested two hundred men for this trip. There will be two centuries of light cavalry, one hundred men each. I want ten men in each century to be proficient in archery. Cratus will lead one of the centuries. I also want a tribune to ride with me and a centurion to ride with Cratus. I have picked Tribune Gius and Centurion Maximus for these duties. I expect we will return in one week's time. Any questions?"

One of the centurions Joseph did not know spoke up. "General, who is leading the second expedition?"

"Did I not make myself clear, centurion? The leader of the second century and the overall commander of this expedition will be me."

The same man responded, "Is that wise, considering how this is a small operation and you are our general?"

The centurion did not receive the death stare that Joseph expected the General to give the man. Instead the General replied in a retrospective manner to the man and the group as a whole, "I understand your comment, centurion. But as I have said earlier, these Suevi have insulted me personally, and it is up to me to dispense what they deserve."

Joseph listened to this dialog and thought, *There is something more than the General's honor at stake here. He seems so focused at times and then his mind seems to wander at other times.*

Another centurion spoke up, "I too think it is not worthy of your position to assume command of such a small detail. Wouldn't the limitanei be better placed to handle this problem?"

"No, the limitanei will not handle this. My field army, the comitatenses, and I will. Are you questioning my decision, centurion?"

"General, I would never question your orders. I'm just wondering why a general of your stature would be so intent on carrying out this expedition."

"Because I have to. That is all we are going to discuss on this subject."

The General turned to Braxus. "Give me the report on the progress of Gul since he was adopted into the army seven months ago."

"General, he has progressed nicely since he joined the ranks. He has developed into a decent swordsman. He is a natural leader, and we have promoted him to squad leader."

"Good. He will serve as my apprentice on the expedition."

There were murmurs from the assembled officers. With no hesitation the General now brought his sword down hard on the wood table. The strong sound of the smack against the wood traveled throughout the room and commanded everyone's attention without the General having to speak a word.

"I do not need to be second guessed. I want to see if Gul is officer material."

"On the other hand, he may want to kill you and then flee back to his homeland," spoke a voice hidden in the anonymity of the large room.

"My information indicates that is not likely, and I trust that to be the case. Besides, I think I can defend myself. Is there anything further? Braxus and Cratus, stay here. The rest of you are dismissed."

The men hustled out of the command room. No one said a word until they were outside. One centurion said to another, "Is the General going mad? Why would he want to command such a small expedition into the countryside when there are so many larger areas of unrest along the frontier that need his attention?"

The other centurion responded, "I don't know if it's so much madness or a desire to get out into the field again—and away from this damn fort. I'm tired of being here too, kept like bear in a cage. I wish I could go with him. I want some action."

A figure emerged from the shadows. It was Bukarma. The men were surprised and shaken. The General could be very volatile, and they were questioning his decision. They knew Bukarma was the right hand of the General and could report their conversation. But Bukarma was not one of the General's spies.

"Are you going to tell the General about what we have been discussing?" one of the centurions asked.

"Of course," Bukarma answered.

The centurions' faces went blank as they were guessing what punishment awaited them. One was thinking demotion while the other one thought he would be going to the mines.

"What I will tell the General is that you have volunteered to make the fort ready for the spring games when he returns. That is why I am talking to you now, and that is the only reason I am talking to you. Now, you have some action."

"Are you going to tell the General about—"

Bukarma cut him off, "Do a good job with the games and this conversation never happened."

With that Bukarma did a one-hundred-eighty-degree turn and was gone into the night. Both centurions felt a strong need for wine or mead.

After the room had emptied out, the General asked Braxus and Cratus to join him at his table. Mead was brought in and the men drank the first glass quickly. It had been a long day. A servant poured another glass, and the General settled back into his chair.

"As I previously said, we leave tomorrow at first light. Normally, I would have a tribune conduct this operation, but it is something I must do, Cratus. I need you with me as second-in-command. I will take Revious when we depart, and you will have his second-best scout. We will take as many scouts as we need. I do not want mistakes. Braxus, if you are feeling envious, don't. You are to take my command here while I'm away. You are to conduct two operations. Prepare for our spring departure from this fort. I want my army to travel northeast, where I have heard there is a large number of Goth barbarians amassing. I hear they are from the tribes of the Tervingi and the Greuthungi. I want to stop them from crossing the Danube. We will meet with a force of limitanei before we reach the Danube to make our plumage appear even larger and more intimidating, like one of those ground birds when it mates. The barbarians will see us and drop their weapons and run back into their woods."

Neither Cratus nor Braxus knew the type of bird the General was referring to or whether his last statement was in partial jest, but they understood his concept. The more inflated a force can look to an enemy, the more likely that enemy will back down. This appeared to be particularly true for most barbarian tribes, including the Goths.

"Braxus, I also want you to prepare a boisterous spring contest when I return. I want the men to be entertained."

As the General spoke, Bukarma entered the room and whispered something into the General's ear, followed by a laugh by the General. It was laughter tinged with sarcasm. Joseph guessed the joke was barbarian related. He was wrong, it was about the two centurions Bukarma had just spoken to.

"Braxus, I believe two officers have already volunteered to help you prepare. They were here for our earlier meeting. Ask Bukarma who they are. Use whatever or whoever you need to help complete my order. You can use my seal to carry out my command."

The General continued, "We should return in about one week. The men will travel lightly, but I have ordered them to bring warm clothes. Revious tells me a late winter storm may be coming. Good night, generals. I will see you in the morning."

Braxus and Cratus left Bukarma, Joseph, and the General in the room. Joseph had been in the background the entire meeting and said nothing. Even if he wanted to, he wouldn't know precisely what to say and how the General would react.

"Priest, while I'm gone, I want you to go through my history and see if there are any errors or gaps. We are almost done, and it is important that it makes sense to a reader."

Joseph nodded but added, "I can't fill in gaps when I don't know anything about the subject."

"I do not want excuses, priest. I want my order carried out. I will review your work as soon as I return. Now go."

Joseph retired and the General confided to Bukarma, "Here are my orders, should something happen to me. Give them to Braxus. He will be my replacement—until those dogs in Milan or Constantinople replace him. You may dispose of my possessions as you wish."

"You have doubts, General?" Bukarma looked directly into the General's eyes and was worried.

"I don't know and I really don't care. Now leave me. Tomorrow, you will become General Braxus' primary guard and follow his command."

Bukarma did not even blink during the General's statement, but as he left the room, he was clearly concerned about the mental state of his commander.

The next day when Joseph arose, the General's cavalry had already left the fort. This was an accomplishment, as Joseph was a light sleeper. He did not know that the General wanted it this way, as this would be practice for a surprise visit on the Suevi. A surprise that would not be good for the Suevi.

The two cavalry units under the General made excellent progress on the first day and traveled almost forty miles. The storm never materialized, which led the General to comment to Revious that he was a much better scout than a weather forecaster.

Revious just laughed and said, "There is a lot more to this trip than the first day."

The General and Revious then made a small wager if they would see snow during their expedition against the Suevi.

At the end of the first day, they made camp by a small stream. After dinner was eaten, the General went over to the creek and took a piss in it. It was his answer to the image he saw in another creek several months ago. He then called a meeting of Cratus, Tribune Gius, Centurion Maximus, and Gul. Revious was present too, and he spread a map on the floor.

Revious opened up the discussion. "At the end of today, my scouts told me where they think the Suevi are and where they are headed. Here is a drawing of the area, showing where we are now and where we think the Suevi are located."

The men all peered at the map, which was covered with a shade of evening darkness that made it difficult to see.

"More candles," ordered the General, as he could see the men were having trouble viewing the sketch. The General had a very low tolerance for poor communication, in particular errors that were caused by guesses over facts. Two junior soldiers appeared each carrying a bag of candles. Because there was no longer a covered tent or a room with walls, the lighting still was not good and a breeze curled smoke around the men. This lack of progress on what the General thought was a simple task made him angry, and he cursed the air.

Eventually a glowing light appeared around the map so that it could be read. Even so, it took much maneuvering before every man could read it with any accuracy.

"Revious, continue."

"We have this range of hills here that splits two narrow valleys. The Suevi are in the southernmost valley. They continue to move largely northeast but at a very leisurely pace."

"They have such a leisurely pace because they don't know of anyone who would come up here at the end of winter to engage them," the General interjected. "They spit in my face. We are about to turn their victory walk back to their land into a death march."

Pointing to an area after the two valleys merged, the General continued, "I will take the first century and we will travel fast through the northern valley. It is my hope in two days' time we will be here. Cratus, you will take the second century and move up behind them. You will need to take your time. I don't want the Suevi to see or smell you until we are ahead of them. During the second day, after we have separated, I want you to begin to press them—to let them know that you are on their trail. You will need to disguise yourselves a bit to make it appear that you have more soldiers than you really have. I want the Suevi to fear that the Romans are pursuing them and so they will need to quicken their pace to escape a conflict. I wager they will flee with their ill-gotten takings rather than risk it all to stand and fight against your century, Cratus."

"What if it snows, or we encounter another obstacle that slows us down, and we get behind schedule, or what if you—" Tribune Gius started to question the General.

The General, as he was apt to do in circumstances like this, when a junior officer questioned his tactics, interrupted the soldier. "Do I look like a fool or someone who just assumed his first command? General Cratus . . ." The General was on the verge of speaking sharply to the young officer, but he caught himself and threw the dialogue over to Cratus. The General meanwhile tried to control his temper. He knew it was foolish to antagonize a subordinate during a campaign.

Cratus responded, "Tribune Gius, the only thing we need to concern ourselves with is carrying out orders. It will work out; you will see. Now prepare the century for tomorrow's work."

"Thank you, General Cratus." The General had regained his composure. "Normally, I would listen to counsel's opinion, but not on this campaign. Do not be concerned, Tribune Gius. Revious has said it will snow, which means it will not, and therefore our time schedules should be met. If something should happen to slow down our schedules, you must keep pushing. Do not worry about me; instead, worry about Revious' wager with me."

Soft chuckles murmured through the camp at the General's light humor. For whatever reason, the General liked to tease Revious, which was sometimes returned to the General. No other person, not even Braxus and Cratus, would try to joke with the General except Revious during a campaign.

The General became serious again. "Cratus, assume we will be in position in two days. If it snows, we will push harder to reach our scheduled stopping point. Besides, I have brought our most trusted scouts—and Revious—who will carry information between our cohorts about our locations and those of the Suevi." The General paused to let the information sink in. Then he continued, "Once the Suevi realize that they are now the prey of

Cratus, I believe they will head right into my position here." The General pointed at the drawing. "The Suevi will be so concerned about their rear guard's exposure to Cratus that they won't suspect my century is in front of them. With us here, and Cratus there, we will pinch them from the head to the ass, where we will quash them like the carrion flies that they are. Do I have any comments now from my officers? Maximus? Gius? I'm listening. Gul, do you have anything to add?"

"No," was the simultaneous reply from the two officers and the young Goth.

"I see you are learning quickly." The General smiled, as did the rest of the soldiers at the meeting.

The General was never this lighthearted during a campaign. The humor from the General made Cratus feel uneasy, but he did not show his concern on the surface.

There was a pause in the conversation as the men looked at the General. The mood shifted, and the General's smile had left his lips as he was turning his knife into the dirt.

"I want us to be at our best as we pursue the Suevi and then punish them. *Punish them severely.* There is to be no mercy, no quarter granted. Murderers and thieves shall suffer with their lives! See that you are prepared to depart at first light. Double the guards tonight. I do not want to be the object of a surprise. Do not disappoint me."

The meeting was over and some of the men went to sleep. Others conducted last-minute preparations. Gul was anxious and could not sleep. The General immediately fell asleep. But it was a short sleep. He soon awoke and thought of things besides the upcoming battle.

XIX

Battle Scars

Light snow fell silently on the men as they prepared to depart at first light. The General was in his saddle, followed by Tribune Gius. Gul was behind the General and Gius. As they rode north, the General could be heard cursing Revious as the snow began to accumulate on the ground and in the trees. Cratus' century cleaned the campground and removed all traces of the Romans' presence. After a few hours of this work, the second unit under Cratus was off to the southeast to place his century behind the Suevi.

The General and his century rode hard to the northeast to locate the northern valley. The men would first have to ride through the series of low-lying hills to reach this valley. The hills were thickly wooded with areas of minor brush cover. As they moved north, they came across a small pile of branches. This was the entrance to a trail that would eventually lead them to the north valley. The General was pleased with the existence of the trail. Gul looked hard at the pile and wondered out loud who had cut and put the branches on the ground.

The General noted Gul's inquisitive look and said, "While you were asleep last night, Revious and his associates left the camp to scout our way forward, to let us know where to go."

Gul gently countered, "But I didn't sleep, General."

"Then you were not very attentive to what was going on around you. If you are going to be an officer in the Roman army, you must be aware of all things going on around you—at all times. If you don't, you will find how easy it is to become a member of the legions of the dead."

With those words the conversation ended. Gul was ordered to the back of the line to manage the group of supply horses needed by the century.

By the end of the day, the General's century had woven its way through the hills on the trail marked by Revious. The woods were quiet, and the troop's movements matched that silence. Snow continued but most melted into the ground like a forgotten dream. The General again observed that some of the trees were growing out of rocks, and he wondered how that could happen. He had seen the same phenomenon many times before, and still these types of trees caught his attention. The General thought the roots of those trees must be incredibly strong to puncture the fractures in the rock and find the nutrients to not only survive but to thrive in such conditions. He imagined himself as one of the trees and what it took to make him what he was today. The General continued to daydream along the trail when an image emerged from the snow. It was Revious.

The first words from his mouth were directed at the General. "Unless I'm mistaken, General, you have some solidi that belong to me—because it sure looks like snow to me." The General groused a bit about the luck of a certain poor scout, and he told Revious to see him when they returned to the fort.

However, Revious would not give in. "General, I'm sure your coins will give me and us good fortune in our encounter with the Suevi."

"I can't afford to debate this all day with a man the likes of you." And with that the General tossed a small bag of coins to Revious.

Revious then responded, "Excellent choice, General. You are wiser than the spirits that haunt these woods."

"I doubt if anything haunts these woods, except your bad breath."

Revious knew the amount of solidi in the bag was the correct amount. He understood that to open the bag and count the money in front of the General would be an insult, and insulting the General would be a very bad thing.

The General turned serious, "To business, scout."

Revious responded, "The snow, although not bad, has slowed the Suevi's progress considerably. In fact, they stayed an extra day at their camp in the south valley. Cratus' century was close behind them, and yet the Suevi have not detected Cratus' presence to their rear."

The General was pleased. "Good. Now we won't need to travel so far to set our trap. Revious, send your man to Cratus with this message—it is too wet out here to write my orders, so he will have to remember them—tell Cratus to wait one day. Then he shall give notice to the Suevi that he is approaching from the south. I believe the Suevi will panic. To save all their plunder, they will head immediately northeast to their home country. However, they will encounter us . . . and their hell on Earth."

"General, you still need a full day's ride to reach the point where we initially anticipated meeting the Suevi. You are now near the north valley. Most of your day will be spent moving eastward beyond where the valleys merge. I suggest, General, that you change your battle plans and ambush the Suevi at the point just where the two valleys merge. This is feasible because of the slow pace of the Suevi."

"And what do you say about the weather? Will it stay the same? Will it get colder?"

"General, you know I don't know the answers to your questions—at least not well enough to avoid the chance for me to get sideways with you or lose a bet, if I should miss something. That is not likely, but the weather is fickle."

"What do you think?" The General was serious this time and was in no mood to word parry with Revious. The snow had diminished, but the cold was moving in from the north.

"It is what you think, General. Snow won't be the problem; it will be the cold."

"We are not equipped to handle too cold of a temperature. I've changed my mind. We must accelerate our schedule. When your scout rides to Cratus, he must tell him to push the Suevi as soon as possible. We will ambush them before the two valleys meet—as you suggest, Revious. We will wait for them in the woods at that point. Let's move, *now*."

Revious gave his assistant his instructions, and he left immediately for Cratus' camp. The General gave the scout an extra horse to switch to when his first horse became tired. It was going to be a tough hard ride for this individual. He then ordered his century to pick up the pace so they could make the merge point in plenty of time. The men could rest there before the approaching fight.

Hurried traveling by the General's century marked the remainder of the day. The cavalry stopped for the night near the point where they expected the Suevi to ride through in the morning. The soldiers huddled with each other in small tents to stay warm. The General did not want any fires to alert the Suevi of their presence.

Cratus was fortunate, as his century could light all the fires they could maintain. The fires would serve two purposes: first, to create an unwelcome surprise to the Suevi and second, to keep his men warm—at least those who did not perform camp security. In any event it was time to give away their presence to the Suevi.

The Suevi did see Cratus' fires in the distance to the southwest. The number of fires appeared to represent a large force, and the Suevi chief guessed it was associated with a Roman encampment. The Suevi chief viewed this as a serious threat, and he sent two warriors out to see how many Romans were in the encampment. They did not return. Cratus was waiting for them as they neared the Roman camp.

Before first light, the Suevi chief had his warriors up and moving northeast, at first slowly as to not create noise in the darkness, then they began to move more urgently. The chief ordered some of the plunder they had taken be cut from the line. *This will improve our progress,* he thought.

Cratus' century also moved at a quickened pace, and they began to close the gap. The Suevi chief was a true warrior, but he was conflicted. Part of him wanted to stand and fight. However, he knew most of his men had been over-celebrating for days and not in shape to take on what the Suevi chief correctly thought was a battle-hardened army. He thought he was right to choose the fleeing option. Unfortunately, he had no idea what awaited him as his band of Suevi arrived near the point where the valleys merged.

Cratus and his troops pushed the Suevi toward the left side of the south valley. He knew the General would have his troops camouflaged at the base of a large hill facing the valley. Cratus was right.

The General had his unit into position well before dawn. They were hidden among the trees and rocks. The dawn carried a heavy mist as the temperature surprisingly rose and visibility fell. This seemed a little strange to the General, given the previous night's cold and because the early dawn was usually the coldest part of the day. In the past he had frequently used the weather to his benefit, and now by accident the weather was his ally again. As the time for battle approached, he ordered Tribune Gius to bring him Gul. In a few minutes Gul rode up from where the supply horses were being held.

"Gul, you shall accompany me into battle today. You shall be beside me and act as my guard. Any questions?"

Gul's mind was spinning. One minute he was outsourced to working with the supply horses, and now he was to be the great General's bodyguard in a battle with real warriors.

"Are you ready for your new role, Gul?" the General asked as he looked straight ahead at the approaching band of Suevi.

There was only one answer Gul could give. He nodded in the affirmative.

"This is reality. This is life and death for the Suevi, and they will kill you if they get the chance. Don't give them that chance. We will see if you have your father's instincts."

The General turned to Gius. "You are my second. Use this opportunity wisely."

The Suevi chief had sent out scouts to survey the area before the main group of Suevi passed by. None of the scouts came up to the hillside where the General was stationed, though. They appeared to be more interested in taking the valley that opened in an eastward direction. They never thought there would be another Roman force so close.

The General ordered his archers to dismount and move as close to the edge of the hillside as possible without being noticed. After the General issued the command to launch the arrows, they were to quickly reload and fire again. The purpose of this action was to create more confusion to an already confused Suevi. Between the first and second volleys, the main Roman force would move out of the hillside and strike the Suevi in a broadside attack. Cratus would then move quickly and hit the Suevi from behind. Cratus' men were now in full gallop toward the Suevi.

The plan worked to perfection. The Suevi were about one hundred yards out when the General gave the command by hand signal for the archers to launch the first volley of arrows. Several of the arrows hit the Suevi and their horses. The General then gave the command to attack, and the force of ninety men emerged from cover. As the Suevi turned to meet the General's force, the second volley of arrows struck. Again more Suevi and their horses were killed or wounded. Before most of the Suevi had removed their weapons, the General was on top of them.

The General's century carried both a short spear or javelin and a spatha, or long sword. The sword was kept either in a sheath on the man's back or strapped in a holster on the man's side. This was because most of the Romans threw their spears first when they were a short distance from the enemy. The sword was then used in close combat. The Roman cavalry also used small oval shields. In this way the Romans always had at least some protection. The General's life had more than once been saved because of a shield.

The Suevi at first outnumbered the General's forces, but the Suevi were disorganized and the General's cavalry was disciplined. Soon the General's archers, who now were mounted on their horses, joined the battle as his century drove as one unit into the heart of the Suevi mass.

The General was equally adept using a spear and sword, and he used both to kill a number of Suevi. Gul was locked up in a hand-to-hand brawl with a larger Suevi who was clearly the better fighter. However, Gul was a scrapper whose quick movements prevented the Suevi from locking onto Gul and dealing a mortal blow. The General watched the fight out of the corner of his eye, but he had his own issues. The Suevi were regrouping and beginning to take the fight to the Romans. The tide of the battle was about to turn when Cratus' century slammed into the Suevi from the south. The Suevi now had to contend with a new threat. It was too late, though. Having lost a large number of men to the General's unit, the Suevi's strength and desire to fight waned.

During a quick break in his fighting, the General again glanced over to where Gul had been waging his personal battle with a Suevi. Gul now stood over the Suevi with his bloody sword in his hand. The General did not know what had caused Gul to be the victor, but there he stood.

The Suevi leader tried one last effort to organize his warriors, with no positive result. A few Suevi were with him, while most were spending all their efforts at staying alive. The result was a breakout free-for-all in all directions. The General yelled for his men to go after any fleeing Suevi. Pandemonium ensued among the Suevi.

The General noticed the Suevi chief head in the direction of the hill and trees from where the General had launched his attack. Another Suevi followed his leader into the hillside. The General commanded Gul to find a mount and follow him into the forest after the two Suevi. Gul located a nearby horse and both man and horse ran after the General. The woods in this area were thick with undergrowth. In one way, the brush made it difficult to travel through, but at the same time it was easy because choices were limited to the few trails.

The General found his way on one particular trail because it showed recent horse prints. He thought the Suevi were nearby and probably watching him. Gul was a few yards back of the General, sword in hand but no shield. He found it odd that the General had picked up a spear to go along with his shield. The General's sword was not apparent to Gul. Suddenly, the General's shield fell to the ground. Gul thought it must have been caused by the narrowness of the trail through the trees. He also fantasized that the General was following his example of not needing a shield.

For several minutes the General and Gul wound their way through the thick brush. Finally the brush thinned and tall trees became dominant as the canopy blacked out the sun for the lower vegetation. The opening spaces in the trees allowed the General to see what was going on around him so he could pick out a Suevi in ambush mode. Further up ahead on the trail a rock formation wedged into the side of the hill. He thought the Suevi would be behind the rocks waiting for him to get closer. Gul trailed in the background on hyper alert, which made him ineffective.

At this point the General was not concerned about Gul. All his attention focused on the rock formation. Suddenly, but not totally unexpectedly, a Suevi spurted out between the rocks. He had a bow and quickly aimed his arrow at the General. The General sat on his horse and didn't move. He dropped his spear to the ground. He then held his arms down along the sides of his body and opened the palms of his hands to the Suevi. It appeared to Gul that the General was asking to die.

Gul yelled something, but it didn't matter. The Suevi launched his arrow straight at the General's chest. Gul pressed forward but it was too late. The arrow was about to strike the General. Yet he didn't flinch or seem to care. At the last second the arrow glanced by a pine knob and was deflected into the tree next to the General. The Suevi gazed at the General, refilled his bow, and got ready to fire again. Only this time the General was off his horse. As the Suevi looked up, he saw an angrily distorted face staring at him. This was unnerving, and the man fumbled in handling his bow. The General's spear was now in his right hand. The Suevi backed up a couple of paces to move partially behind a twelve-inch-diameter pine tree. Two more trees were positioned between him and the General. This maneuver added more protection to the Suevi's cover and gave him a firmer foundation upon which to shoot his second arrow. Still, there was an opening between the Suevi and the General, and both could see each other.

The General's face showed he was fully focused on what he was going to do next. Almost effortlessly he reared back and threw his short spear at the Suevi. The spear was a missile, the harbinger of death. Its direction was perfectly horizontal to the ground, neither rising nor dropping as it moved up the slope. Amazingly, and much to the dismay of the Suevi, it threaded the three trees like an owl homing in on a rodent. The spear hit the Suevi on the upper right side of the rib cage, penetrated through the lungs and heart, and pushed out through the left side. The Suevi was dead before he hit the ground.

Gul was about twenty feet behind the General, whose throw of the spear he would always remember. The Suevi was about twenty-five yards from the General, and it was a perfect throw that few men could have made.

Gul had become so fixated on the General and his actions that his eyes did not see the movement coming at him from the side. The Suevi chief had stationed himself in the brush off to the side of the General and Gul. The Suevi too had watched the General's actions. He knew the General was an opponent that he would like to fight, but Gul was closer and he became the target.

Gul turned to face his Suevi, who was a mere ten yards to his right and charging fast. Gul noticed that the Suevi carried a large ax with red on it, no doubt blood from a Roman. There was nothing Gul could do. In an instant he thought of his childhood and father. He imagined an afterlife.

Within five yards from Gul, the hoof on the Suevi's horse was unlucky enough to catch an extended root hidden beneath inches of pine needles. The Suevi's horse buckled into Gul's horse. Gul instinctively ducked his body as both horses collapsed into each other. The momentum of the charge sent the Suevi chief headlong through the air and just over Gul as he was crumbling to the ground with his horse. Gul grabbed the mane of his horse and the Suevi passed over him. As he skimmed over Gul's body, the Suevi swung his ax. He missed giving Gul a full blow, but he did inflict a deep cut on Gul's right shoulder. Gul let loose a howl at the resulting pain. His horse started to press down on his leg. Fortunately, the full impact by the falling horse was minimized by Gul's quick reflex to move his leg. He thought for sure, though, he was dead as the Suevi was likely on top of him and ready to drive the ax through his brain.

He opened his eyes and there stood the General.

"Where is the Suevi?" Gul asked.

"Over there," answered the General, his sword now in his hand.

The General had been quick to try to help Gul, but the Suevi had been too fast on the attack, and that is what helped Gul. The speed of the Suevi's horse and the force at which the Suevi was thrown from his horse had carried the Suevi head first into the large, knotty tree directly to the side and left of where Gul lay.

"He has a broken neck. It is interesting, don't you think, Gul? Here is a true warrior who dies and a non-warrior who lives. Sometimes things work out the way logic says they shouldn't."

The General turned and looked down the hill. Cratus and several members of the cavalry were riding in hurried motion to the General's location. When they arrived, they found the General standing over Gul and looking at the dead Suevi chief. It was hard for the General to believe that a tree could kill a warrior such as the Suevi leader. The Suevi's horse had a broken leg or legs, and was also dead. Gul's horse was also on the ground and had pinned Gul's leg underneath its body. His horse was still alive.

Cratus immediately asked the General how he was and the General answered, "Fine, but your man here seems worse for wear."

Cratus looked at Gul and then the General. *"Sapor est victoria! Adhuc esurient!"* [Savor the victory! Hunger for more!]

"Yes," the General responded. "Now help Gul and mercifully take care of his horse."

Cratus turned to his men and barked out orders, and several soldiers went to work freeing Gul. Cratus dismounted and walked over to the General. He looked up the hill to where the dead

Suevi lay. The hilt of the spear could be seen protruding straight upward. Cratus focused intently on the line the spear had traveled between the General and the Suevi. He squinted through the trees from point A (the General) to Point B (the dead Suevi) and was highly impressed. Even a soldier with the fighting skills that Cratus possessed knew only one person could make that throw, and he was standing next to him.

"That was an amazing throw, General! How did you thread the spear through those trees and kill that Suevi?"

The General was not interested in discussing that subject.

The General's silence made the necessary impression on Cratus. "Your orders, General?"

"First, the casualty report."

"Five dead. Thirteen wounded. One seriously."

"And the Suevi?" The General turned to look at the dead Suevi chief during this conversation.

"We think all are dead, per your order."

"None escaped or ran into the hills like these two?"

"No, General. We think we got them all."

"Then, that is that." The General spoke coldly and gave no indication of whether he was pleased.

The Tribune Gius, who was in charge of the General's century, joined the group. "Congratulations, General, on your great victory. *Sapor est victoria! Adhuc esurient!*" [Savor the victory! Hunger for more!]

"Was it, Tribune? They were only a bit more challenging than Gul and his band of misbegotten boys—accompanied by a Christian priest who didn't know his place in his religion or in the world. Whereas Gul and company were led by stupidity, these Suevi were led by greed. They should never have come into my territory, they should never have raided villages under my protection, and they should have moved on as fast as they came. Each one of those was a fatal mistake. But the worst mistake they made was underestimating me and what I am capable of. Now they know—in their afterlife."

The General stared at Gius, who had backed away and was looking at the ground. Cratus and the other men focused on the General, and the General issued his orders.

"Tribune, proceed to Centurion Maximus, from the other century. Take the heads from the Suevi and mount them on Suevi spears or swords or whatever weapons you can find. Line this valley with their heads. Do not remove the head of the Suevi chief; he was a warrior. Leave the headless Suevi bodies as they lie, but build a pyre for the chief. Also, take the Suevi horses. Tell the men to take whatever souvenirs they want from the Suevi corpses. Under no circumstances are the men to take anything from the Suevi packhorses bearing their plunder. We will return those items to the proper village—or any nearby village. Select a party to build a large pyre to honor our slain Romans. It is too far to the fort to transport their bodies there. I order their funeral pyre because I don't want to bury them and then have wild animals dig them up and eat their bodies. Cratus, see that my orders are fulfilled—to the details I have specified. *Go.*"

The General's orders were succinct, as always. Cratus had been with the General long enough to understand him, and so following through on what the General wanted was easy. Gul was now up on his feet, but the horse's fall had damaged his ankle and he was notably limping. The General also gave an order for the wounded Romans, including Gul, to be seen by the medic who accompanied the General's centuries.

All the soldiers, including Cratus and Gul, left the hillside. The General walked up the hill around the three trees where his spear had traveled through and looked at the dead Suevi. He was an average-sized man with no discernible marks except a small scar on his left cheek. He was young in appearance, and the General thought this may have been his first raiding party. This

Suevi was about the same age as Gul, only dead. The General pulled the spear out of the dead Suevi and walked down the hill to the valley, blood dripping from the spear.

The men worked quickly to complete the General's orders. The pyres were finished and ignited. The heads of the Suevi were impaled on swords and spears and placed so that they crossed part of the valley floor. This was a grisly task, but the soldiers were all veterans and the work did not bother them. It was clear this was a warning to those who would come by this way as raiders that there was a steep price to pay for bandit activities. Gul had been exempted from these activities. The General thought it best that Gul not be involved with the dead Suevi. Instead he ordered Gul, after his wounds were treated, to return to the task of marshaling the Roman and Suevi packhorses with the villagers' items strapped on their backs. Most of the wounded Romans could ride on their own; however, litters were constructed for the severely wounded soldiers.

XX

Anastasis

The journey back to the fort began at a slow pace. The weather continued to play a role in the guessing match between the General and Revious on whether it would snow again, how much it would snow, and what the temperature would be. The General, though, seemed to have little spirit, and after awhile Revious rode on ahead to escape the gloomy atmosphere that surrounded him. This feeling traveled down to the soldiers. Occasionally the General gave a curt order to Cratus.

Cratus did not understand why the General was acting so sullen. Usually after a victory the General was buoyant and went among his men to congratulate them personally for their efforts. This didn't happen here, and Cratus knew it would be his responsibility to lead the expedition back to the fort.

When Revious returned from scouting, he reported to Cratus that the village that had been destroyed by the Suevi was nearby. The General, who was riding near Cratus, overheard their conversation and immediately ordered the centuries to the village.

The completeness of the destruction was evident. There were no smoldering fires; too much time had elapsed and the fires had died without a source of energy. Piles of blackened rubble were everywhere. No signs of life were evident, either people or wildlife. The General stared at the scene all around him, and a quizzical look replaced the gloom on his face.

"General, what do you see?" Cratus asked.

"Cratus, Revious, what do you not see?" answered the General.

There was a pause of silence, and then both men at the same time said, "There are no bodies."

"That is correct. The Suevi took no prisoners and reportedly killed all the villagers. Except they did not."

The General sat up high on his horse and shouted, "I am General Augustus Marcus Valerias, Commander of the comitatenses and limitanei legions of the Roman Army. The Suevi that attacked and destroyed your village are dead. They will not come your way again."

He sat back on his horse and waited. Soon an old man with scraggly, dirty hair emerged from behind a group of trees at the left of the village limits. The General dismounted and walked over to him.

"I am Orses. I am glad you are here, General Valerias. We have heard of you. The Suevi destroyed everything. They took everything that was not living. They killed my wife, and my son, his wife, and one of my grandchildren. Entire families have been lost. Everyone has lost someone. They showed no mercy even though we offered them everything we could. They tortured men and raped the women—even the little girls—and then killed those they could catch."

Orses continued on and the General listened patiently, a trait the General did not exhibit often. The man finished, "I prayed to the gods that Rome would have protected us from them—"

The General cut him off, "So did I! It was Rome that failed you . . . I failed you."

The two men talked for a few more minutes, and Orses grew comfortable that the General's intentions were not to harm him.

Suddenly he put fingers to his mouth and emitted a loud whistle in three bursts. After a few minutes, the most ragged people the General had ever seen emerged from the forest.

Orses answered the General's question even before it was asked. "These are the remaining people from my village. They are all that is left. Most were out hunting for food or gathering firewood when the Suevi attacked. Some were at a nearby village. That is where I was. The Suevi spared no one or anything. All they could grab were killed, burned, or both. They took everything they could steal. My people are now scared of the dark—of their own shadows."

The General looked at the mass forming before him. Most were old men and women. There were younger women, children, and a sprinkling of men of fighting age. The General thought, *These people couldn't protect themselves now from a band of Gul's worst fighters.* He made an instant decision.

"General Cratus, inform the soldiers we camp here tonight. Make the necessary preparations. Build fires, prepare extra rations for our guests, and tell Gul to bring forward the Suevi packhorses."

He turned to Orses, "You are under my personal protection until we transport you to the nearest village that you want to go to. You cannot stay here. The stench of death . . . I cannot imagine what it is like for you."

"Good, General. We do not want to stay here, either. There are too many bad memories here from the Suevi. We will go to the village down the valley, about a quarter day's walk from here."

"The Suevi will not bother you again. We put them in whatever hellish afterlife they have. By the way, I see no dead bodies."

"We burned what was left of them after the Suevi left. It was important to have the Earth take them as dust rather than wild animals tearing at them or digging them up from the Earth, as we have no one to guard the gravesites."

The General nodded, thinking of the Romans who had been cremated after the fight with the Suevi. Gul rode up with about forty horses, most of them packhorses loaded with bags of stolen items from the village.

"Orses, these bags contain what we could find from the Suevi that are yours. Have your people go through them and take what is theirs—or not even theirs if no one is here to claim the items. You may keep the horses. We leave tomorrow at first light, so you will want to attend to this now."

Just then, a little girl came running over to a packhorse. There was a small bag protruding from the larger bag attached to the horse.

"Mine—mine—my mama's," she said.

The General nodded at a soldier who had dismounted, and the soldier pulled the bag out and gave it to the girl. She ran over and hid behind Orses. The General bent down and asked the girl her name. At first she was shy, as many young children are, but then she peeked around Orses' legs and said, "Anastasis."

The General asked, "Did you find what you needed, Anastasis?"

"Yes." She was swaying back and forth, holding onto Orses' legs in a mixture of shyness and curiosity. She had never met a man like the General. It had also been a long time since the General had talked to a child.

The General rose to his full stature and spoke to Orses. "Tell me."

"They are all gone, killed by the Suevi. She is what is left of her family. Anastasis is my grandniece."

That night food was prepared, and the villagers ate like they hadn't eaten in days, which was true. Afterward fires were lit and the villagers mingled with the soldiers. At the General's fire were Cratus, Revious, Orses, Anastasis and several others. The girl could sense the security of the General and sat right next to him. He was puzzled by this behavior rather than her sitting with her own people, but he said nothing.

Once she asked him, "Are you the king of all these soldiers and my uncle's village?"

"No, I am a general, General Valerias. You may call me Marcus."

"Are you the top general?"

"Yes, I am the first general. Cratus here is my third general and Revious over there would like to think he is a general, but he is not."

"What is he?"

Revious answered this question before the General could—and Revious was full of bluster, as usual. "I am Revious. I am the General's chief intelligence officer. I do all the brave work. I go out ahead of the General and look behind all the trees and rocks for our enemies and then I report to the General what I've found. The General then takes all my knowledge and forms his plan—all because of me and my men. It takes great courage to do my job. You never know who or what is behind a tree."

The General could not wait any longer: "I know what is behind a tree—a good spot for you to sleep and dream of your weather gods."

The group erupted in laughter and even more teasing resulted. It was the first time the General had seen Anastasis laugh—and it was the first time he had laughed hard in what seemed a very long time. The General continued to smile after the laughter had ended. He thought to himself, *It took a child.*

The night passed quickly. When the first real hint of spring arrives, time seems to accelerate. The cold of previous nights was finally being edged out of the way.

The General wasn't thinking of the weather, though. Instead he was focusing on the future of residents of the old village and particularly, the girl, Anastasis. She was so innocent of the evil that had descended on her village. She might end up having a short life, experiencing little that was positive. Yet last evening she had laughed and smiled. He on the other hand, had lived a relatively long life. His innocence was long since spent, and there was blood on his hands. He did not deserve such longevity, while hers could be so short. In the quiet of the night, the General knew what he had to do.

When the bulk of the soldiers awoke, they found the General talking to the sentries. He called for Cratus, and Cratus gave the command to break camp. The villagers had spent a majority of the night securing their belongings and preparing for the trip to the nearby village. There was consternation among a group of villagers who disagreed with Orses. They believed that the nearby village would not accept them because of their poor condition and lack of coin. The General did not have time to spend on this matter and told them unequivocally that would not be a problem. They quietly dispersed without argument.

Orses and Anastasis came into the dawning light. They had slept well. Obviously the presence of the General and his men was a major reason for their good night of sleep.

"Orses, tell your people to gather themselves and their belongings. We break camp in one hour. General Cratus, tell the men to look sharp for the ride to the village. I want us to look like the finest troops that Rome can provide. Impress me. One last thing—Orses, you and Anastasis will ride with me at the front of my centuries."

It was apparent to Cratus this was a changed General. The sullen, quiet General Valerias who had stayed in the background for much of the expedition against the Suevi was now clearly the leader. His charisma had returned, a charisma that silently said, "I'm the one in charge. Follow me."

Cratus was pleased with the return of the "old" General, at least for the short term. He still worried that the General would revert to the morbid-acting General. Meanwhile, the General proceeded to finish cleaning and organizing his gear for the upcoming ride. Anastasis sat by his side, helping him by giving him items that he requested. When he finished sharpening his sword, she put it in the back sheath; then he ordered the soldiers and villagers to prepare to ride. Orses came by on a horse, and the General helped Anastasis on Orses' horse.

With the horses taken from the dead Suevi, there were more than enough horses for the villagers to ride, even though many villagers chose to ride two to a horse. Everyone mounted their horses, and the trip to the nearby village went quickly. The General rode side by side with Orses and Anastasis almost the entire trip. This behavior seemed odd to Cratus and the soldiers. Typically he rode at the front of a column, only preceded by two elite horsemen carrying the banner and eagle of the legion. He would occasionally have a general or tribune or other officer ride up for a command, but now he allowed an old man and a young child to ride alongside him.

Revious and two soldiers rode ahead of the column to tell the targeted village of the approaching Romans and of the survivors from the destroyed village. This was not an occasion for a surprise visit, and the General wanted to give the new villagers time to prepare for the Romans' and their guests' arrival. The terrain to this village was hilly and wooded, which provided concealment from those who were unaware of its presence. *No wonder the Suevi didn't attack this village,* thought the General, *and instead focused their attention on Orses' more open village.*

When the Romans and survivors arrived, the entire village greeted them. Usually occupants of a village would be cautious in welcoming Romans, as they were viewed as occupiers in the land. And now the Roman occupiers had failed to protect Orses' village. This time, though, their reception was different. The Roman, General Valerias, was observed leading the Romans, and riding with him was Orses and the little girl, Anastasis, and the displaced villagers. The Romans' reputation had improved with the villagers, though, because it was obvious they had aided Orses and killed the Suevi.

Orses dismounted and walked over to the leader of the village; they hugged and talked for a minute. Orses then returned to the General with the man and said, "General, this is my distant cousin, Barca. He is the chief of this village.

Barca addressed the General. "Orses told me how you have helped salvage what was left of his village. How is it that Rome let Orses' village be consumed by the damned Suevi?" Barca was being very direct with the General.

Cratus and Revious stood close by, anxious to see how the General would react. In the past such a tone may have resulted in Barca being flogged.

The General was calm. "I am sorry this happened to Orses and his village and little Anastasis. We cannot be everywhere, and this was a relatively small raiding party. The Suevi paid for what they did—you can see the results where the two valleys meet. They are all dead and in whatever hellish afterlife they have. They now—or what is left of them—will serve as a warning for anyone who thinks they can come into my territory and do as they wish."

The General's voice grew sterner and was more forceful as his response continued, and he looked directly at Barca when he spoke. The General was not someone to be lectured to, as Barca had done. Now Barca was fully intimidated.

"I now ask you, Barca, will you take in what is left of Orses' village? And give them shelter and comfort?"

Barca knew he had only one answer to give, and that answer was, "Yes." He wanted to add a comment about how poor his village was and this would be a significant task for his village to undertake. However, he was the village leader because of his wisdom, and as a result, he said nothing. The fact that the General glared at him and was backed by two hundred well-seasoned Roman soldiers also helped him with his decision.

"Good," the General responded. "Now let's make a plan for this to work."

Barca, Orses, and the General went into a private dwelling for several minutes. The men talked in hushed tones, and yet for those outside the structure, the General could be heard doing most of the talking. In the dwelling the General gave each man an equal amount of Roman solidi. They were to spend the money on the necessities for the village to accommodate the extra persons who would be living there. The coin and most of the horses taken from the Suevi would help ease the transition for both sets of villagers to integrate into one village. The money came from the General's private account. He asked both Barca and Orses not to mention the origination of the coins except that the money was a gift from Rome. When the meeting concluded, the three men exited the tent to speak to the assembled villagers.

The General announced, "Barca has agreed for a quick and painless merging of his and Orses' villages into one village. With the merger you will both be stronger, and maybe together you can prevent another attack like the one just committed by the Suevi on Orses' village—if I am not available."

Valerias then ordered Cratus and the soldiers to remount and prepare for the ride to the Roman fort. Before he mounted his own horse, the General walked over to Anastasis and got down on one knee.

"Orses has agreed to take care of you and treat you like his own daughter. I believe him. I have known you for a very short time and you me. I wish you good fortune in your life ahead."

With that he gave her a chain he wore around his neck.

"Keep this safe, Anastasis, and think of me when you are in times of distress."

She had nothing and could give him nothing in return, which made her frown. Just then Orses handed her a leather wrist strap that he had. She gave it to the General and he put it on next to

Jacob's strap. She looked into the General's eyes and saw a sadness that only a child could tell. "Be happy, Marcus," was all she said.

The two hugged for a long time. He then stood up and walked back to Barca and Orses.

"If you need anything or want help, send a rider to any Roman outpost and ask for Generals Cratus, Braxus, or me. We will come."

He paused and quietly added, "Do not let harm come to the girl." The General looked into the eyes of Barca and Orses. This was not a hard, threatening look but one of a wishful request. Both men nodded.

Cratus and Revious had a difficuilt time believing what they had just seen. One of the most feared Generals in the Roman army was on the ground and hugging a little girl. This was a different general than the one they were used to. They didn't have much time to think about this strange event, as the General quickly mounted his horse and gave Cratus the order to move out and return to the fort. To Revious all he said was, "How will the weather be on our return to the fort?"

"Clear and warmer," was the response.

"Then let us go. And if you are wrong . . ." The General laughed.

XXI

CONSOLIDATION

THE FUNERAL FOR Drago was over and the mourning period ongoing. Zestras, leader of the Southern Hun tribes, made the trip to Drago's village to say farewell to his old friend. Numerous chiefs traveled with Zestras along with a large contingent of warriors. Zestras was a few years younger than Drago and commanded great respect from both inside and outside the Hun community. Uldric and Rao dared not propose consolidation or other business matters during Zestras' visit. They were concerned that when Zestras heard the news of Drago's death, he would suspect Uldric's and Rao's involvement.

As a result, Uldric and Rao kept a very low-key, respectful profile during their father's funeral. They planned to approach Zestras four weeks after the mourning period ended. The brothers' primary long-term goal was to mount an attack and either capture Constantinople or extract tribute from the city by the threat of attack. For that goal to succeed, they needed many things, the greatest being an accumulation of a large force of fighters that included the confederation of Southern Hun tribes now under Zestras.

Post-mourning quickly morphed into an ambition time for the brothers. When they felt the appropriate time had come, they organized a visit to Zestras' village. They had originally conceived a plot whereby they would take a large number of fighters with them and overthrow Zestras. Rao rethought that idea and proposed traveling with a small force, and if the opportunity became available they would take Zestras' command by force. If this option was unavailable, they would play nice and promote the idea of consolidation of the Hun tribes to Zestras. Their pitch would be to emphasize strength in unity. When the consolidated Hun force was at maximum strength, they would move against Constantinople. The initial prize would be to obtain the spoils of such a campaign. These riches would then be used to seize the long-term goal of establishing a Hun empire, second to none, including the Roman and Persian Empires.

When the brothers arrived at Zestras' village, they were taken to a large camp outside of it. Zestras had assembled several chiefs of associated tribes of the Southern Huns. More importantly, he was surrounded by a large contingent of heavily armed bodyguards.

Rao glanced at Uldric, and they immediately knew the option of assassinating Zestras was no longer feasible. Zestras too had suspected the purpose of the brothers' visit and wanted to be well prepared for anything that could happen during the visit.

"Welcome, sons of Drago," Zestras began. "Again, please accept our condolences for the death of your father. We held him and his principles in high esteem. He was a respected leader. He more often than not sought peaceful solutions to problems. Did you, Uldric and Rao, learn these techniques from your father?"

This was a clear message to Uldric and Rao that Zestras was aware of the purpose of the brothers' visit.

Zestras continued, "We have assembled a full council of the southern tribes. Tell us, what brings you here?"

The brothers clearly had to go to their second option. "Great leader Zestras, we have come to talk about an arrangement that would be beneficial to all our tribes."

"And what is this arrangement?" Zestras leaned forward as he asked this question. When he did, it was revealed that he carried two daggers in his belt, a sight not lost on Uldric and Rao.

Rao answered, "We propose that our tribes unite under one leader—maybe you or maybe me."

"No, that leader would not be either of you. It would be me." Zestras' tone was condescending, like a father to errant sons. "I know that you have been quietly working with the tribes in your territory to join as one and march against Constantinople. Now you are here to ask us to join you in the quest for your greatness."

Uldric started to speak, but Zestras cut him off. "Have you ever seen Constantinople?"

"No." Rao answered this time.

"I have," Zestras quickly answered. "It is well fortified, has a very capable army under the Emperor Valens, and has the ability to wait out a siege, if need be. I foresee your forces being destroyed and you two dead or taken prisoner. Out of deference to your father, I will speak my final judgment of your plan before you continue."

"You have not heard our plan yet."

"I don't need to because I know what it is. We don't have the numbers or experience to attempt to take the capitol of the Eastern Roman Empire or even make a viable threat—separately or in unison. I will not expose my people to such a campaign without a promise of victory. Can you promise me victory?" Zestras was toying with the brothers.

"Yes, I think we can," Uldric said, but before continuing, he was again cut off by Zestras.

"I will not listen to any more of your fantasy. You are not ready for this endeavor, and I will commit no resources to it. That is my decision." The council all nodded in agreement.

Uldric and Rao were clearly set back by such a quick decision. Both of their options were eliminated. There was no way they could get to Zestras with his army of bodyguards, and there was no way they could persuade him or his chiefs to join them. They also did not realize that Zestras considered the brothers as rivals. He wanted them not only out of his camp but also no longer as leaders of the loose confederation of the northern tribes.

Before dismissing the brothers, Zestras offered them a small piece of fruit. "You are sons of Drago, and that is why I gave you this audience. You are more ambitious than your father, and that is not all bad. Thus, it is my decision that you go to the base of Rome in the Western Empire and lay siege on Rome for one month's time and return to my camp. Only then shall we talk about our joint assault on Constantinople. You do not have to take Rome, but you have to advance on Rome and be successful against the Western Roman armies. That will show me that you are seriously capable of carrying out a campaign against Constantinople."

The brothers started to say something but, of course, were stopped by Zestras. "Go now. Return to me and then we can plan our war against Constantinople."

Stunned, Uldric and Rao left Zestras' camp. They had badly underestimated him. They thought he was an old man who could be easily persuaded to go along with their plans. If he didn't, they could remove him from power and take control of the Southern Huns. Instead, he was clearly in charge. There was no way the southern tribes would go along with the brothers as long as Zestras was in power.

It was clear that Zestras commanded strong loyalty among his men. The brothers never would have gotten close enough to engineer an assassination attempt. Even if they had been successful, there was no doubt it would have been their end. They also didn't have the forces to overthrow Zestras even if they returned to their camp and put together an assault force against the Southern Hun leader.

It was back to initial planning stages for Uldric and Rao. On the way back to their village, they talked intensely about their options. They had little knowledge of Rome except what they heard from the various merchants who traveled through their territory. They knew Rome was a weaker target than Constantinople because of infighting and the pressure from the Goths and other barbarians that were pushing the boundaries of the Empire. They had also heard of a Roman general named Valerias who had a reputation of ruthlessly crushing all of his opponents. He would be a formidable foe if they pushed toward Rome or even Constantinople.

Uldric and Rao realized they had three choices: advance against Rome as advocated by Zestras, take the fight to Zestras, or do nothing and return to their village and live the status quo. The latter two options were unacceptable to the brothers. Creating an enemy out of Zestras instead of an ally was a losing option and would not advance their cause. To do nothing was out of the question. The brothers had too much ambition to sit back and not be part of something great. That meant they would assemble a force and strike Rome. The overall objective was clear. Addressing the details of conquering that objective was the focus of their discussion back to their village, including how to manage the Roman general, Valerias. The trip went very fast.

After Uldric and Rao had left the camp, Zestras gathered his advisors, elders and chiefs from other Southern Hun tribes. Zestras opened the meeting with a question. "What is your opinion of Drago's sons from the north?"

Several men gave opinions that ranged from "They are weaklings whose tails dropped like a beaten dog's today" to "Why not go after Constantinople?"

Zestras gave each attendee a time to speak. When all had finished, Zestras took a moderate path. "I believe what they said warrants consideration. Constantinople would be a great prize, no doubt. But we can't do it in our current state; we are not strong enough. We will see how our Hun brothers fare against Rome. Hopefully well. If they are successful against Western Rome, then Eastern Rome will be more agreeable to our terms. If the brothers return alive from their Rome campaign, they will lead the assault against Constantinople. They will be heroes."

What Zestras said and what he thought were two different things. First, the brothers would have to do the work of organizing a unified Hun army from the northern tribes. Even if that should work, he did not think the brothers would fare well against the Roman armies, particularly those led by Valerias. The northern tribes would be so weakened by this effort that he could move against those tribes, take over as their leader, and form a unified Hun empire. Other outlying Hun tribes would also be inclined to join him. With a consolidated Hun empire, he would then mobilize the attack on Constantinople.

Should Uldric and Rao successfully return from their campaign against Rome, as a reward he would let them lead the initial assaults on the Eastern Roman capital. Such an assault would lead, hopefully, to their deaths. The brothers had no successors that Zestras knew of, which eliminated a successor problem if both were to die. This would leave Zestras in charge of the Southern and now Northern Hun tribes. *Ambition is what drives us to victory,* he thought. *Not blind ambition, but ambition with forethought.*

Zestras declared the meeting over. One of the attendees stayed behind. It was his son, Braga.

"Nicely done, Father."

Zestras answered, "Events have now been set in motion, without one Hun death caused by another Hun. The sons of Drago will do the work for us, and we will reap the rewards. Bring me the Eastern Roman ambassador. It is time to plan our strategy against Eastern Rome, even as we talk to the Eastern Romans."

XXII

Seeking Freedom

Taking the back roads or even single file trails proved to be both good and bad for Claire, Erik, and the other three escapees. The good was that Argus and his men would not think to pursue them in this area for the time being. Thus, the group could slow its escape and save their horses and themselves for what could come in the future. The bad was that the country they traveled in was rough. Bandits and rogues of ample quantity were frequent inhabitants of the woods. The group also had to ration food. Sometimes they were lucky and successfully found and killed live game. Claire was proficient at locating edible wild vegetation. As a result, the group was able to find food and was not starving.

Claire and Erik, however, could never relax. The thought of Argus and his spies lurking behind every tree was nerve wracking. Mary, Anne, and Elizabeth also felt the tension. All it would take is for someone to recognize them and report the findings to Argus, and they would likely be finished.

In one village, where Mary had friends, they rode in at night and were not seen. There they ate a good meal and quietly rested.

Before dawn they were back on the trail, before any villagers knew there had been visitors to the village. Slowly they were making their way to the western tribes and the home of Claire's exiled brother, Eustice.

Three weeks had passed since Claire's escape. Argus was still furious that this could have happened to him. He believed he was surrounded by incompetents. He chastised Flavius for missing the signs that Claire was plotting an escape and then followed through with it. Argus' frustrations boiled over and infected the men around him. Anyone even suspected of helping Claire was severely punished, which included many executions. Flavius carried out the punishments, but he silently disagreed with this approach. Other officers under Argus' command were using Claire's escape to carry out their own personal vendettas against their enemies. Blood was flowing and nothing was being accomplished.

Argus then generated an idea. He ordered leaders of as many villages he could readily locate to meet in the large great room of his castle. Flavius and his officers also attended the meeting.

Argus spoke: "As you have heard by now, the woman who was to be my queen, the former wife of Gerhard, fled like a coward into the bush. Not only is she a traitor, she is a fool. Giving up marriage to me was a mistake. Now instead of being a queen and living in my castle, she is a fugitive hiding in the hinterlands. I will pay five hundred Roman gold coins to whoever finds her and brings her back to me alive. I will take it from there. She will not have a good ending. As for her brood, and anyone who is traveling with her or hiding her, they are yours to do with as you want. Now go forth and find her and bring her to me, *GO*!"

The attendees all yelled back, "Yes," in unison and the rally was over.

Argus turned to Flavius. "That is how you get things done."

The room quickly emptied out. Most of the men who were sent on Argus' mission were hungry for the money and driven by greed. Yet some were sympathetic to Claire. They either went home and avoided the hunt or left for the countryside to find and warn Claire of the impending danger.

After the villagers had left, just Argus and Flavius remained in the room. "Now, Flavius," Argus said, "I am placing you in charge of finding that witch. You are the only one I can trust to do this job and complete it successfully. Take whatever you need. Where do you think they are now—or are going?"

"North or west, Lord Argus," was Flavius' reply. "She may go north. However, I am thinking west. I heard her brother resides with the western tribes. She won't go south."

"If that is so, you must get them before they reach those tribes. They are a nasty people, if you can even call them people."

"Lord Argus, I will send one column of troops to the north country. I will take a second column and proceed west."

"Good."

"We are organizing now for our search and we will leave at first light. We won't return until we have her."

"Good."

The two men had a drink and then Flavius left to prepare to hunt Claire.

Claire and company were at the edge of a dense woods. To the west was an open area like a moor. They were not as familiar with this area as the woods they had previously traveled through. The moor-like area was lightly populated. They began to run low on food, and food was scarce in this area. Even though they knew Argus would soon be on their trail, the group decided to rest and try to increase their food stores. They made a camp to last two days. On the night of the second day, they would set out. Their plan called for night travel with rest during the day. This was a risky strategy because the moor was best traveled in the daylight when hazards could be seen.

On the first day two rabbits from the woods were caught and prepared as travel food. Claire also collected edible plant material.

While searching for food in the woods and away from the others, Claire said to Erik, "If we ration carefully, we will make it across the moor to the hills. The land will then alternate between woods and open areas until we reach the western mountains and my brother."

"You know this country better than I, Claire, but I still don't like traveling at night. If one of our horses should fall or break a leg, we will have to double up. And doubling up will be a problem if we need to ride away from Argus' men."

The two returned to camp to find a figure sitting on a log with his back to Claire and Erik. The girls and Mary were sitting in front of him, and they had concerned looks on their faces. Erik quietly drew his sword and Claire pulled her knife from its sheath. Both looked around for any other people who would be with this stranger. They saw no one.

As they stepped closer to the figure, he spoke up without turning his head. "Put your weapons away. You do not need to fear me."

Claire recognized the voice but could not place it. The figure stood up and walked a short way into the woods. As he did so, he kept his hood up, covering his entire head so no one could identify him.

"Claire, come," was all the voice said.

She hesitated and then began to follow him into the woods. Erik also started to follow Claire until the voice said, "Stay where you are. No harm will come to her—if you stay there."

Erik felt only slightly reassured, but he stopped and went over to Mary and the girls. His eyes never left Claire and the strange man. Claire followed him into the woods and away from the rest of the party. When they were out of sight, he pulled back his hood. He was a large man, with a bushy brown beard. He carried a large ax in his right hand. He had deep creases in his forehead that indicated he was a seasoned outdoorsman.

"Edgbart, it is you! I didn't recognize you from behind and your voice seems different."

Edgbart looked at Claire. "I didn't want any of your party to be able to recognize me by appearance or by my voice. That is best for all involved here."

He then waited for Claire's questions, and she did not hesitate asking them. "First," she asked, "what are you doing here? And second, how did you find me?"

She was careful in her questioning—the weeks in the country-side had made her skittish. It had also been several years since she had seen Edgbart. He had always been loyal to Gerhard, but he may have changed allegiances and had begun working for Argus. She quickly decided that wasn't the reason Edgbart was here.

Edgbart smiled at the questions. "I'm here to help. You have made a very powerful enemy, my queen. Argus is going mad over your escape. I came from a meeting with him and other village leaders—involuntarily, of course. He was rabid with hate, and he set a large bounty on you. The ones who travel with you are worth nothing more than sport. Argus has offered five hundred gold coins for your capture. That has unleashed a flood of bandits, thieves, and deserters, and even those who I consider as good people are looking to hunt you down.

"I come here as your loyal subject and friend. Argus is ruining your dead husband's kingdom. You still have many loyal subjects and Argus has many enemies. We look forward to the day when you return to the throne. If Argus found out I was helping you, he would kill my family, destroy my village, and then kill me—slowly. I can handle the latter, but not the other two. That is why your party must not know who I am. I know, if captured, you would eventually give up my name. But we do not want you to get captured. At the edge of the clearing, you will find several satchels of food for your journey. I do not want to know where you are traveling to and please do not tell me.

Claire said, "What can I say to you so that you know how much I appreciate what you are doing for us?"

Edgbart humbly replied, "You can make it to wherever you are going and return someday to defeat Argus. That is what I request."

"What are you going to do now?" Claire asked.

"I am going to return to my village and organize a hunting party to look for you—but in the wrong direction. One last word of advice, my queen. Argus has hundreds of men looking for you. Make haste and do not stay here long. They will be here soon, and once they pick up your presence here, you will be in peril. Argus' lapdog—*Flavius*—will likely be put in charge. Do not underestimate him. Take care, my Queen."

Edgbart left Claire and walked into the deep woods. Claire could hear a horse trot off and then there was silence. The silence brought to her mind what she already knew—not to underestimate Flavius. He was a very dangerous foe.

Erik came up behind Claire. "Who was that?" he asked.

"A friend. At the edge of the clearing over there are some satchels with food. Get them and load the horses. We need to leave soon. Argus' men are coming, and I do not want to be here when they arrive."

The group packed up and broke camp. They would try the moor in what was left of the daylight.

Crossing the moor proved difficult enough in the fleeting light and was very difficult at night. Fortunately there was a full moon to provide some light. The group still had to dismount and walk carefully. They dared not light a torch as that could be seen for miles and possibly alert those who were in league with Argus. When daylight reappeared, they made it to a pocket of forest. They were so exhausted that they all took a short nap that was surprisingly restful. Claire had always liked the early moments of dawn as a time when new beginnings were the theme. Now she welcomed the day in her sleep.

Flavius winced as he saw the various groups of riders leaving Argus' castle in search of Claire and the reward. He thought of them as dancing in chaos. Sometimes they would bump together, like fisherman concentrating at a hot fishing spot. Other times the greed aspect was too much and they tended to separate in miserly ways. Then if something interesting was found, they lumped back together again as a group.

Flavius took a small group of approximately twenty highly trained men with him as they went west. Other groups tried to stay with him, but they were soon left behind. Flavius was convinced Claire and her group were headed west, and he was going to beat them to their destination. He was traveling lightly to make up time in pursuing Claire, as he did not think he would be in the pursuit very long. He viewed Claire and her company as easy prey.

XXIII

BRAXUS

AFTER THE GENERAL and his centuries had left to go after the Suevi, Joseph gathered up the volumes that composed the General's history and read them cover to cover, including the part he had written. Joseph wanted to find out in more detail what Jacob had written for and about the General. Overall Joseph had a true fear of the General, but he also had admiration for him. The General had a strict moral and ethical code, and he expected his men to adhere to it. The General set the example and expected nothing less from his men. Punishment could be severe for those who strayed from his values. On the other hand, he was loyal to his men and made sure they were compensated well for their service.

Joseph found the history based in chapter form, constructed around the several commands the General had held. There was nothing in the history that discussed the General's birth, childhood, or adolescence. It began when the General became an officer in the Roman army. The reading was dry and consisted primarily of the General discussing the campaigns he had led or when he was a subordinate (which was not a long time). Joseph knew the General dictated and Jacob wrote the words, and that is the way the General wanted his history written. However, every now and then Jacob took a little liberty and added some flesh to the skeleton.

For example, Joseph learned the General was apprehensive about traveling on open water. If the General could travel by land to a destination, that is the way he traveled, even if it added extra miles to the trip. One time Jacob wrote of a campaign where the Roman navy was to ferry the General and part of a legion from one port to another port. The navy flotilla was attacked by a band of pirates from Africa. During the battle the General's ship was sunk. Fortunately for the General, a raft composed of a destroyed ship's remnants passed by and the soldiers on the raft pulled the General onto it and to safety. The General could swim, but swimming was not among his best skills.

The next day after editing chapters in the General's chronicles, Joseph visited Olivertos. When Joseph arrived, the rooms overseen by Olivertos were empty. Only Olivertos and two staff people were there, and they looked bored.

"Why is your area so vacant?" Joseph asked.

"I don't know. I think it is a bad omen."

"Why? Do you think it has something to do with the General's campaign against the Suevi?"

"I don't know," Olivertos repeated.

"Isn't the General a careful planner who would not allow himself to be in a position where he would suffer a defeat?"

"Oh, that is not it at all," answered Olivertos.

"Well, what is troubling you, my friend?"

"I will tell you, Joseph. The General that I know would not have led such an expedition against the Suevi."

Joseph felt confused, and he didn't have anything to say, so he waited for Olivertos to continue.

"When you talk about General Valerias, you are talking about the supreme general in this area. He has two comitatenses legions under his direct command. Additionally, several other legions, both comitatenses and limitanei, answer to his command. Other top generals ask him for advice. As a general, he has never gone off on a wild chase for some minor bandits like these Suevi."

Joseph still looked confused. "But the Suevi burned villages and killed their occupants. Are you saying it was beneath the command of the General to go after these savages?"

"No, the General hates to his core what the barbarians did and he wanted them punished. Under normal circumstances, he would send a tribune, a minor general, or even Cratus alone. You need to remember, the General has assembled a very capable staff around him. Braxus and Cratus are legion generals. They and his other officers are first rate and any of them could carry out this mission for the General. It is just that he decided to be the leader on this campaign. Having the General be the commander of an expedition so small is unnatural, and that could lead to unexpected results. I am not a particularly superstitious man, but things are changing. By the gods"—and then he looked at Joseph—"or God, I hope that is not the case."

After that short speech, Olivertos asked Joseph, "Has the General been acting strange lately? After all, outside of Bukarma, you have been around the General more than anyone else during the past months."

"I just try to do what he wants and not irritate him more than I already have; however, he seems to carry a very gloomy attitude with him, and much of the time he is in a reflective state. He did tell me on the last night that we were almost finished with his chronicles."

"I don't like to hear that," Olivertos responded, looking at his feet when he spoke. "I think he went after the Suevi to die . . . to die in battle."

Both men said nothing until a knock came on the outside frame of Olivertos' room. Two soldiers were at the door. For a minute neither Joseph nor Olivertos knew the purpose of the surprise visit by the soldiers.

One of the soldiers spoke, looking at Joseph, "General Braxus orders your presence in the command quarters—at once."

Joseph looked lost for that moment as his gaze wandered around the room. Olivertos got Joseph to focus and said, "Go at once. We can discuss this later."

Joseph and the Romans disappeared in a late morning fog.

Joseph was calmly apprehensive as he walked with the soldiers to the command center of the fort. Of the General's officers, Braxus had always been the most humane to him. Even after Joseph had experienced bad rounds with the General, it was Braxus who usually spoke to him and tried to provide the explanation for what had just happened. Braxus even provided a security escort for Joseph if he had to travel at night. Still, Braxus was the General's right-hand man and top general.

Perhaps the General is using Braxus to test me while he is away from the fort, mulled Joseph as he walked to Braxus' offices.

So it was with mixed emotions that Joseph entered Braxus' command area. Bukarma was there as always, now as Braxus' main bodyguard. Joseph had grown accustomed to Bukarma and did not fear him, although Bukarma still possessed an intimidating presence. Braxus was sitting in the General's chair reviewing documents when Bukarma announced Joseph's entrance.

"I really don't like sitting in this chair," were the first words that Braxus said. "But this is the job I was ordered to do. Please be seated."

Joseph couldn't recall a time in the Roman camps when anyone said "please" that applied directly to him. This relaxed him a little.

"How do you think General Valerias is doing up in the countryside, chasing the Suevi?"

Joseph was thinking hard about all the possible answers to this question and which one was the correct one. "I am sure the General will be successful in what he wants to do."

"And what does that mean—what he wants to do?" Braxus was now sitting more rigid in the chair.

Joseph knew immediately that was not the answer Braxus wanted to hear. "I mean, my experience with the General tells me he will defeat the Suevi and return triumphantly to the fort."

"Quit trying to be a politician, Joseph. He has been acting oddly the past several months and we are concerned." Braxus looked at Bukarma when he said "we." "In your time with him, has he said or done anything that might help us figure out what is bothering him? Is he sick? Olivertos won't divulge anything."

"Honestly, I do not know. When I am with the General, I try to stay out of his way. I am always afraid of doing something or saying something that will cause him to get angry. I do what he wants, and hopefully I will live long enough to leave this fort and him behind."

"But you are a Christian, a man of God. How is it that you seem to have given up your faith and become subservient to him?"

"Not any more than you, General Braxus." As soon as Joseph said that remark, he was overcome with fear. A response like that to the General would be met with hard retribution. However, Braxus was not the General. Braxus sat back in the chair and looked at Bukarma again, and then smiled at Joseph.

"Ha, there *is* a man in there." He pointed at Joseph. "I understand what you say, Joseph. Not many men can stand up to him and still stay standing. He does listen to opinions, but when the decision is made, that is it, and one learns not to debate the point."

This time it was Bukarma who spoke, which was a rarity. "So you don't wish to martyr yourself for your faith in the presence of General Valerias?"

"I don't have the courage of Peter and the other disciples," Joseph responded meekly.

Then in a remarkable statement that caught Joseph off guard, Braxus said, "You don't need to—the mission of your new life and faith is just beginning. It would be a loss to the people whom you have and will encounter to die now. Such a premature death would be a waste."

Joseph felt both relief and new concern. Braxus spoke kind words, and yet Joseph always kept in the back of his mind that the General would trick him through others to talk of his Christian faith when he was ordered not to do so.

Joseph thought it better not to pursue the subject, and there was a pause in the conversation. Both Braxus and Bukarma were looking at him, which made him think this was a trap, particularly when Braxus added, "I want to hear more about your Christian religion."

Joseph knew he did not want to go further in this line of the discussion and a thought came to him, which he passed on. "Tell me, Braxus and Bukarma, why does General Valerias hate Christians so intensely?"

That was an excellent question, asked at the right time. Braxus sat back in the chair and rubbed his right hand fingers across the short dark beard that covered his chin. Braxus' beard was such a thick mat that one could not see the skin of his chin when he rubbed it. Braxus no longer thought about Joseph, but how to best answer the question.

Finally, he answered, "There are several reasons. Which ones do you want to know about? By the way, what *we* say here stays in this room. You can't even discuss this with Olivertos—although he knows the reasons."

Another pause and more chin rubbing ensued. In that time, Olivertos appeared at the door. Braxus looked up and sighed.

"Come in. You might as well add your thoughts. Joseph here wants to know why the General hates Christians."

Olivertos piped in, "That could take some time."

Braxus looked at Olivertos, then Bukarma, then at Joseph, "You should know that the General achieved the rank of general by order of the Emperor Julian even before Julian became Emperor. Do you recall your history, Joseph?"

"Wasn't Julian a pagan, Julian the Apostate?" Joseph responded.

"That depends on your definition of 'pagan.' Actually, Julian was a follower of the old gods, and the Sun God, Helios, in particular. So he did believe in a god, just not your God. General Valerias served under Julian, so Julian was a mentor to the General. I think you can understand that the General did what Julian expected his officers to do. I was with the General during this time in the same position I am now, his chief officer, only at the time he was a junior general. We sometimes carried out the orders of Julian, which was to 'manage Christians' for whatever reason Julian demanded."

"Then is the General a pagan? I mean, a follower of the old gods, the Sun God today?" Joseph was trying to understand the General's background.

The other three men responded in laughter, and at the end, Braxus said, "For a supposed learned man, you do not see what is around you. Do you think he is a follower of the Sun God? Have you seen him pray to Helios? Does he have carvings of gods in his room?"

"No, I have not seen any such things."

"Has he ever talked about religious matters, or have you heard him talk of any religion in all the time you have been around him?"

"Very little. No."

"Then you have answered your own question. He follows no religion, not the old gods, not the Christian God, not any god. I can tell you that he did not like the order to harass certain Christians, but he did it because that was an order from the Emperor, and he obeys his orders. He much preferred to wage war on the enemies of Rome—the ones that were armed."

Olivertos then spoke, giving Braxus a break, as Braxus was becoming agitated, "One thing that haunts the General, is that he wasn't at Julian's side when the Emperor was killed at Samarra in the Persian campaign. Julian had sent him, along with Braxus, to Africa to deal with a tribal problem. Africa provides much of the grain for Rome, and Julian did not want that resource to be affected in any way. Even today the General feels remorse because he thinks if he had been there at Emperor Julian's side, Julian would not have been killed. There were rumors that Julian was killed by one of his own solders, a Christian. That is one of the reasons why Braxus stays close to the General most of the time."

"To protect him?"

Braxus, in a more calm manner spoke, "Perhaps, but more to the point, to take over and complete the General's agenda if he should fall."

"What if you are killed because of your close proximity to the General?" countered Joseph.

"That should not happen," Braxus continued. "We are close, but not that close."

Now Bukarma interjected, "I protect the General. I always stay close to General Valerias."

Braxus couldn't resist and added, "Then more bathing is needed by you than by me, Bukarma, and that is a good thing."

Braxus, Olivertos, and Bukarma all laughed.

Joseph just smiled as he readied another question: "If all of what you say is true, then why is the General off chasing bandits in a far-away location when you are both here?"

Joseph knew what he had said was ill advised as soon as he'd spoken the words. Braxus looked hard at Joseph, and Joseph knew

Bukarma was glaring at him as well. He looked over at Olivertos, who was staring at the door.

"Sometimes insolence yields a reward that is earned," Braxus said in a staccato rhythm.

Joseph was in trouble, and he reversed course as quickly as he could. "I apologize to you, General Braxus, for my ill-spoken words. I should not have spoken them. Please forgive me." Joseph then looked directly at Bukarma and said essentially the same sentence.

Braxus eased slowly back in his chair without taking his eyes off of Joseph. Joseph knew he had crossed the line and insulted great soldiers. He hung his head and the room became very quiet.

Braxus broke the silence. "I expect—no, I demand—that you show me the same respect that you show General Valerias, whether I am acting in his place or when he is here. And Bukarma is unmatched in his fighting skills, and his work as a bodyguard has been perfect. If you had spoken to the General as you just spoke to me, I promise you, you would most likely be dead. Although, maybe, the General would have shown mercy and given you twenty lashes and sold you to the mines! Keep that in mind!"

Braxus' next words were surprising. "I forgive you." But he added, "Think before you speak and act. The next time forgiveness to you will have a short memory."

"I understand, General Braxus." Joseph's understanding was on many levels. One, he wanted to survive, and to do that, he needed to use smarter choices of words. Two, Braxus had always looked out for him and on more than one occasion had taken actions that ended up saving his life. He should not insult Braxus' soldiering. Three, Joseph had questioned his own Christianity. Here he was—alive—but unable to conduct any kind of mission work. And he knew that he couldn't dare do so, not with the General and his anti-Christianity stance looking him straight in the face on a daily basis. If he performed his mission duties, he would die; if he didn't, his mission would be a failure. He was frustrated, and that may have resulted in his poor choice of words.

Bukarma broke into Joseph's thoughts, "Do you want to hear more about the General and his experience with your religion?"

Joseph could tell there was a message in Bukarma's question that indicated Bukarma was not quite yet in the position to grant Joseph forgiveness. Bukarma had moved on, however, and wanted Joseph to hear another story from Braxus.

XXIV

The Bishop

Joseph asked Braxus, Bukarma and Olivertos if they wanted more mead. It was also an offer of humility that did not go unnoticed. After it was poured, Bukarma looked at Joseph and smiled. All seemed back to normal, at least to what Joseph wanted.

Braxus took a deep drink and then swallowed slowly so that he could enjoy the taste of the liquid. It also allowed him time to recreate in his mind the story he wanted to tell the group. Bukarma and Olivertos were there when the event unfolded, but they still wanted to hear Braxus' version.

"Several years ago a Christian Bishop by the name of Casio came to a Roman fort like this. He was short and heavy, with black hair and a black beard. His eyes were coal black and could stare for minutes without blinking, and yet he never seemed to hold eye contact. He always wore a thick grey tunic that was too small for him and made him itch—he was always scratching. For his stature he was energetic and always moving. What was worse, he said things that many times did not correspond to what would take place. He was someone I did not trust.

"If I did not trust him, what do you think the General thought?" Braxus inquired.

"Who was he and where was he from?" Joseph was immediately interested.

"As I said, his name was Casio and he was a Christian Bishop, I believe from your sect, the Nicene Creed Christians. He said he came from Antioch, but we didn't know whether to believe him. As we later discovered, Casio and Emperor Valentinian's cousin, Protius, were in business together. Protius wanted to wear the purple of the Emperor, and to do so, he needed to rid himself of the Emperor. He figured that the General was the main obstacle to his plans. So the first order of business was to get rid of the General. Then they would replace the General with a general sympathetic to their plan. With his own general in command, Protius thought he could readily assume the throne. The Bishop also wanted to become Pope. Protius had said that when he became Emperor, Casio would be appointed Pope. Greed was their common denominator.

"I repeat, the first part of their plan was removal of General Valerias. Casio took the lead. Casio said he came to the General's legions on behalf of Emperor Valentinian to evaluate the General's adaptation to Christianity as the state religion and religion of choice for his legions. It was to be a survey, not actual proselytizing.

"The General was quiet at first as he listened to the Bishop. He was loyal to the Emperor, as he had been to previous Emperors. That is the primary reason emperors sent him to put down rebellions. He was good at it, he was ruthless in doing so, and he was always loyal.

"So he let the Bishop and his men do their work. At first things went well for Casio. The Bishop stayed out of sight and the General gave him little thought. You have to remember, General Valerias was never interested much in religion, whether it was the Emperor Julian's Sun God, Helios, your Christian God, animists, or whoever. His role was to use his legions to fight barbarians from the outside and to eviscerate usurpers from the inside.

"Casio's and Protius' plan proceeded. Their goal was to sow discord in the General's ranks through a couple of ways. First, they knew the General would not accept what the Bishop told the General. So the Bishop brought with him several men who acted as agents to quietly proselytize throughout the ranks, particularly in cohorts that were not under the daily supervision of the General. When certain targets did not 'agree' to join the Bishop, they were persuaded by heavy-handed means.

"The second way involved the Bishop's efforts to bribe targeted officers to join him. The Bishop had money and was ready to spend it. Both ways worked—but only a little. You see, the General's troops are quite loyal, and soon what the Bishop was up to reached our ears. In fact, Casio even offered Cratus the General's position after the General had been removed from his post. Cratus—after conferring with the General—accepted Casio's offer.

"After several days, the General began hearing rumors and complaints about the heavy-handedness of the Bishop and his men in addition to the bribery attempts. Casio was pushing his view of Christianity hard on some of the cohorts. In response the General sent Revious to the area where the Bishop had said he was monitoring and talking to the men. The Bishop did not know who Revious was, as he had been out hunting renegade Lombards with a centurion dispatched by the General. Revious reported that the Bishop was not mildly conducting his work, as he had promised the General; instead he was trying to convert as many soldiers as he could, and he was using very threatening measures to secure his conversions. There seemed to be a bounty on the number of souls he saved.

"When the General heard Revious' report, he was furious—and would have killed Casio. However, we suggested another way. The General summoned the Bishop and ordered him to stop his proselytizing. The Bishop gave an insulting response to the General that he, the Bishop, was acting on the order of the Emperor and the General needed to submit to the Bishop on this matter.

"Needless to say the Bishop and his minions were thrown out of the camp. Threats were made by both sides. The Bishop said he would go to Constantinople and ask Emperor Valens to relieve the General of his command. The General told the Bishop that if he or his lackeys ever returned to his camps, he and they would be executed on the spot.

"The General immediately left for Milan to discuss the events with the Emperor. The Emperor was not eager to lose his primary general, and as a result, he exiled or banished—however you prefer—Protius to a small Greek island. He may still be alive, but I heard he had died. The Emperor also pressured the Pope to appropriately handle the Bishop. So the Pope ordered that Casio be defrocked and sent back to Antioch for retraining.

"The Bishop did not give up, though. He never made it to Antioch. Instead he went to Rome. There he met allies of the exiled Protius. Together they put a plan in place whereby a team of assassins would strike and kill the General at one of his summer camps. The plan was for seven assassins to schedule an audience with the General. The assassins were disguised as villagers who had a tax conflict with another village and they wanted a Roman decree to resolve the dispute—in their favor, of course. The General was a proponent of proper taxpaying and would focus on tax issues instead of on assassins ready to strike. The General usually had these audiences with two or three guards, and thus Casio thought this assassination would be easy. He was obviously wrong.

"The General surmised the villagers' attempt to schedule an audience with him was made under false pretenses. He had Bukarma, myself, and several soldiers hide in the back room of his tent. The guards the General selected were the finest in his legions, besides yours truly," Braxus looked at Bukarma when he said this.

"Then he made the seven assassins-turned-villagers wait. The more they waited, the more they became restless, and the more likely they would deviate from their plan and strike quickly when brought before the General. Finally, with all in place, the distressed group of 'villagers' was led in to see the General. The main speaker had just started talking when one of the assassins launched himself at the General. The General had held his sword behind him but still had enough time to slit the attacker's throat in midair.

"A second attacker reached the General and both men fell to the ground, each fighting for position. This attacker also had a dagger that became entangled within the two men's hands. The General could not use his sword, but as you have seen, the General keeps a dagger strapped to the inside of his ankle. He pulled the dagger out while wrestling with the man and stabbed him through the side. The man collapsed, and the General threw the assassin's dying body off of his own. When he looked up, he saw both of his guards engaged with the attackers. At that point we had entered the room and finished off the assassins. We left one alive. After a short time of persuasion, the prisoner said this was Casio's planned attempt to kill the General.

"The prisoner made a deal with the General. He would be spared if he would help lure the Bishop into the Roman camp. As it turned out, the Bishop was waiting in the country outside the camp for word of the General's death. The prisoner, with a group of Roman cavalry, approached the Bishop's camp. He announced that the General and I were dead. Cratus was waiting at the camp for his installation as the new commanding general.

"When Casio arrived at our camp, he was led to the headquarters, where Cratus was waiting for him. As Casio entered the room, he saw the General sitting in a chair with both Cratus and me beside him. The Bishop quickly figured out the ruse and tried to rush out, but was stopped by Bukarma.

"I won't bore you with the details, but the Bishop was executed that day. It was a death that was quick, but not so quick that the Bishop could not think of the consequences of his actions prior to death. He was hanged in an upside-down position. A small hole punctured an artery in his neck and he bled out slowly. When he looked out, he saw the heads of the six dead assassins on posts in front of him. Their eyes had been propped open, and in the mouth of each man was a gold coin. A fitting end for a corrupt man, wouldn't you say Joseph?"

Joseph was silent. The story he had heard through the Church was of a general who went insane and executed a bishop.

"Does this contradict what you have heard?" Braxus' question penetrated the thoughts of Joseph, who was thinking about what he knew of this event.

"Ah, yes," was the response.

"We know what some have said, but we know the truth. Note that neither the Emperor nor the Pope took any action against the General. That should tell you something."

"Why did he make such a gruesome scene instead of conducting a quick execution?"

"In reality, it was quick, about two hours. In the end, the General wanted to make two statements: 'Don't take me on unless you can win' and 'Corruption will pay the deserved price.'"

"What happened to the Bishop's body?"

"After the Bishop had died, his body was hung from a tree for two days as a showpiece. The General then cut it down and gave it to local clergy with the directive that the body be buried at an unmarked location. Perfect for a man who should have been an example of good but instead was governed by greed and evil."

Mead was poured for each of the four men in the room. Braxus added a toast, "Life is fragile. It is good to live it wisely."

Joseph took a drink and thought of Braxus. He was very intelligent, and seemed to have a softer side than what he had seen with the General and Cratus. However, Joseph thought that Braxus must be able to control that side in his dealings as a general. Joseph was pleased that Braxus was like a guardian to him. Olivertos was a friend; Braxus was a guardian.

XXV

RETURN

BEFORE THE GENERAL returned to the fort, he ordered the two cavalry centuries into military dress. This command even applied to the wounded soldiers who could function on their own. Uniforms were cleaned and horses washed and brushed. Weapons were polished. This was typical of how the General expected his men to appear when returning to camp after a campaign. Even before the order the men were already under way to prepare for their return. It had been a successful mission, and the General wanted a demonstration showing that success. "Victors should look the part," he always said.

General Valerias had always admired the previous Roman conquerors and their welcome as they returned to Rome after a victory. It was not a reward that he wanted for himself in completing a successful mission, but he wanted the people to appreciate what he and his men had accomplished. This time though he wasn't returning to Rome and he didn't have slaves captured from battle. He also didn't have plunder to give to his rulers. Valerias knew all this and yet he didn't care. The General had another reason besides the obvious one for this triumphant entrance into his fort. This reason was his alone.

Revious rode ahead and alerted Braxus to the General's impending return. The fort quickly materialized into anthill-like action. Soldiers and staff moved in every direction with purpose to their activities. Braxus wanted the fort's occupants to provide the General with a hero's welcome, an objective also shared by the legions. Braxus also had the ulterior motive of trying to uplift the General's spirits, which Braxus felt were in a poor state when the General had left in pursuit of the Suevi. Braxus believed there was something wrong with the General, and he thought he had the solution to correct it. There was definite anticipation in the air at the fort. Braxus and his men's efforts were notable.

Preparing the garrison to welcome the General was a mirror image of the General's readiness for arrival at the fort. This included assembling the infantry inside the fort while the cavalry moved to the outside. The General's command could always pass an inspection, which was the situation now from both ends.

At a short distance before the General and his command reached the fort, Valerias summoned Gul to his side. Gul had been assigned the task of looking after the soldiers who were wounded from the fight with the Suevi. This was a tedious but important task. All the wounded soldiers had lived during their return to the fort.

The General began the conversation. "What do you think of your first campaign, Gul, small as it was?"

"It was good, General. I learned much."

"For example?"

There was a pause as Gul tried to think of something positive that the General would want to hear.

However, the General guessed what Gul was thinking, and he interjected, "I want to tell you two things that you are to remember."

Gul said nothing, but his nod told the General he was ready to listen.

"First, you are never to tell anyone what you saw on the hill in the forest between the Suevi and me. In return, I will not disclose what happened between you and the Suevi chief. Is that agreeable?"

Gul nodded again, but the General made a motion to Gul that indicated he wanted Gul to verbally respond.

"Yes, General, I agree."

"Good."

"Second, I have watched you over the past several months. My men have watched you also and have reported back to me. I'll be blunt with you, Gul. You are not a soldier capable of fighting, or leading infantry or cavalry."

Gul immediately protested the General's conclusion. He quickly realized what he had done, though, and became worried about the consequence of debating the General.

The General acted like he had not heard Gul and continued, "I didn't say you are a worthless soldier or incompetent. You are not a warrior conditioned for battle, and I don't think you ever will be. Let me tell you, two of the finest people who serve me are not soldiers either. They are Revious and Olivertos. Jacob also—when he was alive. You have seen them. I value their trust as much as my warriors Braxus, Cratus, and Bukarma . . . and my officers."

Gul straightened up in his saddle and looked the General in the eyes, wondering about the end result of this dialogue.

The General continued, "You are organized and a thinker and a planner. I would like you to become an engineer apprentice. I noticed on this campaign you prepared devices to help the injured so they could ride more comfortably. When we return to camp, I want you to report to the Chief Engineer, Tribune Tentrides. Trust me, I have been doing this for a long time. The Empire is better served with you as an engineer than as a warrior."

Gul expressed a look of both disappointment and puzzlement.

The General anticipated this response. "You think you will disappoint your father, Mostar Gulivus. Maybe, initially. You think he wants you to be a true warrior leader like himself, and to be an engineer is a lower class—not even a soldier. That is a false presumption. If you successfully carry out your tasks as an engineer, you will provide more value to the legions than as a soldier. Your father will come around. I will talk to him when I see him again. Besides, you will get to see your wife on a more frequent basis, and your children may even get to know you."

The General laughed softly and Gul smiled. Gul, too, noticed a dual meaning in the General's last sentence. On the one hand the General was trying to be lighthearted with Gul, something that had never happened before. On the other the General's words carried a hint of regret.

"Return now to your injured. After we arrive in camp, take them to Olivertos." With those words, the General gave a slight kick to his horse and he galloped ahead to the front.

Gul returned to his post as caretaker of the wounded, and he wondered about his exchange with the General. Was the General looking out for him, to keep him safe and removed from the battle scene? Or was it was because he (Gul) was a poor soldier? In that case he was a disgrace to his father and his tribe. Or was it because he could be a worthy engineer? He thought back to the time when he had led a group of young, unprepared Goths against the General and shuddered about what could have happened to him. After a quick assessment of his options, Gul concluded the engineer route would be his choice.

As the General's troop began to round the bend in the road that led into the fort, the General gave a sharp command. The soldiers moved into a tight formation of two riders side by side and quickened the pace. The banners and standards of the centuries were prominently displayed in the front. The General rode first, followed by Cratus and Tribune Gius and Centurion Maximus. Gul, the injured, and the supply horses were in the rear.

A great cheer arose when the General and his centuries appeared to the fort's occupants. Braxus had all the soldiers positioned to provide the maximum visual impact for the General's arrival. Almost on cue the soldiers shouted, "*Sapor est victoria! Adhuc esurient!*" [Savor the victory! Hunger for more!] The General rode briskly through the open gates of the fort in a completely natural manner. This was his world—he owned it and all knew it.

The General dismounted, and immediately two servants took his horse away. He walked up to Braxus and they "shook hands" the way the General preferred—hand to forearm. The General smiled broadly, as he was obviously pleased with the welcome at the fort and particularly pleased with Braxus. Braxus looked into the General's eyes as they greeted each other and saw the General who looked familiar to him—a general who was at peace with himself.

The next day the General attended the games that Braxus had organized for his benefit. There were contests of strength, speed, and athleticism that pitted cohort against cohort. At the General's command, there were no contests involving real weapons. The General showed great enjoyment as he watched the contests. Braxus sat on his right and Cratus on his left, and the General liberally sprinkled comments about what he was viewing. Bukarma, as usual, stood behind the General like a statue. Olivertos was busy attending the wounded and made it to only about half the contest time. Joseph watched the games across the field from the General's stand. He was fascinated by the action. Even from a distance he could see a change in the General's demeanor. He was relaxed and smiled more on that day than in all the time Joseph had previously spent with him.

At the end of the contest, the General himself awarded the winners with prizes. They were gold medals engraved with the General's likeness. *Braxus had truly outdone himself,* the General thought as he looked at the medals. *The Emperors would be jealous.*

Afterward the General retired alone to his rooms. He asked for three parchments and a writing instrument. He then asked all to leave, including Bukarma, who stood outside the door to the General's quarters. The next morning, the General emerged with three documents marked with his seal. He called for the Centurions Maximus and Tyrol. When they arrived, the General gave each simple commands.

To Maximus: "Take this parchment marked with purple and deliver it to the Emperor Valentinian himself in Milan. Then take this parchment marked with blue and deliver it to lawyer Anguillo Claudius in Rome. You will then return to me with documents confirming that these documents were received by the Emperor and lawyer Claudius. That is all. Go."

To Tyrol: "Take this parchment to the Emperor Valens in Constantinople. You too are to return with confirmation that the Emperor received my letter."

"Yes, General," both men replied, and they proceeded to leave the fort for their destinations.

The General turned to the nearest officer. "Bring me the priest."

Joseph was with Olivertos at the opposite end of the fort from the General's headquarters. Several soldiers were being treated for various wounds obtained during the fight with the Suevi. Other soldiers had a strange stomach ailment that forced them into cots. It was a busy area, and Olivertos needed Joseph's help in addition to his own staff. Joseph thought the stomach problems were caused by bad water or food, and this illness would pass. Olivertos agreed, but telling that prognosis to the soldiers provided little comfort, and a good amount of loud cursing was heard in the makeshift hospital rooms.

It was at an inopportune time when the General's soldiers appeared at Olivertos' door and demanded Joseph's appearance with the General. Olivertos protested mildly but did not try to force the issue. Joseph had a good idea what the General wanted and told the soldiers that he first would need to go to his room. Once there he gathered up the journals and made his way with them to the General's rooms.

When Joseph arrived, he found the General sitting in a large chair eating lunch. He motioned Joseph to stand in front of him.

"I see you have my history, priest."

"Yes, General, I have done what you requested."

"Then my journals are done," the General paused for effect, "to your satisfaction . . . and to my satisfaction?"

"I trust you will find your journals in the manner that you requested."

"You mean as ordered?"

"Yes, General, as requested."

It was clear that Joseph would try to not use the word "ordered," which was his indirect rebellion to the submissive role that the General had forced upon him. The General noticed this new attitude from Joseph, only this time he did not care.

The General pointed to a table on Joseph's right. "Good. Leave them on that table."

Joseph complied and said, "As you wish, General. Is there anything else, as I would like to return to Olivertos' hospital. There are several wounded and ill men there."

"You may leave, priest. But return to this room one hour after sunset tomorrow night."

Joseph started to leave the room but froze as the General added, "For your sake, I hope your work on my history matches your confidence."

No more words were spoken as Joseph exited the room. He did not see the slight smile on the General's face. The smile emanated from the General's recognition that finally Joseph had showed a willingness to stand up to him—without being insulting. *He is learning, but hopefully not too late,* the General thought. He left his chair for the journals that were neatly placed on the table. He pulled the top journal from the pile, went back to his chair, and started reading the words. After a short while of reading his past, he was looking at the wall in front of him, focusing on the future.

XXVI

Small Empire

After their meeting with Zestras, Uldric and Rao spent the next several days trying to recover their pride. Their ambitions had been temporarily crushed. They were naive and had badly underestimated Zestras. Both vowed not to do so again, with Zestras or any other friend or foe. Neither man consumed any alcoholic drink for days as they planned their next actions.

"I think I have a workable plan," Rao offered to Uldric during a midafternoon horse ride.

"What is that?"

"We have been thinking too big. We can't conquer Zestras, Eastern Rome, Western Rome, or anyone else without first starting with small steps."

"You have to think big to accomplish what we want to accomplish."

"Uldric, how many men do we currently command?"

"Maybe five thousand."

"You are dreaming, brother. Try closer to five hundred. That number would be only the size of Zestras' bodyguard. So how could we carry out an operation against Rome?"

Uldric immediately protested but soon backed down because he knew his brother was correct—Rao always was when it came to doing the numbers. "So what do you suggest, brother?"

"Let's start with the tribes and their leaders in our immediate area. Most are friendly to us. They too want the same things as we do."

"They do? Most seem happy enough wandering around their livestock and trying to avoid stepping in shit."

"And daydreaming about their next meal or time with their women or counting the fleas on their dogs."

Both men laughed at their visions of the slow-minded leaders of the other tribes. Yet Rao knew that they should not underestimate these leaders.

Rao summarized his thoughts. "We need to convince them to join us. The days of small raids by small minds are over."

"What if they don't want to come?" Uldric questioned what he envisioned would be recalcitrance from even those leaders the brothers viewed favorably.

"Well, brother, we need to come up with something that will get them to come here. Perhaps we could hold a festival in their honor. We can have drink, food, women, and gifts. Who could resist that? And then we will present our plan to them."

"What if they don't share the vision of our plan? What then?"

"Then they don't make it back to their camp." Rao's half-serious tone took a dark twist. He continued, "I believe this group will quickly come around to our position. It is the outer tribes that I'm more concerned about. What we really need is a chieftain who does not agree with our vision. We then combine our forces with those who do and make an example of the lone dog. Eliminating him could be persuasive to other resistant leaders and to the outer tribes. As a reward to our allies, we can give them some worthless titles and more livestock. I am hopeful that there are men in the other tribes who have leadership qualities and can become true leaders of men in our movement."

The two men returned to their tents and prepared a schedule of milestones they would need to meet. At the conclusion they each decided to have drinks. It began with a toast by Uldric. "Us against the world."

"For now," Rao concluded. "Soon it will be the world that fears us."

The next few weeks were planning weeks. The brothers split duties. Uldric's role was to work with the sub-chiefs within their own tribe. This was a tricky task, as the brothers wanted to keep the number of men knowledgeable about their plan to as few as possible. The Hunnic tribes in the immediate area were well dispersed and also integrated. Tribal members originally from one tribe lived with other tribes. Most of this movement was from arranged marriages. Any mention of the brothers' plan that found its way to the wrong ears in one tribe would likely be the common gossip throughout the area. If other tribal leaders found out what Uldric and Rao were thinking, then they could create an undesirable ending for the brothers.

Uldric eventually informed four sub-chiefs of his plan. All were in some way related to himself and Rao, and he trusted them. Still, he left out parts of the plan to keep them off balance in case something didn't go quite as expected. It was important that he and Rao maintain absolute control. They knew that they couldn't control everything, like the weather, but what they could control they would—relentlessly.

Rao's task was to invite and politely convince members of the nearby tribes to attend a special council in celebration of Drago's life. This effort proved easily done, as all but two of the tribes responded in the affirmative that they would attend the council. Rao knew it was the benefits to be provided at the council meeting and not the words and plans of the brothers that prompted the chiefs to attend. So far the brothers' plan was working.

The day of the council meeting arrived. Activities were well underway before dawn. Both Uldric and Rao had competent servants who were put in charge of the event preparations. As the day arrived, the sun was out to greet leaders of the nearby tribes. Some chiefs came with their wives and other relatives, others with slaves, and many had bodyguards. It was to be a festive occasion, and Uldric and Rao did not disappoint the guests. Food and drink were plentiful. There were many toasts to Drago and wishes for good fortune to the brothers.

Rao was the last to stand for his toast. First he spoke of his father and of his great leadership. He proceeded to acknowledge that his brother, Uldric, and he had been faithful sons. The tribal leaders made various grunts and sounds that affirmed Rao's talk to that point. Rao then journeyed ever so slightly into the real meaning for the festival. He had to be careful not to tip his hand. However, at the same time he worked to gradually persuade the tribes' leaders not to think of their future as solitary tribes, but as a group.

Rao spoke of his tribe first, noting the tribe was typical of the Hun tribes. Rao proceeded to describe the best aspects of the other tribes that were represented at the council. It was a "praise you" speech for the ages. The council attendees were feeling good when Rao promoted the idea of a confederation of the Northern Hun tribes, similar to Zestras' confederation of Southern Hun tribes.

Rao noted such a confederation would have better economic power when dealing with other tribes, including Zestras' confederation. This sounded good to the attendees. Most important (from the brothers' viewpoint), such a grouping would harness the military power of the many tribes into one large force—a force that would have to be taken seriously. The approval from the council members was crucial for Rao's plan to succeed. Several leaders raised questions about how this confederation would be maintained—in one central location or multiple locations? Who would pay for keeping the military portion of the confederation? Did Rao have a military objective in mind? Most important, who would lead this confederation?

Rao deftly handled all questions. They would have one headquarters and several field stations. The central quarters would be located in Rao's and Uldric's village. The field stations would be the other tribes' villages. Money to support such a force would be contributed by all the tribes. Because this was Rao's and Uldric's idea, their tribe would contribute the most to start the confederation. He said they would also approach some of the outlying tribes, including the Alans and others, and "request" they join the confederation, and pay a tribute to the confederation. The alternative for these tribes was to be attacked and destroyed, with the plunder going to the confederation's treasury. Regarding the choice of leader, Rao wisely said they could vote on the leader. He thought to himself that the council would nominate Uldric because Uldric was the son of Drago and was a great warrior—likely the best warrior of the tribes. All leaders of the nearby tribes would be appointed as generals and would attend all council meetings, including war council meetings led by Uldric.

After Rao finished speaking, the participants broke out into animated discussions. Borgas, one of the other tribal chiefs, asked Uldric and Rao to leave the meeting. The brothers went outside and waited.

"You did well, my brother. You prepared and offered the package," Uldric summarized.

"It did go well," was Rao's reply. "Unfortunately, we cannot act without them." Rao pointed to the tent that currently housed the other tribal leaders. "If they agree, we can gradually take control.

If not, we will need to start removing any adversaries. There is much risk to this approach, my brother."

The meeting of the council was over quickly, and soon the brothers were in front of the tribal leaders. Borgas stood up and walked over to Uldric and Rao.

"We agree with your plan. For too long we have fallen short of what we could be. I'm jealous—and my fellow chiefs are jealous—of Zestras. We agree that Uldric is to be the supreme chief."

The council meeting went well into the night about conditions for the confederation and other matters. In the morning agreements were reached and drink flowed. Rao and Uldric had completed a monumental step of their plan.

After the tribal leaders had left, Uldric told Rao, "That went better than I could have imagined."

"Zestras will rue the day he treated us like children. We will be the true founders of the Hun empire, and Zestras will be the goat farmer that he is. Someday we will feed him to his goats."

The brothers knew they had much work to do to reach their next milestone, which was to have the outlying tribes join the confederation peacefully or by force.

XXVII

Running

Edgbart had told Claire about the way to get to the western hill country of Britannia where they would reach safety. They first needed to pass by Durobrivae and then Ratae. They followed Edgbart's route, although it was very slow going. Anne and Elizabeth had grown weary of the trip. Camping outside in cold nights, during rain events and burning sun had taken a toll on the girls. Mary wasn't doing much better. Erik's and Claire's nerves were also frayed trying to show the rest of the company all was well when it wasn't. Claire knew Flavius would soon be on their trail, and then it was a matter of time.

"What can we do to quicken the pace?" Erik asked Claire when they were out of the hearing range of the Mary and the girls.

"We can only go so fast. We still have some supplies. And we are not far from where we need to go. I think the best thing we can do is cover our tracks and walk in the streams whenever possible. Maybe that would throw them off."

"I hope so." Erik noted, "Flavius is as dogged and ruthless as any man I have known. Argus' power and reach would be much less without his lapdog to do his bidding."

Claire looked back and watched as Mary and the girls slowly advanced up the trail. Even the horses they were riding looked exhausted. Claire knew the inevitable and told the party, "We rest here tonight." Dusk was beginning to add its presence to the day. Erik reluctantly agreed and they made camp.

Claire said she would take first watch. Soon it was night and all were fast asleep, including Erik. A sharp crackle like a deer stepping on a branch emanated from the forest about one hundred yards from Claire. The sharp sound awoke her. A second crackle now came from a closer location. Then a third snap closer, but off to the side of the first two. Claire held her breath and gradually pulled an arrow from her quiver and peered into the dark. Now a crackle came from behind. She was all nerves now and turned to fire the arrow at the sound. Fortunately she held her fire, as it was Erik right behind her. She relaxed her bow in a jerky manner. The darkness around the two was confining. Claire wished she had better nerves to handle this situation.

"I heard it too," he said with his sword drawn and hands shaking slightly. "Something is out there and I hope it is not human." Silence joined darkness to take over the forest. A silence that was complete. Both Erik and Claire slowly turned back to the forest where the crackles had originated, bracing for anything. As they did so, they turned back into Flavius, who was right behind them.

Before Claire could breathe, Flavius had his left hand over her mouth. The pressure of his hand was firm but not violent. With his right hand and arm, he pushed her bow down so it was facing the ground. Erik froze for a moment, but soon gathered himself and brought his sword up to waist level. As Erik looked up, he saw Flavius peering at him only a few feet away, with his right hand out telling him to stop his movement. Flavius was also shaking his head back and forth. *Even in the dark, Flavius' eyes seem to glow as if he is possessed by a demon,* thought Erik.

"Put your weapons down," the soft-spoken words from Flavius still rang like an order.

Claire and Erik did not move and looked like statues in the square. In front of them stood Argus' brutal henchman. They were about to die or worse.

"I repeat, put them down," he said, followed by, "I will not hurt you."

Flavius' eyes moved back and forth between Claire and Erik. Claire was the first to drop her bow. Erik reluctantly did also with his sword, but he felt relief. Flavius was a very intimidating man.

"If I had wanted to, I could have killed you in your sleep—or both of you right here. I could take you captive, Claire. I did not, though. See, I am even unarmed." With that, Flavius stepped back for both Claire and Erik to view him. They saw no weapon in his hand or on his body that was readily apparent in the night.

"You are fools to travel this way. There are ambushes just down the trail you are following, about two miles from here. Someone set you up."

Claire's head was whirling. How and why would their mortal enemy be assisting them?

"Focus, woman." Flavius spoke bluntly, but it worked and brought Claire back to reality. "I am here for one reason, for Mary. Quietly, and not to wake your children, get her for me."

"What will you do with her?" was Claire's response. None of this made sense to Claire. Her mortal enemy was not killing them and now he wanted her chambermaid. This was totally illogical.

"Now," was all Flavius said.

"Yes," was Claire's response as she gathered herself enough to disappear into the dark and to her camp.

Flavius turned toward Erik, making Erik very uncomfortable.

"Do you love her?" Flavius asked Erik as he stared into Erik's eyes.

"Who?" was Erik's response. He had become so flustered by Flavius that he wasn't thinking clearly.

"You are a fool, but at least you have guts. Few men would do what you have done. Ride off alone into the wilderness with your Queen without a force of men or a plan and expect nothing in return. You are either her most loyal subject or you are in love with her. You choose. I should have looked at you more closely at the castle."

Erik finally got a hold of his senses and hesitantly said, "How did you find us? How could you track us? I thought we covered our tracks well."

"You did a fair job of hiding your presence. The fools I ride with couldn't tell a human's tracks from a deer's. They are like you—amateurs. I was trained by a man who was exceptional at tracking animals, including humans. It was not only his ability that stood above others', but also his instincts that made him so good. I swear, he could smell an enemy before seeing him, and then he could anticipate what that enemy would do or where he would go. His name was Revious. He later became a scout for a Roman general named Valerias. Ever hear of either of them?"

"No, not really. I did hear sometime ago of a Roman general stationed in the south along the Danube. I heard he had a black heart."

"Tell me, Erik, do I have a black heart?"

"I don't know anymore. You have my mind twisted in knots."

Flavius mumbled, "Hmmm."

There were several minutes of silence between the two men. Finally Claire and Mary emerged from the dark with a slight rustle. Mary covered her mouth for a quick moment when she saw Flavius. She then ran to Flavius and they tenderly embraced. Claire had no idea what to think of this completely unthinkable action. Everything expected had become unexpected.

"Mary will come with me so I can keep her safe." Flavius then threw Erik a satchel containing food. "I strongly suggest you get off this trail and travel north to the forest—very large trees and several lakes. From there go west and you will reach safety. I will keep the fools who travel with me off your trail—if you choose to go that way. However, there are hundreds of others looking for you, and I can't control all of them. If you go west from here, you will be captured. I guarantee that. If you are captured, I will have to kill you to keep our meeting a secret. You see? We now have a secret between us. That is why I don't want your children to see me. The fewer people that know I was here, the better. In fact, I was never here."

With those words, Flavius gave a call that echoed a night bird. A horse appeared and Flavius lifted Mary onto the horse. He then walked over to Claire before he mounted the horse.

"Mark my words, Claire! I have no reason to lie to you. Go north and then west."

Mary added, "Trust him. Good-bye, Claire. Good-bye, Erik. God speed."

As they turned, Claire asked, "What about Argus?"

"I will worry about Argus. You concern yourself with protecting your daughters."

Flavius took his horse over to Erik. "This is what love is." Flavius, in one motion, mounted the horse. Mary put her arms tightly around him and they melted into the night.

Claire had lived a life that was full of surprises, some that went well and others badly, but she had never experienced anything like what had just occurred. Several thoughts were spinning in her head. *Was Flavius telling the truth? Did Mary use them to get free from Argus' castle and then reunite with Flavius? Who should she believe, Edgbart, a friend, or Flavius, an enemy?*

Erik joined her as she pondered these questions. "I think we should follow Edgbart, as he was an ally of Gerhard. Flavius is an enemy."

"True, but I don't think I agree with you this time. If Flavius had wanted us captured or killed, he would have done so. You heard him. He could have killed us a few minutes ago but he didn't. I will wake the children. Gather up our camp. We must not leave a trace that we were here. We will travel north, as Flavius suggested. I don't know about Flavius' relationship with Argus. But I do know Flavius is clearly fond of Mary. He is telling the truth. I sense it. I have made my decision. We travel north, and may the gods be with us."

Erik didn't argue—Claire had made up her mind. For better or worse, they were traveling north, into a country they knew little about.

XXVIII

Decision

General Valerias had called a meeting of his council, which was typical after a battle. Unless there was a good reason approved in advance by the General, his generals, commanders, and officers were to attend the meeting. There had been one time when a subordinate did not show up as ordered without reason, and the next day that individual was no longer in the General's command. It was a lesson learned by all his subordinates.

Braxus and Cratus walked to the meeting together. Dusk approached, but the air was still warm on the spring day. Both men had been out of the fort on various strenuous but routine missions. They were lightly sweating as they walked to the General's meeting quarters.

"I'm not sure what the purpose of the meeting is, are you, Cratus? You were in the field with him. What do you think?"

"With him anymore, I just don't know. One minute, he is ordering the beheading of dead Suevi, then he is hugging a little girl. There was also something about him chasing a Suevi up a hill. I don't know what that was about, but Gul was almost killed."

"By whom?" Braxus asked, mostly in jest.

Cratus rolled his eyes. "He is not mad, at least not totally. No, it was the Suevi chief who gave Gul a surprise he will never forget. Maybe his god came to his rescue . . . because Gul should be dead. Only a raised root stood between him and the afterlife."

"I'm sure we will do a mission debriefing and then we can all have a drink. That sounds good to me. Overseeing the operations of the fort during his absence gave me great stress. I would have rather entertained the Suevi like you did."

The two men reached the entrance to the meeting room, which was guarded by Bukarma. They exchanged greetings and went inside. More commanders filed inside shortly thereafter. Joseph was not there to take minutes as he had been for previous meetings. Braxus noted this absence, but said nothing.

Members of the council discussed several subjects in a normal manner, which the General let continue for several minutes. He took this time to look upon the face of each member, absorbing all he could. Finally he stood up and the room became quiet. The General typically sat for the meetings unless there was an important point he wanted to make. Eyes focused on him.

"We have been together a long time. Some of you"—and he looked at Braxus—"for over fifteen years. I believe over this time, we have served well, both Rome and Constantinople. I have no regrets."

This was not how these meetings went, and the opening statement by the General caused everyone in the room to wonder what was happening. When the General spoke these words, alternatives spun through the brains of the council members as spiders build webs.

"I have tried to be honest with you in our time together, and I will be honest with you again—for the last time."

The council emitted sounds that seemed to be a combination of sighs and groans. At this moment the General had everyone's complete attention.

"I have resigned my position with the army and I am retiring. I have served Rome for over thirty of the forty-five years that I have been alive. I have finished my work with the army. Yesterday I sent officers to Constantinople and Milan. They are carrying letters to the Emperors informing them of my decision. Once the Emperors send confirmation of the receipt of my letters, I will leave you. I have firmly requested of the Emperors that my replacement be Braxus—an excellent example of a loyal, intelligent, and brave Roman soldier. Braxus will carry on my legacy of maintaining the Empire. Cratus is to be his second-in-command. I know of no reason why the Emperors will not grant my request, as it is the only one I have made to them. That is all."

The room was immediately in an uproar. This was totally unexpected. No one thought this statement would be the outcome of the meeting. Everyone had questions for the General, and all were shouting at once, which made hearing any single question impossible.

"When was this decided?"

"Did Rome or Milan cause this action?"

"Did Constantinople?"

"Are you ill?"

"Where are you going—back to your villa in Rome?"

These were a few of the questions hurled at the General. However, the most consistent and frequent question was, "Why?"

For several moments the General listened to this chorus—like a flock of songbirds that had encountered an owl—and then he raised his right arm. That motion quieted the room.

He spoke in a reasoned, emotionless tone. "This was my decision and mine alone. Rome or the like did not order me to step down. It was *my* decision. Why am I leaving and at this time? Because it is time for me to go. I have served the two Empires *for over thirty years.* I have given my all to the Empires and the legions that I have commanded. I am not ill, but I'm tired. Not of you, but of this lifestyle. A lifestyle I chose in younger days and would choose again. But it is not a lifestyle I want any longer. I have not made a decision as to where I will go. Maybe to my villa in Rome. Maybe to Spain. I don't know. It is Braxus' turn to take command of my legions. I know he will do well and I wish him well. I trust that you will give Braxus the support that you have given me."

As he said the last part of his dialogue, the General looked at Braxus and smiled. Braxus reflexively nodded back, although in shock about what had just happened. The General then looked to the back of the room and clapped his hands once. Several servants appeared carrying large cups of mead. Every member of the council received his cup.

The General raised his cup in the act of a toast. All eyes were on him as he looked upward. "I lift up my cup to Rome, to the Empire. May Rome continue to be the beacon of civilization that it has been. May the citizens of Rome work to revive the West to its former greatness." Interestingly, the General focused on Rome and the Western Empire instead of including Milan and both the Western and Eastern Empires in his toast. There was no doubt the General preferred the West in general, and Rome specifically.

He turned and faced the back wall. A doorway was located in the center of the wall. "I toast the soldiers who have served me these many years. Their fortitude and bravery have been my lifeblood."

After that toast he turned back and looked into the faces of his council. "Lastly, I salute you my council. Your loyalty cannot be surpassed. I could not have accomplished what I accomplished without all of you by my side."

The General drank from the cup until it was empty. The members of the council also found their cups were empty. They expected the General to order the servants to refill the cups.

However, the General waved the servants off. "We will have more time to reminisce and talk about the future later. I have another meeting shortly. Leave me and we will reconvene at a later time."

The council members argued but in a quiet manner. When they realized the General meant what he said, they filed out the room. Only Bukarma remained.

"What do you think, Bukarma?" The General asked in a quiet voice.

"The General does what he wants to do," was the reply.

"I want to leave this life behind. I can't take the death that comes with this position any longer. I do not want the responsibility."

"I understand, General. You have not been yourself for months and I—we—are concerned about you, about your health."

"I'm concerned about my mental state more than anything else. It is the right time to step down. Braxus is ready for the command. Even if he is not—he will learn, as I did many years ago."

"Where will you go?"

The General changed the subject. "Bukarma, I am granting you your freedom. No one has served me better than you through my many years as a general. You are also a good friend. I will have the papers prepared. You are a free man! Now, what will *you* do?"

After a few moments of silence, Bukarma responded, "I need to consider my options. You have sprung this on me and I'm not prepared to answer. Maybe Braxus will need a guard. I really do not have anywhere to go."

"You have time to gather your thoughts. Now bring the priest to me."

With that, the conversation was over. Bukarma left the room. He was still feeling shock at the General's decision. He was also thinking about the conversation he had just had with the General. In all his years with the General, he had never talked to him in such a personal way. As he reached the outer door of the

General's headquarters, he found Joseph waiting. Joseph had a puzzled look on his face. He knew something was up, and yet no one would tell him about it. He knew this was typically not good news for him.

Bukarma had an odd face and body language that was not normal compared to his usual straightforward and stoic manner.

"The General will see you now," he said in a low voice that was difficult for Joseph to hear.

"What is going on? I have never seen the council so agitated."

"You will find out soon enough," was all the large man said as he pointed to the General's council room.

XXIX

Revelation

Joseph entered the room and found the General at his table with his "history" books sprawled out in front of him. Joseph thought for a moment that the General looked older, but he shook off that feeling. He was more worried about his own life. When the council members had left the General, not one of them stopped to speak to him. This action was very unusual to Joseph, as he had become friendly with several members. The General's attitude toward him was always variable; thus, Joseph was suffering severe angst because he did not have confidence in his thoughts regarding how the General would treat him.

The General sat in his chair, rubbing his beard on the right side of his face in an up-and-down motion. The General had not shaved since the campaign began against the Suevi. Other than his beard rubbing and the occasional turn of a page, the General sat perfectly still in his chair. His eyes focused intently on the manuscript. He made no sound. The longer this went on, the more nervous Joseph became. He tried not moving or making a sound, but he knew he was beginning to breathe heavily. Joseph also didn't realize that he was swaying back and forth. He had to relieve the intense stress somehow. The General sensed the nervousness, and without looking up, he pointed to a chair just off to his right, then to Joseph and then to the chair. Joseph sat down reluctantly because he was so near to the General and yet he was glad to be off his feet.

Another thirty minutes of silence slowly went by. Joseph's mind was now wandering. He was alternately thinking about his childhood and then his future, if there was one. Finally, the General closed the last book and looked Joseph in the eyes. This was not the typical hard glare Joseph experienced but close to a look of kindness.

"My history is complete. You have done well, priest. I would almost say the spirit of Jacob was with you. I am pleased."

Joseph was stunned. He had expected the worst and received the best. He could only muster a "Thank you, General."

"I have vastly underestimated you—which is something I rarely do—but I did so with you. When you were brought to me, you were a traitor to Rome, and I would have executed you for your traitorous acts. Then I learned about your past and that you had been a traitor to your parents. I gave you an order not to proselytize my soldiers. I even wagered with Bukarma that you would not last a week before I had you killed. But here you are, at my side. You have done all that I asked. Not only that—you have befriended several members of my council—and, of course, Jacob. All speak highly of you. Because of your actions over the last several months, I am granting you your freedom. You may go wherever you wish, and you may go at any time. You are a free man!"

Again, Joseph was stunned—and this time speechless. He looked at the General and then at Bukarma at the end of the room. He imagined he glimpsed the slightest of grins present on both men's faces. Joseph thought that this was a cruel joke. Yet after a moment, he realized that this was real. He relaxed, which was conveyed by his body slumping further into the chair.

As he thought about what had happened, he mumbled to the General, "Why?"

The General continued to rub his bearded cheek and chin and answered, "Because you have earned it."

After a long pause the General, who had been staring at Joseph, looked away. "I have resigned my position with the Empire and its legions. As soon as I receive confirmation from the Emperors, I will leave this place. Braxus is to be my replacement."

"Why?" Again, the only word Joseph could muster.

The General looked at Bukarma and then at Joseph. "I am tired and no longer desire to carry out my duties. I have done enough. That is all you need to know. Come back at the same time tomorrow night. I want to get my history documents ready for travel. Go."

With those words Joseph left the room and made as straight a line as possible for Olivertos. The General watched him leave and then said to Bukarma, "Off to Olivertos, I'll wager. Now bring your game. Maybe I'll win this time."

Bukarma responded, "Maybe I'll let you win this time."

The General was correct; Joseph went straight to Olivertos in his quarters. Olivertos was standing over a table examining a dead animal of some type. Olivertos had a made it a hobby to compare the anatomy of animals to that of humans.

As Joseph rushed in somewhat breathlessly, Olivertos didn't even turn his head. "Shocking, isn't it?"

"Yes," Joseph responded hesitantly, not sure if Olivertos was talking about the General or the animal.

Olivertos put down his instruments and looked at Joseph. "I found out last night before the council meeting. I knew even before the council."

"Why is the General giving all this up? He is the most powerful man I have ever met, maybe even more so than the Emperors."

"I don't think that is the case—powerful, yes, but not more so than the Emperors."

"Then why? I do not understand."

"Only the General knows the true reason . . . or reasons. And he won't tell us. I have noticed over the past year, though, a difference in his demeanor. He has lost his vigor, his swagger. His temper, which he always had, is worse . . . yet he has extended mercy to people who—in earlier years—he would not have. This is a complicated man."

Olivertos eyed Joseph, implying that Joseph himself was just such a beneficiary of the General's mercy.

Olivertos continued, "Sometimes he seems to drift far away from the matter at hand. He is looking for something else—at least that is my hunch. He certainly has appeared to mellow toward you. And I can understand that. You have become friends with many in his inner circle—Braxus, Bukarma, and me. Most important, you have not disobeyed him and have done good work for him. You put your religion under your sleeve—not on it. You have not only stayed alive here, but you have matured here. So where will you go, now that the General has released you?"

Joseph was thinking how—in minutes—he had gone from the depths of despair to the heights of exhilaration and now to reality. *Where will I go and what will I do?*

"I don't know yet. I'm not going back to the Goths. I am also not returning to Rome. There are too many bad memories in both places. I am possibly thinking about going north to Britannia. There is a fellow priest there that I got along with, as we trained for priesthood. I'll go there, I think."

"I have never been there, Joseph. I have heard parts of Britannia are beautiful. Be warned, though, Joseph, it is a dangerous place. The Roman forces there are not strong, and tyrants rule the land. And more good news; raiders from both the east and west plunder the land and leave much blood in their wake. It will be dangerous, even for a man of God."

"I hope you are wrong, my friend. If I can survive the General, I am confident I can survive Britannia."

Olivertos paused. "Remember, Joseph, don't let hope exceed expectations."

The two friends then further discussed Britannia, and the animal Olivertos was dissecting.

The next morning brought an air of gloom to the fort, as the new spring took a backward step to old winter. Joseph spent the morning walking around, viewing the fort through the fog for the first time since he was captured by the General's troops. Now he was a free man. The fort had a much greater size than he remembered. As he walked, Braxus came over to him with a new bodyguard trailing him. "Good morning, Joseph, I trust you heard the news?"

"About the General?"

"Of course. What do you think?"

"First, congratulations, Braxus, on your new command. You will do well."

"Thank you, but Milan must approve the appointment. Constantinople must also second the approval, as the General served both Empires."

"How can they not? You have been the General's second-in-command for years."

"My friend, they appoint whom they want. I could get the position—or I could be sacked. I just don't know."

"Surely the General's recommendation carries much weight."

"Yes, it does. But the General has enemies too. I hope you are correct."

Joseph thought of his recent conversation with Olivertos about hope and expectations, but he said nothing to Braxus.

"Anyway, Joseph, the General would like to see you—now."

As Joseph started toward the General's quarters, he heard Braxus say, "Pray for me, Joseph."

"I will." Joseph walked away with another startling revelation to consider.

XXX

Recollections 1

Joseph hustled to the General's quarters. Joseph was a free man, but he was not going to keep the General waiting. Once he entered the General's set of rooms, he found Bukarma standing outside the doorway to the council room.

"Good afternoon, Joseph. How are you doing today?"

"Fine, Bukarma. Where is the General?"

"He is in the council room. Go in."

Joseph walked quickly in the room and found the General standing by a table. His books were on a table directly at his right side.

"I see you have a bounce in your step, priest. Must be the feel of a free man."

"I feel good today, General."

"I trust all is well with Olivertos?"

"He sends you his greetings."

"Hmm," was all that the General muttered. Joseph now had a confident attitude that the General seemed to admire. Joseph thought it was about time.

"I want you to wrap my books in such a way that I can easily transport them a long way without any unraveling. This will be the last task I ask of you."

"Good, General. It will be done."

Joseph went over to the table to pick up the books. Altogether the books weighed enough that Joseph grunted as he lifted them up. The General laughed at Joseph's exertion.

"Do you need assistance? Perhaps Bukarma can help you."

"I can handle them, General."

However, before attempting to lift them again, a thought crossed his mind. It was something he had always wanted to ask the General while working on the books.

"General, I have read your history—all volumes—from cover to cover, and there is nothing in them that conveys information about your childhood, your time as a young adult, your thoughts about various events. It is a marvelous compilation of your military history, but there is little of your personal history in them."

The General looked at Joseph amusedly. "Are you asking me what created me? What happened to me that made me what I am today? Did events shape me or I them?"

Joseph was surprised by the General's surprisingly philosophical reply. Joseph had taken a gamble posing his comment to the General. He was very aware that the General guarded his personal life very tightly. Only a few close friends knew much of his life, and that was primarily because they had experienced the same events with him. The General went over and sat down in his chair. He rubbed his ever-growing beard, slowly looking at the floor, then at Joseph. He motioned for Joseph to sit, which Joseph quietly did.

"I was born to wealthy parents. My father was an owner of substantial land in Italy, Gaul, and in Africa. My mother was an heiress to even more land holdings. When I was about five, they took me to Africa, to a place near Carthage. I was young, but I fell in love with the warmth and the people of the land. Unfortunately, my father chose the wrong side of a dispute. I don't know about what, I was too young, but it was enough to get him killed. But my father's enemies didn't stop there. They raped my mother and took her away to be a slave. The gods were merciful, as she died before they got very far. A servant told me this. I don't remember much about my parents except they were good to me, and there are times I feel their loss. To this day I will not tolerate raping by my soldiers, including of enemies. If you want a death sentence, commit rape. I find rape and desertion equally contemptible—crimes resulting in swift execution by whatever means I choose."

The General sat in his chair and paused. He was looking at the floor again. Joseph was transfixed and uttered no sound during the pause. This was the first time he had seen the General in even a minor vulnerable position. "My father ended up being crucified. Can you imagine that? I didn't see it, but the servant told me years later. And this happened in a supposedly Christian Empire, where crucifixion had been banned.

"Somehow one of my father's servants managed to hide me during the chaos and took me to the household of a general named Hyperion, where the servant had a relative. Hyperion was a secret ally of my father. He showed me mercy and took me in. Over time I became his adopted son, as he had no heirs. As I grew into my teens, I was an apprentice for several of his officers. I performed my tasks well enough that I rose through the ranks and became an officer-in-training. At fifteen I was given a special assignment. I was to take confidential documents from Hyperion to another general located at a fort about thirty miles away. If I succeeded, I would be one step closer to achieving full officer status."

Joseph observed that the General was completely absorbed in his story, and it had drawn him in also.

"When you rise through the ranks as quickly as I did, you make enemies. I had two in particular, Marcellos and Semelis. I did not view them as good soldiers, as they spent more time seeking pleasurable avenues than on work tasks. Hyperion knew that, but he had to be careful. Marcellos and Semelis were both sons of wealthy landowners, and Hyperion promoted the two of them along with me so as to remain in good standing with their families.

"Marcellos and Semelis were just a little older than I and they were jealous of me. See, I was younger, but had reached a higher level in the junior officer ranks than they had. They wanted me to disappear so that I would no longer be their rival. The thirty-mile journey to the other general's fort went through a country inhabited by wolves. You could hear them wailing away on some nights. The wolves had caused some concern to the civilians in the region. In response Hyperion sent out a wolf-tracking squad to find and kill the wolves. After a couple of weeks in the forest, the squad emerged, tired and defeated. They were only able to catch and kill one old wolf. The packs proved to be smarter than the men. The wolves did not like soldiers anyway, and we had very little contact with them. They preferred the countryfolk's livestock. That is why Hyperion sent me on my mission—safety was not much of an issue, as the potential for a wolf attack on a human was rare. For whatever reason, maybe the topography, Hyperion wanted me to walk instead of ride a horse.

"So I started out, satchels in hand. I had a limited food and water supply as I expected to cover the thirty miles in approximately ten hours. The terrain was largely forest with areas of hills. There were rock outcroppings on the tops and sides of several of the hills. Streams were located in small valleys. I had done this trip three times before, so I knew my way. I had my sword and also my knife that I had placed in a foot sheath, where I still keep it today. The sword was heavy, but I had practiced using it daily and didn't think its weight was a big issue, at least initially.

"I wasn't aware of many things back in those days. I tended to daydream during some of the more mundane tasks that I had to carry out—like this one. What I didn't realize was Marcellos and Semelis had put some kind of food or potion in the satchels as well as on my cloak. It was odorless to me. Whatever it was, it attracted wolves. About ten miles into the walk, I began hearing footsteps coming from behind. They weren't human footsteps, and they were moving quickly toward me. The time for daydreaming had ended, and now I was instantly on full alert.

"I was walking from a wooded area at the time and entering a meadow. It was fall and the trees were beginning to lose their leaves. The leaves were dry and crunched under my feet. I had always liked fall . . . until that day. The footsteps I was hearing were those of wolves, and they weren't wasting any time in getting to me. When I turned around, I saw at least four of them in full run. There was a wolf on each of my flanks and two behind me. Fortunately, I was thinking clearly at the time and dropped my sword and went into a full run. I guessed the wolves were about one hundred yards from where I'd first sensed their presence. I was a fast runner in those days, but it didn't matter. They were closing fast and I had to make an instant decision. Over to my left was a large fir tree. A little further away, but straight in front of me, was another similarly sized tree. If I could make it to one of those trees, maybe I could climb high enough to avoid being butchered. The trick was—which tree. Which one would you have chosen, priest?"

The question surprised Joseph, who was fully involved in the story, and all he could say was, "I don't know. Neither option seems like a good choice."

"I had to make a split-second decision and my life depended on that decision. It was a tree or death! I saw the wolf on my left was moving too quickly for me to reach the tree on my left, so I ran to the center tree. I lost track of the two wolves behind me, but the two on my flanks were heading in a sharp diagonal straight at me—and were now within twenty yards. I was almost at the base of the tree. My life depended on reaching the first branch—reaching it and climbing higher to escape those jaws of certain death."

Joseph imagined himself in the position in which the General had found himself. First, he didn't know whether he would have made the choice to go to the left tree which was closer than the center tree, but where he would have likely met the wolf on the left. Second, he didn't like his chances to make it up the center tree before being grabbed by the wolves and then torn to shreds. He might have nightmares over this dilemma.

The General wasn't paying attention to Joseph at this time. He too was clearly living in the past. "I reached the lower branch at the same time as the left wolf. My weight on that lower branch—especially when I leaped to the next branch—that branch smacked the wolf in the face! He yipped—and I had enough time to climb to another branch. And then another. When I looked down, I was missing a boot, and I bore a small bite on my foot. My arms and hands were badly scratched from climbing the tree as fast as I did.

"However, I was alive. Somehow, I had made it. The wolves jumped at the tree's trunk, but they soon stopped jumping, as I was just out of their reach. I climbed up to another branch and looked down. A fifth wolf appeared, black and large—it seemed to be the general of the other four—the alpha male. The others behaved submissively toward this alpha. I imagined being torn apart—with this alpha taking the first bite. I saw the wolves seemed agitated. I had seen wolves before—but not like this! They paced around the tree, and looked up at me snarling. They were incensed! I was glad to be in the tree.

"I took stock. I had my knife, and two satchels. One satchel contained the document I was to give to the general and the other carried my supplies, food and water. My cloak also still clung to my shoulders. I sat looking at the wolves. They paced around the tree, sometimes looking up at me. They seemed to be grinning, like they knew I was on borrowed time.

"I was thirsty and reached into the supply satchel to retrieve my flask of water. I would have a drink and then I would try to figure a way out of this dilemma. When I pulled the flask out, a piece of cloth was attached to the flask. It smelled odd. Not bad . . . just different. I looked into the satchel further and there were more pieces of cloth. I had not packed these cloths. While I was searching for more of them, the first cloth fell to the ground. The wolves were on it in an instant, tearing it apart and fighting over it. Then I checked the other satchel with the documents I was supposed to deliver. Again, I found several pieces of cloth.

"It didn't take a smart man to figure out that someone wanted me dead, and this was the perfect scenario. I would disappear and my body would never be found. Wild animals would be blamed. For some reason I checked my cloak. Woven in along the edges were small pieces of cloth that had the same smell. The wolves didn't want me—they wanted what was on those cloths. I pulled out or took off anything that smelled like the substance. I wiped my hands on the inside of my tunic. I took the documents I was sworn to deliver and shoved them inside a wedge in the tree. I then wrapped up just about everything in the cloak—including the two satchels and their contents. I threw it as far as I could without falling out of the tree. The wolves tore the cloak and the satchels into bits. I never learned what substance had been smeared onto those cloths, but its power over the wolves was truly great.

"Watching this savagery unfold beneath me, I was truly scared . . . to this day, I have never been more scared. I was too young to know that feeling when my parents were killed. But I was fully aware of my condition now!

"After the wolves had finished their work on the bundle that I'd tossed to them, they returned to the tree. However, their interest in me was waning. Soon four of the wolves left the area, including the alpha. The gray one stayed behind, though, circling the tree. It was getting cooler and I needed to make a move or die in that tree. Interestingly, the tree that had been my safe harbor during the day, would become my tomb during the night."

The General sat deep in thought. "I took out my knife and threw it at the wolf. The wolf was lucky, though, as I had not yet attained the knife-throwing skill that I have today."

The General looked at Joseph and both men knew what that meant.

"The hilt of the knife hit the wolf on its snout. Today, I would throw the knife, so that it would pierce the inside of the neck, causing the wolf to bleed out. Like I said, the wolf was lucky. It gave out a yelp and took off into the forest. I waited several minutes before leaving the safety of the tree. When I felt as comfortable as I could that the threat from the wolves was over, I started to climb down, with Hyperion's documents fully secured in my possession. As I did this, I saw a flash of light in the distance. The sun was beginning to set, and it glinted off something shiny. I was suspicious, so I as climbed down, I looked for a place where I could hide but still see if someone was coming. Someone obviously was trying to kill me, and I wanted to take no chances that the source of the glint was that someone.

"After several minutes had passed, one horse, then a second horse, and finally a third horse appeared in front of me. The horsemen were Marcellos, Semelis, and someone I did not know. They circled the area near the tree and found numerous bits of clothing and satchel material. There was even a spot or two of blood. I thought it was from the gray wolf.

"Marcellos said, 'The wolves must have got him here. What a mess,'

"'They must have dragged him off into those woods and devoured him there,' Semelis added, pointing to a dark area of forest.

"The third man noted that that was the likely outcome, but he was troubled by the lack of body parts and blood. 'I would think we'd see something of his remains . . . and yet, not even a finger.' This man was clearly the biggest threat of the three.

"I crouched down even lower as he made a wider swath of the area, looking for more evidence. He came within a few feet of me. Fortunately, it was becoming darker, and he couldn't pick out my shape in the brush.

"'Come on, uncle,' Marcellos said impatiently. 'He could not have survived the wolves. The special potion from the witch that we inserted into his satchels and clothing would have driven them crazy. It is getting late, and we need to make it back to the camp before Hyperion's guards figure out something is amiss.'

"Semelis smirked. 'Yeah, his precious son couldn't carry out an order.'

"'No, jealous Semelis. Hyperion will not know of his disappearance for days.' The uncle spoke confidently.

"The uncle kept riding back and forth, searching for evidence of my death.

"'Uncle, even if he did survive the wolves, he would surely die tonight from the cold. We will return to camp and act as if nothing had happened to poor Marcus.'

"The uncle acknowledged Marcellos' comment, and then the three men rode off back to their camp. None of them had dismounted while roaming about the tree. If they had, they may have found clues that I had climbed into that tree . . . and was now hiding in the brush.

"They were lazy, and I thank the gods for their laziness. Now came the next hard part—surviving the cold night without much clothing. I did that, though, and I made it to the general's fort in the morning. I ran through the night to keep warm and complete the task.

"The General at that fort asked me what had happened. I told a lie. I said bandits had ambushed me so I tossed the satchels to them—after removing the documents—and then ran away and hid in the forest. The general gave me a horse and I returned to Hyperion's camp. That general had wondered why Hyperion had not given me a horse in the first place.

"I did not want to be seen when I approached Hyperion's fort, so I waited until dark. I knew the night sentries at the gate and they let me in. I went straight to Hyperion's quarters. His bodyguards let me in his private chambers. He had been pacing and was worried something had happened to me. We were glad to see each other. I told him about what had happened, with Marcellos, Semelis, the uncle, and the wolves. He remained calm, like any good Roman general when faced with a problem.

"'We need to do something about this,' he finally said. He then paced some more.

"I asked him, 'Why did you have me walk to the other camp, when I could have taken a horse? The other general asked me that, too.'

"Hyperion looked at me in surprise. 'Do you think I had something to do with you almost getting killed? You are my son. Maybe it was foolish that I let you walk, but I want you to become a man. And you have done that.'

"'I am sorry for doubting you. I'm just tired.'

"'I understand, Marcus. But a soldier does not get tired. Enemies will use that as a weakness and strike when you are too tired to react. You will stay here tonight, while I go and take care of what needs to be taken care of. One thing I do not understand—how did wolves find you in those woods, and what drove them to try to attack you so viciously? The few wolves I have come into contact with are shy and do not attack humans. I think evil was involved with this plot to kill you. I will see you in the morning and this evil will be resolved—permanently.'

"I fell asleep almost instantly and had a good sleep. When I awoke, it was mid-day. I left Hyperion's chambers, and I found Hyperion and several soldiers sitting in a large meeting room.

"'It is a good day, Marcus,' Hyperion greeted me.

"'Why?' I responded.

"'It is warm and dry today. But we had an accident this morning. Marcellos fell off his horse outside the fort and was killed. Tragic. There was also a death in the nearby town of a man that may have been a relative of Marcellos. Villagers say he was drunk and fell down some stairs. Semelis was transferred this morning to an outpost in Gaul. Before he left, he gave us some information that solved a mystery involving two other people. Both of them have left the area, I believe. You may go outside. I have a new assignment for you.'

"I went outside, not sure of everything that Hyperion had said. As I reached the outside door, two soldiers were standing with the most beautiful horse I had ever seen. Hyperion told me it was mine. I was also to be second-in-command of a small section of cavalry in the legion.

"'You have become a man during your last mission, son. This is what men do now. Congratulations, Centurion Marcus Augustus Valerias.' A cry in unison went out from the assembled men.

"I accepted my new role readily and never looked back."

Joseph asked, "Did you ever find out what really happened to everyone in the group that tried to kill you, and why?"

"They were jealous of my standing with General Hyperion. And no, Hyperion never told me anything more about what had transpired with Marcellos' crew, and I never asked. My problem with them was solved. Hyperion was a great man. I learned much from him. He died of some disease, fifteen years ago."

The General paused. "Do you know what I learned from this experience?"

Joseph did not answer. The General looked deep into Joseph's eyes, not blinking or wavering in his stare. "Be very selective of whom you trust, priest. There are liars and fakers and pretenders that you think you can trust, but in the end you cannot. I thought Marcellos was my friend and he ended up trying to kill me. This set of events also pushed me into manhood. It taught me many things that I have carried with me into my professional life. Now a question for you, priest. Do you trust me? I said you could go and be a free man. Do you trust me to let you go and be a free man?"

Joseph did not hesitate. "Yes, I trust your word."

The General sat back in his chair and gave his now customary pause. "Good answer. You are correct."

At that moment, Bukarma appeared at the door. "The council is assembled, General."

"Good." Then, looking at Joseph, he said, "Return here in five days at the same time. I have more to discuss."

Joseph left. He had never seen the General so relaxed and talkative. Joseph felt, for the first time, that he and the General had almost become equals. This was a feeling, though, that he would not admit to anyone.

XXXI

Recollections 2

FIVE DAYS PASSED, and Joseph showed up at the General's quarters at the requested time. The General was busy with an administrative function, and Joseph had to wait. When Bukarma admitted Joseph, he found the General in a foul mood. He barked orders at some staff members, and he signaled for a servant to bring him wine. He drank it quickly and ordered a refill.

He then looked at Joseph. "Would you like some wine?" he brusquely asked.

Joseph thought it would be a good idea not to argue, and so he said, "Yes."

The servant poured the wine into a cup for Joseph and gave it to him. The General signaled to the servant for his refill. After the cup was filled, he sat back in his chair and spoke to no one specifically. "Damn Milan. I sent my resignation days ago and no response yet. And I don't know if they will accept Braxus as my successor—damn! I'm glad to be finished. Oh, and nothing yet received from Constantinople."

"General, there has not been enough time for Milan or Constantinople to process your request and send a response."

The General said not a word and rubbed the edge of his cup. He was not drinking this cup of wine as fast as the first one.

"Perhaps you are right, priest. But this waiting is making me apprehensive. I usually have immense patience, but not this time."

Joseph knew that statement by the General was not particularly accurate, and he wanted to change the subject. "There is good news, General. We have found a way to bind and wrap your history parchments so you can easily carry them wherever you go."

"Yes, that is news that I want to hear. Imagine that—I get better news from a Christian priest than I do from my commanders in Milan."

The General leaned forward and, almost whispering, told Joseph, "As you know, I sent out a set of documents to my lawyer in Rome."

A pause in the discussion occurred. Joseph had to break the silence and asked, "What were those documents for?"

"If you tell anyone this, it will be your last words," was the General's reply.

Joseph was both nervous and eager for the General to tell him. "Yes, I agree not to say a word of this to anyone."

The General peered at Joseph with a gaze that implicitly showed he meant what he said. "The other document was the deed to my villa in Rome. The lawyer, Claudius, is someone I *trust.* He is to transfer ownership of my villa from me to Jacob's family. It is my gift to them for Jacob's years of service and loyalty to me. I won't be needing my villa anymore, and they should have it."

That was the end of that topic. The General quickly eased into a more relaxed manner and started telling stories again. Some were in his books and some were not. One particular story caught Joseph's attention.

The General began, "When Emperor Julian was killed, Jovian took the purple of Emperor. I was stationed in northern Gaul. The Empire was in a state of unrest; however, the area I was in charge of was fairly tame, with little fighting. I tasked my soldiers to complete several civil projects in the area, including road construction. My second-in-command was a man named Gratus. Braxus, at that time, was a tribune and my third-in-command.

"Now, Gratus was the nephew of a powerful General stationed in Rome. Don't concern yourself with his name. Gratus was ambitious, like myself, and two overly ambitious officers do not make a good team. One day I received an invitation to attend a reception given in my name, based on my recent appointment as legion general in the area. The reception would be held at the home of a wealthy landowner named Perocitus. I had to accept; if I didn't, the declination would be viewed as an insult. The invitation noted I should come with only a few soldiers, as space was limited and Perocitus did not want a heavy military presence in his home. I understood his concern. His concern and my concern, though, were as different as white and black.

"I left Braxus in charge of the legion in my absence. Gratus was also invited and would accompany me. When I arrived at Perocitus' home, something didn't feel quite right. There were many guests, and I noted some of them were allies of Perocitus. Without looking too hard, I observed weapons hidden throughout the home, particularly in his great room and in the gardens outside. Perocitus was friendly, but only superficially so. Gratus seemed edgy.

"The party was a festive affair. The drink was freely flowing. Naked men and women were everywhere, and I thought an orgy was planned for later in the evening. My eyes filled with all of the spectacle—like a carnival.

"If it had not been me, I would have been easy prey. You see, priest, even back then, I had a very good intelligence network. Perocitus and his family and Gratus' army allies wanted Emperor Jovian removed from power. A good start would be to eliminate me, because I was a general sworn by loyalty to Jovian. They then would assume control over my legion and join it with other forces in a revolt against Jovian. However, I had learned of Perocitus' and Gratus' plot several weeks before the reception. I informed Jovian, who trusted me to put down the revolt even before it started. Did I mention Jovian was a Christian?

"You should know that even at the apprenticeship level, I never wanted to lose control of my mind. I did not drink to excess, use 'herbal remedies,' and spend time with women I did not know. See, priest, when you lose control, you are weakened in the body and mind. If you are weakened, you become vulnerable, and from there you may end up dead or subject to blackmail schemes. I was not going to indulge myself in lost inhibitions at this or any celebration. The men who accompanied me from my legion were superior soldiers and were to follow my lead.

"The atmosphere of the party was becoming so overwhelming it was easy to succumb to the temptations. On several occasions I had to intervene between the party's temptresses and the sobriety of my men. But they maintained a solid footing. Prior to the beginning of the festivities, I had a man who supplied food to Perocitus' home secretly bring in and hide our weapons under blankets stored along the north wall of the great hall of his home.

"Timing was critical for my plan to succeed. I had my men inside the home pretend that they were falling under the spell of Perocitus' vices. As I said, this proved more difficult than I had anticipated. The line between what I wanted to happen and what *was* happening was becoming blurred. I watched Gratus closely, as he would be the one to initiate the action. When he thought we were sleeping or engaged in other activities, he and his men would pull the weapons they had hidden and would strike us. We were to be easy prey. Imagine an eagle going after a wounded hare.

"I witnessed Gratus move over to a position by Perocitus. Slowly he pulled a sword from behind a curtain. Other men in his command were moving over to where their weapons were hidden. My men and I were already along the north wall, feigning apathy and even drunkenness. Suddenly Gratus issued a loud, one-word command. Instantly Gratus' men were up and moving to retrieve their weapons. Only we were quicker. With our weapons, we advanced on Gratus and his men. They were fumbling around trying to find their weapons when we struck. It also helped that my allies inside the house had hidden most of Gratus' men's weapons. At that time, the rest of my soldiers waiting outside burst into the room, and now our numbers matched theirs.

"It was easy, priest. So easy. Soon all of Gratus' men were dead, except Gratus himself. We took his weapon from him and he begged for his life. Perocitus tried to flee with some poorly trained bodyguards. Again it was easy. Soon we had Perocitus kneeling next to Gratus. The fear in their eyes equaled the shock they were feeling. Just think—one minute you are about to be in favor with the new Emperor, and the next minute you are begging for your life from a soldier of the current Emperor. Can you imagine the power one has over another at that point?"

Joseph could not wait any longer. "What did you do with Perocitus and Gratus? Did you—"

"Do you think I executed them in some horrible manner? Or better yet, in a manner suitable for their crime? If you thought the former, you are wrong, priest. Jovian wanted Gratus in Rome. So I sent him to Rome as a prisoner. What Jovian did with him is something you do not need to know. Perocitus was another matter. He had many connections within the Empire, and executing him in public would have not been wise."

"So you let him live?"

"In a manner of speaking, yes, priest. I let him live."

"But he was a traitor, was he not?"

"Oh, yes, he was a traitor. Like I said, *I* let him live. But I turned him over to his servants and slaves, whom he had abused and mistreated for years. There was a fire in the villa that night and he perished. The cause of the fire was blamed on the excess festivities that got out of hand. Too much excess is not something to desire."

"You said Perocitus had allies besides Gratus—what happened to them?"

"Many suffered the same fate as Perocitus and did not live. They disappeared in the house fire as well. Just call it a variation of being burned alive."

Joseph now remembered why he feared the General. *What an utterly ruthless man,* he thought.

"Priest, there is an epilogue to my story. Gratus' fate was claimed just before Jovian died—it was Jovian's last act. If Jovian had died just a day or two earlier, Gratus might still be alive. Maybe haunting us in the flesh."

The General sat back in his chair, thinking of his story. He finally told Joseph, "Go. You have reminded me of a memory I did not want to remember."

XXXII

HIDING

THE SKY RAINED cold. For a late spring day, it felt more like winter. The wind was especially brisk and caused hands to go numb. Claire, Erik, and the girls slowly made their way north into the icy currents of the wind. Snow showers came and went. Claire, though, was pleased with the weather. Argus' hunters would lie low and not venture out until there was an improvement. The girls were wrapped tightly and sat in the front of horses steered by Claire and Erik. The warmth of the girls provided a small cover to the adults from the front. The other two horses were tied behind Claire's and Erik's. These horses held the packs that contained supplies. If needed, they could switch horses to give the more burdened ones a rest.

At the end of the day, they came to a thick woodlot, which would provide cover from the weather.

"We will camp here tonight," announced Claire. She pointed to a dark mass of vines and brush. "Erik, tie the horses up to that brush."

Erik took care of the horses, while Claire built a makeshift shelter. A fire would be too risky, so they huddled within a blanket and ate cold food. Everyone was too tired to care about the state of the food. Soon the entire party was asleep and no one stood guard. The group was fortunate, though, because the hunters who were tracking Claire were flailing about in all directions. Only Flavius knew their location.

The next morning they arose early. The sun was about to shed its light on the cold world, and, hopefully, warm the land. Claire and Erik took a short walk away from the girls.

"We must leave soon, Erik, even if the girls are tired. If we stay here, we die."

Erik's mind was in another place, as the previous encounter with Flavius had disturbed him. "What are Flavius' intentions? I don't understand his motives," he blurted out.

"I don't know what to make of him, either," Claire answered. "I hated him in the castle, and yet he saved our lives."

"I think he is leading us into a trap, telling us to go north instead of west."

"I have to go with my instincts, Erik, and my instincts say we go north. I know it is against reason. Let's get going. I don't want to debate this any further."

Claire turned to walk back to the camp. Erik gently took her arm and pulled her back. He looked at Claire with intensity. "I will do as you say, Claire. Provided we do not die and reach safety, I want your word that you will give me a chance, an opportunity for me to try to become your husband. I believe I have earned that right. I love you, Claire."

Claire was taken off guard by Erik's statement. She was fond of Erik and most appreciative of his help in escaping Argus. She did not love him, though. Her marriage to Gerhard was arranged. Her love of Gerhard was forced on her, and not natural. Claire did not want to go through the same thing with Erik. However, she did not want to lose him—could not lose him.

She diplomatically responded, "Erik, no one could be a better friend and potential suitor than you. I do not want to discuss this topic any further. We first have to reach safety, and after we do that, then we will discuss what our future might be. I do not want to speak of this again until we are safe."

This wasn't quite the response Erik had wanted from Claire. An unequivocal "yes" would have been ideal. He wasn't completely disappointed, though; she could have said "no." With limited hope in his heart, he helped pack up the camp, and they were on their way north within minutes. Claire wasn't thinking about Erik. She was thinking about the odds of making it safely to Eustice. And her only real hope was trusting an enemy.

Several groups had created a line of small encampments blocking the area west between Claire and Eustice. It was getting dark as Flavius rode into one of these camps.

"Who is in charge here?" he briskly asked.

A large man who had been sitting on a log arose. "Who are you to ride into our camp and demand an answer?"

A couple of men behind the large man recognized Flavius and stepped back in a semi-bow. The large man did not see this movement and persisted in his questioning of Flavius.

"Answer!" He reached for his sword.

"You idiot peasant!" was Flavius' answer. "I am Flavius Magnetious from the court of Argus." Just then several riders appeared behind Flavius, obviously his men. He continued, "I have come to secure the capture of the fake queen Claire. How are you progressing with this task?"

"I apologize, Lord Flavius, for my insolence. I did not anticipate your coming to our camp. I am Edgbart, and these are my men."

"Well, here I am too. Now, how are you progressing on this matter of grave importance to our King? And why are you resting?"

"My lord, we have spent many days going up and down these hills and have found no sign of her."

"You are a fool, Edgbart. A woman with two children and a chambermaid is outwitting you." Flavius, of course, knew Claire's location.

"She has a captain of Argus' guard leading them. He is making it tough to track them."

"Ha!" Flavius responded. "You apparently know very little. Erik, the man you speak of, is not an expert on escape and flight. He is a simple soldier. It really doesn't matter, though, as the whole bunch of them is outsmarting you!"

Edgbart's face showed signs of both subordination and rage. Flavius had achieved what he wanted.

"I see that I have been too harsh with a servant of our King Argus. It was not my intent to do so." Flavius could see Edgbart relax. "Go back and search the hills. All my intelligence still says she and her wicked brood will try to make their way to Eustice the shortest way possible." Flavius pointed to the west. "Through there."

"Will you stay with us?" Edgbart inquired.

"No, I'm going north in case they decide to flee like sparrows before hawks. I want to be sure we have all escape avenues cut off. Remember, we want the bitch queen *alive*. You can do what you want with the rest of the brood. Twenty extra gold pieces to the man who brings Argus that bitch."

Flavius and his contingent then rode off. The two men who had first recognized Flavius came up to Edgbart.

"What a bastard," one said. "I'll wager he would carve up and eat his own young."

Edgbart looked into the darkness where Flavius and his men had ridden off. "I would like to carve *him* up," he said, still smarting from their exchange.

"I wish you good fortune on that one. I have heard Flavius is one of the best swordsmen in the land."

Edgbart continued staring into the darkness. "I hate this work. I want to be home and be warm, with my wife."

"We all do, Edgbart." The three men joined the others and they sat around a fire that grew larger as the men added more wood.

At dawn on the following day, Edgbart and his men returned to their village.

Being on the run was proving to be too taxing for the girls, and both became ill. Claire had some knowledge of the medicinal arts, but the girls' illnesses were more than she could handle. She needed help from a physician. There were villages in the area, and yet she knew no one. Erik tried to provide whatever comfort he could; however, comfort does not cure an illness.

Finally, after three more days in the wilderness, Claire announced she was going into the nearest village to find a physician. Erik was to stay with Anne and Elizabeth.

"I still have several gold coins. Hopefully I can quietly bribe a physician to come out here and look at the girls."

Erik disagreed. "You are far more recognizable than me. I'll go into the village. I'll come back and let you know what I find out."

Claire resisted, but this time Erik prevailed. Both knew he was right. The next day at dawn, Erik made his way slowly to a nearby village. It was quiet as most mornings in the spring were; the planting of crops had not begun, so the men were sleeping in late. A few of the village people were out and they looked at Erik suspiciously. He approached an old lady who was walking from one hut to another.

"Excuse me, woman," Erik began. "I have a pain in my stomach and I need a physician. Does your village have one?" Erik rubbed his belly to reinforce his claim.

She looked at him, glanced away, then looked at him again. She said not a word but pointed to a large building in the center of the village. Erik was not a novice, and he suspected the old woman was leading him to a trap. Usually the largest buildings served as barracks either for the Romans' or a warlord's troops. Without displaying any doubt to the old woman, he thanked her and moved down by the building. He was nervous now, and the closer he moved toward the building, the more apprehensive he became. He walked by the building and saw some movement. A group of men were playing what he thought looked like a game. He could not make out if they were Romans or Argus' men. When he turned around to see if the old woman was watching him, he was face to face with a strange man. The man had a uniform and was a Roman.

"Why are you slinking about, savage?" he said with a sneer.

Those rough Roman words sounded sweet to Erik's ears, for Erik had a better chance with any Roman than he would ever have with Argus' men. "I am sorry, sir, to bother you so early. My children have taken ill and I need a physician. Can you help me?"

"Savage scum," the soldier retorted. "Move on, or I will make you ill as well—with my sword."

Erik was not deterred. "I will give you a gold coin for your help—and one for the physician."

Another Roman had joined them and was watching their interaction. The guard was proving troublesome.

"What if I take both gold pieces, slice you up, and tell the other guards you jumped me?"

Erik reached for his sword. The other Roman now spoke, "Relax, Briton, and give the man his gold. You have found your physician."

Erik was relieved, but still on edge. He didn't know whether he could trust this Roman physician.

"You can pay me after we are done. Take me to them." Erik looked into the eyes of the physician. They had a kind, pleasant look—certainly not like the eyes of an angry or greedy Roman—or Flavius.

"We are in the country, so you will need a horse to ride to them." Erik was not yet willing to divulge the location of Claire and the children.

"I am Proterous, physician for the Roman barracks in this town and the next. On second thought, bring your children to that hut over there." He pointed to a large hut beyond the building. "I am not much for horses. Bring your children to the backside of the hut."

Proterous expected Erik to introduce himself, but Erik did not. He said he would return later in the morning with the children.

Erik returned to the woods where Claire and the ill girls were hiding. Claire was becoming desperate as Anne and Elizabeth each had fevers that were becoming worse, causing the girls to become delirious at times. The situation was not only bad for the girls, it was also bad for the group as a whole, because the noises from the girls could give their position away. With so many bands of all sorts of characters looking for Claire, their position was fragile at best.

"Can you trust the Roman physician?" asked Claire.

"I don't know. I am pleased he is a Roman and not someone in league with Argus."

"Yes, I know the Romans and Argus do not get along well. But do you think you can trust him?"

"I think he can help us. He does not appear to be hostile to civilians like other Romans I have met."

"We don't have a choice, anyway. Our trust is with one man we do not know—like our relationship with Flavius. Let's wrap up my daughters and place them in the hands of this Roman."

"Only we do know *him*," Erik retorted, meaning Flavius.

Claire didn't want to waste time discussing Flavius.

Erik continued, "We must enter the village from the back. I do not have any faith that the villagers will help us. I don't know if they are pro- or anti-Argus."

Erik and Claire bundled up the girls and rode quietly to just outside the village. Hoods covered their heads to prevent anyone from recognizing them. They passed a few villagers who had no interest in their presence. At the village limits they wound their way through the back until they reached the hut where Proterous had told them to go. Erik and Claire each dismounted and carried a girl. They were entering new territory, and were apprehensive. Proterous might be in the hut alone, or there might be Roman soldiers, or, worst of all, villagers friendly to Argus. With deep breaths, they pulled back the cover that was located in the rear of the hut and hunched themselves through a hole into the hut.

"Welcome, visitors," Proterous said to Erik, as he, Claire, and the girls entered the room. "Bring the girls over here."

Claire and Erik allowed themselves to relax a little. The hut was warm with a contained fire located in the center. Fuel for the fire looked like peat. Smoke drifted up through a hole in the roof. The hut was divided into three rooms, rooms that were larger than one would surmise when looking from the outside. Proterous had cots in all the rooms. Once the girls were laid down, he removed their outer layer of clothing and quickly conducted a series of physical tests on each.

"I would guess they drank some bad water, and that is the cause of your girls' sickness," he concluded.

"But we all drank from the same sources," countered Claire.

"They are more susceptible to the corruption in the water than you two. I have been a physician for over twenty years and have seen the same symptoms before—on both civilians and soldiers."

"But they are not adults. How did they get sick and not us?"

"I need to restate: many of the civilians were children and the soldiers were drunk and not careful with their behavior." Proterous said this in such a matter-of-fact tone that Erik and Claire felt a warmth from the man. Perhaps he *could* help Anne and Elizabeth.

Proterous pointed to some stools. "Sit over there. This hut is for villagers, but few come here. They don't trust a Roman, and instead rely on the shaman . . . or whomever. The Roman infirmary is in the large building that you are familiar with." He said this looking at Erik. "You may stay here. In fact, I highly recommend you stay here. The girls should be well in two or three days' time."

Proterous proceeded to do his work. It was almost magical watching him. Proterous mixed various herbs into a broth that each girl drank. He also applied cold compresses and still managed to carry on a conversation with Claire and Erik. He never asked them who they were and what they were doing in the country. Instead he liked to talk about himself, his family and home in Spain. In one more year, he could retire and return to his homeland.

For Claire and Erik it was easily the best time they had experienced since Argus took power. They were exhausted and slept almost as much as the girls. When they awoke, Proterous brought food and conversation with him. He told the girls stories that were so interesting it was difficult for Claire and Erik not to listen. Claire thought that Proterous was the kindest man she had ever known, and he was a Roman. *So much for my thinking that all Romans are bastards,* she said to herself. Someday, if she should ever return to power, she would like to reward him appropriately for his kindness, skill, and generosity.

After three days, the girls were well and ready to travel. Proterous gave Claire a flask of the herbal medicine in case the fever returned. She in turn wanted to give him some of the gold coins she had brought with her, but Proterous refused.

"Your company is payment enough. Now go, and may the gods look after you."

First thing the next morning, Claire, Erik, and the girls gathered their horses and rode out of the village—from a speck of serenity into a world of uncertainty.

Part II

"We are given our place in time as we are given our eyes: Weak, strong, clear, squinting, the thing is not ours to choose. Well, this has been a squinting, walleyed time to be born in."

— *Julian*, by Gore Vidal

XXXIII

Departure

Joseph received word that he was to appear in front of the General within one hour's time. He was mulling over the stories the General had previously told him. Joseph realized he could never understand the General. He was now fine with that conclusion, as he knew his time with the General was limited. Joseph also thought maybe that was what the General wanted as well.

As he walked to the General's headquarters, he observed an unusual amount of activity. He stopped one of the soldiers he knew and asked what was the cause of this energy.

"We are breaking camp and moving into the field. Reportedly the Emperor wants to start a spring campaign against a large group of Goths gathered near the Danube, and we are being ordered to provide support for the operation."

Joseph gave no further thought to the soldier's statement and entered into the General's chambers. He was surprised by what he found. The General had moved out. In his place were Braxus' belongings. However, Braxus had also packed for the field. Joseph was quietly pleased that he was not going on the campaign against the Goths. When Joseph turned around, he was face to face with the General. That abrupt meeting was not quite as shocking as what the General was wearing—civilian clothes. He had never seen the General wear anything besides military dress.

Joseph took a step back. The General offered no apology for startling him. "The Emperors have agreed to my terms of retirement. I am pleased. My legions under Braxus have been ordered to proceed near the Danube and await the Emperor's orders. Have you decided where you will be traveling to, priest?"

Joseph hesitated but said, "Yes, General. I know a fellow priest who is serving in Britannia. I'm going there to join him." Joseph knew he should not say for missionary work.

"Does he know you are going to be joining him?"

"Not yet, but I sent correspondence to him, telling him my plans."

The General's questions continued for a few more minutes. He seemed to be taking a strong interest in what Joseph was saying, and Joseph became uncomfortable with the line of questioning.

Joseph decided to turn the dialogue back to the General. "And where are you retiring to, General?" Joseph was pleased that he could change the subject.

The response was surprising. He answered, "For now, Britannia as well."

Joseph showed no reaction to the General's comment; however, he wasn't initially fond of the idea of the General being in the same region that he wanted to settle in.

The General continued, "I want to go to Hadrian's Wall. I want to see it for myself. I have been to so many areas in the Empire. Britannia is one place that I have not traveled."

"I assume the General will have a cavalry escort for his journey?"

"You assume wrong, priest. I am traveling by myself, *alone*."

Joseph did not expect this response. "You are going to a new region traveling without an escort. Isn't that dangerous?"

The General stepped back and looked reflective, "I want to do this alone. I do not want an escort. I want to blend in and be a part of the populace. I do not wish to live the life of a soldier and, particularly, a general anymore. I don't have to explain myself to you, of all people. Do you understand?"

"Yes," was the response, although he didn't understand what "understand" meant. This was odd behavior from such a powerful man.

"Good. We leave at sunrise tomorrow morning. Braxus has told me that he will provide us with a small cavalry escort until we reach the port at the end of Gaul. From there we take a ship to Britannia. I'm first going to Londinium. You can travel with me there if you so choose. At Londinium, though, we will go our separate ways. You can go your way to wherever and I will go to Hadrian's Wall. When we board that ship, I am no longer the General or Valerias, I am simply Marcus Augustus and you will be Joseph. Do you have any issues with what I have said?"

"No," was Joseph's timid response.

"Good. Now go say your farewells. I imagine you have many to say. As I told you, Braxus has been ordered to the Emperor's campaign on the Danube, so they leave tomorrow as well."

The General turned and left the room. Joseph observed that in civilian clothes the General had the sword inside the sheath that was strapped to his back. Even in civilian wear the man still looked formidable. Joseph had mixed feelings about joining the General on the journey to Britannia. On the one hand the General would provide security and company. On the other he was and always would be the General to Joseph, a person whom Joseph still feared and, until recently, loathed.

Joseph gathered his belongings and said his farewells to a number of people in the Roman fort including Braxus, other officers and soldiers, and administrative staff. His last stop was to Olivertos' quarters. When Joseph walked into the room that Olivertos used for treating patients, he saw no one. There were no patients in any of his recovery areas. Finally Joseph went in the back where Olivertos lived. He saw several bags packed and placed on his bed. The room also looked empty.

Olivertos came up behind him with no intent of startling Joseph, but he startled Joseph anyway.

"First, the General, and now you sneak up and surprise me," Joseph noted half-jokingly.

"Where you are going, Joseph, you will need to be on alert at all times." Olivertos was not joking.

"What is happening with you, Olivertos?"

"I have been 'invited' to join Braxus and the group in our adventure to the land of the Goths," Olivertos said half-sarcastically. "They think they will need a number of physicians to address the casualties anticipated to be generated by this undertaking. Actually, I am looking forward to the campaign. It gets me out of here, as the fort becomes claustrophobic, and I can hopefully learn new treatments. One must always look to expand one's expertise."

"Isn't it about time for the legions to leave the fort anyway, as spring is here?"

"Well, then, that only gives me one more reason to look forward to the campaign." Olivertos spoke as he continued to pack. Joseph observed he was in a pensive mood.

Joseph had always found Olivertos to be mild mannered and thoughtful. How Olivertos and the General got along was a mystery to Joseph. But outside of the departed Jacob and Bukarma, Olivertos was the General's closest friend within the world of the legions. The General and Braxus and the other military figures were friends by their military bonds; Olivertos' friendship with the General was non-military based and a true friendship.

Olivertos and Joseph talked about many things in the final hour they would spend together. The tone of the conversation was tempered by the fact this was likely the last time they would see each other. Joseph was off to the wilds of Britannia, and Olivertos was about to enter a theater of war. Death as an individual or in a group seemed a genuinely possible outcome for each man.

As Joseph left, he told Olivertos, "May God be with you and keep you safe."

Olivertos was not a Christian, but he appreciated Joseph's thoughts. Olivertos then added his final words, "Joseph, seek advice as you need it and measure that advice carefully; however, it is more important to obtain wisdom and do good with that wisdom."

With those words, the two men quickly hugged each other. Joseph returned to his tent for a few hours of sleep. Morning would come quickly.

General Valerias was also saying his farewells. A feast was prepared, and he and his officers enjoyed food and fellowship. Braxus, Cratus, Bukarma, Revious, and a score of Roman officers and administrative personnel who had served with the General were present. Everyone there was tied in some way to the legions of the General. Olivertos came late and joined the General at a seat on his left side.

Multiple toasts were made during the evening, although, no one drank enough to become drunk. Tomorrow would be a difficult day, and being hung over was not the preferable option. The men clearly admired the General. He had been a tough, driven leader. He could be difficult, and yet he was fair to those who earned his trust. Also, importantly, he had won every battle and campaign that he had led. The General too, fully appreciated those who had served under him. They had been loyal soldiers who followed orders and carried out his commands.

When the meal was over, the General rose to speak, and there was silence in the hall. "Men, we are about to part company. We will soon enter a new phase in our lives. You will play a major part in the campaign to be led by our Emperor against the Goths. It has been my honor to serve our Emperors and the Emperors before them. But just as important to me, it has been an honor to have served with you."

This toast was followed by shouting, foot-stomping, and table-thumping by the men. There were shouts of "Hail, General Valerias!"

The General continued, "You have my utmost respect." More shouting and approval erupted from the attendees.

From the crowd someone lofted a question at the General, "Why are you leaving now?"

The General quickly answered, "It is simple. I want to know who I am outside of the army. I know what I am here, but this is all I have done in my life. Leaving is something I must do while I still can."

Puzzled looks appeared on the faces of most of the men. A few who were the General's confidantes understood the General's reasoning, but it still made little sense to them. Only Olivertos clearly understood why the General was doing what he was doing.

The General put his arms up for silence. For the last time this gesture worked. "Braxus will now take command. He has been my second-in-command for almost a decade. I have full confidence in Braxus to continue my leadership in the service of Rome and the Empires. Hail, General Braxus!"

The men returned the cry. "Hail, General Braxus!"

The General required all feast participants to swear a new oath of loyalty to Milan, to Constantinople, and to Braxus. A final toast was made and then the men filtered out of the hall. The General held back his five closest friends for a last word.

"Several years ago I had the finest blacksmith in Rome create several swords and daggers for me that are incomparable in quality. I will take one sword and one dagger with me to Britannia."

The General turned and slowly walked over to an old wooden trunk that he always carried with him. The trunk was worn from its travels. He carefully pulled out four swords, which were sheathed in the original covers and wrapped in cloth. It appeared the swords had never been used. The General then walked over to Braxus, Cratus, Bukarma, and Revious and gently placed the swords on the floor by the feet of each man.

"You have served me and the Empire with a distinction that cannot be fully repaid. I could not have succeeded in what I have accomplished without each and every one of you. Over the years I have had tens of thousands of good men serve me in a brave and loyal manner. But I have counted on you to be the leaders of those men. And for that I am grateful."

The General reached down and put both of his hands around the sheath of one sword, lifted it up, and presented it to Braxus. He followed in the same manner as he gave swords to Cratus, Bukarma, and Revious. Each man expressed deep gratitude to the General when presented with his sword.

After the General had given the swords to the four men, he turned to Olivertos, "Old friend, I know you do not want a sword. What would a physician do with such an instrument of death?" He reached behind himself for a magnificently designed dagger.

He then gave it to Olivertos and said, "This is more attuned to a physician's work.

"Don't you want this dagger?" responded an astounded Olivertos.

"No, it's yours. I want you to have the dagger."

The men could not believe their gifts—they were more works of art than weapons of war. Each hilt was crafted to allow the holder to maintain a firm grip during fighting. Each blade was perfection, with a smooth surface and razor-sharp edges. Words gently imprinted on the surface of one side read *Fortitudinem* [Strength] and on the other side *Victoriam* [Victory]. The swords and dagger were balanced like no blades the men had ever touched. The General did not disclose the metals that comprised the weapons. All that he said was, "The swords and dagger were crafted by the greatest weapon maker in Rome who used the finest materials."

After a few minutes of evaluating the swords and dagger, Braxus commanded the attending servants to bring in a beautifully made carrying case to hold the volumes of the General's history. The case could be easily attached to a horse, and its construction was solid. Anything contained inside could not be damaged. Even better, it was waterproof, so the travel to Britannia could be made without concern that damp weather could ruin the documents. The General was pleased. He smiled as he gently examined the outside and inside of the case.

The men exchanged gratitudes and farewells. The General was never one for sentimentality, but this was an occasion that required a soft change in tone. At that brief moment they were equal brothers. Then it was over, and the men began to leave.

As they left, the General offered a final recommendation, "I have heard that Emperor Valens is assigning a man named Trojax to assume Cratus' old position as third-in-command. He is an appointed general. Beware of this man and keep surveillance on him, because he is not to be trusted. He works more for a politician in the Emperor's court than for the Emperor."

After they left, the General told Bukarma, "Fetch your game, we will play one last time."

Joseph awoke early the next morning. He heard rustling outside through the night and into the morning, but thought little of it. He quickly went through his morning routine to prepare for the day. As he left his quarters to find the General, he was startled. In front of him were the General, Braxus, and ten soldiers in a cavalry formation.

"I see the world must wait for you, priest." On paper the General's words could be considered humorous; however, the General's mood was serious as he spoke them. The General then nodded to a soldier who brought forth a smallish, brown horse.

"She is yours, priest. It is your responsibility to take care of her." Joseph had wanted to walk, but he knew arguing with the

General would be poor idea. Joseph believed if he expressed his desire to walk, the General would just as likely tie him to the back of a horse, and that is how he would travel to Britannia, following the ass of a horse. So Joseph thanked the General. As he did so, several servants quickly placed Joseph's belongings on the horse. Braxus moved close to Joseph.

"I picked her out myself for you. She is young, strong and rides well. You will have no problems with her, and hopefully she will last more than just this ride."

"Thank you, Braxus." Joseph then very quietly added, "You will be in my prayers."

The General commanded, "Let's go." And the group left the fort. A bright sun emerged from the tree line to the east. For the second time in minutes, Joseph was startled. In front of him were the General's legions in full battle dress. The infantrymen marched in their travel formation. The cavalry would follow. As the General rode out, everyone stopped. The sun shone behind him and reflected off the shields of the soldiers. The reflection was so bright Joseph needed to cover his eyes. As he looked through the cracks in his hand, he saw that the General was not even blinking. He had commanded the army in many situations like this one—this moment, though, was his last, and he was soaking in the glory.

Braxus, who was riding to the left side of the General, grabbed the General's forearm. The General took Braxus' forearm with his hand and said, "May good fortune be with you, my friend."

"As with you," answered Braxus.

The General and Braxus released arms, after which the General proceeded to drive his large, black horse into three full circles. A thick cloud of dust rose from this activity. The soldiers in the legions responded by pounding their spears against their shields, shouting, "*Sapor est victoria! Adhuc esurient!*" [Savor the victory! Hunger for more!] "Hail General Valerias!" Joseph witnessed this tribute and was in awe. He even found himself applauding.

The General and his group then rode away from the fort in the opposite direction of Braxus' men. The General was headed north and Braxus to the south. As the General rode north, he passed by Braxus' support forces, including the engineers, cooks, and slaves. The General saw Gul as they rode by the engineers and smiled to himself.

A large, dark forest loomed ahead for the General's group to travel through. The General showed unflinching confidence while Joseph was concerned about the coming unknown. He began to doubt himself and his upcoming mission. He now wished he had stayed with Olivertos. The General too was having second thoughts, but these were different thoughts than what Joseph was thinking. The General was concerned about the fate of his legions and particularly Braxus and his other officers. Yet his face showed no sign of doubt or concern. He had traveled this road before.

XXXIV

Erik

THE WARMTH OF Proterous and his hut were soon a memory as Claire, Erik, Anne, and Elizabeth continued in a northward route. Their spirits were high because of the kindness of one who was a stranger. There were also few travelers on this road. They passed a couple of men on horses whose eyes never wavered from the road.

At a fork in the road, Proterous had told them to take the right fork. It was less traveled, and they would still reach the lake country that Flavius had spoken of. The road soon become more of a trail. The terrain became more hilly, with steep ridges and valleys. If one wanted to stay alive, staying on the trail was the first step.

The warm thoughts vanished into the cool air that seemed to flow down from the hills and through the trees, which formed ambivalent sentries lining the trail. Claire heard what she thought was a man's shout in the distance. Erik confirmed he had also heard the voice.

"Someone is at the fork," he observed.

"Are they looking for us or just some wandering travelers confused by the fork?" she asked mainly to herself.

"We can't take any chances, Claire. Let's go up to that spot, and there I will climb that tall tree to see if someone is actually coming up our trail."

They quickly made their way to the tree, and Erik proved himself a good climber. Claire tried not to appear worried so that the girls would not get upset. Unfortunately, unspoken fear can transfer, and the girls started asking questions. Claire put her hand over her mouth to signal all should be quiet. After a few minutes Erik descended from the tree and the color in his face was white.

"There are about five or six of them, all men." Then he lowered his voice so the girls would not hear. "I believe they are looking for us."

Claire, without hesitation, said, "We must ride as fast as possible up ahead. Hopefully there is a bridge from where we can defend ourselves. We both have bows and can send plenty of arrows their way."

Erik nodded in agreement. Claire and Anne rode first, followed by Erik and Elizabeth. Bushes, trees, and rocks flew by. Portions of the trail became narrow, bordered on both sides by steep slopes. It would be the end of a person's life if he or she inadvertently strayed off the trail. The men following the group were quiet; however, Claire could sense they were drawing closer, even though her group was going as fast as possible.

When they rounded a sharp curve, they came upon a bridge. The first thought Claire had was *we are going to be saved.* This elation was quickly followed by utter despair. Erik had ridden past Claire to the beginning of the bridge. Upon his inspection, the bridge was damaged and uncrossable. Fog was gathering on the bridge emanating from the valley floor below. They were trapped, and a feeling of doom was setting in, as with prey when cornered by a predator. Erik assessed the situation and made an instant decision.

"Back about twenty-five yards, there was a path made by deer. I caught sight of it by accident."

He dismounted and removed Elizabeth from his horse. He requested Claire and Anne do the same. She wasn't sure what Erik was going to do, but she did not say anything. Erik removed the food and supplies that Proterous gave them and handed the goods to Claire.

"Go back to this pathway and hide on it. They will assume the worst, and I am counting on this for you to be safe. Go quickly, they are almost here."

"What are you going to do?"

"It is important for the Queen and her daughters to be safe and for the Queen to eventually return to the throne. It is your rightful place and the kingdom needs you much more than me. We must defeat Argus. You must defeat Argus—that is what must be done."

Claire was assimilating all that was transpiring. "I don't want you to forfeit your life for me. Maybe there is another way. Do you think Proterous betrayed us?" Claire spoke the words but did not believe the answer was *yes*.

"No, he did not—it was not in his nature." Erik was showing a sense of wise maturity. "And I am not forfeiting anything. I am simply doing my duty for my Queen. There is no other way."

He then gently pushed Claire and the girls down the trail to the path. "Go now, get out of sight. After they are gone, return to the trail. I advise you to return to Proterous until things settle down. I trust Proterous. May God be with you, my Queen."

Erik gave Claire an impression of calmness. She started to form tears.

"I love you, Claire," he said, and then he took some branches and wiped away Claire's and the girls' footprints from the trail. Erik mounted his horse and grabbed the reins of the other three horses and then looked at Claire.

Claire was having difficulty formulating an appropriate sentence for the moment and emotions overwhelmed her. She was fond of Erik, like Gerhard, but it was not love. Tears streamed down her face, with both girls clutching at her side. They too were crying because their mother was crying. They didn't have a sense of what was coming. All they knew was that Erik had been a friend to them, and now he was leaving them. Claire's tears told Erik all he needed to know.

Erik made a gesture they should disappear back into the path. "It is fine Claire, your face—I will take it into eternity." He smiled and grabbed the reins from the horses and started down the trail toward the bridge. Claire pulled her children back down the tiny path for several yards and hid behind a group of rocks that was a continuation of the ridge that rose behind them. The fog was becoming thicker as the cool air spilled down the upper ridge. She could hear the riders coming closer on the trail by the path.

Over there, I see them, she thought to herself.

The riders picked up the pace as their prey was close. Erik approached the dilapidated, fog-covered bridge at full gallop. His horses thought the bridge was safe and entered onto it without fear. About halfway across the bridge, the weight of Erik and the horses—and the condition of the bridge—caused a rupture in the main line holding the ropes on the far end. The ropes let go like a man hanging on a cliff without hope and Erik plunged to his death in the deep gorge.

The band of men rode by the path and up to what was left of the bridge and stopped just in time. They peered down into the darkness of the gorge as the fog moved up to meet them at the same time it flowed down from the tops of the ridge. The result was such limited visibility that the men began to have a hard time seeing each other. Curses were hurled into the air. These men were superstitious, and what they surmised was the Earth had swallowed Claire and her group. None of the men had ever seen a fog that flows up and also down. It was eerie.

Even though Claire had a bounty on her head, none of the men wanted to face the unknown at the bottom of the gorge in the deep fog. There could be trolls down there, and they did not have the courage to face a troll, especially in this fog.

After milling about, a man said, “Back to camp, I need to think about what to do.”

More cursing in vile tones followed this statement. However, soon all the men left the area. Once they were gone, Claire waited for several minutes and she and her daughters hurried down the trail back to Proterous' hut. The fog had lifted enough so they could see their way out and yet provided cover.

Claire thought about many things as she walked back to the village. What would she have done differently with Erik? Could she have done anything differently? She now had had two men who said they loved her. She, though, did not love them the way she thought love should be. Maybe she was cursed. It didn't matter anyway—the survival of her daughters was her sole objective. She also wondered at the same time if her son was still safe and alive.

When they reached the village, it was dark. They took the back way to Proterous' hut. He was just finishing with a patient. After he left, Claire knocked quietly on the rear entrance portal. Proterous quickly opened the hatchway, and in stumbled Claire and the girls. All three were in a poor state—physically and mentally. Proterous brought them warm broth and clean clothes. They huddled by the fire. The girls were quick to fall asleep. Claire recounted her story. When she mentioned Erik, tears filled her eyes.

Proterous was sympathetic but cautious. “You can stay here, but you must remain in the hut. Going outside is too dangerous. There will be a flurry of activity now that they think you are in this area instead of in the west. Fortunately, the local scoundrels will believe you are dead and in the belly of trolls or some other beast and will not pursue you further. However, my Roman colleagues tell me Argus' captain, who is a living terror, is nearby. He is someone you do not want hunting you."

"Did you get his name?" asked Claire. She already knew the answer.

"Flavius," answered Proterous.

XXXV

Empire Builders

Rao rode into the Huns' main encampment with a contingent of twenty riders. He advanced to the main tent and dismounted. Uldric came out of the tent to meet him.

"Welcome, brother. I trust you had a fruitful trip?"

"First, a drink and a bath." Rao spoke in as short a sentence as possible. He didn't say which was the priority.

"Are you particularly dirty?"

"Yes, and I particularly want to wash away the stench of some of the cowards I sat with."

Rao waved off his riders, brushed dirt from his clothes, and went to a smaller tent adjacent to the main tent. A man came up to greet him.

"Welcome back, my master. I understand you desire a drink and bath." The man then issued sharp commands. Soon Rao was in a tub-like fixture with a strong beverage in his hand. The warm water of the bath and the drink relaxed him. Rao was the more stable of the two brothers, so when he was upset, those who were around him took notice. When he finished his bath, he took two women from the camp and disappeared into another tent near where he had bathed. Uldric paced outside the entire time, becoming more and more irritable. After two hours, Rao emerged; he had returned to his usual self.

Uldric was now the one on fire with emotion. "So, brother, are you comfortable and rested from your trip? Can we talk now or do you want to have one of your women clean your toenails? How about a music lesson?" With every word Uldric's sarcasm was evident.

"I see, brother. You must have been having a hard time sitting around camp, playing head chief and exercising occasionally with the men," Rao responded, equally sarcastic.

Rao continued. "I have spent the last month visiting our cousins and trying to get them to join our cause. I breathed much dust and dirt, slept on hard ground, ate food that would cause you to spend more time sitting in the shit house than riding a horse, and on top of that—meeting with so-called leaders who would just as soon flay me as a piece of their livestock. And you have the balls to complain about my taking a short break after my return to camp! I don't understand, brother, why such an ass?"

Uldric was typically the more impatient of the two brothers, and he certainly had the worst temper, but he knew it was time to back off, as Rao seldom expressed anger like this outburst.

"I apologize, brother, for being impetuous, but I was anxious to hear of your trip."

Rao looked at his brother and realized he had the upper hand for the moment. He turned to a servant. "Get us a drink and let's talk in the command tent."

Uldric also waved to a nearby slave, who followed the brothers into the tent with a container of drink and cups.

When it was poured, Rao took a deep drink. "After what I drank on my trip, this is the gods' nectar."

After another drink he shouted for one of his officers to bring the map. In a short time a smallish man arrived in the tent. He wore a necklace made of teeth, a combination of human and animal teeth. The necklace rattled as he walked.

"I hope you don't try to ambush someone wearing that thing," Rao chided the man.

The man answered with a sly smile on his face, "I put a spell on it. Then I am as silent as the night bird to surprise my woman."

All three men laughed. Produgas was the acknowledged jokester of the tribe, but he was a superb tracker, so he could get away with words others would dare not say. Produgas spread the map on the table. The men spent hours reviewing the various markings sketched on it and what they meant.

Rao concluded, "My meetings with the Hun chiefs proved only partially successful. My meetings with the Alans did not go well. The Alans are very skeptical at joining us. They think this is a foolish attempt at glory for us. Rome is too far away, and we don't have enough men to take on the Roman army. There is also that damn Roman general, Valerias, whom they fear."

"Valerias again! Who is this man?"

"The Alans tangled with him on several campaigns. They didn't triumph and paid a heavy price."

"Well, now they have the backing of the Huns, so that should remove their fear when they join us."

"You are confident, Uldric, but it will be no good without the Alans. We must first target other tribes, and maybe the Alans will change their minds and join us."

"What other tribes are you thinking about? The Goths are fleeing from us now, and we haven't even begun our quest."

"Let me gather my thoughts."

Uldric had enough of this banter and said sharply, "No, we are not planning a wedding—this is our future, and I seem to be the only one who gives a damn."

"Wrong, brother, I do care about *our* future. But we are not going off on some half-brained scheme. We just can't move without ten or twenty thousand warriors. And we need solid support, with supplies and prisoner control and—"

"Enough. We leave in a month when spring arrives—whether you agree or not. If you don't go with us, maybe you should sit in the camp and wash clothing with the women."

"You are a foolish man with a brain like one of our goats. No thought in preparing for war—just go out and do it and hope for the best."

Uldric and Rao were face to face, with a tight tension between them. Produgas had become concerned there would be blows. He stepped in and made a silly joke, "This reminds me of the time I had to separate two women who were fighting over me."

Uldric and Rao didn't know what to think of the joke. Did he liken them to women? What should they do with such insolence? However, it worked, and the brothers' focus was now Produgas. There were numerous oaths and threats directed at Produgas, and he smiled, which made the brothers even angrier.

Produgas pointed to the map, and as he did so, he said, "Now that you two have settled down, I have a suggestion to remedy our problem. Rao, retell us about your trip and describe to us the villages and camps you saw and particularly the Hun and Alan chiefs you met with."

Rao took a deep breath, which seemed to calm him. He took another breath, looked at Uldric, and then discussed in detail everything he could remember. Rao could read and write, but he preferred verbal communication. When he finished, Produgas ask Rao which chief had the most power and which one was the weakest.

Rao opined, "Dimondes seemed to be the primary Hun chief of the largest outlying tribe. He is also the man who exhibited the greatest resistance to our plan. Jutikes appeared to be the weaker of the chiefs. Dimondes' camp was located at the base of a small salty lake. Jutikes and his tribe were more nomadic and had less organization than the camp of Dimondes. You should also know that Jutikes has a close relationship with the Alan tribes."

"Perfect!" Uldric exclaimed. "I know what we are going to do. We will attack Dimondes, defeat him, and install Jutikes as head of the outlying Huns. Then the Alans should follow him and he will do our will."

"You think this is so simple?" Rao responded.

"Actually, it is, Rao."

"It's not," countered Produgas. "Dimondes has several hundred men at his direct command, with many more in the country who will come when he requests it."

Uldric's face showed frustration. "Everyone seems to have more soldiers at their beck and call than us. Damn, damn, damn." Uldric continued this tirade with more cursing.

Rao then asked a question directed more toward himself than at either Uldric or Produgas. "Did you get a sense how loyal Dimondes' men are to him?"

Uldric broke Rao's train of thought. "I don't know, fool, you were there."

"I know that, *brother*," Rao hissed.

Produgas saw the tension between brothers manifest itself again, so he quickly said, "They are loyal to a point. But they are more loyal to themselves than to the group as a whole."

"Where did you get such great insight?" Uldric again turned his displeasure to Produgas.

"I have a relative who is in the village of Dimondes, and he knows the pulse of Dimondes' tribe." Produgas, to show he was not a lackey of either brother, added, "I don't speak unless I know what I'm talking about."

Rao noted, "Unless you are hiding from all your women—it is amazing you can be the warrior you are with so many women problems."

Produgas realized Rao was also trying to defuse the situation, and they both laughed. It was a hearty laugh, and after a moment Uldric joined in.

Rao turned serious. "One thing you must realize, Uldric, is that we both have the same objective—to build a Hun empire that will rule more territory than Rome, or at least as much as Rome or Constantinople. Maybe toss Persia into the mix also. Produgas, here, is too busy in building his empire of women." Again the three laughed at Produgas' expense.

Rao called in the treasurer for the tribe. With Drago's fortune, Uldric and Rao had a considerable sum to spend, and Rao intended to spend it to accomplish their objectives. The rewards would come later, he hoped.

"Brother, Dimondes sometimes travels to other camps. I'm sure our good friend here," and he looked at Produgas, "will get his schedule for us. We will ambush Dimondes when he is traveling. We will not strike in our own clothing or be recognizable. We will disguise ourselves as robbers and kill Dimondes. I don't want the Alans involved.

"Afterwards, we will return to our village. When we hear of Dimondes' ill fortune at the hands of unidentified robbers, we will ride to Dimondes' village. There we will offer our sympathy to Dimondes' kin and then propose our plan. We will also take gold and offer wages to any Hun who will join us. Once that is in place, we will gradually purge those who do not agree with our plan."

Uldric responded quickly, "I like your plan. Let's get started."

"Wait, a little patience is needed." Rao looked at Produgas. "You know what to do."

Rao turned to Uldric. "Now is the time to prepare the men for ambush training. The group that will strike Dimondes must be few, great fighters, and very loyal. Otherwise we will be strung up on some post."

As Produgas exited the tent, he spoke of a subject that neither Uldric nor Rao was fond of discussing. "Remember, you don't have an heir, either of you. There will come a time when you will need one. Look at how you are counting on Dimondes' heirs to join you."

Produgas pointed to his head, then his frontal part, looked at the brothers, and disappeared into the sunlight.

As he left the tent, Rao observed, "Perhaps we should elevate him to the chief—he has plenty of heirs."

"I'll wager he has heirs that he doesn't know he has."

"Or bastards."

"Probably both." The brothers laughed again. All was now well in the land of the Hun.

Three weeks went by as the brothers planned their move. Finally word came to them that Dimondes was traveling to a village east of his main camp and away from the Hun encampment of Uldric and Rao. Dimondes would be traveling with a light escort because he had grown blithely unconcerned about any hazards that would be encountered in such travels away from his camp.

Dimondes disliked these travels and frequently required stops to rest. Rao, Uldric and a loyal, trusted group of ten men attacked Dimondes at midday when Dimondes' guard had relaxed for a break. The surprise worked, and Dimondes and his escort were slain quickly.

Once this task had been completed, Rao took charge. He wanted to make the area of the attack look like a robbery. Bodies were left scattered about without sign of mutilations. Dimondes and his men were stripped of all valuables, including gold coin and jewelry. When the purging of valuables from Dimondes was completed, Rao sent Uldric and the rest of the Hun warriors out of sight. He then moved to an undisclosed area and dug a pit. He placed the valuables in the pit and carefully covered it up. When he was done, Rao was convinced no one would ever be able to find the plunder.

As Rao rode up to meet his group, Uldric commented, "Did you hide it well enough? I may want to go back and secure some gold for our treasury."

"We talked about that, Uldric. We do not want any jewelry or other items that could be identified as belonging to Dimondes to show up on our men and in our camp, including with you, brother. You know I'm right."

Uldric mumbled something that sounded like an affirmative response. They then rode back to their encampment.

News of Dimondes' death spread rapidly in the area. Rao and Uldric sent their condolences to Dimondes' family and tribe and attended his funeral. They also paid a visit to Jutikes with Produgas. Jutikes and Produgas were old friends and got along well. Rao was pleased to have Produgas at his side as they embarked on their plan, because he didn't seem to have an enemy anywhere.

The thought of a leadership position and the gold offered by the brothers was too much, and Jutikes joined them. With Jutikes in the fold, other outlying tribes joined the brothers, and eventually the tribe previously led by Dimondes did as well.

Uldric patiently explained the brothers' master plan to Dimondes' heirs and tribe. The elders were reluctant at first. However, the young men of the tribe were enthusiastic about following Uldric. Uldric had the charisma that could persuade young warriors to join his cause. The elders did not wish to be estranged from their young soldiers, and after minor haggling between themselves and the brothers, they agreed to join the Hun banner of Rao and Uldric. Thus there was a growing Hun confederation that featured several thousand men of quality fighting ability. Now the brothers could turn their attention to attracting other tribes, such as the Alans, to join them.

Outside their main tent one night, Uldric and Rao looked over the camp. Smoke swirled randomly up from the numerous campfires like moths that had lost their innate compasses.

Rao concluded with a piece of grass in his mouth, "So far I am pleased with how this is setting up. Soon we will advance west."

Uldric looked at him and nodded, "Sometimes I get too impatient, brother. We are a good team. The earth shall hear of the mighty Hun, and it will shake at our arrival."

Rao mumbled an agreement. Both men entered deep thoughts that considered divergent points of view. Rao fumed to himself, *His acting with little thought could end our plan before it begins. I get tired of wasting energy trying to keep my brother in check.* Meanwhile, Uldric was thinking, *My brother is way too cautious. We will die of old age before meeting our objectives.*

Trust and loyalty are essential for a successful campaign, especially the campaign that will be led by twin brothers who do not always agree. Distrust is the negative factor. If events take a turn for the worse, a campaign based primarily on distrust will unravel, and failure will result. The relationship of trust between Rao and Uldric would dictate whether their planned assault at the Roman Empire would be a success or failure. Both men were aware of this necessity.

XXXVI

To Britannia

Valerias, Joseph, and the cavalry escort rode hard on the first day. The Roman-constructed roads in this area were good, and the General wanted to make time. They traveled in a northern direction and passed through villages, fortified cities, and wilderness. The General did not speak a word to Joseph on the first day. In fact, he barely spoke to the captain of his Roman escort. Joseph had ridden horses before, but as the first day progressed, so did the soreness in his legs. By the night he could barely stand the pain and welcomed the rest. Joseph had a restless night of sleep, and in the morning he had great difficulty walking. Joseph did not complain, but it was evident to the General and the other soldiers that he was suffering.

The second day was a different matter. The General spoke at length with the captain at the beginning of the day. He even laughed at a comment made by the captain.

At the end of the day, he walked over to Joseph. "Not used to riding a horse, are you, priest?"

"No, I am used to walking."

"Where we are going, and the distance to reach there, will require you to do more than walk. You need to learn how to ride for distance."

The captain and a cavalryman came over to Joseph. The captain showed Joseph exercises to perform, and the soldier gave Joseph a balm for healing. Joseph went into the woods and applied the balm where his muscles were sorest, covering most of his lower body. He started to feel better. The next day when he awoke, Joseph found the General and the rest of the men mounted on their horses waiting for him. Joseph's horse had already been prepared for the day's ride. Joseph gingerly climbed onto the saddle and felt the pain return to his legs, but it wasn't as sharp. He looked around and was surprised to observe that there was no sign of a camp ever having been present at this location.

The captain rode up to him and added, "We try hard to conceal our presence. The woods are full of bandits, and we are a small group, effective but small."

Great, bandits, thought Joseph. *Sore legs and bandits.*

As they started on the day's ride, Joseph daydreamed about his time in Rome and how great it would be to return. He was suddenly jolted back to reality when he found the General riding at his side.

"Tired, priest?"

"Yes, a little. My lack of riding skill has caused some pain in my legs. But I will be all right."

"Yes, you will, you have no choice, unless you want to navigate these roads by yourself."

As they rode further, the General unexpectedly spoke to Joseph, "What kind of Christian are you, priest? I served the Emperor Julian and he referred to you all as Galileans. Julian believed in the 'Old Gods.' I did too, from the time I was born until Julian was killed. But I learned that things are not quite that simple. The 'Old Gods' were a huge disappointment to me. Their most faithful follower, Julian, my mentor, lasted less than three years of wearing the purple. They failed him. To me this indicates they never really existed, or if they did, they have disappeared. Julian put much faith in the Sun God, 'Helios.' Now I see so many cloudy and overcast days. If the Sun God is so powerful, where does he go during those cloudy days, or at night? Does the Sun God need a rest? If so, then that is not a god, or a god to be concerned with."

Joseph was surprised by this monologue from someone who seemed to have a passionate hate for anything involving Christianity. The General also seemed to have no faith in what he called the Old Gods of the Roman Empire. Joseph wasn't sure if the reference to cloudy and overcast referred to the weather or to what the General had experienced. Joseph also was unclear about how much the General knew about his religion. As Joseph passed these thoughts through his mind, he looked up to make a comment to the General, but he had already advanced up to the front of the group.

The next day at almost the same time, the General appeared at Joseph's side. "I have learned there are many sects of your religion. I am aware of Mithras. Are you one of the followers of Mithras?"

"No," Joseph answered. He also had a feeling the General knew the answer too.

"What about Arius? Are you an Arian?"

"No," Joseph answered again.

"Then you must be an adherent of the sect that believes the trinity, as you call it, are separate forces. That includes your God, his son the Jewish rabbi, and a ghost?"

"No again," Joseph spoke more forcefully this time, as he believed the General was playing with him. "I believe in the Triune

Godhead: the Father who is the Holy God; Jesus Christ, His Son; and the Holy Spirit. They are one and the same."

"That is impossible, you cannot have three entities in one."

The two men continued to debate the subject for several minutes, and then, as yesterday, the General abruptly rode up to the front. Joseph was frustrated with the conversation. *What is the General's point with this talk of religion when he forbids me to talk about it in his camps?* He asked himself.

The next day, at the same time, again the General approached Joseph. "You say your religion is based on love and peace, is this not so?"

Joseph nodded, not knowing where this subject was going. This was typical of conversations with the General.

"And your hero, a Jewish rabbi, died on the cross, so we all could be forgiven. Is that true? And he also rose from the dead?"

"Yes, Our Lord Jesus did suffer for the good of mankind when he was crucified, so that there could be hope for all of us. That means forgiveness and salvation for us. And that includes you as well, General."

"Ha," the General threw his head back when he responded. "You think I will be given salvation? Did you know the first Emperor who became a Christian was Constantine 'the Great'? Did you know he killed several members of his own family? Was he given salvation?" The General almost spit out these comments, particularly the mention of Constantine.

Joseph didn't know what kind of situation he had created, given the General's response. The General had a history of volatility. Would Joseph be killed, with his body tossed off the road in a ditch or some other forlorn location to become supper for wild beasts? However, nothing happened. The General had relaxed and looked at him in a soft way and again rode up to the front. Joseph's insides churned. He did not like these question-and-answer sessions, and he especially didn't want to spar with the General over inane comments. Yet he had to, to stay alive.

The next day the General did not come back to Joseph's position until they stopped and set up the evening camp. Joseph didn't realize how much ground they had covered over the five days since they had left the General's main fort. He was surprised to learn they had traveled over half the trip to the channel and then Britannia. The conversations with the General had upset him so much that he forgot about his legs and the pain associated with prolonged horse riding. *Maybe that was his strategy all along,* mulled Joseph.

When the General's group encountered a Roman encampment or fort, it was awkward. On one hand, it was good to have the protection of Roman troops. On the other, the General did not want it known to the Roman garrisons that he was heading north. Unfortunately the winds of rumor were sometimes more fleet than a Roman horseman, and soldiers often saluted the General as he rode through their encampment.

On the sixth night the group camped in the wilderness. As he prepared for camp, Joseph saw the General off to his side, sitting on a large, fallen tree. The General motioned for Joseph to come over. Joseph, of course, obeyed. The skies showed that a deep dusk was settling in for a brief stay. Fires were kept to a minimum to prevent bandits or other unsavory persons from locating the camp. Even though this was Roman territory, bandits and rogues frequently sought out innocent travelers and small Roman escorts.

The General looked at Joseph and took a deep breath. "I do not believe in any of that nonsense that goes with your religion, Christianity. I have seen so much. I have done so much. Much of what I have done you would consider a sin. There have been actions that I have taken that I am sorry about; however, I regret nothing.

To regret anything, to feel guilt, is a sign of weakness. And priest, in the arena in which I exist, I cannot show weakness or timidity. If I do, I will be brought down, and as a result, I would be replaced by someone who could be much worse than I. That is the world we live in."

The General waved his hand in the motion of a circle. "Everything I have done was for the continued glory of Rome and the Western Empire. Constantinople and the East are secondary to me. Rome has always been my utmost priority. I have sacrificed much as a soldier and General for Rome. And I would do it all over again, if I were given that choice or chance. I have no regrets!" he repeated. The last sentence was spoken with a firmness that caught Joseph off guard.

The General turned the subject to Christianity. "In all my travels I have never seen a man rise from the grave, as they say your Jesus did. I always thought if anyone could leave the grave, it would be Emperor Julian, with all his gods behind him, and that didn't happen. I believe in life and then death; nothing more and nothing less comes before or after your life. There is the light and then black. The hereafter or Heaven and Hell, as you call them, are merely myths, just like the stories of the old Gods."

"That is where faith comes in, General. You don't always have to see something to believe it is the truth. For instance, you are not with Braxus and Olivertos, and yet you know Olivertos is helping Braxus as much as possible on the transfer of power from you to Braxus. And you have faith that Braxus will do his best to keep your legacy with the army intact. It works for me as well. I have never seen God or Jesus, but I know they exist—right here," and Joseph pointed to his heart.

Before Joseph could continue, the General growled slightly at Joseph and then headed for the makeshift camp the cavalry members had pieced together. That was the last communication between Joseph and the General for the night.

The next day the General's group was on the road early and heading north at a fast pace. A light river of fog was hovering in the lowland areas of the road. At midday the group slowed to a walk.

The General rode back to Joseph. "I understand your savior says that if someone strikes you, that you should turn your cheek and prepare to receive another blow. That is so misguided that it makes me laugh. If someone takes a sword to me and I do nothing and let him strike me, I'm dead. And to let it happen again, I am a dead man twice. I presume I could go to Heaven and Hell in that case. Same goes with you. What good are you if you're dead or can't function? There would be no proselytizing."

Joseph ignored the General's sarcasm and responded, "My interpretation of that reading is more of a metaphor than what is expected in a real situation. I think what Jesus meant is that under adverse conditions it is better to take a step back and think of one's options before striking to hurt people. This is kind of like the old saying—think before acting."

Joseph added his own interpretation to Jesus' teaching to mollify the General. He knew the General could not understand the real meaning behind Jesus' words—after all the General was a Roman soldier of the old ways. The General rubbed his increasingly bushy beard. For the first time that Joseph could remember, the General did not debate him or gesture angrily in response to something he had said. Instead the General looked at Joseph quizzically and rode back to the head of the column.

The next few days hurried by quickly; however, the pace of the General's group slowed notably. They stopped at several Roman forts. The General uncharacteristically even went inside and talked to Roman officers. He was interested in what the officers knew about conditions ahead and those in Britannia. At one location he said a long goodbye to another officer whom Joseph did not know. Joseph bided his time at these stops and focused his conversations with locals about churches and clergymen in the area.

Joseph increasingly enjoyed the time in the day when the General and he would talk about religion and life—sometimes in general and sometimes specifically. Joseph learned that the General stated a rigid philosophy about life but there were instances when he went against that philosophy. For instance, he had been stationed in areas that were subject to drought or barbarian raids. When the time came to pay the taxes owed by the locals, those taxes were mysteriously paid or were substantially reduced. It was the General who orchestrated these developments. On numerous occasions he granted leave to his soldiers so they could attend a family celebration or emergency. He was demanding of all those who served him, but he could also be flexible.

What Joseph learned in his discussions with the General was that the General had a keen knowledge of religions, both Christianity and paganism. His adopted father, Hyperion, believed in the old gods, and the General followed Hyperion in the same manner. As he served with Julian, he continued that belief. However, that lasted only as long as Julian was alive. After Julian died, the General had become an atheist. He harbored a deep dislike for the hierarchical structure of the Christian Church and its many divisions. Much of his dislike was centered on certain Church officials who had the audacity to tell him what to do, even though they had no authority over him. And, of course, there was his encounter with the Bishop Casio, which still weighed heavily on his mind. Joseph learned that the General, while being reserved about his religious knowledge, was actually quite astute.

The General also learned a few things about Joseph's character. He knew Joseph had had a troubled background, due mostly to his actions. However, the General believed Joseph was earnest enough about his new calling to warrant the opportunity to become a valuable member of his faith, someone who would do something good and not just take from the good. The General thought Joseph's biggest problem was not the desire to do well as a Christian priest but figuring out how to accomplish his goals. His running with Gul, for example, had been a very poor decision. Joseph told the General he wanted to find a community and to do what was necessary to help that community. The help would also consist of providing God's word, at least Joseph's interpretation of the word. The General did not dispute Joseph's goals and did not tell him what to do. His only advice was to stay away from the coasts, particularly in the east, where Saxon raiders seemed to be everywhere, like a bad infestation of diseased fleas.

When they arrived within a few miles of the coast, the General could smell the ocean air. Joseph had been raised in Rome and on the Mediterranean Sea, but it took a little longer to grasp how close they were to leaving Gaul by sea. They reached a small village that also acted as a port, where there was a boisterous amount of activity for such a small village. The ship that would take the General and Joseph to Britannia was a fishing vessel. The captain of the ship was a large man with long, brown, shaggy hair and beard. Joseph wondered to himself how that beard could function on a sea voyage—would it keep the man warm or get in the way? He looked at the General's beard and thought the captain of the vessel and the General could keep good company, beard wise.

The captain was concerned about a front that was coming through, so he delayed embarking for a day. The General seemed unconcerned and spent the day walking through the village, sometimes by himself, other times with the soldiers, and once with Joseph.

When he was with Joseph, he asked, "Is this the type of village you want to settle down in, or do you want to travel throughout the entirety of Britannia?"

"I'm not sure yet. My friend is located in central Britannia, so I'm going there first."

"I am warning you as I did earlier, stay off the east coast. The Saxons won't care if you are Briton, Roman, or Christian. You have come too far to be sacrificed so easily." The General looked straight ahead as he spoke, as if he did not care if Joseph heard him.

Joseph looked straight ahead as well. His eyes were watching an old woman trying to clean a fowl of some type. Yet his mind focused on the General's words. The General had never spoken to him in such a manner.

"I understand, General, I mean, Marcus." After almost a year with the General, Joseph was having a difficult time not calling him "General."

The General just sighed, and without turning his head continued through the village streets, which were more like muddy paths.

XXXVII

Separate Ways

The Roman cavalry troop left town at dawn of the next day. The General shook the hand of each man in the ten-member group. He also gave each a coin from his pouch. Then they were gone as the sun rose in the east through a haze. The General was free from Rome's presence. His traveling companion was Joseph, a Christian priest.

Joseph awoke and prepared for the day. He went outside and found the General staring off in the direction of Britannia. He had changed his clothes again and now had lost all outward vestiges of his past. He was a soldier in disguise as a civilian and was anxious for the ship to leave port. The captain approached him and told the General that they would leave in an hour.

The General turned around and was not surprised to see Joseph standing behind him. "We leave in an hour. Prepare yourself for travel."

"Yes, I'll be ready, Marcus." Joseph thought, *How did he sense I was there?*

This time a slight grin formed on the General's bearded face, which masked his old appearance. Yet his eyes were the same as always.

When it came time to board the ship, Valerias hesitated slightly, which Joseph noticed. After the ship had left port, and when they were alone standing near the railing, Joseph asked, "I noticed you did not jump on board like I expected. Are you feeling well?"

"I'm fine," Valerias responded. Then he added after a long pause, "To be honest with you, I don't like the water or being on a ship."

Joseph stared at him. This was a statement he did not expect to hear from the great General. Joseph had heard it from others, but he didn't think Valerias would utter those words—indicating a weakness.

Valerias looked back at Joseph and then at the dark water, which seemed to have no clarity. "I don't like what I can't see, and I can't see below the surface. It is not like being on land. Even if you don't know exactly where your enemy or ally is located, you can find out. Here, I don't know what is down there."

Valerias took a pebble on the ship's deck and dropped it into the water. It disappeared in the blink of an eye. "I don't believe in sea monsters or those kind of beasts, but there are creatures that come up from the depths and pull you under for food."

Valerias paused again: his mind was clearly in the past. "Many years ago I was on a fleet of Rome's finest ships set for Africa. As we were about to reach the shores, enemy pirate ships attacked us from behind. It was a sea battle that raged for an entire day. My ship was set upon, burned, and sunk. Many us of managed to jump off the ship beforehand. As we waited for help, a number of men scrambling in the water screamed and disappeared into the dark. I was told by some of the sailors afterward that sharks were the killers. Other sailors said mermaids were the cause of death. They would come up and grab you. And all we could do was float on any objects that were left over from the sunken ship and hope we would not be next. We won the battle, and eventually our ships pulled us, the survivors, out of the water. I will never forget that day. It has been the only time as an officer that I have been afraid. Besides a few other short trips, I have not sailed since. I would much rather be on land, even if greatly outnumbered. I will be grateful when we arrive in Britannia. I've arranged for the captain to take us directly into Londinium."

Joseph joined the discussion. "I used to travel all around Italy as a boy. My father, the merchant, needed to travel to obtain the goods he wanted to sell. A ship and the waters it travels on never bothered me. I actually prefer traveling by water rather than land. There could be something or someone behind that rock or tree you don't see on land. On the sea you can see what is coming even if that is not good."

It was a fine day to sail. There was a light breeze from the west that toyed with the seawater, creating small waves that gently rocked the boat. Joseph noted the light wind would slow the trip to Britannia. He also observed that Valerias' fears of being in a shipwreck had abated.

Valerias turned the conversation to religion. "You believe in the 'do unto others as you would have them do unto you' mantra and 'turn the other cheek' philosophy? I want to hear more about these Christian thoughts, priest."

Joseph knew Valerias was not serious when he asked this, but he nodded, "I believe those are goals we strive to attain in an ideal world. But I know that achieving those goals is something that cannot be true in every event or action we undertake."

"You can't control the actions of all people with your goals, priest. Even as a Roman general I know that is not attainable with soldiers under my command. People may wish or even crave for peace at one moment, and in the next moment, for whatever reason, they may slit your throat. My experience tells me the latter action will prevail over the former. You can live in an ideal world and die soon, or you can be realistic and live. Placing your trust solely in the hands of your God or other people is for fools."

"I said it was a goal, not reality yet. If we all try to follow these concepts, yes, I do believe the world will be better, regardless of your cynicism."

Valerias was intent. "Again, you can try, but you can't manipulate others to follow what *you* want in life. You can only control yourself—controlling others only goes so far when dealing with men."

"Maybe a positive influence can be persuasive and initiate a chain reaction of good intentions."

Valerias replied, "Good intentions are not reality. Just be sure you can control yourself first—even then one can be involved in situations where maintaining control becomes difficult, and your chain of good intentions falls apart. Instead, I believe that you lead, set the example you want to set, and the other men will follow you. But sometimes you have to bring the sword, and that is a better influence on behavior than a few words. The reality is that the sword controls men better than your hopefulness."

Joseph was enjoying this conversation immensely. It had been a long time since he could converse on the subject that he believed in, and it was with the one person who had restricted him from projecting his beliefs. This was almost like training for a practice ministry. Valerias was proving to be an excellent foil for Joseph to make up for the lost time and reengage his Christian knowledge that had been temporarily buried by the General. Joseph would now be better able to start his ministry in Britannia. Valerias too was pleased that he could have a conversation that didn't involve military matters.

As the ship reached the coast of Britannia and the captain entered the River Thames to Londinium, Joseph couldn't resist. "Why are you doing this, Marcus? Why are you giving up everything? You are the great General Valerias. Some people in your camp think you could wear the purple, if you chose to. You have power and all that goes with that power. It makes no sense to me."

"That person is no longer here. I am a citizen, Marcus Augustus, retired soldier of the Empire. That is all."

"That didn't answer the question, Marcus." Joseph was becoming bolder in his questions.

Valerias glanced at Joseph, then looked to the shore. "Don't think yourself free to say anything you want to my face, priest."

"I apologize, Gen . . ." Valerias as usual had rattled Joseph, and he resorted to identifying Valerias as the General instead of Marcus Augustus.

Valerias waved his hand in a dismissive manner, but at the same time said, "Could I have tried to become Augustus? Yes, I could have tried. However—*however*—that is treason to the Emperor and Empire. I do not commit treason. In fact, much of my life has been spent tracking down and eliminating usurpers to the Emperors. Do I always agree with the Emperors' decisions? No, I don't. But I obey their commands. It is like the control issue we just discussed. The Emperors I have served think they control me, and they do. If I were a lesser man, though, I doubt the Emperors would have such control."

Then, as an afterthought, Valerias continued, "I do exercise some flexibility in how I obey my orders—nor do I expect my officers to follow everything I say completely. I may not be out in the field with them, and in such cases, I expect them to do what is best for Rome and for me."

When Valerias had completed speaking his thoughts, Joseph added, "I don't want to force people to accept my religion. I want them to respect my religion. I want them to accept Christianity on their own."

"That is not what I have seen from your religion. I have seen greedy, self-serving bishops exert control over their followers and rob them blind. It is not what I expect from piety. In fact, I have seen much more bad come from your religion, priest, than good, and that is sad."

"I don't agree with that statement. It is not what I have witnessed."

"That may be so, priest, but I see your religion as corrupt as any other religion I have come into contact with. The best religion I know is that of the legions, the army, the sword."

Joseph ignored that comment and wanted to get the conversation back on subject. "You still didn't say why you retired and are losing yourself into the wilderness of Britannia?"

This time Valerias slowly cleared his throat. "Braxus is ready to lead, and he is now capable of performing his duties better than I could. As I told you before, it is time for me to find myself a life outside that of a Roman officer. That is all."

It wasn't all, though. Valerias had other important reasons for his withdrawal from the life he has always known, and no one else, including Joseph, needed to know those reasons. For one, Valerias had always believed it was a soldier's greatest honor to die for the Emperor. He had lived many times while others had died. Why this had happened was very troubling to him.

When the ship pulled up to a pier, Valerias was first off of the ship, besides one of the crew, who tied the vessel to the pier. It was clear to Joseph that Valerias did not like the water. After they unloaded the horses and supplies, the two men stood briefly on the pier together.

"It is time we part ways now, priest. You must go your way and do what was intended for you. This is a second chance for you to do what is right. You may not have a third opportunity, so do well. Think of it this way: if your messiah came back today as has been foretold, no doubt by charlatans, what would you tell him about how you have lived your life? Like I said, take this opportunity—it is yours to succeed or fail, it is up to you."

Joseph was surprised by this mini-pep talk from Valerias, of all people. Joseph decided his response would be succinct,

"Good-bye, Marcus, I hope you find what you are looking for too—and may God look after you."

Valerias just smiled a wry smile, mounted his horse, and turned down a street in Londinium. Joseph took his horse and walked away in the opposite direction.

Valerias wound his way through several streets to a shop a couple of miles from the pier. He unloaded the case containing the volumes of parchments that constituted his history and entered the shop.

"General Valerias, my old friend, I have been expecting you. I trust you had a good trip." The older man was sitting behind a desk in his shop.

"Yes, Bradicus, I did. The water was calm, and I was not eaten by a fish or captured by a mermaid. Please call me Marcus Augustus, as I do not want anyone to know of my presence in Britannia."

The two men talked for several hours. Bradicus had been a chief accountant for Jacob and retired several years ago. He moved to Londinium and opened a shop for copying and publishing documents. They reminisced about Jacob and discussed the state of the Empire in general and Britannia, specifically. Valerias believed the Empire was at a tipping point. Internal struggles and external pressures were squeezing the life of the Empire. The next few years would yield the future of Rome. Finally they got to the reason for Valerias' visit.

"I need you to make a complete copy of my parchments here. When done, send one set of documents to the chief librarian in Rome. I know the chief librarian, and he is expecting the documents and will know what to do with them. You may keep the other set here with you."

"It shall be done as you wish, General, I mean, Marcus. This will take several months to complete."

"Take your time and do it right. Just see that it is done. I trust you as I trusted Jacob."

That was the highest compliment Valerias could give, and it showed on Bradicus' face. "Thank you, General, Marcus, do not worry. I will complete your project."

Valerias took out a bag of coins and gave several to Bradicus, who objected about being paid for this work. Valerias cut him off. "Your family will appreciate this gift. As a bonus, Bradicus, I am giving you my horse. I believe your son would like a horse. In return, I want you to sew a small pouch to place this in the bottom of my tunic."

Valerias took off the signature Roman ring from his finger. "It goes with me everywhere and will continue to do so as I travel in your land. I don't want to forget Rome."

"Absolutely, General Valerias—er—Marcus." Bradicus took the ring and the tunic from Valerias and disappeared in a back room. Several minutes later he returned with a smile on his face. "You will not know it is here."

Valerias took the tunic, and the ring was indeed difficult to find. Bradicus had sewn a small inner pocket in the lower edge of Valerias' tunic. "Well placed. I know it is there, Bradicus. It is good as long as no one else knows it is there but me."

The men talked a little longer, and Bradicus brought some food out from a back room. They ate slowly, and afterward Valerias left the shop, pulled two satchels off his horse, and walked down the street alone as dusk approached.

Joseph walked through Londinium and felt free for the first time in over a year. There would be no general to serve or even to fear. It felt good to be free. And then he remembered all the people he had met who had become his friends, and the knowledge gained from his time with the Roman soldiers and even the General. He would take the good he had learned and apply it to his ministry. First, he thought he would enjoy his freedom. With that thought Joseph mounted his horse and rode out of Londinium to see an old friend at his church. *I will be walking soon enough*, he thought, *and it is becoming dark.*

XXXVIII

Desperation

Claire and her daughters were fast asleep, and Proterous was in a bind. He was a Roman physician and served both Roman soldiers and the local population—in that order. However, because he was quartered in an area with a large native population, he provided more daily care to civilians than soldiers. Proterous worked primarily out of his medical "building," also known as his hut, and through service calls. He also had quarters in the nearby Roman garrison.

Proterous' worry was that one of the local people would enter the hut and recognize Claire, and then they could be in substantial trouble. However, his concern for himself was superficial compared to his concern for Claire. Proterous was a skilled physician with a calm manner and a sense of humor. He was popular with the Romans who served in the area. If he were caught, Roman justice would be light. His likely punishment would be a transfer to another location outside Britannia, as the quality of his work was valued by Roman command. Also, the people he was hiding were not Roman deserters. Rome cared little for the locals and their petty quarrels, and many Roman soldiers and staff welcomed an exit out of Britannia.

For Claire, though, it was a different matter. Argus would undoubtedly take her and the girls and execute them as traitors. There was also the distinct possibility that they would be severely tortured before execution. That possibility weighed heavily on Proterous the most; he didn't want Claire and her daughters to be harmed.

Proterous was a heavyset man with a short clipped gray beard. He was not good at covering up a problem and he knew it. As a result, he could feel the perspiration accumulating on his back as he sat and watched Claire and the girls sleep, with dark thoughts on his mind.

Proterous conceived an idea while he sat. He would move Claire and her daughters to one of the separate rooms of the hut and announce to anyone that asked that the "person" in the room was a stranger being quarantined. Proterous knew that option was a short-term solution. The young girls and maybe Claire would have an issue being confined to a small room for very long period. His patients would also get suspicious about who was in the back room. However, this option would have to suffice for now.

Argus recalled Flavius when news spread that Claire and her daughters, Erik, and Mary, the chambermaid, had ridden to their deaths in the canyon. When Flavius rode through the gates of the castle, Argus immediately met him.

"Tell me, Flavius, is what I have heard true?" were the first words uttered by Argus.

"I spoke with the men who saw them fall into the chasm. It was a deep gorge, a deeply etched canyon, so I don't think there is any question that they perished in the fall. You don't need to worry about Claire any longer. You are the rightful king and I salute you. Hail, King Argus."

"It is truly amazing that I, Argus the King, must do all the thinking for my kingdom. Flavius, I am surprised that you of all people would return to me without proof verifying that they are dead."

"The men I spoke to have sworn to me that they saw Claire and her brood and the traitor, Erik, on the bridge, and that it gave way under their weight and collapsed into the canyon. It was well over one hundred feet to the bottom. There is no way they survived."

"Are you sure of that Flavius? Did anyone see their bodies at the bottom?"

"No, it was foggy and the bottom could not be seen. Besides, no one could have survived that fall."

"Take your sorry ass and return to that canyon, as you call it, and come back to me with proof they are all dead. Don't come back unless you know this as a fact, not speculation."

Flavius showed no emotion when given this order. He called for a fresh mount and one was brought to him. His saddle and supplies were already placed on the horse. It had been a tiring ride to the castle. Now he was back in the saddle.

As he was leaving the fort, he heard Argus call out, "Don't fail me, Flavius, or don't come back."

Flavius did not say a word. When he was out of earshot, he let out an ear-piercing scream. Afterward he gathered himself and rode to the nearest town. There, he found a group of six men in a local tavern.

The smallest man spoke to Flavius when he entered. "Lord Flavius, what did you hear from King Argus? Are we free to go back to our villages now?"

"Our new king has decided that our, or my, word isn't good enough. So no, no one is going back to their villages. You will be coming with me."

Flavius walked over to the bar and grabbed a mug of the thick beer served at the tavern. "We will return to the canyon and find our enemies' bones, bag them up, and then present them to Argus as proof they are dead."

There was much grumbling among the six men.

"Shut up. You all sound like you were assigned for a month's work doing latrine duty. Develop some backbone. We will ride back to the canyon that they fell into, and I will descend into the canyon depths and pick up what I can find. We will need to do so at noon, when the trolls are sleeping."

Flavius knew the men were superstitious, and he preyed on that fear. "Don't worry, it will be me who goes into the bottom of the canyon, not you. All you have to do is hold the rope that I will take to get to the bottom. I may need to climb up fast, if I should awaken a troll. Now take care of your horses and any supplies you need. We leave tomorrow at dawn."

Flavius left the crew and walked over to a boy who was waiting for him.

"You know what I want, don't you?

"Yes, Lord Flavius, I will take excellent care of your horse, like the gods would take care of their steeds."

"Good." With that word, Flavius tossed the boy a couple of coins and disappeared in a back room of the tavern. He took his off armor and boots and fell fast asleep on the bed. He hoped there were bones or some relics of the dead at the bottom of the gorge.

Claire and her daughters hid in Proterous' hut for one week. They were cool days with little sun. Every now and then a mist would douse any dryness left in the area. Gloom ruled the weather. It was warm in the hut, and Claire did not need to work hard to keep the girls inside and out of sight. Fortunately this was a period of little action, so the volume of soldiers needing aid was low. Civilian patients were also few. When he could, Proterous conducted his physician business outside of the hut. Claire and Proterous, when available, played games with the girls and told stories, but in whispers so as to not give notice to anyone passing by the hut that they were inside.

At the end of the week, Proterous rushed into his hut. He was out of breath, and perspiration was clearly evident on his face.

"Flavius and six men just rode in. They are looking to stay overnight at the inn down the road. You must be careful and quiet and discrete . . ."

"Yes, Proterous," Claire stopped him in mid-sentence. "We know what to do. The most important thing is for you to relax. You must not give any indication that there is something abnormal going on here. Flavius can sense things others cannot."

Claire's statement did not soothe Proterous, whose composure was now under vigorous attack.

Claire went up to him and took him by the hand to sit down. "We have come all this way, and we are not going to fail now. You have been like a rock to us and twice saved us. We need you to continue to be our rock. You can fool Flavius—I did it for over a year. I know that sometimes a physician must handle patients by playing with the truth. That is what we have here. I don't know if you will see Flavius, and if you do, remember you are the rock here, a stone that cannot be overturned, by Flavius or by anybody."

Claire continued to talk to Proterous, and he listened to her intently. He was calm now and focused on what he must do in the event he came into contact with Flavius, which didn't take long.

At about midnight, there was a knock on the door. Proterous' heart skipped several beats, and he anticipated about what was to happen. He first made sure Claire and her daughters were in the back room. Claire had her hands over each girl's mouth. He then slowly walked to the door and opened it. A tall, thin man with curly black hair stood before him. Proterous saw the sword dangling slightly on the man's left side.

"Good evening, Physician Proterous."

"Good evening to you as well," Proterous answered back. "Who are you and why are you awakening me from sleep in the middle of the night?"

"I am Flavius, senior military officer to Argus the King."

"And why are you here in my medical hut at this time?"

Flavius was never shy about saying his thoughts. "If you are asleep, why are you not in nightwear?"

"Oh, I was doing some paperwork." Proterous pointed to stack of papers on a desk. "And I fell asleep."

"I don't care about that. My problem is that I have traveled over 50 miles in two days. My legs are chafed badly, which causes me much pain when I ride. And I need to ride many more miles."

"Are you in pursuit of the brigands that haunt the woods outside of town?"

"No—we are looking for the former queen of Gerhard. She ran off and we are trying to find her. We need to reunite her with the new king, Argus, in an arranged marriage, if you will. Have you seen anyone traveling through this area with two small children in the last few days? There is a large reward for information leading me to them."

"We have many travelers through this area, but I haven't seen anyone that meets the description you just gave. Maybe the woods have them."

"Perhaps—it is rough country up there," Flavius said, pointing north.

Proterous was starting to sweat, and the more he tried to maintain his cool, the more perspiration he emitted.

"Physician Proterous, are you feeling well?"

"Oh, yes, sometimes I have night sweats, and this is one of those times."

"Can you help me, physician?" Flavius bluntly steered the conversation back to the subject of treating his sore thighs. The sores didn't look too abrasive to Proterous, and he wondered if Flavius was playing him. But Proterous pretended the sores were painfully bad and returned to his physician mode.

"I have something for you that should reduce and then cure your ailment. Of course, the best thing would be to take several days off from horse riding."

"That is not going to happen, physician."

Proterous nodded, walked over to a trunk, and pulled out two trays. He then reached in one of the trays and brought out a bottle. He squinted at the writing.

"I'm going to give you the entire bottle. I can get more." Proterous was trying to get Flavius out of the hut. He pulled out a clean cloth from a nearby drawer and then two longer pieces of cloth from another drawer. He shook the contents of the bottle onto the first cloth. He took the salve and rubbed it slowly into the small sores on Flavius' legs. Flavius never made a sound, but he stared at the wall that separated the physician's main room from where Claire and the girls were hiding.

When Proterous was finished, Flavius took the bottle and cloths and looked at Proterous in a way that caused the physician to sweat even more.

"I appreciate you treating me, physician. As a Roman you didn't have do this for me. I will give you adequate payment tomorrow. By the way, we leave tomorrow for the place where my men saw some traitors die. We will return hopefully tomorrow night or the next day. When we return, I will visit you for a check-up. I hope some of the clutter in your hut is cleaned up by then." Flavius paused for effect, and then added, "So I can sit more easily."

He then gave a quick glare at the wall protecting Claire and left the hut. A few minutes later, the sounds of Flavius giving orders and horses leaving the area outside the hut lingered in Proterous' and Claire's ears.

When Proterous was sure Flavius was gone, he opened the small cover to the room hiding Claire and her daughters.

"I have never met a man like that before," said a tense Proterous. "He is everything I heard about him. He also looks Roman to me."

"He is," answered Claire.

Proterous was unsure if Claire's response was for the first, second, or both statements. "I think we fooled him," he said hesitantly.

"No, we didn't, Proterous. He knew we were here before he even entered your hut. For some reason he seems to be protecting us, or at least guiding us somewhere. I just do not know. His message was clear though. We need to leave here at first light. Otherwise, Roman or not, you would be in danger if it is discovered that you were hiding us."

"I am not sure where you would go, though."

"I'm not sure, either, something to think about tonight. But tomorrow we must leave."

It was a restless night. Claire was awake, thinking about what they would do. She fell asleep at almost dawn and was awakened by Proterous.

"Claire, come quick, you have to see this."

Claire was still drowsy as Proterous took her to the door of his hut. Outside and tied to a rail was a large brown horse, complete with an enlarged saddle and satchels with supplies.

Attached to the front of the saddle was a note from Flavius that read, "Physician, thank you for your kindness last night. Here is a gift of gratitude. Be sure to use it well."

Proterous read the note and looked at Claire, "He left the horse for you."

Claire hurriedly awoke the girls. Dawn was starting to creep over the eastern horizon, and not a single person stirred in the village. Proterous helped each girl onto the horse. Claire gave Proterous a hug he would always remember, because its meaning was real. He handed her Flavius' note, and when he did so, he noted on the back was a sketch.

"He drew you a map of where you should go. I don't understand what has happened."

Claire mounted the horse and took the reins. She had Elizabeth in front and Anne behind her. "I don't either. It is ironic, our lives are in the hands of a brutal man who serves a ruthless king, a king who is sucking the life out of our land."

Claire left Proterous and rode down the streets of the village and out into the country covered by a dreary fog.

XXXIX

Contentment

Valerias traveled north by foot from Londinium to Durobrivae. He stayed off main roads and trails to avoid people. He didn't want to engage anyone, and he wanted to avoid any situation where he would be forced to face a gang of thugs. The first several days of his travels went exceptionally well. The weather was warm and dry except for a few stray showers. Vegetation was thick so he could camouflage himself from other travelers. Food was also plentiful. Valerias had learned the skill of selecting edible plants from his many campaigns, and he snared an occasional rabbit. He used fires only for cooking rabbit.

In his campaigns Valerias had looked at the land as a tool either to help his forces or to be used against the enemy. When he had to take grain and livestock from an area for his troops, he would give back the excess to the affected locals and would pay them for what he had confiscated. Valerias did not care for the idea of natives sabotaging his campaigns from behind, so he generously provided reimbursements. That way the locals would side with him and not the enemy. Alternatively, when he was in hostile territory, he used the "scorched-earth" approach. That way the enemy forces' supplies would be eliminated, resulting in the subsequent reduction of the effectiveness of that force.

One day he came across a deep pool of clear water in a secluded part of the forest. A natural dam created the backup of water that formed the pool. A small waterfall gently plunged into the pool. Valerias could not resist. He stripped off his clothes and climbed into the water. The water was refreshing. It was at the perfect temperature, where one could stay immersed for hours and not become chilled. He watched birds at first dart quickly around him, no doubt in primeval fear that he was a predator. After a time they relaxed their guard, and one even walked within inches of Valerias' hand.

Valerias was also fascinated by an insect trying to climb up the almost sheer face of rock on the side of waterfall. Several times it tried climbing up the wall only to reach a certain height and then fall down into the grass next to the waterfall. Valerias thought the bug lacked intelligence, but it was persistent. The bug reminded Valerias of himself, at least the persistence.

Valerias looked up to the sky. It was mostly blue except for a white cloud that morphed into a horse and then was gone. The sun was partially blocked by trees, as their strong limbs acted as arms that lifted their leaves into the heavens. Valerias thought of Joseph, *I wonder if he thinks Heaven is up there, in the sky? What a fool.*

He looked at his reflection in the pool. It didn't have the harshness of what he had observed in the creek a year ago. He smiled to himself. Valerias lay his head back on some soft grass that had grown on the edge of the pool. He was perfectly content with himself for the first time since he could remember. There were no responsibilities or cares to consider. No men to condemn or judge. Every part of his body was fully relaxed. The sun, light breeze, and water contributed to a feeling of pure contentment.

A thought then entered his mind and his brow formed a crease. He was a realist and knew this feeling of absolute contentment wouldn't last, and then what would happen? Life was so rarely this good that he thought few people could feel what he was experiencing at this moment. He knew it would end and soon, and he was right. He pulled himself from the pool, air-dried his body, put on his clothes, grabbed his belongings, and headed north back on the trail he was following.

XL

Awakening

Joseph, like Valerias, found the first few days of his journey north to be quiet and with good weather. Joseph had always liked the sun and the warmth it brought to the Earth. He remembered that on cloudy, cool days his mood could match the weather. This was not the case on the trip so far. Joseph knew that maintaining an even-tempered personality would be important if he was going to be a good Christian and priest.

Joseph didn't want to travel alone for any part of the trip. He also wanted to stay on the main roads, which had been constructed by the Romans many years ago. When he left Londinium, he noticed a group of merchants also traveling north. He asked them if he could join them and they agreed. The merchants thought a pleasant priest would be good company. They didn't want a sullen priest who would spend the travel time lecturing them on the ways one could end up in Hell. They were correct about Joseph's personality.

On the fifth day of the travels, the sun was particularly warm and Joseph's disposition was equally sunny. The landscape they traveled through was bright, the road was in good condition, and the woods, when they closed in on the road, didn't seem foreboding. Joseph led his traveling companions in a medley of songs as they sauntered down the road in no real hurry to get to their various destinations. Alcoholic beverages were also consumed, which helped make the singing sound even better—to the drinkers. Not only could he sing, Joseph found out he could be a good storyteller as well.

Joseph and his companions occasionally encountered squads of Roman cavalry, which added to their feelings of security. However, the patrols gradually dropped off, and they began seeing armed vigilantes who were providing security for a price. These ruffian types were also looking for a small band of traitors who had fled a warlord named Argus. The vigilantes harassed the merchants with questions about whom and what they had seen on the road. The payment of gold eased the pressure from these rogues. Other groups ignored the presence of Joseph's group entirely, like they were ghosts.

At the end of the fifth day, the group reached a village and found an inn to lodge in for the night. During supper the landowner told Joseph and his merchant friends about Claire and her escape from Argus. The landowner superficially supported Argus, but on a deeper level Joseph could tell the man had a great dislike for Argus. They had now entered the territory controlled by Argus. Although Rome still had a presence in the area, it was Argus who exerted real power.

The next day Joseph's group woke to early morning showers, which diminished into a cool mist. As they left the village, they encountered a Roman patrol. One of the merchants was apprehensive of his situation and bribed the Romans to escort him to another village several miles to the north. The rest of the group followed that man's initiative and chipped in money. Joseph only had a few coins, and he did not want to use them unless absolutely necessary—which did not include this situation. Because he was a priest and good company, the merchants paid for Joseph's way.

As they made their way north, Joseph could tell there was a change in the countryside, and not all of it was weather related. The ground vegetation looked like someone had just sat on it and there was no energy left for the plants to bounce back. The people they encountered appeared to have no life. They were a cheerless lot, and Joseph found it depressing trying to talk to them. Joseph was glad to have the Romans as an escort. He changed his mind and gave the Roman captain one of his few coins.

Two days later Joseph, the merchants, and Romans reached the village that was the final destination of the first merchant who had paid for the Roman escort. That village and villages that they had passed through earlier in the day gave an impression of thorough depression. Joseph, who had been lost in his thoughts for much of the day, awoke to overhear one of the soldiers say this village was called Bergen. This is the village where Joseph's friend and fellow priest, Brother Timothy, had been stationed.

Joseph inquired from a villager, "Where is Brother Timothy?"

"Brother Timothy," the villager responded and spit at the same time, "left the village weeks ago. He said he had business elsewhere, but we know he wanted to escape from our wretched plight. A dedicated man of God," the villager said with biting sarcasm—particularly felt by Joseph.

"Do you mean the rule of Argus is wretched?"

"No. I said nothing about King Argus, long may he reign."

The villager's statement was made with the same enthusiasm as one about to take an ice bath. All around the village despair hung like the mist. Joseph observed that the clothing worn by villagers was a dark shade of drab. The villagers shuffled as they moved about, and there was little talking among them. Joseph had never before seen people with so little hope, but surprisingly he did not feel pity for them.

The merchant who wanted to travel to this village said he no longer needed to be there. The Roman squad shortly completed its business in the village and was ready to head north, out of the area ruled by Argus. In a repeated scene every merchant added to the coffers of the soldiers so that they could stay with the Romans. The perceived or real risk of staying in the village or traveling without an armed escort was too much for these men. The Romans provided a real feeling of security.

Joseph stood by his horse as the Romans and merchants mounted their horses.

"Are you coming with us, Joseph?" One of the merchants asked.

The Roman captain also motioned for Joseph to get on his horse. Joseph had made many friends in the short time they had been together, and there was concern in the group about Joseph's hesitation.

There are times in life when a person reaches a crossroad. In this case Joseph's choices on that crossroad were simple. He could go forward in the physical sense with his friends. If he chose this route, no one would question his thinking, and in the short run he might be better off. The alternative was that he could stay and take over Brother Timothy's role. This choice was a spiritual one. As he weighed his decision of physical or spiritual options, Joseph thought about his life, about his religion, and about his time with General Valerias.

Joseph thanked the Romans and merchants for their concern for his well-being and for taking him to the village of Bergen. He believed he was being called to this village and that he would stay and do what he could to help. He knew his decision created a substantial risk, and he might die for that decision. For the first time in his life, Joseph believed he was doing what was the perfect action for him.

The Roman said something about coming back this way and checking up on him. He noted the merchants would likely be traveling with him when he returned. Several of the merchants nodded as the Roman captain spoke. Then they departed and soon were out of sight. Joseph felt alone, but he also felt an inner strength that he had never felt. The villager he had initially talked to had started to walk away.

"Villager, I am Father Joseph. I have come to take Brother Timothy's place. Can you take me to his church?" Joseph didn't like to be called "Brother." "Father" seemed more appropriate.

They slowly walked up a road and then onto a side street. On the left was a wooden building in serious disrepair. The villager pointed to the building. "There is the church, or what was the church."

Joseph looked at the church and then at the villager. "Thank you, what is your name?"

"Names aren't important in these times. 'Villager' is fine with me."

"Very well, Villager, is there an inn where I can stay in the village until I can get my church rebuilt, cleaned and organized?"

The Villager pointed to a small building just down the street from the church. "They sometimes rent rooms. They probably will for you."

Joseph turned around to look at the church. *This is going to take much work*, he smiled to himself. He turned back to ask the Villager another question, but he was already gone. *May not see him again* was Joseph's next thought. He went inside the church. Essentially just the frame of the building still stood. It appeared most its contents had vanished, most likely by robbery. It was a small building that could not have held many parishioners. Joseph started to form ideas on what he could do to get the church back into providing Christianity and, hopefully, the business of saving souls.

When he turned around from the entrance, he was face to face with a young woman. She was covered in splotches of dirt and grime, which seemed to be the attire of most villagers he had seen. Joseph could tell that she had brown hair and green eyes, and underneath the filth she was an attractive woman.

"I am Ruth," she said before Joseph could say a word. "I am here to help you, because you will need it."

Joseph nodded and said, "I am Father Joseph. Your help will be appreciated."

Ruth left the church, saying she would return shortly. For the first time in over a year, Joseph fell to his knees and prayed. It was a prayer of thanks for having survived the past year and, more importantly, a prayer to help guide him through what was to come.

XLI

DECEPTION

Flavius was satisfied with himself as they left Proterous' village about what he had secretly accomplished with Claire. However, he was highly irritated with Argus' demand of returning to the place where Claire, Erik, and the daughters supposedly had died. As he rode in silence, he thought to himself that Argus was nothing except a moron with a crown who had the intelligence of a mad dog. Without him Flavius thought Argus would not last long. He was tired of being tied to Argus. Yet he had no feasible alternative. He thought of Mary and wanted to be with her much more than with the thugs who rode behind him.

Flavius and his men periodically stopped on the way to the gorge of Claire's death site. It appeared to the men that the farther away from Argus they were, the more Flavius' personality seemed to lighten. Flavius brought out a large flask of some type of spirit, and the men drank its contents.

Flavius began to ask questions. None of the questions pertained to Claire and her group. Instead Flavius focused on the potential presence of fierce wild animals and the trolls in the steep canyon. Had the men ever seen evidence of trolls? Were strange sounds coming from the gorge after Claire fell in? Did they think trolls and possibly even ogres inhabited the rocky areas around the canyon? What about the stories of a man who could turn into a wolf at night and savagely slay all those it encountered?

Flavius' men grew edgier as they drank and he talked. They started asking the questions. Had he (Flavius) ever seen a troll? Answer: "Yes." Had he ever killed a troll? Answer: "No." Do they ever eat humans? Answer: "Yes. They particularly like the flesh of men because they are more muscular. Sometimes they will take a woman captive to be a slave." How strong are trolls? Answer: "Strong enough to break a deer in two with one quick snap of the wrists."

The men were clearly already cautious regarding trolls, but this dialogue with Flavius on the matter sent them into a near panic.

One man spoke. "We think we can just go to that canyon, take a quick look down, and then leave that enchanted place. If we all stick to that story, how will Argus know what we did and saw?"

Several grunts approving this approach were heard from the men. Flavius looked at the men with a sympathetic eye. He had them right where he wanted them.

"I hear you, but Argus wants us to do more than just look. Since I am the leader of this group, I will descend into the canyon and see for myself if there are any remains left of Claire and her allies. I will want two ropes lowered so several of you can pull me up in case I locate a troll or, more importantly, in case he sees me. I do not want to be skewered and cooked, so you men will need to be at your strongest."

The men were more than happy to oblige Flavius' great sacrifice.

As they rode closer to the canyon, the atmosphere shifted. It was now definitely cooler with a slight breeze. Fog slowly rose from places that one would not expect fog to appear. It covered the trail in spots and caressed the rocks and trees on the sides of the trail.

Flavius' men were on full alert. Several men drew their swords, and some men carried spears now at the ready. It appeared to these men a repeat of the events when they pursued Claire. The gorge and its surroundings appeared to be enchanted.

The gloom became worse as they arrived at the edge of the canyon. The fog at the former bridge lifted up a little and then down again. Even Flavius was becoming apprehensive. *What an eerie place,* he thought to himself. Flavius looked at the remnants of the old wooden rope bridge that once had allowed persons and their belongings to cross the canyon. He thought it had been a long time since the bridge had seen any maintenance. Flavius dismounted and peered down into the gorge. He saw nothing but fog that stood as a stationary guard toward the bottom. Flavius' men had dismounted and were looking at the canyon. They were all standing a little further back from the edge than Flavius. Everyone was listening for sounds, especially the sounds of trolls. Unfortunately, no one knew the sounds made by trolls.

Flavius ordered the men to remove ropes from the horses. Two sets of ropes were tied to trees. Flavius wanted to make sure there was enough rope so he had the men measure out well over one hundred feet of rope on each line.

When the ropes were secure, Flavius asked the men if there were any volunteers to accompany him down into the canyon. A groaning sound came from somewhere in the upper part of the canyon. A light mist covered in fog drifted around the bridge and the men. Flavius' men were fully convinced the area was haunted. As Flavius had predicted, there were no volunteers.

Flavius took a large canvas bag, secured his sword, and descended into the chasm. One minute the men could see him, and the next he was immersed in the fog and gone from sight. Flavius' descent down the canyon took several minutes. Finally he reached the floor, which was very uneven. Boulders intermixed with smaller rocks were strewn throughout the floor. A small creek with a flow that had a hard time pushing a leaf downstream was situated on one side of the canyon bottom. Opportunistic scrub plants found locations on the rough floor where they pried their way through the rocks and gave a stunted presentation. It was very quiet.

Flavius was neither a superstitious nor a religious man, but this place was something he had never seen before and was truly eerie. In response to this uncomfortable feeling, Flavius drew his sword. He started to see images deep in the fog or was it his imagination? He knew that if he stayed at the bottom of the canyon for much longer, he would become part of what he was seeing. He quickly made his way over the rocks looking for one thing—the body of Erik. Flavius knew that Erik was here and that Claire, her daughters, and Mary were not. It wasn't long before he found what was left of a human skeleton. He thought that there might have been some flesh left on the bones, but all flesh had been removed. Additionally, the skeleton was not whole. The bones were scattered about. Flavius also saw bones from the horses. He gathered up the skull and several bones from Erik and small bones from the horses as quickly as he could.

Another groan-like sound came from upstream along the canyon walls. Under normal conditions, Flavius knew the sound was from a natural source. However, this was an unnatural situation. As he turned to the ropes along the wall, he stumbled over some debris. When he jerked his foot loose, Flavius pulled out a mass of an old skeleton. The skull was still attached to what was left of the rest of the body. The eye sockets of the skull were looking at Flavius like someone who was telling him that it would be good to join him in death.

It took every bit of his self-control for Flavius not to let out a scream. He knew if he did scream, his already frightened men would run away from this place. He then could be stuck forever in this most horrible of places and end up like this skeleton mass.

Flavius regained his composure. He added the skull and bones from the mass into the bag. This skeleton had been at the bottom for some time. Flavius wondered about the story of this skeleton. It was a fleeting thought.

Flavius tied the bag of the remains onto one of the ropes and gave the rope a tug. There was no movement on the bag. Flavius gave the rope a strong pull this time. Shortly thereafter someone up at the top began pulling up the bag. Flavius looked around for signs of other bodies but did not see one. He thought he saw a large image huddled behind a boulder in the fog. The image was close to him. He thought he saw it move, but not in a particular direction. Flavius' heart had started to beat faster as he began this mission on the canyon floor; now it raced even faster. He no longer could reason well. Was his mind playing tricks on him, or was what he was seeing real? He didn't care to answer his own question.

Flavius sheathed his sword quickly as he tied the rope around his midsection with a loop going around his right shoulder. He gave a hard tug and his men began pulling him upward. He climbed to the top as quickly as possible. When Flavius reached the top, his men were waiting for him. Sighs of relief were heard. They were elated that it was a live Flavius and not a half-eaten, dead Flavius, or worse, a troll. One of the first questions the men asked was whether Flavius had seen a troll. Flavius wasn't sure if he had, and he told the men that conclusion. This time he was truthful, he wasn't playing the men. One of the men offered Flavius a drink, and he took a deep draw from the flask.

"Anybody else want to go there and confirm my findings?" Flavius said as he pointed to the canyon floor. "I swear it is haunted with the dead."

No one offered an affirmative response, and Flavius then added, "Let's go."

They all quickly mounted their horses and rode out of the area of the canyon as fast as anyone could leave the place. The return to Argus' castle was accomplished in near-record time. The men stopped only as long as needed to rest the horses and grab some food. They avoided any tavern along the way, and Flavius did not stop in the village where Proterous was stationed.

Argus was not waiting at the gate for Flavius this time when he returned to the castle, so Flavius dismounted and took the bag of bones up to Argus' sitting chambers. The rest of the men took their horses to a stable and then hurried to a tavern. They wanted to tell anyone who would listen what they had seen and heard.

"I saw you return," Argus started out. "I trust you had success this time."

"Enough to confirm they are dead."

"I see you brought evidence of the dead bitch. Show me."

Flavius undid the bag and dumped the bones on the floor. The two skulls fell out last.

"I thought there were four or five people in Claire's party?"

"We know there were four, King Argus, however, these two skulls were all I could locate. I think animals took the others and some of their bones."

"We are still missing at least two skulls, Flavius."

"I did not want to mention this, but I saw what I thought was a troll. He was watching me while I searched for the bodies in the fog. I didn't want to be meat for the troll. As you know, I don't fall for superstitious beliefs or supernatural myths. But I tell you as I stand here there was something evil about that place. The men believe it is haunted. You are welcome to enter the canyon with me and we can see what is left to find. Just know neither of us could kill a troll."

Flavius knew Argus was very much afraid of what he couldn't see. He also knew that Argus, himself, would not want to go to the canyon.

"No, I take your word. Wrap up the bones and bury them somewhere out and away from the castle's walls. I never want to talk of this matter again."

"Yes, King Argus. Celebrate the fact that the witch, Claire, is dead and will not be a bother to you. It is time now for us to move forward and consolidate your rule."

"Of course, that is what we shall do. By the way, I retained a man to share your position as my chief general and counselor. His name is Morguard. Now there shall be two of you."

Flavius was taken completely by surprise. "Why are there now two of us when I was managing very well with what needs to be done?"

"Because, the job has become too much for you, Flavius. Look how you failed the first time in bringing me proof of the bitch's demise. And then I had to send you back. Don't worry, though, there is more than enough for you two to do."

"It is yours to decide what to do and who should do it. I just obey your orders, King Argus. I would like to take my leave now to bury the bones and take a rest. Maybe two people doing my position's duties is a good idea."

After Argus dismissed him, Flavius gathered up the bones and buried them outside the castle in a grove of trees. Later he joined the men who had traveled with him at a nearby tavern and drank until he was drunk.

XLII

Mary

The map Flavius drew for Claire was remarkably clear. She was to travel on a side road to another village called Abrador about thirty miles to the north. She initially encountered few travelers, and these were of questionable merit. She became worried when two in particular appeared to be following her. By luck or good fortune, a Roman patrol came by and invited her to travel with them to the village Claire sought. She gave the Roman leader made-up names for her and her daughters and told him a story that they were on their way to visit a friend in the village. Both Anne and Elizabeth had been through this drill before, and this ruse worked again.

The Roman gave Claire a short lecture about traveling alone on this road with young children. Argus, the new leader of this land, was a cruel despot, and by his actions, he had created an entire new underclass of impoverished people that looked to steal or rob anything that wasn't tied down. Claire and her daughters would be ideal targets. She already knew what the Roman was advising, but she kindly accepted his suggestions. As she listened to him, Claire thought that since leaving the castle, the entire trip undertaken by her had been a huge risk.

When they arrived at the village, the Romans went on their way and Claire asked a townsperson the way to the end mark on the map. After traveling a hundred yards to the west, through a scattering of huts and brick houses, they arrived at their destination. The house where they stopped was larger than most of those in the village. They dismounted, tied the horse to a post, and knocked at the strong wooden door. Claire had no idea what awaited them inside. She was still wary of Flavius, and yet she had a strong undercurrent of trust in his actions. She was very tired, though, and essentially sleepwalking through the motions. She simply put all her trust that who or whatever was behind the door was not the enemy but a friend who would help them. She said a silent prayer to herself: *Please let this be good.*

A minute later the door opened and it was Mary, Claire's former chambermaid. Without hesitation, Mary looked past them, pulled the three travelers inside, and quickly closed the door. She then looked Claire straight in the eyes and after a brief pause gave Claire a massive hug similar to one given to a long-lost relative or friend. She then embraced each girl.

"Claire, it is so good to see you! You made it. And you too, Anne and Elizabeth. I have thought of you often and prayed to God that you would be all right and make it safely here. It is God's will." Mary had tears in her eyes.

"I'm not sure what God you are referring to," Claire responded. "I am so glad to see you also."

After weeks of hard arduous travel, Claire had finally reached a place where she could finally let her guard down, and she too started to weep. However, she quickly caught herself, as she would not allow herself to cry in the presence of her daughters. This was a sign of weakness.

After Claire regained full control, she asked Mary, "How did you come to this place?"

"It's either Flavius' house or a friend's house, I don't know for sure. The family that normally stays here is on a long-term diplomatic mission at the request of the Roman general in charge of Britannia. I was retained to keep the estate clean and free of vagrants that seem to be everywhere these days. Argus has ruined your husband's kingdom."

"Yes, he has, but what of your . . ." Claire paused. "Flavius. I do not understand his motives. Twice now, maybe more, he has saved us from certain death or I think even worse—capture. I have thought as Argus' chief enforcer—Flavius' actions are worse than what Argus does."

"You will not believe this, but Flavius does have good inside him. Yes, he has done very bad things. He has to stay alive. Argus can have him killed as easily as any of his subjects. You must understand this—he has no intention of hurting you or the girls. He would be much happier fighting the Saxons or Picts than acting as the schoolyard bully for Argus. You do what you must do to survive."

"Then why doesn't he just kill Argus and end the charade?"

"Well, the primary reason is that he has done bad things that have created many enemies. Argus does have his supporters, and if Flavius should slay Argus, then that creates another class of persons who would want to kill him. There would be a long line of potential executioners for him and no support. Remember, Flavius is also Roman, and that does not sit well with the native Britons."

"What about me or Eustice taking the crown and pardoning him?"

"He thinks that is too dangerous. If you pardon him, there may be a revolt, and such a revolt may be led by the remnant supporters of Argus' rule or by enemies of Argus and Flavius. Many people view Argus and Flavius as one and the same. Whether he is helping you to somehow save his own life or because he is actually good, I like to think the latter. He has always treated me very well."

At that moment, Claire felt exhaustion take over her mind and body. "Where can we rest?"

"You will stay with me for several weeks' time. After that, a trusted man will take you west to Eustice. Flavius will pay him very well to successfully complete this task, even more money than is on your head as a bounty."

Claire was shown to a back bedroom. There she and the girls went instantly asleep for almost a full day.

XLIII

Seeds of Terror

The brothers were pleased with the development of their fledgling empire up to this point. Dimondes was no longer a problem. Jutikes, their handpicked leader of several tribes of outlying Huns, was settling into his role as the unsuspecting doormat for the brothers. It was time to begin the move west into the land of the Goths and eventually into the Roman Empire. Uldric and Rao called for a war council. Also present were Produgas, Jutikes, Borgas, and several other chiefs from the Hun tribes. Representatives from several Alan tribes were also present.

"It has come to our attention," Uldric started the council meeting, looking at Rao, "that our Roman enemies have titles for their chiefs. We want to do the same. Rao, tell us what you have found out."

"Romans have Emperors who are supreme leaders. We don't have one of these, and we don't want an Emperor or even co-emperors. They do have a number of officer ranks. I don't fully understand what these are and their purposes. For instance, they have generals, tribunes, and centurions, and many different levels within each rank. We don't want that either. So we have decided to divide our ranks as follows. Uldric and I will be co-master generals. Jutikes, Produgas, and Borgas will be given the title of general."

Rao added one more name to be general: Oxanos. Then Rao listed several names to the rank of sub-generals, which included both Huns and Alans. He promised an Alan would be selected as a general, should the Alans join the Huns. Each general was given a name for the tasks he would be responsible for carrying out. For example, Produgas was the General of Intelligence. Borgas was General of the Cavalry. Jutikes was co-General of the Alans. Oxanos was the general responsible for various logistic tasks. Each general would have Hun and Alan troops assigned to him.

The real power, though, rested with the brothers. Their objective was to have the leaders of the tribes gather under the Hun banner of Uldric and Rao. At the same time the brothers felt it was important for the generals and sub-generals, and, most important, their troops to be a part of the effort. That way there would also be less chance or desire for a rebellion. The plan worked, at least initially.

At the end of the council meeting, Rao gave each of the four generals the names of their sub-generals. The sub-generals were to be known as pro-generals. This was a symbolic gesture to help key personnel feel part of the leadership group and, thus, become allies. The tasks assigned to each general and his pro-generals were suitable to them and would best help the brothers' cause. For example, the brothers thought it would be difficult to manage the Alans with the Hun general, Jutikes, so they chose an Alan leader named Turkson to be co-general. It was up to each general to discuss with his pro-generals the organization established by the brothers and what was expected of each man and his unit.

Afterward the generals and pro-generals attended a second meeting with the brothers. Uldric and Rao went over their future plans at the meeting, including a schedule highlighted with plan milestones.

At the meeting Rao stated bluntly, without warning, "We leave in three weeks, so prepare now. We don't know how long we will be gone, so say goodbye to your wives, concubines, families, goats, whomever or whatever, because we may be away from here for over a year."

Uldric added, "We want to take a supply unit that is as small as possible. We want to travel fast and live off the land. That is why we are traveling without wives or children."

In just those sentences Uldric was becoming excited about their mission, and he continued, "We are no longer a bunch of backwater tribes that others look down on." Uldric looked at Jutikes as he said that. "We are no longer children. We have grown up. Now it is time to show that we are men. Zestras has given us a challenge to complete, and complete it we shall. Now we are on the fringe of embarking on that task. We will ride to the outskirts of the Roman capital and put the fear of Hell into the Romans. When we return victorious, we will join Zestras and move against the Romans at Constantinople and take that city. All plunder, whether taken alive or not alive, will belong to your men. It is time for the Hun nation—with our friends, the Alans—to rise up and be included with the Persians and Romans as the greatest Empires on the Earth!"

As Uldric finished his last sentence, he was in full lather, only to be brought down by words from Oxanos.

"We only have twenty thousand men. To get to Rome, as you indicated our target to be, we need to go through the land of the Goths and then armies of Rome. Each one can field over one hundred thousand men."

Uldric tried to show patience even though it was rare for him. "You will see, Oxanos. Our fighters are better than their fighters, and we have surprise on our side. We want to first set the

Goth world on fire and spread panic so that they flee to their fortresses instead of engaging with us. We are not going to lay siege to any fort or walled city. That takes too much time and lives. They will be so pleased that we did not attack their city that they will leave us alone. We will make deals with other Goths and not attack them if they too leave us alone. I think the image of fire raining down on their heads will take care of the Goths. Maybe some Goths will march under our banners. Also, from our intelligence I understand that Persia is currently weak and the Western Roman Empire is in disarray. Constantinople is afraid of us."

Uldric was interrupted by a pro-general who appeared more knowledgeable about the lands to the west than either Uldric or Rao. "My Goth spies told me of the Roman army centered in the area by the Danube. Should we get through the Goths, we will have to face this army. We hear a Roman general named Valerias commands it. He has a reputation that cannot be overlooked, and he will not go down easily. And if we defeat him, we will not have the forces necessary to defeat the other Roman armies sent against us."

Uldric looked directly at Rao and said, "Your concern is well taken, pro-general. However, Produgas has given us the information that we need to initiate our advance late this spring. This General Valerias you speak of has retired and disappeared."

"What about his pro-generals?" the same man asked.

"They have been sacked. Valerias' command has been taken over by a weak officer named Trojax. Valerias will not be a problem. See, our intelligence is very capable of finding out what we need to know."

From there the discussion was free flowing. Everyone felt excitement about the coming hunt. The beginning of the campaign produced positive attitudes that were contagious in the camp. No one had yet experienced casualties, physical hardships, mental trauma, or financial concerns. Victory seemed assured. In a huge moment for the brothers, the Alans agreed to join the Huns—provided the Alan chief, Turkson, was confirmed as a general. Rao agreed to this request.

Rao tasked each Hun and Alan unit to develop its own name. Several suggestions were promoted, including the Dragon, the Serpent, the Eagle, and others. Rao was pleased with the names, primarily because it would be a source of pride for the unit. He particularly liked the name advocated by Produgas—the "Death Chasers." The symbol would be a skeleton with a cape tacked to its head. The cape showed effects of being wind driven to symbolize the movement of the Hun/Alan forces as they moved west. *A perfect symbol for our campaign,* he thought. Once the designs for the standards were chosen, the village blacksmiths created the original standards that would be kept at the front of each unit in the coming days.

The few weeks to prepare for a year's campaign seemed like the wind quickly rushing down a mountainside valley. On the day of the departure, all the Northern Hun warriors were assembled outside the camp of Uldric and Rao. There were at least twenty thousand men, and most were cavalry. Uldric and Rao led the procession out of the camp and to the west. Once the warriors were free of the camp, the pace quickened.

The first few days were uneventful. The main units of the cavalry could not proceed as fast as desired because the supply wagons and their supporting infantry were loaded down and traveled slowly. They rode without incident by several villages and farms that were Sarmatian and not hostile to the Huns. Several Sarmatian units even joined the Huns. Finally they arrived at the gates of the first fortified city that was not friendly to the Hun forces, an eastern Goth city.

The leader of the city had heard of the Hun approach and prepared the city's defenses for an assault. It never came, at least initially. The Huns requested a parley with the city's mayor, and he reluctantly agreed. The meeting occurred just outside the gates of the city. Rao, two bodyguards, and an interpreter represented the Huns, and the mayor with a contingent of guards acted on behalf of the city. The mayor was a tall, thin man about sixty years old. He had a dark beard that appeared dyed and a thin moustache. His most notable feature was a large, dark mole just off of his right nostril. Rao couldn't take his eyes off the mole. The mayor's eyes darted around like a moth trying to escape a bird, so Rao knew he was nervous.

Rao presented the terms for the city's surrender. The city would be spared if it provided the Hun forces with substantial supplies of food, gold, livestock, and one hundred men to be used in a support service role to the Hun/Alan warriors. Rao thought this was a reasonable request.

The mayor did not, though. He forcefully declined Rao's offer and pointed up to the battlements. "We have repulsed larger forces than yours. We can defeat you too."

He then invited the Huns to ride off into the distance and leave the city alone. The mayor made no insulting or inflammatory remarks. He simply said the short meeting was over, and he and his contingent went back inside the walled city. After the door closed, Rao returned to the command tent where Uldric was waiting.

"He is scared of us, brother, but the fortress is impressive. We cannot take it without major casualties. I suggest we move on as we have before. The main Goth camps are what we want to save our resources for. These people will not bother us." Rao was hoping that his brother would agree.

"I agree, brother," Uldric added nonchalantly. "We camp here tonight and then in the morning move west deep into the land of the Goths."

Rao did not know that his brother had initiated a secret operation. Days before the Hun arrival at the gates of the city, Uldric had sent a half dozen Alan spies into the city. Alans were frequent visitors to the city, so the arrival of six new Alans was not scrutinized by the local security. Inside the city Alans found and bribed other non-native city occupants to learn about back entrances to the city. Surprisingly, penetration was accomplished with only minor effort. A grate that blocked a storm water and sewer outlet from the city was easily removed out of eyesight of the guards on the fortresses' walls.

Deep into the night Uldric sent a force of over fifty Huns into the sewer system. The sewer tunnel was large enough to accommodate only one man at a time, so the men had to walk single file. The tunnel was dark, the walls slimy, and there was a powerful smell. The Huns hurried through it. The men followed a rope left inside the tunnel by an insider; the sewer gas and its explosive potential prohibited the use of torches. Several points in the city could be accessed from the various branches of the sewer system. The Hun commander of the force inside the sewer, however, decided they should emerge only from one location instead of several, and that location was inside a stable. The Alan spies quickly dispatched the few guards inside the stable.

After the stable area was secured, the Hun strike force entered the stable from the sewer line. From there they quickly made their way to a secondary gate that was known to only a small segment of the city's population. The main gates were too heavily guarded to be breeched. Thus the secondary gate became the target.

The secondary gate was lightly guarded, and these guards were quickly killed. The Huns quietly lifted the gate. Uldric had massed a large force of the Huns and Alans close to the gate but at such a distance that they could not be detected from the city's walls and battlements. The Huns inside the city quickly moved to the city's main gate to distract the city's security away from the open secondary gate.

Rao had been asleep, but the commotion around his tent woke him up. When he went outside the tent, he was surprised and highly annoyed at what was before his eyes. It did not bother him that they were trying to take the city; instead what truly irked him was that Uldric had not consulted or even briefed him about the attack. Rao was angry, and he started to briskly walk toward the city's main gate where he thought Uldric's forces were centered. At that moment he heard a great yell off to his right. A thousand-member Hun force rushed the secondary gate. Resistance from the city forces proved light at first, then grew steadily heavier as the breech in the gate was discovered.

It was too late. The city fell within hours. The Huns showed no restriction on degree of violence they exerted on the city's population. Men, women, children, and even animals that were not of high value to the Huns were slaughtered. Everywhere people pleaded for mercy, with none given. Men were disemboweled in front of wives, women were raped and then killed in front of their children, and the children impaled on sharpened posts. The level of savagery was unmatched in terms of time and locale of the city. Uldric led the assault on the city, and at the end his entire body was covered in the blood of his victims. The Alans and even many of the Huns were uneasy with the overwhelming gore they had inflicted on the city.

Several prisoners were found in the city's dungeons. Uldric promptly killed two of the prisoners and then asked the remainder if they would join his army. They all replied yes and were given weapons, and they too committed violence on the population that had imprisoned them. Several of the former prisoners later deserted the Hun force as it marched west.

As the slaughter began to wind down, Uldric left the city for the Hun camp. There he found an incensed Rao.

Rao sharply marched up to Uldric and gave him a hard blow to the face. "Do you feel better, brother?"

Uldric staggered back but did not fall to the ground. He pulled himself up and drew his sword. "You attacked me, brother—without cause—and now you shall pay the highest price for your actions!"

Rao already had his sword drawn and was ready for battle with his brother. His crimson face bespoke his rage. "I did not agree to undertake our mission so that we could spend time butchering women and children and old men. Look at you! You are a disgrace! You are to be a leader—not a blood-soaked monster!"

Uldric was now in full rage too and he shouted, "And now I shall add you as part of my bloodied self!"

The two men rushed at each other and were about to strike blows when several Hun warriors grabbed both from behind. Weapons were taken from both Uldric and Rao and they were forced to sit down. Both men hurled curses at each other like air daggers embalmed with fire, and also at the men who were holding them. After a few minutes the energy that had propelled Uldric and Rao against each other began to subside.

Between the two men a familiar figure walked in, Produgas. He looked at Uldric and Rao in a slow motion gaze and then spoke. "We just secured a great victory."

Rao started to protest; however, Produgas continued undeterred, looking at Rao. "I understand that our action didn't need to yield the result that we just witnessed."

Produgas pointed to the city. "I understand your concern, Rao, but what was done is done. We can't go back and undo what just happened. So we take what happened and use it to our advantage. We want to use this episode to frighten all who stand in our way. We will send our Alan spies to the Goth villages, cities, and lands to the west, and they will tell the stories of what happened here today. I think you will see panicked populations, which will add to our reputation. We want as little resistance and casualties as possible until we hit the Romans."

Both Uldric and Rao looked at Produgas as if he was claiming leadership of their army.

"Don't worry, brothers, I have no aspiration to be the leader and take your places. However, any more fights, or if one of you kills the other, we will have another council meeting to determine whether either of you is fit to be our leader. Release them."

Uldric and Rao were set free, and both men put their swords in their sheaths. Neither man said a word, and they walked away in opposite directions.

As Uldric and Rao left the area, a pro-general spoke to Produgas, "Perhaps you should be our leader. I don't know if we can trust them to carry out our mission without first destroying each other."

Produgas responded brusquely, "Put those words away like they did their swords. That is treason. Until they show us they are unfit to lead, they will be our leaders."

Another pro-general had a question. "If they were to fight each other, who would win?"

Produgas replied, "Uldric is bigger and more forceful and bloodthirsty. However, Rao may have better skills as a fighter, and he is clever and patient. It all depends on the day. We need to keep watch on both of them. It would be such a waste to lose either of them before we begin our campaign against the Romans. Whether you think the pillage of the city today was good or bad, one thing is clear, from here on out the seeds of terror have been sown. We just need to nurture them to fruition."

That night Produgas met Braga in the woods outside camp. Produgas updated Braga on the day's events, including the destruction of the city and the near fight between Rao and Uldric. Afterward Braga returned and informed his father, Zestras, of what had occurred at the city. Zestras was pleased. One or both of the brothers would die fighting each other, and then either the Goths or the Romans would crush them. He, Zestras, would be left to pick up the pieces of the short-lived Northern Hun empire. Zestras was a schemer, and so far his plan was working perfectly.

The next morning the Huns proceeded to burn and raze the city. When they were done, there was nothing left but rubble and smoldering wastes. The Huns moved westward. As they moved out and away from the city, Uldric never looked back; his focus was to the west. Rao, who had not spoken to his brother since their altercation, could not take his eyes off the ravaged city and the spiraling smoke streams that were being emitted from the remnants of what once had been a historic city. Then Rao turned toward the west. He realized there were other cities and countrysides to burn and Goths and Romans to slay. The most important task, above all others, lay ahead.

XLIV

Edith

Several days and weeks jogged by and Valerias lost track of time. There were days and nights, but how they added up to weeks and even months he didn't know. He was aware fall was in the air. He withstood spurts of poor weather associated with fall. Cool fronts blew in from the north and brought rain and a chill that made one even with the fortitude of Valerias shiver. When it wasn't raining, the dampness penetrated through his skin and made him crave the heat and dryness of a fire. That craving most times had to go unfilled. He had to be careful about fires, as he didn't want to alert anyone in the surrounding area of his presence. The worst part, though, was that there were times he couldn't perform the act of starting a fire. Valerias had been an officer for so long, he now lacked the rudimentary field skills, such as fire starting.

Valerias had another problem besides staying warm and dry. He found that food was becoming scarce, particularly food he could readily secure. The rabbits and other food animals seemed to know what he was up to and disappeared when he appeared. Edible plant species that he knew seemed to vanish the further north he traveled. Valerias was quite aware of the source of the problem: He had been at the top of the command chain for years. He'd had officers, soldiers, servants, and slaves for his every need. He had lost touch with the soldier of his youth that could subsist in the wild for long periods without effort. Now he had to be his own servant, and he fared poorly.

At first Valerias had no desire to communicate with humans. He had grown tired of dealing with personalities and conflicts. Being the General made it all the more necessary to successfully manage disputes among his men and the local populace. So often it seemed that the locals approached him and wanted him to resolve their problems. Yet he preferred these disputes to military ones because the potential consequences of alienating a local were much less than creating a festering resentment among officers who thought they were being slighted by his decision. A knife being plunged into his back was always a concern.

Now in the wilderness he began to forget the past conflicts and remember the good relationships he had had with his officers, Bukarma, Olivertos, and Jacob. When he had left for Britannia, Valerias thought he wanted to be nonsocial and avoid humans. He was regretting that lifestyle choice.

During one particular nasty cool front when Valerias thought he saw snow instead of rain, he came down with a fever. The fever gripped him hard, like a wrestler who has an opponent in such a stranglehold that the opponent cannot move no matter the effort he exerts to escape. The snow may have been an illusion, but the cold steady rain was not. Valerias attempted to find a shelter like a cave or natural enclosure and could not, so he built his own makeshift shelter with branches and tree boughs. When finished, Valerias thought it was a good shelter, but in reality it wasn't even adequate.

He positioned himself under the roof of the shelter. Still the rain found pathways through it and dripped on Valerias, creating a new form of torture. In this state Valerias became delusional.

He recalled events that were real and then slid into fantasy. In one image he saw all the men he had killed in battle standing on one side of a river waving for him to come over and join them. Valerias thought it was a bad idea to do so, but there was an irresistible urge to cross the river. In another spurt of delusion, Anastasis called to him to save her from a sea monster. She had grown up, with golden hair and eyes that gleamed in the darkness. The sea monster was too large, and he couldn't save her.

On and on throughout the night, he had these visions. He felt he was going to die, and he would accept death. In a moment of clarity, he imagined what kind of animal would feed on his corpse after he was dead. *The great General Valerias reduced to being eaten by rats.* He laughed to himself in a humorless way at how he ended up in such a state.

And then he had a vision. Only this vision was all in black. There were no images or figures. In the dark a voice called out to him, "Valerias, I need you still." The voice repeated, "I need you still." Over and over again it said those words. They were delivered in monotone, and Valerias couldn't tell if the speaker was a man or woman. When the voice stopped, Valerias woke up. The sun was shining and rays of light penetrated the shelter, as the rain had gone in the night. The fever had broken. Valerias lay in the sunlight and thought of the words he had heard. He was ready to die, thought he would die, and now he was alive. He felt good again. The remorse he had been feeling subsided. He looked at the poor shelter he had constructed and again laughed to himself. Valerias gathered up his few belongings and headed north, anticipating how he was to be needed.

Valerias walked onto a small road that appeared fairly well traveled. It wasn't a Roman-built road, but it wasn't a deer trail either. As he traveled on the road, there was an occasion when he could hear riders coming up to him. He quickly darted off the road to a heavy cover of bushes as the riders whipped by fast. They didn't see him, and he got a quick glance at them. There were several horsemen headed south at a fast pace. They all looked like Britons, except possibly the leader, who had physical characteristics of a Roman. The riders seemed to have a singular focus of speed without taking in the surroundings. Valerias wondered what was driving the men south, as he continued on his way north.

An hour after he observed the horsemen, he came to a fork in the road. The main path ran northeast and the smaller, less traveled path curved off to the northwest. Valerias gave a quick assessment of the situation and decided to take the less traveled pathway. It was quiet on the path, and after about a mile he noticed fewer birds and other wildlife. Soon the pathway gradually became wider, and it appeared that the vegetation along the edges had been planted. Valerias became so interested in the pattern of the vegetation that he didn't notice the house that appeared to spring out of nowhere in front of him.

He looked at the house, and the first item that caught his eye was that it was situated between several large pine trees. It was obvious to Valerias someone had sawed the limbs on the sides of the trees adjacent to the house, as the tree trunks formed parts of the corners and sides of the house. The house was one story high with a steep peak rising up in the front like a steeple. A strange symbol had been carved into the wood in the middle part of the peak. The front door of the house had a dark red color that was different than the brown texture that covered the rest of the structure. The symbol in the steeple was also colored red. The area in front of the house was bare of vegetation and consisted of a gravelly substance instead of dirt. Two windows had been cut into the house on both sides of the door. Shutters had largely closed the windows. *This is a unique structure,* thought Valerias.

Normally, Valerias would have left the house alone and continued on his way, but something drew him to the door. He was reluctant, but gave in to this feeling. He knocked and there was no response. He knocked again and still no response. He knocked a third time, and to his surprise the door swung open in front of him. Valerias' senses were on alert, and he drew his sword. He slowly entered the house. Straight in front of him was a circular fireplace. The fireplace was cold. To his left was something that resembled a kitchen with a small table. Straight back was a hallway that extended into what appeared to be small rooms. To his right was a set of chairs. It was dark; the only light was filtered sunlight peeking its way through holes in the shutters of the windows on the south side of the house. When Valerias' eyes adjusted to the light, he could see a figure sitting in one of the chairs.

"Come in, Roman warrior, and sit," the figure called out to Valerias. "Put your sword away. You have nothing to fear here in this house."

Valerias could tell by the tone in the voice that the speaker was an old woman. She motioned Valerias over to the chair that was set in front of her. He could not clearly see her face, although she had white hair tied behind her head. She spoke in a tone that was quiet and firm and showed signs of old age. Valerias sat down, but kept his sword at his side.

"Who are you, old woman?"

"I am Edith, daughter of Marta and Jergens. And I know who you are, General Marcus Augustus Valerias."

"How do you know my name? In fact, I am not admitting that is my name."

"I know many things, General Valerias."

As she spoke those words, Valerias raised his sword to her throat. "What do you know now? Do you see your death?"

"You will not kill me, General. It is not in your nature."

Valerias thought this old, arrogant woman should feel some steel, but he knew she was right and lowered his sword. Still, he kept his sword at his side with the point down slightly indenting the floor. Valerias was wary, as he didn't know what to think about this strange woman. In any event he wanted to be able to spring into a defensive mode against any human and nonhuman entity she could conjure against him—if she could actually conjure something.

"Don't worry. You are safe in my house," Edith repeated.

"Maybe so, but my sword will not be sheathed while I am here." He slightly changed the subject. "How did you know my name? Very few people here know who I am and where I am, and you are out in the wilderness. Very little gossip could reach you here."

Actually, gossip and loose lips frequently made their way to her. Yet she seemed to have knowledge that would be very hard to obtain, including the presence of Valerias in her house.

"I have my ways, General, and that is all I'm going to tell you. Kill me now, if you desire that path."

"You are right. I'm not going to do that. However, I will ask you not to call me General or Valerias. I want to be anonymous here in Britannia. Call me Marcus, and I am a retired soldier of the Roman army. If you insist on calling me General or Valerias, you will pay the appropriate penalty."

Valerias was dead serious when he spoke those words, and Edith appeared to agree. "As you wish, Marcus."

"Who are you and what are you doing out here all alone?"

"I am Edith, and I am a Druid priestess. You have heard of Druids before, have you not, Marcus?"

"Of course, I have heard of the Druid cult, yet I give little credence to religion—whatever religion that may be, Hellenistic, Christian, or Druid. I think all religions are pointless. One lives and then dies—the end. Religion is the way a weak man seeks relief from the unknown or even known forces that are in some way affecting him. Weak men use religion as an excuse to explain the unnatural or to conduct evil under the banner of religion. As I said before, I believe in life and then death, period. I also thought Druids were extinct. And here you are."

"I am not surprised about your skepticism, Marcus. There are many people who would disagree with you, though. We believe in an afterlife, an afterlife of reincarnation."

"You mean I could have been Caesar in another life?" Valerias rolled his eyes.

"Perhaps. Who is to know who we were previously?"

Edith could tell this conversation was not going anywhere. "Would you like some stew and tea, Marcus?"

Valerias hesitated to answer. He was beginning to believe that the old woman was some type of witch or shaman. Maybe she was just crazy. Yet he was hungry. The bout with the fever had caused his stomach to rumble not so quietly.

Edith picked up on the pause. "I will not poison or drug you, if that is what you are thinking."

"Then I will take you up on your offering."

Edith stood up and walked to the small oven that was to the left when Valerias had entered the house. She was a small woman, wearing a white flowing robe. Valerias had not observed the oven when he entered the house. Edith took a ladle and dipped it into the pot and poured the warm contents into one bowl and then another ladle worth into the second bowl. She then reversed the order to pour a second ladle of stew into the bowls. After the bowls of stew were prepared, she reached for a kettle and poured two cups of tea. Valerias watched closely how she prepared the stew and tea to assure himself that there was no poison or trickery involved. She brought the bowls and cups over to a small table. Her final act for the meal was to grab a loaf of bread. She pulled a chunk for herself and offered Valerias the loaf. Valerias took a chunk of bread for himself. He now noticed her hair was no longer tied behind her head and was free flowing and long down the sides of her face. She looked younger.

"See, no need to worry about me trying to poison you. I would not have done such a thing to you." She then proceeded to eat portions of the stew, tea, and bread.

With that action Valerias ate and drank heartily. He was too hungry to worry about what the old woman would do to him.

Edith quietly asked, "Why, great Marcus, did you give it all up to wander around this island like a lost dog, when you could have had the best of everything?"

Valerias was grateful for the food and drink. He took a break from devouring what was before him. "There were many reasons. Why do you want to know?"

"Tell me a reason for what you did. I know of no man who would do what you have done."

"I became very tired of what I was doing. I had done it for so long. I wanted to see the world from an individual viewpoint and not from the vantage point of what a general sees. I never had a social life or a real family. My family was the army. It was all business to serve Rome. You are wrong, woman. Even though I had everything, as you indicate, I missed out on much. And that I can never get back. I am happy to fade into the countryside and let it go at that."

"Oh, it is not so easy to do what you want, my general. Your destiny in life has not yet been completed. You still have much to accomplish."

Valerias thought about his dream the night before. Maybe his path was not to obscurity after all. He did not acknowledge this thought to Edith. "Well then, woman, just what is my destiny?"

"I don't know what your ultimate destiny is—I just know you haven't fulfilled it yet."

Valerias sat back in his chair and looked at Edith. She almost seemed to glow with a fine light. Valerias was again uncomfortable around her. Edith had conducted actions reminiscent of witchcraft, such as pulling stew from a pot placed not on what he thought was a stove but a shelf. Yet she had a presence that evoked a certain calm in him. He did not feel physically threatened, and he finally put his sword in the sheath. Valerias was also not mentally threatened; instead, he was intrigued by her. *So I'm not going to ride off into the sunset as I had hoped. What is the alternative then?*

Edith continued, "We are all sucked into the vortex of time. I believe I will come back out of the vortex and begin a new life as someone else. You believe once you enter the vortex there is nothing, but the end."

"We are all caught in the realm of time—including you old woman."

"Well, I just guess that shows our differences."

The two talked on for another hour in a deep discussion about life, death, and the afterlife. Finally Valerias saw that the day was fleeting away into evening, and he told Edith that he needed to take his leave. He thanked her for her hospitality and company, and returned to the path through the woods. As he left the house, he felt a little confused. He looked back at the house and wondered if it was enchanted. Valerias didn't believe in such things, but this house and Edith had a different feel to him. The more he walked away from the house, the clearer his thinking became.

After Valerias had gone, two figures came up behind Edith. They were her sons. Both men were of average size and shape except that they smelled like men who had been confined in a livestock barn. Both men were unshaven and unkempt, in contrast to their mother who was dressed in a white gown.

"Ma," one of them said. "I think that is a Roman deserter. We have heard Titus, the Roman general in Britannia, is paying well for deserters."

"They are worth more dead than alive," the other son chimed in. "Titus likes others to extend punishment to deserters."

"You boys are fools. How would Titus know they are truly deserters unless they were alive? Woe to the man who kills a Roman and then finds out in front of Titus that the dead man wasn't a deserter."

"We will take our chances on that, Mother."

One son told the other to get the horses out of the barn so they could ride after Valerias, who was on foot.

"Stop right there, you two." Edith had become very angry quickly. "Neither of you two is going after that man."

"We can take him, Mother, with surprise on our side."

"No, I said. He walks with the shroud of death over his head. If you try to take him, he will add you to the shroud. No mother wants to lose her sons to that."

She knew Valerias was a much better fighter than her sons, and she would surely lose them if they proceeded to try to take him. Her sons realized she was serious and temporarily backed off. Her visions were usually accurate, and to challenge her would be fruitless.

"We will do as you ask, Mother."

"Good, now finish your chores."

The two sons retreated to a nearby shed, softly grumbling as they walked to it. Edith looked at the woods where Valerias went after he had left her house. She too wondered about what was to come. Later that night Edith's sons assumed that their mother was asleep. They crept into the shed that held the horses and led them silently out of the shed to a grassy area located at the side of the house. They mounted their horses and began to slowly ride down the trail where Valerias was last seen. Suddenly Edith appeared in front of them. Her white gown and hair seemed illuminated in the night.

"What did I tell you boys? Don't you listen to me?"

"Sorry, Mother," both sons replied in unison.

Then one of them added, "We want to capture the Roman. We need the gold that he will bring to us."

"You are fools," she responded. "This is not meant to be, and it is more than gold you are after—it is the thrill of the kill. I'm telling you, the only killing there will be, will be you. If you die, it will break my heart."

One son said, "We will be fine, Mother. There are two of us, and we are on horses. He is nothing but an old Roman deserter on foot. The world will be better without him."

Both men then gave their horses a kick and were off past their mother and into the night.

Edith slowly walked back into the house. She lit a candle, turned to go down the shallow hallway and was abruptly startled. It was Valerias sitting in the chair she had sat in earlier in the day when they had talked.

"Good evening, Edith. Have a seat."

She sat down and asked him, "Why are you here?"

"I noticed evidence of two men when I was in your house. Where they were when we were talking, I don't know or care."

"Please don't hurt my sons." Edith's eyes were no longer that of a Druid priestess but those of a concerned mother.

"You were kind to me today, so I will return the favor. I will not kill your sons if they do not follow me. If they do, I cannot deliver on any promise I make to you. You are in my world now, where life and death are daily matters that I must deal with."

Valerias sat straight up in the chair and looked Edith deep in her eyes. "Now you know why I chose to do what I have done—to walk around your country like a lost dog, as you said, instead of enjoying the life of a general."

Edith felt the power of Valerias and could only say, "Thank you for your understanding, Marcus."

"It all depends on your sons." Valerias took the rest of the loaf of bread that Edith had left on the counter. He looked at where the stove was located when Edith had earlier taken the stew and he saw nothing but a shelf. "Damn," was all he said and then he was off into the dark.

Edith slouched back into her chair and said a short prayer to the Druid gods.

She didn't need to worry. Edith's sons tried to track Valerias and gave up. A tavern was located a short distance from where they were searching. Soon they were at the tavern having drinks and telling other local people embellished stories driven by alcohol-fueled imaginations.

XLV

Juncture

Over the next several weeks, Mary took good care of Claire and the girls. They regained their strength and began to relax. The stress of the past several months faded. Balanced against the fading past, Claire felt the need to be constantly on guard for future problems. In her mind, Argus' men or other bandits posed a continuing threat. It mattered little if the threat was real or imagined, they were the same. Claire pretended all was well to Anne and Elizabeth, and yet her mind could not settle. Mary sensed Claire's ill feelings and tried to reassure her that it was only a matter of time before she would be safe with Eustice. However, when there is a knife at one's throat for a period of time, the feeling remains that the knife is still there even when it has been removed.

After the girls went to bed at night, Mary and Claire would talk about the past, present, and future. Claire was very fortunate to have a friend like Mary. Mary was someone whom she could trust even at the castle, and that was a valuable commodity to Claire. They had become close friends, as their relationship had advanced beyond that of master and servant. The combined feeling of former servant and now-friend drove

Mary to help Claire, even if it meant sacrificing her own life. They knew that after they parted ways, it would be unlikely they would ever see each other again.

The end of the time in the house proved bittersweet for Claire, Mary, Anne, and Elizabeth. The young girls grew to believe that Mary was their aunt. Claire immensely enjoyed her secure time in the house with Mary, but if she and the girls were to reach true safety, she had to leave soon and reach Eustice before winter.

Almost three months from the day Claire arrived at the house, a man knocked on the door. He introduced himself as Stephen. He was as new to Mary as he was to Claire. Stephen carried a paper with instructions. He was to take Claire and her daughters to a place in western Britannia where Eustice and his men would be waiting. It was not a far journey, but a very dangerous one. The countryside was wild with all sorts of outlaws and people who had nothing to lose. Argus and his men were a secondary threat, although Argus was the cause of the unsafe countryside.

Flavius chose Stephen for this task because he was a master at hiding and escorting people through the assortment of bandits and rogues in the country. He was not tall, only a little taller than Claire. Stephen had a bushy brown beard, and his eyes never seemed to set in one position. Claire found that to be irritating and unsettling. Stephen also smelled of a distinct earthy odor. He appeared to have just emerged from a slumber deep in the ground covered with rotting leaves. *Maybe it was supposed to be that way,* Claire thought.

Mary had previously discussed Stephen's impending arrival with Claire, even though Mary had never met the man. Flavius had spoken highly of him to Mary; thus, she was confident that Flavius would pick the best person and pay him accordingly to successfully complete the assigned task. The meeting between Claire and Stephen was the easy first step. The hard part was to transport Claire and her daughters across the dangerous countryside to Eustice.

Stephen was a man of few words, and he was that way with Claire and Mary. He didn't even initiate an opening greeting to them, it was all business to him. Flavius gave him a task to perform and he was going to do it—within reason. He would attempt to complete his mission, although he had no intention of sacrificing his life for a woman and her children because they knew Flavius. The time was too rough and turbulent for such guarantees. In the end he chose to take his chances with Flavius rather than Argus and, of course, because Flavius would pay him.

"We leave tomorrow night," he said directly to Claire. Then to Mary, "Do you have the payment?"

Mary answered, "I do, but you know the deal. You get one-half now and one-half when you finish the mission. Eustice will pay you when Claire and the girls are safely delivered. Let me repeat—safely delivered."

Stephen was also a rogue, a smart rogue. It had crossed his mind that he could take the money from Mary and disappear, leaving Claire to survive on her own. Yet he wanted the rest. A full share was much better than one-half share. Additionally, Flavius had faith in him, and that was a positive boost to Stephen's ego.

"I understand, that is the deal," Stephen spoke directly at Mary.

"You will get your down payment share when you leave tomorrow night."

Stephen grunted in the affirmative. "Be ready tomorrow night." This time he looked directly at Claire. "We need to avoid Morguard, the new Flavius."

With those words Stephen was gone.

"Where do you think he is going?" Claire asked Mary.

"Only God knows. He is crafty though. He will stay out of sight until you leave. Now let's rest. After tomorrow night you will have little time for rest."

Flavius stood at the corner of the castle stolen by Argus and looked to the northwest. As he did this, Morguard with two hundred men rode forcefully through the castle's gate in a northwesterly direction. Morguard's mission was to crush a rebellion in the corner of Argus' kingdom that seldom garnered attention. A secondary goal was to test the resolve of a warlord in the next kingdom to the north. Argus considered that man nothing more than a small-time bandit and not a true king like himself. Argus calculated that his forces were superior to those of the warlord. In case of war, Argus' troops would win and his kingdom would be enlarged.

As he watched the cavalry stream toward the northwest, Flavius was spun with emotions. The predator in him wanted to lead the expedition and crush the rebels, as he had done many times. Yet he was relieved he was not given the command, as he was becoming reluctant to harm innocent lives.

Then there was Mary. If he commanded the expedition instead of Morguard, he could assure Mary's safety and also that of Claire and her daughters by guiding his force away from them. By sitting in the castle, he could not perform that function. He hoped his planning would be enough to save Mary and also Claire.

As Flavius stared out at Morguard's men, a figure approached him from behind. It was Argus. Today he was dressed in a splendid robe of bright purple, with slashes of white across the chest. Flavius thought for a moment he was looking at a Roman Emperor. The robe was too large for Argus. Flavius did not say a word about the robe to Argus, but he was thinking to himself, *This man is no Emperor.*

"Tell me, Flavius, do you wish that was you leading my cavalry?"

"Of course, King Argus, haven't I always faithfully led your troops, and always with success?"

"Yes, you have, until this latest venture. I think you have become too old for completing all of my tasks. It is time we brought in new blood to help take over your responsibilities. Don't worry, Flavius, you are still my first officer."

Argus turned his back on Flavius and walked away. Flavius had never fully trusted Argus and he did even less now. He knew his days were numbered with Argus, particularly if Morguard were successful. *Everyone is expendable,* he thought as he turned back to view the cavalry that was now about out of sight. He wasn't worried for himself, he was worried for Mary.

Claire and Mary spent the next day organizing and packing their belongings. They had to be careful not to leave a trace of Claire's and the girls' presence in the house. At some point there would likely be a search of the house. Any sign of Claire would bring disaster to the owners of the house, and Mary did not want the owners harmed. Anne and Elizabeth played quietly in a back room all day. They sensed the seriousness of the situation and stayed out of the way.

At dusk the four had a last meal together. The conversation was forced. There was no more happy talk to exchange. Claire and Mary knew that it was time for the final push. Either Claire would make it to Eustice, or she and her daughters would die or, worse, be captured. It was an odd situation. Claire and the daughters were supposedly dead, and yet hunters still roamed the country searching for them. The bounty Argus had put on Claire was too great, and many in the countryside maintained a hope that they would be the ones to take Claire and claim the reward.

After dark embraced the land, a quiet knock was heard at the door. Mary knocked back twice. On the other side a progression of three knocks followed. Mary opened the door. It was Stephen. He had a slight smell of alcohol but did not appear to be drunk.

"Is the package ready?"

"Yes," Mary answered. "Is it a good night for a delivery?"

"Oh, yes—there is no moon and the breeze should help mask our trip. We leave now."

Mary nodded to the back of the house. First Claire emerged, then the girls. Stephen had already packed Claire's horse. He would take Elizabeth and Claire would ride with Anne. Before mounting the horses, the girls gave Mary firm hugs. Claire followed with a long embrace. Whereas only several months before Claire's and Mary's relationship had been of a queen and a servant, now it was that of close friends.

Stephen looked bored and finally told Claire to get on the horse with Anne, which she did. He mounted his horse after he placed Elizabeth on it. Mary walked up to Stephen's horse and gave him an envelope. Stephen looked inside and gestured a quiet smile.

"Take care of them," Mary said quietly.

Stephen looked at her and then the money and smiled. He did not say a word. He pointed to a direction and they left silently into the dark. Mary went inside the house and prayed.

The path they took was almost straight west. Stephen led the way. Travel was exceedingly slow due to the dark. Claire thought they covered only about five miles in the first night. Along the way they occasionally heard distant noises. Some were animals, others were human, and the rest were too hard to identify. At the first hint of dawn's arrival, Stephen searched for a place to stay during the daylight. He preferred heavily vegetated areas off the trails and roads where it would be extremely difficult for anyone looking for them to find them. They dared not have a fire, as a fire would attract those who they didn't want to attract—like insects to a light.

The girls were brave without fault. They did not whine or talk unless spoken to, which was seldom. Claire thought to herself that it was foolish to think younger people could not follow instructions, especially when their lives were at stake. Stephen said very little unless there was an order to give. Claire thought that his bad scent was more than his body odor. She also kept in the back of her mind that Flavius was setting them up, but first taunted them with their lives. Yet she believed in Mary and Mary's trust in Flavius. This belief kept Claire going.

Morguard had laid waste to the countryside where the rebels were supposedly carrying out their rebellion. It didn't matter if the people were innocent—they were guilty in his mind. Besides, he wanted to impress Argus that he, and not Flavius, could lead Argus' troops.

When he arrived at Abrador where Mary was staying, there were only a few villagers left. The majority had fled into the countryside. That didn't stop Morguard—he found a few males, whom he promptly tortured and then executed. If there were women who were not old hags, in his mind, he had his soldiers rape them. The children were left alone. He wanted them to remember what happened to those who rebel. At the end of the village's main road was the house where Mary was staying. One of Morguard's captains, with several men, advanced on the house bearing torches.

As they approached the house, Mary emerged from the front door. "What do you want here?"

The captain looked at his men and laughed. "We want the house and also you. We want to show the rebels who roam about here what happens to those who disobey King Argus."

He motioned to one of his men with a torch to set the house on fire and to another man to take Mary.

"Stop!" Mary stated firmly. "I am Mary Selenies. And I am taking care of this house for the Roman nobleman Alexander and his wife. I am their niece. Alexander is the brother of the Roman General Titus, and he is on an ambassador assignment for Titus. You destroy this house or harm me, and you will incur the wrath of Titus and also my uncle."

The Britons stopped in their tracks at these words and looked to the Captain. He looked puzzled. This was a predicament for which he was unprepared.

Mary waved a parchment in front of him. "This is proof of what I speak."

The Captain looked behind to a horseman and whispered an order. The horseman quickly disappeared. He turned to Mary, "If what you say is not true—" He didn't finish the sentence but smiled slyly at Mary.

"I wouldn't do that as well. I am their niece and a Roman citizen. I know my uncle, General Titus, personally. Woe to the man who harms me in any way." Her statement was all bravado.

The two stared at each other for a few minutes. Mary had learned long ago never to back down or show weakness to a male, and this was a perfect time to practice her situation management skills. Soon several other men rode up to the house, leaving a trail of dust in their wake. The leader was a man dressed all in black except for a blue cape. Mary sensed an aura of evil around this man. He and the captain spoke in quiet tones out of her hearing. Finally the man in black rode up to Mary.

"I am Morguard, General to Argus, King of this land." Morguard had inflated his position with Argus. "My captain tells me that this house is a Roman house—in the land of the Britons, no less. And you are a Roman. Is all this true, woman?

"Yes, and I have the documents to prove to you what I tell you." Mary's face was resolute as she spoke, but she was bluffing. The house was indeed Roman owned, but she was not Roman and did not know if she had permission to live in the house while the occupants, Alexander and his wife, were away. How Flavius had arranged this set-up, she did not know.

A soldier came up and grabbed the parchment from Mary. She was worried but showed no evidence of stress.

"I would like those documents back when you are finished reviewing them. My Uncle Alexander will want those documents."

Morguard gave Mary a hard look. She did not flinch. He looked at the parchment for several minutes. After he was finished, he resumed his threatening facial expression to Mary.

Finally he spoke. "Unfortunately, what you say is true. If I had my way, I would destroy this house and you as well, but Argus does not want a war with Rome and Titus, *yet*. We will leave you alone."

Morguard and his soldiers slowly turned around and left the area. Mary retreated into the house and collapsed. After a few moments, she offered a prayer of thanks to God. Mary was a fortunate woman. First, Morguard could not read, and he faked reading the document to not embarrass himself in front of his men. Second, a large patrol of Roman soldiers was in the area. Morguard did not want to engage the Romans when he could take on easier targets such as unarmed villagers. Third, she did not recognize any of Morguard's men from her time in the castle now inhabited by Argus.

Morguard left Abrador a smoldering ruin. As he camped nearby, a rider approached him. It was a scout and informant for Argus.

"Hail, Morguard," the man said as he rode up to Morguard.

"Greetings, Kretawac. Do you like my work?"

"Exquisite, Lord Morguard, King Argus would be pleased. Soon the rebels will be destroyed."

"Where are the remnants of the rebels?"

There is a group of them about twenty miles west of here. Word has it that they are looking for sanctuary with Eustice in western Britannia."

"How far is Eustice from where the rebels are situated?"

"No one can answer your question. It could be one mile or fifty miles. We have seen their scouts in the area, but we have no idea where his main force is located. Eustice is proving to be very elusive. Wherever his force is, it is larger than yours. So my advice is not to engage them or be tricked into a fight. Report back to King Argus, and then he can launch his full army at Eustice. Eustice can then either choose to fight Argus and be destroyed, or he can retreat into the hole he came from."

"I'll decide what we do, Kretawac."

"You also need to put this into your calculations, Lord Morguard. Within five miles of here the Romans have a large force of cavalry. We do not know what Titus is up to, but be on alert. Titus can turn on you with little notice. We have heard he is not a supporter of Argus, and he doesn't like what you are doing to these villages. It is his elite cohort, so under no circumstances should you engage his force."

"You don't know much, do you, Kretawac? Be that as it may, I'm not afraid of the Romans or Eustice, and I don't like the thought that I could not defeat them either."

"Lord Morguard, if you want to replace Flavius, you have to stay alive and show your fighting and strategic thinking ability to King Argus. At this time—*at this time*—chase after the small rebel group and report to King Argus. He will then appoint you to lead the army against Eustice."

Morguard was impetuous but not stupid. What Kretawac said was true.

"I understand what you are saying, Kretawac. We will hit the rebels and report to Argus. This is my chance, and I do not want to end up like Flavius."

"Good choice, Lord Morguard. We can be at the rebel camp by tomorrow, hit them hard before they can melt away into Eustice's territory. But if we tangle with Eustice, I will not mind that either. Just be smart about that."

Morguard gave the signal to his troops, and they were off to the western hills.

Edith's words bothered Valerias as he walked through the land west of the provincial capital, Ratae. He had been traveling with many thoughts, which diminished his usual attentive manner. He let his guard down and tripped on a rock, reinjuring the same ankle he had twisted back at the reflective pool, in what seemed like a long time ago. The ankle was not hurt so badly that he couldn't walk. The assistance of a staff he created out of a fallen branch helped him navigate through the woods.

As Valerias walked and then rested, he continually thought of Edith. The thoughts were more than just the words she had spoken, but that she had spoken them to him. He wondered what role was left for him and how she knew this.

Valerias was also beginning to feel lonely and missing company. His food supply had dwindled to almost nothing after he had eaten the food he had taken from Edith's house. The skills he used to catch small animals and identify edible plants had vanished. He knew some insects and worms were edible, but he couldn't bring himself to eat them. Valerias concluded that it would not be acceptable to die in the wild and have the worms eat him when he couldn't eat them. *What an irony*, he thought.

His appearance had deteriorated. The beard and hair were long and unkempt. Even the Emperor Julian would not have approved of his beard. His clothes had turned into rags, and the rags were filthy. He hadn't bathed in weeks, and he knew his odor was strong, and that bothered him more than anything. When he found a pool of water, he would bathe.

One sunny fall day he sat under a large, smooth-barked tree in the midst of a grove of similar trees. He began to yearn for his old life, not the life of a general but as a citizen of Rome. The life of a lost hermit was not for him. He wondered how Braxus, Cratus, and his legions were doing. Were Bukarma and Olivertos and Revious serving Braxus, or did they retire like him—only into a better lifestyle? He knew none of them were hermits contemplating feasting on bugs and worms.

The more he sat under the tree, the more he contemplated changing what he was doing. A small brown-shaded bird flew about him and favored a branch to his left. The bird seemed to have no purpose in its actions. Valerias didn't move; his eyes fixated on the bird. He had noticed in previous observations of wildlife, there was a purpose to the actions of animals, such as a predator, or as prey, or for finding food or mating. The bird's odd behavior had his full attention. Then in an instant the bird flew to the bark of the tree, snared a moth that was the color of the tree bark, and disappeared out of his sight. The bird's actions were for a purpose.

The bird pleased Valerias, and he smiled to himself. His stomach growled. Valerias arose from under the tree and decided it was time to travel to the nearest village. He wanted a bath, new clothes, and, most important, food. He still had coins to pay for these necessities. With that in mind, he ventured forth to the nearest village, which he figured was about five miles west of his current position.

When he arrived at the outskirts of Abrador, he found a state of pandemonium. The residents who were left were all hastily packing whatever belongings they could carry and fleeing out of the village in a westerly direction. He tried to ask several villagers what was taking place. Because of his appearance, no one stopped to answer his questions. *I must really be in a hideous condition,* he thought to himself. *Maybe they think I'm an ogre. In a few short months I have gone from a supreme general in the greatest army the world had ever seen to a bum.*

Finally an old man stopped long enough to tell Valerias that Morguard was on his way and the village would soon be destroyed. Any inhabitants found in or near the village would be killed.

"Who is Morguard?" Valerias asked the old man.

The old man looked at Valerias curiously. "Did you climb out from some cave, old man?"

Valerias bristled. He was being called an old man by an old man. "Yes, who is Morguard?" Valerias repeated himself.

The old man again carefully looked at Valerias and gave a quick answer, "The devil's keeper. Watch yourself, old man. Morguard cares not if you are young or old, man or woman. He will put the sword to you. He is worse than Flavius."

The old man picked up his pack and took off for the forest west of the village. Valerias watched him disappear. *If there is a devil's keeper, then who is the devil?* he thought. He pulled up his own filthy pack off of the ground, which contained the few remaining items he owned, and, using his staff, walked briskly into the same woods as the old man. He would follow the villagers and see what happened to them. Maybe this is his destiny as foretold by Edith. Or was she a crazy woman trying to get inside of his head? It really didn't matter; he felt alive again.

Claire had followed Stephen for several days now, and it didn't seem they were moving closer to where Eustice was reportedly situated. She was even unsure of what direction they were traveling. At this moment Claire hated her life. She always seemed to be at the mercy and will of men, most of whom did not seem to have her best interests at heart. Claire had always been an independent woman. Her father had taught her to be able to think and act on her own initiative. Now she was subject to the whims of men, and she didn't like the feeling of subordination.

She thought, just two years ago she was married to King Gerhard and was a Queen. He was now dead. Erik could have been a fine suitor, and now he was dead. Argus wants her dead. Flavius' motives were unclear to her. Now she had to deal with Stephen. Flavius was a mystery and Stephen, who was hired by Flavius, was of questionable character. Furthermore, she heard that Argus had a new enforcer, Morguard. She wasn't even sure anymore if she could trust her own brother, Eustice. Claire was extremely uneasy with how her life was unfolding. Yet she had to trust Flavius; that was the only way through this quandry.

As they traveled at night, they frequently rode by camps of refugees. Most of these people seemed to be running away from their villages. Obviously Argus was the cause of this misery. He had managed to take the kingdom under the proud rule of Gerhard and herself and turn it into madness. The prosperous land that once formed the northern and western part of their kingdom had fallen into a pit of despair under Argus and Flavius, and now, a new bringer of terror, Morguard. She felt sorrow for the people of the woods, and yet she couldn't help them.

A couple of groups they encountered were clearly outlaws. It was doubtful they had ever been "good" citizens of the kingdom. Stephen was very cautious around these men. The displaced villagers would likely leave his group alone, but these outlaws would not show a similar attitude.

The longer they traveled, the more people they had to avoid. They could see smoke from fires in the distance, as Morguard was burning any village he could find. When Morguard had completed his mission, the rebellion in the north—real or imagined—would be smashed to pieces so thoroughly that normal life could not be put back together in this country for years.

Stephen always behaved carefully around Claire. He talked little and explained less. They slept during the day so they could travel at night. On their tenth day together, Claire awoke to find Stephen missing. His horse was gone as were all his belongings. She looked around the camp for any sign of what happened. When she turned back to find the girls, she saw a note plunged through a branch stub of a tree. It read:

> *I am sorry the risk of traveling with you is to great if Morguard find me with you there will not be enuf of me to find Eustice is 30 miles west I trust you make it I will take my chances with Flavius*

An arrow on the note pointed straight ahead.

This was about the worst thing Claire could have imagined. Her heart sank to a depth below despair. Morguard would certainly catch them now. Claire wept bitterly about her situation. Flavius was not the judge of character he thought he was. Stephen had turned out to be a huge disappointment. If they were so close to Eustice as Stephen indicated on his note, then he should have completed his mission and been paid the rest of his commission. She felt Stephen's note was a lie.

She looked at Anne and Elizabeth sleeping soundly. She thought, *This is how the Christian priests would describe angels.* Claire wiped her eyes, took a short walk around the campsite, and woke the girls. She thought she would head in a westerly direction, but that was a guess. It was make or break time for her. She had had enough.

As Claire was waking the girls and packing up the camp, she observed a number of people quickly moving toward her. At first she was frightened, as she thought they were Morguard's men. Then she observed that women and children composed the bulk of the group. She ran out to meet them. On the spot Claire made up the name of Clarissa for herself. The girls could keep their names. She told the apparent leaders of the group that she had become separated from her village members and was lost. She was trying to flee Morguard and asked if she and her daughters could join them. To her surprise they accepted her immediately and said she could come with them. They too were attempting to reach hopeful sanctuary with Eustice.

The members of the group told Claire to prepare herself and her daughters quickly, as they were sure Morguard was close behind them. Claire gathered the girls, and quickly packed their camp. She put the girls on the remaining horse and walked the horse to meet the group. When she looked back to see if anyone was coming, she noticed a solitary individual following the group. Her first impression was that of a mad hermit trailing the group for whatever crumbs they left behind.

The mad hermit was Valerias.

XLVI

Temptation

On his first night in the village, Joseph fell soundly asleep in the church. The clutter and debris in the building did not bother his sleep. The structure and roof were actually still in fair shape and provided a dry shelter, as a rain shower had blown through the area during the night. Joseph was thankful for these conditions. Camping outside was the less preferred alternative. He said a prayer of thanks to God when he awoke and surveyed his surroundings in dry clothes. Joseph had always been one who did not like to be part of a harsh environment, and he avoided getting soaked and cold at every opportunity.

The church had a small main sanctuary and three small rooms on the west side. There was no balcony or second floor. He looked at each room and decided the medium-sized one would serve as his quarters. The largest room would be for guests or other people who were suffering ill fortune. The small room would act as a prayer room or another guest room. These rooms and the sanctuary were in a state of deterioration, including rotting floorboards and a roof with small holes. The church would require much repair and cleaning.

First things first, though, which involved Joseph touring the village to obtain an understanding of the environment he would experience. Bergen was located on the northern border of Argus' realm. The village was poor, with no outward show of wealth by its inhabitants. An accumulation of wood-structured huts and block buildings was set in a haphazard pattern. Along the main road of the village stood a larger building that appeared to be vacant. Joseph asked a resident about the status of the building and was told Romans used it when they come to the village. The villager noted that occasionally the Romans stopped here on their way to other sites and used the building as a resting place. If the force was large enough, the officers used the building, and regular soldiers slept in tents outside. When it was vacant, no one from the village dared use the building for any purpose.

Once a poor villager decided to sleep inside the building. The Romans surprised him, and the man found himself on the end of a rope hanging in the main square of the village. That was a sufficient message for the rest of the villagers. Joseph asked the villager where the mayor or leader of the village lived. The villager pointed to a house located at the northwestern corner of the main square. It was a well-built building with two stories. Joseph walked to the house and politely knocked on the door. After a minute a woman answered the door. She looked familiar.

"Good morning, Joseph."

"Good morning, ma'am," Joseph responded. He was still not sure who she was.

"You don't remember me, do you?"

"Yes, I do. How are you doing, Ruth?" It came back to him quickly, but how could the poor woman who he had seen at the church the previous night look as fine as she did now?

"I know what you are thinking, Joseph. How the woman you saw last night could be the same woman in front of you today?"

"I just had that thought, yes."

"Our village has been the site of much violence of late. I spend much of my time working to help the poor. Many live in wretched conditions. When I return to my house, my father expects me to clean up from this work. And frankly, I do not disagree."

At that moment a large older man came from behind Ruth and gradually edged his way in front of her.

"I am Garth, the mayor of this poor village and, as you may have surmised, father of Ruth."

"I am . . ." Joseph was cut off in mid-word.

"I know who you are—Joseph, the Christian priest, who just arrived yesterday."

There was an awkward silence as the three stood in the doorway. Finally Garth asked Joseph if he wanted to come in. Joseph nodded affirmatively and entered the house after Garth and Ruth.

"Ruth, prepare tea for us."

"Yes, Father," and Ruth proceeded to go to the kitchen area of the house.

"Have a seat, Joseph. We need to talk."

Joseph sat in the chair Garth pointed out to him. Garth sat in front of him. A few minutes of silence followed, with Garth staring at Joseph. Garth had thick silver hair that bushed out on the sides of his head and included hair from the front that had been pushed back. He had a large forehead and a prominent nose. Garth's yellowish teeth were quite noticeable when he spoke. Joseph tried not to look at them. Even at his age Garth looked very strong. Joseph thought Garth's overall physique was much better than the condition of his teeth. Joseph hypothesized that at some time Garth had been a farmer or even a soldier.

When Ruth came back with a tray of tea, Garth thanked her and then invited her to sit down beside him.

"Both Ruth and I have seen tragedy within the last two years. I lost my wife of thirty years—Ruth's mother—to some disease last year. Ruth's husband was killed almost three years ago this fall. He was a farmer."

"How was he killed?" Joseph asked.

Ruth jumped in, "Gerhard and his rival to the north, Wendover, were fighting over territory, and my husband got in the way." Even though she had previously cried about his death several times, tears formed in her eyes.

Garth added, "You see, Joseph, this village was on the fault line between two kingdoms led by despots. I thought of them as warlords and butchers rather than kings. Ruth's husband had been drafted into Wendover's army. He was not properly trained and was killed by Gerhard's soldiers in an early battle. Training is very important if you are going to fight a war. I know, I was once a soldier in the Roman army and we were well trained—over and over again until it became such a habit, you knew what to expect and how to react to any situation. Ruth's husband had no such training and the result was his death. It is very sad, he was a good farmer."

"What happened as a result of the war?" Joseph quietly inquired.

"Nothing," Garth answered. "Gerhard was killed by Saxons in a far-away district. Wendover just died and his kingdom disintegrated. Now we lie on the cusp of the rule of a man who I think is mad, named Argus. He has proceeded to ruin this part of the country. Prosperous villages are now dirt poor. The country, which was safe, is no longer so. It is a sad time in which we live. So welcome to our village, Joseph."

Joseph sat back in his chair. He looked at Garth and then at Ruth. Even though he did not know these people, he felt he needed to speak from the heart. Joseph spoke in a slow and clear tone, "During the past couple of years, I have given much thought to what it takes to be a good and true servant of the Lord. To be blunt, I have not done so. I have not had the courage to do what must be done, whether it be with the Goths or the Romans. If I had truly stood up for my principles of faith, I might have been killed, but then I would have stood up for what I believe."

Garth interrupted, "How does being dead advance any principles? It is a waste to be buried with your principles. Then what do you have? What do those around you have after you have died? Nothing!"

Ruth added, "Sometimes one must do what is needed to survive so that your ideas are not forgotten, and are carried out."

Joseph was listening to the same conclusion coming from two different people. Now civilians were politely lecturing him. Joseph felt embarrassed by his lack of faith that was on display to Garth and Ruth. This time, though, he was determined to show he was a man of God. "I don't care about the past. The only element of time that I am interested in is the present. If the present is managed properly, the future will take of itself."

"It will take all the courage and faith you can muster to stay here and accomplish your goals," Garth answered.

"And perseverance," added Ruth.

"I know times are tough." Joseph spoke, stating the obvious, "I will need some help, volunteers with know-how to repair the church so that we can have a village center and also a place to have a church service in relative comfort—thinking of God instead of what an awful place it is to worship. I promise no one will need to help to any large extent. I can learn fast and take over most of the work myself."

"I will see what I can do to find you volunteers," responded Garth.

The three continued their conversation that lasted long into the night. They discussed philosophical topics, declining Roman power, and what the future would hold in the event of likely Roman pullout from Britannia. Garth sounded depressed, while his daughter was more hopeful. Joseph thought the young or, in this case, younger, adults are usually more optimistic about the future. Joseph also spoke positively, and at the end of the discussion, Garth appeared to come around a little to Joseph's and Ruth's views.

The next morning Joseph awoke in his makeshift bedroom in the church. He was groggy from staying out too late with Garth and Ruth. After finishing his morning prayers and dressing, he went outside to test the weather. When he opened the door, several men were preparing to work on the church. Garth was front and center.

"After speaking to the men, we decided it was better to have a strong church in our village and surrounding area. The church will give people hope in these dark times. We will work on the church until it is finished. Are you ready to get to work, Joseph?"

"Yes," nodded Joseph.

Garth gave orders to the assembled villagers. They broke into teams and delved into working on specific tasks. One team was assigned the roof, another was to stabilize the walls and foundation of the building. A third team began work on the inside.

The teams worked hard for a week, and then, amazingly, they were done. Joseph watched the villagers as they worked to pick up tips so he could perform his own repairs going forward. Unfortunately, the pace the men worked was quick and involved several areas, so that his working knowledge of repairs improved only a little. When the work was completed, Joseph was amazed at the transformation of the church. It had gone from a dilapidated hulk to a usable and safe building. While not a new, pristine structure, it was viable for Joseph to conduct his church duties. Joseph felt a deep pride when observing the repaired church. Even his temporary quarters were redone to provide him with a permanent bedroom/study.

Joseph wasn't sure how to thank the villagers besides "feeding" the men spiritually. While thinking about a reward, Ruth approached him.

"I am guessing that you are thinking how you can repay the men for their work."

"Yes, Ruth, how did you know?"

"I know how a man thinks."

"But there are different kinds of men and they think differently. I was once in the employ of a man, and most of the time I had no idea what he was thinking." Joseph was talking about General Valerias and was liberally using the word "employ."

"You are a good man, Joseph, and a good man would think, how can I give something back to the people that have helped me? A not-so-good man would think, how can I get more from these people without them expecting anything from me in return?"

Joseph felt warmth with these comments. Few people had paid him compliments, and these words were nice to hear. He liked Ruth. She had the characteristic of resilience that he did not see often.

"We will have dinner in the church for all those who helped with the church."

"Maybe we should also invite their families?"

"Why not the entire village?" Ruth one-upped Joseph.

"I don't have the means or the ways to host such a dinner, and the church will likely be too small to handle such a crowd."

"Leave it to me," countered Ruth. "But I will need your direct involvement."

Joseph learned quickly that Ruth was a great planner. She was organized and, most important, could think ahead. She contacted most of the village, it seemed to Joseph, and she also obtained a fairly accurate estimate on the attendance. It was a drab, mean time before winter, so most villagers readily agreed to attend. For those who planned to attend, Ruth assigned them tasks to complete. These tasks involved bringing food, drink, and ancillary dinner items.

Joseph was present when she met with the villagers, and at those meetings he was introduced to those he had not met on earlier occasions. When he wasn't with Ruth during the planning events, he was at the church reading his Bible or working with villagers on renovating their homes. At scheduled times Joseph led church services. With the church more usable, immediately the attendance increased. Also, the more the people of the village became comfortable with Joseph, the more they began to talk to him about their problems as well as for spiritual guidance.

When the villagers learned Joseph had physician skills, his popularity skyrocketed. The village had not had a physician in recent memory. Although Joseph was not a true physician, he had learned much about the profession during his pre-priest days. His time with Olivertos had extended his knowledge and skill tremendously. After only two weeks in Bergen, he had successfully delivered two babies.

The party to celebrate the completion of the church's repair was held three weeks after the work was finished. It was a large celebration. The entire village turned out, as they had wanted to feel positive about something. Everyone was dressed in his or her finest clothes, even though many of those clothes were quite worn. Joseph said the blessing to open the festivities. All was going well, and Joseph was very pleased. He could not believe what had happened to his life since he said goodbye to General Valerias. He was enjoying the moment, so much so that he didn't see Ruth come up behind him and gently squeeze his shoulders.

"You have done well, Joseph."

"We have done well," he responded.

As he felt her touch, another feeling came over him, a feeling of strong affection toward Ruth. He quickly changed his attitude. He was a man of God now, and this feeling for Ruth was very troubling to him. While she was still holding his shoulders, Joseph suddenly stood up from the table and walked over to an area where several villagers stood. They greeted him upon his arrival and continued on in their conversation regarding the amount of crops harvested this year. Joseph had little comprehension of the subject and instead was consumed by thoughts involving Ruth. *What was he going to do?* He couldn't, even in the slightest way, acknowledge Ruth's flirtation with him. He had been taught that Christian priests should be celibate. He, as a priest, had to follow the tenets of the church. Coveting a female was not allowed if he desired to remain a priest.

Yet he was attracted to Ruth and had been since he had first observed her in the village. She was pretty, intelligent, and worldly enough to converse with him about any subject.

Likewise, Ruth was attracted to Joseph since he had visited her father's house. She thought, *Finally, there is a man in the village who not only is kindhearted, but is well versed on any number of subjects and has traveled.* Most of the men in the village had not traveled much outside it or the surrounding villages, and their favorite conversations seemed based on how many chickens a man had or other nonsense. Ruth was bored with these topics of livestock, crops, and politics. Also she was of childbearing age and wanted to have children.

Joseph and Ruth had not discussed their feelings toward each other or with anyone else. They knew in their hearts there was a chemistry between them that was more than that between a woman and a priest. This situation needed to be handled delicately. Ruth watched Joseph across the room talking to the villagers, knowing why he had made his move away from her. She picked up several items from the dinner and disappeared outside of the church. Joseph stood with the villagers until the end of the dinner. When the people had left and the church was moderately cleaned, he closed the door to the church. He sat on a bench and prayed for guidance until he fell asleep.

XLVII

Alpha

The group of villagers Claire had joined moved through the land like domesticated cattle. They were loud and without focus instead of blending in with the landscape. Claire worried about the attention the group would attract. She estimated there were about five adult males, several elderly people and females, and at least fifteen children. She wasn't sure where all the males were—probably dead or rebels in hiding.

One of the males in the group was clearly the dominant one. He barked orders and bullied the elderly. Claire silently named him "Alpha." He initially left Claire alone because she was new to the group, and she had a presence that signaled she wouldn't accept his tirades. The hermit she noticed previously continued to follow them, but he maintained a discreet distance. Others in the group also observed him, and there was talk in the group that he was a spy for Morguard. That talk was quickly dismissed. Why would an older man with a limp who needed a staff to aid him in walking be a spy?

Anne and Elizabeth kept looking at him as they wound their way through the forests and glens. They seemed to pity him. Claire, though, thought he was a poor specimen of a human and told the girls not to look at him. At the end of the second day, Claire became distracted by Alpha berating one of the older men. At that moment the girls took the opportunity and brought food to the hermit. He first thanked them and then ate ravenously. He finished in a minute and smiled. He said his name was Marcus and asked the girls for their names.

"I am Elizabeth, "said the youngest.

"And I'm Anne," Anne piped in, not to be outdone by her sister.

"I can tell you are intelligent girls. You don't look like the rest of that group. Where are you from?"

This time Anne spoke first, "We are from . . ."

Claire rushed in and cut her off. "That is not your business." She had seen the girls talking to Valerias and hurried over to them.

"I apologize. I was too forward. I miss the company of intelligent people."

Claire was surprised by his response. It was not of the substance typically spoken by a hermit or a bum.

"Where are you from?" she asked him.

"A long way away. I originally came from Rome, but I have traveled far distances in time and land since my days in Rome."

"So you are Roman then." Claire's response was part question and part statement.

"Yes, I am a citizen of Rome."

Valerias was not about to disclose many details of his past, so he kept his answers short and vague.

"We get few Romans up here in Britannia who are not attached to the Roman military or Roman bureaucracy. So what brings you here by yourself?" Claire had in the back of her mind that Valerias was a spy for Argus.

Valerias sensed her trepidation. "I am here of my own free will and because I choose what I want to do. I didn't plan on how things have ended up—my appearance even causes me concern."

"What do you mean? You are acting on your own?"

"When I came to your country, I just wanted to live off the land and be by myself. It has not been easy, and I have regretted my decision on more than one occasion." Valerias changed the subject. "Now, what are you doing out here? Shouldn't you have a male escort?"

Claire sharply spoke, "I do not need a male escort. I have done well on my own."

"I see that." Valerias spoke with a hint of sarcasm.

Claire looked at her daughters and saw images of children who had been thoroughly exposed to the wild, as the warmth of Mary's hospitality wore off. Claire and her daughters were beginning to morph into a similar state as that exhibited by Valerias.

She angrily responded, "What I'm doing and what we look like is my business, not yours. And I have had male and female escorts for my travels." Claire thought of Erik and Mary when she responded to Valerias.

Valerias growled, "Then we don't know much about each other or our purposes, and that is fine with me. I think I will join your group, as they appear to be going in the same direction as I."

"What direction is that?" Claire reactively questioned Valerias.

Valerias did not say a word, he just pointed vaguely in a northwesterly direction. He then reached into a pouch in his worn clothing and pulled out two figures. They were small but intricate woodcarvings of Roman soldiers he had created while traveling alone in Britannia. He gave one to each girl and noted they were given in appreciation of their bringing food to him. Each girl politely thanked him and he smiled in return.

Valerias had become a superb wood carver because of all the vacant time he had during his traveling, particularly waiting at forts. The very sharp dagger he kept strapped to his calf was the instrument of the carvings. Claire had noticed the dagger as well and the sword sheathed on his back. She began to think he was not the person shown by his appearance.

Claire still felt there was a possibility Valerias was a spy or informant for Argus sent on locating rebels and informing Flavius or Morguard of their location. She had her doubts about whether Flavius was as evil as she originally thought, and now she wondered about Marcus. She decided to test Valerias.

"Have you heard of a man named Argus?" Claire looked intently into Valerias eyes.

"Not really. I have tried to avoid people when I arrived in Britannia. I know he is a nobleman of some type. That is about it. Should I know more?"

"What about Morguard?"

"No. But I did hear his name mentioned when I was recently in a nearby village."

"Flavius?"

"I know many people by the name of Flavius. It is a Roman name. I don't know anyone by the name of Flavius in Britannia."

The conversation turned back to Claire. Valerias asked, "Tell me why I should know these persons? Are they your kin or friends?"

"No, they are not," she answered. She didn't want to give herself away, so she continued, "They are not friends of normal Britons. They helped murder a ruler, stole our resources, and as you have seen, turned our country red with the blood of the people."

She changed the conversation bluntly back to Valerias. "What is your name?" She again studied his face for any sign of speaking untruths.

"I am called Marcus." It was the truth as far as his answer went. She tended to believe him but followed with, "Do you have a last name, or is Marcus your last name?"

"That is the name I go by. Now what is your name?"

This question gave her great concern. As before, she couldn't answer "Claire." Even if he weren't a spy, that knowledge, if it became widespread, would likely be her and her children's death sentence. She again responded, "Clarissa." Both girls looked at her a little oddly but said nothing. The way she spoke the name "Clarissa" was enough evidence for Valerias to know "Clarissa" was not her true name. He didn't care, though, except he stored the thought, *Why is she lying to me?*

"All right, Clarissa, where are you going?"

"We are headed west to where a man named Eustice is located and away from Argus' tyranny."

"You don't look like part of the group you are traveling with."

"Neither do you, Marcus."

"That is correct. I'm not part of any group. I saw this bunch and thought I would accompany them in a fallback position until they reach their destination."

"Hopefully it will be a short journey." Claire became less guarded. "We have traveled far, and now we are almost in sight of our destination."

At that moment a foot came down and pushed Valerias off of the log he was sitting on.

"Leave the woman alone, scum." It was Alpha, exercising his normal bullying form.

Valerias' instinct was to reach for his sword and give Alpha an involuntary tracheotomy. However, he pushed that instinct temporarily aside. Valerias instead tried his best to grovel a little, which was very difficult for him.

"I'm sorry, sir. I do not wish to offend anyone." Valerias continued, "I would like to join your group."

Alpha laughed, "Why would we take you? You look next to worthless. And you could be a spy for Argus."

"I am not a spy for anyone," countered Valerias.

"I assume anyone I don't know is a spy. Can you prove you are not a leech on Argus' back?"

Valerias rolled back the sleeve to his left arm. A Roman symbol had been tattooed on his shoulder. It was typical of a Roman soldier. Valerias was careful not to reveal his right shoulder, where a tattoo showing his officer status had been placed.

"Well, I'll be damned. A Roman soldier that looks and smells of the earth is in our presence. You must either be a deserter or a traitor to be here now."

"I am neither. I served my time and retired."

"Then why are you not dressed in your finest clothes and loafing around some villa where it is warm and sunny? It is simple to me—you are running from something."

Alpha turned to Claire. "And where are you from?"

Claire pointed in an easterly direction and said the name of the village where she had stayed with Mary—Abrador.

Alpha was not very familiar with that village, so he nodded and said, "Do you think this Roman is a spy for Argus? After all, Flavius is a Roman."

"No, I don't think so." Claire had not yet made up her mind about Valerias, but she didn't want to see him killed by Alpha, if there was any doubt he was a spy.

"Okay, woman, you can come with us. We are close to escaping Morguard. I need a mate and you will do." Alpha looked at Claire and then stared at the girls. "You can bring your brats. I'll decide what to do with them later."

Alpha pointed at Valerias. "And you, you will carry our supplies—like an animal. You should feel at home. Time is wasting. Let's move."

Claire's heart sank. Of all the people she had met during her time escaping Argus, Alpha was clearly dangerous to her and her daughters. He was nothing but an animal that had become pack leader by intimidation. She said a soft prayer to no one being in particular, pleading that she be able to find a way out of the situation. Claire looked behind to Valerias as they walked to Alpha's camp. The girls were walking with Valerias and looking at him like he was a novelty.

"So you are a Roman soldier?" Anne quietly asked, in more of a statement than a question.

"I was a Roman soldier. I am not any longer."

"So you know how to fight." Anne continued her questioning.

"Yes." His answer was limited to one word spoken in a whisper.

Claire had heard the conversation between Anne and Valerias. Her mind was thinking ahead. *Perhaps the old man could be of use after all*, she thought.

Alpha's group, including Claire and Valerias, camped by a stream that night. Alpha did not trust Valerias to serve as a sentry; thus he was free, within reason, to inspect the area around the camp. He observed a path that served as a deer trail that paralleled the stream. There was another deer track that wound its way up through a steep hillside. The base of this path was primarily rock.

Alpha's sentries were sloppy in their watch, and Valerias was not seen conducting his survey of the area around the camp. After he had observed what he wanted to see, Valerias went over to where Claire was resting and sat down on a log. The girls were sleeping soundly.

"Did you find your escape avenue?" she said not looking at Valerias.

"I saw what I wanted to see. That is all."

"Are Roman soldiers trained in the art of flight?"

"You Britons have a funny way of thanking those who protect you."

"So, you are now protecting me? From whom, Alpha? Morguard? Argus? Or the Romans?"

"Why the hostility toward Rome?" Valerias responded with a question.

"First the Romans took our land and subjected the people to Roman rule. Now they are so weak that they can barely protect the people that they have dominated." Claire started to speak of her husband, Gerhard, and his fate, but stopped. She didn't want anyone, including this odd Roman, learning her true identity.

"Yes, the deterioration of the Empire bothers me too. What was once indomitable is now mortal. The years of Marcus Aurelius, Hadrian and Diocletian are just memories. Our recent leaders have not been worthy of the purple. And the people themselves have not deserved someone who was worthy of the Emperor's purple."

Claire looked at Valerias. She again felt this was not the typical Roman soldier she had encountered during her life. Also, once Valerias started speaking, the words flowed like a brook. He discussed the Roman hierarchy, Roman life, and his service with Julian. After several minutes of monologue, he stopped. Outside of a few peasants and the druid woman, Edith, he had not spoken to anyone in months, and it showed. He was both embarrassed and angry for talking as much as he had. Claire would suspect he was more than a typical soldier, so he turned the conversation back to Claire, and, more precisely, to her daughters.

Claire went into brief summaries of each child, including what she liked, how she responded to situations, and how brave she had been during their trek to Eustice. She tried not disclosing concrete details about the girls that would give away their identities, but Valerias was easy to talk to, and he listened.

"Do you have any children?" she asked him.

Valerias paused before answering and kicked at the dirt. "No, I don't. I have never been married."

Claire thought that was understandable given his appearance, and yet he had a way about him that did not match his appearance. And the girls seemed to like him.

At that moment Alpha appeared from behind Valerias and gave him a kick and moved himself between Valerias and Claire. "Get out of here, you wretched piece of shit! I have some business with the lady, and I don't want you around!"

Valerias knew it was time to end the life of this bully. As he began to reach for his sword, a cry went out: "They're coming!"

The camp was now in pure chaos. Morguard's scout team had located Alpha's band and had notified Morguard. Lights from torches appeared in the distance. Morguard was on the scent, and the noise coming from the camp gave him all the information that he needed. The race for life was on.

XLVIII

Turnabout

Earlier in the day Stephen had left Claire and the girls because their dire situation became too great of a concern to him. He left the note for Claire because he was afraid for his life. However, once he was away from the camp, he thought of the money he would not receive from Flavius and had a change of heart. Meanwhile, Claire believed Stephen had deserted her and the girls, forcing her to join Alpha's group. When Stephen returned to the former camp, he found that Claire had gone.

He followed Claire's trail to Alpha's camp. He observed the camp and concluded there was nothing more that he could do, as he was not about to ride into the camp and announce he was protecting a queen. *That wouldn't work at all,* he told himself. She would probably be safer with Alpha's group anyway. Stephen reasoned he could explain to Flavius what had happened. He thought the worst that Flavius would do to him was not pay him the final sum of gold that had been promised. Stephen knew his limitations of bravery, and those limitations had now been reached. His desire for safety again outweighed the desire for money. Stephen turned his horse around and slowly moved away from the camp.

Stephen had traveled a leisurely half-day's ride away from Alpha's camp when he decided to take a break. He dismounted and tied his horse to a tree. The woods were silent, which he thought was not unusual for a fall day. He sat underneath a tree that provided much shade. He took a slow, deliberate drink of water from his flask and closed his eyes for a moment, contemplating what he would tell Flavius. Maybe he would ride off to a distant kingdom and not see Flavius again.

A rope tightened around Stephen's neck in an instant. He immediately used both hands to grasp at the rope to try to loosen its grip. Stephen's mind flashed through who would be doing this to him. *Is it Flavius repaying me for my failure to complete the task he had commissioned? Is it outlaws taking advantage of a poor traveler? Is it Romans, although they typically do not sneak up on a solitary traveler out in the country?*

The rope was tight, but it wasn't being pulled tighter. Stephen reasoned whoever was behind the tree wasn't trying to kill him, at least not yet. He had a low threshold of panic, and that threshold had not been exceeded. He knew someone wanted something from him, so he relaxed and waited. After several minutes, he looked up to a man standing in front of him. The man had blond, flowing hair. He wore no armor and was dressed entirely in black. He had bluish eyes and a large mouth surrounded by thin lips.

"I am Morguard, general to King Argus, the Great. And who are you out wandering about in the country?"

Stephen had heard of Morguard and knew he was a rising star in Argus' kingdom. The rope around his neck was still tight, and Stephen choked out a few incomprehensible utterances. Morguard didn't like to waste time, and he gave a look of daggers to whoever was behind the tree holding the rope. Stephen's plan worked, and the rope was loosened.

"I am Stephen." Stephen thought it wouldn't hurt to use his real name.

"Where are you from, Stephen?"

"I come from a rural area outside a small village east of Ratae. I live by myself."

"I can see that. Some of the poorest peasants I have come into contact with are an upgrade to you."

Stephen was pleased that his lack of grooming was for once paying off. Morguard's manner, while calm, did not ease Stephen's concern about his situation.

"Tell me, Stephen, what is a rodent such as you doing out here in the woods? Are you looking for a new den to hibernate in during the winter?" Morguard laughed at his own joke, and Stephen heard several more people in the vicinity laughing as well.

"I am hunting rebels as King Argus has commanded."

More laughter splattered from the group that now surrounded him. A large burly man to his left had an especially obnoxious laugh. Stephen was a proud man, and he didn't think any of this talk at his expense was funny, particularly from the large man. When he turned back from looking at the large man, Stephen stared into the face of Morguard, and the sharp point of Morguard's dagger pressed into his throat. Stephen had been wrong; Morguard's disarming nature was an illusion.

"Tell me, rat man, what rebels are you looking for?"

"Lord Morguard, you have flushed many out this way. I was hoping to pick off a straggler or two and receive my bounty from our king." Stephen had trouble getting these words out with the point of the dagger a hair's width from breaking skin.

Morguard relaxed the dagger very slightly. "Have you located any rebels since they were flushed your way?"

Stephen knew his survival depended on his answer. "Yes, I spotted a group of them over to the west." Stephen pointed as gently as he could in a westerly direction hoping not to feel the sharp pressure of the knife again.

"Then I can assume you will take me to them of your own free will?"

"Of course, Lord Morguard."

Morguard pulled the dagger away from Stephen's throat and put it back into its sheath on his belt. He motioned for one of his men to bring Stephen's horse to him.

"Tell me, Stephen," Morguard spoke in a more cordial manner, "how many rebels did you see in this group?"

"About thirty."

"Men, women, children?" Morguard was fast becoming inpatient.

Stephen concluded that Morguard was a very volatile man. Flavius was much more stable but equally as dark as Morguard. Thus, in a matter of seconds, Stephen now feared Morguard more than Flavius or even Argus. So he knew he had to be very careful what he told Morguard. If he gave up Claire, he would face the wrath of Flavius. On the other hand, if he said nothing about Claire, he could be implicated in helping her. Yet he had to give Morguard something, so he created a half-true story.

"There were not many men of fighting age. There were several women and children and elderly people."

"Was there a woman with two girls?"

"Could be. I saw young girls in the group. I would think there were several mothers." Stephen was proud of himself for walking the fine line and convincing himself of his tale. Hopefully Morguard accepted his story.

Morguard had always been suspicious that Claire had not been killed. Something did not seem right. Her strange demise and the lack of real proof by Flavius were not convincing to him. Unfortunately, his suspicion was more in his mind than from anything factual. Still, the bounty on her life and his future status with Argus made chasing any clue down regarding her possible living existence worth it. Morguard's ideal situation would be to find Claire and give her to Argus. Flavius would be finished, and he would become King Argus' chief commander.

"You will lead us to this group, Stephen. If you are correct in what you have been telling me, I will let you live and maybe even toss you a few pieces of gold. If you are wrong, I will nail you to a tree and the ravens and whatever else that infest these woods can pick your body apart."

After everyone in Morguard's unit had mounted his horse, Stephen began to lead Morguard to the rebel camp. He had no idea how this would turn out. Morguard had already sent out scouts to locate the alleged rebels. Stephen knew he would do well to be accurate in guiding Morguard to the rebels before or at the same time the scouts did. He also realized his chances for surviving this predicament were far less than stellar. He said a silent prayer to no god in particular that he be spared in what was to come.

The scouts returned to Morguard as Stephen was leading Morguard's forces to the rebels. They informed Morguard of the rebels' presence in roughly the same location that had been pointed out by Stephen. This finding pleased both Morguard and Stephen for different reasons. The scouts told Morguard that they could not give an individual count of the rebels because it would soon be night. The rebels were also not hiding their presence because occasional loud sounds were emitted from the camp and by a small fire set by a rebel.

Morguard had about thirty men in his company at that time. The rest of his men were terrorizing other sections of the countryside. Morguard divided his force of thirty into five units to cover and converge on the rebels. One of Morguard's captains had warned that splitting their force into too many groups could weaken them to the point that if they encountered a large armed rebel group, the rebels could inflict damage on Morguard and his men.

Morguard simply told the captain, "You are wrong. The rebels are so scattered and weak that our forces could overcome any resistance thrown by them. If you do not agree, you can ride with your tail between your legs back to Argus." There were no further questions.

Morguard and his men rode quickly and quietly to where the rebels were camped. However, one of Alpha's sentries was awake enough to hear Morguard, and he let out a camouflaged cry like an owl to warn Alpha. Alpha's group was not a military force, and when word spread of Morguard's nearby presence, a structured defense was not the response. Instead, panic spread throughout the camp. Alpha tried to coordinate an escape route along the creek and persuaded many of his group to follow him.

As he was directing the pedestrian traffic, Alpha peered through the shadows and observed Claire talking to Valerias. Both of Claire's daughters were beside their mother. He forcefully ran over to her.

"You will come with me. Grab what you can carry. Let's go."

Claire hesitated. She did not care for Alpha at all, and she was very concerned with what would happen to her and the girls if they went with Alpha. The only alternative besides death or capture seemed to be Valerias. He had his back to Claire and Alpha, listening to sounds coming from Morguard's men. He turned around and faced Claire and Alpha.

Alpha looked at Valerias with disgust. "Old man, we will leave you here. Maybe you can take on Morguard by yourself. Your smell should drive them away. Let's go, woman."

Valerias spoke calmly to Claire with his eyes directed at Alpha, "If you want to live, you and your daughters should come with me."

"You would choose to go with this scum that passes as a man instead of me?" responded Alpha.

Claire was indecisive for a moment. Alpha started to reach for her and was stopped cold. Valerias had drawn his sword and was holding it in front of Alpha.

"She will make her own choice," Valerias said in a measured manner. "Now back away."

Claire looked at Alpha and then Valerias. She now had to make an extremely difficult choice. She had doubts about whether Valerias could handle the situation. He did not seem to be a polished warrior. His trustworthiness was still very questionable. Then she glanced at Alpha. She knew what would happen to her with him *if* they were to survive Morguard.

"We will go with him—with Marcus," she said to both men. Claire stepped toward Valerias with her daughters in tow.

"Foolish bitch. You will soon be sausage to Morguard. Good riddance. I'm taking your horse as payment to me for letting you stay with us."

The presence of Morguard closing in pushed Alpha away from Valerias and Claire, and he disappeared up the path by the creek. Several shadowy people followed him on the path. When they were gone from sight, Valerias sheathed his sword.

"We will go this way." He pointed in the direction of what appeared to be rugged terrain.

"Why don't we follow the path Alpha took?"

"Because," answered Valerias, "so will they." He pointed in the direction of Morguard. "At least this will buy us some time. First, tie this rope around your waist so we don't lose anyone. You too, Anne and Elizabeth." Valerias passed a rope to Claire.

"I'm placing all my trust with you, and I don't even know you. Whatever happens, it is more important for my daughters to escape than me."

"Why don't we all make it through this and not worry about priorities." The rope was now secure on the four. Valerias spoke in a tone that was reassuring, "Now follow me."

Valerias had scouted this route earlier in the evening. It was a rugged, inclined route, but its floor was rock. It would be much more difficult for Morguard to follow them in this terrain than along the creek bank, where footprints would be viewable and the tracking easier. Valerias, Claire, and the girls carefully walked along what was barely a trail. They walked up and down slopes, among hillsides, through primarily forested areas. A full moon graced the sky with enough brightness to light their way.

After a couple hours of the trek, Valerias noticed that the girls were becoming tired. He signaled for them to stop and said they could take a short rest. They had climbed to the top of a hill, and much of the countryside spread out before them. Under different circumstances, it would have been a beautiful night. As they sat there, noises came from the area where Alpha's group was headed. There were screams from Alpha's group and yelling from Morguard's men. Valerias and Claire knew what that meant, and it was likely the girls did also. Valerias didn't want the girls to focus on the cause of the noises, so he requested that they return to the trail and resume their escape.

XLIX

The Cave

Morguard caught up with Alpha's group, and the slaughter began. Anyone of Alpha's people they could find, they killed. It didn't matter if the person was male, female, young or old. Alpha, since he was leading the group, bolted into the underbrush as soon as Morguard assaulted the rear of his group and fled away from the scene as fast as he could. Leaderless and powerless, the group offered no resistance. Stephen watched in horror as the event unfolded. He had seen brutality before, but not like this. He feared for his life now.

When it was over, Morguard commanded, "We camp here tonight. In the morning we will see what we have. We can chase down any stragglers tomorrow. Did anyone see evidence of a woman with two children?"

No one responded affirmatively. Morguard turned to Stephen. "I hope for your sake we find certain bodies tomorrow."

"But..." Stephen started to speak, but the look from Morguard froze his tongue. Stephen did not sleep that night.

The next morning Morguard sent out search parties for survivors. They caught Alpha hiding behind a tree about two miles from Morguard's camp. Alpha's horse had broken its leg as he fled the creek area. He was brought before Morguard, his hands tied behind his back and a rope around his neck.

"Name yourself," commanded Morguard to Alpha.

Alpha said his name in a low voice. He knew his fate.

"Tell me about your rebel group."

With the tiniest hope for survival, Alpha spoke of the elements of his group—the men, women and children. He said they were not rebels and had allegiance to Argus.

"Where are you from?"

Alpha mentioned a village to the east. A smile emerged from Morguard's face. "That is one of the villages I have burned. When I am through, there will not be any rebels or resistance left."

"You were their leader, correct?" Morguard continued.

"Yes."

Morguard pressed on, "Have you seen a mother with children in your group?"

"Yes, we had a few mothers with children. Why do you ask?"

"Just curious. Did any of them not originate from your village?"

Alpha answered, "Yes, we did have a woman and her two daughters join us. They said they were from a nearby village that had been torched."

"Did the woman have a name?"

"I heard her name was Clarissa, why?"

Morguard loosened Alpha's bonds and helped him to his feet. "Look at the dead and tell me if this Clarissa is among them."

Alpha walked around where Morguard's men had brought the dead villagers. Alpha vomited as he looked at the grotesque site. These people were his fellow villagers. He did not feel like an Alpha now.

"No, none of these people is the woman, Clarissa, and I do not see her daughters either."

"Do you know where they are?" Morguard spoke in a calm manner.

Alpha faced Morguard with an air of a defeated animal. "No. They went with some old hermit. I have no idea in which direction they went. They couldn't have gone far—being an old man and two young girls."

Alpha turned back to look at the dead. He was going into shock. He heard a noise to his side and began to look in that direction. The blade of Morguard's knife slit his throat. The last thing he saw was Morguard's men piling the dead villagers on top of each other. Alpha collapsed to the ground and died.

"Put him on top of the pile since he was their failed leader, and burn the bodies."

Morguard ordered his second-in-command to appear at his side. As the bodies began to burn, he ordered, "Split the men into groups and find the bitch, Claire, the old man, and the children. Those who find her will receive a huge reward. Failure will not be so rewarding. Go!"

The man divided Morguard's force into three groups of six. Twelve men were left with Morguard to track any of the other villagers who had escaped. The three groups then rode out in search of their prey.

Morguard would have been surprised to learn how far Valerias and Claire had traveled in the night and now by day. The terrain became increasingly rough, though, and their progress had slowed considerably. They had to be careful where they placed their feet, because a slip could result in an injury or bring death. Even an injury could prove fatal in the long run, if it caused the group to slow their escape and allow Morguard to catch up to them.

After several hours Valerias could easily tell the girls were tiring. He alternated carrying them on his shoulders and became tired himself.

"I need to rest a bit," he announced.

Claire and the girls were relieved to have a break. Valerias scouted along the hillside and found what he was looking for—a cave. He carried the girls up to it. Claire followed the girls inside. Valerias picked up branches that had fallen from trees and covered the entrance. Dusk was calling from the west, and Valerias said they would wait in the cave through the night before resuming their flight from Morguard in the morning. The cave was quite large and could fit as many as thirty people inside. In addition to its roominess, the cave was not cold. Most caves Valerias had seen were usually quite cool. Why this cave was warmer than others he had experienced was a mystery to him, but he didn't care to learn the reason. He was tired too.

The girls fell instantly asleep. Valerias and Claire rested in a sitting position with their backs to the cave wall. Valerias relaxed only slightly. He kept his knees bent and eyes facing toward the entrance. He got up and went outside for a few moments and returned with dry leaves and sticks. He arranged the leaves on the bottom with the sticks on top. He then retrieved some branches, which he broke into smaller pieces and placed near them the sticks and leaves.

"We can have a little fire. These materials should burn fairly clear. I don't want to alert anyone, friend or foe, of our location."

Valerias made several attempts to start the fire and failed each time. Claire finally leaned over, and with a few tricks she learned as a young girl started a small fire. Valerias was embarrassed that he could not ignite a fire and poked at it without saying a word.

"Why are you helping us?" she finally broke the silence.

After a pause, Valerias answered, "Because I want to."

"But you have everything to lose and nothing to gain. You could have been killed. You may be killed."

"On the contrary, Clarissa, I have everything to gain and nothing to lose," he spoke with conviction.

Claire didn't understand this reasoning, so she returned the conversation back to the initial subject, "I still don't understand why you are here."

"Why I am here is my business." Valerias took a couple of deep breaths. "I came here on a quest." More silence followed.

"What quest?"

"I do not know anymore. It seemed easy to think about when I was back with the legions. Now that I am here in Britannia, I have lost my focus."

"Maybe the focus of your quest has changed."

Valerias poked at the fire a little longer. When he looked at Claire, she was asleep from exhaustion. For the first time since she had left Mary, she was relaxed enough to sleep. Valerias gazed at Claire and the girls. He thought to himself, *Life is so fragile. One minute you are in sleep with your dreams, and the next minute you are at the end of a sword.*

When Claire woke the next morning, Valerias was gone. The sun had started its rise, and sunlight filtered through the entrance of the cave, even though Valerias had piled branches at the entrance. Claire panicked and her mind raced through all the possible scenarios of what had happened. Marcus had deserted them and disappeared into the hills. Or Marcus was actually a spy for Argus and Morguard and had left to bring her enemies to her. Or Marcus may have left to find food or water and was returning to the cave. Based on her experiences to date, she feared the second scenario was the most likely one. She knew she had to take the necessary responsive action.

Claire woke the girls and told them they had to leave the cave as soon as possible. The girls were groggy and slow to move which caused Claire to let her impatience show. As she stood up her left foot felt an object on the cave floor. She bent down and picked it up. It was a dagger wrapped in a cloth. It was obvious: Valerias had left it for her. Now the quandary she faced was—did he leave it so she would have it for defense on her own, as he was not coming back? Or was he returning? Claire soon learned the answer.

As Claire was moving the girls along, there was movement in the brush that covered the cave entrance. Someone was throwing it aside. Claire first thought that it was Marcus returning. Her heart stood still for a second when a large man stepped inside and spotted Claire.

"She's in here."

Soon four more men appeared in the entrance of the cave. They advanced toward Claire with a smaller man in front. He appeared to be the leader as he barked commands to the other four men and at least another outside the cave. None of the men was Valerias. She pulled the girls behind her and held the dagger out in front. She was trained to fight with a dagger, but there was no way she could fight off the five men. In the back of her mind, she knew her time was up and what was to come would be beyond brutal, especially for her daughters. Anne and Elizabeth knew the situation was bad and held tightly on to their mother.

The leader spoke through yellow teeth, "You must be Claire, and those are your daughters. The entire country, particularly those aligned with King Argus, have been searching for you. And now we"—he pointed to his fellow men—"are going to be rich. What makes this even better is the reward is for you being brought back dead or alive. And me and my men haven't had a woman or a girl in a long, long time, and now that drought is about to end. You are about to give us a bonus."

Claire thought bitterly about Valerias and why he had deserted her. He was a coward, no better than Stephen. She was convinced Valerias had tipped off Morguard's men of her whereabouts. What also weighed heavily on her mind was the sacrifice that others had made for her and the trials she had undergone to get this far and fail. It was too much for her to bear, and she became weak, and the knife she was holding began to shake.

"Leave them alone!" The call came from the entrance of the cave.

Not all of Morguard's men heard the voice.

"I SAID BACK OFF AND LEAVE THE WOMAN AND CHILDREN ALONE!" He shouted the demand this time so no one could mistake what it meant.

The leader with yellow teeth turned around and the other four men parted so that there was direct visual contact between the two men. Claire looked into the sun, which was beaming into the front of the cave. She had a hard time physically identifying the figure that was speaking, but it was unmistakably Valerias.

The leader spoke in a haughty tone, "What pile of grunge did you emerge from?"

Valerias did not answer.

The yellow-teeth leader decided the silence was a voice of submission from this strange man and continued, "Who are you? What interest do you have with this woman and her brood?"

"She is my friend and I promised to accompany her on her journey."

"Even if her journey's end is death?"

"Yes, even if the result is death."

"You are old and ugly. One of my men could take you without breathing hard."

"One already tried." Valerias moved the sword he had carried in the cave with his right hand from behind his back to his front. He then moved his left hand forward. In the left hand was the head of the man who had been watching the cave. It was dripping in blood. Valerias tossed it on the ground in front of the yellow-teeth leader. "Was he supposed to guard the cave?"

"You son-of-a-bitch!" The yellow teeth leader nodded to the large man and he began to advance on Valerias. "I shall cut your head off and place it on the trail for all to see. You will not make a fool of Morguard or me."

Valerias' sword was held with the point down to the floor. The sun hit the sword directly and the sharp reflection off of it bounded about the cave walls. The large man raised his sword to bring its full weight down on Valerias' body. But Valerias was quicker than anticipated by the large man as his sword swished through empty air. Valerias' sword struck a single blow that pierced through the large man's chest and exited out of his back. He was dead instantly.

Valerias took the dead man for a ride into the other four men, pulling the sword out of the corpse as it fell to the floor of the cave. The four men were temporarily stunned by the maneuver. The large man was one of their fiercest warriors, and he had been killed so easily. Two of the four men had not even drawn their weapons.

Valerias rolled onto the floor and pushed the body of the dead man away. While on the floor he observed the foot of one of the standing men and plunged his sword into the foot. He quickly pulled the sword from the foot and with a slicing motion cut behind the knee of another standing man. Both men howled with pain and became more involved with their injuries than with Valerias—at least temporarily.

In one motion Valerias jumped to his feet and blocked a wild sword swipe by another man. Valerias gave him a kick to the chest, causing the man to fall back into the wall of the cave. His instinct told him that fourth man was behind and ready to stab him in the back. At the last second, Valerias whirled about and knocked the sword from the man's hand with a forceful blow. The fourth man took a step back, but it was too late, as Valerias' sword entered his gut. Valerias pushed him into a wall, and he fell to the floor in agony.

The remaining three men began to recover from their initial injuries. They realized that momentum was no longer in their favor, and their fates were perilous. They grabbed their weapons and in a chaotic motion rushed Valerias. The two men with leg injuries were tenuous though and the third man was quicker to meet his death. Valerias made a simple fake motion to his right. The man fell for it, and Valerias struck him sharply across the throat with his sword. The man dropped his blade, put his hand around his throat, and fell on his knees, and finally forward on his chest.

The man whose foot Valerias stabbed was now starting to make his way to the entrance of the cave, but not before Valerias gave him a kick from behind sending him sprawling on the floor. The other survivor whose knee had been cut shouted and rushed Valerias more out of fear than courage. Valerias blocked the man's sword and hit the man with the hilt of his sword hard in the face. The man stumbled, and Valerias pierced his chest and his heart.

Valerias pulled his sword from that man and now faced his final foe, who had pulled himself off of the floor and was standing with difficulty. It was the man with yellow teeth. Valerias took two steps and was on him. Valerias put his left hand on the blade of the yellow-toothed man and pushed it away from his body. With his right hand Valerias took his sword and ran it up and through the man's front. The man looked at Valerias in disbelief and died.

As the yellow-toothed man died, Valerias in a fit of rage screamed, "I reject rapists and cowards, and now you are all dead and returned to whatever Hell you emerged from!"

Valerias walked to the cave entrance. He raised his arms with the sword dripping with blood in his right hand. He had slain five men in less than a minute, and had splashes of blood covering much of his body. He gathered himself and quietly said, *"Sapor est victoria! Adhuc esurient!"* [Savor the victory! Hunger for more!] After standing in the sun for a moment, he returned to where Claire and the girls were huddled.

Claire still clutched the dagger. She had never seen anything like what she had just witnessed. The utter power and ruthlessness of this man was so unexpected. Although Claire did not want to watch the violence, she could not turn away, as if she was under the spell of an enchantress. She never imagined that this older man, who looked like a hermit, could fight in the manner she had just witnessed.

"I can fight when I need to Clarissa," Valerias firmly stated and he dropped the sword on the cave floor. "I have never deserted any one or run from any event in my life."

He kneeled before the girls. Their faces exhibited shock from both the arrival of the five men and their subsequent brutal deaths.

He spoke slowly and quietly to the girls, knowing what they had seen. "I am very sorry for what has just happened. They were very bad men who had to be done away with or they would have hurt you and your mother. I do not take another man's life easily, but I didn't want them to hurt you. You have been through so much for being so young. I will do anything in my power to get you safely where you are going. Do you trust me to do this?"

"Yes," both answered without wavering. They had in their eyes a look of trust, which Valerias had seen once before—with Anastasis. He gave them a broad smile.

"Good."

Claire had now regained her composure. "You are not just a soldier, are you?"

"Clarissa, I am Marcus, retired soldier of Rome. That is all you need to know."

After a moment of silence, he continued, "And you are not just a village woman, are you?"

"That is all I and my daughters are—people of the country. And that is all you need to know."

"Then we both have our secrets." Valerias was smiling again. This time Claire smiled back. Both smiles were not of the "happy variety." Instead they were more of, *I have secret information that you don't have.*

Valerias' smile was brief. He felt a dull pain in the upper part of his back left shoulder. He removed his tattered shirt to examine the source of the pain; however, because of its location, he couldn't see it. Claire stood behind him and asked that he move to the front of the cave where there was sufficient light. Claire noted there was no cut, but a deep bruise was forming in the area between Valerias' neck and shoulder. The area was turning dark, and a knot was forming in the muscle. Valerias was trying to recall the source of the bruise and came up empty. It must have occurred when he was on the ground with the dead man and someone had wildly struck at him. Fortunately, the strike was not from a sharp blade.

Claire said, "If we had some cool water, we could soak the wound, and then I could make a bandage for you that could ease the pain."

"There is a stream just down the hill from the cave. I was there when these men found the cave. I will go there and clean up. You should stay here and prepare the girls for the rest of our journey. I will be all right, just sore for a few days. Thank you."

Valerias disappeared out of the cave. Claire had also noticed several scars on his back when she looked at his wound and thought he must have fought in many battles. As she walked back to her daughters, she observed Valerias' sword on the cave floor. She picked it up and moved it around gently, as if she were in a mock fight. She noticed it was beautifully crafted, with perfect weight and balance. This convinced her further that Valerias was much more than the old, retired soldier that he pretended to be.

Claire walked over to one of the dead men and saw that he had a clean cloth in a pocket. She took it out and wiped the sword down and cleaned it of any blood residuals. She examined the dagger given to her by Valerias. Again, it was more a work of art than a weapon. She gave it a quick wipe down and placed the sword and dagger up against the wall. Her daughters watched their mother go through these activities with interest but said nothing.

Claire looked around the cave and finally settled her gaze on the girls. "Anne and Elizabeth, let's get ready to go. I feel we are close to being with your Uncle Eustice. I believe we have found someone who we can complete our journey with—successfully."

Anne answered, "He is a good man, Mother. I like him."

Elizabeth nodded in agreement.

Valerias found a small pool in the creek and took the water in his hands and washed his face with a splash of cool water. He repeated the act several times, then washed his shoulders and legs. The water felt refreshing, but he knew the pain in his shoulder would be a problem for several days. He thought of Claire and her daughters and a warm feeling came over him. Maybe this was the destiny that the old witch Edith had talked about. He again thought of little Anastasis. Valerias told himself that he would do all that he possibly could to take Claire, Anne, and Elizabeth to safety—even if it meant he would die.

After a few minutes of air-drying, he walked back up to the cave. Just outside the entrance was the headless body of the sentry that the yellow-toothed man had stationed at the cave. He was an easy kill for Valerias. Valerias put the body on his right shoulder and carried him into the cave. He told Claire the man was just another casualty and tossed him on the floor with the other five dead men.

He looked at Claire. "Let's move. Morguard or his men will be here soon. This will be a surprise to them, and they will want to find us with even greater expediency."

Claire and the girls exited the cave. Valerias took the branches he had originally used to cover the cave entrance and placed them back over it. With another branch he swept the area in front of the cave to remove any footprints or evidence anyone had come there. Unfortunately, he could not remove all the blood from the headless sentry.

When satisfied with his work, Valerias tossed the branch down the slope, smiled at the girls, and said, "You will have to be strong—I can't carry either of you for the rest of this trip."

L

DEMONS

JOSEPH HAD MADE it a habit to pray first thing in the morning after he awoke and at night before he went to sleep. In the morning he prayed for the blessing that it was good to be alive and to guide him in the day's activities. At night he prayed for what had happened during the day and for guidance in what was to come tomorrow.

For comfort he carried with him words from Paul in his letter to the Romans.

For none of us lives for ourselves alone, and none of us dies for ourselves alone. If we live, we live for the Lord: And if we die, we die for the Lord. So, whether we live or die we belong to the Lord.

The day after the community dinner, Joseph spent the morning cleaning the church. He didn't want to venture outside in the event he would see Ruth. At lunchtime there was a knock at the door. Joseph reluctantly opened the door and his fears were realized. However, it was not Ruth at the door, it was Garth.

"Have you seen Ruth, Joseph?" Garth politely asked.

"Not since last night, Garth. Did she not come home last night?"

"No, and I'm worried. She rarely does not tell me what she is up to."

Joseph was torn. He didn't want to find her and have to relive his feelings of last night. Yet it was more important to search for her. That would be the right thing to do, and he secretly wanted to see her again. Besides, any hesitation would make it obvious to Garth something was wrong.

Once Joseph gathered his coat, they were off to first search the village. If that yielded no results, they would enlist other villagers to search for her in the countryside. They had visited two homes when Garth spotted Ruth and a friend coming back into the village from the nearby woods. Garth was elated to see that his daughter was fine. Joseph also found himself very grateful and said a short prayer of thanks to God.

"Where have you been, child? We have been worried." The "we" implied both Garth and Joseph.

"We?" Ruth answered, looking first at her father then focusing on Joseph. "I'm pleased you were concerned about my safety." Ruth did not take her eyes from Joseph's. "I stayed at my friend's home last night." Ruth pointed to her partner. "Then this morning we went a little ways into the woods to search for special fall herbs. I am sorry, father, I should have told you. I won't let my failure to communicate with you happen again." Ruth stared at Joseph as she spoke these words.

Joseph wished he could disappear, but Ruth reduced the pressure by saying she would go to the friend's house and divide up their morning haul of herbs. She would be home soon. With those words both women walked away.

Garth and Joseph watched them walk down the main village road and turn off on a side road.

"My daughter is falling in love with you. Do you know that, Joseph?"

Joseph's heart raced extra beats, as their formative relationship was apparent to another person, Ruth's father. There was a definite budding chemistry between Joseph and Ruth. If Garth had noticed something, it was likely others would have also observed the impact Ruth was having on Joseph. He had to be very careful about what he said.

"I have also noticed. It's like a young girl's crush."

Garth was sharp in his response. "Do not pretend with me, Joseph. She is not a girl. She was married previously and knows about life and love—probably more than you do."

The last phrase was a slight insult whose purpose was to have Joseph open up about what he thought of Ruth.

Joseph looked around to see if anyone was near and saw no one was within earshot. "Yes, I have feelings toward her. Please know that I know what it was like to have loved and not just in a spiritual, priest-like way. I have not always been a priest."

"But you are now a priest, correct? And doesn't a priest have only one true love—the love of Jesus Christ and God? I mean, you are to love your fellow man, and even the enemy. However, I have heard there can be no love between a man like you and a woman in your religion, correct?"

The conversation was disconcerting to Joseph. He was being verbally grilled by someone who Joseph wasn't sure was a true Christian, and yet knew some basic tenets of Christianity. The General came to Joseph's mind as someone who knew about Christianity but not about being a Christian.

Joseph knew that he was the keeper of the Christian faith and spoke back sharply. "Yes, I know what a priest can and cannot do. I have subjected myself to Christian principles and applied them to my life to be a good example to those around me."

"No one doubts your principles, Joseph. During the short time you have been here, you have accomplished much, and the people have begun to adopt you into the village. You behave like a good Christian. And yes, Joseph, I know what you're thinking—I am a true Christian.

Garth looked at Joseph in a sincere, fatherly manner. "It comes down to this—I want what is best for my daughter. She was very hurt for some time when her husband died. He was a good man as far as men in the village go. I know she is fond of you and you of her. So how does this play out? A priest cannot take a wife as your sole allegiance is to Christ and God?"

"And to the people I serve. I don't know, Garth. You are right. It is something I have to work out."

"It is something you both have to work out. Whatever the outcome, I want my daughter handled with compassion."

Garth said his good bye to Joseph and returned to his house. Joseph stood in place for several minutes and looked at the road that previously held Ruth.

Joseph spent the next several days caring for sick villagers. He wasn't sure of the cause of the illness, but guessed it was a disease emanating from the change from fall to winter. A makeshift hospital was set up in the church. Most patients recovered relatively quickly; others took more time. Amazingly, no one died. Joseph's stature in the village was steadily rising to a top berth, next to Garth. Joseph never thought much about accolades; instead, he was thinking more of Ruth and what he could and should do. Those would lead to different paths.

Ruth was unlike any woman he had known. She was bright, pretty, a tireless worker, and could easily carry on a conversation with anyone at any time on almost any subject. She did not show up in the church/hospital for the first few days of the epidemic and then, seemingly out of thin air, she appeared one day and directly asked Joseph if there was anything she could do to help. Joseph bumbled around with his response and finally said "Yes." It had become too much for him to manage, and many of the villagers who could have helped him stayed away from the church to avoid the disease. Joseph knew that was largely nonsense; however, he did not want to alienate any of the villagers and potential parishioners, so he said nothing.

Ruth was a fresh summer breeze in early winter. She handled caregiving tasks with ease. She was already well thought-of in the village because she was a genuinely nice person with status. She may have exceeded Joseph and Garth as the most popular person in the area. Joseph admired her. Ruth was also becoming an excellent physician's assistant. Together Joseph and Ruth made a good team.

After one particularly arduous day, the two sat together on a bench outside the church. It was unseasonably warm for the time of year.

"Thank you, Ruth, for all that you have done here. You are a godsend."

"Are you thanking me for my caregiving or about not talking to you about us?"

"Both I guess, Ruth. I just don't know what to say. Yes, I like you. I like you very much. You have to know that. Why do you think I have been avoiding you? And yet I have taken a vow of celibacy to God. My church leaders advocate such a role. God and Christ should fill my soul."

Ruth asked, "Did you take your vow to a man or to God?"

"To God, through a man."

"Why do think you need to take this vow? If every man took this vow, the population of man would die out, would it not?"

"Yes, I suppose so. But not every man is a servant of God."

"We are all servants of God, Joseph. I joined the Church when the first missionary came to our village. He was a good man. Some of those who followed him were not good men and had been corrupted by earthly temptations. That tends to dampen one's faith in God."

"When I first became a priest to the Lord, I was not ready to serve. I did not act as a servant of God should act. I'm trying hard now; it is difficult."

Ruth reached over and held Joseph's hand. "You are a very good man. You have God within your heart. I ask that you include me in your heart as well. There is room for both of us."

Tears were in Ruth's eyes as she spoke, and Joseph felt a deep, thoughtful sadness. He had to think about what to do. He knew he was falling in love with Ruth, as she appeared to have already crossed that threshold with him.

"I am going to Ratae in a few days. There is business I need to attend to there. I will think about us and our future during this period. I understand what you are saying. I just need to sort things out. Please give me some time."

"Take as much time as you need, Joseph. I will wait for you."

Joseph looked into her eyes, gave her hand a soft squeeze, and went back into the church. He felt utterly torn. He believed he had to make a decision between Ruth and God. Maybe there could be a middle ground. The more he thought about his situation, the more upset he became. He didn't sleep that night. He ended up "caring" for the last few ill people still at the church—even though they were asleep and did not need any care.

A week later, after the church was empty of patients, he left for Ratae. He gave Garth the job of holding whatever church service he wanted to hold. There really was no business for Joseph to take care of in Ratae, except to come to a decision about his feelings for Ruth.

LI

STANDSTILL

THE QUARRELING WAS loud. Dishes, equipment, and other tent-ware items had been hurled against the sides of the tent and onto the ground. Servants had either fled the tent or hid. One of them ran to Produgas, who was talking to colleagues. "Produgas, they are at it again!" the servant shouted.

"What now?!" Produgas was obviously annoyed at being disturbed.

"They are arguing about schedules. Uldric wants to advance, and Rao says we should stay put for the winter and consolidate our territory."

"Have blows been struck?"

"Not yet, but they will be. Please do something, Produgas. You are the only person the brothers will listen to."

Produgas waved for his friends to follow him. He was not about to break up this fight by himself. As they entered the tent area where the brothers were fighting, Produgas heard screaming. Not screaming that indicated pain, but screaming of intense anger. This was serious and he took immediate action.

Produgas opened the tent covers. He noticed neither brother had drawn a weapon. That was the good news. Uldric's face was crimson red and Rao's complexion was a shade lighter. That was not good news. Produgas quickly summed up the situation, revised his thinking, and dismissed his comrades. Under these circumstances, he believed it would be prudent if it were just the three of them in the tent.

"Please tell me this quarrel is about a woman?" Produgas spoke as he entered the tent.

Uldric looked at Produgas. "No, you pompous ass. Why do you think that?"

"Because your caterwauling is carrying on so loud that the reason had to be a woman. Now who is the woman?"

Rao took a step back and relaxed slightly. Uldric followed Rao's lead.

Produgas continued, "You two are the leaders of this expedition, our mission. We are now far from home. How do you think the men are taking this—their two leaders fighting all the time and not using restraint that leaders should express?"

"We don't need to explain anything to the men, because we are their leaders," retorted Uldric.

"I'm glad you said we, Uldric," Rao interjected. "Because without the 'we,' we will perish on these plains."

The emotions had now calmed significantly, and Produgas pointed to blankets so the brothers could sit down at the same table. He ordered a servant who had been cowering in the corner behind a table to serve drinks to him and the brothers.

"Winter is in the foreground and we must be prepared." Produgas was starting to lecture the brothers.

"I know the time of year, you old fool." Uldric still had acid on his tongue.

"Good, I'm glad you do." Produgas said, businesslike without a morsel of sarcasm. He continued, "Let's resolve our problems now and then we can plan for the future. Now what is the issue?"

Rao spoke first. "I say with the arrival of winter we set our camp in a protected area and wait winter out. Uldric wants to keep moving west and south. We first need to secure our supply line and check with the home base that all is well and coordinated before proceeding further."

Uldric disagreed. "We need to keep progressing and not let our enemy build up strength when we should be pounding them. Hibernating like rodents over winter is not the way to drive our invasion through the Goths and then into the Romans."

"I understand what both of you are saying. Now let me add my own little suggestion."

Both Uldric and Rao were paying close attention to Produgas. "We do need to strengthen our position here and back home as Rao suggests; however, we can still launch raids from our base here and do damage to the areas outside of our base. That way we can keep the Goths apprehensive and off balance before our major invasion in the spring. I am anticipating—as you both are—that additional tribes will join us over the winter."

"I assume you are going to suggest that it is me that stays in camp and conducts all the logistics for the spring invasion, while Uldric conducts his raiding actions," Rao noted in a mildly mocking tone. Secretly that is what he wanted his role to be, because traveling about the countryside in winter was not his first choice.

"You assume correctly," voiced Produgas. "Doesn't that make sense?"

The brothers nodded slightly at Produgas' suggestion indicating they agreed. They spent the next several hours discussing who was going to conduct what task and when. Finally, at the end of the long evening, the brothers shook hands and went separately off into the night. Both were ambivalent about their agreement, but there was now peace in the land of the Northern Hun.

Produgas watched the brothers leave the tent with disdain and said to himself, *I am the real leader of this force. I just do not have the power. The ones that have the power do not know how to use it.* He had the servant pour another drink and he continued to look into the darkness.

For the next three months, peace prevailed in the Northern Hun camp. Rao put his disdain for winter traveling behind him as he journeyed back to the homeland. He even met with Zestras and provided him with an update of Uldric's and his progress toward the Roman Empire. Zestras had spies in the Northern Huns, but he listened intently to Rao about information he already knew. Rao was also suspicious that Zestras was not as uninformed as he pretended. Rao always felt that Zestras had underlying motives for nudging his brother and him to go on the expedition to the west.

Rao suspected that Zestras all along had had his eyes on the Northern Hun territory. Without he and his brother's presence, taking the territory would be an easy task for Zestras. Rao was correct in his suspicion, and it was in that line of thought that made Rao more conservative in his approach to the Roman campaign. Uldric did not see this side of Zestras. Uldric was more interested in achieving his goals of conquest and plunder. He was more accomplished in pursuing the physical side of warfare while Rao preferred the mental considerations, such as planning operations.

Rao was in a bind and he knew it. He had a brother who was marginally out of control and continually needed to be reigned in. Zestras was a manipulator, and he had the power to back his manipulations. Finally, there was Produgas, who seemed to have his own agenda. Maybe it was Produgas' intention to let Uldric and him kill each other and then he would step into the leaderless void. Rao thought about his life in a contemplative manner. He now would rather be in the home country living a simpler life. Murdering his father with Uldric and waging the current bloody campaign had taught him that his "previous" life was the preferable one. That was no longer possible, though, as he had passed the point of no return.

In this web Rao found himself. His first act was to challenge Zestras to back the campaign with something besides words. Zestras initially resisted, but eventually Rao convinced him that if they were to work together in the future, they needed to start their joint venture now. Zestras reluctantly agreed and said he would provide up to one thousand of his best warriors and substantial gold for the spring campaign. Rao, in a parting remark, told Zestras there would be no campaign unless Zestras actually followed through in providing resources.

Rao rode back to the Northern Hun winter camp. He was initially pleased to see Uldric at the camp instead of conducting raids in the hinterlands. Uldric had done his best to carry out waves of destruction in a large area. However, Rao, through Produgas, learned that when Uldric had recently raided a nearby city, a group of his best fighters had been ambushed by a freak late fall blizzard, and all the men perished. *It was a shame to be killed by snow and not man,* thought Rao.

Other raiding parties were struck by the same blizzard. Several men suffered frostbite and gangrene poisoning. Subsequently there were amputations, infections, death, and permanent disabilities for many of these men. The men didn't like Uldric's inadequate leadership, and there had been talk of a revolt. The whole event tempered Uldric's warring behavior until spring returned.

For his final action regarding his potential detractors, Rao, with Uldric's concurrence, promoted General Produgas to senior advisor to the brothers. Rao knew Produgas did add value to the brothers' plan. With his promotion Produgas would constantly be with the brothers. Rao believed this would keep any quarreling between himself and Uldric to a minimum. A secondary and important benefit was that in his new position Produgas had to stay close to the brothers and, thus, Rao could keep an eye on him.

The Northern Huns stayed busy over the course of the winter. They trained and consolidated forces during that time. Sarmatian and Suevi tribes and additional Alans joined them. Rao even let Uldric out for raiding now and then. At the end of winter, Rao had emerged as the clear leader of the Northern Huns—at least that was the unspoken consensus in the camp.

LII

SACRIFICE

VALERIAS TOOK SEVERAL steps away from the cave thinking that the six men came to the cave by horseback, so there must be horses nearby. It didn't take him long to find the horses tied to a long tree branch. Valerias was initially concerned that the yellow-tooth man may have had a guard stationed at the horses. That was not the case, though. Valerias observed that the horses were not prize trophies, but would suffice for his group in leaving the area of the cave.

Valerias took Anne and Claire rode with Elizabeth. The other four riderless horses were tied together in a line that trailed behind Valerias and Claire. The terrain was hilly and alternated between forested and treeless slopes. After about an hour of riding, Valerias stopped in a heavily wooded area and told Claire and the girls to take a rest.

Valerias dismounted, took rope that was attached to one of the horses, and disappeared into the woods. He thought where the trail narrowed in the trees was a perfect place to set a trap. The trap required a rope, a sharpened stick, and a sturdy branch. A snare was positioned in the trail to be triggered by an unwary enemy rider. The rope holding the branch would then be released, and the sharpened stick would hurl toward the rider and hopefully kill him.

Claire dismounted and walked up to Valerias, watching him as he worked.

"I see what you are doing." She couldn't wait any longer to comment.

Valerias turned around and saw Claire. "I am buying us time. It won't be long before Morguard locates the cave, sees what has happened, and then catches our scent. If we can make them a little wary and thus slower, that will be good for us."

"What if an innocent person comes down the trail and meets your surprise?"

"That would be a casualty of war, Clarissa. And after what I just witnessed, we are in a state of war. Those men were after more than just a peasant woman back in a cave. You have special significance to Morguard and, I assume, his master. Do you want to tell me about that?"

"No, not any more than you want to tell me about yourself."

"Fair, but I'm not being hunted."

"You are now, Marcus."

"You are correct, but it isn't the first time. That is why I am taking this precaution."

After a brief pause, Claire returned to her original line of questioning. "Does it bother you that a casualty of war is so insignificant to you?"

Valerias finished the task and gave the trap a few tests without setting it off. He stepped back and seemed pleased with his effort. Without looking at Claire, he said softly, "When you have been a soldier as long as I have, the life of unknown nonmilitary people loses its significance, especially when compared to one's own life or those that person is trying to protect. As I said, a casualty of war."

He turned and faced Claire, "Would it bother me if I knew my trap killed a young child or other innocent? The answer is yes. But I would keep on going. And I promise you that it will be Morguard's man or even Morguard who will face his maker when he meets this trap. We need to get going."

Valerias and Claire returned to the horses and remounted them. Valerias' instincts told him urgency was the best course of action. He spurred his horse down the trail to the west. Claire thought about her children and the closeness to safety. Thoughts of the innocent vanished from her mind. She wondered if she had found the man who could take on Argus.

Morguard's scouts found the cave and reported back to him. He walked into the cave and looked at the six dead men. He then conferred with the scouts.

"How many men are we dealing with here?"

"Lord Morguard, we have searched the cave and area around the cave with great thoroughness." The scout expected his next statement would bring a harsh rebuke. "We have found only one man was here. He did a good job of covering up his tracks. One man did all this."

Morguard felt that the scout was right, but he unleashed a torrent of vulgarities directed at the dead men, the scouts, and anyone within earshot.

"You lie, scout. One man could not do this. My men are good fighters, and there is barely evidence of a fight here. There must have been more than one man. It must have been an ambush."

"Maybe." The scout was being coy. "But we find evidence of only one man. And a woman and two children."

Morguard immediately stopped his movements and thoughts about the mystery man. "Say that again."

"We found tracks that there was one man, one woman, and two children."

Morguard knew immediately that the woman was Claire and the children were her daughters. His thoughts of Claire back in Alpha's camp had been confirmed. Who the man was, he had no idea, except he was a man skilled in fighting, maybe a guard hired by Claire. Morguard walked back to his horse and called for his scouts to begin tracking the quartet. He looked at Stephen from the side so as not to attract attention, and as he mounted his horse, he thought to himself, *This man, Stephen, knows more than he is saying.*

The group found the trail used by Valerias and Claire, and they were quickly after them. This time he would get to them and expose Flavius as a traitor or at least as incompetent. He would be promoted as Argus' top general and enjoy all the benefits that position would yield. Morguard smiled as they began riding down the narrow trail, thinking solely to himself, *Argus said find and bring them back—dead or alive. And that is what I will do.*

Valerias picked up the pace of his group as they headed to the land of Eustice. Even though Morguard's men had been easily defeated in the cave, he never liked to underestimate anyone, and he was not going to do it this time. He believed Morguard's men were bandits, not well-trained Roman soldiers, so under normal circumstances, Morguard's men would be easy fodder to defeat. But it was only himself with a woman and two tired children, so making a stand was not an acceptable alternative.

The wilds of western Britannia were just up ahead. Once they reached that wilderness, he might be able to lose Morguard, or, better yet, Eustice could come to their aid.

"Do you have a meeting location with Eustice?" he asked.

"No," Claire answered, "I didn't have time or the method to arrange that."

Valerias was frustrated with that response but showed little emotion. "How are we going to find him? This is a big country, and Morguard will likely catch up to us in one day's time. We don't have much time to find Eustice."

"I have put my faith in that he will see us, through locals or his scouts, and he will come to us."

"I knew a man who said he had faith." Valerias was thinking of Joseph. "But his fate depended on my faith in him and what he did." Valerias caught himself before explaining further, and giving away his past as a Roman general. He was pleased with himself for succinctly summarizing a complex thought. Claire, though, did not know what he was talking about.

"Is that a riddle?" she asked.

Valerias just grunted an unintelligible response.

As they rounded the top of a hill, they heard a scream in the distance.

"That will slow them down a bit. Sometimes a well-set trap works." Valerias was looking in the direction of the scream while talking to Claire in a slightly condescending tone.

"Yes, it did appear to work on Morguard—*this time*." Claire's response back to Valerias was equally condescending.

As they rode deeper into the wilderness, the oldest daughter, Anne, who was riding on the horse with Valerias, began talking to him. She had never been shy with him since their initial meeting, and now she turned on a fountain of thoughts and questions.

"Are you afraid of anything, Marcus?"

"Only your Mother." Valerias laughed at his comment.

"No, really, does anything scare you?" She was serious with her question.

Valerias looked at her as she turned her body and head around to look him in the face. "No, Anne, I am not afraid of any man, living or dead." He paused a few seconds before continuing, "I am afraid of something, though, and that something is time. I mean, time comes and goes, and there is nothing I can do about it. I'll be a day older tomorrow and so will you. But to me the concept of time is real. To you, it isn't yet."

Valerias continued, "I can control people to some degree. But I cannot order time to stop, because it won't. It is important to get done what you can when you can, because tomorrow you are older and may be gone." Valerias had turned philosophical and was speaking in a tone that was hard to hear unless you were sitting right in front of him.

Anne looked confused and interjected, "Were you an Emperor?"

"Why do you ask that?" Valerias was surprised with the question.

"Because you sometimes talk like my father, and he was a king." Anne very quickly followed with, "Forget what I just said—*please.*"

Valerias now realized that the woman Clarissa at one time had the status of a queen. He stored the information in his mind and quickly answered her question, "No, I'm not an Emperor—not in the past, not in the present. Like I told you from the beginning, I'm just a retired Roman soldier, that is all I am."

Anne looked at him with round eyes, the size and shape of large coins. Her look indicated she did not believe him.

"I believe there are some things that should stay a secret between us, don't you?"

"Yes," she answered.

Claire, who had been lagging behind because Elizabeth was growing tired of riding on the horse, suddenly spurred her mount up to Valerias.

"What are you two talking about?" Claire was brusque in her question.

Anne was quicker than Valerias with a response.

"We were talking about horses and how long we have been riding and how much more there is to go."

Claire was not convinced and gave Anne a stern look. Valerias did not see the expression on Claire's face, but he could tell by Anne's look that it was time to change the subject. The trail was wide at this point, and Claire moved up to be parallel with Valerias.

Soon both girls dozed off, and for the next hour Claire and Valerias discussed many things, including the rigors of parenting, trust and Eustice—the elusive brother of Claire. It proved to be a conversation of equals. Both Valerias and Claire were pleased to finally have a similar mind to talk to, but they avoided discussing specifics regarding either person.

Finally Marcus pulled the reins of his horse tighter and abruptly said, "It is time to move quickly. The horses are rested and Morguard is at our backs." He could instinctively feel Morguard's approach.

They traveled into the rough country with deep forests and narrow valleys. Valerias had given up trying to hide their trail. Instead he was not concealing their tracks at all. He wanted to make it appear that they were running and not being careful anymore. The quartet reached a shallow but wide creek.

"This is where we part, Clarissa."

"Why now? What are you doing?" Claire seemed stunned. She thought Marcus would ride with them to the end, either to Eustice or their capture or death.

"I fear Morguard is within two miles of our current position. He will catch up by nightfall. I can't let that happen."

Valerias looked into the eyes of the girls and then Claire. "We are going to split up. You and the girls will take one horse. You will ride up the creek bed for at least one mile. When you come to any rock outcropping after that distance, you will leave the stream and ride west as far as you can."

"Where are you going?" Claire hesitantly asked.

"I am going to take the four extra horses and ride downstream away from you. I will try to make the trail hard to follow, but not too hard. My plan is to lure them away from you long enough that Eustice will find you. I hope, for your sake, he really is out there." Valerias pointed to the dark hills to the west.

Valerias rode alongside Claire and lifted Anne onto Claire's horse behind Claire. Elizabeth remained sitting in front of Claire. The horse was strong and could easily handle the weight of Claire and the girls. Valerias smiled at the threesome.

"You two," Valerias pointed at Anne and Elizabeth, "have been brave soldiers throughout your ordeal. As brave as any man I have served with. Now you are almost done with your journey. Help your mother through the next day just like you have done for so many days." Then he spoke to Claire, "Clarissa, may you find your way to safety and happiness."

"Will we see you again, Marcus?" she asked.

Three pairs of eyes were locked on him for his answer. "I don't know. If it happens, it happens."

Valerias gave a satchel of food and flask of water to Claire. His final act was to give his dagger to Claire. "You may need this, now go." With that, he gave Claire's horse a mild swat and it and its three riders disappeared around a curve in the creek. Valerias turned his horse, now tied with the four other horses, and disappeared in the opposite direction of Claire's horse.

LIII

Morguard

Valerias rode part way in the creek bed and the rest on the creek bank. The creek was shallow in most areas, but along the banks of the creek, where it curved, there were deeper pools. Valerias observed small fish in the pools. *They too are trying to hide from Morguard,* he thought.

Valerias was riding the fine line of disguising his trail, but not so much so that a decent tracker could not follow him. Valerias also hoped he could camouflage his tracks enough so that Morguard and his men would not know whether they were following five or six horses. And it worked. Morguard and his men came to the spot in the creek where Valerias and Claire had gone separate ways. There was no sign of anyone going upstream. After several minutes of searching, one of Morguard's men found Valerias' trail and the entire group was after him.

Morguard was clever too. He guessed where Valerias was heading and split his group up in two, twelve-man units. One unit would follow Valerias along the creek bed while the other group would ride away from the creek but parallel to it in an effort to try to cut him off.

Valerias rode the horses back and forth through the creek, creating substantial splashing action that was meant to distract and confuse Morguard. Morguard's scouts were indeed confused and couldn't figure out why those up ahead were pursuing this tactic. They also couldn't figure out how many horses they were tracking. Morguard didn't like the information he was being given and let out a constant barrage of cursing and criticism. Morguard was not well liked by the men he traveled with, and his actions alienated them further. They were not afraid of Morguard; however, the imagined presence of the dreaded Argus and Flavius behind Morguard kept the men reluctantly faithful to him.

Because Valerias had four horses in tow, he lost speed. He realized this put his position in jeopardy. He decided he would go with the extra horses as long as he could and then take three of the horses into the forest. He would use the remaining horse as a backup in case the horse he was riding became overly tired. He also figured by traveling with one extra horse he could outrace his pursuers, including those who might try to attack him from a side or downward position.

Valerias came to a clearing surrounded by woods to the west and south, and he rode the horses into the woods. Initially there was a decent canopy with little underbrush. The fall leaves blanketed the forest floor. Valerias took the horses deeper into the woods to an area with pockets of thick underbrush. *Perfect,* he thought to himself. He untied three of the horses from his horse and from each other. He gave the lead horse a sharp slap and it and the other two horses quickly disappeared into the forest. The horses were all a shade of brown, and they blended in with the color of the woods.

Valerias headed back to the creek where he would ride downstream and then go straight south. He reached the stream and followed it a short way. It was becoming deeper as the water frequently pooled. Valerias decided to leave the stream at this point.

He climbed out on the bank, maneuvered through thick brush, and everything turned black.

Valerias regained consciousness slowly when one of Morguard's men threw cold water on him that was obtained from the nearby creek. He was lying on the ground. His left shoulder was very sore from the fight in the cave and from his fall off the horse after being struck on the head. His ankle still hurt him. Valerias' head throbbed from the surprise blow he had taken, and it took time for him to regain a sense of what was happening around him. Another bucket of the stinging cold water splashed onto to his head and upper torso, and this time he was brought fully back to reality. He looked around and saw a number of figures peering at him. One in particular stood out, the man dressed in all black.

"Welcome back," the man in black said in a voice that reminded Valerias of the cold water he had just "enjoyed." "I don't have a lot of time, which means you don't have time either. Tell me, who are you and what are you doing in this place?"

Valerias looked at Morguard with an expressionless gaze.

Morguard kicked Valerias in the sore shoulder. "Answer me, swine."

"What do you want me to tell you?" Valerias muttered back in pain.

"Who you are?"

"I am called Marcus."

"That is a Roman name. Are you Roman?"

"Yes."

"Are you a soldier of the Roman occupation of our land?"

"I am a soldier, yes, not of this land."

"You're too old to be a soldier?"

"I am retired."

"You mean you are a deserter. No Roman I know would retire to a life in a foreign land, live the life of a rat, and look as disgusting as you do. You should be enjoying retired life in a sunny warm part of your Empire."

"I am not a deserter. I retired."

"Enough of this talk." Morguard had little patience and that was gone. "I know you somehow killed six of my men and were running with a criminal wench and her two little bitches." He was guessing this was the case.

"I don't know what you are saying. And who are you?"

Morguard kicked Valerias again. "I am Morguard, chief general to the king—King Argus. You are an ant to me. Now, where did the woman go?"

"I do not know. As you can see, she is not with me." Valerias was speaking the truth at this point.

Morguard did not know what to think of Valerias. He looked old and worn and yet he was obviously an experienced and tough fighter. He also obviously had been with Claire. He decided to apply some torture techniques to see if Valerias would talk. At the end of an hour, all Morguard got from Valerias was grunts. Finally he concluded, "Damn Roman" and gave Valerias another kick.

Morguard then looked at Stephen. He walked over to Stephen and in a flash of explosiveness hit him hard in the abdomen. Stephen vomited and fell to the ground. Morguard ordered Stephen to be lifted up and hit him again. Morguard guessed Stephen knew something of Claire.

Stephen was an excellent guide and a man of the earth, but he had a lower threshold for pain than Valerias. It didn't take long for Morguard to crack that threshold and get Stephen to talk. One of his techniques was to place Stephen's face into the sediment of the creek until he couldn't hold his breath any longer. Another technique was to pull his fingers back to the breaking point. Morguard carried out the interrogation in stages. First he learned that Stephen had been retained to take Claire and her daughters to Eustice. Morguard was pleased with this information. *So Claire really is the person I have been pursuing for the past several days,* he thought.

Second, it was Mary who had helped provide a sanctuary for Claire in the village. This was the same Mary who served Claire in the castle now under Argus' rule. Morguard did not know Mary, but he quickly put the puzzle together. She was the same woman who had pulled a ruse on him in the village telling him that she was Roman.

I will take care of her shortly, he thought to himself. The information provided by Stephen made Morguard feel good, and now Argus would recognize him. The negative side was that he hadn't caught Claire yet.

The last stage was to get Stephen to name the person who had hired him. Morguard eagerly hoped it was Flavius. On a personal basis, Morguard didn't know what was more important—to find Claire or stick Flavius as the instigator of the Claire mystery. Stephen tried hard not to reveal Flavius, but the pain was too much and he did name Flavius. Morguard then looked like a man who had been freed from prison. His mind was spinning, *What is the best way to tell Argus? Should it be in person or by messenger?*

As he reviewed these thoughts, one of his men rode into the clearing. "We found their trail," he shouted to Morguard. "It is several miles upstream, and they are only hours ahead of us."

Morguard cleared his thoughts and focused on his priority task of taking Claire dead or alive. "Keep these two here under guard," he shouted to a trio of men stationed near Valerias and Stephen. "If either tries to escape, and I doubt they will, kill them."

Morguard put his face inches from Valerias' face. "You and I are not done, Roman. I know you helped the bitch. When I catch her, I'll make her give you up, and then you can meet my king—King Argus."

Morguard and the rest of his men rode off up the streambed and out of sight. Valerias was in much pain, the greatest emanating from his shoulder. He thought Morguard was a fool. If he could get free, Valerias would quickly dispatch him by liberating his head from his torso. However, when he looked over at Stephen, he knew who had received the worst of Morguard's efforts.

"You too were helping Clarissa or Claire?" Valerias asked Stephen.

Stephen could barely speak, but mumbled, "No matter what happens, I, Stephen, am a dead man. Morguard will kill me as a rebel . . . and now Flavius, if he somehow avoids his fate from Argus as a traitor, will also kill me. Stephen kept saying to himself, *My life is worth little.*

"Who is Flavius?" Valerias was curious.

"Don't you know him? He was once a Roman officer. Maybe you served under him."

Valerias didn't answer, immediately. He was distracted by wondering where Claire was at this moment and hoping she would escape Morguard. He also searched his mind for the Flavius he had known and which one of those Flavius' would have ended up being a nobleman under a Britannia king. He could recall nothing on the matter. "What?" he said to Stephen.

Stephen repeated, "Do you know Flavius?"

"I know several men named Flavius, but I don't know which one you are talking about."

"They are going to take us to Argus and kill us." Stephen's voice was fatalistic.

"Morguard is a bully that is hiding his cowardice. I'm not afraid of him anymore than that tree over there." Valerias pointed to a half dead tree. "He will not find Claire and then have to explain his failure to Argus. I think Morguard will have to tread carefully if he wants to live."

"But if he gets Claire, we are doomed."

"We will see if that happens." Valerias grew tired of Stephen's negativity and told Stephen he was going to rest and that Stephen should rest also.

Claire had left the creek and was climbing up a small deer trail that appeared to end in a clump of bushes. Without a trail to follow, she worked her way up a slope and then down to another small valley. The daughters were very tired and begged their mother for a rest, and she obliged. She was tired too. Again, it was her against poor odds. Claire looked down the valley and saw no signs of life. She sat by a tree with no low branches and a thick upper canopy. Sitting in the shade would have normally been an enjoyable experience. Today she lost the ability to care. She wished she and her daughters could fly up to the top of the tree like birds and be unseen. Claire looked at her daughters, and their faces were pale, with dark circles under their eyes. She didn't know if they would elude Morguard, and if they should escape, would they lose the rest of the childhood they had left?

Claire heard a noise coming from behind her. It may have been an animal or a branch rubbing against a tree. After all, the breeze had picked up. Or it may have been Morguard now on their trail. She couldn't wait any longer. Claire told the girls to get ready to ride and they complied. After they were settled on the horse, she urged it forward at a quickened pace—a slow gallop—which is all the terrain would allow.

Claire rode the horse hard for a couple of hours and noticed her horse was becoming exhausted. Foam appeared at the corners of its mouth. Claire slowed the horse to a slow walk and listened for signs of life behind her. Many thoughts were flowing through her mind. Foremost, what would happen if Morguard caught her? Would he let the girls live? She doubted it. She couldn't think of those thoughts anymore and turned to thinking of the men who had tried to help her—of Erik, who was dead, of Proterous, Stephen, Marcus and, of course, Flavius. Was Flavius an ally, or was he putting her through all of this so his men could capture her at the end? *A brilliant game of fortune hunting*, she thought.

Claire heard another unnatural sound coming from the east. She feared Morguard would soon be upon her. Hiding the girls was not an option. She grabbed a hold of the dagger that Valerias had given her. She seriously thought about taking her girls' lives as the alternative to becoming prisoners of Morguard and whatever he would do to them. Her options were few, and desperation was setting in. More noises and she turned to face the enemy behind her. Her heart raced and sweat began to run down her face.

Then she heard Elizabeth say, "Look, mother."

Claire turned around to what was now in front of her. She expected the worst and she gripped the dagger hard. She looked straight into the eyes of a man dyed green, with small branches stuck to his back.

"What?" was the only word she could utter.

Out of the corner of her eyes she saw several more like-colored men emerge from the ground. There had to be well over ten such men. The man in front of her grabbed the reins of her horse and did not say a word. None of the men said anything. Claire initially believed they were Morguard's men. That thought quickly vanished, as she knew Morguard would not allow his men to go without horses.

Claire was helpless as she kept hearing sounds of men behind her. She took her eyes off the green man who held her horse and looked back again. The girls were scared and holding tight to Claire. Claire turned back and peered into the woods. A man followed by several armed men emerged from the forest on horses. The lead man was Eustice, her brother.

LIV

TRIBULATION

MORGUARD FOLLOWED THE scent of Claire well into the dark hills of western Britannia. He knew he was close to her—it was only a matter of time. He ordered his scouts out to find where she was located. They would report back to him and then he would swoop in on her like the triumphant bird of prey and all the resultant rewards would be his. It was to be a good day—his day.

Morguard was thinking what it would be like to become Argus' second-in-command and even possible heir to the throne. One of the returning scouts disturbed his daydreaming.

"Why are you back so soon? Is the she-bitch just up ahead?" Morguard was a bit hazy in his return to reality from dreaming about his career path.

"We have been gone for hours, Lord Morguard." The scout was mystified at Morguard's behavior.

"Fine. What is your report?" Morguard was now fully engaged.

"Not what you want to hear my lord."

"Why is that? Did she escape you?" Morguard was becoming exasperated.

"Well, yes and no."

Morguard interpreted the scout, "If you are playing riddles with me, you will soon find yourself stripped naked and buried alive in the creek bed back at camp."

"No, my Lord. We know exactly where she is."

Morguard glared at the scout in a manner that caused the scout to speak very fast, "She is with Eustice."

Without hesitation Morguard responded, "Let's go and get them both."

The scout knew what he had to say and he cringed when he said it, "We could as you wish, my lord—but please know that we counted at least one hundred fighting men with Eustice and we only have twenty-four. Remember, we lost six to the Roman. The rest of your force is scattered. We are good fighters and will do as you command, but we will not succeed if we have to carry out your order."

The scout waited for the cursing and possibly a light beating. However, that did not occur. Instead Morguard sat back in his horse and said not a word for several minutes.

Finally he spoke, "We will return to camp. I will send a messenger to King Argus and tell him what has happened. He will need to send his army with Flavius to Ratae. From there we will launch our assault on Eustice. With the army we will certainly outnumber Eustice, and then either kill or capture the traitor Eustice and his bitch-queen sister. Send men to locate the rest of my force in the countryside. We go to Ratae."

The scout nodded and then frowned. "I thought Flavius was a traitor to King Argus."

"Oh, he is. Yet, we will not speak of this until Flavius is in Ratae. We shall show the prisoner, Stephen, to him in front of Argus. It's a multiple point win for me . . . for us. Flavius is exposed and executed, Eustice and Claire are caught and killed, and I become Argus' second. Get the men and let's return to camp."

Argus sat with the scrawled letter sent by Morguard. Because Morguard was illiterate, one of the men in his camp wrote as Morguard dictated the letter. After finishing reading it, Argus summoned Flavius.

"Flavius, I received word from Morguard. Claire is with Eustice in the western hills. He gave the size of Eustice's force. Assemble two hundred cavalry. Include my personal guard. We leave for Ratae in the morning. We will travel light and obtain supplies in Ratae. I am going with you. If you succeed with this mission, Flavius, you can regain your post under me."

"Yes, my King." And Flavius took his leave. Ever since his demotion, the relationship between Argus and Flavius had become distant. Neither one trusted the other, and with good reason. This mission would be a test. Flavius was relieved as he left Argus' chambers. Stephen had completed his task and delivered Claire to Eustice. Yet he did not relish the thought of now trying to capture her. He was also worried about Mary. Yet, if anyone could survive this situation, it was Mary. He called for his captains and explained Argus' orders. The men nodded. They would be ready to leave the dark castle of Argus in the morning.

By the time Morguard returned to his base camp where Valerias and Stephen were prisoners, his mood had become one of self-satisfaction. He had not captured Claire, but he had a new mission. He approached Valerias and Stephen and told them Claire had reached safety with Eustice. He also announced they would be leaving shortly for Ratae. Valerias was perplexed by Morguard's change of attitude. He suspected something might have happened to Claire that Morguard wasn't saying, because Argus would not be pleased that Claire had escaped.

Morguard at first ordered that Valerias, Stephen, and two other men be tied behind horses and forced to walk to Ratae. These other men were suspected rebels seized by Morguard's men in a raid. The two men were actually villagers who had been in the country looking for food when they were captured.

After a few miles of this journey, the rebels and Stephen could not keep up with the pace set by Morguard and were now being dragged on the ground. Valerias with his injured shoulder and ankle was close to joining the three men. Morguard's captain grew concerned that the men would be casualties, which would not serve Morguard well with Argus. The captain gently persuaded Morguard that the better option was to let the men ride into Ratae, show them off to Argus, and let the men receive their punishment from Argus. Morguard agreed, and soon the four prisoners were riding packhorses.

When Morguard's troop reached Ratae, the prisoners were placed in a stockade. Before they entered the compound, Morguard beat all four with a whip. He would not kill them. However, they were rebels or Roman scum and they deserved his contempt, carried out in a physical manner. Some of the existing prisoners in the compound shared water and bits of food with the new prisoners. Valerias appreciated their kindness and fell fast asleep.

He awoke in the night when the air was still and the compound was silent except for an occasional cry of an animal or a soldier moving around in the distance. Valerias was surprised to see Stephen staring at him.

"Why are you looking at me? Why are you not asleep?" Valerias was troubled by Stephen's action.

"I have heard from the other prisoners, and overheard guards talking, that Argus is arriving tomorrow. We will all be tortured again and then executed. You, though, may have value.

Sometimes Titus, the Roman general of this land, buys Roman deserters from the locals—including from Argus too—and then you will meet your fate with Titus."

"Tell me about Argus," Valerias asked.

Stephen told Valerias all the embellished stories he had heard. Valerias asked more questions about Claire and Eustice and the state of the kingdom now ruled by Argus and also of Titus. Stephen spoke in hushed tones not to give himself away, and several times had to stop when a guard walked by. At the end Valerias had learned what he needed to know and thanked Stephen.

"Be brave come tomorrow, for it is how we leave this Earth that is remembered. If we have a stay from death and our time is extended, it will lead to better days." Valerias grabbed Stephen's forearm as a soldier does and smiled.

LV

Fortitude

JOSEPH AROSE EARLY on Sunday in Ratae. His heart ached about how to deal with his feelings toward Ruth. He was becoming too close to her for his and her own good and that of his supposed complete devotion to God. Yet his attraction to her was strong. He had spent the past week visiting churches in the area, but his mind the entire time was on Ruth.

The sun hovered on the horizon as he dressed and ate a small breakfast. The sun didn't rise high in the sky this time of year in Britannia. He was new to the area and unaccustomed to such a low sun. Still, it was a warm sight for Joseph, and fortunately it was going to be a warm day for November. Joseph thought he would cross the city and visit a small church on the far outskirts of Ratae. During his time at Ratae, Joseph helped as he could at the local churches, primarily doing medical care. He felt nameless, though, as these were not his patients as they had been in his adopted home village of Bergen. He knew his stay in Ratae was limited, and he would have to decide what he must do in his relationship with Ruth and return to the village.

Morguard heard that Argus was coming to Ratae bringing upward of two hundred cavalrymen. They would organize in Ratae, and then their joint forces would take the field against Eustice. As a gift to Argus, Morguard would bring the prisoners out of the holding compound and march them near the gates where Argus would enter the city center. He especially wanted Stephen in the front, followed by Valerias as his special prizes. Morguard was salivating at the thought of seeing Flavius' face when he entered the city and saw his co-conspirator in front of him. Morguard, through Stephen, would expose Flavius as a traitor and he, Morguard, would be the beneficiary.

Morguard wanted to prepare Stephen for his role in the upcoming drama by threatening and then beating him.

"When you see Argus and Flavius, and I ask you a question, you will answer it truthfully, so all can hear—particularly King Argus and Flavius. Do you understand?"

Morguard was about to hit Stephen again when he heard a clear voice off to his side.

"You are a gutless coward, beating on people who can't defend themselves because you have tied us down. Free me and I will teach you about answering questions."

Valerias knew it was a mistake to say those words to Morguard. He was just tired of witnessing Stephen being brutalized by the bully, a man who disgusted him. Morguard stepped back from Stephen and grabbed the whip from one of his men. He proceeded to whip Valerias to the point that Morguard's men thought he would kill Valerias and shouted, "Stop!" in almost unison. Valerias was worth more to them alive than dead. Morguard did stop. His breath was heavy and his talk was punctuated with short gasps.

"You, Roman dog. You, Roman dog. You are in no position to tell me anything. I should kill you now, but Argus may not understand my temper. I must show control. Just know that if Argus or your Roman master, Titus, doesn't want you, you will be mine to do with as I want."

Morguard gave a barely conscious Valerias a kick to the midsection of his torso and told his men to take the prisoners to the front by the main gate. Two men had to help Valerias to his feet and then shoulder to shoulder carry him out of the compound. Morguard stopped at a well and ordered that the prisoners be washed and given water by a group of slaves. He didn't want them to look in too awful of a condition before being presented to Argus. The break and water helped Valerias regain a foothold on reality. Stephen, who was sitting by Valerias, thanked him for his courage in standing up to Morguard. Valerias said nothing, but he gave Stephen a faint smile.

The men were then taken through the city. The inhabitants of the city lined the street. They said not a word—not a cheer or a jeer. Argus was not popular, and some of the rebels were well thought of in the village. Morguard sensed the hostility and occasionally whipped a bystander who was too close.

Valerias looked at the people as he was dragged through the city. To his astonishment, he saw a familiar face just off to his right. It was Joseph on his way to the small church. Without hesitation, Valerias extended his arms and made a weak lunge at Joseph. Morguard's guards were caught by surprise. Joseph instinctively reached out his hands in return. He initially thought the prisoner was a Christian asking for a prayer of forgiveness. The shock in Joseph's face when he saw that the prisoner was Valerias was sharp but short lived. Valerias shook his head at Joseph in a sign to say nothing. Joseph quickly complied based on his past association with Valerias. Valerias asked Joseph for a prayer and Joseph started one. However, Morguard returned to Valerias and gave him a quick whipping.

"You, priest." Morguard was pointing his whip at Joseph. "You should leave Roman dogs alone. You should know that. Your history with them is not a good one."

Joseph thought, *Morguard doesn't have his facts correct, as the Emperor Constantine became a Christian many years ago,* but he thought it unwise to disagree with this foul man. Morguard pulled Valerias away from Joseph and continued dragging him down the street. Joseph stepped back and then moved into the shadows. He opened his hand and stared at Valerias' ring.

Joseph was overwhelmed at this change of events. A minute ago he was on his way to a church and thinking about Ruth. Now he had the ring of the person for whom he had conflicted feelings. Valerias almost killed him more than once when he had been in Valerias' camp. Valerias didn't respect his religion or his profession in the Christian church. Yet through all the harsh treatment of him by Valerias, Joseph saw a complex man with a good center. Many on Valerias' staff had become his friends, and these men were a reflection of Valerias. It was Valerias who had granted him basically a free range in the camp. Most important, Valerias ultimately freed him and let him come to Britannia.

Joseph's mind shifted to Valerias' ring. Why did Valerias give it to him? What did it mean? Joseph was puzzled. It was still early on a Sunday, but the city square was busy. Merchants and their customers were out in force. There was a steady hum in the air. Joseph sat and thought about the meaning of the ring and why he had been given it. The garrison in the village had been vacated by the Romans. However, he was aware of the Roman garrison located several miles outside of Ratae that housed Roman soldiers. Further in the distance was an old castle. *Someone of real Roman power must be centered in that castle,* he thought.

More questions popped up in Joseph's mind, like a weed giving birth to hundreds of seeds. They all came down to three questions: Why did Valerias look and dress like a beggar—after all, he was a general, even if he was retired? Why was Valerias being treated like a common criminal? How would the Romans in Britannia treat him, a Christian priest, if he were to take the ring to them? Further, a corollary question: Would the Romans believe that he had seen the General and he was not setting a trap for vengeful Britons? He had found some Romans still hostile to Christianity, such as General Valerias, while others were actually Christians. Joseph's mind wrestled with answers to these questions without resolution.

He believed if he asked any native civilians about Valerias' current condition, it might end badly for both the General and himself. He might also find the Romans would not believe that a former Roman general could end up as a prisoner of Briton barbarians. Or that the Romans in Britannia would view Valerias as an enemy. All the political possibilities were too confusing for Joseph. He decided to walk to the church at the end of the city and decide what to do then. As he walked to the church, he silently prayed the entire way.

Joseph's prayers gave him his answer, and he decided what he had to do. He must travel to the Roman garrison and tell the Romans about Valerias. Joseph's concentration was so strong that he walked into the steps of the church without seeing the church.

A priest was present at the church and he engaged Joseph in light conversation, after Joseph said he was not hurt from tripping on the steps. Joseph finally asked the priest, "How far is it and how can I get to the Roman garrison south of here?"

The priest looked oddly at Joseph, so Joseph felt he had to say, "Brother, I need to make the visit for a parishioner of mine." The priest quickly drew up a map and gave it to Joseph.

When he was finished with the map, the priest blessed Joseph: "May God be with you on your journey."

Joseph responded, "As you pray for me, I shall pray for you and thank God for your help."

Joseph felt he could make the trip in less than a day if he walked fast. He packed a flask of water for his journey and was off down the road and away from the city. After a few hours of walking, he realized he was not in the shape he once was in, and that troubled him. He wished he had brought his horse with him; however, he had loaned the horse to a family that he was staying with in the city.

Occasionally people approached him on their way to Ratae. Joseph found these people provided a diverse mix of personalities. Some were friendly, others were not. Several were in groups, although there were a few single men. Also, most of the people had animals, either riding them or walking beside them. Joseph wanted his horse more than ever now.

As the day wore on, Joseph became more worried. He still had a substantial distance to travel to the Roman garrison. He doubted that he would make it there by nightfall. That meant he would have to stay in a building or other shelter that he could locate. The thought of spending a night along the road without decent shelter gave him much discomfort.

By late afternoon Joseph walked by an old building. He took the short path to its entrance and gave a quiet knock to the door. No one answered initially, so he knocked again. He was about to give the door a push, when it did open and a man appeared.

"What do you want?" The man asked in a gravelly voice. He was a small, thin man with a ragged black beard. The hairs of the beard seemed to have no uniform directional purpose. Joseph could tell he was not a pleasant man.

"I'm looking for shelter, for the night."

"Well, there's none here. Say, aren't you one of those Christian types?"

"Yes, I'm Father Joseph. Any kindness would be appreciated. Where else could I go?"

"Nowhere, you are in no-man's land. The authority of Rome or Argus does not reach here." The man had a mocking attitude as he addressed Joseph.

Joseph could hear men's laughter behind this man, which told Joseph there were several men in the building. The small man held the door in a mostly closed position, but Joseph could still peer inside for a look. And he didn't like what he saw. The room was mostly dark. On the floor and off to the right, Joseph thought he saw the bottom half of a human torso. He took in an inward gasp. Now he wanted out of this situation and fast. His mind went wild thinking about the origin of the body. Was it a drunken man passed out? Were these men body snatchers of corpses? Or, worst of all, had he come upon a house being robbed and pillaged by robbers and now murderers?

Joseph decided it was time to leave. He politely said thank-you to the small man with the ugly beard and hurried down the short path to the road. Once he reached the road, adrenaline took over and he practically sailed down the road toward the Roman garrison. When he slowed down for a breather, he sensed something or someone was behind him, so he gave a quick look over his shoulder. It was the small man with several partners. Fortunately none of these outlaws had a horse, but they were coming fast.

Joseph picked up his pace again and began running. He could feel his heart starting to race. He knew he was in trouble. He was the deer being pursued by wolves. He knew if the outlaw men caught him, he would be robbed, beaten, and left for dead somewhere off on the side of the road.

Joseph was not wrong—that was the intention of the outlaws. They thought Joseph had valuables, and they didn't care for Christians, so robbing and eliminating Joseph was their plan. Joseph did not think he had any real valuables with him, and then he remembered Valerias' ring. It had a large red stone, perhaps a ruby, set beautifully in a gold setting. Roman sayings were carved in tiny print around the stone. It had to be worth considerable coin.

The small man and his associates were within a few hundred yards of Joseph. His sides started to hurt. He silently cursed his clothing as the cloak slowed him down. He had placed the ring in an inner pocket, so at least the outlaws would have to look to find it if they caught him. As he ran, Joseph had contrary thoughts. He thought to himself, *I made it alive out of his grasp and now Valerias will get me murdered anyway*, and laughed sarcastically. Then a feeling of calm came over him. *I will succeed and save Marcus. This is what God intended.* He said one of his favorite short prayers as he ran, hoping God would give him the strength to save himself: *Lord, let me reach great heights, so that I may serve You as You have served man. Give me strength to do great and honorable things in Your service.*

Another mile went by and the small man and his outlaw accomplices were within one hundred yards. Joseph guessed he had run for about two miles since the house. His only hope was that the outlaws would tire and give up. What troubled him as he ran was that the men appeared in better condition than he. *Valerias would be disappointed*, Joseph mocked himself.

He saw a small bridge up ahead. Strangely, there were no other travelers on the road, as it was becoming dusk. Joseph believed if he made the bridge, the outlaws would stop and return to their normal abode, wherever that was.

Joseph reached the bridge and turned around. The outlaws had slowed down, except now the small man was not leading the group. A much larger man was running at full speed. It was a matter of seconds before he reached Joseph.

Joseph had nowhere to go. He couldn't outrun the man who was almost on top of him. To his left and right were the edges of the bridge. There were fragile railings on the edges that could not stop anyone from going over. Joseph's only hope was to turn and run as fast as he could and hopefully outrun the large man. As Joseph turned to make his dash across the bridge, he slipped and the momentum carried him to the left rail of the bridge, which he easily broke through. His left leg went out from under him and he found most of his body dangling over the edge. He reflexively turned and grabbed a log plank that formed the left edge of the bridge.

Joseph looked down and saw the fall would be about twenty feet. At the bottom were a series of sharp-edged boulders beckoning him to join them. Joseph quickly thought of Roman mythology and the sirens luring sailors to their doom on rocks. He thought that might be a better ending than what the outlaws had planned for him. The large man stood over Joseph and insulted him while he waited for the small man and the others to join him. The small man came up beside the large man. The others of the group were close behind.

Joseph was calm as he went through his options: death on the rocks below or death with these men. He decided the rocks were preferable. Joseph said a silent prayer, the Lord's Prayer. Joseph was ready to die.

He looked up at the men as they reached for him. Joseph was about to release his grip when a low whistling sound swept through the air and ended with a sharp thud hitting the large man and tearing into his flesh. Joseph saw the source of the sound was a spear thrown by someone on the other side of bridge. The large man feebly tried to remove the spear but to no avail. He struggled to the left edge of the bridge just above Joseph and fell head first onto the rocks below. He made almost no sound when he died.

The small man turned and ran, along with his comrades, back across the bridge, followed shortly by several horses. There was much shouting at this point. Joseph recognized the military tone of some of the men while cries for help emanated from others.

Joseph was too weak to pull himself up, and he was about to join the dead man at the bottom of the gorge. Then two sets of hands reached down underneath each of Joseph's arms and pulled him up in one motion onto the bridge. Joseph collapsed and closed his eyes for a second. He hoped he was in Heaven. When he opened his eyes, he saw two Roman soldiers standing over him. A command came from behind. "Bring him some water." Soon a canteen of water was offered and Joseph took a long drink. When he had finished, the two soldiers helped him to his feet. He opened his eyes and looked into the face of a young Roman officer.

"What in the hell are you doing out here at this time of day?" were the first words spoken by the Roman. "Don't you know this area is full of bandits and other unsavory characters? We usually run our patrols to this bridge and then return to garrison for the night."

"No, I didn't. I'm still new to the area. I should have thought this out better."

"Damn right. You are very lucky. We almost turned around before the bridge tonight, and then you would have been very unlucky. These sorts don't tend to take prisoners or hostages if you aren't a man of means, which certainly you are not."

"What happened to the outlaws?" Joseph was curious.

"We killed most of them. I think a couple got away into the wilds and we lost them. That is not a big issue. Now, to repeat, what are you doing in this area tonight?"

"I must see the commander of your garrison."

The young officer looked around at his men that had now joined them at the bridge, and smiles were notable on the faces of the men. "Now, why do you want to see the commander? Aren't you a Christian priest?"

"Yes, I am, but I need to be taken to your commander. I want to show him something."

"What could a priest want to show our commander?" Again, there were smiles and even some laughter from the Romans.

Joseph reached into his inside pocket and was relieved to feel the ring. He pulled it out and gave it to the officer. The officer took the ring and stared at it for a long minute. He put the ring in a pocket and then looked at Joseph, "Where did you get this?"

"A man I know gave it to me. It was his ring. I decided I must show the ring to your commander. Maybe he can decide what to do. I have come from Ratae to do this."

The officer pulled the ring out and looked at it again and then at Joseph. He was not laughing or smiling now. He gave curt orders and horses were brought to end of the bridge.

"You will ride with me, priest. The general will want to see you."

LVI

TITUS

THE MAN LOOKED in the mirror. He was proud of his beard. Any stray hairs were neatly trimmed with careful precision. The beard was gray, almost white, which reflected the man's age in the lower fifties. He kept the beard short cropped for a reason. He had served with Julian and at one time had facial hair in a similar fashion as the Emperor/General. Since Julian had died, he alternated removing his facial hair or keeping a short beard. The beard reminded him of Julian.

It was dark out, and he was waiting to hear from the patrols he had sent out during the day to learn about the mood of the natives in the area. He had been assigned to Britannia most of the past three years. Before that, he had spent four years in Palestine. He felt those assignments were punishment for his support of Julian, and they were. However, he was an effective administrator and good soldier, so he became indispensable to Rome—in faraway territories.

Conducting patrol work was dangerous, especially in the time since Gerhard had been killed and Argus took the throne. The country was wild with rebellion. Refugees, bandits, invaders, and, of course, Argus' men carried out their brutality on the population. He had to double the size of the patrols for their own protection. The constant strife was tiring to him, and he planned to retire in the coming year and return to his villa south of Rome.

Such was the life of General Titus. To his friends and equals, he was called just Titus. To all others he was General Titus. Titus was a robust man with energy that usually outlasted whomever he was working with at the time. He was an inch or two taller than average but not a towering figure. However, he was burly and had a voice that could cut through walls and men, if need be. He was known as the "king of the Romans" in the Britannia he administered. He also had the grudging respect of the local populace. They hated the taxes the Romans placed on them, but the protection he provided was sought after and appreciated.

After he finished trimming his beard, Titus dismissed all but one of his servants and an officer. Titus and the officer then discussed strategy to address the Saxon problem in the east of Britannia. Titus preferred the large castle south of Ratae as his headquarters and rarely liked staying in a tent or smaller garrisons. Normally his senior officers and primary guard also quartered with him at the castle. Other soldiers, when not out on missions, stayed in tents in the fort near the castle. He also had stationed several thousand men in satellite forts, garrisons, and camps across the country. Titus took good care of his men and was rewarded with their loyalty.

On this night he was thinking about his patrols. All but one of the patrols had returned for the night. The missing patrol was the one that had to travel in the wild country where he had little control. Titus kept looking at the gate to the castle for any word of the last patrol. He turned around and finished a thought with the officer, when there was a commotion at the gate. When he turned back, he observed the patrol that finally returned. Titus would now get the report from the patrol's commander, and then he and his officers would go over tomorrow's activities. He was a little perplexed that the entire patrol and not just its captain had come to the castle. Normally the patrol would stop at the nearby garrison.

It was different this time. The captain of the patrol, and several men, made their way to Titus.

After the obligatory salute, General Titus questioned the commander, "Why are you not following protocol?" Protocol meant only the captain of a patrol would report to Titus and conduct the day's briefing.

"We, I mean, I have something to report from our patrol that was a surprise. That is why I have asked certain of my men to accompany me to your office."

Titus was intrigued with this response. "What is this surprise?"

The men parted and brought forth Joseph.

"Is this a joke?" Titus was suddenly irritated at his men. "You bring me a Christian priest? What crime did he commit?"

Titus, as a past follower of Julian, was a self-proclaimed pagan, and he knew his assignment to far-off Britannia was due to his pagan history. Titus hadn't embraced Christianity as the religion of the Empire, and he was not generally fond of mixing with Christians either. Yet over time, activities involving Christians became more of a daily routine, and he had gradually evolved to accept them.

"No crime, General," was the reply of the officer. "He was almost killed by a group of robbers. We saved his life."

"Great." Titus said half-facetiously, then focused on the patrol's mission and asked the captain, "Are the bandits dead?"

"Yes," he said initially to please Titus. Followed by, "A couple may have escaped."

"Hmmm." Titus then moved on to the next subject. "So tell me, what have we here." Titus pointed to Joseph. "Who are you, and why did you end up almost in the hands of outlaws?"

"I am Father Joseph, priest of the Village of Bergen. I have traveled to find you, to give you this."

Joseph looked at the captain, who stepped forward with the ring in his palm. Titus looked at the captain, and then picked up the ring and examined it. He called his chief clerk, who was in one of the nearby rooms.

"Read me the name inscription on this ring."

The man read a couple of words and came to Marcus Augustus Valerias.

"Read the name again," ordered Titus, and the man reread the name.

"Damn. In the name of the Gods."

"Come here, Joseph." Titus' demeanor changed slightly.

Joseph came closer and was right in front of Titus.

Titus asked, "Do you know this man?"

"Yes. I was his clerk in his headquarters near the Danube." Joseph thought it was prudent to not go into details about his relationship with Valerias. He was also leery of the relationship between Titus and Valerias.

"Where did you get this ring? Who gave it to you?"

"He did—the General, in Ratae, this morning."

"Why did he give it to you?" Titus was focused very intently on Joseph's answers.

"He was a prisoner of Morguard, one of Argus' men. He was being treated very roughly to the point he may be severely injured or may even be dead as we speak. I know Morguard was waiting for King Argus to arrive at Ratae to deal with a rebellion to the west. I imagine the General will be dealt with at that time."

Titus stood back away from Joseph without taking his eyes off of Joseph's face. The silence continued for several minutes. No one in the room moved or spoke. The silence was particularly eerie for Joseph, and he became very uncomfortable. Finally, Titus called over a servant. "Bring us some wine." The servant complied immediately.

Titus motioned for Joseph to sit. Titus sat immediately to his right. Joseph took a long, deep drink of the wine. He was very thirsty—most of which was stress induced. Titus ordered another cup of wine be poured. Joseph didn't drink this time. Instead, Joseph looked around the room. Several men were present, and all eyes were on him. He was nervous, and drinking the next cup of wine would be of no benefit to him. He looked again at Titus. The face was pure Roman and intense. Joseph was reminded of Valerias. *These Roman generals must all be cut from the same cloth,* he thought to himself.

Titus interrupted the silence, "Tell me again everything that happened to you today. I want you to focus on what you observed with General Valerias."

Joseph recounted his story in detail. No one spoke, and when he finished, Joseph did take a drink of the wine.

Titus was still staring at him when he said, "I believe your story."

He turned to the men behind him. "I want five cavalry centuries ready to travel fast to Ratae tomorrow. We leave at first light. They should pack for conflict."

The men disappeared into the night beyond Titus' council room. It was now just Titus and Joseph. Titus stood up and bent over just a few inches from Joseph's face. "If you are lying to me about any of this, I will disembowel you and then cut out your heart while you still live. Do you still stand by your story?"

"Yes, General, what I tell you is true." Joseph had a similar feeling as when Valerias had stood over him with a knife to his throat. This though was different—he knew what he was doing and was firm in his reply.

Titus relaxed at this point. "Good. You will ride with me tomorrow. You may want to say a prayer for us."

Titus was a pagan, but he had been around Christians enough to occasionally ask them for spiritual help.

Joseph asked Titus, "Is General Valerias friend or foe?"

"I didn't say, did I?" was Titus' response. Titus was expressionless as he answered Joseph. Titus motioned for Joseph to leave, signaling the end of their conversation. A servant took Joseph to his sleeping quarters. Joseph did not sleep that night.

LVII

Ratae

Argus and his cavalry arrived in Ratae early in the day. Argus entered the city gates and beside him was Flavius. Morguard met them just inside the gate. There was little fanfare, as the city had had little warning of Argus' visit. It wouldn't have mattered anyway. Even with adequate notice, any cheering would have been subdued, because Argus was not highly thought of in Ratae. There also would have been no jeering.

"Greetings, King Argus and Lord Flavius. Welcome to Ratae." Morguard announced their arrival.

Argus gave a halfhearted salute. Flavius made no movement. Morguard invited the group to the predetermined location inside the city. As they advanced into the city, they came upon an open area that was the old city square. In the center of the area was a row of wooden stakes planted deeply into the ground. Several men were attached to the stakes by short chains that were tied behind their backs. Valerias was tied to one stake. One stake was vacant. The rest held suspect rebels whom Morguard had captured and were now awaiting their fate.

Argus and Flavius dismounted and handed the reins to aides. Argus' guards and the rest of his cavalry dismounted and the guards stood behind Argus.

"Who are these men?" Argus asked Morguard in a dismissive voice.

"Traitors to your kingdom. We are wiping out the rebellion, and we captured these men in the process."

Argus walked down the line of staked men. They all looked like normal farmers and certainly not like anyone attached to a rebellion.

"Your rebels are a motley bunch, Morguard. It is amazing to me that you could not defeat them and you let Claire escape."

As he spoke, Argus walked by Valerias. Argus carried a switch, similar to that carried by Morguard. Argus lifted up the clothing covering Valerias' right arm and stared at the tattoo.

"Where did you find this man?"

Morguard answered, "He is the one who helped the Claire-bitch escape to Eustice. He is a Roman deserter."

"What is his name?" Argus inquired.

"Marcus Augustus, King Argus."

"Do you also know he is a Roman officer?"

"No," Morguard sheepishly answered.

"A Roman officer who deserted is worth much money to Titus. He does not favor deserters."

Valerias was badly hurt, but he followed the conversation between Argus and Morguard. He also glanced over to Flavius and did not recognize him.

Argus put Valerias' sleeve back down and hit him with a backhand across the shoulder. Pain seared through him.

"If Titus won't pay me for what I am asking, you will pay dearly for helping the bitch escape." Argus angrily spoke.

Argus marched over to the empty stake. "Why is this empty?"

"A gift for you, King Argus."

Morguard motioned for his guards to bring forth a prisoner who had a sack over his head. It was clear the man had been severely tortured as two men had to carry him and place him by the empty stake. When his hands were secure, Morguard removed the sack. The beaten man was Stephen. Flavius' instincts were to reach for his sword, but it was too late. Morguard had positioned men around Flavius, and they jumped him as soon as Flavius saw Stephen.

Morguard walked up to Argus and pointed his switch at Flavius. "He is a traitor to you, my King. He arranged for this man," Morguard pointed at Stephen, "to take Claire and the bitch's daughters to Eustice. He would have failed, if it weren't for this man." Morguard pointed at Valerias.

Argus looked at Flavius. "Is this true—what Morguard has alleged you to have done?"

Flavius said nothing. Argus crisply walked over to Stephen and lifted up his head. He asked someone to bring Stephen some water. Stephen drank a couple swallows and put his head down. Argus lifted the head up again and asked his question. Stephen answered in a very low tone with a muttered, "Yes."

Argus slowly rose and spoke to Morguard. "What do you suggest I do with Flavius?"

"Stake him and execute him tomorrow after he has had time to think about his traitorous behavior to you."

"Where will I stake him, as you put it?"

Morguard walked over to the man that had been placed between Valerias and Stephen and promptly beheaded him. Soldiers removed the body and head from the area, and Flavius was tied to that stake where the blood of the fallen man was warm.

Argus snarled at Flavius. "I had suspected for some time that you were a traitor. Now it is confirmed. You will regret your actions, very, very much."

Argus turned away from the staked men and spoke to Morguard. "I am pleased you have stepped up and showed your loyalty to me. Tomorrow take half of the men and establish a camp in the western hills. I will join you the day after tomorrow with the rest. From there we will commence the operation to crush Eustice and maybe, maybe take care of Claire once and for all. When this is done, you shall be my second."

Argus strode back to Flavius. "You have no idea what will befall you tomorrow, traitor." Argus took his switch and sharply struck Flavius across the face and walked away.

The afternoon sun warmed the prisoners. It was unusual to have sun in November, and today had been an exception. Night was a different matter, and the cold set in with a grip tighter than the handclasps on the men. Valerias had gone to sleep or was passed out much of the afternoon and through the dusk. He was awake now, as the pain and cold overpowered his sleep threshold. He looked over to Flavius, who was watching the activity in the yard. Men with torches were walking back and forth and talking to each other. Stephen, beyond Flavius, was a limp rag who showed no sign of life. In the distance there was a commotion.

"Morguard and his men are preparing to depart at first light," Flavius said in no particular direction, yet directed at Valerias.

Valerias shrugged off his pain and tiredness. "Did I miss anything?"

"No, we are just a few more hours closer to our maker."

"You seem calm, for a dead man. You are Flavius?"

"Yes, and you are?"

"Marcus Augustus." Valerias continued his stratagem of not revealing his identity.

"Where did you serve? You are a Roman officer."

"Many places. Can't you tell by my age?"

"You didn't desert, did you?"

"No, I retired, but no one believes that. What about you?"

"I deserted, Marcus Augustus. I was in a hellhole in Africa. My superiors had the intelligence of insects and were leading us to ruin. I spent more time fighting idiotic civil wars than the real enemies of Rome."

"You are a deserter?" Valerias was still having a hard time accepting such comments.

"Yes, Marcus Augustus. If I had not deserted, I would be dead and my bones leaching into the sands of Africa. I came to Britannia because it was as far away from Africa in the Empire that I could go. I ended up being Argus' second. It is strange how things happen. So, why are you in Britannia?"

"I once said I have no regrets—I do now. I left the legions because I became worn out with my life and was unhappy that I had spent my entire life as a soldier. So I left—on my own terms. I made it my personal quest to venture to Hadrian's Wall—after all, he was a great general and Emperor.

"The wall is overrated. Be glad you were never given an assignment there. I heard you helped Claire—along with this man to my right, Stephen." Flavius turned his head to the right slightly.

"Yes, I did. She needed the help. I didn't know at the time she was a queen. But I don't regret helping her. And you?"

"I knew who she was and served her—poorly. It is complicated. I fell in love with her chambermaid. It changed my view of things, so I too extended my help to Claire."

"And now we will both die—along with Stephen—for what we did."

"So be it," answered Flavius. "I can die for that reason. Maybe in some way that will help me in the next life."

"If there is one," countered Valerias.

A guard walked by and delivered light blows to both Valerias and Flavius and told both men to stop talking. The blows were soft, as if the guard wanted to show he was delivering punishment for the talking and at the same time not inflicting any damage. Valerias wondered about this. Was the guard sympathetic to them, or was he deliberately not trying to hurt them so they would be in better shape for their execution? Valerias knew he would be executed and not sold to the Romans. He recalled his recent conversation with Flavius. In the past he would never have had such a talk with a man he didn't know, particularly a deserter. But then, the boundaries for dead men are not the same as in normal life. He too began watching the activities around him.

The morning proved a true mid-November day, cloudy, misty, and cool. During the night someone brought water to the men tied to the stakes. Valerias was resigned to his fate, and it appeared Flavius was as well. Valerias thought Argus would bring the ax, sword, or whatever weapon of death down on the group first thing in the morning. Argus, though, was of a different mind. He wanted to savor the moment, which included making the men anticipate their approaching doom.

At certain intervals Morguard would walk down the line. He seemed to take great satisfaction in taunting Flavius, but he received no response in return. Morguard told Flavius that Stephen had given up Mary. He had also dispatched men to the location where Claire had sought refuge with Mary. When she was caught, Mary's fate would be worse than that of Flavius. Flavius again said nothing; internally he was vigorously hoping Mary had left that house and moved to a safe location.

Valerias was watching Morguard. Previously he had wondered where his sword had gone when he was taken prisoner. This morning he didn't have to look far. Morguard was carrying it around like a prize. *It is a pity that idiot has my sword,* Valerias thought to himself. *He couldn't serve as a stable boy in my legions.*

Finally, at what seemed high noon on this November day, Argus came from somewhere in the city with approximately fifty guards, including Morguard in tow. Obviously Morguard hadn't left for the hills at dawn.

"Good morning," Argus shouted to the staked men. "Your time has arrived."

Several of the men to the right of Valerias groaned and others begged for their lives. Valerias guessed most of them were innocent civilians who had been caught in Morguard's show. Argus nodded, and the man furthest to Valerias' right had his head removed. The sobbing grew louder, and the next man was executed. Down the line death came to the prisoners, until it was Stephen's turn. He was as close to the ground as the rope from the stake would let him lie prone. The executioner stood over him, but there was no movement and no verbal noise. Something was not right, and the man behind the executioner bent down and shook Stephen's shoulders. Again there was no movement.

The man continued to examine Stephen and then stood up and spoke to Argus, "This man is dead."

Valerias watched the death march and prepared mentally for his end. When it was announced Stephen was dead, Valerias felt pity for the man. *He died a warrior in his own way*, Valerias thought.

Valerias wondered if after death he would join Julian in the Elysian Fields. Or would it be in the priest's Heaven, or would it be Hell? He wasn't sure what category he would fall in, and he laughed to himself about the absurdity of the choice. Or would life just end and what is light would turn to black, as he had always envisioned death's reward?

Valerias looked over to Flavius. He also seemed calm in awaiting death. Only Argus would torture him to some horrible degree before finally executing him. Flavius was a Roman officer, though, and he showed the temperament of an officer. Flavius even smiled at Valerias to show him there was a code between Romans. Valerias had always figured he would die in battle or from the executioner's sword from some conqueror after a lost battle. He was fine with the way his end would turn out today. It was certainly better than dying of a disease in old age, like his adopted father, Hyperion.

Argus grew bored with all the death while Morguard grew more animated with each death. Suddenly there was clamor at the gate. One of the gatekeepers ran and gave Argus a message. Argus had a quizzical look on his face. "I suppose we will have to let them in." He spoke to no one, although Morguard was in hearing distance.

"Who, my King?"

"The Romans. It appears the Roman, General Titus, is conducting a visit to the area. He has five hundred cavalrymen behind him. Don't stand in their way."

"What do we do with these two?" Morguard pointed Valerias' sword at Flavius and Valerias.

Argus sneered, "He can watch, or he can pay me for the Roman. I don't care which. Flavius is mine, though."

Shortly several Roman horsemen entered the yard carrying the banners and standards of the centuries under Titus' control. Titus followed these men, and after him came his primary guard and well over one hundred cavalrymen. The city yard was filling up with Romans, and they were heavily armed, a fact not lost on Argus.

"Welcome to Ratae, General Titus."

Titus just smiled sternly and said nothing.

"What brings the esteemed Roman general to our city?"

Titus dismounted and two aides took his horse. He looked around the yard and at dead bodies as if he were bored. He was not. "I hear continually of the rebellion in your kingdom, Argus. This rebellion seems to go on and on. The casualties are striking even for me. It is time for the rebellion to end."

Argus thought for a moment that maybe Titus would be an ally against Eustice. Argus motioned to Morguard, and he and about twenty men mounted their horses and prepared to leave the city.

"I have prearranged for Morguard, here, and some men to leave and begin my campaign against the rebel leader off to the west."

Argus' dithering had put Morguard almost a half of a day behind schedule. On one hand Morguard was upset that he couldn't witness the demise of Flavius, but his desire to please Argus was his primary motivation.

"Do you mind if my second leaves now to start my campaign to rid this land of the rebel named Eustice?" Argus was only asking Titus this question as a formality.

"No. I have no issue with that." Titus was focusing on the staked men.

Morguard saluted Argus and rode out of the city. As Morguard left, Argus thought to himself, *This damn Roman is causing me a major delay. At least Morguard can commence the operation of eliminating Eustice.*

Titus had watched or had partaken in multiple executions throughout his life, so looking at the dead men attached to the stakes did not cause him concern. He looked at the two survivors and asked Argus who the men were.

"Ah, one is called Flavius. I believe he is of Roman descent—one of you. A deserter, I believe. The other man is a Roman officer who also deserted your army. He is a *traitor* and gave aid to the rebel's sister, a traitorous act."

"What is his name?" Titus asked in a staid manner.

"He is called Marcus Augustus. And he is an officer, as I said before."

"I can see that."

"What is he worth to you, General Titus?"

"He is worth much to me, Argus." Titus had drawn his sword and was standing over Valerias. Argus moved closer to both men. He anticipated Titus killing Valerias on the spot.

"You can kill him here or take him with you. The price will be the same, Titus."

"I cannot pay you for what he is worth. But I will give you what you deserve."

Argus didn't have much time to contemplate that statement. Titus' sword punched through his chest and heart, the sword tip pushing through his back. Titus retracted the sword and grasped the dying Argus by his clothing just below his neck and growled, "The rebellion is over! You are deposed!"

Argus fell to the ground with a mystified look on his face, blood running out from his chest and mouth, and then he was dead. At that moment the Roman units engaged themselves into action. Any of Argus' men who resisted were slaughtered on the spot. The remainder surrendered peacefully.

Titus motioned for soldiers over to the stake that held Valerias. Titus gently lifted up the Valerias' head and looked into his eyes. At that instant he confirmed this wretched prisoner of Argus was Valerias.

Titus turned and faced his men. "This man is General Marcus Augustus Valerias, commander of the legions on the Danube and my friend. He will be treated as the Roman general he is, of the highest ranking."

A murmur spread through Titus' troops. Valerias' reputation was well known throughout the Empire, and it was not lost on the troops who were in the yard at that time. Aides quickly rushed in, broke his shackles, carried him over to a shaded area, and gave him water. Between the fight with Morguard's men in the cave, the beatings, and lack of food and water, Valerias was in poor shape and edging close to death. Titus ordered a special room in the unused garrison in the city be prepared for Valerias.

Watching the events unfold before him was a surreal experience for Joseph. He even set aside thoughts of his own future.

Titus was in process of giving an order for his primary physician to be summoned, when Joseph, who had stood behind Titus the entire time, politely spoke, "General, I would like the opportunity to administer care to General Valerias."

"Why? What are your qualifications?"

"I am a physician." Joseph could see doubt in the face of Titus. "I served with Olivertos in the General's headquarters."

"Who was more skilled, you or Olivertos?" Titus was testing Joseph.

"He would tell you he was. I am telling you I was."

"He cannot tell me his side because he is not here." Titus liked Joseph's answer. "All right, you can be General Valerias' chief physician. Pray to your God that nothing happens to him."

Joseph thought to himself, *That comment sounded like something Valerias would say*. Joseph countered with, "Something will happen, and it will be good."

Titus gave a quick laugh. It was Joseph who had saved Valerias' life, a thought not lost on Titus, and he would give Joseph a long leash. "Hard to believe General Valerias has a Christian priest as his savior and physician. Ironic, I would say. Did Valerias join the ranks of the converted?"

"No," Joseph said shaking his head. "He is a remnant of Julian."

Titus tilted his head sideways and squinted his eyes at Joseph and waved him off. Titus then ordered two of Argus' men to be brought before him. After a short period of questioning them, Titus called for one of his officers.

"Take two hundred men and track down and kill that ass, Morguard." The officer exited the city, and the sounds of a large group of cavalry were heard heading west where Morguard had gone.

Titus called for a scout of Britannic origin. "Go to Eustice and tell him that he is now the right and just ruler of his kingdom—a kingdom he should have inherited with his sister, Claire. Have him meet me here. I will not go anywhere until I know General Valerias will live."

Finally Titus turned his attention to the final staked man, Flavius. Flavius had been generally unharmed from Morguard and Argus, so he was fully aware of what was occurring in front of him. "So, Flavius, we meet again. Last time I saw you, I recall you being Argus' enforcer. Did you have anything to do with Gerhard's death?" Titus did not believe in small talk.

"No."

"What should I do with you? You are a deserter from the Roman army. You cooperated with Argus in turning this kingdom into a foul land and killed many people. I hear many things, and you are not on the good end of any of the stories. It is sad what has happened to you, Flavius. You have changed from a noted Roman officer to a disgraced man. I will place you in prison and decide your fate later. Although I wouldn't place a wager on your future lasting longer than the cycle of the moon."

Flavius knew what Titus meant. He would be executed by Titus or turned over to Eustice. Flavius didn't put much hope in his future either way.

LVIII

Revitalization

THE NEXT COUPLE of weeks went by quickly. December arrived, and the grip of winter descended upon the land. Valerias gradually recovered under the watchful eye and care of Joseph. Titus made frequent visits to Valerias' quarters, and the two generals talked at length. Titus and Valerias were friends, and both men found it refreshing to have someone of similar stature with common experiences. Both were generals under Emperor Julian. Titus served with Julian at Samarra when the Emperor was slain, while Valerias was stationed in Africa. Titus had always been suspicious that a Roman in the guise of a Persian had killed Julian, but he had no proof to substantiate his belief. The assassin was also rumored to have been a Christian; thus both Titus and Valerias blamed Christians for Julian's death.

Since that time Titus had moved further down his path of forgiveness of Christians than Valerias. Maybe that was because Valerias thought that if he had been with Julian at Samarra, he could have saved him. Titus had long ago come to the realization there was nothing he could have done to prevent the tragedy, and the subject no longer bothered him.

One day in the middle of December, the two were seated by a fire at the reclaimed Roman garrison in Ratae. Valerias was almost to the point he could walk normally and had started light weapon training to regain his strength. Joseph had done a fine job in Valerias' rehabilitation.

Titus squirmed in his chair. "I need to return to my headquarters soon. I can take only so much of messenger service and you." After they laughed, Titus continued, "What will you do, Marcus, once you fully regain your health? Or do you expect me to take care of you forever?"

Valerias glanced at Titus and smiled. Then he became serious. "I have somewhere I need to go—to find something out for myself."

"You wish to see the Lady Claire. I've been watching you, Marcus, since you have been here. You are not acting like the man I knew when we marched together with the legions."

"You are making that up, Titus. I am who I always have been."

"We will see. I have invited Eustice down from the hills where I can formally extend Rome's friendship to him as the new leader of Britons in his region. Former Queen Claire had abdicated the throne to her brother. Eustice doesn't seem to trust me yet, and I don't know why. We are the ones who opened the throne to him. He will be here tomorrow. I'd like you to join me, arm in arm, to acknowledge King Eustice." Titus purposely forgot to mention he had also extended his invitation to Claire.

"Yes, I would like to join you. I would like to meet this Eustice. Hopefully he is a better man, a better leader, than Argus."

The two men resumed reminiscing about the past and speculating about the future. Titus was interested in Christianity and joked with Valerias that he would pull a Constantine on his deathbed and be baptized at the moment of his death. He knew Valerias' short temper on the subject, so a lively discussion of religion followed. They would also tease Joseph about God, Christ, and the Holy Ghost as the triune Godhead versus individual spiritual entities.

This time, though, relationships had changed. Titus frequently reminded Valerias that Joseph had saved his life, not once but twice. Valerias remembered back to the time when he had almost killed Joseph and treated him poorly in his camps. Then, when he could have let Valerias die, Joseph had risked his life to save him. Valerias had an awakening and treated Joseph as an *almost* equal.

For his part Joseph could come and go as he pleased. If he talked religion, specifically with Titus' men, he would not be punished. Joseph felt good about his place among the Roman army for the first time. Yet in the back of his mind, he continually thought of Ruth. His time with the Roman army had provided him with a reprieve, but he knew he would have to make a decision and face her soon.

The following day dawned. It was winter-like, and a breeze of cold chill sifted through the city. It was sunny, but the sun barely rose above the horizon. Titus had ordered a full honor guard to be present for the arrival of Eustice. He had neglected Flavius for the most part of the past three weeks until today. Flavius was treated well enough to keep him alive in prison. He figured Titus wanted him in good shape for his execution.

Valerias visited Flavius several times. He was interested in what had turned a loyal Roman officer into a deserter and killer for hire with a despot. This didn't make any sense to Valerias. This was a complicated situation, even for one who thought he understood most issues; yet he did not understand Flavius. He talked to Titus about Flavius; however, Titus appeared resolved to execute Flavius, and Valerias had no reason to intervene to save him. The date of the execution was the only variable. Being in control of events was something Valerias missed. When he was the commanding General, the world revolved around him. Now he was just a well-treated observer, but a pawn in this game of life.

At midday Flavius was brought out of his prison cell and chained to the same stake where Argus had placed him. Titus told Valerias he was going to make a gift of Flavius' execution to Eustice.

When Eustice arrived, he sent a small squad of men to the city first. They were received by one of Titus' officers and were escorted to the city garrison. When they were satisfied all was adequate, one rode back into the hills. A few moments later Eustice and a large force of about one hundred men emerged from the hills. They were shown to the garrison yard where Titus and Valerias waited for them. Both Titus and Valerias observed that they were not dressed for war, but for conference.

Titus was unarmed, as was his personal guard. Eustice dismounted and in a symbolic gesture of peace, handed his weapon, a symbolic war club, to one of Titus' men. Titus faced Eustice. "Welcome, King Eustice."

"Please accept my greetings, General Titus."

Eustice moved closer to Titus so only the two men could hear each other. "I thank you for returning the throne to our family. Yet I must show a certain dislike for you and the Romans to my countrymen. Even though you have done good things, it is my position that we are not friends. We are not enemies either."

When he had completed his opening statement, Eustice looked over to Valerias. "Who is this man?"

"King Eustice, this is Marcus Augustus Valerias, soldier of the Roman legions on the Danube." Titus purposely did not use the word "general" when introducing Valerias.

"Retired." Valerias finished Titus' introduction.

Titus and Eustice engaged in small talk for a few moments when the sight of Flavius tied to a stake caught Eustice's eye.

Eustice walked over to Flavius. "Well, Flavius, good to see you again. Last time I set eyes on you, you were plotting with Argus to take the throne. He won, and I had to flee to the country. Now it appears your time on this Earth is about over."

Valerias noted that Flavius now looked haggard, having been in prison for weeks. His clean-shaven, crisp appearance had given way to a disheveled, bearded man who looked like an emaciated priest. He had not been beaten. Valerias strangely felt a bond toward Flavius as a fellow officer, but there was nothing he could do or even wanted to do.

As he had been with Argus in November, Flavius was resigned to his death with Titus. He hoped Titus would execute him instead of turning him over to Eustice. A quick death from Titus was more welcome than torture and then death with Eustice. Flavius also contemplated his past and his role with Argus. Flavius was a soldier and did what was ordered. He did commit evil deeds, but he had never done so with malice or pleasure. It was a business, and that was what it always had been with him. Flavius thought it ironic that what he did as a Roman was rewarded and yet the same actions he conducted for Argus would result in his death.

"I have decided to execute Flavius for his crime of desertion against the Empire, and I would like to you watch."

"What is he worth to you, General Titus?"

"He is not for sale, if that is what you're asking, King Eustice. He is a Roman and he shall die as a Roman. He shall pay for his offenses, both against Rome and against your kingdom."

Titus looked at Valerias in part while he spoke to Eustice. Valerias nodded slightly to Titus to let Titus know he concurred with Titus' decision.

Eustice protested a little longer, but he knew he would not win the debate. Titus was too strong to be confronted. Titus motioned, and a large man wearing Roman execution dress approached Flavius. Flavius turned his back to the man and was on his knees. The large man raised a sword vertically above Flavius. He would bring the sword down and through Flavius' back. It would be a soldier's death, and Flavius was grateful.

Just before Titus gave the word to proceed to the executioner, there was a cry from behind Eustice. The cry was "Stop!" followed by "Stop this execution!"

A woman emerged from behind Eustice. It was Claire. She had traveled to Ratae with Eustice upon Titus' invitation. She had not wanted involvement with the Romans, and now she was involved. All parties on the scene were in disbelief. Titus thrust out his right arm to the executioner and the man stopped and stepped back. Flavius looked at Claire with a blank stare.

"Are you Claire?" Titus knew the answer.

"Yes, and you are General Titus."

"Why do you want me to halt the execution, Claire? After all the terrible things he has done to your people?"

"Because I owe this man my life. He is not evil."

There was an initial silence in the crowd and then murmurings and finally loud talk among the audience. Titus raised his hand for quiet.

Eustice was dumbfounded. "When did he save you? This man after all was in the employ of Argus who had your husband slain and took your kingdom. This does not make sense."

Claire answered, "I know it doesn't, my brother. Flavius seemed to appear out of nowhere when we were trying to get away from Argus. We would never have made it without him. I believe he had a change of heart. His sentence of death should be commuted. I ask the great General Titus to free him."

There was more commotion in the audience among the city dwellers. Titus ordered his guard to secure the area around Flavius, and no one had the desire to confront elite Roman troops.

Titus looked at Claire. "I will take your request under advisement. We will discuss this matter further at dinner tonight in the relative quiet of my quarters."

He turned to his guards. "Take the prisoner back to his cell." Titus then ordered the crowd to break up, and if anyone disagreed, they would join Flavius in prison. In response the crowd quickly dispersed.

Claire looked at Flavius, then Titus and Valerias. She did not recognize Valerias in his current condition. He was clean-shaven and well dressed. In Rome, he could have been taken for a senator. He had no resemblance to the man who had apparently sacrificed his life for her and her children. But he knew Claire, and when their eyes met, they locked for several seconds. She turned away to talk to Eustice, and when she looked back to say something to Valerias, he had gone inside the garrison with Flavius. She felt she knew this man but could not place him. For his part, Valerias was experiencing a feeling he rarely, if ever, had—a genuine heartfelt attraction to a woman.

Later that day Claire visited Flavius. She wanted to ask him why he had helped her. He responded that he wanted to change, and helping her was the best way he knew how to accomplish this goal. Mary, a Christian, had been the catalyst for his turnaround. He had also grown weary of Argus' brutality.

Flavius asked Claire if she knew anything about Mary. Claire said she did not. She had heard there was a group of refugees that had fled the village where she and Mary had stayed. Several of the refugees had been captured by remnants of Argus' army led by Morguard and were being held for ransom. There was no money in the kingdom to pay the ransom. She was going to ask Titus for his help, but she didn't know how Titus would respond.

Flavius was convinced Mary was now in Morguard's hands, just as he was under the control of Titus. His feelings for Mary were deeply intense, and he wanted to find her. Claire said she would do whatever was in her power to help, as Mary was her close friend. She would petition both her brother and Titus for their counsel and help. There was even a Christian priest with the Romans, and she would ask him for his prayers in helping Mary. Claire was not a Christian, but she would seek all measures to help her friend.

Claire returned to her camp just outside the garrison but within the city walls. She was planning for her dinner with Titus and how she would approach the subject of Flavius and Mary. While she waited, a guard announced himself and entered her quarters. He said there was a Roman at the entrance to her camp who had requested a visit with her. She knew that the man wasn't Titus, and she was unfamiliar with the other Romans she had seen earlier in the day. Claire was perplexed but interested in who this Roman could be. She told the guard she would see this man. Eustice had trouble trusting Romans, and he required any Roman who entered their camp to be escorted by two guards.

The Roman entered a visiting room in the camp's main tent followed by the two guards. The Roman was unarmed.

Claire glared at the Roman. "Greetings, Roman." And not wasting any time, "Why do you wish to see me?"

"I am very pleased that you are well and that you and Anne and Elizabeth safely reached your brother."

Claire was now intently looking at the Roman. "Do I know you?"

"I am Marcus Augustus Valerias, the man who helped you escape Morguard in the countryside."

Claire moved very close to Valerias. He did not move or blink.

"I see the resemblance to that man. You were the man in the cave and in the creek. You clean up very well, Marcus Augustus Valerias."

"So do you, Claire."

She ignored his comment and continued, "Why are you here? Do you have a relationship with General Titus?" Claire had many questions.

"I am here at my own choice. General Titus and I have been friends and colleagues in the Roman army for many years. It was General Titus and the priest, Joseph, who saved my life when

Morguard captured me. I was captured after we separated in the western hills. I wasn't as clever as I thought."

Valerias didn't want this line of questioning to continue, and he changed the subject. "I understand from Titus that you were the queen before Argus overthrew you and your husband."

"You do not know the entire story. Argus was an aide and relative of my husband, Gerhard. He had my husband killed in a false mission against the Saxons. He planned his coup for some time. Flavius, your Roman friend, was the instrument that carried out Argus' work. I feared for my son's life and sent him away. I didn't think Argus would harm my daughters, but I was wrong. Titus did a very good thing when he killed Argus. Now my brother is on the throne. He will be a much better king for this land than Argus."

"Flavius is not my friend. I did not know him in the Roman army. Why did you save Flavius' life?"

"He saved mine, and I'm returning the favor. We are even now. I imagine he will serve prison time within the Roman system."

"If he is sent to the Roman system, as you describe it, he will likely be executed."

At that moment Eustice, with several bodyguards, entered the room with Valerias and Claire. Since assuming the throne, Eustice upgraded his wardrobe and wore clothing of a king.

"You have found my sister, Marcus Augustus Valerias. Are you coming to the banquet tonight? Titus has invited only a few guests, and I have heard you are one of the invited."

Valerias answered, "Yes, Eustice, I will attend."

"Titus must hold you in high esteem. I didn't think Roman generals invited soldiers to dinner, especially those who retire or desert."

"That is between General Titus and me." Valerias did not care for these questions. He thought to himself, *Why is it so hard for so many people to believe I retired and wanted to change my life?*

Eustice and Claire, with selected bodyguards, and Valerias made their way to Titus' banquet. It was a very small affair. Besides Titus and Valerias, there was only one other Roman present, one of Titus' senior officers, a tribune. Joseph joined the small sitting and gave a blessing.

As the meal progressed, Eustice asked Valerias what his rank had been in the army. Valerias hesitated, so Titus jumped in with the answer.

"My friend here *is* a general." Claire and Eustice looked at Valerias and he felt embarrassed. Joseph watched with interest. "Not just any general." Titus looked at Valerias and laughed. "No, this is General Marcus Augustus Valerias, undefeated in battle and feared by Emperors."

"My friend exaggerates, I am retired." Valerias tried to be upset with Titus, but he was embarrassed even more. He had wanted to keep his rank a secret.

"Now I have heard of you," Eustice interrupted. "Your campaigns in Gaul and along the Danube are legendary. I have heard you have a ruthless heart."

Valerias was becoming angry, although not visibly. Joseph broke the tension. "I served with the General along the Danube and found him to be respected but a poor player at bones. And they said his scouts did all his work."

Titus erupted in laughter. Something in his past with Valerias was reawakened. "He never changed. I won so much money from him in our wagers that I paid for all my scouts and his scouts. I had to, otherwise Revious would have joined the Goths!"

The rest of the dinner went more smoothly. Valerias regained his even temperament and fended off any further irritating questions from Claire and Eustice. The subject of Flavius came up toward the end. Claire was concerned that he would be executed at some time in the future. Titus said that there were no guarantees.

Just then the officer of the guard entered the room. "Flavius has escaped."

"What do you mean?" Titus firmly asked.

"He is just gone."

"Are any of his guards dead or injured?"

"No. It is like he vanished from his cell. Some of the men are nervous that he is a demon."

"I can assure that he is not a demon, and when I find out who helped him, they will wish that I was only a demon."

Joseph again interjected, "I heard through some travelers that remnants of Argus' army have taken to raiding pockets of areas in the countryside east of here. A man named Morguard may be involved. There was a group of refugees fleeing from the village of Abrador that were captured by these bandits. I suspect Flavius had an interest in this event, as he heard this information as well as I did."

"Mary!" Claire said out loud. "He is going to find Mary. I pity any man who has mistreated her."

Claire explained that Flavius and Mary were romantically linked and that it was Mary who had turned Flavius away from Argus. Claire said Mary at one time was her chambermaid, but since the death of Gerhard, she and Mary had become close friends. Mary had saved her and the daughters' lives.

When Claire had finished her story, Titus stood up and spoke to the officer who had brought the news of Flavius' escape to the dinner party. "Take a century of cavalry and bring back the refugees, including Mary. Kill or capture any of the bandits that you find. I do not care which option you choose. I will not have men escape from my jails, but I will tolerate even less bandits in my territory associated with Argus. Try to bring Flavius alive—I need to reconsider his fate."

The officer saluted Titus and vanished into the night.

Eustice also excused himself to deal with a problem that had arisen during the day. He had previously been scheduled to return to the castle where he would serve as king. Unfortunately, rooting out the remaining adherents to Argus was proving more difficult than Eustice had originally thought. His advisors had urged him not to return to the castle and claim the throne until the last vestiges of Argus' command were eliminated.

Claire was very worried about Mary, and she expressed her concerns to Titus from a military viewpoint and to Joseph from the moral side. Titus said the cavalry century he had dispatched would find her, and asked her not to worry. Joseph added that he would add Mary to his evening prayers. Joseph's ritual of saying evening prayers before bed cleared his mind.

Valerias noticed that Joseph seemed more spiritually oriented than when they had been together, and, strangely, he felt good about this transition. *At least Joseph will be an honest Christian priest,* he thought. At the end of the dinner, Valerias volunteered to take Claire back to the Britons' camp. On the way back to the camp, he and Claire talked about many subjects.

"I should have known you were more than a regular soldier, not only by the way you fought in the cave but by the way you carried yourself when we were riding together."

"And I knew you were more than a simple village woman."

"How did you know that?"

Valerias laughed. "Your daughters told me. I didn't know precisely who you were, except someone of noble status. I doubt I would have concluded you were a queen. By the way, are Anne and Elizabeth with you? I have not seen them."

"Yes, they are with me, just out of sight—Roman sight. Also, I am like you—retired. Eustice is the king now. He will have to find his own queen."

"I still would like to see your daughters again. I think we got along well together, don't you?"

"Yes, we did. I will make arrangements tomorrow. Someday, maybe you can meet my son."

"Thank you. Do not worry about Mary, Claire. Titus sent his best cavalry after her. And the wild card is Flavius. I imagine he knows this area of Britannia quite well and the habits of the bandits."

Valerias found himself holding Claire's hand. "If I knew Britannia like Flavius, I would have gone after Mary too." He wasn't sure why he had said such a forward statement.

By now the two had reached the Briton's camp. Claire and Valerias faced each other. Valerias spoke first, "I look forward to visiting Anne and Elizabeth tomorrow."

"What about me?" Claire asked coyly.

"That goes without saying, Claire." They parted for the night. Valerias walked swiftly back to the Roman garrison and felt like he was twenty-five again. Claire smiled as she walked to confer with Eustice. She had retired as queen, but she was still Eustice's confidante.

LIX

Vengeance

Valerias was up early the next day. It was a cold day, but this cold did not bother him. He went into the city market and purchased two small bracelets from a merchant. One was gold and one was silver. He also purchased two bottles of another merchant's finest wine. Finally he spoke to a blacksmith who was also a weapons maker. Valerias bought the finest knife the man had in his shop. He paid for these purchases with money loaned to him by Titus. Valerias had saved substantial sums of gold and silver from his time in the army and from his inheritances, and had placed the money with a trusted friend in Rome. Titus would get his money when Valerias retired to Rome.

After procuring his gifts, Valerias paced the grounds until it was midday. Then he left for Eustice's camp. Once there he gave the wine to Claire and the knife to Eustice. When he finally saw Anne and Elizabeth, he presented them with their bracelets. Valerias was already a star in the girls' eyes, and the gifts enhanced his standing even further.

Eustice was skeptical at first about receiving the dagger. He noted that the only contacts he had ever received from the Romans were in the form of tax bills or firm requests for some service or other unreasonable demands. Thus Eustice thought that there were strings attached to the knife. Valerias assured Eustice that the knife was simply a gift. Claire teased Eustice that if he didn't want the knife, she would take it for herself. Eustice said that would not happen and gave an abbreviated "thanks" to Valerias in the form of a grunt. Eustice was slowly warming up to Valerias.

Eustice took his leave to address other tasks. The girls then took center stage, and Valerias played with them using the carved figures that he previously gave them during the escape from Morguard. Once playtime was over, Claire scooted the girls off with a nanny and suggested she and Valerias take a walk.

"You are a natural with children, Marcus."

"I have no experience with them. I am not sure how to act. I had no childhood and I have no children. I appreciate their innocence. I wish I had more of that, but the world is cruel, and innocence equals death in most of the environments I have traveled."

"Have you ever had a wife?"

"No, I have never had a long-term relationship with a woman. I was too busy being a soldier, then officer, then general. You could say Rome was my wife. I do not regret that life though. There were advantages."

Valerias, as he often did, turned the questioning around to Claire. "Tell me, Claire, about your life."

Claire went into detail about her childhood as a noble. When she arrived in adulthood, she was married by arrangement to Gerhard. He was for the most part a good man, and she bore him three children, with the son being the heir to the throne. Because of the children, she thought she loved him, but she now believed that was a false love. Gerhard had been a naïve man with a streak of arrogance. Argus had used those characteristics to persuade him to fight the Saxons who were raiding the kingdom's eastern lands. She knew Argus was manipulating her husband, but he wouldn't have listened to her anyway. Moreover, Gerhard was only an average fighter, and subsequently he had been slain either by Saxons or Argus' men. It didn't matter now. In the end she thought she had never experienced love either.

Claire and Valerias talked for hours. The subjects were varied but interesting to both. When evening came, Claire invited Valerias for dinner and he accepted. It was a quiet dinner with just Eustice, Claire, Valerias, and the girls. After dinner more conversation ensued. At the end of the evening, Valerias said he would return to the garrison. Claire took his hand, and said he would stay the night with her.

The next morning Claire rose first and met Eustice by chance in the camp headquarters.

"I don't think it is a good idea for you to be fornicating with the enemy," was his brusque opening.

"He is not the enemy, Eustice. He is a good man. You make simple assumptions."

"I have asked the Romans about him, and he carries an utterly brutal reputation. He served on many campaigns as the Roman Emperors' enforcer—like Flavius did for Argus."

"He saved my life against steep odds when he could have chosen not to. And I need to remind you that he sacrificed his well being for us to escape Morguard and find you. The girls adore him. He has shown nothing but kindness, and I want you to respect him." Claire was unusually forceful in her statement to Eustice.

Eustice backed down slightly from his position. "I understand what you are saying. It will take time for me to accept a Roman soldier or general or whatever he is now."

"He is retired."

Valerias had arisen and joined Claire and Eustice. He had heard the end of their conversation. "I understand your concerns, Eustice. My intentions toward your sister are only good. I have nothing to gain, nor do I want anything. I have retired from the Roman army. You are now the king of this land. Titus is the general."

With that Valerias made a gesture that consisted of a very short forward motion. Valerias would bow to no one, except an Emperor, but he wanted to acknowledge that Eustice was indeed the king. Eustice in turn gave Valerias and then Claire a forced smile.

During the exchange between Eustice, Claire, and Valerias, there was commotion in the Britons' camp, followed by an equal disturbance along the city walls that were manned by Romans.

From a distance there appeared to be a solitary man riding a horse with several horses strung behind him. As he came closer, it was clear the man was Flavius. He had a woman riding directly in front of him on the horse. A cloak covered most of her features. The horses behind him were carrying bodies, each strung across the horse with their front sides facing down. There were five bodies. The last three horses contained sacks of unknown contents also tied across them. It was a parade of death.

Flavius was despised in most quarters of the kingdom, and the area around Ratae was no exception. However, no obstacles were placed in front of him and no one jeered as he carried his cargo into the city. He rode through the city to the Roman garrison. Several soldiers stood in front of the gate to the garrison, and Flavius halted his march. Titus had been summoned, as Flavius was a wanted man by the Romans, and he soon appeared at the gate.

"You returned, Flavius. I did not expect this."

Flavius wasted no time. "I need help now." He removed the cloak, which revealed a woman who was Mary. Her eyes were glassy.

Valerias and Claire had watched the procession and followed Flavius into the city. When Claire saw the woman was Mary, she cried out, "Mary!" Then speaking to Flavius in a rush, "What happened?"

"The remnant factions of Argus did this. She needs help, now. She is alive, but barely."

Valerias spoke to Titus, "Bring Joseph. He may be a better healer of bodies than minds."

Titus beckoned to a guard, and soon Joseph was in the courtyard. Claire was over by Mary. Titus summoned his guards to gently take her from the horse and lay her on clean sheets on the ground.

Claire spoke directly to Joseph, "I need you to help her as best you can. Marcus has spoken highly of your physician's skills."

She looked up at Flavius and saw a worn person with exhaustion in his eyes. This was not the Flavius she was used to seeing.

Joseph also looked at Flavius. "Tell me what has happened to her."

"I will tell you inside. We need to be away from the crowd, and it is cold."

Titus again motioned to his men, and they carried Mary as she was lying on the sheets into a room inside the garrison, heated by a small but glowing fire. Soldiers placed more wood on the fire, and it grew like a dragon on special herbs. Joseph gave Mary a limited drink of water. She looked very pale and seemed quite thin. Joseph looked over to Flavius. He was warming himself by the fire. Flavius turned around and slowly gazed at the people in the room.

"She was helping the remaining villagers of Abrador flee from Morguard's force, which had occupied the village. The people were trying to make it here, to the Roman garrison. Morguard's men plundered the village, murdering anyone who resisted and raping the women. It is what you expect from those beasts associated with Morguard. Somehow Morguard's men found out about the refugees. They caught up to Mary and the others. All were killed or were left for dead, including Mary. She and the other women were raped repeatedly before being put to the sword. For whatever reason, Mary was not killed.

"I tracked them and killed all of them that I could find who had stayed near where the refugees were massacred. Unfortunately, most of those bastards had dispersed. I could not find Morguard and have no idea where he is. I brought Mary here as fast as she could travel. I also brought some of the men with me that I encountered, so you know what I speak is true."

Joseph looked at all those gathered in the room and spoke up, "I'm pleased so many of you care about Mary, but you must leave now. I need time to do what I can do, and she needs quiet. Take your talk of death out of this room. I will care for her and I will pray for her. Flavius, you are her friend. You can come back tomorrow morning. Same with you, Claire."

Joseph looked at Valerias, who had just entered the room. He and the others reluctantly exited.

"Joseph seems to have taken command," summarized Valerias.

"Was he like that when he served under you?" asked Claire.

"No, he wasn't. He has matured." Valerias also thought but did not say, *And I too have mellowed.*

Valerias then spoke directly to Flavius as Titus stood beside him, "Under whom did you serve in the legions? You seem to have been trained well and are an expert in combat. I should have . . ." then Valerias looked at Titus and continued, "we should have heard of you."

"I served most of my time in Africa where there was much conflict. We had to adapt quickly or we would be dead. Many of my colleagues died in that land. One of the commanders I served was General Gallus."

Both Valerias and Titus nodded at the same time.

Titus added, "I recall that this was the Gallus we heard was touched with the illness." Titus pointed to his head. "I'm surprised you survived."

Flavius looked at Titus and then Valerias with a strong glare. "The strong survived." Flavius changed the subject. "Do you think that Christian priest can make Mary well again?"

Valerias answered, "Mary is fortunate, Flavius. Joseph is a skilled physician and Christian priest. So she is getting a two-for-one treatment. I would trust anyone to his care."

"I hope you are right. Mary is a Christian, so his prayers are welcome."

"You can pray too, Flavius. She will need it." The speaker was Joseph, who had just entered the room. He told Titus he needed certain supplies and then made a quick comment. "She has undergone a terrible experience. She has been raped, brutalized, and stabbed. She may lose an eye. She will need both physical and mental care." He walked straight over to Flavius. "Can you provide what is needed to get her and keep her well?"

"Absolutely. I swear on my life," answered Flavius. "I love her."

"Good. That should be of enormous help. Now, please obtain the supplies that I need."

Titus spoke in a commanding tone, "Yes, and if you need anything else, come to me." Then to Flavius, "Flavius, even though you are my prisoner, I will let you stay as near to her as Joseph will allow. I guess in my old age I have become soft."

No one believed that sentiment. Joseph went into the room where Mary rested. Just after Joseph returned to the room, two men appeared and brought him the requested supplies. Claire said she was going to stay as near to Mary's room as possible for the rest of the day and through the night. Valerias agreed to join her and keep her company. Flavius sat with Claire and Valerias.

Titus left and found Eustice outside. They discussed the day's events and when each would return to their headquarters. Eustice would leave in two days for the castle that formerly housed Claire and Gerhard and then the devil, Argus. Titus said he was preparing to leave for his own castle soon. The weather was fit for traveling, even at the end of December.

LX

Serenity

January came and turned into February and then March. Titus returned to his castle headquarters, and Eustice began his reign from the castle that previously belonged to Gerhard and Claire. Mary was making a recovery, although it was slow. She was a strong woman, but the damage inflicted upon her was severe. Joseph was correct that her spiritual wellness needed as much care as her physical recovery. Flavius stood by her side full time or was nearby, doing what he could to help her. It was a sight that affected Valerias. He persuaded Titus to relieve the prison sentence that had been placed on Flavius. The theory was that Flavius would not leave Mary, and he did not.

One day Valerias came to the room to see how Mary was progressing in her recovery and to also spend time with Claire. Flavius was there as well. When Flavius saw Valerias, he motioned for the two of them to leave the room. Flavius picked up a cloth-wrapped item as they left.

"When I was disposing of those rogues who had assaulted and violated Mary and killed the other villagers, I found this."

Flavius pulled out a sword, a spatha, from the wrapped cloth.

"It is a Roman sword that belonged to an officer. Not just any officer, but one who knows fine weapons, a general such as yourself."

Valerias looked at the sword and took it gently from Flavius' hands. He carefully inspected it and did a few short fighting moves. He looked at the hilt and smiled broadly.

"This is mine, Flavius. The most talented master craftsman in Rome specially fabricated it. He made five of these swords. This is the only one I have left. If you look carefully, you can see my name."

Valerias gave the sword back to Flavius and pointed at the small engraving at the base of the hilt. It read "M.A. Valerias V." "The V stands for the fifth sword made by the weapons maker."

Flavius read the inscription and repeated, "M.A. Valerias. It is a beautiful sword, General. I thought it might be yours when I found it."

"Please do not call me General. That is not my calling anymore. It is Marcus or just Valerias." Valerias had made his point and hurried into his next question. "Tell me, Flavius, why didn't Morguard have my sword? He was the one who took it from me."

"I truly do not know what happened to Morguard. If he had been there, I would have killed him. But he wasn't. This was in the hands of an ordinary fool who thought he was a fighter and was not, and now he is dead."

Valerias examined the sword again. "It appears to have made it through our separation in fairly good shape. I shall take it to a weapons maker tomorrow for a thorough cleaning and repair. Do you have any recommendations for this job?"

"No. I am sure your Roman friends know someone in the city. Perhaps one of them is good enough to do the work for you."

"I won't forget your gesture, Flavius."

Flavius went back into the room with Mary. Claire joined Valerias in the outside room.

"What is the story with the sword?" Claire asked.

"It is mine. Flavius retrieved it when he killed the parasites that attacked Mary. The only bad thing is the bastard Morguard wasn't on the other end of the sword when Flavius took it."

"Does the sword mean much to you?"

"Very much. It was my constant companion when I was a Roman general." Valerias knew he needed to reduce his happiness about the return of his sword. "When I *was* a general," he repeated. "And I had it with me in the cave."

Later that day Claire returned Valerias' dagger to him. "Your sword and dagger are now reunited," she announced. "I should not need it any more." Valerias was pleased both of his weapons of choice were back in his possession.

When Mary was strong enough, Joseph took a leave and journeyed back to his adopted village of Bergen. He told Ruth what had happened. When Joseph returned to Ratae, Ruth came with him to assist with Mary's recovery. There was also an infectious disease sweeping the area, and Joseph needed help administering to the sick in addition to his care for Mary. Ruth would provide the assistance. Ruth and Joseph made the trip mostly in silence. Joseph was afraid to say much of anything that would give away his feelings for her. For her part Ruth was smart about the situation, but she was nervous. She did not want to prod Joseph into any decision-making about their relationship.

During this time Valerias and Claire became very close. Valerias had found part of what he had been missing in life when he devoted everything to the army. He loved Claire and her daughters. He wanted to meet Claire's son, Douglas, but he had signaled his intentions to stay with the monks at the monastery for the time being. Douglas was technically the heir to the throne, but he preferred the safety and solitude in the monastery to a life of political intrigue. He was just too young and weak to become a king. Valerias recognized that Douglas was a threat to Eustice, but he kept his thoughts to himself. *We will see how Eustice adjusts to holding power,* he thought.

Claire had fallen in love with Valerias as well. He was a true leader, fearless and yet with a soft side that had been exposed during his time in Ratae. Even though he was no longer in the commission of the army, the soldiers at the garrison carried a strong respect for him. His reputation and friendship to Titus made him a pseudo-general in Titus' absence. The natives of the city also began to trust Valerias, and he became a de-facto arbitrator of civilian and even a few Roman disputes.

In late March Valerias felt his life couldn't be better. His love for Claire was deep. Mary had largely recovered, and the weather was turning from winter to spring. Valerias found he no longer cared for the cold. In the past cold was something to adjust to and then not be concerned about. There were always other issues that were more important. Now on cold days his joints hurt. He considered escaping winter some day for a warm climate.

On an unusually warm day he took Claire and the girls on a picnic to a serene location by a lake. The ice had just fled the surface of the lake, and the water was clear. Valerias pointed out fish hugging the bottom of the lake near the shore. The breeze was warm and moist. He sat back using a tree trunk as a brace. A feeling of contentment came over him. He shut his eyes, and then a thought he had had many months ago rolled back into his mind. *True contentment does not last. It is a fleeting feeling. It is the preface to a storm. It is not human to be truly contented, except in the short term.* He frowned on the inside. That thought was soon forgotten, as the girls had awakened an amphibian and their giggling brought the smile back to his face.

PART III

"The Romans quickly learned what lay behind all the mayhem. Again in Ammianus' words: 'The seed-bed and origin of all this destruction and of the various calamities inflicted by the wrath of Mars, which raged everywhere with extraordinary fury, I find to be this: the People of the Huns.'"

— *The Fall of the Roman Empire* by Peter Heather

LXI

Horizons

Rao felt good about how life was going as he sat in his tent and watched the stars. It was a cold day, but he didn't care. He had solidified his hold over the Northern Huns and their allies. Uldric, after some persuasion, had accepted his role as second-in-command, at least through the winter. He was still overall commander of the army, but it was Rao who set policy and schedule and was the final decision-maker. Uldric was free to go as he wished to conduct raiding operations. He was content with those responsibilities while the Huns remained centered in their main camp for the winter. However, Rao knew that when spring arrived, he would have to temper Uldric's desire to march west into the land ruled by the Romans.

Rao had become even more suspicious of Zestras' push for the brothers to tackle the Romans while he, Zestras, sat back and let them take all the risk and do all the work. The more Rao thought about the situation, the more he wanted to return home and take on Zestras. Rome and Constantinople were overly big obstacles for the Huns at this time. If they survived their journey west, the brothers would be too weak to fight Zestras, and then he would be in position to assume control of the Northern Huns. Rao saw through Zestras' plan now. He just had to convince his brother of his revised plan. Rao knew that once Uldric wore out his famous temper, his brother would agree with his conclusion, and they would adjust their plan.

Rao had held weekly council meetings with his generals, pro-generals, and officers to discuss their schedule and ways to maintain their troops' morale. A secondary agenda item for Rao was to wean the men away from wanting to attack the Romans and Goths to focusing on Zestras. Slowly the men began to believe in Rao's war philosophy. Uldric attended about half of the meetings. Rao always reserved a place beside himself for Uldric, whether he attended or not. When Uldric was present, Rao steered the conversations away from Zestras, and so far his strategy was working.

It was a late February day, and Rao decided to take a ride around the camp and meet personally with his men. Uldric was out with another raiding party as usual. Rao was popular with his troops with his cerebral approach, and the visits were morale boosters. He spent the entire day in the various areas of the camp meeting the men and watching several training exercises. Rao was not quite as good a fighter as his brother, so he did not participate in many of the drills. There were times he wanted to be a better fighter, but a Hun general once told him, "We need your intelligence and leadership. Your brother can be the fighter."

In the evening he took a back trail on the way to his tent. The air was silent, and the moon shown above the horizon to the east. It was a full moon and pale as the snow on the ground. The moon appeared to float, and Rao thought about what it was like this night in Rome. He wondered what it would be like to be the first conqueror of Rome. He laughed to himself about this fantasy.

The quietness of the time was interrupted by a soft swish, followed by a thump. The arrow slammed into Rao's back. He instinctively reached behind to grab it. A second arrow pierced his hand and also dug deep into his back. Rao looked at the moon with a grimace and fell off of his horse into a small pile of snow. Blood ran from his wounds, and the snow around his back began to turn red. Rao could hear footsteps coming toward him. If he could reach his sword . . . but he was too weak and life was flowing from his body into the snow. He looked up and the last thing he saw was the face of Produgas.

After confirming Rao's death, Produgas walked back to his horse. He made no attempt to cover his tracks. Once on his horse, he removed his boot coverings and placed them in a sack. He then rode off to the east. He came to a swale with a small stream snaking its way through the countryside. A rider appeared downstream from Produgas. It was Braga, son of Zestras.

"Is it done?" Braga questioned with no emotion.

"It is," replied Produgas.

"Good. Now give me the sack with the boot covers and any leftover arrows you have. We do not want anything traced back to you regarding what just happened—do we?"

"No, we don't." Produgas' horse sauntered slowly over to Braga. Produgas handed Braga the sack with the arrows and boot covers.

"You only needed two arrows. You must be a good hunter."

"Good enough for what we needed done."

Braga continued, "So, based on your belief, Uldric will go mad trying to find Rao's killer or killers, and in doing so, will destroy himself. You will then assume leadership of the Northern Huns. We will merge and proceed to take Constantinople under joint command."

Produgas looked at Braga's face. It was so young looking, with no lines or cracks. *He hasn't learned about life and death on the steppes yet,* Produgas thought to himself. Produgas turned to thinking less of Braga's features than of the opportunity to command the Northern Huns. Here he was, not long ago a jester to Rao and Uldric. Now he was in position to be the leader and the brothers, with all their power, would be nothing. The more he thought of the possibilities, the more he cared less for Braga. He even thought of marching against Zestras and Braga for control of a consolidated Hun empire.

Snow started to fall over the swale.

"See what good fortune you have, friend Produgas. The snow will cover both of our tracks so we will not need to do that ourselves."

Produgas said goodbye to Braga who, as they separated, told Produgas that he would contact him shortly. Braga quickly disappeared behind a bluff that formed a curve in the stream.

When Rao did not return to his tent, his guards became concerned, and several spread out over the camp. It wasn't long before one of Rao's scouts tracked the place where Rao was lying. He had been dead for over an hour, and his body was becoming frozen. Calls went out, and soon a large contingent of men arrived and carried the body back to his tent. Several parties began searching for the assassin. The Hun generals gathered in Rao's tent and tried to form a strategy. This was not a strategy of how to manage without Rao; instead, it was centered on who would be the unfortunate man who would tell Uldric of his brother's death.

When Uldric found out about his brother's assassination, his rage was pure. A scout had brought him the information, and Uldric promptly killed him. He swiftly rode back to the main camp as if the dogs of hell were chasing him. He would find the murderer and flay him into a thousand pieces. Uldric arrived in the camp as more snow covered the earth. He jumped from his horse and quickly went inside Rao's tent, where Rao was in a state of repose. Several Hun generals were in the tent, along with servants. Produgas had just entered the tent and feigned disbelief at what was before him. A number of women were wailing.

Uldric wasted no time in dissecting the situation.

"What happened!"

No one said anything. Most of the persons in the tent seemed to have become part of the shadows that formed along the edges.

"NOW!" Uldric smashed his fist against the table. Cups and bowls flew through the air. He stared at those in the room with a glare that would stun any animal.

Finally Produgas stepped forward. "We are all sorry about what happened to Rao. He was a great leader."

Before he could continue, Uldric swore several curses. "I didn't ask if you were sorry, I asked what happened? How did my brother die? Who committed this violation against me and, more important, insulted the Northern Huns? There are no more jokes, Produgas."

One of the scouts in the tent spoke hesitantly, "We believe the assassin was a Goth."

"What?" was the only word spoken by Uldric and he stared sternly at the scout.

"Yes, General Uldric, a Goth." Uldric had ordered his men to call him General, Commander of the Army. The scout continued, "We found the two arrows that killed Rao had Goth markings. We have seen them before when we scouted the area west of here three months ago."

"A Goth here, do you jest?" Uldric sternly addressed the scout.

"Yes, General Uldric, a Goth." The scout repeated himself.

The scout removed the arrows from a sack and gave them to Uldric. Any blood that had been present was removed before Uldric could inspect them. Uldric looked at them carefully.

"How did a Goth get so close to our camp and not be detected, particularly by my elite guard? And why was Rao out on his own and without his bodyguard?"

Uldric smashed the table once again. He looked at Rao's face and chest area. "He was shot by two arrows, in the back, correct? Cowards!"

Uldric was very upset but surprisingly maintained his composure. "Let me summarize. My brother was out for a ride, without his guards. A Goth or Goths sneaked through our sentries and guards without being detected. And my brother was killed by Goth arrows shot into his back. Any of you have anything to add to my summary?"

Not a word was spoken, so Uldric continued, "Did anyone track his killers? There is snow, and the assassin's tracks would be traceable, wouldn't they?"

The scout answered again, "We tracked for the signs, but the snow had covered all the tracks. I would have found the tracks if I could have. The tracks were headed west when they disappeared."

"At least one of my men has guts. Your performance is poor, but speaking up to me saved your life. Bring me Rao's guards."

Several guards were brought into the tent. Everyone in the room knew Uldric would administer some type of punishment, and they were correct. To whom and the type of punishment were the only questions. No one was immune.

Uldric had a dagger in his hand and walked up to the leader of Rao's guard and stuck the knife in his throat. Blood gushed out and sprayed onto Uldric. He did not seem to mind. He then called for one his guards, who brought out Uldric's weapon of choice, the spear with two curved blades. The blades had been mounted into each end of the spear handle. Uldric referred to this weapon as a scimitar. With two extraordinary moves, he sliced off ears of the two nearest guards positioned next to Rao's chief guard who was now dead on the ground. Both men winced in pain and put their hands over the places where their ears used to be. Uldric handed the weapon back to his guard. He walked over to Rao's remaining personal guards.

Blood covered his chest, and he walked down and stared at each man. They stood at attention, although each was shaking as they pictured their death administered by Uldric.

"I don't think of you as cowards, but you let my brother down and me down, terribly. I will let you live, but if for any reason you cause me to doubt you in the future, you will die. Is that clear?"

The men all nodded with relief in their eyes. Uldric did not execute or harm any other man that night. During the next day, though, the man in charge of sentries was hung tightly from four trees with an arm or leg tied to each tree. Uldric thought he could keep watch over the camp from that position. He perished in that position, and Uldric left his body in the trees as a warning to others.

After Uldric had finished with Rao's guards, he left the tent in disgust and went directly to his tent. No one, not even Produgas, accompanied Uldric to his tent. It was best to leave Uldric to mourn on his own and keep his wrath to himself. Uldric entered his tent and sat down in a large, soft chair sown from a compilation of animal hides. His servants hid in the dark. Uldric sat in that position for several hours, hardly moving a muscle.

He and Rao had had their issues and they frequently clashed over policy and timing of events. But they were twin brothers, and close. As much as they disagreed about various matters, they always seemed to come together at the end, when it mattered. Rao's death was a huge blow to Uldric. He would now have to be the sole leader and do everything alone that he and Rao would have accomplished together. In a small way he was grateful for Rao's death. Now only he would know the cause of their father's death.

As he sat in the tent, the sun began to enter the horizon with the first rays of the day. A woman emerged from the dark and brought him an enclosed letter sealed by Rao. The woman was a trusted harem girl who had served Rao. She told Uldric the letter was to be given to him at the time of Rao's death—whenever that time was, and it was now. The woman said it was only for Uldric's eyes.

Uldric was literate, but not to the degree of his brother, so Rao wrote the letter to Uldric's comprehension of the written word. Uldric quickly became immersed in the letter. The contents of the letter flowed almost poetically. Rao reminisced about his childhood with Uldric, what he had seen, and what they had achieved together. It almost seemed like Rao expected to die and to die before Uldric. Uldric developed tears as he read the letter.

The last part of the letter was more ominous. A frown and the associated wrinkles formed on Uldric's face in place of tears.

> Brother, when you read this, I have gone to our celebrated afterlife. I do not mind, as I know it is better where I'm going than where I have been. I do not trust Zestras. I have come to believe that he has sent us on this mission so that we become so weakened that he takes control over our confederation. Be wary of him, brother. You may want to consider stopping your advancement to the west or south against the Romans and return to our land and seek out Zestras. If I were still alive, I would give you this counsel. You must make your own way. But that is the way I would choose.

The letter concluded with sentences wishing Uldric good fortune, and that they would see each other in the afterlife. After reading the letter, Uldric sat in his chair a short time before calling his primary servant.

"Put this letter with my special belongings and seal it with my seal. Anyone who breaks the seal will die."

The servant bowed and took his leave. Uldric called for his guard to have his officers assemble in his tent. Produgas and the rest of Uldric's generals soon arrived in the tent. Uldric was very calm.

"My men," he began. "We all will miss my brother, the great Rao. No one more than me."

All in the room gave a hearty shout and banged their weapons together.

"I am now the leader, the sole leader, and I will determine what direction we go. Now, gather all your men and weapons and prepare for war. In two days' time we take the field against the Goths. I want them destroyed in any way or manner it takes. They shall be our dogs. Whatever you want with the Goths, you shall have. There will be no quarter for any Goth. Death is the only way out for those animals. Go forth and bring the Suevi, the Sarmatians, and the Alans into the fold and anyone else who wants victory, glory, and plunder. Go!"

The men continued with their salute to Uldric and his mission. All pledged their undying support and left Uldric's tent with renewed passion. They had become bored sitting around the camp for the past few months. Even though it was still winter, war was the better alternative to sitting like old women.

After all the men had left, only Produgas remained with Uldric.

"General, what about the Romans?" Produgas asked.

"First the Goths, then we will deal with the Romans."

Produgas left Uldric's tent satisfied about how the future would play out.

What Uldric failed to tell Produgas was that he had no intention of chasing Romans to Rome or Constantinople. After the Goths were crushed, he would take his enlarged army and march against Zestras. Uldric trusted no one after what had happened to Rao, and his plan would be his plan alone.

The next months proved to be disastrous for the Goths and Produgas' ambitions. Hell reigned on Earth in the form of Uldric's annihilation of any Goth who crossed his path.

LXII

Reversal

THE DAY WAS sunny and warm. It was one of those early April days when the wind from the south blesses the land with signs that spring is at hand. Valerias frequently trained with the Roman soldiers at the garrison to keep his skills up and reflexes sharp. Yet he had no intention of entering again into formal combat. On some days Flavius joined the men. He had impressive fighting abilities and was gradually being accepted back into the Roman ranks. Technically he was still a prisoner; however, Valerias and Titus let him pursue his own path, which revolved primarily around his devotion to Mary. Unfortunately, he was still despised by a large segment of the local population for his role with Argus.

It was midafternoon, Valerias' favorite time of the day, and he and Claire were out for a walk. The girls ran and played alongside them. Valerias had reached the point that he wanted to ask Claire to marry him. He was nervous, though, because he had never come this far with a woman. Rejection of his proposal would be unbearable. Valerias would know it as a defeat—which was something he rarely experienced.

For her part, Claire loved Valerias like no other man she had known. Gerhard was her husband and father of their children. However, he was often distant and shared little with her. She had a soft spot in her heart for Erik, who had sacrificed his life for her and the girls. But Erik had always been too eager to please and was too carefree for her. Valerias was who she thought her ideal man should be. He was intelligent, confident, and had a sense of humor that emerged when he was near her. His fighting skills were exceptional, and after what happened to Gerhard and Erik, she wanted a man who could take care of her children. They also could talk for hours and shared much in common.

Valerias was a Roman, though, and Eustice constantly reminded her of that fact. Further, what was he going to do now that he was retired? He had no trade or skill besides conducting warfare. Claire informed Eustice that Valerias as general had been an administrator over an area larger than Eustice's kingdom. If he wanted to, she thought Valerias could be a consul to Eustice. He could provide military and financial advice without having to engage in combat for the king. Valerias certainly would not be a usurper of Eustice's crown.

She did not know, though, that Valerias was in control of a large sum of money held back in Rome. The money had accumulated in part through inheritances from his parents and adopted father and in part by compensation for his position as a Roman general for several years. He had spent little of the money while in the army, so he didn't need to work to earn money.

As they walked through the field near Ratae, a large contingent of Roman soldiers entered the city. Even though the soldiers were far away, Valerias could tell Titus was riding in the group.

"Titus is here for a reason," he mentioned to Claire. "We should go and find out what that reason is. I suspect it may be related to Flavius or your brother."

Titus was a man with a purpose, and he had not come to Ratae this time to socialize with Valerias. Valerias and Claire hastily returned to the city. When they arrived, Titus was sitting on a chair inside the fort with a cup of mead.

Valerias and Claire walked into the room.

After the customary greetings, Titus cut to his point, "I'm glad you two are here. Now I don't have to come and find you."

With that introduction, he handed a sealed letter to Valerias. Valerias inspected the parchment. It was sealed with two wax seals. One was from the Emperor Valens of the Eastern Empire. The other was sealed by his brother, Valentinian, Emperor of the Western Empire. Valerias had no idea why two Emperors would send a retired general a letter. He looked at Claire quizzically and then back at the parchment. He pulled the seals off and read the letter. It took Valerias only a minute to read it. Comprehending its meaning would take a longer time.

> To General Marcus Augustus Valerias: It has come to our attention that a great menace threatens our Empires. Our scouts and emissaries have informed us that an army of pronounced multitude is massing a month's worth of days' ride east from the Danube. This army is centered around a tribe of Huns that we know little of. The Hun army has created chaos in the land of the Goths. As a result, the Goth barbarians have fled west and congregated near the Danube. We understand the Hun army is set to assault either or both of the Western and Eastern Empires after they destroy the Goths. What is more, the Huns have created a refugee crisis among the Goths, which threatens to cause massive immigration of the Goths into the Empires. This invasion of Goths would have enormous consequences for the stability and longevity of the Empires. We request your return to active duty and field an army to meet and defeat

the Huns. Whatever you need to undertake this task shall be given to you. General Titus will escort you to the coast. Time is imperative.

The letter was signed by each Emperor, Valens and Valentinian. Valerias, maybe for the first time in his life, looked stunned. He handed the letter to Titus who read it.

"Did you know about this, Titus?" Valerias added.

"By the gods, I did not. I don't understand. I have heard nothing."

Claire reached for the letter and looked at it with an initial questioning gaze. She had been educated in the classics and could read Latin.

"What does this mean, Marcus?" The magnitude of the order had not yet set in with her.

"I have been called back to serve the Empires." Valerias' voice sounded deeply resigned to the situation. He knew that when he reached that pinnacle of contentment days ago, it would not last, and it hadn't.

"Do you have to go?" Claire asked with a little desperation in her voice.

Valerias said nothing and looked at Titus.

Titus answered, "He received a direct order from not one but two Emperors. He must serve his Emperors. To not comply would mean death."

Claire responded, "But they said this was a request."

To which Titus replied, "It is an order—and cannot be discarded."

"But the Emperors are so far away. They could not possibly enforce their order."

Titus looked at Valerias, and now Valerias responded, "Titus has received his orders as well. If I do not comply with the order, Titus must carry out my punishment for treason."

Claire followed up with Titus, "I thought you said you were not aware of the contents of the letter before it was read by Marcus?"

"It is implied what Titus must do if I do not rejoin the army and resume my command, Claire."

No one said a word. Valerias waved the letter in the air. "I can never escape from my destiny—because now I know my destiny." A forlorn Valerias then said softly, "Leave us."

Everyone but Claire left the room. Valerias reached for Claire's arm and pulled her close.

"I love you, Claire, more than my own life. It is so unfortunate that this happened, but I must follow the orders of the Emperors. To not do so would be the ultimate treason. I will not commit treason."

"We could run away to the western hills where Eustice hid from Argus." When Claire spoke those words, even she didn't believe them.

"My dear Claire, Titus would follow us to the end of your island. My best guess is Titus would grant Flavius a full pardon if he would track us down. As you know, Flavius is an excellent tracker."

Claire sat down, crushed, and Valerias sat beside her. Just when she had found her true love, that love was now going to leave her and might never return. She thought about her daughters and son. She thought about Valerias. Valerias just looked at her. She arose from the chair. The events of the last few minutes seemed to age her, and it showed in her face.

"Come to our quarters tonight as usual. I must think this matter over."

With those words Claire left the room. Valerias was motionless and stared into the corners of the room, focusing on nothing in particular. Titus returned.

"What do you want me to do, Marcus? I can let you leave and pretend not to find you."

"You are a very good friend, Titus. I will not put you in that position. You may lose your retirement and may even be executed for not successfully carrying out the orders from not one but two thrones. You are too old to chase me around the countryside. You need to spend your old age on a beach south of Rome." Valerias smiled as he said those words.

Titus remarked with a sly grin, "You are correct, I'd rather spend time on a beach or evaluating my estate than chasing you or some damn Hun around."

Titus ordered wine brought to the room. After each man sampled the contents of the flask, Titus inquired, "What are you going to do with Claire?"

"This is a problem. If I hadn't met Claire, I would probably follow whatever command I receive from an Emperor. Claire has changed my life. Finally, after all these years, I have found something, someone, who has shown me an alternative to military life. Frankly, Titus, Claire has pulled out of me that which I didn't know I had—the ability to love another person. I am also very fond of her daughters. I have a family now. I was going to ask Claire to marry me."

"I understand your issue."

"What about your family in Italy, Titus?"

Titus sighed softly. "Sometimes the concept of family is not what it seems. I have not been home in over three years. I have received occasional correspondence from my wife, which is not the same as seeing her on an every day basis. I understand our oldest son just had a baby, at least his wife did. I don't know if my wife has been faithful. I have strayed a couple of times myself. But I do love my wife, and I look forward to getting out of this wretched place. I do believe Rome will withdraw its forces from here shortly. When you think about it, our occupation here is a losing proposition. You have the Saxons to the east, the Celts and

Picts to the north and west. It is becoming a wreck. I actually feel sorry for the Britons."

Titus became embarrassed. He had started a monologue of his feelings when he preferred brevity. Valerias caught Titus' meaning. "I worry about the entire Empire. Back in the days of Marcus Aurelius, Rome was the king on the hill."

"Seven hills, you mean," interjected Titus.

Both men laughed at the correction.

Titus changed the subject. "Marcus, do you think what we have done for this place, for the places we have been and for the Empire we have served, will be remembered? Will we be remembered for our great deeds?"

Valerias sensed sarcasm in Titus' voice. "I would like to think so," Valerias responded honestly.

"Are all the great acts of Caesar remembered for what they actually were? Or have they been modified or forgotten over time? Will we be forgotten, Marcus?"

"I have been keeping a history or account of what I have experienced in my life as an officer, so future officers and soldiers can learn what I have learned."

"Where is this history now, Marcus?"

"In safekeeping in Londinium. Maybe a set has made it to Rome by now."

"I truly hope that your documents are kept in good hands and are evaluated in the future as you have intended them to be evaluated. I have done no such history. My legacy, if you will, will be as others define it. I'm hopeful it is somewhat positive, but I will have no control over that and neither will you. What we have done will be as others interpret those actions. But in my opinion, Marcus, what we have thought, what we have said, what we have done, and most important, what others around us have thought of our words and deeds, will all be lost over time. Scholars may read your history and know what you did on a certain date and maybe why you did it, but they won't know all of the reasoning for your actions and what others thought at that time."

Titus and Valerias finished their cups of wine in silence. Titus finally spoke, "Sometimes I talk too much; however, I believe in what I have said." He motioned for more wine.

After it was poured, Valerias looked at Titus as if he had an awakening. "You are wise, Titus. I think it goes with your old age." Both men laughed.

At that moment Joseph entered the room.

"Would you like wine, Joseph?" Titus asked.

Joseph looked at Titus and then Valerias. Valerias nodded and a cup was poured. Joseph looked at them expressionlessly and then took a drink from the cup.

"Titus, I have asked Joseph to come here. He became my chief accountant and scribe during my last year as general. He was responsible for the final preparation of my history that you have so readily discounted."

Titus grunted after that statement, letting Joseph know that he did not agree with Valerias.

Valerias ignored Titus and continued, "I want Joseph to take my dictation as the response to the Emperors."

Valerias handed Joseph a parchment and writing instrument. "The first letter will be addressed to Emperor Valentinian. Then make a copy of that letter with the proper adjustments for Emperor Valens. I would like these to go by courier at the first sign of dawn."

Valerias began with his salutation to the Emperor Valentinian. He made several complimentary statements, some of them true, but some were enhanced. Then he began addressing the heart of the matter.

> I, your humble servant, will once again take up the standards of the legions to campaign against the Hun. I will

need men and supplies from you who have commissioned me for this task. I will be providing you with a list of these items as the campaign begins. I also need to request your consideration of a few conditions, which I pray you will approve. These are:

My officers and legions that were once under my command are to return to my command. This includes my Generals, Braxus and Cratus. Trojax, and whoever else is in place of my former command, are to be transferred elsewhere.

A one-time amnesty be granted for all soldiers in my legions who deserted the army since my retirement.

The former Roman officer, Flavius Magnetious, be granted amnesty and be allowed to exile in Spain.

General Titus be granted an early retirement and be allowed to return to his villa in Italy.

I do not demand or state that these are my conditions for returning to the army, or that I will not serve unless granted. These are requests from your loyal servant.

Marcus Augustus Valerias

Magister Militum

General, Danube Legions

Titus was surprised by these requests from Valerias. "You ask nothing for yourself. You also used the word 'pray.'"

"The Emperors are Christian. They will like the word and Joseph will like to write it. As for my requests, no, I don't have any. My only request would be to be near Claire. I don't see how that can be worked out now. Joseph, prepare the copy to Emperor Valens. When you have finished the letters, both Titus and I will add our seals to the letters."

"Yes, Marcus," Joseph replied.

"Soon it will once again be 'General' when you address me," Valerias said, with weariness in his voice.

Titus and Valerias left Joseph to prepare the letters. It was now dark in the land outside the garrison. Valerias left the garrison for his place with Claire. His heart was heavy, as if it were being pressed by a great slab of rock. He needed to tell his love that he was going to leave her, likely forever.

LXIII

Adjustments

Valerias returned to the quarters he shared with Claire. He was already mentally worn down by the thought of the future and his conflicted feelings. A part of him looked forward to the campaign against the Huns. He was a military man and would always be one to some degree. Further, the thought of another challenge intrigued him. And yet he felt guilty for having those thoughts. He truly looked forward to a future life with Claire without the continuing pressure of being the General.

Claire was sitting on the edge of their bed.

"I put the girls to bed early tonight. We need to talk."

"Yes, we do."

Without hesitation Claire said distinctly, "I am going with you when you go against the Huns."

Valerias was shocked. He had not anticipated this response. He assumed Claire would stay in Britannia and help Eustice as her brother established himself on the throne. Their relationship would likely end at that point.

"What?" was the only thing Valerias could say.

"I imagine it is hard for you to comprehend, a woman leaving her children and traveling with you into the heart of the enemy."

"Yes, it is, my dear. First and foremost, I do not want my love in any way harmed. I have been through many of these campaigns and they are savage. Soldiers die and civilians, who have no interest in the war, die."

"What do you think I have just been through? To have your husband killed. To almost be forced to marry the man that had your husband killed. To have your children threatened. To be hunted across the countryside like an animal. Think again, Marcus." Claire was angry now, angrier than Valerias had ever seen her.

He was on the defensive. "What about your daughters?" he meekly asked. "If something happened to you, they would become wards of Eustice. Is that what you want?"

"Anne and Elizabeth will travel with us. Douglas will stay where he is currently located."

Valerias cut her off, "No, that will not happen. I will not be responsible for the girls when we go on campaign."

"You are a fool, Marcus. Do you think I would put my girls into harm's way after what they have been through?"

"No, on second thought."

"You are correct. Now listen to me. I have already made arrangements. Mary is now almost back to full strength. She will take my daughters to your Roman city of Milan. Flavius knows the city and will provide protection. I trust he will be better off in Milan than with Eustice. After the Huns are defeated, we will call for them. One other thing, Marcus, you forget that I'm an excellent handler of the bow. I recall beating you in a contest."

"A contest in friendly confines is not the same as in combat, Claire."

"I have been in combat."

A servant entered Valerias' and Claire's quarters.

"A man named Joseph is here to see you, Marcus."

"Of course, let him in."

Joseph walked slowly into the room. He had heard the heated discussion between Valerias and Claire and did not want to interfere.

"We are fine, Joseph. A healthy discussion is good. Did you bring what I requested?"

"Yes, Marcus," and Joseph held out two scrolls.

Valerias took them and read through each thoroughly. When done, he said, "These look fine to me."

Joseph handed him a quill and ink and Valerias signed each document. Joseph handed a seal to Valerias and he sealed the parchments. Joseph turned to leave and was halted in his steps by Valerias.

"Have Titus also seal the parchments. And one more request, Joseph. I would like it if you were to accompany me back to my legions. Olivertos will need your physician skills, and I could use your presence in the camp. You will not need to hide your Christianity in my army—just act discreetly. You may return to Britannia as soon as we defeat the Huns."

Joseph was silent and did not know what to think. If he had had ten guesses as to what Valerias would ask of him, this would have been number eleven.

Valerias added, "This is not an order, only a request—and not from an Emperor. I also think you will need the time away from your lady friend to sort your relationship out."

It was no secret in the garrison about the chemistry between Joseph and Ruth. Valerias was very astute about how Joseph and Ruth acted toward each other—even though he, Valerias, never had a serious relationship with a woman before Claire.

"I will let you know in the morning, Marcus."

"That is fair, Joseph. Good night."

Joseph started backing out of the room. He watched as Valerias spoke to Claire. "I would welcome your company on the campaign. I only hope your daughters and son do not become orphans."

When they were alone, Claire spoke softly now to Valerias, "When I was reunited with my brother, a feeling of extreme relief came over me. Starting back when my husband, Gerhard, was killed, it had been such a long journey. It was so arduous for the girls and me to get to Eustice. Many people died along the way—and you could have died. When we reached safety, I took a walk in the woods alone and I cried like I never have cried before. I am a strong woman, Marcus—I've had to be for my people and my family. You are the only one I have told this to. I don't want to be without you."

Claire looked at Valerias' face, and it was awash in sympathy. He pulled her close and said, "I know, I know. I feel the same way." After a few minutes of silence he added, "It is not all bad. If these events had not happened, Argus would still be alive and we would have never met."

Valerias embraced Claire on the edge of the bed for an hour. There was no moving or talking—both were lost in thoughts.

A servant knocked quietly at the door, and Valerias reacted first. A second round of knocking aroused Claire. Valerias looked at her and said, "Now you are with a general—so you need to get use to these interruptions."

"Yes, come in," Valerias said to the servant.

The servant poked his head around the entrance. "General, there is a lady to see you."

Valerias turned to Claire. "I know who this is, it is Ruth, Joseph's friend. I must speak to her, alone. I will return."

Valerias put on his cloak and left the bedchambers. He went to an outer room where a woman was standing.

"Good evening, Ruth—I thought you would be coming to see me."

"Thank you, General for your time—I'm sorry that this is an inconvenient time."

"It is not, and call me Marcus."

"Yes, Marcus." Valerias could tell she was uneasy about calling him by his first name.

"I talked to Joseph, after he left your quarters. You asked him to accompany you on a war mission far away from here."

"That is true, Ruth. I have developed a respect for Joseph. He is a fine physician and administrator, and he seems to be good at his religious duties."

"You are not Christian, are you—Marcus?"

Valerias wanted to avoid any discussion of religion or priests or marriage with someone he barely knew, so he quickly changed the direction of the conversation. "No—what do you want to say to me, Ruth?"

"Withdraw your request of Joseph. I know he will agree to accompany you. He respects your opinion."

Tears formed in Ruth's eyes. Valerias felt pity, but with years of training as an officer and general, he showed no emotion.

"Ruth, it is up to Joseph as to what he will choose to do. I will not order him to come with me or stay—it is Joseph's decision. As I said, I have gained respect for him."

"I don't want to lose him."

"You and Joseph need to work out your relationship, Ruth. He is a good man, and I can tell that you are an equally good woman. I will promise you this—if Joseph decides to come with me, I will make it my personal responsibility to see that he returns to you. What happens after that is between you two."

Ruth looked into Valerias' eyes and saw a man who does what he says. She knew her time was up, and said, "Thank you, Marcus, for your time and wisdom. I pray this works out."

"It will," answered Valerias as Ruth left the tent.

Valerias returned to Claire and he recounted the conversation.

"I hope it works out for them," Claire added.

"The future is difficult to predict. I hope so, too, Claire." Then he added, "For all our sakes."

LXIV

From Britannia

THE NEXT DAY was April 10 in the year 374 A.D. The birds decided to more heartily welcome spring on this day than any day so far in the year. Flavius arose early and quietly left the bed he shared with Mary. She had almost completely physically recovered, although her mental recovery lagged. Flavius was aware that this part of her recovery would take longer. As a gift to Mary, Flavius had become a Christian. That was what she wanted, and he agreed to convert. Joseph performed the service and the baptism. Instead of casually adopting Christianity, Flavius embraced the religion with enthusiasm. He and Joseph spent many hours discussing theological questions and concepts. Joseph didn't fully understand the cause for this change in personality from essentially a killer for hire, first for the Romans and then Argus, to a converted Christian. Was it because of Mary, or was he running from his past, or both? Joseph didn't have the answer. But he was pleased to have such a man devoted to the faith.

When Flavius emerged early from his quarters, he was surprised to see Valerias waiting for him.

"General, I'm surprised to see you so early this morning."

"I do not sleep sometimes. Last night was one of those nights."

"I know why you are here. Claire and Mary have already talked, and Mary talks to me. I cannot campaign with you. It would go against my religious beliefs. I must add, though, that the old Flavius would fight for you."

"Flavius, I do not want you to fight against the Huns. Yet you cannot stay here without me. I am your buffer against Eustice and even Titus. And that is fine with me. I do want you to do something for me."

"I know what you are going to say, General."

"Good, then it won't take long. Claire is going with me on the campaign against the Huns. Mary will take the girls to Milan for safekeeping. I want you to be their bodyguard, so to speak. I have many friends in Milan, and I have also asked the Emperor for your amnesty. These are strange times, and allegiances are broken easily. Therefore, I want you to look after Anne and Elizabeth while we are away."

Flavius looked at Valerias and said, "I have already agreed to this task through Mary when she talked to Claire."

Valerias nodded. "Your services would be for defensive purposes only. I know enough of your religion that, in principle, killing other humans—particularly innocents—is not to be tolerated. We could debate how innocent the Huns are, though. You can talk to Joseph about this matter if you want. I believe he will agree with me, at least on this matter."

"I have already spoken to Joseph, General. I accept your order. Moreover, I swear on my love for Mary and on the Holy Cross that I will protect Mary, Anne, and Elizabeth with my life.

"Good. That is what I expect from a Roman officer. We will leave in less than a week's time for Londinium, and then Gaul. You and Mary will come with us for part of the way. You will likely be leaving Britannia forever."

With those words, Valerias returned to the Roman garrison. Titus was waiting for him.

Valerias greeted Titus, "Good morning, Titus."

"Good morning to you as well, General Valerias. The documents left earlier today for the Emperors."

Valerias was anxious. "I cannot wait until we hear back from the Emperors. I plan to leave shortly for Londinium. From there I will go to Calais on the Gaul coast and begin organizing operations."

Titus responded, "I and an escort will take you to Calais, as ordered by the Emperors. Eustice is king of only one area of Britannia. The rest of the country can be wild, as I'm sure you found out. I believe it is only a matter to time before the country implodes. The barbarians seem to be everywhere—and that includes the locals. I also understand Claire will accompany you against the Huns."

"That is true, Titus. I am still completely bewildered as to why she would leave her children and come with me. To me, it does not make sense."

"Yes it does, Marcus. She is in love with you. Embrace that fact, for true love can come at any age."

Valerias still looked confused and muttered, "I can't understand what I don't understand." As he started to leave, he added, "I need to return to Claire before it gets too late in the day. I also await Joseph's answer as to whether or not he will join me in the campaign."

Titus had the last words: "Of course he will, Marcus. For some reason he admires you—and you, a pagan, no less."

Titus laughed mirthlessly, and Valerias motioned goodbye to him.

The day passed without a word from Joseph. However, when the next morning came, Valerias was the one surprised this time, as he found Joseph waiting outside his quarters.

"You are up early this morning, Joseph."

"I am. Someone taught me the virtues of early rising and what can get done in the morning." Joseph gave Valerias a wink.

Not wasting time, Valerias questioned Joseph, "And what have you decided, my friend?"

"I'm skeptical of this campaign. Could it be that there is a secret mission to it?"

"What would that be, Joseph?"

"To acquire more land and taxes for the Roman Empire? Subject more people to Roman rule?"

Valerias let out a hearty laugh. "The Empire cannot even maintain the land it possesses. Look at Britannia and tell me this is an enlarging empire. You can see that this is not the situation. The southeastern portion of the Empire is always under threat from the Persians. I think Julian found that out. Yet the Emperors do not bring retired generals out to face the Persians. No, something has made the Emperors nervous, and that must be the Huns. Our mission is to stop the Huns before they further threaten and kill the Goths and the other tribes."

"Won't your actions also eliminate the threat to the Empire from the Goths, if the Goths are kept under control and do not migrate en masse into Roman territory across the Danube? So in the end isn't it a double win for the Empire if you prevail?"

"Yes, you could say that. But my campaign is to stop the Huns. Anything else is secondary to me. I have no will, nor do I have orders from the Emperors, to take more land. My only charge is to stop the Huns. I have no other agenda. Once this mission is over, I intend to disappear with Claire and for her to be my wife."

"I have prayed and thought hard on this matter. I will go with you. You might as well know anyway that I would have gone with you, no matter how you answered my questions, because the Marcus I now know would have answered them—with honesty."

"Good. Now what will you do about your friend, Ruth?" Valerias suspected that Joseph wanted an excuse to postpone dealing with Ruth and his feelings for her.

"Is it that obvious? How did you know that I have un-priestly thoughts about her? I am a Christian priest and I cannot have these feelings."

"Because we are all human, and that includes you. Have you acted on your feelings?"

"Absolutely not." Joseph thought his answer was firm, but Valerias just looked at him.

Joseph continued, "Sure, I have thoughts. My prayers, though, have carried me through the temptation."

"Joseph, what do you ultimately want from this relationship with Ruth?"

It was a question Joseph could not answer. He had fallen in love with Ruth and yet he did not want to betray his religion. *Life is so complicated,* he thought. *Valerias' world is black and white and mine is gray.*

"Perhaps your coming with me avoids your decision on this matter. Am I right?"

Valerias had deduced Joseph's reasoning on the matter, which made Joseph angry.

"I said I would go with you, and that is enough!"

Valerias backed down a little. "I know she is a good woman. She visited me two nights ago and she is concerned about you. You and Ruth will need to work out your future relationship. Now, I will need you to prepare a list of items that we have and those that we will need. Work with Titus' chief of staff. Let's reconvene tomorrow. Thank you."

Since they had met, it was a rare event when Valerias spoke those two words to Joseph. Joseph replied, "You're welcome," and left the room.

The next few days hurried by quickly. Titus returned to his castle-fort, as he liked to call it. Valerias met Eustice with Claire at his side as they discussed Valerias' campaign and how Claire was going to manage Anne and Elizabeth. Surprisingly, Eustice thought taking the girls to Milan was a good idea. He didn't want to spend resources protecting them when the kingdom was in such a troubled state.

Eustice had developed a favorable opinion of Valerias and his seasoned, controlled manner. He offered Valerias a position in his court when he returned from the campaign against the Huns. Valerias in turn said he appreciated and would consider Eustice's offer. Most of all, Eustice was pleased to get rid of Flavius. He had developed a deep hatred for the man when he became Argus' instrument of terror against the people. The majority of Britons in the kingdom also shared that feeling.

Finally, Eustice made Valerias swear that he would do all he could to protect Claire. Eustice and his sister had always been close. Her leaving again after they had just been reunited was difficult for both of them. Claire promised she would return, and she made Eustice promise to be a wise ruler. Eustice acknowledged he would do his best to accommodate her wishes. Valerias stood in the background and wondered how the accession to power would affect Eustice. *Power can create an evil man out of a good man,* he thought.

The morning came when Valerias and company were to leave the Roman garrison in the city of Ratae. Valerias knew it would take several more days and maybe weeks to hear back from an Emperor and especially both Emperors, even if the couriers rode day and night. He was also anxious to find out about how his former legions had done during the previous year without him. He hoped for the best.

When it was time to depart, Titus rode up with one hundred cavalrymen in parade dress. *Titus knows how to create a scene,* Valerias thought to himself.

As they prepared to leave, Valerias saw Joseph with Ruth. When the two said their goodbyes, Ruth embraced Joseph with a passionate hug. Joseph returned the hug but with a reluctant enthusiasm. When they were done, Joseph climbed on his horse and rode to Valerias' group.

Ruth looked totally forlorn. Valerias left the group and rode over to her. "Will you be all right here in Ratae without us?" he asked. "Would you like a guard?"

Ruth shook her head and whispered, "My father, Garth, and other men from our village are coming to the city today. I will soon be with them."

"Good." Valerias seemed relieved to hear that information. "I confirm my promise to you—to keep him safe so he can return to you."

"I'll pray for you, General."

Valerias nodded to Ruth, smiled, and said, "I hope you do." He turned his horse back to Titus and the rest of the departing group.

For the first time Ruth felt confident that the future events would equal the hope in her prayers.

Valerias and his group joined in with Titus and his men. Several Roman cavalrymen would lead the way, with the leaders carrying the standard and banners of Titus' legions. Valerias and Titus would ride just behind, followed by Claire, Claire's daughters, Joseph, Flavius and Mary, and the rest of the cavalry. It was an impressive sight as they traveled through the Britannic countryside. Valerias again felt proud to be a Roman soldier.

As Valerias and his group left Ratae, they met Eustice with a large force of cavalry. Valerias was unsure what to think; however, Eustice quickly dispelled any worry.

"I have thought about what you are about to do." Eustice looked at Claire, but he was also speaking to Valerias. He continued, "In a small way I would like to contribute to your campaign. Thus, I'm lending you twenty cavalrymen who will accompany you. They are all fine soldiers."

Claire responded, "Thank you, brother—this is a kind gesture."

Eustice rode up to Valerias until their horses were touching side-by-side and their faces were inches apart.

Eustice spoke quietly to Valerias, "I prefer they act as Claire's personal bodyguard. Please take care of my sister."

"It shall be as you wish—and I wish," Valerias said equally softly.

Eustice looked into Valerias' eyes and added, "May the gods be with you." Eustice then clasped Valerias on the shoulder and returned to his men.

Claire later asked Valerias what her brother had said to him. He told her that Eustice had said that the men were to be used as Valerias wished against the Huns. Valerias did not mention they were to be her bodyguard. It was the truth with an angle.

The roads were good and the weather favorable; the group made quick time, and soon they were in Londinium. They stayed five days in the city. Valerias took the opportunity to visit Bradicus with Claire and the girls, while Titus and the rest of the soldiers stayed in the Roman fort. Bradicus was pleased to see Valerias. He was a grandfather, and gave each girl a small treat. He showed Valerias the history volumes that he was working on and keeping for Valerias.

Valerias remembered his conversation with Titus and was satisfied that his history was well cared for—at least for the time being, he thought. Valerias knew he needed to rethink his plan of sending a copy to Rome. He requested Bradicus keep all his documents in Londinium until he received word from Valerias.

The group took three ships from Londinium to Calais. Titus took only a select group of his men and their horses across the channel. On the principal ship there was time for several discussions to occur among the parties. Titus took the opportunity to tease Valerias about his fear of sailing. At one time Titus swore he saw the arms of the mythical sea monster the Kraken rise out of the water in the distance. Valerias saw visions of being caught in the tentacles of the beast and being torn to shreds by the Kraken's beak. Claire and Flavius were amused by Titus' stories and Valerias' feelings about water. Indeed, Valerias had a much different appearance on the ship than he did on land—he appeared like a feeble old man.

When Valerias had gathered his "sea legs," he asked Joseph what transpired between Ruth and him. Joseph said they parted in good spirits, and he told Ruth he would decide his course of action when he returned to her. He told Valerias that he would use the time for meditation and prayer to help him make the best decision. "You should already know the answer to your dilemma," Valerias told Joseph.

Valerias and Claire also took this time to discuss with Flavius and Mary their roles in caring for the girls while Claire was away with Valerias. When the discussion was completed, all parties felt confident about the future care of the daughters. Valerias secretly hoped Milan was the safest place for them. In this time, though, a safe place might be a mirage. Meanwhile, "Uncle Titus" was a happy man, showing all his knowledge, both accurate and faulty, with the girls as they thoroughly inspected the ship.

When the ship was close to land, Valerias was pleased to make it to Calais, and not in the bowels of a sea creature.

LXV

Deserters

When they arrived at Calais, a Roman officer awaited them. Valerias was first off the ship.

The Roman officer addressed Valerias: "I need to speak to General Valerias or General Titus." He apparently didn't think a general would be first off the ship, but then he didn't know about Valerias and sailing.

"I am General Valerias. With whom am I speaking?"

"I am Quintos, Tribune to the Court of the great Emperor Valentinian."

Titus disembarked and walked up to the two men. "I am General Titus. Why are you seeking us?"

"I have something for you both." Quintos held out two parchments and gave one to Valerias and one to Titus. Each man opened up the sealed document and read it carefully.

Valerias spoke first. "Good news, Titus," and then he saw that the others had formed a circle around him. "The Emperor Valentinian has agreed to my requests. Flavius, you are free and can go to exile in Spain."

Flavius grinned. "After your return, of course, General."

Valerias continued, "Titus, your retirement awaits you in Rome. You will soon be drinking wine by the seashore, just like the elite and old men do, and reminiscing about your conquests."

Titus was frowning. "My letter from the Emperor says I am to accompany you to the Danube and assist you on your campaign."

"What?" Valerias was incredulous. "That is not what my letter states. It says you are granted retirement."

Titus countered, "True, mine does say I can retire, but after you finish the campaign against the Huns."

"Let me read your letter," Valerias requested as the pitch in his voice rose.

"No, my letter is for my eyes only. The Emperor decreed this. I too can write to the Emperors." Titus folded up the letter and placed it inside his cloak. "The matter is closed, Marcus."

Valerias protested to no avail. Finally Titus suggested the group go to a nearby tavern that Titus was familiar with for food and drink. As they were walking to the tavern, another man rode up with a contingent of Roman cavalry.

"General Titus, I am General Magnus Maximus. The Emperor Valentinian has authorized me to be your replacement as General to Britannia."

Titus pointed out a building to Valerias where the tavern was located and said he would join them at a later time. Titus was surprised that Valentinian had acted so swiftly in authorizing his replacement. He knew there was a motive behind such action, which initially concerned him. The feeling, though, quickly disappeared. Titus' thoughts were more focused on the upcoming campaign against the Huns.

Titus wanted to brief Maximus, so they walked over to a private area to talk. Titus told Maximus several strategies and tips for managing his command in Britannia. He added that he had written what Maximus would need to know on documents maintained by his scribe in the castle he used as headquarters. Titus was a detail man, and he passed that information on to Maximus. Whether or not Maximus listened was not an issue for Titus. His history was brief, not as important to him as Valerias' history was to Valerias. Titus could tell that Maximus was a very ambitious man and that Britannia, even in the shape that it was in, was not a big enough country to keep Maximus very long. *The Emperor will need to deal with him at some time,* Titus thought.

Maximus told Titus he could choose a company of ten men to ride with him as a security force. Titus quickly chose the ten, all from his personal bodyguard. Maximus boarded the three ships with his contingent and the remaining soldiers that had accompanied Titus from his castle. Titus then joined Valerias and his group at a tavern called the Dragon's Tooth. The Britons assigned by Eustice to accompany Claire also entered the tavern.

Valerias had not wasted any time. When he walked into the room, he observed several men who were likely Roman army deserters. Some left quietly when he walked in, while others just pushed their chairs deeper into the tavern's darkness. Valerias recognized a couple of the men who had belonged to his legions. He pulled out his parchment and opened it.

He looked around the room and made an announcement. "I am General Marcus Augustus Valerias. I have here a letter from the Emperor Valentinian. In his letter the Emperor has granted amnesty to anyone who deserted the army and now wishes to return to the legions with me. I know my reputation has not been kind to deserters. It is a moot subject now. I want anyone who is willing to join me in a campaign against Huns on the Danube regardless of your military status. You will be well paid and receive amnesty. I promise this on my life. This is a very good deal for you that I ask you to consider. I want to repeat what I just said—there are no repercussions for coming forward and returning to the army. You have amnesty and you have my word."

Valerias sat down and folded the parchment. Soon two ragged-looking men began to slowly approach the table where Valerias was sitting. Titus and the rest of the group were sitting at a separate table. As the men approached, Titus and Flavius became uneasy and reached for their swords. Valerias, though, showed no evidence of any worry. As they reached the table, Valerias stood up and extended his arm at the first man. The man grabbed Valerias' arm, and smiles erupted from Valerias and the two men's faces.

"Hermides and Pyrin, last time I saw you, you were doing centurion duty in my legions. I would have thought you would be promoted to senior officers now under General Braxus. Why are you here?"

Hermides answered, "General, Pyrin and I are so pleased to see you return. We thought you'd retired."

Valerias nodded with a grin.

Hermides continued, "Soon after you retired, General, Trojax sacked all of the officers who had served under you. We guess he was jealous and wanted to remake your legions according to his whims. As a result, Braxus was imprisoned. Cratus and Bukarma didn't agree with the new leader and were sent to the mines. The rest of the officers were demoted, put in prison, or sold to the mines. Your legions deteriorated after that. You would not recognize them. Trojax likes gold, and his focus was to accumulate as much wealth for his family and his primary officers as possible. When the Goths began to accumulate along the Danube, he became even less of a general and more treacherous. We left the service then. We don't know the status of Trojax and your legions now, except it is not a good situation."

By the time Hermides had finished, with complementary cursing by Pyrin, Valerias' face was red with rage. Claire was worried that he would become physically ill.

Valerias took several deep, slow breaths and looked around the room as all eyes were on him. "Trojax has become irrelevant.

I have orders from both Emperors to meet and defeat the Huns. I shall regain my legions and return them into the fighting force they were before I retired. Should I encounter Trojax as I carry out these tasks, he will be held responsible for what he has done."

Titus knew what Valerias meant when he said "held responsible." There would be a quick execution for Trojax, even if he had some relation to the Emperors. The Emperors had spoken, and Trojax was now a casualty.

Valerias continued speaking to Hermides and Pyrin. "You two are hereby granted amnesty. Once we reach the nearest fort, we shall get you outfitted in proper officer dress. First, though, I would like you to go among the populace here and where we travel and try to persuade others who left the army after Trojax assumed control over Braxus to rejoin me." Valerias was careful not to use the word "deserter."

Valerias finished and walked over to the table with Claire and the rest of the group. He was calm now, focusing on what needed to be done.

LXVI

Revious

Valerias and his group slowly made their way to an area east of Milan. The weather proved to be trying as spring weather sometimes does. Valerias wanted Anne and Elizabeth to make the trip without undue stress, so they took frequent breaks. They stayed overnight mostly at Roman forts along the way. Valerias was also not in a great hurry, because the slow pace allowed Hermides and Pyrin to recruit a number of veteran soldiers back into the ranks of soldiers that Valerias needed. Most of the men were leery at first about joining him. However, over time they realized he harbored no ill will toward them, which resulted in nearly three hundred men reenlisting by the time they reached a point within one hundred miles east of Milan.

Finally, the fork in the road was reached. Here Flavius and Mary would take Anne and Elizabeth west to Milan. Titus and his ten chosen men also were to provide an escort for the foursome to Milan, and from there they were to go to Rome or to the Danube. Valerias let Titus choose his option. Valerias and his reconstituted band of veterans, Claire and her escort, and Joseph would begin their journey to Valerias' former command center near the Danube.

As expected, parting proved to be a difficult time for Claire and her daughters. They had known this day would come, and as the day drew closer, thoughts of the future separation became more stressful.

The girls would frequently ask, "Why are you and Marcus leaving us when we were having such a good time in Ratae?"

Claire consistently responded that she needed to help Marcus and that they would have to go away for a few months. When they returned, they would never be apart again.

Valerias could see the separation from her daughters was very stressful for Claire, and he tried hard to convince her to go with the girls. He would join them as soon as his campaign with the Huns had been completed. She would have none of it, though, and Valerias always let the subject drop. Claire took comfort that Mary would look after the girls. Mary had been almost like a second mother to them since they were born, and Valerias took comfort in that he fully trusted Flavius to serve as their bodyguard. Titus would also accompany them to Milan. Besides being a fine soldier, he was becoming almost like a grandfather to the girls. Titus could spin colorful stories by the hour, which enthralled the girls and even soldiers, who voluntarily stayed within earshot of Titus.

When it was time to say good-bye, emotions spilled over into tears. Claire, who rarely cried, wept. Mary kept her emotions under control, which was good for Claire. Mary again told Claire not to worry; she and Flavius would do everything to provide a safe environment for Anne and Elizabeth.

Valerias, who usually did not succumb to such feelings, felt real sadness. He asked Joseph to do something, and Joseph offered a prayer for safe travels and future reuniting. Then each group rode off in different directions and to different journeys. Valerias never said anything, but he was deeply troubled with the prospect of Claire never returning to Milan.

For the first several miles after they began the trip to the Danube, no one said a word. Finally Joseph began telling a silly tale that made Claire and Valerias smile and think about something else besides leaving the girls behind. Valerias admired Joseph—he was a man who had many talents.

After the separation Valerias and his force of former deserters were met by a contingent of cavalry sent by the Emperor Valentinian consisting of slightly over two hundred men. Valerias now had roughly five hundred men under his command. Several bureaucrats were also traveling with cavalry. Both the soldiers and administrators were to provide support for Valerias' mission.

"The Emperor gives you a gift," chimed in Hermides as the two forces joined together.

Valerias answered crisply, "We will need much more than this."

Then he thought to himself, *I particularly hope we will have all the resources needed to successfully run this operation.*

The remainder of the trip to Valerias' old summer camp by the Danube was arduous but uneventful. The weather was unpredictable. One day was warm and the next day cool. There was even a very late season snow squall that produced much cursing from the ranks. By mid-May they had reached the point where they were about one day's travel from his former camp. Valerias decided to stop at a small Roman garrison. He wanted to assess the situation at his former headquarters. He figured his approximately five hundred soldiers would be against three legions of several thousand men under Trojax. The unknown factor to Valerias was the status of his former legions and whether they would fight for Trojax.

It was night and Valerias was tired from the trip. Claire and Joseph had held up better than he had, and he silently cursed his age. His men were also tired, which was a good thing. It would be a quiet night at the garrison. Valerias poked a log on the fire and turned around to sit down when he found a man sitting in his chair. Valerias' instinct was to reach for his sword and then he saw who the man was. The man was Revious, his chief scout for many years.

Valerias and Revious embraced. Both men were clearly pleased to see each other again.

"Revious, I thought you had returned to your old country—or even suffered an unpleasant fate from Trojax. You look well."

"As do you, my general."

"I see you are already sitting."

"Yes, your chair is comfortable. I may take it with me back to my old country."

"You're not going there yet?"

"No, I think when I retire, I am going to Britannia too. I have heard it is a better place than my old country. I would like to become a Druid."

"I think you need to come back to this century. There are no more Druids." Valerias remembered the old woman, Edith. "At least that is what I have heard."

Both men laughed at their banter. Suddenly Valerias started to talk, but Revious cut him off and he walked over to Joseph. "Joseph, so good to see you again." Then Revious pointed at Valerias and Joseph and said, "You two do make an odd couple!"

Joseph added, "Yes, he," pointing to Valerias, "has come a long way."

"Maybe in more ways than one," Revious added, sensing a change in Valerias.

"Enough, you two. Revious, I would like you to meet Claire. She is my . . ." Valerias paused.

"My what?" Revious asked. "Are you having trouble with your speech, like many old men?"

Valerias was flustered. Everyone that he had recently been with knew who Claire was. He hadn't thought how he would address her to those who did not know her. He had not asked her to be his wife yet. He and Claire had discussed the subject but nothing formal had been decided. It was an awkward moment for Valerias and Claire.

Joseph eased the silence. "Revious, Marcus and Claire are very good friends."

"Damn!" Revious interjected loudly. "I can't believe the General found a woman who could put up with him. This is an amazing day. I think we need a toast." Revious had always been the one man who could tease Valerias and get away with it, and he had done so again.

There were no servants in the camp, so Valerias found four cups and poured wine that one of the bureaucrats had brought from Milan.

Revious led the toast. "To good friends, may we all find our way through the forest that we are about to enter."

Revious' toast harbored the thoughts all four of them had about what was to come. For Valerias the first step was to reclaim the legions he once commanded. Valerias turned serious.

"Tell me, Revious, what happened? Everything was in place for a proper succession from me to Braxus. What happened?" he repeated himself. "I have heard Hermides' account. Now I want to hear yours."

"I will tell you, but you will not want to hear it." Revious recounted much of what Hermides had said. "Trojax had slyly usurped power from Braxus by himself and through proxies. Once he seized control, anyone who was an officer and didn't renounce loyalty to Braxus and swear allegiance to Trojax was ousted and typically met a poor fate. The legions are now shadows of what they had been, and the remnants are poised for rebellion. Trojax is in power only through the brutal ways of his Bucellarii guard."

Revious paused and then continued, "Trojax is aware through his friends that the Emperor has ordered you, General Valerias, to replace him. What Trojax would do in response to the threat you pose is anyone's guess. My opinion is that he will not give up the legions and will try to kill you."

Revious ended his narrative with the statement and a question: "You and I have seen several of these types of men. How do you suggest, General, that we handle this man Trojax?"

Valerias called out in the camp for Hermides and Pyrin, who quickly appeared.

"Good. I'm pleased you are here. This is what we are going to do. First, Hermides, your task is to free Braxus and any other of my men who have been imprisoned. Take up to fifty men to accomplish this task. Revious will tell you where to find Braxus."

Hermides answered, "General, it should not be a problem, and we can get by with fewer men. I have previously talked to Revious about this. The head jailer of where Braxus is being kept is actually your ally. I will need a letter from you and some solidi coins to bribe the other guards."

Valerias looked at Joseph. "I will need your help in a minute."

He turned his attention to Pyrin. "Pyrin, I want you to take up to fifty men and free Cratus, Bukarma, and any other of my men from their imprisonment in the mines. Talk to Revious about what you need. And I will prepare a letter and provide solidi for the guards at the mines."

"Yes, General," Pyrin responded.

"Revious, I need you to slip back into the fort of Trojax and spread word that I am coming and that Trojax is doomed. If you fear you will be spotted, use your most trustworthy associate."

"But General," Revious noted, "Trojax has spies too. Won't the rumor of your return have made it back to Trojax, with or without me?"

"I am counting on that, Revious. But, I want you to reinforce that thinking. I think Trojax is a weak leader, ruled by the god of greed instead of his duty to the Empire. I want him to worry."

Valerias asked Claire and Joseph to leave the area for a minute to discuss a confidential issue. After they were gone, he told Revious, Hermides, and Pyrin, "Do what you think is needed to secure success for your given task. If that means killing those who get in the way, then so be it. Do whatever it takes to succeed. Do you understand? Also, Hermides and Pyrin, if you succeed in your missions, I will promote you to positions of senior aides to me. Now go, time is important. The sooner we can retake the legions and remake them back to my standards, the sooner we can begin our campaign against the Huns—our real mission."

After the trio left, Valerias called Joseph and Claire back. "I didn't want you to hear the full charge I gave to my officers. I do not plan on excluding you from my plans in the future unless I need to, and this was one of those times. Joseph, please sit and let's write the letters that Hermides and Revious suggested I prepare. Claire, feel free to provide comments."

Within an hour the letters were finished and given to Hermides and Pyrin. Then they and Revious left the camp in various directions with the men each selected. Afterward Valerias called for the head of security to the camp. The man was very quick to respond.

"I am sorry, General, about that scout getting through the guards and into your room. I will accept your punishment."

"Relax. I am not going to punish you for this offense. Revious is the best at appearing and disappearing. I am used to it. Just be sure no one else can get into this camp without you or your men finding out what is going on. Trojax attained the rank of general because he has some talent. I hope I am clear."

"Yes, General," and the man left. Valerias could hear him yell out, "Double the guards!"

"Well done, Marcus. I would have thought the old General would have given some horrible torture or death reward to that man," Joseph observed.

"I gave him another chance. That is all. Now, I'm tired."

The rest of the evening provided a short reprieve for Valerias and Claire.

LXVII

Reclamation

THE SECOND HALF of May arrived, and Valerias became anxious. Timing was important. He knew he had to begin his campaign against the Huns by no later than early July if he wanted a resolution with them. He particularly did not want to be bogged down by winter. Revious was the first to return, and he brought good news.

"The rank and file of your legions will back you against Trojax," he announced after taking a drink of mead. "Trojax and his guard are basically hunkered down on top of the hill where you used to keep the command tent at the summer camp. However, your old legions *won't* move without you. Also, I don't need to tell you that you have five hundred men with your command to try to take him. And even though they are Roman soldiers, those men are not well-trained fighters at this point. That is not going to be enough."

"I know," replied Valerias. "I'm hoping to hear from Hermides and Pyrin any day now."

Revious noted, "I doubt that the actions of Hermides and Pyrin, if successful, will produce enough soldiers to help our cause. Trojax has at least one thousand highly trained soldiers who have sworn allegiance to him."

"Damn this situation," a very frustrated Valerias said. "We will wait for two more days. With or without Hermides and Pyrin and the results of their missions, we will move on Trojax. There is no other option. Damn."

"I'll do what I can," answered Revious. "It would be nice to have a miracle of some sort."

"I do not believe in Christian myths. Maybe you should talk to Joseph."

"I already have, General. He is praying for us."

Valerias ignored the comment, "It is said that to save an empire from an outside threat, you first have to save it from itself."

Claire, who was in the room at the time, added, "I know from my experiences that the worst enemy can be an enemy you thought was an ally."

The next two days produced results that were the opposite of the gloomy weather. Hermides was successful in freeing Braxus. Money was a factor, but the head jailer wanted to keep Valerias as a friend in the future, so it was an easy decision for the man. The reunion between Braxus and Valerias was warm, like two friends who did not expect to see each other again and were now face to face. Valerias introduced Claire to Braxus, and he bowed to kiss her hand. Valerias teased Braxus about being a servant with his bowing. Braxus joked with Claire that he had thought Valerias would end up being a lonely old man. Braxus had been treated well and looked fit.

Unfortunately, only a few other men had been imprisoned with Braxus, so eight additional soldiers made the trip with Braxus and Hermides to Valerias' camp. Valerias recognized two of the eight as officers in his legions. The others he did not know. It didn't matter to Valerias, though, he was pleased to have Braxus back at his side, and the two talked about Braxus' time in the jail. When Braxus observed Joseph in the camp, he rushed over and asked for Joseph's blessing. Braxus had become a secret convert to Christianity when Valerias was in command. Now he didn't care if Valerias knew it.

Valerias didn't care anymore either, but noted to Braxus, "I hope your new-found religious belief will not affect your generalship. I need you in the campaign."

"I can assure you, General, that I can keep my beliefs separate from my command duties," Braxus replied.

Valerias was pleased to hear that, as he had Flavius and his Christian pacification in mind.

Valerias was curious. "What happened to your campaign with the Emperor on the Danube?"

Braxus replied in an agitated manner, "The campaign never materialized. We were recalled back to the fort. That is when Trojax began his deceit and plotting."

Valerias sighed in response to Braxus' statement. An hour later, Pyrin surprisingly entered the camp. He also had several more men accompanying his troops than when he left for the mines.

"General, I have returned from my mission. I wish I could say it was a success, but we had difficulties."

Valerias grew concerned about that comment. "What happened that proved difficult?" At that moment Cratus and Bukarma rode up and both were wearing full smiles. After the initial greetings Valerias noticed both men were scarred around their necks and had lost notable weight.

"What are these?" Valerias asked, pointing to the men's necks.

"Just some left over effects from the mines," answered Bukarma.

"You should have known what happens to those you sent to the mines," Cratus answered with a smile. "It is not my favorite place to be. Thanks be to the Gods for freeing us."

Valerias frowned and turned to Pyrin, "What happened?"

"When we arrived at the mine, the guards welcomed us like long-lost friends. Then either because they wanted more slaves or they were in league with Trojax, they ambushed us. But we were ready, General, and fought the bastards off. We either killed them or they ran away. We also lost several men. We freed whomever we could find. We didn't know your men from others, including criminals. We asked all those who we freed if they were your men. Of course they said yes. The ones who wanted to come with us did so, and those who didn't turned tail and ran off in the opposite direction."

"And the fate of the chief of the mine?" Valerias' question was asked to anyone in the room who could answer.

"He is now a permanent part of the mine, a new formation, so to speak," answered Pyrin.

"That is how it should be," Valerias opined.

Before saying anything more, Valerias noticed that both Claire and Joseph had seen the commotion associated with Pyrin's arrival and joined the group. Valerias thought it best not to discuss anything further regarding the fate of the mine's chief and his guards.

Later that day, Valerias summoned Hermides, who appeared with Pyrin before the General. Valerias praised each man for his courage and ability to carry out a successful mission. In a quick, nondescript ceremony Valerias promoted the two men to their new senior aide rank, as he had promised.

Valerias now had his two primary generals, two senior aides, and numerous other officers to go along with the approximately five hundred soldiers who were with him in the camp. Bukarma didn't have a rank, but everyone knew his position was similar to a tribune's rank. Valerias thought to himself that his force was becoming top heavy with officers to soldiers. In this situation he decided a meeting at his camp should be democratically based.

Instead of having an officers' meeting and then having the officers meet with their assigned soldiers, he declared a meeting for all military personnel in the camp.

The soldiers assembled, except for the sentries and staff. Valerias summarized what had happened and who the leading officers were in the camp. Most everyone knew Braxus and Cratus, but it was good to reintroduce them, along with Hermides and Pyrin. Valerias turned his focus on the near future. Based on Revious' information, he described the main camp controlled by Trojax and how he planned to take the camp from him. Because this was a democratically held meeting, soldiers could ask questions of Valerias. One asked how a few hundred men could overthrow three legions. That seemed an impossibility—even for Valerias.

"It will not be easy," Valerias answered. "But I do have information that the soldiers—except for Trojax's guards—will support me when we appear. Trojax will be outnumbered and surrender. Or he will run for his life."

Another soldier asked, "What if Trojax sends his guards out to meet us first? Won't that keep the legions, your legions, under his control and out of the conflict?"

Valerias had thought of that possibility. "That is why we must strike first, at dawn tomorrow, and catch Trojax off guard."

More questions and much grumbling ensued among the soldiers. Few wanted to be part of an operation where five hundred men could potentially fight three legions comprised of over ten thousand soldiers.

Valerias was displeased with the attitude from some of the attendees and dismissed the meeting. *Democracy has ended,* Valerias mused to himself. *Democracy does not work in the military.*

After the meeting was over, Braxus, Cratus and Bukarma stayed behind with Valerias. Braxus took that opportunity to speak up to Valerias. "I must be candid, General, this is either a very brave or very risky strategy you are advocating here. I do not mind dying for you, but I prefer better terms on which to die."

"Sometimes there is no choice, Braxus, and this is that time. My orders are to conduct a campaign against the Huns, and the only way I can conduct such a campaign is to take back my legions from a man who does not have the standing to command them. The Emperors can only provide limited help; we must do this ourselves."

Changing the subject slightly, Valerias asked Cratus, "Do you think others that you freed from the mine will be ready tomorrow to move against Trojax?"

"They will be ready, General, but their effectiveness will be another matter. The mines were not kind to them."

"Yes, I see that. Perhaps I should have kept better focus on what went on there. Get cleaned up, and we will have another meeting tonight."

Valerias allocated additional sentries as he began to worry that Trojax might try a surprise move against him. Revious was also ordered to scout for any of Trojax's approaching forces. Valerias felt strangely tired and suggested to Claire that they take a walk to clear his head. It was a good idea; Claire always made him feel better.

They walked around the camp as the afternoon drizzle gave way to sun. The air warmed considerably as the sun muscled its way into the sky. Valerias was going over his strategy to take back his legions, and he wanted comments from Claire.

Claire inquired, "Did you know things would be like this when you agreed to return from Britannia?"

"No, I did not. When I left, everything was in place. Braxus was set to take charge. Cratus was next in line. My other generals and officers were to remain in place. The only change was me leaving. Within one year it has all fallen apart. No one warned me about the present status of my legions."

"Why did your command unravel?"

"It was Trojax. He must have had a plan to remove Braxus and the rest of my command before he even came here. Trojax is a cousin of some sort to the Emperors. My experience has been the ranks are full of usurpers, all poised to strike if there is an opening. Braxus and the rest were naïve to let Trojax become entrenched. But the biggest fool is me. I should have seen this coming. I knew Trojax was going to be a replacement officer of questionable character. Instead I was so intent on retiring and getting away that I failed to notice Trojax's potential for evil."

"It is not your fault," Claire said. "As you just stated, there are many people who have the potential to plot against you. One cannot know all. Look at me. I should have known about Argus and Flavius at the time I was queen. Both men upset me, but I didn't press Gerhard to dispense them away from the kingdom. I am not a foolish person, and yet I was fooled. Now, let's forget the past. Let's focus on today and tomorrow."

"This is why I love you, Claire. You are so grounded. You are correct. I have a plan for tomorrow."

Valerias called a soldier who was standing nearby. He told the soldier to inform all the officers that they were to report to Valerias as soon as possible. Then he told Claire that she and Joseph could attend the meeting. They had become part of his circle now, and he did not want to exclude them.

As they gathered for the meeting, a warning sounded from a sentry. "Riders coming! There are many!"

Valerias' first thought was of Trojax sending his cavalry down on his camp. Valerias ordered his men to form defensive positions. Unfortunately, many of the men were new to his system, and the scene looked more like an out-of-control circus event than military formations established by seasoned soldiers. Valerias yelled to Claire and Joseph to take their horses and run into the deep woods and hide, but neither would follow his order. He worried about what was transpiring and drew his sword. Valerias was more angry with himself for having such a ragtag operation under his command when he was used to perfection.

As the riders came into clear eyesight, the leader was a white-haired, older man, who Valerias immediately recognized—the man was Titus.

Titus rode up to Valerias, and taunted, "Your army has arrived!"

Valerias was stunned for a quick moment. Behind Titus was a large number of Roman cavalry. These were actual soldiers, not former deserters who had come back to Valerias.

"I know you can't speak, General, so I will summarize for you. This is a 'gift' from the Emperor Valentinian. He 'donated' two full legions, or sixteen cohorts, totaling eight thousand men to your cause. Eight of the cohorts are cavalry and eight are heavy infantry. I think the Emperor prefers you to his cousin, Trojax."

Valerias regained his wits. "I thought you were headed for retirement after you finished your escort of Claire's daughters. Have the beaches lost their appeal?"

"When I can spend time with you in the field, working in the fine weather, living in tents, eating culinary delights, fighting Romans and then Huns—why would I want to spend time on a beach drinking wine?"

Both Valerias and Titus laughed, and Titus dismounted.

"Good to see you, my friend," Valerias said sincerely to Titus.

Titus sighed and looked upward, and both men laughed again. Claire joined them and Titus bowed deeply, and they all laughed some more. Titus and Valerias then became serious, as the subject at hand needed to be addressed.

Valerias summarized, "With your eight thousand men and my five hundred men, we can launch our attack on Trojax tomorrow."

"Good to see your army has grown. Have the former deserters multiplied at a fast rate?"

"Not fast enough," replied Valerias.

Titus continued, "The infantry is about a half-day's march from here, but they should be here by late tonight. We can go on the attack tomorrow by midmorning. I also want to inform you that I heard Emperor Valens was also donating at least a legion, but they won't be here for a few more days."

"I am still counting on more former deserters to join us. We get a trickle daily. Unfortunately, that is not a flood. I realize my reputation has not helped in this regard. I have also sent out officers to my former limitanei, with positive results. I think they will provide us with a legion's worth of soldiers as well. They are worried that the Goths will cross the Danube and overwhelm them unless we can eliminate the source of the pressure—the Huns."

Valerias called a meeting of the officers. Roles were assigned, tasks given, and responsibilities defined. The camp was loud and became louder with the arrival of Titus' infantry. Food was provided by Titus' legions, but no wine or beer. The camp was organized chaos, and Valerias felt back at home.

The next day came quicker than Valerias had wanted, but he couldn't control time. Valerias and Titus decided to split up the forces. Valerias and Braxus would take the cavalry and advance to Trojax's fortified camp in the morning. Titus and Cratus would bring up the infantry. Claire and Joseph would stay with the administrators back at camp. Valerias reasoned that his cavalry would be enough to win over those legions only nominally under Trojax's control. Those units, along with Titus' and Cratus' infantry, should be able to strike a decisive blow against Trojax and his Bucellarii.

At midmorning Valerias and his cavalry advanced on Trojax's position. As Valerias neared his former camp, he grew anxious. The possibility of a conflict always started his adrenaline flowing.

This time, though, the fight was for his legions. He was ready for battle. As he approached camp, Valerias was surprised for the second time in two days. Stretched out along the roadway were soldiers forming lines on both sides of the road to the camp. The soldiers were standing at full attention. It was a sign of respect for their former general.

Valerias stopped and told most of his cavalry units to wait. He took Braxus and a century of his best cavalry up the hill to his former headquarters. A man came out from the tent. He was unarmed. Valerias did not know him, which caused some concern of a possible ambush.

"General Valerias, I am General Proctur. We have been anticipating your arrival to your camp. We are pleased you are here."

Valerias could only say, "What happened? Where is Trojax?"

Proctur answered, "Oh, he fled, like the coward that he is. He heard you were coming with an army. He did not want to fight a man of your reputation, so he left."

"So. Who are you, again?"

"Proctur. I was an officer under Trojax. I didn't agree with him on some issues and so I was imprisoned. Being the highest-ranking officer after he and the others fled, it is my duty to welcome you here."

Valerias dismounted and kept a wary eye out for an ambush, which did not materialize. He quickly became more comfortable and went to the edge of the hill that overlooked the camp. He gave a Roman salute and was answered back with roars from the troops. The rest of the cavalry joined the mass of soldiers, followed by Titus and his infantry. He was back on top of his world. Valerias felt contented for just a brief moment. Then the moment fled as it always did. Another thought crossed his mind—*many people have helped me get to where I am today; it was not a solo effort.*

LXVIII

THE DANUBE

BY NIGHTFALL ALL of the troops had arrived at the old camp. Valerias declared extra food for the troops, while the officers scheduled a banquet for their general. Valerias did not know about the banquet beforehand, so he was surprised to see all his officers present and standing as he walked into the General's dining tent. There was Braxus, Cratus, Hermides, Pyrin, Proctur, sub-generals, tribunes, and centurions. Of course, Bukarma and Olivertos were there. Valerias formed a bright smile when he saw Olivertos.

Claire, Titus, and Joseph accompanied Valerias to the banquet hall, and the rousing salute the men gave to Valerias left an impression on them. It was a deep respect that the men showed their general. They were very appreciative of having him back, especially after the failed generalship of Trojax. Valerias tried to keep the event at a modest level, but that was not to happen. It was a raucous night they all enjoyed. In the back of his mind, though, Valerias knew the celebration would end and the future would bring a most difficult challenge.

The next morning Valerias woke early. Claire was at his side, looking at him.

"When I first met you, you were a scrounging, hermit-like man. Somehow, and with good fortune, I chose you over that Alpha man. I had no idea you were this man that I was with last night. I believed you were some tired, old soldier or a spy or deserter. Yet you carried your own in the fight in the cave. Now I am with an elite general beloved by thousands of men. Why did I not see this?" Her tone was not angry, but she again questioned her ability to know people. She thought of Argus and Flavius.

"When I met you, Claire, I was the man you saw. I had left the life of a general behind, and I thought I would not return to it. But here we are today. I didn't ask to return to this life. It happened."

Valerias thought he would make one final attempt to persuade Claire to leave this mission. He did so halfheartedly. "Do you want to leave now and return to Britannia after you gather your daughters in Milan? There is still time."

The question caught her off guard, and she paused before answering. "No, of course not. You are my love. The man I met in Britannia is the man who lies beside me. You are not some young man who will change over time. You are now who you will be. I go with you regardless of the circumstances."

"I wish I could have met you earlier in my life."

"Why? You would have been a different person—wedded to your legions—and I would have been with Gerhard. Life is fine now the way things are."

They heard a shout at the entrance to Valerias' quarters. It was Olivertos. Valerias rose from the bed and met Olivertos outside of the bedroom. The two men hugged each other and talked for over an hour about what had happened in their lives during the last year. It was good to catch up with Olivertos, probably Valerias' oldest friend. When Joseph showed up, Valerias knew the new day had begun. He called for his officers and laid out plans for their expedition to the east. These plans included training and the prompt organizing of his force.

The remainder of the day was crammed with a multitude of military and administrative tasks. Titus was assigned the role of supreme commander, and he and Valerias divided up responsibilities among the generals and other officers. Braxus was placed in charge of training.

At the end of the second day and the night meal, Valerias stood outside his tent and looked east. Claire was beside him with Titus and Joseph. Bukarma stood in the background, posing in his usual position. Valerias liked having his friends with him. A shooting star rocketed toward the eastern horizon. Valerias sometimes wondered about the origination and destination of these bright shooting lights. Were they some god hurrying across the sky or debris sent from the moon? These were questions he knew would not be answered, so he moved onto something more tangible.

Revious had been with Valerias earlier and gave him his description of what he knew of the Huns. The discussion didn't take long, but at its end Valerias knew he would meet a very formidable foe. Valerias also knew that to defeat the Huns would take an excellently trained and disciplined force. What was currently before Valerias now was not yet such a force.

As they looked to the east, Valerias said to assembled friends, but to no one in particular, "Out there is the Hun. It will be the Hun that will give me my greatest challenge."

After several minutes he asked Bukarma to get his game. He wanted a different kind of challenge.

The following weeks went by at a feverish speed. Valerias' focus was preparation and training, and both involved multiple divisions of labor. There was only a short time to prepare, and Valerias wanted every minute used wisely. Joseph was assigned administration duties, which included the treasury, accounting, and procuring and providing food for man and horse. Joseph was given a large staff to assist him with his duties. Olivertos was named Physician-in-Charge. He could consult with Joseph as needed.

Finally there was the engineer division, which included Tribune Tentrides and Gul. Valerias worked closely with the engineers. He wanted a pontoon bridge constructed across the Danube, and these were the men who had to accomplish this task. Valerias considered Gul more Roman than Goth. When Valerias was convinced his engineering division was ready, he sent them to the Danube with a highly trained military escort of four thousand men—a Valerias-defined legion. Valerias was concerned the Goth tribes situated along the Danube would interfere with his mission, and the strong military presence would prevent any interference. Cratus commanded this unit.

More men who had deserted continued to return one by one into the camp. Several cohorts of limitanei, the troops located along the border, also arrived at the camp. Braxus was charged with training the deserters and the limitanei cohorts into two cohesive legions. Valerias felt Braxus' personality was more suited to the temperament of these men instead of Cratus, who could be unforgiving. Valerias knew that sensitivity, even extended to a minor degree, was needed to meld this group into even an average fighting unit. He designated these legions as the pseudo-comitatenses.

The rest of Valerias' soldiers were from his former legions and those legions provided by the Emperors, including two full legions sent by the Emperor Valens from Constantinople. These seven legions formed the comitatenses, the field armies. Even though the use of "legions" was becoming rare in describing army units, Valerias preferred this designation to describe his main army divisions.

Valerias' approximate count of men under his command had grown to over thirty-six thousand. He knew he had nine full-strength legions at four thousand men per legion. Four of these legions were cavalry based and the other five were infantry. A large percentage of the infantry were also archers.

Claire had become good friends with Olivertos and spent much of her time helping him prepare for the campaign. The rest of the time she spent with Valerias. He liked her by his side as she provided him with a calming influence. Some of the men did not understand her role, but no one outwardly dared question the General on the matter.

It was the beginning of August and the state of preparation was good. Valerias decided it was time to start the campaign. The night before they departed on to the east, Valerias gathered his officers in the meeting room. There he covered many details. When he reached the end of his talk, he announced, "When we reach the Danube, we will cross the river and move east against the Huns."

This announcement was a revelation to the officers. They had thought that once they reached the Danube, they would construct fortifications along the river, on both sides, and go no further. To cross the Danube into territory inhabited by the Goths and then to go further east against the Huns concerned them. Valerias, though, laid out his strategy and ordered it to be carried out. Valerias had never been wrong before, and that carried great weight and provided a consensus from the officers.

At dawn the next day, Valerias and his legions left the fort to begin the campaign. It was a warm and sultry day. Even though the men had confidence in Valerias, he had internal doubts. It is tough to carry the ring of invincibility forever, and the ring was becoming a yoke to him. He was confident he could defeat the Huns, but he wondered in the back of his mind how much longer his good fortune would last. He thought about Edith and her comment on his destiny. Valerias looked at his officers and men and hoped there would be few casualties from the campaign, even though he knew that would be a false hope.

Crossing the Danube proved to be relatively easy. Revious and Tribune Tentrides had selected a good location to construct the pontoon bridge. It had been a dry summer in the area, so the river was at a low level and the current was light in the selected location. Still, constructing a portable bridge over a large river is a formidable task. Tentrides was a master engineer, and with the help of his staff, including Gul, he managed to complete the task in approximately a week and before Valerias' arrival.

The army and support groups crossed the pontoon bridge over to the east side of the Danube in two days' time. The operation occurred during both day and night. When the army had finished crossing, there was a concern in the ranks regarding what to do with the bridge. They could leave the bridge intact or dismantle it. At least one officer wanted the bridge left intact.

"Why do you want the bridge left as is?" Valerias asked the concerned man.

"So when we return, we will not have to wait for it to be reconstructed."

Several other officers offered muted agreement.

"You mean, when you are fleeing from the Huns, you want your escape path wide open? You don't want your flight slowed down unnecessarily? Are you a coward?" Valerias chastised the man and those who had supported him.

This time there was no outwardly affirming agreement by the other officers with the officer who had spoken. Valerias did know some of his men were concerned about having a way back should the mission fail.

"You recall the Emperor Julian burned his ships when he was campaigning against the Persians. I admit that proved to be a bad decision. No, I am not going to destroy the pontoon bridge now that we have crossed on it. That would be foolish. But I am also not leaving it intact as is. I will order the bridge be deconstructed, with the parts stored across the river on the west bank. When we need it reconstructed, I or one of my generals will order that action. And it will be rebuilt quickly."

Valerias still observed that some of the men did not understand that proposed action and he continued, "There are many Goths camped along the riverbank. More are coming every day. They are obviously fleeing the Huns. Why would I want to create a passageway for them to cross the Danube and possibly take over Roman territory when our position on the west side of the river is weak now that we are on the east side?"

The officers all nodded in response to Valerias' logic. Valerias also did not feel he had to explain his orders any further. He turned to Tentrides. "Carry out my orders."

"Yes, General," Tentrides returned to the bridge.

"Does any other man here want to stay and help guard the bridge while we are out on campaign?" Valerias asked in almost a sneer.

No one volunteered. However, Valerias wanted a group of soldiers to guard the sections of the pontoon bridge that were to be taken back to the west side of the river. He singled out an officer and ordered him to take two hundred fifty men with their only assignment to not allow the bridge to be stolen or used for reconstruction without the General's or a subordinate's permission. Valerias was concerned that two hundred fifty soldiers might not be enough men to keep the Goths at bay, but he counted on the river to block the Goths' migration westward.

LXIX

PRELUDE

THE SCOUT SQUATTED in front of Uldric, who was seated in a large chair. This gave the appearance of a cat hunched over a mouse. The scout's name was Arb.

"Tell me, Arb, tell me of the happenings to the west."

"Great General, the Goths are in complete disarray and filled with panic from fear of the Hun. They run like rats from the flames of the firestorm."

"Yes. Radic to the north, and Sardich to the south, are carrying out my orders with the greatest of success. And, of course, we are cutting through the Goth middle like a sharp knife through warm fat." Uldric, since Rao's death, had promoted two of his favorites, Radic and Sardich, to the posts of lead generals, over the other Hun generals and pro-generals. Both men were of a similar mold as Uldric. As such, they were more likely to carry out Uldric's agenda on the Goths. And they did.

"The Goths, General, are fleeing in vast numbers. Only the Danube River is blocking their path to the west."

"Good. We shall soon rid the Earth of that race."

"There is one matter, General, we need to discuss."

"Yes."

"A large Roman army has assembled and it has crossed the Danube."

"Is this army after the Goths as well?"

"No, General. My sources tell us they are coming to meet our great army in battle."

"Why would the Romans send an army to meet us in battle? Are they aware of our plans?"

"The Romans are afraid of the Hun, great General."

"They will be, and you didn't answer my question." Uldric sat back in his chair and rubbed his chin, forgetting his last exchange with Arb. After thinking to himself for a few minutes, he spoke thoughtfully, "When we defeat their army, that will open up the land south to Constantinople and all the riches that the city has. I am more interested in Constantinople than Rome. I think Zestras was trying to trick my brother and me in chasing a far off Rome, when Constantinople is much closer. Zestras will pay for his treachery."

"Yes, General. Your logic is sound, as always."

Uldric rose from his chair and called for Produgas. When he arrived, Uldric ordered, "Produgas, send messengers to Radic in the north and Sardich to the south. Tell them to return to me with their armies. The Goths can wait. We have a new enemy on the horizon. There is no power on Earth that can stop our army from doing anything we want. I want to show the world the power of the Hun."

Uldric retrieved a sketch of the region. He pointed a spot out to Produgas. "Tell my generals that we will meet here. Tell them to reach here in as few days as possible. Go now."

With those words Produgas left the tent. He knew this was one order he had to follow. Any errors and he would be held responsible. That in turn could unravel his plans. He went directly to a messenger area and talked to two men. Soon they were off riding in opposite directions in great haste.

Arb was still in the tent with Uldric after Produgas left.

"You have done what I ask, Arb. Now I want you to do more. Split your scout team. I want one group to give me a sense of Constantinople. The other is to obtain as much information as possible about the Roman army that crossed the Danube. You are to lead the men who will ride and give me the information I need about the Roman army. I need the information fast. Do not disappoint me."

"Yes, General. I will do as you command."

Arb left the tent to locate his scouts, who were enjoying time playing a local game comprised of bone fragments and pebbles and ingesting a beer-like drink. They did not want to go to the field again, but a direct order from Uldric must be obeyed without question.

Valerias had also sent his scouts led by Revious to conduct reconnaissance on the Hun army. Revious' task had two purposes. The first was to obtain information about the Huns. Any information was valuable, as Valerias knew little of the Huns. Second, the mission was to locate a suitable area where the Romans could establish a defensive position to block the Huns' path.

While Revious conducted his work, Valerias continued to drive his troops north and east of the Danube and south of Carpathian Mountains. His men were finally coming together as an army. He didn't want to wear them out, so a typical day was to travel a set distance. After setting a camp, training was conducted. At night the men could relax or play various games. As time progressed, alcoholic beverages were provided less and less to the men.

Two weeks passed when Revious returned to the camp. He complimented Valerias on how far the army had traveled since he had left. On a map Revious pointed out where the Romans were, where the Huns were currently located, and what he thought was a favorable site for the Romans to set up fortifications against the Huns.

"I agree with your choice of location, Revious. One day you will become a general."

Both men laughed at the statement, because the likelihood that would happen was the same as a hawk turning into a plant eater. Revious had no intention of becoming a permanent member of the army, particularly if he had to serve anyone but the General. Valerias would also find it difficult to appoint a scout to a general's position.

"Tell us about what you learned of the Huns, Revious."

By now the General's officers had joined Valerias and Revious. It was a very short meeting.

From the camp a loud call went out directed to no specific person. "An army is coming! An army is coming!"

There was incredible hustling in the camp as soldiers ran to retrieve their weapons and officers tried to organize themselves and their soldiers. Some of the men thought it was a surprise attack from the Huns, others believed it was the Goths, but most were confused about who the enemy was. However, all were focused on preparing for battle.

Valerias was angry with himself. He had given so much attention to what was transpiring in the east that he had left the western approach to his army open to attack.

Valerias came quickly out of his tent, with several officers, including Titus. They squinted off to the west and shielded their eyes with their hands from the sun at what appeared to be a large contingent of men coming toward the Romans. The force contained infantry and cavalry. Valerias gave his officers orders, and he and Titus walked down a trail, where aides had their horses waiting for them. Valerias mounted his horse and with Titus rode in the direction of the approaching army. As Valerias reached the edge of the Roman camp, Revious rode up to the generals. Valerias wondered how Revious could have traveled so far ahead of him when he was just at their meeting.

"General, it is Mostar Gulivus and a large army of Goths. They carry the white flag."

Valerias looked around and ordered an aide bring him a white flag as well. Once he had the flag in hand, he rode off with Bukarma and two aides to meet Mostar Gulivus. He requested that Titus stay behind in case Mostar Gulivus planned a trap. Titus would take command in that case.

There was no trap. Mostar Gulivus gave an inaccurate version of a Roman salute to Valerias, and Valerias returned the salute.

"What brings my friend Mostar Gulivus to the Roman camp?"

"We heard of a great Roman army marching east to meet the Huns, our sworn enemy. We want to join you. The Romans fight for us, so we must fight with the Romans."

"I was surprised the Goths let us into Goth territory so easily."

"We know your reason for crossing into Goth territory, and it is not to punish the Goths. Besides, we learned it was you, General Valerias, leading the army, and we believe you do not wish to harm the Goths."

"True, my only order is to stop the Huns. Whatever happens after that is what the Fates decide. I was *asked* out of retirement by both Emperors to lead this expedition."

"We count you as a friend, and you are my friend and protector of my son, Gul. The Goths who I have assembled will fight for you. Do you want us?"

Without hesitation Valerias responded, "Of course, you are a great leader and fighter, Mostar Gulivus, and I accept your offer. How many men have you brought?"

"We have twenty-five thousand men under arms. That is all we could bring. There are twenty thousand infantry and five thousand cavalry. The Huns have scattered us in many directions—those who they have not killed. We are not trained or disciplined like the Romans, but we will fight until we die against the Huns. You have no idea the harm that they have inflicted upon our people."

"No, I don't, but I intend to have it stopped soon." Valerias turned and gave a signal to the Roman camp. Braxus joined the group.

"Mostar Gulivus, you remember General Braxus?

"Of course, General."

"Good," answered Valerias. "I want you, General Braxus, to work with Mostar Gulivus to try to integrate our two armies so that we can be best prepared to face the Huns."

"Yes, General," Braxus answered. Although he thought, *This is not my favorite assignment, working with an enemy.*

Valerias spoke again, "Good. I want both of you and one aide to meet in my tent in two hours. I want to go over our strategy and logistics."

Mostar Gulivus had one final question. "How is my son doing?"

"Gul is doing quite well. He is almost my second-in-command in the engineering division. He serves directly under my 'general' of engineering, Tribune Tentrides. Your son is a natural. I will have him come to our tent tonight for our meeting.

Valerias returned to his headquarters. Once he dismounted, Valerias spoke privately to Titus, "Titus, my old friend, we now have an ally against the Hun. Mostar Gulivus is an old enemy who is now my friend."

"Who is that?"

"He is a leader of the Goths."

Titus had an expressionless look, which prompted Valerias to laugh. "It is a strange world we live in, Titus. I can use the Goths against the Huns."

When the meeting occurred, it was very dark outside. There was no moon and stars, and the campfires burned low. Valerias had changed his mind and invited the core of his officers, so Valerias' tent was full of officers and their aides. Claire decided not to attend, as she said she would feel suffocated in a room full of men. She was more comfortable assisting Olivertos. Valerias requested Joseph to attend, as he wanted Joseph to take notes of the meeting.

Valerias began, "Fellow officers, the purpose of this meeting is to plan our strategy for engaging the Huns. First, Revious will tell us what he found out about the Huns."

"Actually, I found out little specifically. They remind me of a swarm of locusts centered around their leader, a man named Uldric. His own men fear him. Uldric had a twin brother named Rao. Rao was the brains of the Huns while Uldric brought the hammer. Rao was assassinated by Goths, which unleashed this maelstrom upon the Goths. Without Rao, Uldric has metamorphosed into an effective leader. And he is exceptionally brutal. We cannot underestimate him."

Mostar Gulivus interrupted, "I have talked to many Goths, and no one claims any responsibility for Rao's killing. We can't get anywhere near Uldric or Rao. Just ask your spy here." Mostar Gulivus pointed at Revious.

"I prefer the term Intelligence Officer, Goth," was Revious' reply.

Tensions rose in room, as many of the Romans did not like the Goths' invitation to the officer meeting. Valerias quickly extinguished the tension with a terse comment, "Our goal, our number one and only goal, is to stop the Huns. We are all allies in this room to accomplish a successful result to my goal and the Emperors' goal. Are there any problems or other concerns you have, or can we get on with the briefing?"

The question raised by Valerias was a statement, and no one spoke. This was the General that all present in room remembered.

He had a commanding presence, and it would have been unwise for anyone to speak out at that moment.

"Continue, Revious."

"When I was conducting my *intelligence*, I stopped at a tavern in a small village. I met a man there who was also an Alan, but of a different tribe. His name was Arb. I knew immediately he was a *spy* for the Huns, and we talked. I picked up some information from him and him from me. The information I gave him was largely an exaggeration or falsehood. For example, I told Arb, that our General Valerias was invincible and related to the Sun God, Helios."

Revious told other tales he passed on to Arb, and the room broke out in laughter.

Valerias frowned, though, and offered, "Do you think he believed any of your stories?"

"Does it matter, General? I want Arb to pass on to Uldric whatever he wants to. I want to keep the Huns off balance as to our intentions and capabilities."

"Did you obtain good information from him?" Valerias was referring to Arb.

"He was smart and cagey as well. We know so little about the Huns. So I don't know what is fact and what is fiction, either."

"Do you know what his intentions are? Where is he going to strike?"

"I'm fairly sure the original intent of him and his brother, Rao, was to raid either Rome or Constantinople. That changed with his brother's killing. Now I think he wants to destroy the Goths and then focus on Constantinople."

Mostar Gulivus was growing impatient, as the discussion seemed to ignore important details. He bluntly interjected, "I can tell you personally about the Huns. They fight almost exclusively on horseback. They are expert bowmen. In hand to hand they are very good with their sabers. They are fearless and not afraid to die. And, most important, they are utterly ruthless. I have witnessed much, but I have never seen anything like the brutality they inflict on anyone who is not in league with them. They will kill, rape, and plunder until there is nothing, not even a blade of grass, left in their way."

There was silence in the room as several officers looked down at their feet.

Valerias slammed his sword on the table, and everyone's attention turned to him. He was suddenly angry. "I don't care if they spawn in the underworld and can fly. We are Romans, now joined by our Goth allies. We will show the Huns our fighting ability, our discipline, and our bravery. I'm not afraid of dying either, and neither should any of you or our men be. We live for this chance to battle enemies of Rome, and this may be our greatest opportunity. Are you with me?"

The men shouted their agreement. Titus banged his sword on the table. "I will follow you to the Gates of Hell and beyond, General Marcus Augustus Valerias."

All the men again roared their approval. Joseph was reminded of the days when he was the General's accountant. Valerias had a way with his soldiers, and Joseph was impressed.

After a few minutes of the boisterous reaction, Valerias urged his officers to calm down.

"I want Uldric to focus on us. I want him to come after us. Not the Goths, not Constantinople, not Rome. Here is my plan. Revious, you are to take whatever scouts and resources you need. Pick one hundred soldiers. Go to the Hun camp of Uldric and cause any kind of disturbance you choose, even a minor one. When you are done, I want Uldric to think of only me and our army. He will accept this challenge and come to wipe us out, but we will defeat him."

Valerias continued, this time to all his officers, "Prepare for battle within the next two weeks. All training and preparation must be completed. Double the sentries. We move east tomorrow to the location Revious has selected for our defense against the Huns. Go and prepare!"

After all of the officers had left, Valerias pulled Revious aside.

"You have done much for me, as you always have. What I ask now from you is of great sacrifice. This is more than a request. Your life and the lives of your men will be at serious risk. Our mission may depend on your results. Whatever you want to call yourself, Chief Intelligence Officer or Head Spy or General, I don't care. You are my most trusted advisor. May you return safe and your mission be a success."

Valerias had concern on his face and in his voice. He was very serious this time. It was not lost on Revious, who had become used to rigid commands from the General. This was beyond one of those commands.

"I serve you, General, and salute you."

Revious smiled, and the men gripped each other's forearms; then Revious left the tent.

Every night Valerias ended all business at a set time and returned to the tent he shared with Claire. He explained everything that had gone on during the day with her, and she told him what she had seen. Valerias was pleased that Claire was with him. She made him feel human.

When the sun rose on the next day, Revious had already selected his men and departed to the east. Valerias' legions shortly thereafter broke camp and marched eastward.

LXX

Skirmish

Uldric was pleased. Both Radic and Sardich were within one day's ride from his central camp. Arb had returned and was giving him a briefing on what he had seen.

"So you met one of the spies of the Romans?"

"Yes, great General. He may have even been the Roman's chief spy. He told of fantasies sprinkled with some grains of truth. The way he told his stories, one would think their general is a god."

"He is no god," countered Uldric.

"True, great General, but he is one of Rome's best—they brought him out of retirement, just for you."

"Should I be grateful to the Romans for putting forth their best just for me—a retired general no less? Or are they trying to stop me from completing my right to destroy the Goths?"

"I don't know, great General. The Romans and the Goths are not friends."

"This is perplexing. I must think on this, Arb." Uldric paused for a moment of thought. He continued, "What do you believe Rao would have done in this situation?"

"He was more cautious than you, great General. He would think about the best action to take—like you have chosen to do now."

"I will wait until my generals have returned, then I will decide whether to go after the Romans or finish the Goths or both. Go get rested, Arb. You will be needed again soon."

The next day the armies of Radic and Sardich returned to Uldric's camp. Uldric treated them like heroes. They both had destroyed Goth resistance to the north and south. Most Goths had fled further south or west to the Danube or had been assimilated as slaves into the Hun army. The celebrations were wild with excess drinking and debauchery. The Goth women who were captured and made slaves were put to good use from Uldric's viewpoint.

Several miles from the Hun camp, Revious waited for night. His plan was to plant a bee sting into the Huns. To that end he would conduct a raid on the part of the camp where the Huns kept their horses. Throughout the night Revious placed his men at strategic locations near the Hun horse corrals. The Huns had significantly let their guard down celebrating the arrival of Radic and Sardich, or just for the sake of having a celebration. They never thought that anyone, Goth or Roman, would attack them.

Approximately two hours before dawn, Revious struck. He had his best scouts kill the Hun sentries who ringed the horse corrals. Once this was done, Revious and his men advanced into the corrals with impunity. At a set time three archers shot fire arrows into the tents of the sleeping Huns near the corrals. The arrows were a signal, and Revious' men began escorting the horses out of the corrals. Horses ran first in a guided direction by Revious' men to the corral gates. Once through the gates, Revious ordered his men to let the horses loose. The horses took advantage of their freedom and tore throughout the Hun camp, creating pandemonium. The initial few Hun defenders who arrived at the corrals were quickly struck down. Revious' men picked up torches from the remains of Hun fires and used fire to scatter the horses and burn Hun tents.

It wasn't long before Hun regulars began arriving from the main camp. Small skirmishes erupted, and Revious knew it was time to abandon the camp. Another archer launched a single flaming arrow deep into the dark sky, and Revious' men disappeared out of the Hun camp. At a set meeting point just outside of the camp, he met his squad leaders and obtained a casualty report. Two men were confirmed dead and several injured, but no one was missing.

"How bad are the injured?" Revious inquired.

One of the squad leaders answered, "Two men are hurt badly; I don't think they can ride far. The rest are good enough to make the return to camp."

"Where are the two injured men you speak of?"

"Here." The squad leader took Revious over to the two men.

Both men lay next to each other with their backs resting up on a slight slope. One of the men was barely coherent; the other appeared to be unconscious.

Revious bent down and looked at each man closely. He asked each how they were doing. The coherent one answered he could not see and the other man did not answer. Both were bleeding profusely. Revious told the men they had served Rome well and the mission was a success because of them. When finished, he nodded to the squad leader. Revious and the squad leader pulled their knives and simultaneously slit the injured men's throats. There were sharp gasps from some of the Romans near the scene.

Revious looked at the men. It was dark, but he could still see their eyes.

"There are to be no prisoners left for the Huns. What they will do with these men as prisoners will be unspeakable."

Revious placed a Roman shield by the dead men and mounted his horse. The group rode hard to the west. After an hour's ride, the men stopped to rest their horses. A man wearing a hood was brought before Revious. Revious removed the hood and looked at the prisoner. It was an Alan. Revious was disappointed. He had hoped to capture a Hun.

"You won't give us any trouble, will you, Alan?"

"No," was the reply. "I wanted to get away from that devil."

"Good. I will keep you in restraints, but the hood can stay off."

A scout with a very thin appearance came up to Revious.

"They are not following us." The thin scout spoke quickly.

"Interesting," answered Revious. He gave his horse a quick kick, and his group finished their hard ride back to the Roman camp.

Uldric arrived at the horse corrals shortly after the Romans had left. The chaos in front of him was disturbing. He issued a few sharp orders. The camp was soon back in control except that many of the horses were still missing.

"Where is the head of my sentries?" Uldric impatiently asked.

"Dead," was the response.

"That's good. Saves me from an execution."

One of the Hun guards rode up to Uldric.

"What can you tell me?" Uldric pointedly asked the man.

"They killed over twenty men and wounded many others, General."

"Did they capture any of our men?"

"I don't think so, but we are still conducting our review."

"Did they capture any horses?"

"Again, General, we don't think so, but we are still counting the horses."

"And who is 'they?'"

The guard motioned and another man brought forth the shield that Revious had left. It was a Roman shield. Uldric grabbed it and gazed at it from top to bottom.

"What was the purpose of the raid by the Romans?" Uldric asked the question to anyone who was within earshot.

No one spoke at first. Finally Arb, who just arrived at the corrals, broke the silence, "He wants your attention, great General."

Uldric spoke sharply, "The old Roman has it, and that will be his undoing. As soon as this disaster is cleaned up, I want all my generals and pro-generals assembled at my tent. I am clear now as to what we must do. We are going after the Romans—the Goths can wait."

Revious and his men returned to the Roman camp in haste. Valerias was waiting for him in the main tent with his officers. Claire and Joseph were also there to take what they learned to Olivertos, who was preparing to treat the wounded men. When Revious entered the tent, Valerias beckoned to him from the General's chair.

"Welcome, Revious. Back from your mission in one piece, I see."

"Thank you, General. It is good to be back at our quarters—alive."

"Your mission was successful, was it not?"

"Yes, General. We raided the Huns' horse corrals and caused quite a disturbance with them."

"Casualty report, Revious."

"We lost four soldiers with about ten wounded. We had to kill two of our own men or they would have fallen into the hands of the Huns or slowed us down too much on our return to camp."

"Tell us, what did you learn about the Huns?"

"They were surprisingly lax in guarding their camp. I think they were in the midst of celebrating something. It was easy to penetrate into the corrals and accomplish what we wanted. I doubt they will be so loose in security from now on. But we learned very little about them."

Valerias looked disappointed. Revious sensed this emotion and waved his hand to the front of the tent. Two men entered accompanied by a hooded man. Valerias motioned for the hood to be removed.

Revious spoke, "This is an Alan we captured during the raid."

Valerias arose from his chair, walked over to the man, and surveyed his face. "I can see the similarities between you two." Valerias smiled at Revious, who in turn gave Valerias a mock frown.

Valerias' gaze at the Alan turned into a glare. "You can tell me what I need to know now voluntarily, or you will be persuaded to tell me what I need to know. I will let you live if you choose the former. The latter choice won't be so good for you." Revious translated for Valerias.

The man proved to be a fountain of information. He had no love for the Huns. He had been conscripted as a youth years ago after the Huns separated him from his parents. The man assumed the Huns at some point had killed his parents.

"You ask me about the Huns. I will tell you all that I know. Their world is centered around their leader, Uldric. He is a great warrior who fights with the scimitar, a deadly weapon that can kill two men at the same time. Around him are his primary guards. They number about two thousand men. They are very tough, seasoned warriors. Then there is the remainder of the Huns. They number about twenty-five thousand. You must be prepared for them. They fight almost exclusively from horseback. They are bowmen who can accurately shoot well over one hundred yards from horseback. The arrows they use can penetrate most shields even at that distance. If you get them off their horses, they are skilled fighters on the ground. It doesn't matter much if they are on a horse or not. Finally, around them are the Alans, Suevi, Sarmatians, and factions of other tribes, including Goths."

The man looked at Valerias after he said his speech. "There are about forty to fifty thousand non-Hun men who serve Uldric. Many are infantry." Valerias returned a look that indicated he wanted more, so the man continued his monologue. "These other men do not have the fighting skills of the Huns or the loyalty. But they have sworn blood oaths to Uldric, and woe to the man that breaks his oath. Their numbers make the Huns powerful."

For the next hour the man continued talking. Valerias tended to believe this man, and he knew much of what the Alan said could be employed in constructing a defense against the Huns. When the Alan finished, Valerias asked Revious what should be done to him. Valerias had given his word that if the man talked, he would be spared, and he would keep his word.

There was always the alternative of sending him to the mines. Yet Valerias considered that as a poor alternative, considering the trouble he'd had with the mine operators during the imprisonment of Cratus and Bukarma. Revious requested that Valerias grant the man amnesty, and Valerias did so. The condition was that Revious was responsible for the man. As a result, Revious would take credit for the good things the man did and the blame if he failed. The Alan was more than happy to be spared and, not surprisingly, became very loyal to Revious. He became known around the camp as "Alan."

LXXI

Harbingers

While Revious had been away, Valerias and his forces had reached the location on which Valerias would establish defensive fortifications against the Huns. The next days proved to be a flurry of activity. Officers were assigned specific responsibilities.

Braxus was reassigned from working with the Goths to taking total charge of the Roman infantry. He had the patience and knowledge to handle this group. Valerias considered the infantry to be the heart of his defense.

The lead general for the cavalry legions was Cratus. His more fiery nature was suited to the cavalry.

Valerias gave Titus the responsibility of working with Mostar Gulivus' Goths. He was about the same age as Mostar Gulivus, which Valerias theorized would work well, as the Goths would not accept a younger Roman with command duties over them. Titus and Mostar Gulivus seemed to get along, considering one was Roman and the other Goth.

Titus was also given title as second-in-command to Valerias. Braxus and Cratus and some of the other senior officers initially resented this appointment, Valerias persuaded them to accept Titus' leadership command. It was to be only temporary. As

Valerias noted, "Titus yearns for Rome." Valerias explained to his officers that his own return as General was temporary as well.

The men worked around the clock. Defensive positions were first set up and then reinforced. Several long-range catapults and shorter-ranged bolt-throwers were constructed. Training became redundant. Valerias took frequent trips to the physician's tent to check on Olivertos and, of course, Claire. All but one of the men who participated in the raids on the Hun camp had been released, so the atmosphere in the physician's tent was one of boredom.

Valerias was pleased that Eustice had sent the guard contingent of Britons with him when they departed from Britannia. Valerias assigned the Briton guards to the physician area to provide security for Claire. He also placed some of his own guards to provide security to the physician area.

Valerias admired Olivertos. Nothing seemed to upset the physician. He was a good person for Claire to be around in this time of approaching turbulence. Joseph usually went with Valerias on his trips around the camp. Valerias liked to have Joseph at his side. Similar to Claire, Joseph provided a calming effect on him.

After weeks of intense preparation, Valerias was satisfied they were ready. It was not a moment too soon. When dinner was finished one night, Valerias left his tent and looked at the eastern horizon. It was now the middle of October, and night spread itself across the land at earlier and earlier times. Chilled air also accompanied the dark. Off to the east a glow extended across the horizon for a great distance. Revious joined Valerias outside the tent.

"The Huns approach," Revious said quietly, his voice almost reverent.

"When will they arrive, Revious?"

"The day after tomorrow—at the latest, General."

"And then the battle will begin."

"Yes, General."

"Bukarma, please bring me Joseph."

Joseph, who was in the next room, quickly appeared.

"Joseph, I need your writing skills. I am going to write a letter to both Emperors, informing them of what has transpired and what is likely to come."

Joseph left and quickly returned with two parchments and a quill. Valerias dictated a letter to the Emperor Valens. He asked Joseph to make a copy of the letter for the Emperor Valentinian. Valerias sat until Joseph completed the second letter. They were signed, rolled, and sealed. Messengers quickly departed to reach each Emperor.

"Thank you, Joseph. You have accomplished much for me during the past months."

Valerias stared off into space as he spoke. "You can leave any time you like. You have earned that right. If you go, I want you to take Claire. I don't want her children to be orphaned because of me."

"She won't leave you, Marcus. She loves you."

"And I love her, but that doesn't mean she has to die."

"What makes you think you are going to die?"

"I don't know, Joseph. Sometimes your destiny appears before you . . . the Huns are my destiny . . . *Uldric* is my destiny. I know this now. I have heard this and I have dreamed this. I think it is my time. I don't know if there is anything beyond that."

"I believe there is."

"You have to; you are a Christian priest. And you believe that if you are good and follow the tenets of your religion, you can sit at the feet of your god after you die. You believe there is an afterlife. I don't believe in an afterlife. I've seen too much, most of which you would not consider good, for me to believe in any afterlife, good or evil."

"I have learned to put faith in man as well as God. I have faith in you, Marcus. In your men, in Claire, Olivertos, and this mission."

Without giving thought to Joseph's words, Valerias spoke, "I was once in the mold of Uldric. The role of my legions was to inflict utter domination on our enemy. And I made sure the enemies of Rome ultimately became subordinates to the Empire, if I allowed them to live. Much of me feels the same way today."

"Marcus, I know you are not the same man as when I met you."

"I am, though. I just have good people who influenced me to become a more moral man. But I am still the same soldier, the same general, that I was when we met, and I always will be. If you are going to stop someone like Uldric, you have to be like me—or like him. I can promise you that if you 'turn your cheek' to Uldric or any of his men, you will be killed, and killed viciously."

"I am not going to leave, Marcus. I will stay with Olivertos and Claire and pray that you can defeat the Huns."

Valerias looked at Joseph and spoke intensely, "What will you do, Joseph, if the time comes and you have to choose between your beliefs and saving a life? Will you raise a sword and kill an enemy? Or will you let the enemy kill you and the innocents around you?"

"You ask a very tough question, Marcus. I don't know."

"Very well, Joseph, that is a fair answer. The men look up to you. You survived my rage and became an important part of my organization within a short period. The men see that. Many of them think you are blessed. You have my permission to bless anyone who requests such a blessing tomorrow or before the battle. I imagine Braxus will be first in line." Valerias smiled.

Joseph nodded. Claire arrived at the tent with her Britannic escorts. She had heard the last part of the conversation between Valerias and Joseph. Valerias wanted to rest and said it was time to retire to his chambers.

He remarked to no one in particular, "Tomorrow will be the last day before our destiny comes to be."

Later as Claire and Valerias walked to their tent, Valerias started, "I want you to consider—"

"The answer is no. I know you're going to ask me to go. I will not. My place is at your side."

"If the battle goes badly, I do not want you harmed or taken prisoner."

"That won't happen. I had a dream that we won the battle and defeated the Huns."

"Did you *live* in your dream?"

"We won. That is enough."

"That didn't answer my question."

"I don't have an answer to your question. I didn't dream about you or me—just the result of the battle. Maybe Joseph should offer a prayer for you?"

"That is something you can do on your own, Claire. I believe in the man, not his religion."

Valerias had a restless night. He had dreams, but he couldn't remember them.

Uldric always started and ended his day looking west. It helped him focus on the objective of tomorrow. October was a favorite time of year for him. Mild days and cool nights were preferable to the hot summer. He also did not view October as the harbinger to winter and the death of the land. Today was the day his soldiers would leave for the Roman position less than thirty miles west of his camp. He was anxious to get moving, and he grew more impatient as the morning eroded into midday and his troops fell behind schedule. They would travel light and carry the bare minimum provisions with them. He anticipated they would reach the Roman army within one day. He envisioned the resulting battle would take one day. Uldric was fully confident and believed the Romans would quickly crack under his onslaught. The remainder of the Goth kingdom and the Roman Empire would then be his to take.

His daydreaming ended when a guard called out to him. "General, riders are coming. It is Braga."

Uldric uttered a loud curse. *What does that vermin want here*? he thought. *To take our glory for himself and his damned father, Zestras?*

Braga rode up to Uldric, dismounted, and gave a halfhearted greeting. There was a palpable distrust between them.

"What brings the son of Zestras to my camp?"

"I come to assist you, my general."

"Why would the son of the Southern Huns want to help the Northern Huns?"

"To help you advance on Rome or Constantinople—your choice, General Uldric."

"Do you realize that not more than thirty miles from this spot the Romans and the weakling Goths are waiting for us?"

Braga appeared truly surprised at the news. He didn't believe the Romans would field an army north *and* east of the Danube. After a moment of thought, he said, "Good. This will give us some practice for when we face the Roman army that guards their major cities."

"I agree with you, Braga. We will crush this Roman army, crush the Goths, and then the world shall open up to us. I predict the Roman cities and their remaining armies will capitulate to our demands. We shall be rich and victorious."

"And I brought five hundred of our finest warriors to help you in this cause," Braga announced.

Uldric looked at the men Braga had brought, and he was not impressed. He decided not to say anything to Braga about the quality of his men. But he knew how he was going to use them.

"Braga, take your men over there." Uldric pointed to a large meadow in the distance. "I have decided you will be in Radic's command. We will talk about what your role will be. Go, and meet me in my command tent in one hour."

At that moment Produgas entered the tent. After giving a false greeting of surprise to throw Uldric off guard, Produgas volunteered to escort Braga and his men to the meadow.

On their way to the meadow, Braga said, "The appearance of the Romans so close is a surprise."

"It will work out," answered Produgas. "Uldric and the Romans will weaken each other, and then the Southern Huns can rise up and take this entire country. Maybe the entire world."

"We will see. You are quite optimistic, Produgas. Your general's preoccupation with the Goths has proven to be a distraction. That is why I came—to put Uldric back on course."

"I think his course has been set by the appearance of the Romans."

Uldric and his officers held their meeting to plan strategy for the upcoming battle. Approximately one hour later the great Hun army was on the move, heading straight for the Romans.

LXXII

Toasts

The Huns did not waste time and were soon at the doorstep of the Romans. Valerias could see in the distance a dust storm of humanity headed straight toward him. Because it was almost night, he did not think the Huns would attack. Still, he ordered triple the usual guard as sentries. Additionally, one half of his force would rest the first half of the night, while the other half maintained vigilance. The second half of the night was a reversal of the resting and guarding positions for the other half of the army. Valerias did not want a repeat of his earlier attack on the Huns being repaid on his army by revenge-seeking Huns.

Valerias had spent the daytime hours riding through the various areas of the camp checking on the status of his defense positions and boosting morale. Titus and Joseph accompanied him on these rounds. He wanted the men and Titus to become more familiar with each other. He allowed Joseph to conduct his Christian services for whoever wanted them. As he predicted, Braxus was one of the men. Cratus was not. At the end of the day and in private, Titus even requested Joseph's blessing. Titus was beginning to feel his mortality and wanted the blessing just in case Joseph's cause was the right one. He jested with

Valerias that it was the spirit of Emperor Constantine in him that influenced his request for a Christian blessing.

Valerias made no comment or even negative facial gestures during Joseph's work. He simply did not believe in Joseph's faith, but he would not try to stop anyone else from his or her belief. Valerias sometimes wondered what would have happened to Julian's reign if Julian had been more accepting of the Christian faith or even became a Christian. Would he have lasted as Emperor longer, or would the end result still have been the same? It didn't matter, though, now, tomorrow or even tomorrow's tomorrow.

That night a simple pre-battle dinner was prepared for Valerias and his officers. In an odd gesture he had Olivertos and Joseph sit with Claire and himself. It was strange, because none of the three was a military commander. As dinner ended and the men were about to head back to their stations, Valerias stood to make a toast. He held his cup in his left hand. Valerias had shaved off his beard since the start of the campaign, as he didn't want any gray whiskers to show. His eyes were intense, with a glint of reflection.

"As sure as the sun will rise in the heavens tomorrow, we will be in battle with a group of men we know little about. Do not be concerned about these Huns. You have battled the Huns' allies before—the Suevi, the Alans, and rogue Goths—and have been successful. This is just another tribe of barbarians who have fought women and children . . . but not the Roman army.

"I have always been proud of the men I have served with, and I am proud of you. We will fight and defeat the Huns tomorrow and send them back to their hellholes in the east. It is my destiny . . . and it is your destiny. I am convinced that this is fact. And I'm convinced that triumph will be ours. With our brothers, Mostar Gulivus and his Goths, we will prevail. For those who die, you will be revered as heroes. For those who live, you will be hailed as victors. There is no greater honor than to fight and die with great men! I toast to us—to Rome—to destiny!"

At the end of his short speech, Valerias lifted up his cup and took a long drink of wine. He held up the emptied cup, and the men let out a lusty roar.

"Now go out to your commands and talk to them as I have to you!"

The men let themselves out of the tent and only Braxus, Cratus, Olivertos, Joseph, Titus, Bukarma, and Claire were left. Valerias spoke softly to Olivertos and Joseph, wishing them good fortune, and they left. He put his hands on the shoulders of Braxus and Cratus and told them that they were his brothers. Valerias and Titus went out of the tent and looked east. A deep, reddish orange glow was present on the horizon.

"Looks like a false dawn." Titus spoke first.

"Tomorrow the Hun will meet his match and will be defeated."

"Yes, he will, Marcus, with your leadership."

"And yours, my friend. To fight the dragon, one must know the dragon. To kill the dragon, one must understand it. I may not personally know this dragon, this Hun, for I have never met him. But I understand him. He is ambitious and cunning, and will act with brazen fury. Yet he is an impetuous bully. We will meet that fury with patience and intelligence—and a fury of our own. And, of course, we have the greatest soldiers ever assembled on Earth."

Titus knew instinctively what Valerias meant and nodded in agreement. Titus took his leave. Valerias told Bukarma to rest. Claire and Valerias retired to their tent. They talked quietly into the late hours of the night. Valerias did not tell Claire that he had ordered her Britannic escort to get her out of the area if the physician's tent came under attack. Claire did not tell Valerias that she had asked Joseph to pray for his well-being. Those were their secrets. Neither wanted the other hurt, and so they did what they thought was right.

As Valerias held Claire close, he said, "I truly don't know if we shall prevail tomorrow. I used to be supremely confident of my abilities to defeat any of my enemies. Now I do not feel so confident. I suppose I feel like a real human."

"Did I do this to you, Marcus?"

"Yes, and I love you all the more for it. There have been times recently that I wanted to die and couldn't. Now I don't want to die, but I may. But I am content with that. I am content now, truly content. You have shown me what have I missed. Now that I have found that, anything can happen and that will be fine with me."

"Don't you want to live anymore?"

"Of course I do. Tomorrow, when I take to the field, living will be more important to me than ever. It's just that I don't know if my destiny will carry me through tomorrow. But I want you to know . . . that I love you more than my life. I am a very happy man."

Claire looked at Valerias with understanding eyes. "Sometimes Joseph speaks of finding salvation. We may find that tomorrow."

Claire put her face into Valerias' shoulder, and he held her tightly. They lay in bed for over an hour until Claire fell asleep. Valerias put a blanket over her and returned to his command tent.

Bukarma was there, and sitting on the table was his game of bones. "Are you ready to lose again, Marcus?"

"Of course, my friend—losing in your game will be good luck for us. Just so we do not lose tomorrow."

Uldric, as was customary for this time of day, was looking west from his tent. This time, though, instead of darkness there was a reddish glow to the west. *The Romans also burn fires,* thought Uldric.

A voice came from behind. "Tomorrow you shall have a great victory, great general." The speaker was Produgas. Uldric was increasingly aware that Produgas was two men: an advisor and a traitor. He also knew Braga was up to no good. That is why he had either Radic or Sardich with him at all times. He trusted both generals implicitly.

Uldric had previously told Radic to take Braga and his men and place them in a vulnerable position when the battle begins. *We shall see if they are the great fighters Braga says they are,* he thought to himself. Likewise, he wanted Sardich to do the same with Produgas and his command.

In an earlier conversation with Radic and Sardich, Uldric had sarcastically said, "The two conspirators shall see what a battle is really like up close. With life seeping from their fallen bodies, the two traitors will experience what it is like to die. We will suffer no loss with their deaths."

Uldric believed there was an afterlife, and if he died, he would be reunited with Rao. He had no fear of death and wanted to fight the Romans. It would be the test he had wanted. Uldric ordered all to leave him, besides Radic and Sardich. Both generals were at his side, looking at the red night sky.

Radic observed, "The Romans are not Goths, General. They will not flee and hide behind walls. They will stand and fight. I have heard so from others that have fought them in the past."

"Good," Uldric grunted.

Sardich commented, as if Uldric had not spoken, "We will face the great Roman, General Valerias. The Alans, Suevi, and our Goth allies are afraid of him. They say he has no heart."

"We shall see when I open his chest and cut out his heart. Do not be concerned about the Romans and their general, Sardich. Victory shall be ours. When we are done, we shall impale their great general on a stake on the banks of the Danube. The Goths and the Romans will know how great the Huns are—and shall provide us with the tribute we demand."

Radic said, "Great General, our men await your command. We will follow you into Hell—if that is what we need to do!" Sardich nodded enthusiastically.

Uldric knew that his generals were ready. He ordered drinks from a servant. They looked to the west and toasted the upcoming victory. As they drank, Uldric clenched his fist.

LXXIII

Death's Shroud

DAWN ARRIVED CLEAR and cool, as on many October days. The Romans were at their battle stations before the sun began to crest over the hills in front of them. Valerias and Titus had already ridden to Braxus' and Cratus' commands, where they discussed final strategy in the fight to come. Valerias had also decided to assign General Proctur to support Braxus. Proctur was the holdover general from Trojax's command. Valerias had watched Proctur over the last several weeks and trusted him to serve under Braxus.

Valerias enjoyed Titus' company. With his well-trimmed beard and hair, Titus had a fatherly presence. For an older man he had a remarkably full head of grayish hair with a tinge of brown. Titus had a spatha sword similar to Valerias', but it was longer than the typical Roman spatha. He carried a shorter, dagger-like sword at his side, a gladius. Titus also carried a heavy shield. Like Valerias, he had the charisma of a commanding general.

The men had an affinity for Titus. He could tell stories by the hour and not be boring. However, no one could tell if they were truth or fantasy. One story Titus frequently told was about his grueling encounter with a large serpent in Africa. In the story Titus was half-swallowed by the serpent before he slew the beast. Valerias knew it was a fabrication, but he always looked interested when Titus spun the tale. And most of the men believed it.

After their visits to Braxus and Cratus, Valerias went with Titus to the forces of Mostar Gulivus. These men were noticeably more apprehensive than the Romans. Valerias was concerned about the state of the Goths and whether they could hold their position. Mostar Gulivus informed the two in a blunt fashion that his men were ready. Many of the Goths had painted their faces with war markings. During the past several days, Titus spent substantial time with the Goths to prepare them for the Huns. He had also become friends with the Goth leader.

Valerias told Mostar Gulivus that he was very proud of the courage of the Goths—although inside he was less confident. *When the battle comes, they must hold their position,* he thought. He left Titus with Mostar Gulivus and the Goths to act as an advisor. However, if something were to happen to Valerias, Titus would take full command.

As he was leaving Titus, Valerias asked him one final question: whether he, Titus, on second thought, would rather be in his Roman villa looking out at the sea instead of on his horse awaiting the upcoming battle.

Titus answered forcefully, "There is no place I would rather be than right here and in this position. I was born for this and I will die for this!"

Valerias answered back, "We will defeat the Hun—and then you can chase women on the beach in full view of your wife!"

"There would be no need for that. My wife still looks good after all these years. Either way you look at it, I will be in paradise soon."

The men laughed together, and Valerias rode off to the center of his command.

Uldric had not slept that night. He spent the early morning hours discussing with his generals how they would attack the Roman positions. He was supremely confident in Radic and Sardich and their abilities to lead and fight. He also wanted the two generals to be sure that Braga and Produgas received a serious dose of combat experience. At dawn he divided his army into the three familiar segments led by Radic to the right, Sardich to the left, and Uldric in the center position. Once the divisions were completed, the combined force of the Huns and their allies began advancing forward on Uldric's command.

Before launching the attack against the Romans and Goths, though, Uldric had made a special request he kept to himself. He had one of his guards fashion a white flag, which he knew meant truce. Uldric ordered Arb to go with him. Then Uldric, Arb, and the flag-carrying guard rode out ahead of the Hun army.

Valerias was watching the scene before him, and he too ordered a white flag brought to him. He requested that Revious hold the flag. He ordered a messenger to bring Joseph to him. When Joseph arrived, Valerias asked Joseph if wanted to be a part of the "truce" party to meet Uldric. Joseph said he would. Bukarma had brought a lion pelt, complete with a headdress, and placed it on the back of Valerias. Valerias wanted to put a seed of doubt in the Hun's mind as to his own sanity, and he thought the lion skin would be useful.

The group of three from each army met at a halfway point between their forces. All weapons were left behind. Arb and Revious were to be translators. Valerias could not speak the Hun tongue, and Uldric did not speak a word of Latin. However, Revious spoke

Latin and Arb spoke the Hun language. The Alan tongue was the common language between the two scouts. So with translators in place, Valerias and Uldric could speak to each other. Revious and Arb, as a sign of mutual respect, nodded to each other as they took their places.

Uldric spoke first. "Greetings, Roman leader, from the Hun people."

"I too extend my greetings from the Roman Empire to the Huns."

"You look older than I thought you would be." Uldric was almost insulting.

"And you are exactly what I expected," countered Valerias.

Uldric didn't know whether to take that remark as a compliment or insult.

"Why do the Romans want to save the Goths? They are a lecherous band of half-men and half-swine. I thought the Romans killed Goths. That is what I have heard." Uldric took on a mocking tone.

"It is a different time. Other enemies have become a priority."

"I assume we are now your enemy," Uldric continued, in his mocking voice.

"You have assumed correctly. My men have learned you have aspirations beyond the Goths. Could it be that you have interest in Rome or—more likely—Constantinople?"

"What you think doesn't really matter to me, Roman. Soon the Goths will be mine—and then you, the finest Roman force ever assembled, and then the gates of whatever city I want—all will be mine. It is in the stars, Roman."

"I don't see that in the stars, Hun. When I look up, I see all the great Roman generals and Emperors looking down on us. They will not let the Empire be destroyed by someone like you."

Uldric looked at the lion skin robe. "What is that that you are wearing? I haven't seen any animal like it."

"The animal is the great cat of Africa. It is the symbol of power. Like Rome. A power you shall soon know."

"Did you kill that animal?"

"Yes—with my hands. As my army shall do to you today."

"I think at the end of today, your head will be planted on a stake outside my tent."

"The day will be ours, Hun. I have never lost a battle, and I have fought better men than you."

Undeterred, Uldric continued his range of subjects, "My allies tell me that you are a God with no heart. I just wanted to see who you are before your army bleeds into the earth under our feet."

Valerias sat on his horse and did not say a word. He looked at the Hun soldier, then at Arb, and finally at the face of Uldric. He did not blink or change expression. The Hun tried to look equally expressionless, but he could not. Instead, he looked at Joseph.

"Who is this thin 'soldier' you have brought here? What is that robe he wears?"

"He is our spiritual guide. He will pray for your salvation, if you ask."

"Salvation! Ha!" Uldric glanced at Arb and the flag-bearer, and they rode back to his army.

Valerias, Joseph, and Revious turned and headed back to their stations.

On the way Joseph asked, "Why did you bring me to this meeting, General?"

"I wanted you to see the devil." Valerias smiled and looked at Revious, who looked incredulous, as did Joseph. Valerias continued, "He is not the devil as imagined in your religious books, Joseph. He is simply an overly ambitious man who can and will die soon. That is all."

As they rode up the ridge, the three saw the splendor of the Roman army in full battle dress. The legions before them were comprised of heavy infantry and cavalry. They looked magnificent. Even the Goths to the left gave the appearance of a disciplined force.

"What a beautiful sight!" The General looked at his over sixty thousand Roman and Goth men in battle formation. The red of the Roman uniforms shone brightly, and the sun glinted off their metal, creating an aura.

"Some may say they are merchants of death." Joseph was taken in by the likely ramifications before him.

"And others may say saviors." Valerias had a relaxed but earnest expression. "Go now to Olivertos' group and give that field hospital any blessing you want. It will need it. Take care, my friend—we shall see each other again. Revious, return to my command post."

Joseph did not know what to make of that last comment. The General sounded almost wistful as he said it. Valerias took his sword from his sheath. He proceeded to ride his horse up and down in front of his army, raising his sword in a pulsating rhythm. The men cheered in simultaneous replies as he rode by them and let out the Roman war cry. Joseph watched this sight unfold with a certain awe. This was an awe not based solely on appearance but also of the singular purpose the General possessed.

When Valerias had finished his review of his troops, he rode back to his command area. He gave the lion skin to Bukarma. "It is yours now, Bukarma."

"Did you kill this cat?" Bukarma asked.

Both men knew the answer.

The General replied, "No, I didn't. Remember, Mostar Gulivus gave it to me as a gift for letting his son, Gul, live." Valerias winked. "But the Hun doesn't know that."

LXXIV

APOCALYPSE

Uldric returned to his army. Radic and Sardich were there to meet him.

"The Roman leader is a man I can respect. He has no fear of death. That is true of us. But it is he who will die today. Return to your forces. It shall be the Huns' day."

Uldric turned to one of his nearby commanders and nodded. A force of two thousand men led by General Jutikes broke from the center of the Hun army and charged at the Roman central position. Jutikes' men were largely Alan and Suevi infantry with scattered Hun cavalry.

"We will see how the Romans react to this charge!"

Valerias, who was watching the charge, motioned to Pyrin, and instantly a messenger was off to Braxus. The front of the Roman infantry legions that would face the brunt of the Hun attack went into defensive formation with shields up and in front. As the Huns grew closer, Jutikes was perplexed by this formation. He expected the Romans to break formation and retreat under attack by his fierce force. His men shot arrows into the formation, but they had little effect against the reinforced Roman shields.

When the Hun force was within one hundred yards of the Roman line, the Romans in the front positioned themselves into a lower position. Hundreds of infantrymen behind them dropped their shields and rose up, bows and arrows in hand. At Braxus' command the archers let loose a fusillade of arrows at the Huns. After a count of ten, they archers fired a second volley.

The arrows had no specific target. They were like ticks in the woods that waited for a host to attach onto. The arrows many, many times found their targets in the lightly armored Huns and their allies. Men and horses spilled over the ground in front of the Romans. A third and then a fourth volley followed. The arrow barrage devastated the Hun attack. Several Huns managed to shoot arrows at the Roman archers, but most failed to hit their mark. A few Huns on horseback reached the Roman ranks. Romans with spears finished off these men quickly. Some fell to the ground and were set upon by infantrymen with their swords and spears. When the Romans let go a fifth volley, Jutikes had seen enough. His troops were either dead or demoralized, and he ordered a full retreat.

As Jutikes and his remaining troops raced back to their original position with Uldric, the Romans gave out a victory cry. The Huns had been defeated—or so they thought. Hermides also cheered.

Valerias looked at Hermides. "You are foolish to reach such a conclusion, Hermides. This was just a test of our strength and our resolve. The Huns lost very little with this attack."

Valerias motioned to Revious, who was with him. Revious disappeared and was soon on the battlefield. After a few minutes of observing the area, he returned to Valerias.

Revious immediately came to the point, "Those are not Huns that were part of the attack. They were non-Huns, such as the Alans, Suevi, Sarmatians—and even some Goths. They were sacrificial cattle. He is saving his best for the next attack."

Hermides' gleeful expression turned dour. Valerias ignored Hermides and focused on Revious.

"When do you think Uldric will attack next?" Valerias asked Revious.

"Soon. Very soon," was the reply.

"He will test the Goths first and then he will test us. Our defense showed a spine. Uldric will now hit us with the full force of his Huns. This time they will use their cavalry. Look for an all-out assault on our infantry."

Valerias nodded and looked at his aides. "Pyrin, go to General Titus and tell him to expect an attack on our right flank. They will attack the Goths first. Hermides, inform General Cratus that the Huns will attack his position soon. They won't attack the cavalry on our left flank just yet, but they will. Revious, inform General Braxus that his training of the infantry will be fully tested after the Huns try their hand against the Goths. You three, return to me after you deliver your messages. You are going to have a busy day today!"

The three departed for their respective generals.

After the three were gone, Valerias glanced at Bukarma. "Give me my battle helmet." It was a typical battle helmet except that it had only a small frill on the top. It was made of lightweight metal with a strip of protective metal that ran down his face to the bottom of his nose. It had ear holes, but they were layered with thin metal strips that protectively covered the open space. Valerias wanted a full range of hearing, and his helmet allowed this to happen. If one were to look at the General's helmet, one would have an impression of an animal face, similar to a big cat, covering that of a human. Valerias admired the lion from his time in Africa, and he'd had his helmet forged to give the appearance of a lion's countenance.

Valerias pulled on his helmet. He left his sword in its sheath located on his back. His ever-present dagger was strapped to the inside of his left calf. He carried a small shield with impressions of his legions painted on the front, a shield that had been reinforced personally by Bukarma. Valerias rarely carried a spear anymore, and he didn't today. He was now ready for battle.

He looked at Bukarma, and he was also ready. The two men smiled at each other. Whatever would happen today would happen. It was in a God's hands, or the Fates, or just in the hands of men, it didn't matter. Valerias now firmly believed this was the moment he had lived all his life for—his destiny. He briefly thought of Claire and his current position and felt a moment of contentment again.

Uldric was not the strategist that his brother had been. He had triumphed over all foes with ease by brute force and now another foe was in front of him—the Romans. He thought that the Romans would present more of a challenge than any previous foe. Still, Uldric had been undefeated and had begun to consider himself to be almost immortal. Besides, his scouts had informed him that his army substantially outnumbered the Roman and Goth contingent. The initial skirmish was but a hiccup. Even though Uldric had lost many men, they were Alans and others—not Huns. Now was the time to unleash his Huns. He gave the signal and down the line it was passed. Sardich commanded his warriors under the Death Chaser Standard to advance on the Roman right flank manned by the Goths. Uldric had calculated they would be the weak link of the Roman army.

Sardich had twenty-five thousand men under his command, consisting of largely infantry and a few cavalry units. The majority of Sardich's force was Hun allies. However, he also had a core force of five thousand Huns under his command. They were hungry for battle. Turkson, the Alan general, rode with Sardich.

Titus had worked hard with the Goths and Mostar Gulivus for several days. Although they were not Roman-ready for battle, Titus felt they could hold their own against the Huns' troops. The

Goths were also a combination of infantry and cavalry, but largely infantry based. Groups of the Goth infantry could shoot a bow.

Part of the land defended by the Goths was forested, and Valerias had had his men build platforms in the taller trees. The better bowmen from the Goths and even some Romans were placed in the perches. Their sole objective was to punish the Huns with arrows from the sky.

Valerias and Mostar Gulivus knew a strength of the Huns was their ability to shoot arrows accurately from a distance while riding their horses. Valerias thought this was an impressive skill. As a result, the Romans and Goths worked to protect themselves from the Hun archers by reducing the target space as small as possible with larger, reinforced shields. This approach worked initially, as Goth casualties were low during the initial Hun approach, which consisted of an exchange of arrows.

Eventually the first wave of Sardich's Huns slammed into the Goths and began taking a toll on those troops. Conversely, the Goth and Roman archers in the trees targeted clumps of Hun riders, causing death or injury to many Huns. This allowed the Goths to regroup, and hand-to-hand fighting between the two forces commenced in earnest. The Goths had their backs to a wall, realizing their homeland was in jeopardy, and they fought valiantly. Their desire for victory equaled the Huns' fighting skills, and neither side had an advantage.

Valerias watched from his position and was pleased that the Goths were doing well. He thought the Huns would then attack the Romans' left flank held by Cratus' roughly four legions of cavalry. He was correct again. Radic and over fifteen thousand cavalry comprised of a mixture of Huns and their allies under the Green Serpent Standard advanced on Cratus' position. Cratus had become well versed in the Huns' abilities, and his forces were trained to limit damage from Hun arrows. At the far edge of the meadow where Radic was advancing, there was a forest area. To prevent the Huns from outflanking Cratus, Valerias had ordered hundreds of traps be set in the forest. He also stationed archers' platforms in the trees. One advantage for the Romans in this area was that the further in the forest one went, the more nature had set its own obstacles in the form of rock walls and chasms. It would be very difficult for any cavalry to proceed though this area.

Radic did what was expected and tried to outflank Cratus' position, which proved to be a dismal failure. So many men were being killed or wounded by the traps and archers that Radic called his men back and directly attacked Cratus. Cratus had always been a warrior's warrior, and his men rallied with him and fought Radic to a standstill.

Uldric's next move was to send his central force under his leadership, and the Standard of the Dragons, straight at the Roman infantry. He had over thirty thousand men under his command, and almost half were Huns. Valerias' defense had over five legions, or twenty thousand of the best infantrymen in the world. He also had about fifteen hundred cavalrymen to back up the infantry. Uldric's strategy was to bull-rush both of the Roman flanks by Sardich and Radic and then directly charge the center. With the Huns' overwhelming fighting capability and superior numbers, he thought this attack would produce a quick and successful outcome. He was wrong. The Roman flanks held, and now it was his turn.

Uldric sent his first wave of Huns under Borgas and then a second wave commanded by Oxanos toward the heart of Valerias' infantry. At first there was no movement from the Roman infantry. As the Hun cavalry advanced to within one hundred yards of the Romans, hundreds of large, sharpened, wooden stakes rose quickly up from the ground and were set in pre-dug holes for stability. The stakes were set into the ground at a height to rupture the undersides of a horse. This action caused Borgas to become confused, and he slowed the progress of his force. At that moment hundreds of arrows from Roman archers again fell onto the Huns. The first wave of Huns stopped advancing. Those soldiers were then hit from behind by the second wave. Borgas was hit and killed by arrows. Chaos ruled the Hun attack. Uldric had seen enough and ordered a third wave of cavalry led by Jutikes to charge. The sound of the third wave coming at them forced the neutralized Huns in the first and second waves to regain their momentum and return to the attack. No one wanted to face Uldric through a retreat.

For the Huns the initial results of their attack bore little resemblance to what they typically encountered in advancing on their enemies. Valerias saw the disorganization in the Hun ranks and ordered Tentrides and his engineers to let loose volleys from the Roman artillery, consisting of stone-throwers and bolt-shooters, into the Hun mass. The payload in some of the catapults was set on fire before it was launched, so when it hit the ground it would cause maximum damage. Additionally, before the battle, Valerias had ordered dried grass be placed on the field where the Huns would attack. A source of tar had also been found by a Roman unit a few days before, and it was intermixed with the grass. When the incendiary load from the catapults hit the ground, areas of fire soon spread. The fires created fear in the Hun horses, resulting in multiple cases of the horses not obeying their riders by revolting and throwing them.

Hun casualties were mounting by the minute, and victory seemed imminent for the Romans. Unfortunately, a certain event can turn the fortunes of war in an instant. That was the case for the Romans. Mostar Gulivus had rallied the Goths to the point they were driving the Huns back to their initial point of attack. An arrow fired by a Hun fifty yards away struck Mostar Gulivus just above the breastplate. The Goth king pulled at the arrow but it was wedged deeply into his chest. He feebly tried to sound a command but died quickly and quietly. He rolled off his horse and hit the ground hard. The Goths around him became alarmed. Several men rushed to pull him away from the battle zone. The Huns proceeded to pick off these potential rescuers one by one, and soon there were a number of dead Goths lying beside their leader. A Goth rode over to Titus' position and told him of Mostar Gulivus' death. Titus barked commands, but with only limited success. The Goths started to flee the area. The Huns saw an opportunity and returned to pressing the attack.

Titus rode to the area where Mostar Gulivus lay, and his horse was struck by a Hun arrow. A second arrow hit the horse, and the horse drove itself into the ground. Titus' right leg was lodged underneath the dead horse. Titus knew his leg was broken. As he tried to pull it out from under the horse, a Hun came up on foot. He looked at Titus and with his saber moved to strike. As he did so, Titus' sword struck the Hun through the crotch. The man screamed and fell back. A Goth on horseback rode by and sliced the Hun across the neck. The Hun fell on top of Titus, the Hun's sword piercing Titus' arm. That act, and the pain from his broken leg, caused Titus to lose consciousness. Heavy hand-to-hand fighting erupted around Titus. Another body and then another fell near or on him.

Valerias observed this turn for the worse from his command center. He did not want to lose this flank. He called Hermides to his side. Hermides and Pyrin had recently returned to Valerias' command center. Valerias ordered Hermides to be the commander of one of the two remaining cavalry cohorts to his side.

"Get Gul from the engineers. Take him and your cohort of seven hundred and fifty men and ride to the Goths' position. I need you to shore up our position with the Goths. I am counting on the Goths seeing Gul and rallying behind him. Also, if you locate Titus, send him here."

Hermides acknowledged the order and rode off to the engineers. Valerias was concerned for his friend, Titus, and yet there was nothing he could do now. The feeling of contentment he had just an hour earlier was gone, like a songbird at the onset of night, just as he knew it would flee. He looked to his left and could see Cratus' legions battling the Huns evenly. In the central theater the Huns were taking a pounding from his infantry. The combined effect of the disciplined legions, the archers' arrows, and the rain from the artillery had killed well over a thousand Huns. In this area Uldric had been stymied.

Time passed, and the battle in the forest between Cratus' and Radic's forces had turned into a stalemated, wild melee. Cratus was one never to shy away from conflict, even when the odds were against him. It would not matter whether he was a general or an ordinary soldier. To distinguish himself from the other officers, Cratus wore a specialized helmet. At the top of the forehead part of the helmet, Cratus had commissioned a blacksmith to forge a spike into the helmet. Cratus said it was another part of his personal arsenal of weapons, and he had used it effectively in many battles.

As Cratus fought on, he observed that several Roman cavalrymen, including his officers, had fallen. He decided to take the offensive in an effort to end the deadlock. With the cavalrymen who remained around him, Cratus gave the charge command.

Cratus had always led by example, and he led this charge directly into a pack of Huns who were initially confused by his actions. They rallied quickly, though, and the mass of men and horses were engulfed in hand-to-hand fighting. Cratus became surrounded by Huns.

Two Huns directly in front of Cratus felt the sharp sting of his sword and perished. As he engaged more Huns to his front, Cratus did not see a Hun come up on his blind side, who then struck him in the back with his saber. The wound was not instantly fatal to Cratus, as his armor provided some protection, but the saber inflicted severe damage. As Cratus turned to face that attacker, another Hun rushed in from the other side and plunged a dagger into his lower abdomen.

Knowing that his death was imminent, Cratus focused on finishing the Hun who had used the dagger. Cratus turned to that side and locked eyes on the Hun with an unconquerable glare that melted the Hun's resolve. Cratus cursed the Hun and turned his dying energy into fury. With his last breaths Cratus pulled the Hun toward him, and with his helmet drove the spike into the forehead of the surprised Hun, killing him instantly.

Cratus died as he fell forward on his horse. His last words were: "*Fortitudinem*" [strength] . . . "*uictoriam*" [victory].

The Huns knew Cratus was a Roman leader. They took heart from his death and pushed hard into the Romans. Valerias learned Cratus was dead and dispatched his last cavalry cohort, with Pyrin as leader, to reinforce his left flank. Valerias had only about twenty men around him, including Bukarma, to act as guards and messengers. His best cavalry units were deployed on the right and left flanks. There were no more reserves.

Even with the addition of Hermides' and Pyrin's cavalry, Valerias watched as both flanks were starting to show evidence of crumbling. In the middle Uldric was sending wave after wave of Huns against the infantry. Uldric was taking mass casualties, but he did not seem to care. He acted almost suicidal. Valerias' artillery had become useless as the division between the two forces was erased. The last shot from a catapult hit a group of men that consisted of Huns and Romans. Braxus was in that melee and may have been hit. Valerias ordered the catapults be disarmed and destroyed. Then the engineers were to locate their weapons and prepare to fight.

The battle was slowly disintegrating to the Huns' favor. During the confusion, a group of about fifty Huns managed to slip by the Roman defenses and make their way into the Roman camp. The leader of the Britons saw the Huns and alerted his forces.

Valerias heard the shouting and for the first time since the battle began removed his sword from its sheath. He ordered Bukarma to stay in the commander's position and took off after the Huns. Bukarma gave Valerias his shield before he left.

The Huns were wreaking havoc on the camp. They had killed several Britons and Romans although they had suffered multiple casualties themselves. A small group of the Huns made their way to the physician quarters. They encountered a stiff resistance from the Roman soldiers who were carrying in the wounded on stretchers. Four Huns made it near the physician tent where Olivertos and Joseph were tending to the injured. Claire had just left the tent under pleading from the Briton leader to abandon the area. Before she left, she took a sword and drove it into the ground near Joseph with the hilt facing up in case either Joseph or Olivertos needed it for defense.

Joseph, at the time combat had commenced, told himself that he would not use a weapon, no matter the situation. He believed in the Christian principles he had been taught—one of which was that violence was not the solution. Now as danger closed in around him, he became less sure of his principles. Before he had become a priest, he had used a sword, so handling one was not new to him. Olivertos was too busy with the swarm of wounded and dying to be of any help. Joseph prayed that the guards would hold off the Huns. He was wrong. The tent flap opened and in walked a Hun. He was a short man with long black hair. He had a look in his eyes that meant death to anyone in his vision. His eyes first looked at Joseph, then to the physician assistants in the tent, and finally rested on Olivertos. The Hun had surveyed the situation and determined that Olivertos would be the first to die. He raised his saber and began to charge Olivertos. Joseph's focus turned to the sword that Claire had left them. He wrestled with his principles for a second and then reached for the sword.

It was too late. The Hun turned his attention to Joseph and was upon him, knocking him to the ground. As the Hun raised his arm with the saber ready to strike Joseph, the Hun suddenly straightened his body up with his back compressed. He screamed something incoherent and fell sideways on the ground. An arrow was wedged in the upper center of his back that likely had penetrated his heart. Joseph's eyes were wide, and he looked up at the tent flap expecting another Hun. Instead Claire hurriedly walked in and gazed at the scene and at Joseph and Olivertos. The flap opened again, revealing another Hun. Without hesitation, she put another arrow in her bow and shot it into the Hun's neck. The man grasped at the end of the arrow for what seemed like minutes, but was actually much quicker. Before he hit the ground, she had another arrow ready to fire at any other Hun that would come into the tent. The leader of the Briton guard wisely called out to her as he entered the tent.

Claire looked at Olivertos and Joseph. "Keep helping the wounded. We will protect you!"

She walked out of the tent, and two more Huns approached. Her arrow found a fleshy target through the armor of one of the Huns, killing him quickly. As the second Hun watched his companion die, the Briton captain killed him with a thrust to the body.

Valerias rode into the physician area just as Claire was leaving the tent. A Hun on horseback took aim at Valerias with an arrow. Valerias judged where the arrow would strike before it was shot, and he used his shield to block it. He took his horse and charged into the Hun before he could shoot another arrow. The Hun was dead within seconds as Valerias' sword lifted the head from its body. Another Hun rode at Valerias with his sword raised. Valerias had reached down and taken a spear from a dead soldier and threw it through the armor of the Hun, knocking him off his horse, where he was killed by the Britannic guards. After a few more minutes of fighting, all the Huns in the camp had been killed.

Valerias quickly surmised the situation was under control. He looked at Claire and remarked, "If only I could shoot arrows like you! Take care of my physicians!" Valerias hurried back to his command position.

When Valerias returned, he found two additional people in his command position, Revious and "Alan"—the Alan Valerias had placed under Revious' control.

"General, our man, Alan, here has some news you will want to hear."

Valerias saw that the Roman positions were unraveling on all sides of the battlefield. "Tell me what I can do to make this situation better!" Valerias looked first to Revious, then to Alan.

Alan pointed down to the Roman right flank, where the Goths and Romans were desperately fighting to hold their position. One of the Huns leading the charge wore a red head covering.

Through Revious' translation Alan said, "That man with the red headdress is Sardich, and he is one of the two supreme generals under Uldric. Kill him—and you weaken the Huns."

Valerias watched Sardich in the fight. Sardich was not a great fighter. He tended to stay near his guards, who did the fighting while he avoided combat.

"He does not appear to be much of a warrior," Valerias said to Alan.

"No, he isn't. But he is like Uldric's brother, Rao, who was assassinated by the Goths. He knows how to manage the fight. You must kill him."

Valerias had heard enough. "Bukarma, take half of what is left of my command and do as the Alan suggests—kill that Hun, Sardich."

"Yes, General." Bukarma selected his men and immediately left the command position for Sardich's location.

"He will kill Sardich," Valerias said to Revious and Alan without looking at them. Valerias was focused on the left flank. The Huns had gradually picked off most of Valerias' men in the tree platforms, and bodies began falling from the sky as much as their arrows. There appeared to be a mass of bodies mauling each other in no apparent order near one of the tree stands. No one in Valerias' area knew it, but Radic had just been hit with an arrow shot from one of the few remaining active platforms in the trees. The fight to rescue him ended quickly—the arrow had killed Radic.

The Roman infantry in the center had withstood charge after charge by the Huns. Braxus rode back and forth between his units, calmly urging them on and, more important, devising various defensive strategies and counterattacks against the more numerous Hun forces. Even though Braxus was riding on his horse and providing an accessible target for Hun archers, it appeared he had an invisible shield around him, as no arrows reached him.

Braxus was so fixated on his command that he did not notice a wayward blast from a Roman catapult until it knocked him off of his horse. Adrenaline from the battle kept him from losing consciousness when he hit the ground; however, the fall had broken his left shoulder and shattered his left ankle. A deep gash of blood oozed from his left cheekbone.

Even with these injuries, Braxus managed to stand with the aid of a nearby spear, which acted as a staff. He put the pain aside as he focused on encouraging his troops and issuing commands. Unfortunately, the errant catapult blast had exposed and weakened his position, as many of his guards were dead or injured. Multiple Huns were now descending upon him, many more than he could fight.

Braxus realized he was lost and said a prayer to God to receive his soul in the afterlife. Even with one damaged arm and leg and blurred vision, his sword pierced the chest of the first Hun to reach him. A second Hun had little chance as well, as Braxus terminated his life with a slice across the neck.

But there were too many enemies, and he was engulfed by Huns, who attacked like ants swarming prey. Roman soldiers desperately counterattacked the mass of Huns to reach their general, but their numbers were insufficient for the task.

Braxus died looking up to the sky. The Huns knew they had killed a Roman leader and attacked the Roman infantry with renewed vigor.

Another group of Huns was moving between the Roman's right flank of Goths and Roman infantry in the center. The purpose was to surround and decimate the legions fighting in the center. If the center fell, the battle was lost. The death of Braxus escalated the push from the Huns. The leader of the Huns in this movement was Uldric, who had joined the battle. He and the other Huns were, surprisingly, on foot. Valerias could soon see why—Uldric was using his scimitar, and it was killing or wounding Romans at an alarming pace.

Valerias knew what he had to do—stop Uldric. He looked to the sky and said a few words to Julian's Helios, Joseph's God, Edith's deity, or whoever was listening: "Grant me victory. Grant me victory."

The sky was a clear, tranquil blue, not reflective of what was transpiring on the ground. Both forces were in a death grip with thousands of bodies, man and horse, piled all over the field. It was difficult to walk because there was no open space.

Tentrides appeared at his side. Valerias ordered the engineer to take his men and defend the physician's quarters with their lives. Without hesitation Tentrides responded, "Yes, General" and was gone.

Valerias thought of Braxus, Cratus, and Claire, smiled, and said, "Thank you." He turned to his remaining soldiers and asked them, "Are you ready to give your lives to Rome?" He had such an earnest look on his face that they all experienced an inspiration that was hard to describe, unless one was in a similar circumstance. This included Revious and Alan.

"Well, let's go, then. We do this for the glory of Rome—and for ourselves."

The men all yelled something in return, part in excitement, part in courage, and part in fear. Valerias aimed his descent straight at Uldric. When they reached the outskirts of the battle, Valerias easily dispatched any Hun that advanced against him. Uldric had also identified Valerias as the Roman coming for him and quickly moved toward him. By the time they reached each other, both of their escorts were either engaged in combat, wounded, or dead.

As they faced off, Uldric spoke first. "At last—the Hun against the Roman. Soon you shall join the rest of your Roman dogs and Goth rats as part of the earth. I will do you a favor. I will mount your head on a *clean* spike for all the world to see. I will show how strong the Hun is . . . and how weak the Roman is."

"You've won nothing, Hun. You have so many dead by the Roman sword that your army will never rise again. The rest of the Goths will come now and finish you off—unless you return like straggling vermin to whatever hole you emerged from."

Even though neither Valerius nor Uldric understood the words that were spoken by the other, the meaning behind their words was clear. Somehow the thought of Zestras crossed Uldric's mind at that time and then that of Rao. Looking around, he saw all the death and began to feel duped by Zestras into engaging this fight with the Romans. Uldric missed his brother and yet felt angry that Rao had deserted him at his greatest time of need. His thoughts had moved him into a boiling rage. His rage was less against the Romans, more about his fate in life.

The two men circled each other slowly at first. Even when angry, Uldric knew he had to be wary of Valerias' fighting skills.

Each inflicted minor wounds on the other during the early phase of their fight. Valerias realized he likely didn't have the energy to match Uldric in a prolonged fight and moved to attack Uldric aggressively. Uldric returned the effort. Remarkably, the soldiers from both sides let the two men battle without interference. Some even stopped fighting to watch the two men. What they were witnessing was a fight that turned into one of stunning ferocity. Blow after blow was struck and deflected by the two combatants. It was a true fight to the death. No mercy was to be granted—or wanted.

With his scimitar Uldric occasionally inflicted shallow wounds on Valerias, but nothing eroded Valerias' fighting power. Valerias, on the other hand, was using two swords, as he had discarded his shield. The second sword was one that he had picked up from a dead Roman. It was slightly shorter than his own sword. In one sequence Uldric bull-rushed Valerias and knocked him on the ground. Still, Valerias blocked each swing of the scimitar that Uldric took at him, using both swords. Valerias was silently impressed by the sharpness of the blades on Uldric's scimitar and the fact the blades did not break when they struck the ground.

Valerias managed to return upright after he cut Uldric's leg with the shorter sword. The cut was deep and blood oozed from the wound. Uldric still went on the attack. This time both men became tangled in each other's grip and fell to the ground. Uldric was stronger than Valerias, but he was not as experienced in close combat. Valerias managed to head-butt Uldric, knocking him back. Valerias pushed Uldric off of him and started to rise to his feet. He was going to strike at Uldric, but his instincts made him stop. Uldric, in a move that was quicker than anything Valerias had witnessed before, spun his scimitar over the Valerias' head. If Valerias had stood fully erect, he would have been cut in two by the scimitar. Again and again they charged each other, with Uldric blocking Valerias' sword thrusts with his scimitar and Valerias blocking the cuts from the scimitar with his swords.

Several minutes of fighting passed, and the men were becoming fatigued. After another bruising round of in-close fighting, Valerias stepped back to regroup. As he backed up, his left foot became entangled with the corpse of a dead Hun. He lost his balance and fell partially on the ground. He knew what was coming and moved quickly out of the way to avoid the scimitar's blade. To complete this maneuver, he dropped the shorter sword. His efforts were only partially successful. His left hand, which he used to brace his fall, was sliced off cleanly by Uldric. Blood spurted from the wound.

With his hand separated from his body, Valerias rolled to his left. Uldric witnessed the damage he had inflicted, stood in a full upright position, and glared at Valerias.

"Time to die, Roman! Your life ends at this place—at this time—conquered by the Hun!"

As Uldric moved the scimitar back for a mighty swing at Valerias' neck, Uldric felt a dull *thud* against his own neck. He lowered the scimitar and reached to his neck. Blood flowed from the gashed artery in his neck—gashed by Valerias' dagger, the one Valerias always kept strapped to his calf. Uldric pulled the dagger out and looked at it dimly. He was becoming confused as the blood poured out of him. His foggy eyes saw a figure rise, and he heard the words:

"It is your time to die."

A swift blow cut off Uldric's head. The head rolled a short distance away from the body, which remained standing for a few seconds. The hands on the torso released the scimitar, and the body fell sideways on the ground. Valerias knew he had only a short amount of time, as blood gushed from the stump that used to hold his hand. He picked up the scimitar and plunged one end into the ground. The sharp blade penetrated deeply into the soil. The ground was soft from blood that had been spilled and the nature of the soil.

Valerias grabbed the hair on top of Uldric's head and lifted the head up as high as he could. As he rotated from left to right over the field of battle, he shouted, "*Sapor est victoria! Adhuc esurient!*" [Savor the victory! Hunger for more!] He said those words five times, and all those within range heard the words, Romans and Huns alike. Valerias then slammed the head onto the exposed blade of the scimitar. He looked around, turned, and began his walk back to his command center, blood flowing from what remained of his left wrist and with his sword gripped tightly in his right hand.

LXXV

Embers

Valerias didn't remember much after he spiked Uldric's head on the open end of the scimitar. Two men who were remnants from his principal guard came over to him as he walked away from Uldric's body. Valerias slowly collapsed, and the two men caught him. Two more men, Revious and Alan, rushed over to his aid. Neither man had engaged in significant combat and both had relatively clean clothes. Revious removed a strip of his shirt and tied it around Valerias' forearm as a tourniquet.

"Take the General to Olivertos," he said sharply to the three men.

Revious had drawn his sword and was looking for any Huns that would interfere with Valerias from being hustled to the physician quarters. He did not need to worry, though. Without their leader, the Huns were finished. The primary Hun allies, the Alans and the Suevi, had experienced more death than they thought was possible when they joined the Hun expedition. By the time Uldric had died, they were looking for any excuse to leave the battlefield. The deaths of their own leaders, combined with deaths to Radic and Sardich and finally Uldric, gave them an out to flee.

Valerias' victory over Uldric also gave the Romans and the Goths a huge morale boost. They had fought with extreme bravery up to that point, but the tide of battle had begun to go to the Huns' favor. The death of Uldric imparted to them a superhuman fervor to take the fight to the Huns. The Huns had surprisingly lost so many men in a battle that they had expected to triumph easily that they wilted like cut flowers. Leaderless and without their allies, the remaining Huns also decided the best course of action was to retreat under duress.

Hermides was the only Roman officer in a command position who had not been severely injured or killed. He ordered the Romans to pursue the Huns and their allies for a short distance to drive home the point of who was the victor of the battle. He also ordered other Roman forces to check bodies. Any Roman and their Goth allies who were still alive were taken to the physician area. All Huns, Alans, Suevi, and other enemy combatants were killed on the spot. Valerias had ordered no prisoners be taken, and he knew the Huns would have done the same to the Romans should they have triumphed.

Both Braga and Produgas had somehow survived the battle. This was due to luck and because they had avoided any serious fighting. After riding several miles away from the battle scene, they observed that the Romans were no longer pursuing them.

Produgas seemed to have mixed emotions. On the one hand he was genuinely sorry Uldric had been killed. Produgas was an admirer of the great leader. However, this was a temporary emotion. He was more pleased that events were going as planned. He would now be the undisputed leader of the Northern Huns. Produgas envisioned that as leader he would join with Zestras as an equal to form a united Hun empire. They would then return to the lands of the Goths and Romans with even greater numbers and avenge the deaths of Uldric and Rao.

Braga pointed to a far-off landmark to the east as a location where they were heading. Produgas looked east, then turned back to Braga to acknowledge the comment—when Braga's sword pushed through Produgas' abdomen.

Produgas' face twisted as he looked at Braga and gasped, *"Why?"*

"Because there is room for only one Hun leader, and that is Zestras. But he is getting old. Then it will be my turn. Your time is up—before it even started!"

Braga pulled his sword out of Produgas' body. He ordered two of his men to tie Produgas on his horse. When that was completed, Braga turned the horse in the direction of the Romans and gave the horse a sharp crack on its hindquarters. The horse jumped forward in a sprint and ran straight west.

The two men with Braga nodded during this act.

"My father will be pleased with what we have done. Almost all the leaders of the Northern Huns are dead. Uldric, Rao, Radic, Sardich, Jutikes, Turkson, Borgas . . . all gone to the afterlife. The rest will bow before my father and *me*. We shall soon unite all Huns, and then be masters of this world."

The men rode quickly eastward as a report came that the Roman cavalry was still in pursuit.

For the next week, Valerias was unconscious. However, the action around him was a blur. There were so many wounded soldiers that Olivertos, with his staff of Joseph, Claire, and several others, worked nonstop. If a soldier was not involved in handling the deceased Romans and resetting their camp, he was drafted into the physician ranks. The Goths took care of their own, with Gul leading that effort. Tentrides had also been badly wounded fighting off a Hun, so Gul served double duty: as the temporary Goth leader and temporary leader of the Roman engineering division.

Joseph also performed dual roles as priest to the Christian and even non-Christian fighters and as a physician. He also took whatever extra time he could, along with Claire, to look after Valerias. For several days it appeared that Valerias might die, which caused concern throughout the Roman camp. On the seventh day or so after the battle, no one could accurately remember the time, Valerias awakened. No one noticed at first, then a soldier saw the General's eyes open and called for Claire. She ran over to his bedside, followed by Joseph and, lastly, Olivertos. He looked at the three of them and emitted a very faint smile.

"Marcus is alive," was all Claire said, as tears appeared in her eyes.

"Welcome back, Marcus," Joseph observed. "We missed you."

Finally Olivertos provided his opinion, "It is about time, General. You have been tying up one of my beds for too long." He smiled at Valerias. "Good to have you back, Marcus."

Several days passed and Valerias' health gradually improved. He could sit up in bed and was able to talk for longer periods of time each day. One time he spoke softly and said he thought he had talked to Julian. Other persons were present, but he could not remember them. A voice spoke to him in a comforting tone. He remembered no angels or demons.

Claire was frequently at his bed until he asked her to help the other wounded men. One day when he was mentally ready, he requested the summary of the battle and a casualty report. Valerias knew what such a report would bring to his ears, and he was not looking forward to it.

Hermides appeared at the General's bed with a parchment in his hands. He was nervous and started to speak quickly. Valerias asked him to take his time—he wanted to clearly hear the report.

"First, General, we were victorious. *"Sapor est victoria! Adhuc esurient!"* [Savor the victory! Hunger for more!]

"Thank you, Hermides. Casualty report."

"General Braxus—dead. General Cratus—dead. General Proctur—dead. The Goth King Mostar Gulivus—dead. Tribune Pyrin—dead." Hermides also identified by name many other officers as dead. Valerias winced at the mention of Braxus and Cratus.

Hermides continued his report: "Bukarma—severely wounded and still unconscious. General Titus—severely wounded with the loss of his right leg. Tribune Tentrides—wounded and lost an eye."

Valerias interrupted once and asked Hermides to repeat the names. He had expected this report, yet it was still very troubling to him.

At the end of his report, Hermides solemnly said, "Over eight thousand Roman soldiers dead, and another seventy-five hundred wounded. We have estimated around ten thousand Goth casualties . . . dead or wounded . . . we just don't know the counts."

Valerias hung his head. *So many deaths,* he thought to himself.

Hermides changed the course of his report. "We estimate the Huns lost their entire leadership. They, and the Alans, the Suevi, and the Sarmatians, suffered twenty-five thousand dead, and likely many wounded men escaped." Hermides inhaled. "You stopped them, General. A great victory is yours."

"It is ours, Hermides. The dead, the living, the injured, and the dying—it is all of ours."

Claire entered the room. She was tired and sat on Valerias' bed. His right hand caressed her shoulders.

"You should not have been here, but I'm glad you were. I'll wager Joseph and Olivertos and countless soldiers are also glad."

Claire answered, "I have never seen such a bloodbath before. I never thought people could do such butchery to each other."

Claire was a very strong woman, but the events of the past days were too much for her. She broke down, crying on Valerias' shoulder. Valerias wrapped his right arm and the remainder of his left around her, and said, over and over again, "I know. I know."

After a few moments, he looked Claire in the eyes. "I am done with this. As soon as we cross back over the Danube, I want to marry you. Will you marry me?"

"Of course," was Claire's answer, as she looked back into Marcus' eyes, and saw the softness that she remembered before all this had begun.

As Valerias recovered, he received good news about Bukarma and Titus. Both would live, albeit with permanent souvenirs from the battle. Titus' wounds were more serious than Olivertos had initially told Valerias. In Olivertos' opinion Titus' life would be shortened by his injuries.

Valerias soon could get around with the aid of a walking stick. Almost all of the wounded who had lived were now able to travel. As the beginning of November arrived, Valerias knew they had to get back across the Danube before winter set in. He sent Gul ahead with the engineers and the injured Tentrides and a contingent of soldiers to reconstruct the pontoon bridge across the Danube.

For November the weather held, and what was left of Valerias' army that had crossed the Danube weeks earlier re-crossed the river before the first snows of winter fell. No Goths stood in their way. What Valerias had done was told in the Goth camps and had become legend. They let him pass without incident. Whatever food they had, they shared with the Romans. Of course, the presence of Gul, now a Goth hero, in the Roman army also helped remove any potential Goth interference.

After they had crossed the Danube and returned to Valerias' former winter headquarters in the fort, Valerias visited Gul in the engineer section of the camp. Tentrides was still recovering and was not with the engineers when Valerias appeared before them. Gul and his fellow engineers were startled to see the General because he rarely visited them, and there was a rumor he was still at death's door. The appearance of a vital General Valerias dispelled that rumor.

"Gul, I have heard from many sources of your courage during the battle with the Huns. Most important, your mere presence helped to stabilize the Goth army. You never flinched to carry out an order, even at the point of almost certain death. Your father, Mostar Gulivus, was a true leader—and I had great respect for him. In fact, he was the only enemy leader I ever respected. He would be proud of you. I am proud of you."

"What about Uldric, the Hun king?"

"Oh, in some ways, yes. I thought he had good fighting skills and he could lead men into battle. But I'm talking about a *true* leader, and that is who your father was—a true leader. Now it is your turn. You have a real talent for engineering. Tentrides has talked of your essential help in reconstructing the pontoon bridge and in building our artillery and many other devices. You have a knack for that work. I wrote a letter to Emperor Valens in Constantinople asking that you be promoted to Engineer Commander and be given your own division as a tribune. The Emperor has agreed."

Valerias held out a parchment to Gul.

Gul unrolled the parchment and read it. "The Emperor wants me to come to Constantinople and work on a new defensive scheme for the City."

"I also understand your Goth tribe wants you to return as their leader. I'll let you decide your future, Gul. Only you can decide."

Valerias returned to his horse and was assisted by his guards in mounting it. When he was up, he thanked the engineers for their service. Gul had grown to admire the General, and he felt a twinge of emotion for the man as he rode out of their camp.

An engineer friend commented to Gul. "For the General to appear at our camp and offer you such a position is remarkable. He is telling you something, and you should listen."

LXXVI

Beginnings

THE NEXT SEVERAL weeks went by quickly. There was much to do after the battle and upon returning to the old fort. The winter was short but brutal, with snow that never seemed to let up or go away. The cold periods caused several of the Roman men to develop mild cases of frostbite. Valerias had recovered well enough that he could walk without human and artificial assistance, but it was a long recovery. Not only did Valerias suffer the loss of a hand against the Hun, several swipes of the scimitar had penetrated deep into his flesh, and he was continually being watched for infection in those wounds.

Titus died at the fort during a particularly brutal cold spell. He never recovered from his injuries and was living in agony. Valerias, happy that his old friend had gone to a better place, ordered a hero's funeral. Titus had wanted and received a funeral pyre with the soldiers in full military dress in attendance. He had become a Christian at the final moment, and Joseph presided over the service. Titus and Joseph had developed a close relationship after the battle, and Joseph, even though he tried not to, showed emotion at the funeral. Valerias had Titus' belongings bound into a package, which he sent with a personal note to Titus' widow.

What she would do with the articles was her business. Valerias kept Titus' dagger in memory of his friend.

Valerias knew Claire was becoming very anxious to see her daughters again. So as hints of spring broke upon the land, Valerias made plans to leave the fort. Valerias had received word that Emperor Valens was sending a fresh legion under a new general to the fort. The Goths were still migrating to the Danube, and the legion was intended to prevent their crossing the river. Valerias could now retire once and for all. Bukarma had become well enough to travel, and he inquired whether he could accompany Valerias to Milan. There they were to meet Flavius, Mary, and the girls. Valerias heartily agreed that Bukarma could travel with them. He could also stay with them as long as he wanted.

Joseph too was ready to travel with Valerias and Claire to the meeting point with Flavius and Mary. Then he would go by separate route back to Britannia and his village, Bergen. He was worried about Olivertos. His friend had always been a little eccentric, but he was a warm man with a good sense of humor. Now he seemed lost and was just going through the motions. The battle and its aftermath had severely affected Olivertos' mental condition. He had been through several campaigns with Valerias before, but he had experienced nothing equivalent to the battle with the Huns in terms of the overwhelming violence humans could do to one another and the wreckage the carnage left behind. He was an excellent physician, yet the sheer volume of dead and injured soldiers he had faced affected his personality.

Valerias was also deeply concerned about his friend, and after talking with Joseph announced to Olivertos that he, Olivertos, was retiring from military service and would accompany Valerias out of the fort. Olivertos, showing no emotion, agreed. Valerias wanted Olivertos to go to Milan or Rome, open a civilian practice, and get away from the bloodshed of military life.

The journey between the fort and meeting point with Flavius and Mary was uneventful. When Valerias and his company left the old fort, there was no hero's good-bye this time, not because the soldiers did not want to acknowledge their leader but because there were not many of them even at the fort. The remaining limitanei had returned to their posts. Most of the surviving former deserters melted back into the surroundings, as they were through with the army. The battle with the Huns had destoyed the fighting tenor of the Roman legions that had participated in the battle. What were left were a few units that were trying to hold it together until the Emperor's legion reached the fort. Before he left, Valerias said farewell to those he could. Gul watched him leave in the early morning cold.

Claire and Valerias rode together most of the way from the fort to the meeting place near Milan. As they rode toward the city, Claire made a surprising statement to Valerias. "Joseph is a great man."

Valerias partly disagreed. "He has become a good man. You didn't know the Joseph I knew when I first met him. He has done good things since that day. But he has not reached 'great' yet."

Claire continued, "I think becoming great means utilizing your potential to reach the upper limits of the possible. That is what you have done, that is what Joseph has done—just in different ways."

"I'll grant you that he has changed . . ."

"And become more of the man he wants to become—a true Christian and a Christian leader." Claire tried to finish Valerias' sentence.

"You know how I feel about Christians," Valerias replied.

"He possesses a serenity that he brings to all those around him." Claire was ignoring Valerias.

"Are you becoming a Christian, Claire?"

"No, not yet, Marcus. But I want you to know that I prayed for you before, during, and after the battle. And you are here. Maybe my prayers were answered by the Christian God."

"Maybe so, Claire. I understand what you are saying. It will always be a mystery to me why I survived." After a pause Valerias added, "I don't want to talk about Christians anymore today. We will leave it at that, Joseph is a good man—a good Christian."

Valerias turned the subject to Anastasis, wondering how she was doing. Valerias thought of her often and was tempted to travel to her village and check on her status. He had also thought about adopting Anastasis. Unfortunately, it didn't work out, as he didn't want a young girl with them as they traveled to meet the Huns. And after the battle he and his forces were in no shape—and the weather was too unstable—to go any distance out of their way. She had her guardian, Orses, anyway. Valerias hoped for the best for her, and even asked Joseph to pray for her.

The reunion of Claire and her daughters occurred in a small village about one hundred miles east of Milan. This was the village where they had earlier separated, when Claire went east with Valerias to meet the Huns. Claire was so happy to see her girls she couldn't let go of them. The feeling was mutual. The girls looked fit and happy, and Valerias was very pleased to see them in such a condition. Mary and Flavius had been superb as caretakers for them. Valerias made sure to introduce Olivertos to the girls. Perhaps a spark of humanity would return to him.

Flavius was carrying a sword when they met. He immediately said to Valerias, "I heard you killed the Kraken, General. Part of me wishes I had been there."

Valerias smiled slightly, more from painful memories than happiness. "No, you don't. Yes, we stopped the Huns, but at great cost."

Flavius saw that Valerias' left hand was now a stump. He also observed that, for the first time, Valerias portrayed a mortal appearance.

Valerias continued, "I see you are carrying a sword again, Flavius."

"One has to in these uncertain times, General. I am a Christian—with limits. I can live with that. I fear uncertain times are upon us, and I want to be prepared. Mary has come to accept that a sword will always be a part of our lives."

Soon after they arrived, preparations were made for the wedding. The girls were very excited. They were fond of Valerias, as he was of them. In the short time he had known them, Valerias had become a father to them. Joseph was to conduct the ceremony in a nonreligious format. Valerias had asked Olivertos and Bukarma to serve as joint best men, and they agreed.

On the day of the ceremony, Joseph stood with Valerias while waiting for Claire to arrive.

"I heard that during the battle with the Huns, when the Huns invaded the physician's tent, you had the choice to raise a sword in combat. You chose not to, until it was too late."

"You are correct, Marcus. I refused to raise a sword on my own behalf, but then I thought of Olivertos and Claire and all the wounded. I refused to let my failure to act be the cause of so many deaths."

"I understand, Joseph. Sometimes the world is not just black and white; it is less than clear. I have not picked up a sword since the battle. I do not want to use the sword again. Yet I see Flavius carries a sword."

Joseph noted, "Sometimes there are alternatives to conducting violence."

"I agree." Valerias took his sword from its sheath on his back and stuck it blade first into the ground.

"What does that mean?" Joseph asked.

"It means that I too want to find solutions that do not require the sword. I have grown weary of the sword."

As Valerias said those words, he looked over to Olivertos, who stood, head bowed, several feet away. Valerias spoke in hushed tones. "I am worried about our friend, Joseph. I am concerned he may do something to himself."

"So am I, Marcus. We must do what we can to elevate his spirit, and give a meaning to his life, a meaning that he can acknowledge."

"He has a strong spirit, Joseph. We just need to bring it out again. I think it best that you take him back to your adopted village and see if he can regain his mind there."

"I have thought of that, as well, and I will, Marcus. But at some point he may be better off in Rome."

Changing subjects, Valerias asked Joseph, "When you return to the village, what will you do about Ruth?"

"I wish I knew. I have prayed to God for an answer, but have not received one."

"That is because you need to provide your own answer, Joseph. If I were you, and this woman—whom I have met—is as wonderful as you describe, I would go after her. I think you can be a good Christian *and* a good husband. But that is your religion and your decision. I do not care to delve into such things. Just don't let a golden opportunity slip away. You may regret it later."

Joseph asked, abruptly, "Tell me, Marcus, would you do it all again?"

"Do it all again? Your question is open ended. But I will try to answer. Yes, absolutely, I would do it all again. I realize now that I have few regrets. My journey over the past years has been well worth the trip. Besides, I do not have a choice in most matters. Nobody has such a choice. What happens, happens. That is all there is to it. We can try to control events, but we really can't. I can have the best plan in place, and if a quirky thing happens that upsets the plan, the final outcome may not be as I want it to be."

Valerias saw Claire approaching. "If I hadn't come this way, the Huns would be trampling across this land, and who knows how that would have ended? I wouldn't have met you. I wouldn't have met Claire . . . who changed my life. Perhaps you would not have become the man you are today."

As Claire arrived, Valerias smiled at Joseph. "I wouldn't want it any other way. Now help us get married!"

The ceremony was conducted quickly. Marcus and then Claire said their vows, which were based on a combination of experience and hope. These vows were more thoughtful and meaningful than the vows of an arranged marriage, such as Claire's marriage to Gerhard. Claire's vows with Valerias meant something. In Valerias' vows, he mentioned his past and his friends and his loyal soldiers. Claire mentioned her son and daughters. Both Claire and Valerias acknowledged their deep love for each other.

At the end of the ceremony, Olivertos grinned broadly. Valerias interpreted that to be a good sign. Revious stopped by for the service and offered his congratulations. He too was no longer a soldier of the Roman Empire. He and Alan were headed east back to the land of the Alans and a friendly tribe. The group began to split up. Flavius and Mary were leaving soon for exile in Spain. Joseph and Olivertos were on their way to Britannia. As they prepared to ride north to Britannia with a small contingent of Roman cavalry and the remaining Briton cavalry, Valerias grabbed Olivertos' arm and sincerely told him to find a new life in Britannia, away from violence, and to use his substantial physician skills to help civilians.

Joseph looked at Valerias and added, "Be well, Marcus and Claire."

"Do well and choose well, Joseph," was the reply.

Joseph looked at the sword Valerias had stuck into the ground. "What will you do with your sword?"

Valerias smiled, "Believe what you want to believe, Joseph!" Joseph and Olivertos rode down the Roman-built road and out of sight.

The girls each took a turn hugging Claire and Valerias. Valerias spoke to them quietly. "I want you two to go with Uncle Flavius and Aunt Mary. I have something to say to your Mother, and then we can have supper." The girls laughed and waltzed away with Flavius and Mary. Valerias took Claire's two hands in his right hand.

"Joseph restored my faith that a man of religion can be a good man. Before I met him, I would have picked any of my officers or even regular soldiers as having a better moral center than most—if not all—of the religious people I have met. That includes pagans, Christians, and other 'pious' folk I have encountered. I didn't know a man who was more ethical and moral than my former administrator, Jacob—and he was Jewish. I'm sorry you never met him. I miss Jacob to this day. Then Joseph came along. He showed me that a man of faith can have true faith. And then Titus, Braxus, Cratus . . ."

Valerias stopped and stared off into space, as if he was searching to see if any of his friends who had passed on were listening to him. He grew melancholy, reflecting on his past.

After several minutes of silence, Valerias changed the subject, "My dear Claire, there is something else I need to tell you. As you know, I kept a history of my actions as an officer with the Roman army. And I left the volumes with Bradicus, in Londinium. At that time, they meant more to me than my life. Now they are not worth a tenth of my life."

"Time has a way of changing what was and is important."

Valerias continued, "And maybe few would care now, anyway. My friends and colleagues are either dead or gone. Bukarma told me this morning that he'd changed his mind and is going to Africa after the wedding. You are what I have left. I am so fortunate to have you. At one time I wondered what my destiny was. Then I thought it was to meet the Huns in battle. But I lived, when so many died, and now I know my destiny is to be with you. And that is the greatest destiny. Joseph restored my belief in man's potential, but you restored my faith in myself and the life I want."

Tears formed in Claire's eyes. Marcus reached out to her more intensely than ever before. She wanted to be part of him and his life. "Maybe we have more than one destiny, Marcus. Do you want to retrieve your history?"

"Not now. Not ever. History can write about me any way it wants, or not at all. I know what I have done, and I am content with my history. Titus felt the same way." Marcus looked out into the distance at a flock of birds. A feeling of contentment returned to him. He thought to himself, *I know it is a fleeting feeling, and I'm satisfied with that. At least I have had this feeling.*

Valerias turned back to Claire. "Although I may change my mind," he added with a smile.

"What about your sword? Are you going to leave it or take it with us?" Claire already knew the answer.

Valerias walked over to the sword and pulled it from the ground. He wiped it off on a clean cloth he was carrying. He nodded to Claire, and she helped him put the sword back into its sheath he carried on his back.

"I did think about giving up the sword, as Joseph would want me to, but I can't. The world is too violent, too corruptible, and always will be. It is human nature to be violent. Joseph has high ideals—and that is good. If more men could be like him—including his own Christian leadership—I might have hope. I don't, though. There are too many selfish, greedy, violent people, and that is why I will keep my sword."

Claire was not as pessimistic, and gently countered Valerias, "Perhaps the philosophy of peace will be carried forth in the future by people such as Joseph, the converted Flavius, and my friend, Mary, so that peace prevails over violence."

Marcus paused, and then in a conciliatory tone added, "I could live with that."

As he spoke, he watched the birds hovering in the sky. The air became still from breezes and silent without the voices of people. In the quiet Valerias heard a familiar sound to his left, and he took a few steps in that direction. A small creek emerged through the trees and brush. The water in the creek appeared to be in a hurry as it flowed quickly to some unknown destination. Yet even in its haste, the water seemed to gently caress the rocks in its path. Valerias watched the motion of the water as it interacted with the stones for a few minutes. As he reflected on the scene, he smiled to himself.

Valerias returned to Claire, and again he smiled. "Now, let's go have supper with the girls."

A light shower fell on the two as they walked down the road. A cool front was coming and a fog was beginning to cover the land. Soon Valerias and Claire faded from sight as the fog followed them to a destiny known only to time.

THE END

"Finally, brothers and sisters, whatever is true, whatever is noble, whatever is right, whatever is pure, whatever is lovely, whatever is admirable—if anything is excellent or praiseworthy—think about such things."

— *Paul's letter to the Philippians* 4:8, NIV

REFERENCES

Heather, Peter. *The Fall of the Roman Empire: A New History of Rome and the Barbarians.* Oxford University Press, 2006.

Goldsworthy, Adrian. *How Rome Fell.* Yale University Press, New Haven, 2009.

Kelly, Christopher. *The End of Empire: Attila the Hun and the Fall of Rome.* W.W. Norton & Company, Ltd., London, 2009.

Vidal, Gore. *Julian.* Vintage Books, Vintage International Edition, New York, August 2003.

Ferrill, Arther. *The Fall of the Roman Empire.* Thames and Hudson, New York, 1986.

Elton, Hugh. *Warfare in Roman Europe: A.D. 350-425.* Clarendon Press, Oxford, 1996.

The Bible, NIV.

Wikipedia.

The map provided at the beginning of this book is a compilation of information included in the references.

44469407R10368

Made in the USA
Charleston, SC
24 July 2015